As we boarded, appearing as a young Chinese man dressed in a smart black business suit came out from the main cabin.

I handed him the scroll tied with vermillion ribbon that contained the Jade emperor's edict. He perused it quickly; this part of the proceedings was just a formality. He returned it to me and nodded. "Your passage has been confirmed. Please come with me. There is tea and soda inside, if you wish."

As he spoke, the boat and the sky both went black and the surge of waves beneath the boat ceased. The sound of the noisy tourists on the next pier was cut off, as was the noise from the myriad boats moored in the typhoon shelter. The air echoed with the eerie sound of the inside of a huge cavern and the darkness surrounded us. The water was completely still and black as ice, and the temperature dropped.

We were on our way to Hell . . .

Books by Kylie Chan

Dark Heavens

WHITE TIGER
RED PHOENIX
BLUE DRAGON

Journey to Wudang

EARTH TO HELL

And coming soon . . .

HELL TO HEAVEN
HEAVEN TO WUDANG

EARTH TO HELL

JOURNEY TO WUDANG
BOOK ONE

KYLIE CHAN

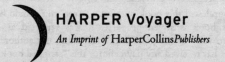

HARPER Voyager
An Imprint of HarperCollinsPublishers

First published in Australia in 2010 by HarperCollins*Publishers* Australia Pty Limited.

HARPER Voyager

An Imprint of HarperCollins*Publishers*
10 East 53rd Street
New York, New York 10022-5299

Copyright © 2010 by Kylie Chan
Cover Design by Darren Holt
Cover images: Woman by Ray Massey © Getty Images; all other images © Shutterstock
Chinese characters supplied by author
ISBN 978-0-06-202143-4
www.harpervoyagerbooks.com

First Harper Voyager mass market printing: October 2012

Harper Voyager and ❭ is a trademark of HCP LLC.

Printed in the U.S.A.

10 9 8 7 6 5 4 3 2 1

The Serpent slides through the
black icy water of the Antarctic,
wreathed in permanent darkness.

The Turtle hides from the weak
Arctic sun beneath the ice.

They cry, but there is no answer.

CHAPTER 1

'Now,' I said gently, 'concentrate. You've done it before. This time, bring the chi out as slowly as you can. Feel the rubber band pulling it back.'

Apple bit her lip and the glowing yellow ball of chi floated out of her outstretched palm.

Emma, emergency, the stone in my ring said. *Some third years have run into trouble. They raided a prostitution den in Mong Kok that was holding sex slaves, and instead of humans running the show they met up with demons. They need help.*

'Let the chi go, Apple,' I said, still very gentle.

The chi floated back down into Apple's hand and she sagged.

'Take a break now, and don't try it again without supervision,' I said. 'I've been called away, so we'll end it there. Head back to the Folly and have a rest.'

Apple nodded. 'Yes, ma'am. Thank you.'

I patted her shoulder, then quickly rose and spoke urgently to the stone as I charged out to the stairwell. 'Get Marcus to bring the car around the front. I'll meet him at the ground floor. Which Masters are free?'

'Sit, Park, Lee and Edwards are there already. The demons are holding the students hostage. It's a standoff,' the stone said.

1

I jumped over the balustrade to the empty space in the centre of the stairwell, twenty storeys to the ground. I fell at maximum speed until the floor loomed below me, then slowed my fall, levered one foot on the railing and jumped down to the landing in front of the ground floor door.

'Demons holding third years? They must be big,' I said.

Do you need us? General Ma said into my head. *The demons holding your students are quite large.*

'Aren't you dealing with a demon attack on the Horse Village?' I asked via the stone.

The Majia are handling it well, General Ma said. *If we bring in the Princess we will be finished very quickly and be back in Hong Kong within the hour to help your students. Western Horsemen are on their way to assist us.*

'Can the Horses and Horsemen handle it?' I said. 'I don't want to take Simone out of school unless it's absolutely necessary, you know that. She's skipping a lot of school with these attacks as it is.'

They can handle.

'Head back when you're relieved, and we'll see if we need your help. How long do you think it will be?'

About an hour and a half.

'See you then.'

My Lady.

It took nearly forty-five minutes to reach the area of Mong Kok where the students were being held hostage. Marcus wound his way through the narrow, busy streets of the area and dropped me outside the brothel, then went off in search of a car park. The brothel had a large sign outside advertising the prices: *White Russian 500; Fair Skin Thai 400; North and South Chinese 300.*

Two of the Masters, Sit and Park, stood outside the brothel with a group of five or six seniors, looking up

2

at the second-storey windows. The brothel was a blackened concrete apartment building, 1950s era, with small barred windows on each floor. The ground floor was occupied by a microscopic mobile phone shop, all pristine white tiles and blazing lights. The brothel's single front door had a steel gate, which now hung open. Plain narrow concrete stairs led up inside.

'Where's Edwards?' I said.

'Around the back in the alley with another couple of seniors,' said Lee.

'What do we have here?'

'Six level fifty to sixty demons. A couple of them appear to be Mothers. They're holding a team of third years who came in to practise on them and were taken by surprise.'

'Mothers? Damn. Anybody hurt?'

'One of the prostitutes tried to escape and a demon smacked her down; she's probably concussed,' Sit said. 'A couple of the students sustained some severe injuries when they were taken — these demons hit them hard with some sort of energy blast.'

'The police aren't aware of what's going on? We won't see uniforms and guns roll up?'

'No,' Park said.

'What do the demons want?'

'Free passage.'

'That's all?'

'Yes. We're just waiting for you to give the go-ahead on either a raid or to let them go. We're prepared either way.'

'Recommendation?'

'Let them go.'

'Can we take them down without hurting any more girls or students?'

Park hesitated, then, 'No.'

'Let them go.'

'Ma'am.'

Park concentrated, and the teams moved into action. Sit and Lee went upstairs to deliver the deal to the demons. A bus appeared around the corner and stopped outside the brothel.

'Demons took off,' Park said. 'Lee has taken a recording.'

'Good.'

Three more of the seniors with us charged into the building and up the stairs. Two of the four third-year students who had been held hostage came limping down the stairs, obviously nursing injuries. They made for the bus.

'By your leave, ma'am,' Park said, 'we'll take the other two injured students directly to the infirmary.'

'Go,' I said.

Park and Lee went into the building.

The seniors who had run up the stairs shortly before came down escorting ten or so prostitutes. The girls were tiny and slim; some of them only looked about fourteen or fifteen. There were no Europeans, only Thais, Indonesians and Chinese. They were obviously terrified as the seniors guided them onto the bus.

A few bystanders watched, curious. One of the seniors jumped off the bus, walked over and loudly told them in Cantonese that this was a police plainclothes operation and to move along. The bystanders grinned but continued to watch, unfazed.

'Update on the Horse Village,' I said to the stone.

Under control. A squad of about fifty demons attacked the village, but the Horses held them off. Three Horses were killed and four were injured before the Generals arrived to help.

'Tell General Ma we have a lid on things here and he's not needed,' I said.

We have been called to another attack anyway,

ma'am, Ma said. *A phoenix has called for help — a Mother is outside her nest and threatening her clutch.*

'Can they make it in time?' I said.

If we move now we may make it, but we will be cutting it close, Ma said.

'Need help?'

Simone could be there immediately to protect these chicks, Ma said. *It is the phoenix's nursery; she thought it would be safe in this remote area, but some Mothers have found it. She and her children are fighting but there is a large number of demons after her clutch.* He hesitated a moment, then, *This looks very bad. Please allow us to send in Princess Simone.*

Help, General Danahuo, a woman's voice said into my head. *All of my babies are here, and a Mother and sixteen of her demon spawn are attempting to break into my nursery.* Her voice became strained. *Help!*

'Can you relay, stone?' I said. 'Let me see.'

'Networking …' The stone's voice trailed off. 'I have a link. The phoenix has a sentient stone Shen as a jewellery item. Oh! It's Glauconite, I know this one. Bringing up an image.'

A phoenix appeared in front of me, transparent against the buildings and people around me. She bowed, spreading her scarlet wings; royal blue and purple peacock-like feathers rippled among the flaming red pinions.

'General Danahuo,' she said. She gestured with her head to her left. 'There they are. They threaten my clutch.'

She was standing on a barren, rocky hillside somewhere in southern China. About twenty metres down the slope, some red-garbed warriors fought with a band of demons. A Snake Mother stood behind the demons; the top half of her body was human, but with the skin flayed off, while the bottom half was an enormous black snake with clear gelatinous toxin oozing from between her scales. She must have been close on four metres in length; a really big one. I gasped when I saw the demons she was controlling — fake stone elementals. They appeared to be made of rough-hewn blocks of granite held together with an invisible force. They were about two metres tall, had featureless faces and moved with disturbing smoothness as they battled the phoenix's defenders.

'More of these things!' Edwards said as he approached me from the back of the building and saw the projection next to me. 'Who's making them? They keep popping up everywhere!'

'I'm surprised they sent stone to fight the phoenix's guards,' I said. 'Wouldn't water be more effective against fire?'

The guards, wearing traditional all-red Chinese armour, were fighting valiantly with both swords and phoenix fire, but the demons outnumbered them about three to two. None of the guards had fallen yet, but they were obviously losing the battle — the stone demons were completely unharmed by their weapons and fire.

'Tell Simone,' I said to the stone. 'Tell her where to go.'

Thank you, ma'am, both the phoenix and General Ma said at the same time. The image of the battle snapped off.

On it, Simone said into my head. *It was only PE anyway.*

'I'll go on the bus with the girls,' I said to the stone. 'Tell Marcus to take the car back. How are the injured seniors?'

In the infirmary back at the Academy, the stone said. *Serious injuries but not life-threatening. There's some debate about whether to send them to hospital.*

'What does Regina say?' I said as I got onto the bus and sat next to Edwards. Edwards, as usual, wore a pair of plain slacks and a business shirt without a tie. His bald head, glasses, and paunch made him look like a fifty-year-old schoolteacher — and deceptively harmless.

The driver pulled away from the kerb and into the traffic.

Regina says hospital.

'Damn, we can't afford this. If they don't go to hospital what are the consequences?'

They will just receive better care in hospital, the stone said. *Regina doesn't have the facilities to deal with this type of fracture.*

I hesitated. We would be asked too many awkward questions if the students were checked into a hospital. 'Stone, get me Bai Hu, please.'

Ma'am, the White Tiger said into my head.

'Ah Bai. We have two badly injured students and Regina wants to hospitalise them. Any room in your clinic?'

Stand by.

His voice returned a couple of minutes later. *Either of them demons?*

No, the stone said. *Human.*

Ah shit, the Tiger said. *Well, okay, I'll take them. A Horseman is on his way to get them.*

'Thanks,' I said. 'Why do you always want my injured demon students?'

The Tiger didn't reply.

'He has a group of his children researching demon nature,' the stone said.

'Dear Lord, he's not doing any genetic experimentation on them, is he?'

Nah, just having a look inside, the Tiger said. *They're moving way ahead of us in breeding research,*

7

they always have. I thought it was about time that we caught up.

'Breeding?' I said, horrified.

'The Tiger is breeding demons?' Edwards said.

No, no, of course not, the Tiger said. *We just collect them as we go along. Some of yours would be fun to have — a few of yours are the results of some very interesting breeding experiments. That's why they have so much free will and have joined you in the first place.*

'You hurt one hair on any of my demon students' heads and your tail is in serious trouble,' I said.

'Hear, hear,' Edwards said quietly.

'He's not breeding them, he's collecting them and doing research,' I said for Edwards' benefit. 'He wants some of ours 'cause they're the result of some "interesting breeding experiments".'

Edwards leaned back in his seat and crossed his arms. 'No way is that bastard laying his paws on any of my students. My kids are not guinea pigs.'

I promise I won't hurt them, Jim, the Tiger said.

Edwards gave an excellent British harrumph. 'The psychological damage of undergoing that level of medical examination would undo all the good work we've done in getting these kids over what they've endured in Hell. The Tiger can piss off, he's not getting any of mine.'

What if they volunteer? the Tiger said.

'Oh, now that's clutching at straws,' Edwards said with amusement.

It's like a holiday for them, Jimmy, the Tiger said. *You know how nice it is out here. Let them come and check it out.* His voice became eager. *How many good demon students do you have anyway?*

'None of your damn business, and shut the fuck up,' Edwards said. He winced. 'Sorry, ma'am.' His tone was amused as he spoke to the Tiger again. 'Get lost. You're not getting any of my demons.'

'You're not getting any of the Academy demons,' I added. 'Get your own. And if I send any over to you for medical attention and find that you've experimented on them, your tail is mine.'

Fine thanks I get for helping you out here, the Tiger grumbled in my head. *Just one or two —*

'No!' Edwards and I said at the same time.

Fine!

'Oh, and Ah Bai?' I said.

What!

'Thanks for looking after these students for me, my friend. Most appreciated.'

Stop sounding like Ah Wu, he said, and went quiet.

'Be interesting to see what he's finding out about them,' Edwards said. 'I've always been fascinated by demons. Never knew they existed when I was back in the UK, but I must have run into a couple of them without realising.'

'You think so?' I said.

'It follows. Demons are often in on the nasty stuff that goes on.' He nodded towards the prostitutes, who cowered in their seats at the back of the bus as the students tried to explain to them that they were no longer slaves. 'We were often called in to deal with this sort of thing.'

'Ever run into any nasties that seemed more dangerous than your average felon?' I said. 'That gave even a group of trained fighters like yourselves a tough battle?'

He thought for a moment. 'Never had anybody that didn't drop when we shot them, and demons would be unaffected by guns.' He hesitated. 'But some of them did seem tougher. We were given extensive training, and it's like they were too.' He shrugged. 'Stronger, faster, smarter. A match for us. Could have been demons.'

'But if you shot them, they fell down,' I said. 'Never had any explode into demon stuff?'

'Never,' he said. 'Must go back to the UK and have a look one day.'

'I'll come with you,' I said.

He harrumphed again. 'Neither of us have the goddamn time, ma'am. We're both flat out keeping our people here safe from the Demon King and his little kiddies.'

I sighed. 'I know.' I touched the stone. 'How's Simone doing?'

'Let me see,' the stone said. 'She's just arriving there now.'

'Can you link me up, please?'

Simone appeared as a small image in front of us, running downhill towards the demons from where the phoenix was standing guard at the entrance to her nest. She was wearing her school PE uniform — a pair of green shorts and house T-shirt — and carrying her father's sword, Dark Heavens. The sword was completely without adornment on either the handle or the blade. It was slightly too big for her but it was her weapon of choice.

As she closed on the demons, she lifted into the air, her tawny hair flying around her. She raised Dark Heavens horizontally above her head, and held her left hand up, her first two fingers pointing towards the demons, ready to use chi energy if necessary.

She flew lightning-fast over the Snake Mother, somersaulted directly above it and sliced diagonally through its skinless body. It fell in two pieces, the snake part writhing across the ground, the human hands scrabbling at the gravel.

Simone landed in a crouch, and I was breathless for a moment thinking she had hit the ground too hard. She spun and rose and launched shen energy at two nearby demons, blinding white blasts that destroyed them. The red warriors that had been fighting the demons stepped back in shock and raised their hands.

About six of the fake stone elementals remained. Simone ran to the centre of the battle, concentrated for a split second, then rammed Dark Heavens into the ground. Her hair flew up, the gravel lifted from the ground around her and a shockwave spread outwards from the blade of the sword, creating a visible ripple in the stony ground. When the shockwave hit the warriors, it knocked them off their feet; but when it hit the demons, it completely shattered them. They fell to the ground in shards of stone.

The shockwave stopped and the gravel that had been flying around Simone dropped to the ground. She pulled her sword free, and walked back up the slope to the phoenix. The red warriors rose and checked the area; the demons had all been destroyed.

Simone shared a few short words with the phoenix, then they touched wing to hand, the flaming feathers doing her no damage. She nodded to the warriors, who saluted her, then she shot straight up into the air and disappeared towards the north, leaving behind a trail of vapour.

I thank you, Madam General, the phoenix said into my head. *You and the Princess have saved my babies. I am your servant.*

'Tell her she's welcome,' I said to the stone, and the image of the phoenix snapped off.

'Never ceases to amaze me how such a sweet young lass can kick so much serious arse,' Edwards said.

One of the seniors called to us from the back of the bus. 'A few of these girls don't speak anything but Indonesian and Thai, and one is Vietnamese. We need your help, Masters.'

Sit moved to the back of the bus where he talked to the girls in Putonghua. Nevertheless, they all understood him.

'I envy the Immortals,' Edwards said.

'Then you'll never join them,' I said.

He shook with a short, silent laugh. 'I know.'

'If you want to take the time to go and cultivate the Tao, it's your choice,' I said.

He considered for a moment. 'One day maybe. They all encourage me to go and cultivate the Tao on the Mountain, living on pine nuts and spring water, but I don't think I'm ready for the Art of Navel Gazing. I'm just having too much damn fun here.'

I nodded. 'Just so you know. If you feel the time is right, then go. They will help you.'

'Thanks, Emma,' he said softly. He shifted to sit more upright. 'Nearly there now. Let's work out what to do with these poor girls.'

CHAPTER 2

The team who'd rescued the prostitutes gathered for a debriefing in the conference room on the ninth floor.

'Four of them can't go home; their families sold them into this and they won't be wanted back,' Sit said. 'Of the seven who can go home, we found only three of their passports in the brothel, the other four passports are missing. We'll have stones tap into the relevant immigration computers to extract their details and make duplicates for them. Something very interesting, ma'am — one of the girls appears to be half-dragon and completely unaware of her nature. One of our dragons recognised her.'

'I'll talk to her,' I said. 'Arrange for her and Amy to meet me in my office after this; and to bring along the four girls that can't go home. But first let's have a look at Mr Lee's recording. I want to see this energy blast that injured the students.'

Lee folded up from human to stone form and drifted to sit in the middle of the table. We waited for him to produce the recording of the standoff with the demons, but nothing happened. He returned to human form after a couple of minutes, obviously puzzled.

'The recording's not there,' he said.

'It's not in your matrix?' I said.

He shook his head, bewildered. 'That area of my structure is clear. Like nothing was ever there.' He looked concerned. 'I've been hacked.'

'Not possible, they were just Mothers,' the stone in my ring said. 'Bring out what you have either side, let's see.'

Lee rubbed his hands over his face. 'There isn't anything there. I recall arriving at the building, going up the stairs, then going into recording mode. Then the next segment of data is me back down in the bus. I've been wiped.'

'Not possible!' the stone said.

'Has anything like this happened to you before?' I said.

Lee shook his head. 'Very disturbing.'

'Time to go back and see what's going on there,' I said. 'Lee, grab a couple of other stones, take a couple of Celestials. See if you can get a dragon if they're free, and teleport directly in. Everybody take a recording. Someone take an old-fashioned video camera from stores; ask Lok for one. We'll meet back here in a couple of hours and see what we can see.'

'Ma'am.' Lee lowered his head and disappeared.

'Has anything like this ever happened before?' I asked the stone.

'It is possible for us to experience damage to part of the matrix, but usually we can piece together the undamaged parts to give us an idea of what went wrong,' the stone said. 'Being erased like that is unheard of.'

'Are you passing it through the stone network?'

'Quite a few stones have dropped what they're doing and are going along with Lee. A few want to examine his matrix. We're looking into it.'

14

'Good,' I said. 'Sit, get a stone to make some duplicate passports for these girls, and let's send them home. I'll talk to the dragon and the four that can't go home in my office. Other than that, I think we're done here.'

'Ma'am,' Sit said, and disappeared.

'I'm very concerned, Emma,' the stone said.

'You're not the only one.'

'So it's your choice,' I said to the five girls. 'Go home to your own country, or stay here. If you stay, we can give you the right of abode and you can find a job and work here. We will give you somewhere to live. It is up to you.'

One of the girls sniffled. The others sat looking down at their hands, silent and disbelieving.

'If you don't know what you want to do, take your time,' I said. 'We will look after you; we won't make you do sex work. We will train you to do office work if you like, and you can find yourselves good jobs back home.'

None of the girls moved or spoke.

'My staff will show you where you're going to live until you decide,' I said. 'The lady who brought you here is waiting for you outside the office. If you want to go, just tell her, she'll take you home. If you're not sure, then you can stay with us until you know.'

I called to Martha and she opened the door and came in. 'I'll do the rest,' she said.

She smiled at the girls and folded her hands in front of her. 'I will look after you, nobody will hurt you any more. I can take you home or you can stay here; either way you are safe.'

The girls sat without moving.

Martha put her hand out. 'Come with me.'

The girls rose like automatons, still looking at the floor, and went out with Martha. One of them sniffled again and wiped her nose on her sleeve.

Martha gently put her hand out to stop one of the girls from leaving the room. 'Not you, you stay here. Madam needs to talk to you.'

The girl stopped, still staring at the floor. The other girls went with Martha without looking back.

I checked my notes for her name. 'Hien. Please sit again, and I'll tell you a story.'

She returned to her seat and glanced up at me through her long fringe. I smiled. Actually looking at me was a promising step.

'About eleven years ago, I took a job as nanny to a little girl named Simone. Her father was a wealthy Hong Kong businessman.'

Hien didn't move.

'After a while, I discovered that he wasn't a businessman at all, but a god. He was Xuan Wu, the black Turtle Snake God of the North.'

Hien glanced at me through her fringe again.

'I don't know how much you know about the gods, but he was the North Wind, an Immortal. He married a human woman and had a child with her. It's a long story, but because of his wife he was forced to stay in human form for a long time and this made him weak. His wife was murdered by a demon before I met him; that's why he needed me to nanny. He and I fell in love and he died about three years after that, murdered by a demon. I've been looking after his daughter, Simone, ever since. I've also been given the job of looking after his martial arts academy and some other stuff related to him being Emperor of the Northern Heavens.' I put my chin on my hand. 'Not exactly what I was intending to do with my life, but one day he'll come back and we'll get married.'

Hien clasped and unclasped her hands in her lap.

'Yep, you're probably thinking: more lies. But this is actually easy to prove because I can have any god or demon wander in here and take their True Form and scare you to death. I won't do that though.'

She studied her hands carefully, still too traumatised to talk. This would take time.

'Some of the staff and students here at the Martial Arts Academy are dragons,' I went on. 'Dragons are fierce fighters with impeccable honour and completely loyal to us. They are also incredibly fickle in love. They tend to love humans and then leave them without thought; not out of malice, just because that's the way they are. We've been working here to explain to the dragons that this sort of behaviour isn't really acceptable where humans are concerned. That if you produce a child with a human partner you're expected to hang around and help care for it. Dragon children hatch fully able to care for themselves, but half-human dragons are generally the same as human babies.'

She sighed gently. I was boring her now.

'One of your parents took off when you were a small child, Hien, leaving the other to care for you. Was it your mother or father who left you?'

She frowned slightly but didn't reply.

'Please answer me, Hien. Was it your mother or your father that left you when you were a small child?'

She tilted her head slightly, still hiding under her long fringe. 'Mother,' she whispered.

'Your mother left when you were little. Your father probably has nothing but good things to say about her, and says that she left because that's the way she was. He might even say that he still loves her.'

She glanced up at me through her hair.

'Your mother is a dragon, Hien.'

She looked down again. Lost her.

'You're a dragon too, if you can learn to transform. You can be very powerful, able to swim and fly. But you must make this hidden dragon nature emerge.

If you can, you will never again have to worry about anybody harming you.'

She remained still and silent.

'I have one of the Academy dragons outside the door, Hien. She's been translating for me. I can't speak a word of Vietnamese.'

A small lie, but worthwhile in the circumstances. Amy wasn't translating for me; all languages were understood within the walls of the Academy.

'Right now she looks like an ordinary young woman. She can transform into a dragon to show you, if you like, and then you can decide whether you want to be a dragon and learn what you are capable of, or whether you would just like to go home.'

Hien sat unmoving, thinking about it.

'Come on in, Amy,' I said.

Amy opened the door and Hien jumped. Amy smiled reassuringly at her, and sat in the other visitor's chair.

'I know this is shocking for you,' she told the girl. 'I didn't know I was a dragon until I was twenty-five years old; my father never told me he was a dragon too. We have a community of dragons here at the Academy and we go out and swim and fly together. It's great fun. And we're fierce fighters too; we never have to worry about being hurt.'

'Amy will look after you now, Hien,' I said, 'and introduce you to some other dragons. All of them will be in human form. When you're ready, you can ask her to show you her dragon form, her True Form. Take a few days, meet the other dragons, then at the end of the time decide whether you would like to learn to become a dragon yourself, or whether you'd like to go home.'

Amy held her hand out to Hien. 'Come with me, I'll look after you. Nobody's going to hurt you any more.'

'Go with her, Hien,' I said. 'And good luck. I hope one day I see you in dragon form. I'd like to see what colour dragon you are. Amy is the most beautiful black dragon with gold fins that I have ever seen.'

I nodded to Amy and she smiled back at me. As she gently guided Hien out, she turned back to me. 'Don't worry, Emma, I think we'll bring her round.'

'I hope so,' I said. 'She's had a lot of bad stuff happen in her life. It would be nice to see something good happen.'

I was about halfway through the end-of-year leave requests when there was a knock on the door. 'Enter.'

Lee came in, looking grim, with Silver, one of the Academy dragons. They took the visitors' chairs and Silver placed the Academy's video camera on the desk.

'What did you find?' I asked.

They both shook their heads.

'Nothing,' Lee said. 'I wasn't wiped this time. In fact, nothing at all happened. We went right through the place and didn't find anything. You can watch the video, but it's basically a tour of a down-market Mong Kok brothel. Four stones and Master Sit came with us, and absolutely nothing happened.'

'Let's see,' I said.

Lee picked the camera up off the desk, flipped open the LCD screen and turned it on. He glanced down at the screen and his face filled with shock.

Silver leapt to his feet and changed to Celestial Form — nearly two metres tall with long, flowing, shining grey hair and scaled silver armour. He summoned a spear and held it to one side in the small office.

'Don't attack,' Lee said to Silver without looking away from the screen. 'That's Lady Emma's serpent form.'

'*What?*' I said.

Lee turned the LCD screen around so that it faced the same way as the lens. I could see myself in the screen; the camera was on record mode, not playback.

I stared at myself. 'Holy shit.'

Silver changed back to human form, but his hair remained long and grey. 'The Dark Lady is a serpent?'

'Nobody knows why, but I can change into a big black snake. Not many people know about it, Silver,' I said, watching with fascination as the enormous black serpent in the tiny screen also opened its mouth to speak. 'We'd prefer not to freak out the students.'

I took the camera from Lee and watched myself. 'I never knew I'd look like that on video; on still cameras I appear human. Wait!' I looked up. 'Stone, Simone took a home video about six months ago when we went to London and I was human in that. What the hell?'

'No idea, Emma,' the stone said. 'Your guess is as good as mine.'

'This information isn't to be shared,' Lee said to Silver. 'Many of the human students would probably take it quite badly.'

Silver nodded. 'I understand. How long have you been able to do this, Lady Emma?'

I paused, embarrassed.

Lee glanced at Silver, obviously sharing the information by telepathy, and Silver's face cleared. 'Sharing mind and body with the Dark Lord. That could very well bring out an inherent serpent nature.'

I could feel my face growing red, and Silver grinned. 'In this respect you are still very human, ma'am.'

'And I'd like to stay that way, thank you very much,' I said.

I changed the camera to playback and watched as Lee and Silver swept through the brothel, pausing to focus on the untidy metal beds in each room with their cheap polyester quilts. 'You were right. Down-market.'

'Very,' Lee said. 'But we didn't find anything.'

'I had a serious look around for anything that would give us more detailed information on the nature of these

20

demons,' Silver said, 'and I too came up blank. No paperwork, no messages, nothing. I'd say it was stripped clean but they never came back to do it. Which means there was never anything there to link the demons to the operation in the first place.'

'Credit card machine? EFTPOS?' I said. 'Any cables you could hook into to get information, Lee?'

'They had an EFTPOS line to the Hong Kong Bank. I traced it back and it was listed to a company registered at the brothel's address, but with names of nonexistent people as the directors,' Lee said. 'Drawing a blank, ma'am. We have nothing.'

'Okay,' I said. 'Let's leave it for now. Warn the third years, and keep an eye on the criminal operations for these demons.'

'They'll probably keep a low profile for a while now,' Lee said. 'But I'd really like to know what they did to me.'

'Are you okay?' I said.

'I've been checked over, I'm fine.' His mouth tweaked in a small smile. 'I've just been erased.'

'We'll let the others know. The stone network is on the lookout. That's basically all we can do,' Silver said.

'Thanks, guys,' I said.

They stood patiently in front of my desk.

'Dismissed!' I said. 'And you know you don't need to wait for it!'

Silver bowed slightly, grinning knowingly. 'Serpent Lady.'

'And don't call me that!'

They both disappeared.

CHAPTER 3

I'd just finished the last of the end-of-year leave forms when I heard a soft sound and a red box materialised on my desk. Thank you very much, Heavenly Bureaucracy: 7 pm, a hell of a day, and this lands on my desk. I hoped it wasn't urgent.

I pressed my thumb to the elaborate gold filigree clasp on the front of the box. Inside was a single scroll, dun-coloured vellum tied with a red ribbon. I opened it and perused the black Chinese characters. Not written in red, so not an edict from the Jade Emperor, but from the complexity of the large square seal at the bottom of the document it was from someone quite high up. I couldn't read the flowing Chinese calligraphic characters but the Celestial nature of the scroll made their meaning apparent as I scanned them. My heart leapt when I saw Leo's name.

Lady Emma Donahoe, Grand Master (Acting), New Wudang Academy of Martial Arts; Probational Regent of the Northern Heavens

Madam,
Your application to attend to the matter of your

Retainer Leo Gerald Alexander has been reviewed by the Office.

In light of the nature of the circumstances it has been decided that this matter will be forwarded to the Secretary for Underworld Affairs for further consultation.

Signed and chopped
Undersecretary for Review of Promotion

Yes. Finally we were getting somewhere. The Secretary for Underworld Affairs was the head of the Department of Hell and Yanluo Wang's second in command. Yanluo Wang, Lord of the Underworld, answered only to the Jade Emperor when it came to the judgement of those found Worthy for Immortality. After eight years of tedious bureaucratic blockades I was close to being able to enter Hell and talk Leo into coming out.

I grabbed the scroll, rolled it up and shoved it into my handbag. Simone would be thrilled. I was meeting her for dinner at a Thai restaurant nearby and then we were going shopping in Pacific Place. I walked to the door, then stopped when I heard a soft sound outside. I listened. Quiet voices. Damn, in this form I couldn't use my Inner Eye to check.

I tapped the stone, then put my hand over it to signal that it should stay silent.

I hear them, it said in my mind. It paused. *Demons, Emma, big ones.*

Not again. And right when I was about to go home. This was becoming ridiculous.

Yep, the stone said. *It's only three weeks since the last bunch.*

I dropped my bag on the floor of my office, strode out the door, down the hall to the lift lobby, and switched on all the lights. There was a soft exclamation, then silence.

I stormed back into the middle of the main office cubicles, stopped in front of the demons, and crossed my arms.

They had taken the form of ordinary Chinese teenagers: two boys and a girl. I studied them carefully. The stone was right: really big ones. The girl was a shape-shifter; the two boys were humanoids.

'Looking for me?' I said.

The demons shared a look, then the girl stepped forward. 'Are you Emma?'

'Yes I am.'

She smiled and tilted her head. 'We found your wallet downstairs and wanted to return it to you. But I left it back at my apartment. Can you come with us and I'll give it back to you?'

Wow, that was lame even by their standards.

'I suggest you leave right now,' I said, 'before you find yourselves in serious trouble, kids. How did you get in past the seals anyway? I just had them reset three weeks ago.'

Her eyes glazed over. 'Seals?'

Great, a genius leading the group.

'Yes, seals. Ours are some of the best. Who helped you to get in?'

A fleeting expression of vicious cunning crossed the face of one of the boys. Ah, the real brains.

'We don't know what you're talking about, Emma,' he said. 'We just have your wallet and want to give it back to you.'

'You were told by the Demon King that if you brought me to him in one piece, he'd let you back into Hell,' I said. 'What did you do to piss him off? You're the fourth bunch of kids since November.'

The girl recovered herself. 'I'm sorry, Emma, I have no idea what you're talking about. Don't you want your wallet?'

'It's in my bag back in my office,' I said. 'And now I'm giving you fair warning. Turn, and I will take you in. Run, and you'll probably starve to death locked out of Hell. If you wish to take the third option, I will oblige but I won't be happy about it. You could attain humanity if you just gave it a try. I'm a generous master to all my demons, you can ask any of them.'

When I said the word *demons* they stiffened slightly.

'Very well,' the smart one said. 'You know what we are. Fine. Come with us and we won't hurt you. Our dad just wants to talk to you, that's all. Come along, and we promise nothing will happen to you.'

'I can take all three of you down, you know,' I said.

The girl snorted with laughter. 'Yeah, right. We're all spawn of the King himself. No chance, lady. Come quietly or you'll regret it.'

The cunning one studied me appraisingly.

'We can take her,' the girl told him. 'Dad said she's just an ordinary human. We can do it.'

I held my hand out. 'Three against one is hardly fair. May I use a weapon?'

The second boy shrugged. He hadn't spoken yet, and his presence radiated apathy. The follower. 'Whatever. We can take you, doesn't matter what you use against us.'

'Anything at all?' I said. 'How about this then?'

I called the Murasame, the Destroyer, and it appeared in my hand. I held the katana in front of me and used my thumb to slide the blade five centimetres out of its scabbard in a visible threat. 'So who's first?'

'That's the Murasame, guys,' the second boy said quietly. 'Oh my God, we are in big trouble.'

'Not possible,' the girl said.

'Why? Because the Murasame belongs to the Dark Lady, head of New Wudang?' I said. 'Check the first floor of this building with your demon vision, kids, and tell me what you see.'

Their eyes unfocused and their faces filled with horror as they saw the armoury that took up most of the floor.

The girl made a soft wailing sound of terror. 'This is New Wudang. He sent us to New Wudang.'

'Let's get out of here,' the cunning boy whispered.

'Join me and I'll treat you well, you know I will,' I said. 'If you run you'll end up dead.'

The girl and the cunning boy disappeared. Running. The follower boy didn't run; he stood and watched me.

I bowed slightly and dismissed the sword. 'Welcome. Kneel and pledge.'

He fell to his knees in front of me and his face filled with wonder. 'I pledge allegiance to you, Dark Lady. I am your servant. Protect me, I am yours.'

'Rise,' I said. 'Someone will have to complete the taming process for me because I really am an ordinary human.'

The demon rose and the expression of wonder faded into contentment. 'As you wish, my Lady.'

'Stone, can you see who is on the night shift for demon duty and ask them to come up and get him?'

'Did it a while ago,' the stone said. 'Nigel's on his way.'

'Now tell me what you did that got the King so annoyed,' I said to the demon.

He sagged, miserable. 'We were on guard duty for the black one.'

I raised my hand to stop him. 'The black one? You mean Leo Alexander?'

He shrugged. 'Yeah, that one.'

A stab of pain hit me. 'Is he okay?'

'Apart from refusing Immortality, ma'am, yes, he is.'

'So, what happened?'

'We were guarding Leo when a hawker came past with sweet bean curd. We all went to buy some, and left Leo's cell unattended.'

'Is Leo alive?'

'Uh …' The boy hesitated. 'Define "alive", ma'am, and I'll be able to answer that.'

'If I were to go down there and talk the Courts into releasing him back to the Earthly Plane, would he be able to return to his previous life?'

He thought for a while, then shrugged. 'I have no idea, ma'am, because nobody's ever done that.'

'Na Zha did.'

His expression cleared. 'Yes, ma'am, yes, he did, I remember that very well. He went in and took his parents out of Hell. So yes, it theoretically could be done.'

Nigel appeared next to me, and sagged when he saw the demon. 'Not *another* one, Emma.'

''Fraid so, Nigel,' I said. 'Have the seals reset as well, please. Three of them broke in without Lok even knowing.'

'Lok's over at the New Folly with the girls we rescued today,' Nigel said.

He held his hand out to the demon. 'Take my hand.'

The demon didn't move.

'Good,' I said. 'Take Nigel's hand.'

The demon raised his hand, hesitated for a second, then strode to Nigel and took his hand. His eyes widened.

'Done,' Nigel said. 'Where do you want to put it?'

'Wait,' I said. 'What number are you?'

'Four Seven Three,' the demon said, its voice weak with awe.

'Okay, Four Seventy-Three,' I said. 'How the hell did you get in here? Our seals are the best.'

'I have no idea,' the demon said, as if in a dream. 'We were just told to come to the top floor of this office building and find a woman named Emma. We were told we would be able to come in, and we did.'

'Someone on the inside?' Nigel said, still holding the demon's hand and studying it appraisingly.

'No, of course not,' I said. 'The Masters are completely loyal, and all the students are examined before entering. We need to recheck those prostitutes' natures — one of them might be the cause of the problem — but the seals are failing all the time. Stone.'

'Yes, Emma?'

'Get together with Yi Hao tomorrow and arrange a meeting about this. Something needs to be done now about the failure of the seals; we can't let it go any more.'

'By your leave, my Lady,' Nigel said. 'I'll take this one down and put it away.'

'One more question before you take it.' I nodded to the demon. 'As far as you know, is your father planning anything against us?'

'No,' the demon said.

He answered very quickly. Interesting. He didn't need to think about it at all.

'Very well, dismissed,' I said. 'Thanks, Nigel. I'm going to have dinner with Simone.'

'And about time too, Emma, it's past seven o'clock,' Nigel said. 'Stop working so hard.' He and the demon disappeared.

I grabbed my bag out of my office, returned to the lift lobby, turned off the lights, and pressed the button to call the lift.

'You should have called for backup, Emma,' the stone said. 'If you'd destroyed those three and absorbed their essence you would have been converted completely to a Snake Mother.'

'Don't worry, I had no intention of destroying them,' I said.

'Just be careful, dear,' the stone said.

The lift came and I stepped in and pressed the button

for the ground floor. 'Reminders,' I said to the stone. 'Have the seals reset on Hennessy Road *again*, have those girls rechecked, and call George about sending his kids here for punishment. What do I have on tomorrow? I might get something from the Secretary about Leo; I want to be free if it happens.'

'Energy novices at ten and three,' the stone said. 'Gold wants to talk to you about the school for dragons — I've scheduled him for four.'

'Lunch?' I said.

'Free. Any particular time you want to schedule the meeting about the seals?'

'No, whenever.'

Its voice softened. 'Don't go in after Leo, Emma, you'll get yourself killed. Or the King will find a way to hold you. Or, even worse, convert you. Don't do it.'

'Leo's been in there for eight years and there's still no sign of him relenting,' I said. 'If I can talk to him, he might agree to come out.'

'You shouldn't even be talking to the King, Emma,' the stone said. 'That bastard wants you and you know it.'

'He's a creature of honour,' I said. 'He won't do anything underhand. If he does try me, he'll do it right upfront. I can handle him.'

'When the Dark Lord finds out he'll have kittens.'

'Turtles or snakes. Not kittens,' I said with grim humour. 'Bai Hu's the one who'll have kittens.'

I walked out of the lift onto the ground floor of the Academy building. The coffee shop occupying one of the shopfronts was still ablaze and the owner gave me a friendly wave from behind the counter. He was a Shen in some trouble with demons and was under the protection of New Wudang. He made a modest living out of the café, which also provided the Academy with cover. I waved back and then walked down the steps into busy Wan Chai street. The pavement was packed with pedestrians hurrying home, and Hennessy Road was bumper to bumper with buses at a standstill in the usual evening rush-hour gridlock.

Are you far away, Emma? Simone said into my ear. *I have a table already.*

As I pulled out my mobile phone to call her, it rang. I pressed the button to answer. 'I'm on my way now, I'll be there in about five minutes. Order me a coconut, will you?'

'That's wonderful,' said the Demon King on the other end of the line. 'I'm so looking forward to it. I own a strip club just around the corner from your Academy and they serve fabulous coconuts. Do you want the address? If you come I'll tell the staff not to put poppy in the coconut, just for you.'

I sighed with exasperation. 'Stop sending your kids over, George. They're making my life miserable.'

'Oh, that's too bad,' he said without a hint of remorse. 'If you come pay me a visit, they'll stop, you know. I won't hurt you, I promise. I just want to buy you a cup of coffee and have a chat.'

'I'm afraid I don't have anything to say to you, Wong Mo.'

'Oh, I'm cut. My title and everything.'

'Loathsome Majesty.'

He chuckled. 'Now you're just rubbing it in, Dark Lady. But I'm serious — come and chat, and the kids will stop. I want to talk to you about Leo.'

I nearly walked into a light pole. 'Leo? Why didn't you say so?' I hesitated, then, 'Can you get him out?'

'He doesn't want to go, Emma,' he said. 'He wants to kill himself. He doesn't understand that's not the way it works. Please, come down and talk to him; we're thoroughly sick of him.'

'I need permission from the Jade Emperor,' I said.

'I've been petitioning him for years, working my way up through the Celestial bureaucracy. I've made it as far as the Secretary for the Underworld. As soon as I have sanction, I'll be straight down there.'

He sounded like a little boy who'd just been granted his fondest wish. 'You'll really come down for Leo?'

'Of course I will.'

'You should have told me, Emma. I'm on good terms with Yanluo Wang, I could have speeded up the process for you. I'll help you any way I can, and I mean it,' he said. 'Okay, the kids will stop. No need now.'

Simone put the scroll down beside her plate and sat back. 'So this means there's only one more step before we can get permission from the Jade Emperor?' she said excitedly.

'Yes,' I said. 'If we're lucky we won't even need to bother the Jade Emperor. This Secretary guy can give us sanction to talk to Leo.'

'I hope that ugly dragon kid isn't hanging around when we talk to them. I heard he crawls to all the most senior Celestials trying to win favour.'

'Geez, that won't work up there,' I said. 'He should know better.'

'Oh, it works for some of the Celestials that are promoted rather than Raised. I heard if you find yourself a good patron up there you can go a long way.'

I sighed and rested my chin on my hand. 'I hate politics.'

She snorted with amusement. 'You need to resign then. You're right in the middle of it, Madam Emma.' She waved her hand. 'Let's not talk about that stuff anyway. When we have Leo back, I don't want anything to do with any Celestials. I've had enough of them, particularly that blue guy.'

'What about Daddy?'

31

'Daddy's different. He's the most *normal* Celestial there is.'

'*Normal*,' I said, pulling out my wallet to pay, 'is not a word often used to describe your father. Very much the opposite, in fact.'

'Same goes for you, Emma.'

'Humph.'

Simone held a CD in front of my face. 'How about this one?'

I pushed it away from my face so that I could see it. 'Boy bands *again*?'

'Hey, these guys are cute.' Then Simone dropped her voice and nodded towards another stand of CDs. 'Have a look over there. In the metal section. Oh my God, that is so *sad*. Chinese can't do Goth, and when they're as old as him ...' She inhaled sharply. 'No.'

I spun to see. It was him. Long hair, black clothes — of *course* he looked like a Goth, he'd *invented* it.

He casually flipped through the disks. Simone and I stood and watched him. It was Simone who snapped out of it first.

'Daddy!'

She raced along the aisles and skidded to a halt about two metres from him. He didn't seem to notice her.

'Daddy?'

He was completely oblivious.

She took a hesitant step towards him and held her hand out. 'Daddy?' She dropped her voice. 'Xuan Wu.'

I strode over and stood behind Simone. He still didn't appear to notice us. 'John. John Chen Wu, will you *look* at us?' I said.

Simone stepped forward and touched his sleeve. Her hand went straight through. She waved her hand through his arm, up and down. He wasn't there at all.

'But he's moving the disks,' she said.

'Look closely, Simone. The disks he's touching aren't moving. It's an echo of who he was.'

'Can he do that?'

'I don't think there's much he can't do.'

Simone sighed and stepped back. 'Is he really that *old*? I don't remember him that old.'

'That's how he was.'

'I thought he was a Goth.' She turned away and slammed her palm on one of the racks. 'I thought he looked *stupid*.'

'You can tell him one day, sweetheart, he'll have a good laugh about it.'

Then I inhaled sharply, and she turned back. He'd selected a couple of disks and turned to purchase them. And saw us.

He looked me right in the eyes, then saw Simone. He smiled sadly.

She held her hand out to him, and he held his out, palm-up, to hers. They rested their hands on each other without really touching.

Nobody around us seemed to be aware of his existence. He dropped his hand and turned to me. He raised his hand again as if to touch my face, then lowered it. He put his hand over his heart, then held it out to me, still smiling sadly.

'Oh God,' Simone whispered.

'He's fading,' I told her. 'Have a last look.'

Tears running down her face, she watched him disappear.

I reached into my bag, pulled out a packet of tissues and handed it to her. She took a couple and handed it back. I took a tissue out as well and we both wiped our eyes.

'I don't feel like buying anything, Emma,' Simone said, her voice hoarse. 'Can we just go home?'

'Sure,' I said, my voice similarly strained. I heaved a huge sigh. 'Let's go.'

She nodded, holding the tissue against her face. 'I want both of them back, Emma. Daddy. And Leo. I miss them so much.'

'So do I, sweetheart.'

'He knew who we were. I wonder how long ago that was. When it happened for him.'

'We can ask him when he comes back.'

CHAPTER 4

Back at home, Simone shut herself in her room, still upset. I went into John's office and sat behind the desk. I sighed, then proceeded to check the email; always a bad idea in the evening. There would be a large number of administrative matters that needed urgent attention and I'd be restless thinking about them until I could deal with them the next morning.

One student's mother was ill and he wanted to return to Cambodia to see her; unfortunately there was a very good chance he wouldn't be let out of the country again to return to us. We'd have to arrange a Celestial to go with him to ensure that he could be brought back. Another student was having major difficulties with his roommate's lifestyle — too much late night music and mayhem when he was trying to study. I forwarded the email to Lok, the building manager, with a note telling him to let the senior involved know that I really didn't have time to handle this sort of thing. Lok would understand.

Yes, I understand, Lok said into my head. *But you still owe me a fresh cow's heart. I have a shocking craving right now.*

'Tell him next time I go through the markets,' I said.

'And I told him to take some vitamins if he's having cravings,' the stone said.

My food contains all the nutrients I need for a healthy and active lifestyle, Lok said. *Says so right on the pack. Shame it tastes nothing like fresh, warm, bleeding flesh. So remember next time you're in the markets! Stone, remind her! Fresh cow's heart!*

'Okay, okay,' I said. 'I will. Oh, what about the girls? Anything show up when we rechecked them?'

No, Lok said. *They are all perfectly normal humans and their presence has had no effect on the seals here in the New Folly. Must be something else that's weakening the seals at the Academy. A couple of Masters are looking into it.*

'Thanks, Lok.'

Fresh cow's heart! And if you happen to see a cow's or pig's head in a basket at one of the butcher's stalls …

'Don't push your luck.'

Lok didn't reply.

I skimmed through the rest of the emails. Problems with the Northern Heavens; the Generals were trying valiantly to keep things running, but without the Xuan Wu to provide the Centre of Power and energy source, the place was falling to pieces. All the vegetation was dying. Residents were moving out, losing us much-needed tax revenue.

I stopped dead and gasped at an email in the midst of the administrative messages.

To: Lady Emma Donahoe, Regent of the Northern Heavens (Probationary), Acting Grand Master, New Wudang Martial Arts Academy <Emmad@newwudang.com.hk>

From: Secretary for Underworld Affairs
You have been granted an audience with the Jade

Emperor two days hence, on 16th November at 11 am Hong Kong time to present your case regarding Leo Alexander.

Ensure that your attire and that of your Retainers is suitable and that you present yourself at least one hour before the audience to ensure correct protocols are observed.

It is suggested by this office that a Mortal such as yourself might consider enlisting the help of a senior Immortal well-versed in Celestial protocol before attending.

Signed and chopped.

'Only two days, Emma? You have a lot of organising to do,' the stone said, then its voice trailed off. 'Oh my.'

'Where's Gold?'

'With Amy.' Its voice softened. 'They're both in True Form and she's carrying him over the mountains of Guilin. They've perched on top of the highest peak. The view must be spectacular.' Its tone changed to one of amusement. 'He just told me to mind my own damn business. I'll tell him how important this is and to get back here.'

'Leave them to it,' I said. 'Where's Jade?'

'At home watching television.'

'Relay the following message for me, stone. Jade, I've just received an appointment to see the Jade Emperor —'

Jade appeared in front of me. 'How long do you have to prepare?'

'How long I have to prepare is beside the point, Jade, because the minute I enter the Celestial Plane I'm dead.'

She opened and closed her mouth a few times, then fell to sit in the visitor's chair across from me, stricken. 'What are we going to do?'

'If I disobey an edict from the Emperor I'm as good as dead anyway. I'll lose the Academy, and maybe even Simone.' I ran my hands through my hair. 'Any ideas?'

'Ask them to see one of your Retainers instead, Emma,' the stone said. 'Jade and Gold can do the job.'

Jade was horrified. 'I'd prefer not to attract the attention of the Celestial, stone. Gold and I are in enough trouble as it is.' She shook her hands in salute over the desk. 'My Lady, I beg you, don't make me go to Heaven in your place.'

'Tell Gold it's urgent,' I said.

'Already did, he's on his way back,' the stone said.

The front doorbell rang.

Jade hesitated, concentrating, then her face went blank with shock. 'Quickly, ma'am,' she said. 'It's the Planet.'

'Oh shit,' I said, and raced around the desk and flew down the hallway to the front door, Jade behind me.

Monica had already opened the door. The Planet Venus, the Jade Emperor's personal emissary, was standing on the other side in full Celestial regalia. Monica stared at him, mouth open.

I touched her shoulder. 'It's okay, Monica, I can handle it.'

She snapped out of it and scurried into the kitchen.

I'm staying in here, Simone said from her room. *I'm not coming out to talk to him unless he orders me.*

I opened the door wide and gestured for Venus to enter. He nodded graciously to me and glided through, floating just above the floor.

Jade fell to one knee before him, saluting, then moved to stand to one side as Retainer. I cursed my torn T-shirt, tatty jeans and bare feet as I saluted him.

Venus drifted to the centre of the room and turned to face Imperial South, which gave him a view out of the windows overlooking Aberdeen. I quickly moved so that I could be seen by him. He wore a Tang-style robe of many layers of transparent white silk over an under robe of palest lilac. A similarly purple cloth crown covered the topknot on his head, and his long black hair swept down to his waist. He glowed gently with ripples of silvery light.

He nodded to me. 'Lady Emma. I bring greetings from the Celestial. The Jade Emperor has asked me to convey this to you.' He held a red lacquer box out to me.

I nodded and moved forward to accept it.

'There is a note inside from the Celestial himself explaining the nature of this item he is lending to you,' Venus said. 'He asks that you guard it with your life and that of your Retainers. In the wrong hands, this jewel could cause a great deal of trouble for both the Celestial and the Earthly Planes.'

'We will guard it with our lives,' I said, holding the box with awe. It was about twenty centimetres a side and intricately carved with a cloud pattern, a dragon on the right and a phoenix on the left.

Venus changed form to an ordinary slim Chinese man with long hair wearing a smart grey designer suit. He drifted down to the floor, his glow disappearing. He held out his hand. 'Lady Emma.'

I shook his hand. 'Venus.'

He nodded. 'Good to see you again, ma'am. Lunch sometime soon? It's been a while. Maybe in the Landmark?' He quirked one eyebrow at me. 'You can take the opportunity while you're in Central to go shopping for some new clothes and some slippers for wearing around the house like a civilised person.'

Jade snorted with laughter at the side of the room and bent double with silent hilarity, her hand over her mouth.

Venus bowed slightly to her. 'Princess.' He turned back to me. 'Don't be a stranger, Emma. We haven't met for lunch in ages. Can my people contact your people and arrange something?'

'Sure thing, just call my secretary,' I said.

He bowed slightly again. 'See you in Heaven.' He disappeared.

I stormed past Jade to take the box into the office, and thumped her arm as I passed her.

She gasped with laughter. 'He's right, you know, ma'am.'

I pressed my thumb against the seal to open the box. A scroll and a small rosewood jewellery box were the only things inside. I took the scroll, undid the ribbon and opened it. It was written in English, in vermillion ink, in the Jade Emperor's distinctive flowing hand.

> *Wear this while you are on the Celestial Plane and you will be unharmed. Make sure you remind me to ask you to give it back though; it's one of my Symbols of Office. See you in a couple of days.*

I removed the tiny box and flipped it open. Inside was a gold ring set with a large oval piece of jade. I took the ring and studied it, wondered if the stone was sentient and, if so, whether I should say hello.

The stone in my ring solved the problem for me. 'Not sentient, just a nice piece of jade.'

Jade came into the office and gasped. 'The Emperor's Imperial Ring. I've never seen it outside the Celestial Plane.'

I slipped it on the ring finger of my right hand. 'It'll stop me from being killed when I enter the Plane,' I told her, 'but I have to give it back. Tell Gold to go back to Amy, we're fine.' Then I sighed with resignation. 'The Jade Emperor knows.'

'Of course he does; he knows all,' Jade said. 'Now, you only have two days to prepare. We'll need to have something made for you right away, ma'am. Can you cancel your appointments and meet me at Mr Li's tomorrow?'

'I'm free after energy class at ten. I'll meet you in Central?'

Jade bowed slightly. 'Ma'am. We will also need to spend the afternoon revising Imperial protocol, if you want this petition to succeed.'

'Damn, Jade, how much do I need to know? All I do is go in, bow to his JEness, and talk to him about Leo.'

Jade smiled slightly. 'I think probably a great deal. We can spend the afternoon going through the protocol. If he meets with you in his rooms, you will need to know specific details.'

'Basic things, like the fact that any seat that the Emperor sits on becomes his throne and no other person may sit on it,' the stone said.

Jade nodded. 'I'll need to write a list of things to remember. By your leave, ma'am, I'll return home and begin.'

'It's after work hours, Jade. No need until tomorrow.'

'It will take me several hours to gather the information, ma'am.'

'Don't work too hard, Jade.'

She disappeared.

I sighed. 'I didn't even ask her how her kids are.'

'They are dragons,' the stone said. 'They are young, troublesome and hungry all the time.'

'Sounds like all kids.'

'You are quite correct. Now go do something else for a while, Emma. Enough worrying about this. You will be fine. And you will finally be able to extricate Leo from this little mess he has put himself into.'

I rose to go into the training room. 'Yes, Mother.'

* * *

I was halfway through a demon-essence kata with the Murasame when the Tiger appeared next to the mirrors, leaning casually on the wall.

'How the hell did you get in?' I said without stopping.

'Your goddamn seals are fading again,' the Tiger said. 'Get a different Master to do it, baby. Whoever is doing it right now sucks.'

I swung the sword in a wide arc, leaving a black feathery trail behind it. 'We have our best Master on it. He doesn't know what's going on either. It's the same at the Academy.' I stopped and lowered the sword. 'Want to send one of your guys over to have a look?'

'Done. I heard you got your audience, and about time too.'

'Yep, day after tomorrow, 11 am our time.'

'You can't go up there though. I've tried to shield you before and it doesn't work. We'll have to arrange for someone to go instead of you.'

'The Jade Emperor sent me a ring that will stop me from being harmed, but I have to give it back when we're done.'

'Good idea.' He grinned broadly, making his tawny eyes sparkle. 'Want a lift?'

'Only if you promise to behave.'

'Never.' He levered himself off the wall. 'Make yourself pretty, Emma. If you blow this, you'll lose the Regency and some Celestial asshole will take over your Academy and your Heavens.'

'Can you hide my demon nature from the public eye?'

'I'll do my best. The Celestial One will know everything, but hopefully the crowd who gather to see you won't see it.'

'Crowd?'

'Yep, this'll be the biggest thing to happen in Heaven in a long time. They'll all want a look at the mortal white chick who's running the Northern Heavens.'

'Very badly.'

'Nah.' He leaned against the wall again and crossed his arms. 'You're not responsible for the energy failure. Ah Wu should have set up some sort of backup plan.'

'We never really had much of a chance to make it work, Tiger.'

'Yeah, I know.' He dropped his head. 'See you day after tomorrow. Meet me underneath the China Resources Building in Wan Chai at about 9 am. That's where the Gateway to Heaven is.'

'The *China Resources Building*? That big office tower in Wan Chai?'

'Yep, ground floor, where there's a replica of the Nine-Dragon Wall. That's the Gateway. Good central location. See you there.' He disappeared.

I changed to an ordinary chi kata. If my demon nature became public knowledge during this visit to Heaven, everything I loved could be taken away from me. The Jade Emperor knew about it and had helped me; but if everybody in Heaven found out, there could only be trouble.

CHAPTER 5

Evening was falling and the sky behind the beach was a flame of sunset colours. Over the ocean the sky was darker, and Venus already shone. The waves crashed and the warm breeze ruffled my hair as I walked on the soft sand, thinking.

I looked up and froze. A dark shape, alone on the beach. Hair lifted by the wind. Watching the waves.

It was him.

I didn't run. I continued to walk towards him, and saw him clearly as I neared. He watched the ocean with longing.

When I was close enough he turned to me and smiled slightly, his noble features serene. His hair wasn't tied back and it flew around him in the breeze. He wore his plain black pants and jacket, and his feet were bare.

I approached him carefully and stopped next to him. He smiled down at me. He reached out and ran his fingertips over my face, and I closed my eyes. His hand came around the back of my neck and pulled me closer and his lips met mine. I delicately held him, unwilling to grip him too hard because he might disappear. The wind changed and his hair wrapped around us, clinging to both of us.

He pulled back and gazed into my eyes. 'Who are you?'

'I'm your Serpent,' I whispered.

'No, you aren't.' He turned to the ocean and gestured. 'My Serpent is out there.'

I turned to see, his hand still behind my neck. The Serpent raised its head in the water out past the breakers. It was enormous; it must have been more than twenty metres long, a black shadow against the darkening sky.

He smiled down at me again. 'I think I know you.'

'Emma.'

He tasted the name. 'Emma.'

'Xuan Wu,' I said. 'John.'

Something changed in his eyes. 'Hello, Emma.'

I ran my fingers over his face. I floated my fingertips along his throat, revelling in the silken skin. 'Hello, John.'

'How long have I been gone?'

'Eight years.'

'You haven't changed at all.'

'Are you ready to return, John?'

He looked out at the surf. 'My Serpent is there.'

'You haven't rejoined,' I said. 'You're still in two pieces.'

He sagged so slightly it was almost undetectable. 'It hurts.'

'I know it hurts, love. Go to it.'

He glanced down at me. 'But then I would leave you alone. You and ...' His face went strange.

'Simone,' I said.

He jerked as if he had been hit, grimacing with pain. He spun and ran to the surf. When he reached the water he changed into the Turtle and pulled himself into the waves.

I watched him go without moving.

Then I woke up.

I shook my hands with frustration as I tried to push them into the voluminous sleeves of the Tang-style robe. Mr Li had made it out of black silk with gold chrysanthemums, which somehow seemed to have become my signature fabric. The sleeves were wider than they were long, probably about a metre wide, and designed to hide a noblewoman's hands as she never needed to use them; servants should do everything for her. Maybe I should have let Jade come into the changing room with me to help after all. I finally found the openings, then quietly cursed as I drew the belt around the robe.

Gold's child appeared at eye level next to the mirror. 'Aunty Jade says hurry up.'

'You should not be in here,' I said. 'This is a changing room.'

The stone grew two long appendages and pretended to cover its nonexistent eyes. 'Can't see anything, Lady Emma.'

'I'm done,' I said, and raised my arms to the sides. Now that I had the robe on, the sleeves added to the volume of the kimono-style dress, making it elegant and flowing. Unfortunately the style didn't suit me at all and I looked ridiculous. My more generous Western shape made me appear fat and my breasts made the front opening bulge out. I looked awful.

I sighed and walked out of the change room. Jade and her three children were waiting for me next to the cushioned seats. The children were in dragon form, chasing each other around the waiting area, but Jade was in human form and wearing a robe similar to mine with willowy elegance.

I raised my arms. 'I look completely ridiculous.' I could see from Jade's and Mr Li's faces that they agreed with me.

Jade grimaced delicately. 'Perhaps a different colour?'

Simone came out of her change room. She wore a robe of dark shining indigo silk with twining golden flowers over a gold under robe and closed with a wide elaborately embroidered gold belt. The gold brought out the hues of her tawny hair. Wide silk ribbons of a brighter shade of blue, embroidered with golden chrysanthemums, decorated the neckline either side of her throat and fell as panels down the front of the robe; similar ribbons edged the enormously full sleeves.

She looked spectacular. She sighed when she saw me. 'Oh dear, Emma.'

Mr Li raised one hand and my robe changed to the same dark blue as Simone's. Jade winced. The robe changed to red and Simone said, 'Ick.'

The robe rotated through a variety of colours and patterns.

'Doesn't work,' Jade said with resignation.

'Well, that's the last acceptable style,' Mr Li said. 'We have to choose one of them. I think the Qing may have worked slightly better than this but it still made her look fat. She is approaching middle age now, and even though she is fit her figure reflects this. Her breasts are too large —'

I snorted with derision and opened my mouth to say something about late thirties not being middle-aged, but he continued unfazed.

'Nothing seems to suit her and I don't have time to adapt a style for her. We should have tried this earlier, I would never have expected this problem.'

I turned away. 'Forget it then. I'm wearing my jeans and a shirt and the Jade Emperor can deal with it. Or better yet,' I turned back and grinned at them, 'I'll wear my armour and carry my sword and let him deal with *that*.'

Jade and Mr Li both lit up.

'Can she do that?' Simone said quickly.

'Even more appropriate,' Jade said. 'Much more suitable than a Tang robe. Lady Emma is a warrior.'

Mr Li eyed the bolts of silk on the wall appraisingly. 'Take that one off. We'll make a lighter under robe for the armour. It'll still need to be Tang style, but I think we can get away …' He wandered off, talking to himself.

'Brilliant, Emma, you'll look magnificent,' Simone said.

'I'll put your hair up in a simple spike, same as the Dark Lord would wear into battle,' Jade said. 'Not —'

'Tortoiseshell,' I finished for her.

'No, ebony, I think,' she said, and we shared a smile. 'When the Dark Lord returns, you two will be a matched set. Dark Lord and Dark Lady, both warriors together.'

I felt a shot of pain and sighed.

'Don't worry, Emma, he'll come back,' Simone said.

'Any sign of him?' I asked.

She unfocused, snapped back and shook her head.

'I'll fetch your armour, ma'am,' Jade said, then called to the baby dragons, 'You kids behave.' She nodded to me. 'Be right back.' She disappeared.

Simone and I sat on the cushioned benches and waited for them to return.

'He visited me in a dream last night,' I said.

Simone sighed and put her chin on her hand without replying.

'What's the matter, Simone?' I said. 'You've been quiet ever since we found out we were going to see the Jade Emperor.'

Simone didn't move or look at me, her chin still in her hand. Her eyes turned inward, remembering. 'When I was very little, Daddy took me and Mummy to Heaven. He thought I'd enjoy seeing him at "work". Mummy stayed in our apartment in the Palace, she hated it. Daddy changed ...' She ran her hand over her face. 'Daddy changed into his Celestial Form, and picked me up and carried me to the Grand Audience Hall. You have no idea what it was like, Emma.' She turned to gaze into my eyes. 'You've seen it, you know how big his Celestial Form is. He carried me so far from the ground, and I didn't know him as Daddy. He was so *huge*! And black, and he didn't look like Daddy, he was just a giant carrying me so high up that I was afraid, and he walked with these huge strides — it was incredibly scary. I cried, and he did something to me to make me quiet, but I was still ...' She took a deep breath. 'I was still terrified. Then he took me into the Grand Audience Hall and it was full of dragons and other Shen — animals and nature spirits, all sorts were there to see me, staring at me — and then we went up to the Jade Emperor, and he was in Celestial Form too, and Daddy handed me over to him.' She smiled wryly. 'Apparently, the Jade Emperor thought I was adorable. I was bound by Daddy, so I couldn't move or speak, or cry. I just looked at the Jade Emperor as he held me. He was bigger than Daddy and way scarier.' She shook her head. 'It took me a long time to get over that. Even now, I think if I saw Daddy's Celestial Form, I wouldn't see it as him, just as this monster that bound me and carried me away.'

'I wondered about that,' I said. 'I remember how scared you were of his Celestial Form.'

'When he took me back to the apartment, he unbound me and I let loose,' Simone said. 'In seven different directions — I wet myself, threw up, everything. I was only about a year and a half old. I can remember Mummy screaming abuse at him. He changed back and tried to console me, but apparently, I would have nothing to do with him for a few weeks afterwards.'

'I can understand completely,' I said. 'If it was me, I would have sent him down to Hell for a few days to "meditate upon his faults". What a rotten thing to do to a little child.'

Simone made a soft sound of amusement. 'Mummy did. Shot him right between the eyes, from what I've heard.'

'You are the equal of any Shen in Heaven, Simone. You don't need to be scared.'

'I just can't help feeling that way right now. I'll be fine once we get there and I can see the Jade Emperor's not a hundred metres tall.'

'Would you like to talk to the Lady about it before we go?'

She waved me down. 'I'll be *fine*. Oh, Jade's on her way back with your armour.'

Jade reappeared and held the armour out for me. 'Ma'am.'

I rose to take it.

On the morning of 16 November, Marcus dropped me and Simone outside Harbour Centre in Wan Chai. Harbour Centre and Great Eagle Centre were two matched towers, that stood side by side right on the waterfront. They each had large neon signs for Japanese electronics companies on the first-floor level and featured in many Hong Kong postcards.

Simone and I took the escalators up to the first floor to use the walkways across to the China Resources Building, then walked along the covered open-air podium that overlooked the water. The adjacent building, the Convention Centre, jutted into the harbour, its flowing finlike shape making it look like a giant sea creature. I remembered another time I had stood watching the water and felt a twinge of pain. But we had seen him. He was searching for me. He would return.

We crossed the walkways, passed a small traditional Chinese garden, and took the escalators down to the open area under the China Resources Building. Two bronze Chinese unicorn statues, qilin, faced the road, and behind them stood a fountain of dragon heads squirting water. Behind the fountain was a replica of the Nine-Dragon Wall in the Forbidden City in Beijing.

Bai Hu stepped out from under one of the supporting pillars. 'You have all your gear?'

I raised the shopping bags I was holding. 'All here.'

'What about your armour, Emma?'

'It's folded up in there as well.'

'Good. Where's Gold? I thought he was coming.'

'He said he's in enough trouble as it is and begged me to leave him at home. Same with Jade.'

'That's true. It's probably a good idea to leave them at home. Gold particularly has been in trouble with the Celestial many times before.' Bai Hu gestured with his head. 'This way.'

We followed the Tiger to the wall. Nobody around seemed to notice us. As we neared the wall, the white stone balustrade in front of it slid smoothly into the ground. The wall grew from two metres to nearly four metres tall, and the nine dragons on it came to life. They writhed across the wall and gathered at the middle.

The gold dragon in the centre stuck its head out and waved its enormous fangs menacingly close to my head. 'Is this the mortal that wishes to enter the Celestial Domain?'

Let me handle them, the Tiger said into my head.

'No need,' I said. I unrolled the scroll and held it in front of the dragon's face, making it jerk its head back slightly. 'The Jade Emperor wants to see us.'

'It is highly unusual for a human to be granted an audience with the Celestial One,' the dragon huffed.

'You are accompanied by no Retainers. How are we to know that you are worthy of such an honour?'

'Cut the bullshit and let us up,' the Tiger growled. 'If I knew you were gonna give us this crap, I would have summoned a cloud.'

The dragon glared at the Tiger with disdain. 'Perhaps that would have been preferable. Then our services would not be used by a *mortal*.' It spat the word.

The Tiger grunted and took a couple of steps forward, but I raised my hand to stop him.

'In this situation the mortal usually flatters the dragon's enormous ego until the dragon is mollified and lets the mortal through,' I said. I pulled the Murasame, still in its scabbard, from my shopping bag and waved its point in front of the dragon's nose. 'I don't crawl to anybody though, so I might try the alternative tactic of whacking you with my little sword here until you let me up. Would that work?'

A white dragon on our right sniggered and the gold dragon glared at it. Then it turned back to me and watched me appraisingly.

'If you're thinking that she doesn't have the nerve, then I can assure you she does,' the Tiger growled. 'She's even taken my head off a couple of times when she got pissed with me. She seems to like killing Celestials.'

The dragon lowered its head to look me in the eyes. 'You have taken the White Tiger's head?'

A couple more dragons stuck their heads out of the wall to look at me.

'He can be a complete dick sometimes,' I said with a shrug.

The dragon hesitated, then threw its head back and roared with laughter. The other dragons joined it in a chorus of loud, high-pitched hissing.

'Welcome, Lady Emma,' the gold dragon said when

it had regained its breath. 'Please, walk on the clouds to a destination that you richly deserve.'

The wall separated in the middle and a stairway of mist appeared in the gap.

'Welcome to Heaven, Lady Emma,' the gold dragon said. 'Anyone who takes the Tiger's head when he's being an asshole can come on through any time.'

'That would mean the Tiger never having a head at all,' a purple dragon said, choking with laughter.

The dragons collapsed into hysterics again, twining around each other with mirth.

I stepped forward into the gap in the wall and put a hesitant foot onto the misty stair. It appeared to be made of thick swirling fog but was also transparent. I relaxed when I realised that it was solid. I put the sword back in my shopping bag and began to climb.

As the Tiger came through behind me, the dragons' heads followed him, still laughing.

'A woman has finally tamed the pussycat, and she is not even his,' one of them said.

The Tiger grunted. 'Let's just get out of here,' he said.

'A collar and bell for the pussy!' another dragon called as we proceeded up the stairs.

At the top was an enormous gate, at least five storeys high, with massive red doors embellished with huge black metal reinforcing studs. A red wall stretched away on either side of the gate, disappearing into the clouds and seeming to go on forever.

Kwan Yin stood at the gate waiting for us. She was in human form, but appeared ageless and wore flowing white robes that floated around her. She smiled at us, and Simone ran to her and took her hand in greeting.

I glanced behind us. The path we stood on also disappeared into the clouds. We appeared to be floating in Heaven.

'Is there anything down there?' I asked.

'Actually, no,' Bai Hu said. 'The Palace sits on a floating island of rock. The only way here is to ride a cloud or use a Nine-Dragon Wall.'

'Where would I go if I fell off?'

'Nobody knows, because nobody ever has.'

A small door at the bottom of the gates opened. It was only about a metre and a half tall and a metre wide and fitted so neatly into the corner of the gate that it was invisible when closed. Kwan Yin moved beside us and the four of us faced it.

An elderly man with long grey hair stepped through; the door was so small he had to stoop to fit. He wore a traditional black robe with an official's hat; a high, square style with long extensions either side.

'Don't step on the threshold, Emma,' Bai Hu said. 'The raised step at the bottom of the door. Careful.'

'I know,' I said. 'What about the seals? There's no way I can go through them without being destroyed.'

'This official is to bring them down for you.'

The official approached, stopped about two metres away, and carefully saluted each of us in order of precedence. 'Lady Kwan Yin. Lord Bai Hu, Lord of the West. Princess Simone. Lady Emma Donahoe, Promised of the Dark Lord of the Northern Heavens. Welcome.'

We all saluted back.

'Please, come this way. We are ready for you.'

As we neared the gate, the official stopped and concentrated. The seals on the bigger gates shimmered into visibility: sheets of paper at least ten metres high with complicated calligraphy and symbolic charms. The paper shredded and dissipated.

The official sighed. 'It took me nearly a year to create those seals when I put them on about a thousand years ago. We'll have to make do with something temporary while I construct some new ones.'

'Good Lord, I'm putting the Celestial Palace at risk?' I said, horrified.

The official smiled over his shoulder at me. 'No, ma'am. The seals don't really do anything, they're just there for show.'

'What is your honoured name, sir?' I asked.

'Just call me Mr Wong, Lady Emma.'

The massive gates opened inward smoothly and silently, revealing the Celestial Palace within.

The Palace was constructed of stone adorned with brilliant cobalt blue tiles. Traditional gold tiles covered the roofs with their upward-curving edges. At each corner of each roof was a glazed ceramic image of a man riding a chicken, with other animals lined up along the edge of the roof behind him and a dragon bringing up the rear.

The Palace was built up the side of a gently rising hill with a magnificent hall at the top, at least a kilometre away. A network of identical pavilions and walkways worked up towards it in perfect geometric arrangement, mirrored on each side. The gold-tiled roofs sparkled in the sunshine beneath the brilliantly azure sky. Green treetops jutted between the walls.

A huge grey stone-paved courtyard, at least two hundred metres to a side, lay between the gate and the base of the hill. Bonsai trees, each about a metre high, were scattered about the courtyard, some of them bearing large peaches, apricots and cumquats; flower pots containing massive chrysanthemums in brilliant colours also broke the monotony of the paving. Larger potted trees, some of them up to five metres tall, flanked the courtyard, also bearing peaches. A wide stream flowed across the courtyard, its surface level with the paving. It was spanned by three arched bridges, and small blue dragons swam within the crystalline water. Brilliant phoenixes with plumage of many colours wandered around the courtyard, like ornamental peacocks. The view resonated with me, then I realised it was similar to the courtyard at the front of the Forbidden City in Beijing.

The official led us into the courtyard. 'The first hall is the Hall of Welcome Contentment. There you will prepare to see the Celestial.'

He raised his head and spoke loudly and clearly, 'Hall of Welcome Contentment,' then took a step forward and disappeared.

'Do the same, Emma: just say the name of the hall and take a step forward,' Kwan Yin said.

'Hall of Welcome Contentment,' I said, stepped forward, and was instantly at the entrance to the hall. Mr Wong stood there waiting. Kwan Yin, Bai Hu and Simone appeared next to me.

'Way cool,' Simone whispered. 'I wish we had this at school. Those stairs are a killer.'

Mr Wong raised one arm. 'Please, enter.'

The hall had large red pillars and its ceiling was covered with elaborately decorated tiles. It was empty except for a pair of rosewood stands, as tall as a man, holding incense braziers.

Mr Wong gestured to the left. 'This way, everybody. There is a preparation room where you can ready yourselves.'

We walked to the end of the hall, where a simple doorway led to a set of apartments with modern furniture. Priceless silk rugs covered the polished hardwood floor. A comfortable set of tan leather couches sat to one side, and an oval rosewood dining table inlaid with mother-of-pearl to the other.

There were doors at each end of the room and another door, paned with glass, that opened to the courtyard beyond. Ming-style rosewood shelves displayed a collection of antique vases.

Bai Hu had a quick, whispered discussion with Mr Wong. The discussion became heated, although still whispered. Bai Hu raised his voice and glanced at me, then lowered it again. Mr Wong shut the discussion off and stormed out.

Bai Hu thundered over to us, his face raw with fury. 'I do not believe this!'

'They can't do this to her,' Simone said. 'It's *not fair*.'

'The Celestial does as he wills,' Kwan Yin said. 'It is traditional.'

'But it isn't her True Form,' Bai Hu hissed. 'They're doing this deliberately to shame her.'

'Oh my God,' I said, and they all looked at me. 'He's going to make me go in as a snake, isn't he?'

Ms Kwan's voice was full of compassion. 'Everybody takes True Form in front of the Jade Emperor. Nobody hides anything. But you were born human, Emma. I have already discussed this with the Celestial, and he agreed to see you as a human. He has just, in this last hour, changed his mind.'

I sighed with feeling. 'This could cost me everything. I hope he protects me when everybody goes after my head.'

'You have to take Celestial Form too, Simone,' Bai Hu said.

Simone's face closed up tight.

'You have a Celestial Form?' I said. 'Why didn't you tell me you could do it?'

'How the hell does he know about that?' Simone said.

'The Celestial knows all, Simone,' Kwan Yin said. 'It appears that Mr Li's time was wasted.'

'Why'd you keep it a secret, Simone?' I said.

'When you see it you'll know.'

'Is it that bad?'

She didn't reply. Her face was still closed up tight.

'Well, whatever,' Bai Hu said. 'Drop your stuff and we'll go on. Mr Wong says we have ten minutes to prepare, to change into the forms, and he'll take us up to the main chamber.'

'I'm still wearing my armour and carrying the sword,' I said. 'I'll change when I'm there.'

'That is unusual but permissible,' Kwan Yin said.

'Is Mr Wong the Jade Emperor, Bai Hu?' I asked. '"Wong" means "King" in Cantonese.'

'Of course he is. Isn't it obvious?'

The Murasame's scabbard had a strap that telescoped out from the top and clipped to the bottom so that I could carry it over my shoulder with it resting diagonally across my back. I hefted it on and returned to the living room.

Kwan Yin and Bai Hu were waiting there in True Form. Kwan Yin's white robes flowed around her, and a glowing aura surrounded her serene face. She stood more than two metres tall. Bai Hu's tiger form was about four metres long.

Simone hadn't taken Celestial Form; she wore the robes Mr Li had made for her, the same as I did. She saw my face. 'I'll do it when I'm there, same as you.'

'Is it reptilian?' I asked.

'No, the problem is entirely in the other direction.'

Mr Wong returned and we all saluted him again. While he was acting as this minor official, we were expected to treat him as such. Everybody had to pretend that we didn't know he was the Jade Emperor, and he pretended that he didn't know we knew. The duplicity made my head ache.

He led us back into the main part of the hall, then towards the centre of the Palace. We entered a courtyard with a single huge tree in its centre.

'Grand Audience Hall, Main Entrance,' Mr Wong said, and disappeared.

Bai Hu stepped forward. 'I'll go first.' He repeated the words and disappeared.

'JK Rowling did something like this in Harry Potter,' I said.

'Well, she can sue the Jade Emperor,' Simone said, recited the words and disappeared.

CHAPTER 6

The Grand Audience Hall was massive, about a hundred metres to a side and a good fifty metres high. Enormous doors glided open before us. A set of stairs led up to them separated down the middle by a sloping ramp of marble carved with dragons. Whenever the Jade Emperor went up he floated over the marble; everybody else had to take the stairs.

Mr Wong had vanished.

'Gone off to turn into the Jade Emperor and embarrass the hell out of us,' Simone growled. 'I *hate* that he's doing this to you, Emma.'

'How about we change once we're in his presence?' I said.

'That is not acceptable, Emma,' Kwan Yin said.

Simone and I shared a small smile.

'Good. Which stairs are we supposed to use?'

'The left ones.'

Simone and I shared another small smile and headed straight for the stairs on the right. The Tiger growled something unintelligible and loped after us. Kwan Yin just floated up the stairs.

A couple of guards appeared on either side of the huge door. Each of them wore a Tang-style red robe and carried a massive halberd, a spear with a broadsword blade on the end. Their True Forms were nearly three metres tall, and the red robes flowed around them. They had goatees, and glared fiercely at us. The one on the left's face was black; the one on the right, red.

'General Qin. General Wei,' I said. I raised one hand. 'Hi, guys, long time no see. How's the family, Ah Bao?'

'Hi, Emma,' said the left-hand door god, Qin Shu Bao. 'Everybody's good. My Number Five Son has just been engaged to one of the Dragon King's daughters, gorgeous purple dragon.' He tapped the bottom of his halberd on the grey stone paving. 'What business have you here?'

'We're here to see the Jade Emperor, mate,' I said. 'Let us in.'

'That is not the correct formal address, Emma, and you know it,' the Tiger said.

'Too bad.' I turned to General Qin. 'Open up.'

'In you go, pet,' General Qin said. 'Don't start too quickly — we want to come in and see the fireworks.'

'Oh, don't worry,' Simone said. 'There'll be plenty to see, I can assure you.'

'I have been looking forward to this for a very long time,' the other door god, General Wei, said. 'Don't tell the Jade Emperor to go to Hell, it's already been done.'

'Don't worry, we'll think of something suitably outrageous,' I said.

'Excellent,' General Qin said.

The Tiger stopped next to Simone and looked up at her; he was so big he didn't need to lift his head far. 'You sure you want to do this?'

'Oh, yes,' Simone said, and we stepped through the doors into the hall.

Massive red pillars intricately carved with phoenixes and dragons held up the roof, which towered above us. A smaller roof was set above some clerestory windows that allowed the brilliant Celestial sunshine to light up the interior of the hall. The throne at the end, with its gold silk cushions, must have been nearly ten metres wide, raised on a dais three metres above the floor.

The way to the throne was marked by a gold carpet on the grey stone, with ornamental lanterns on either side at intervals of about two metres. A large number of Celestials had gathered on either side of the aisle, all watching us.

Well then, let's give them a show, Simone said.

General Qin came in behind us to announce our presence. 'Holy Bodhisattva Kwan Yin. Lord Bai Hu, White Tiger of the West. Princess Simone, only human daughter of the Dark Lord of the Northern Heavens. Lady Emma Donahoe, Promised of the Dark Lord, Regent in His Absence.' He added silently, *Go get 'em, girls.*

'Don't encourage them,' Bai Hu whispered, a throaty rasp.

Simone and I walked towards the throne, the ranks of silent Celestials watching us from either side. Bai Hu and Kwan Yin followed us, also silent. We both tried to appear as casual and confident as possible, but Simone's breathing was as ragged as my own.

Large gold screens carved with five-toed dragons stood behind the throne, and a General guarded it on one side, but I could hardly see the Jade Emperor himself, it was such a long walk.

As we approached, he came into focus. Yep, our friendly lowly official, Mr Wong. Now he was resplendently decked out in a Tang-style wraparound robe of brilliantly gold Imperial silk embroidered with five-toed dragons, and wore an Imperial hat with a square brim and beads that hung in front of his eyes so nobody could see them.

The guard at the Jade Emperor's right hand was the

Second Heavenly General, Er Lang. He was in True Form: a massive three-metre-high young human wearing pale green and gold armour and a war helmet. He had three eyes; his third eye was open and appeared as a lashless eye in the centre of his forehead. He held a halberd as big as those of the door gods. A black dog stood at his side, watching with disdain as we approached.

We fell to our knees at the base of the dais and touched our foreheads to the floor. '*Wen sui, wen sui, wen wen sui*,' we said. I nearly grimaced; imagine wishing an Immortal ten thousand times ten thousand years of life.

We waited for the Jade Emperor to tell us to rise. He didn't.

We waited with our foreheads on the floor, not looking at him, but still he didn't say a word. All I needed: a power game.

'Rise,' the Jade Emperor finally said after an uncomfortable couple of minutes, and both Simone and I pulled ourselves to our feet.

'You are ordered to take True Form in the presence of the Jade Emperor,' Er Lang said loudly.

Neither Simone nor I said anything or moved.

'Take True Form!' Er Lang shouted.

'These are our True Forms,' I said.

'Simone —' Bai Hu began.

'Shut up, Bai Hu,' Simone said.

There was the very faintest rustle of movement through the hall. Nobody said a word, but they were restless and their slight movements made the silk of their robes hiss.

The Jade Emperor's face didn't shift from its expressionless mask. 'Lady Emma Donahoe.'

I saluted him, bowing slightly. 'Celestial Majesty.'

'You claim that the form I see here is your True Form?'

63

'That I do, Celestial Majesty.'

'Princess Simone,' the Emperor said.

Simone saluted. 'Celestial Majesty.'

'You too?'

She bowed slightly and saluted again. 'Celestial Majesty.'

The silk rustle in the hall became slightly louder, then faded again.

'Er Lang,' the Jade Emperor said.

'Lady Emma Donahoe is ordered to take True Form,' Er Lang said without looking at me.

'As the Celestial Majesty wishes,' I said, and didn't change. I just stood quietly at the base of the dais.

'This is not your True Form!' Er Lang shouted.

'This is the way I was born. This is the way I wish to be perceived. This is the true me,' I said. 'This is my True Form. Any other form I could take would not be me.'

The rustling became louder and a series of hushed whispers rippled through the hall then quickly settled to silence.

'Er Lang,' the Jade Emperor said again.

'Princess Simone, daughter of Xuan Tian Shang Di, is ordered to take Celestial Form,' Er Lang said.

Simone hesitated.

'Do it, dear,' the Jade Emperor said. 'You have a Celestial Form. You have been ordered. Do it.'

Simone made a short, clipped whimpering sound and changed. She gathered all of the darkness in the hall and wrapped it around her, completely hiding herself from view. The darkness grew and became more massive. A spreading, seeping cold emanated from her and the air around her filled with ice. The darkness exploded out from her in a silent eruption and dissipated. Her Celestial Form became visible.

The voices in the hall erupted to a roar, then quickly faded.

Her livery was deep blue, almost black, and shining gold. She was nearly four metres tall, and her golden-brown hair swept around her, so long it lay on the floor. Much of it floated in a breeze that wasn't there. Her skin shone translucent in the light; a delicate honey brown. Her enormous golden eyes glowed with wisdom far beyond her years. She appeared to be about twenty-five years old. Her deep blue robes flowed around her, decorated with a thousand tiny pinpoints of golden light, like stars. She was breathtakingly beautiful, more like a force of nature than a young woman.

'Can you call Seven Stars, Simone?' the Jade Emperor said.

Simone held out one slim arm and the sword appeared in her hand. The scabbard was black, the hilt was white, and the sword was nearly two metres long. It fitted her perfectly. She lowered her hand and held the sword in front of her. She truly appeared as a goddess with the sword in her hand and an expression of detached ferocity on her face.

'Good,' the Jade Emperor said. He rose from the throne and stood before us on the dais with his hands clasped behind his back. 'What is it you have come to see me about?'

I bowed slightly. 'Leo Alexander, Retainer of the Dark Lord, is held in Hell at your pleasure,' I said. 'We would like your permission, Celestial Majesty, to go and talk to him about accepting Immortality and returning to us.'

'Why should he do this for you when so many of my staff have been unable to convince him?'

'Because he loves us,' Simone said in a voice of sharpened honey.

He smiled slightly. 'Anything else?'

'I request the freedom of the Golden Boy, child of the Jade Building Block, and the Jade Girl, eighty-second daughter of the Dragon King.'

Simone glanced at me.

'And that's all?' the Emperor said.

'Yep,' I said. 'Uh, yes, Celestial Majesty.'

'Return to your normal form, Simone.'

Simone changed back and we shared a small sigh of relief.

'Meet me in the Imperial Private Offices in one hour, together with your sponsors. Concluded. Dismissed.' He returned to the throne.

We fell to our knees again. '*Wen sui, wen sui, wen wen sui.*'

'Supplicants are permitted to depart,' Er Lang said.

We backed away for about ten metres, then turned and walked out of the hall with every eye in the place boring into our backs. I could tell from the way Simone walked that she wanted to run out of there as much as I did.

'What in Heaven possessed you two to do something like that?' the Tiger shouted. He paced in front of us with his hands clasped behind his back.

Ms Kwan had also returned to human form. She sat at the dining table, as serene as ever. She waved one hand and summoned a pot of tea. 'Sit. Drink tea. All will be well, Ah Bai.'

The Tiger stopped and glared at her. 'Don't encourage them.' He turned his attention back to me. 'What if you'd been ordered to take demon form? What would you have done then?'

'Refused again.'

The Tiger paced once more. 'I'm glad you weren't ordered to then. Defying an order from the Celestial *once* is bad enough; twice would have got you executed. And *you*.' He rounded on Simone. 'You *should* have refused. Or at least taken something less impressive. God, Simone, what a stupid thing to do.'

'That *is* less impressive,' Simone said. 'That's the smallest one I can do. In the full version, I'm more than three metres tall, as big as Daddy's biggest Celestial Form. The robes appear like space; the gold stars really *are* stars. My eyes are even bigger and freaking *black*. And the yin hangs around my hair like some sort of freaking cloak, freezing the air wherever I go. It's *huge*.'

'Shit.' The Tiger began pacing again. 'You sure your mother was human? Every Immortal in Heaven is going to be after your hand, my girl. If I saw you like that, and I didn't love your father like a brother, I'd be after you in a second myself.' He shook his head. 'What a fucking disaster.'

Mr Wong tapped on the door and came in. He smiled like a kindly grandfather and we all glowered at him.

'Well done, ladies. But you should have taken the full version, Simone. Maybe later, eh? Come on up and have some nice tea with me, and we'll talk about it.'

Bai Hu stood threateningly over Mr Wong. 'Don't you dare let anybody grab this little girl, Ah Ting. She's just a child.'

'Calm down, Ah Bai, don't get your whiskers in a twist. I'll protect them, don't worry. I know what I'm doing.' He glanced at me, his eyes sparkling. 'Come on up to my apartment and we'll have a little chat.'

'It's about time someone reminded that bunch of stiff-arsed old farts exactly what it means to pursue the Tao,' the Jade Emperor said amiably. He poured the tea and we all tapped the table in thanks. 'See? You show respect in exactly the right amount required, at the time it is required, and not more. And when the order is a stupid one, you make your feelings clear. The most senior Celestials are aware of your serpent form, Emma. They were fully expecting you to take it, even though you made it clear that you regard your human form as your True Form.' He sighed with feeling. 'So many blindly follow orders purely to avoid taking responsibility for their actions. *Lazy*. Now.' He picked up his teacup, brushing his long sleeve out of the way. 'Leo Alexander. Stupid bastard. Entirely much more trouble than he is worth. I know why you did it, Lady, but he has still been a massive thorn in my side for many years.'

Kwan Yin nodded silently.

He sipped his tea. 'You certainly have my permission to try your best to pull Leo out. Go for it. If you can persuade him out of Hell, I'd be very happy indeed.'

'I wasn't expecting this to be so easy after all the bureaucracy we've had to go through,' I said.

The Emperor smiled slightly. 'We thought we would be able to fix this without the intervention of a mortal such as yourself. It makes us look very, very bad to have to call you in on this. The Celestial should be able to handle this type of thing.'

'Leo's very stubborn when he wants to be,' I said.

The Emperor raised his teacup to me. 'That he is. And thoroughly Worthy. I am looking forward to seeing him take his place here among the Immortals.'

'He's black and gay, Ah Ting,' Bai Hu said.

We all stared at Bai Hu with astonishment, even the Jade Emperor.

'I'm just saying,' Bai Hu said with a shrug. 'He'd be the first.'

I turned back to the Jade Emperor. 'He'd be the first gay Immortal? Is it allowed? I know the tradition ...'

'Humankind is very fond of rules,' the Jade Emperor said. 'Very fond of putting things into little boxes and sticking labels on them. Yang is masculine; yin is feminine. Therefore all males must be yang and be attracted to females. Despite the fact that the universe is obviously not built that way, humans insist on creating their little boxes and pushing things into them even when it's quite plain that they don't fit.' He poured more tea. 'The nature of the Tao is the true nature of all. If a man is attracted to other men and that is his nature, then how can he pursue the Tao without pursuing that nature? Ridiculous.'

'So it's not an issue?' I said.

'Of course not,' the Emperor said. 'There are plenty of gay Immortals, there always have been. The minute you stick a label on something it loses its true nature and you move further away from the Tao, which is nameless.'

'But he's *black*,' Bai Hu said.

'I have the sudden urge to rap you sharply across the nose, cat,' the Emperor said.

'He's not *Eastern*, I meant,' Bai Hu said. 'It's not the colour, it's the *location*. I mean, we've had Westerners gain Immortality here before ...' His voice trailed off. He raised his hands in defeat. 'Okay. I just made my own point. Shutting up now.'

'You aren't just a sexist pig, you're a racist one as well,' I said with wonder.

'The hell I am,' the Tiger said. 'He doesn't belong to this Corner of the World. He should be Raised to Immortality in the United States, his home. He should reside on his own Celestial Plane.'

'What about me?' I said.

'You too. If you were to gain Immortality, you should do it in the South, where you belong, and live in the Southern Celestial Plane.'

'What about me?' Simone said.

The Tiger opened his mouth and closed it again.

'Oh, very well,' the Emperor said. 'But this is strictly for your ears only, you are not to share it with anyone. The Elder of the Southern Shen and I have been in contact for about ten years. We're arranging a conference in a neutral territory, probably Antarctica. As soon as we contact the Western, African and North and South American Shen we'll start making arrangements. We'll probably do it when Ah Wu's back and he can do the security in conjunction with each group's people. We'll thrash out a reciprocal agreement.'

'Not North, South, East and West Shen?' I said.

'No, the Eastern and Western thing is just for convenience,' the Jade Emperor said. 'Actually, each continent has its own Shen, divided by the ocean or desert. So there aren't actually any Northern Shen, unless you count Ah Wu who is the essence of the North itself.' He shrugged. 'Hardly anybody lives up there anyway — people there fit into their own region. So basically it will be a meeting of Shen from the six continents, and when we get together we'll probably start formal naming and reciprocal diplomatic arrangements.'

'What, Shen UN?' I said.

The Jade Emperor made a soft sound of amusement. 'Yes. Now that travelling between the Corners is becoming common, we need to deal with the matter of mortals attaining Immortality in a Centre outside their own. If they choose to reside in a different Celestial Plane, the option to do so should be open to them. Leo is a classic example of this; he is in the first hundred or so black people who have been through our Hell, and the first to gain Immortality in our Centre. Until now, we have had very little contact with other Celestials. The time has come that we should make an arrangement for free movement between the Planes.'

'The demons are moving as well,' I said. 'Look at these stone things.'

'*Precisely*,' the Emperor said with feeling. 'Mixing Western mystical stones with Eastern demons. And the biotech that One Two Two was experimenting with ...'

70

He glared at the Tiger. 'Absolutely not acceptable.'

'I don't do anything like that,' the Tiger said. 'My kids are just studying them. Just having a look. Working out what makes them tick.'

'As long as that's all it is,' the Jade Emperor said. 'Supervise your scientists closely. Interfere with the demons' true nature and Er Lang will land on you so hard you'll think your nose is your tail.'

Bai Hu saluted. 'Celestial Majesty. I agree with you anyway.'

'Jade and Gold,' I said.

'Ah.' The Emperor leaned back. 'Do you know *why* they are bound into servitude?'

'No,' I said. 'They're both obviously embarrassed about it, and I haven't pushed the point.'

'They deserved it,' the Tiger said. 'They should have spent the time in Hell.'

'I didn't see *you* charging out of the West to defend the honour of the Qing,' the Emperor said.

'You issued the goddamn edict telling us not to interfere yourself, Ah Ting,' the Tiger said.

The Jade Emperor thumped his hand on the table. 'That is the third time you have called me that, Bai Hu. Call me Ah Ting again and I will have you executed! I gained this appointment through *cultivation* and *merit* and that story is a *lie*! You are walking a very fine line!'

The Tiger grinned and saluted.

The Jade Emperor turned back to us, serene again. 'In 1843, a young man by the name of Robert Fortune sneaked into China. He wanted to free our nation from the scourge of the opium trade. You know about that?'

Both Simone and I nodded.

The Jade Emperor continued. 'The opium trade was purely because of the tea. Young Robert thought that if he could grow tea in a territory of the British Empire, then the traders would no longer need to sell the opium in China to pay for the tea.'

'He stole the tea,' I said. 'There was a show on the History Channel a while ago.'

'I saw that too, it was very good,' the Jade Emperor said. 'Anyway, he travelled the tea plantations looking for owners who would be patriotic enough to help end this destructive trade. He was aided by a young woman who was both powerful and naïve.'

'Not *Jade*,' Simone said.

'Yes. Jade took the young man to a plantation owned by a Shen. You might say the Shen had inherited the plantation when his demon master was destroyed. The Shen, being just as naïve as the young lady, provided Mr Fortune with seeds, plants and tame demons to cultivate them in the British Imperial Territory of India.'

'Demon master?' Simone said. 'Gold was bound to a *demon*?'

'He lost a bet and was bound into the demon's servitude,' the Emperor said. 'The demon was destroyed, Gold was freed and he escaped with the deeds to a tea plantation the demon owned. He gave Robert Fortune the tea — directly in defiance of an edict issued by me that no Celestial was to interfere in human affairs during that time of conflict.'

'The economy collapsed when the tea trade dried up,' I said. 'And opium addicts with no supply filled the streets. It caused the Boxer Rebellion.' I inhaled sharply as I understood. 'The Boxers worshipped *John*. They believed that Xuan Wu made them invincible. Gold helped *cause* the Rebellion. The civil war afterwards brought down the freaking Qing dynasty.'

'And led to a century of turmoil that our nation could barely afford,' the Jade Emperor said. 'If we had retained control of the tea trade, it is possible we could have salvaged minor economic independence. As it was, we were at the mercy of the rest of the world. The West and Japan both moved in and carved us up. When they left, there was civil war again. You know the story.'

'*Gold* did this,' Simone said. 'He gave Robert Fortune the tea.'

'And Jade helped him,' the Emperor said. 'I knew what I was doing when I issued that order. They should have known better than to defy me; I work only for the best interests of my human subjects.'

I straightened. 'Right. I understand now. They've been in servitude, what? Nearly a hundred years?'

'Not nearly long enough,' the Tiger said.

'Ah Bai's right,' I said. 'Leave them in my service until they have completely atoned.'

The Jade Emperor gazed at me with wonder. I glanced at Simone, she had the same look on her face. 'What?'

'You are so much like Ah Wu sometimes, it's uncanny. Are you sure you're not his Serpent?' the Emperor said.

I sighed. 'I have no idea *what* I am, Celestial Majesty.' I looked up at him, full of hope. 'Could you have a look at me? You might know what I am.'

'What if she is his Serpent?' Simone said. 'If he comes back and they rejoin?'

'Then she'd probably disappear completely into him. You'd lose her, and gain his yang side.' The Emperor smiled at his tea. 'Not an ideal situation for those who love you, I think, Lady Emma, whatever your feelings on the matter.'

Simone glanced sharply at me.

I shook my head and looked down. 'I want it, Simone. I want to be part of him, to join with him. I want it more than anything in the world.' I sighed and looked into her eyes. 'I want to be his Serpent.'

'You aren't,' Bai Hu said. 'We've seen it. The Serpent shows up occasionally, wreaks havoc with the weather and then disappears again.'

'That's true, it's highly unlikely,' the Jade Emperor said. He sipped his tea. 'Even I don't know what you are. I have never seen anything like you before.'

'I thought you knew all,' I said with humour.

'I know all in the Eastern Plane. Something about you is not part of this Plane and therefore beyond my knowledge,' he said. 'Maybe it is part of your Western or Southern heritage. When Ah Wu returns and we have our conference we can find out more.'

Simone leaned over the table and whispered, 'Please don't be Daddy's Serpent. I couldn't bear to lose you when he returns.'

'I'll try not to be, Simone. That's all I can promise.'

'Are we finished?' the Jade Emperor said.

'Thanks, Celestial Majesty,' I said. 'I appreciate your time.'

He waved it down. 'Not a problem, Emma. I nearly came down to see you anyway; I was sick to death of hearing about Leo.'

The Jade Emperor rose and we did as well. Simone hesitated, then went to him and embraced him. She kissed him on the cheek.

'Thanks for everything,' she said.

He smiled up at her; she was about five centimetres taller than him. 'You're welcome, sweetheart. Thanks for showing me your Celestial Form, it's spectacular. Now.' He put his arm around her waist and glanced from her to me. 'I'd like to give you two some little gifts I have for you, but I want to do it with all the Imperial bullshit in front of everybody. Do you mind?'

'Do you have to?' Simone whined.

He squeezed her around the waist. 'Oh, come on, make an old man happy.'

'Promise you won't make me take serpent form,' I said.

'Cross my heart. I never wanted to force you into serpent form; I just wanted you to show them that defiance is the right path to take when it is with good reason. But Simone,' he looked up at her, 'it would be a good idea to take the full version of your True Form. Scare any potential suitors half to death. Pull in all the yin you can, wrap it around you. Make your eyes huge and black, your hair as well if you can. Be as scary as possible. Make them think twice about doing anything stupid to make me give them your hand. Carry Seven Stars, the blade bare. Have you tried to load it with energy?'

'I'm not game.'

'Don't worry about it then. Just take your biggest, scariest Celestial Form.'

'Good idea,' I said. 'Do it, Simone.'

'What are you going to give us though?' Simone asked.

'Just a couple of little things,' the Emperor said. He squeezed her again. 'You'll do it for me?'

She shrugged. 'Okay.'

CHAPTER 7

General Qin announced us again. 'Bodhisattva Kwan Yin. Lord Bai Hu of the West. Princess Simone. Lady Emma Donahoe.'

Why does he keep doing us in the wrong order? Simone said. *You have precedence over Uncle Bai.*

I raised my hand to hush her and we walked down the carpet again. Even *more* Celestials had turned up. The hall was nearly full.

We did the obeisance thing at the base of the dais, and this time the Emperor quickly told us to rise.

We stood and waited.

Er Lang raised a scroll and read from it, sounding unhappy. This time he was in human form, appearing as a normal, good-looking young Chinese warrior. His third eye was closed and undetectable. 'Lady Emma Donahoe, step forward.'

I moved to the base of the steps that led up to the throne.

The Jade Emperor rose from the throne and raised one hand. 'Approach, Lady Emma.'

I bowed slightly, then climbed the stairs to the top. A young woman in a floating pink robe appeared behind the Emperor holding a black and silver cloisonné casket. The casket was about thirty centimetres long.

At the top of the stairs I fell to one knee and saluted again.

You are very good at this, the Emperor said.

I winked at him on the way back up.

He gestured for me to stand beside him and face the hall, and I did. The raised faces of hundreds of Celestials shone below me. Simone watched from the bottom of the dais, her own expression full of pride.

'Lady Emma Donahoe is the Chosen of the Supreme Lord of the Dark Northern Heavens,' the Emperor said loudly.

Everybody in the hall went completely still and silent. The Emperor's voice echoed through the vast space.

'The Dark Lord appointed Lady Emma to be Regent. She has been kept on probation; her performance has been monitored.'

He nodded and the young woman approached with the casket. He opened the lid to reveal a black jade ruyi — a thirty-centimetre long ornamental sceptre shaped like an archer's bow, with a cloud design on one end and a set of pa kua symbols on the other. Twining snakes adorned the centre of the rod. Its flattened body had a central knob on the underside to hold it when it sat on the desk. 'Ruyi' meant 'as one wills'. It was a symbolic representation of the holder's will and a fung shui method of gaining positive outcomes to decisions. Most of the Celestials in the hall held them as indicators of rank.

The Jade Emperor carefully lifted the ruyi out of the box and turned to me. He spoke loudly and firmly as he held the sceptre out. 'This ruyi represents the Dark Lord's dominion. Lady Emma is no longer on probation; we confirm her rank and station as Regent of the Dark

77

Northern Heavens, Ruler of the Celestial Mountain of Wudang, and Acting First Heavenly General.'

I froze. First Heavenly General? I didn't have time for that! Simone had exams coming up, and the students needed to be organised after the end-of-year holiday trips home. *And* it was tax time soon.

Only in name, don't panic, Emma, the Emperor said. *Er Lang can handle it.*

I breathed a quiet sigh of relief, took the sceptre with both hands and bowed.

Turn to face them holding the ruyi, he said, then switched to out loud. 'We confirm Lady Emma Donahoe as Regent of the Dark Northern Heavens. Obey her as you obey the Dark Lord.'

Everybody in the hall, even Simone, silently fell to one knee and saluted me; except for Kwan Yin who just nodded.

I turned to the Jade Emperor, knelt on one knee and saluted him as First Heavenly General with the ruyi resting in the crook of my left elbow. I sneaked a look at Er Lang; he was glowering at me. Uh-oh.

'Dismissed,' the Emperor said.

I saluted him again, rose, and walked down the stairs to stand next to Simone.

Simone was called up next, and another box was pulled out.

'Princess Simone is given Celestial Endorsement,' the Emperor said. He pulled a jade tablet out of the box and presented it to her. 'She may call upon the Celestial any time.'

Simone bowed and returned to stand next to me. The Jade Emperor returned to his throne.

Er Lang read from the scroll. 'Princess Simone is ordered to take Celestial Form.'

'Move back, Emma,' Simone said softly. 'This is going to be big.'

She was right. It was huge. Her robes didn't appear as fabric at all; they were holes in reality, with stars sparkling inside them. She wore the universe as clothing. Her immensely long black hair didn't make it to the floor; it floated in a Celestial breeze. Clouds of yin moved in and out of the strands of her hair, filling the air with sleet that hissed as it hit the floor around her. Her enormous black eyes shone in her expressionless forbidding face. She summoned Seven Stars and held the bare dark blade in front of her. The sword had seven indentations, each centring on a hole that went right through the blade.

A commotion erupted to our left among the Celestials. A young man in human form wearing blue and silver armour stormed out of the crowd onto the carpet and planted himself next to me facing the Jade Emperor. I recognised him: the Dragon Prince that Simone had mentioned. He was one of Qing Long's sons, about number five or six.

'I demand the right to challenge for Princess Simone's hand,' the dragon said. 'As her father is not sentient and present, you are able to grant her hand.'

The Jade Emperor rose to speak but Simone spoke first.

Her voice echoed, as icy as any her father used, sending a chill up my spine.

'I will give you my hand, on three conditions.'

'Name them, Princess,' the dragon said defiantly.

'One,' Simone said, 'You must defeat the Lady Emma in armed combat. Not to the death, as she is not Immortal.'

Quick, Emma, she said into my head. *Pull out the Murasame and do something really impressive.*

I tossed the ruyi to the Tiger, who held it floating above the floor. I whipped the Murasame out of its scabbard — I'd perfected a technique that made the yin

79

blade hiss as it came out. I held the blade in front of me, filled it with chi, and performed the first five moves of the highest-level Wudang sword kata as fast as I could. The chi made the sword trail a golden image as it sang through the air. I stopped and saluted the dragon with the sword, then pulled the chi out and lowered it. He watched, eyes wide, as condensation dripped from the end of the cold, dark blade.

'Lady Emma is the finest human student the Dark Lord has ever seen,' Simone said as if from a million miles away. 'She can take down any level of demon with the sword known as the Destroyer, which was a gift from the Demon King himself.'

Before resheathing the sword I held it over the back of my wrist. *Red*, I willed, *please be red*, and then lightly ran the blade crosswise over my wrist. Red blood welled where the impossibly sharp blade touched me. I raised the blade a few centimetres above the wound and the blood spun up from my arm and disappeared into the dark metal. I returned the blade to its scabbard on my back, then concentrated and healed the wound.

Oh God, Emma, I'm sorry, Simone said into my head. *I completely forgot.*

Tell her, not a problem, I said to the stone.

Yes, a problem! she retorted. *What if it had been black?*

I shrugged imperceptibly.

The dragon had watched me feed the blade with wide eyes. He pulled himself together and turned back to Simone, defiant again. 'What else, Princess?'

'Next you must defeat me in battle,' Simone said, perfectly calm. She raised Seven Stars to the side. 'Again, not to the death, as I also am not Immortal.'

'And?' the dragon said.

'Then, after defeating Lady Emma, and defeating me,

the suitor must embrace me.' She summoned yin over her raised arms so that it floated around her pale hands and the blade of the sword. 'Embrace me, and my nature. Embrace my yin.'

The dragon gasped and took a step back. 'Touch the yin?'

'Embrace the yin,' Simone said, her voice still echoing eerily. 'Embrace my true nature.'

The hall filled with complete silence as the dragon watched the yin writhe over Simone's arms and the enormous blade.

He fell to one knee and bowed his head. 'I withdraw my challenge.'

Phew, Simone said. *He's a good fighter too.*

'Go with honour, Dragon Lord,' Simone said out loud. 'I am honoured by your attention.' She raised her head. 'Those are the conditions for any who wishes to have my hand. Defeat Lady Emma. Defeat me. And then embrace my yin.'

She dismissed Seven Stars, changed back to human form, and nodded to the Jade Emperor. 'Celestial Majesty. By your leave, Lady Emma and I must prepare for a journey to Hell.'

'Dismissed,' the Jade Emperor said. His eyes were full of amusement. *Excellent job. Well done. Bai Hu is going to shout at you for a long time, Simone, but don't worry, it will work out.*

I held my hand out and the Tiger passed the ruyi back to me. Simone and I fell to one knee and saluted the Jade Emperor as senior Retainers, then turned and walked out of the hall together, with the Tiger and Kwan Yin following.

General Qin appeared in the doorway. 'Holy Bodhisattva Kwan Yin. Lady Emma Donahoe, Confirmed Regent of the Dark Northern Heavens, First Heavenly General. Lord Bai Hu, Emperor of the

Western Heavens. Princess Simone, only human daughter of the Dark Lord of the Northern Heavens.' *Great job, ladies.*

Oh. You didn't have the precedence until you were off probation, Simone said. *Way to go, Emma. First Heavenly General! Way cool!*

'You say cool far too much,' I growled under my breath.

A litany followed me down the stairs back to the preparation room. *Cool cool cool cool cool!*

Bai Hu leaned his elbows on the dining table and held his head in his hands. He rubbed his hands over his face and looked at us, despairing. 'I really don't know what the fuck I'm going to do with you two. That was *beyond* stupid.'

'I thought we handled it okay, Uncle Bai,' Simone said. 'At least we won't have all these Celestials trying to marry me.'

'Expect at least two dozen challenges in the next two weeks, Emma,' Bai Hu said.

'No way,' I said. 'If they win, they have to face Simone. And if they win that, they have to touch the yin. They don't have the nerve.'

'Nothing to do with the yin, girls. Simone, you just declared open season on Emma. Anyone who wants to match skills with her can try. Every guy in Heaven who thinks he's halfway good will be calling her out.'

'Oh.' Simone's face fell. 'I hadn't thought of it like that.' She turned to me, full of remorse. 'I'm so sorry, Emma.'

I shrugged. 'Not an issue. I'll be able to practise against some good opponents, it's not to the death, and if they win, they won't dare to take it further because they're all scared to death of the yin.'

'And another thing,' the Tiger said. 'You said that

anybody that wants your hand has to do these three things. What, you plan on never having a boyfriend at all? You gonna be a goddamn *nun*? How many guys out there can actually physically touch yin? Guys that aren't related to you, daughter of yin? You just made yourself pretty much permanently unavailable for marriage for the rest of your life.'

Simone shrugged. 'So? I'll just never marry. If I really like a guy we'll move in together.'

'It's your hand in the sense of your hand in the bond of love, Simone,' the Tiger said grimly. 'More than just marriage. If you want to have a live-in relationship with *anybody*, Celestial or human, they have to touch the yin.'

Simone opened her mouth and then closed it again.

'Don't worry about it, Simone,' I said. 'We'll just cross that bridge when we come to it. It'll work out. Use the declaration as a shield. When you're older and ready, you can change it.'

'You can't change something like that,' the Tiger said, still grim.

'Whatever. Right now it'll keep all those losers off your back.'

'Starting with that little blue creep,' Simone said with relish. 'God, I loved the look on his face when he thought about touching the yin. He's been so arrogant, expecting me to just fall at his feet because he's so *freaking* gorgeous.'

'He's Qing Long's,' I said. 'I wonder if any of his children haven't inherited his attitude?'

'Nope,' the Tiger said.

'So. Hell,' Simone said. 'Help us out here, Uncle Bai. What do we need to take with us?'

Bai Hu leaned back and put his hands on the table. 'Right. Hell. This is what you need to do.'

* * *

I came around on the couch at home, with the Tiger's concerned face above me. I sat up. 'I'm okay.'

Simone sat on the opposite couch, still in her robes.

'How long was I out this time?' I said.

'Only a couple of minutes. It's quicker every time. Soon you'll be able to transport without losing consciousness at all,' the Tiger said.

Monica heard us and came out of the kitchen. 'Welcome back, ma'am.' She saw the armour and the sword. 'Did everything work out okay?'

'It's all fine.' I rose and headed into the kitchen. 'Could you make us some tea? We need to talk.'

'There are a lot of messages for you as well, ma'am,' Monica said.

I pulled off the sword and the armour and dropped them onto the floor next to the pantry. Simone headed towards her room, probably to change out of the robes. The Tiger and I sat across the kitchen table from each other. Monica put a pot of Chinese tea in front of the Tiger and a mug of Ceylon tea in front of me and we nodded our thanks. Notes and envelopes covered the table, and the Tiger picked a few up to read them. I slapped his hand and he grimaced and dropped them.

'Dinner at home tonight, ma'am?' Monica said.

'Yes, thanks, Monica.'

I flipped through the envelopes. Mostly bills, they could be handled later. I checked the phone messages. Three from staff on the Mountain. Two from Generals. One from the bank. One from Simone's teacher, asking me to call her back urgently.

Simone returned in a pair of scruffy jeans and a T-shirt. She had let her hair down without brushing it and it formed tangled skeins around her head. I waved the note at her. 'You been up to anything at school?'

'Nope.' She pulled a box of lemon tea out of the fridge and sat with it. 'As far as I know I'm not in trouble about anything, but I've skipped a few classes lately, and you didn't ring them this morning to tell them I wasn't going to be there.'

'Oh yeah, that's right,' I said. 'You have to remind me, Simone. I have too much going on all at the same time.'

'I've got a bunch of notes for you too.' She jumped up and went out.

'Just bring them directly,' the Tiger said to her back.

'I'm not lazy like you,' she retorted without turning around.

I moaned and leaned on the table. 'This school is solely responsible for the destruction of countless rainforests. She brings home a mountain of notes every week. It's okay for the mothers at home who have time to attend endless morning teas and tennis socials, but I have better things to do with my time.'

'You wouldn't have that problem —' the Tiger began.

I cut him off. 'If she went to Celestial High. I know. But she wants to be normal.'

He snorted, and opened his mouth to say something, but Simone came in with a stack of notes and put them in front of me. 'This is from last week too.'

I quickly flipped through the information and stopped at an envelope with 'Mr and Mrs Chen' typewritten on the outside. I glared at Simone, but she just shrugged. 'No idea.'

'I ring them every time to tell them to address stuff to me,' I grumbled as I opened the envelope. I read the note, then threw it on the table. 'You've been missing too many classes lately and they want to talk to me immediately. They want me to contact your teacher right now for an interview.'

'I don't want to repeat Year Nine, Emma. Please go and talk to them,' Simone said.

'If she went to Celestial High —' the Tiger began.

Simone cut him off. 'I'm not going to any Celestial High full of Celestial freaks. I want to stay down here with normal people.'

'What does that make me?' the Tiger said gruffly.

'The biggest freak of all,' she shot back. She turned to me. 'Please, Emma, talk to my teacher. Give them some excuse. Tell them I have cancer or something and I need chemo ...' She changed her appearance so that she appeared ten kilos lighter. Her cheeks went hollow and her eyes sunk. 'Tell them I'm dying and I can't attend because of that.'

'I'll email your teacher and arrange an interview for after we've come back from Hell,' I said. 'I need to check my email anyway. And don't let me forget to write you a note to say that you're sick.' I sighed with exasperation. 'And change back, that looks awful.'

Her appearance returned to normal. 'I can't hold it for long anyway.'

I rose from the table. 'I'd better check my email, it'll be backed up forever.'

'You two have been gone just a few hours and you still forgot to do a lot of important stuff,' the Tiger said, waving his teacup at the notes on the table. 'You should hire a secretary.'

'Look, the two of us already have two live-in staff,' I said. 'If I hire someone else, it'll just be *more* people for me to manage. And remember, we're trying to keep as normal a profile as possible. We're already unusual in that we have a domestic helper whose husband has a job outside. A home secretary would be complete overkill, especially since I'm just supposed to be Simone's guardian and nothing more.'

I rose, picked up my tea and went to the office. I had nearly two hundred messages. I ran the spam filter then checked the remainder. There were still a hundred and fifty left.

I filed the info memos from the Heavens, the Academy and the Mountain, and flipped through the important stuff. There was a message from Simone's teacher, three situations requiring my attention in the Northern Heavens, and two more about the Academy.

And nearly seventy-five messages of congratulation on my appointment as First Heavenly General. Some of them were obviously grudging.

Wonderful.

CHAPTER 8

When I got home from the Academy the next day, I could hear the yelling from the lift lobby. I hesitated at the apartment's front door, then opened it and went in. The yelling was louder: two male voices, probably in the dining room. I kicked my shoes off and hurried in. The Tiger and Michael both stopped shouting and glared at me. Simone was there as well. She shook her head and sighed with exasperation.

The Tiger thrust his hand towards Michael. 'Stupid bastard wants to go with you.'

I leaned on the back of one of the dining chairs. 'You can't, Michael, you're not Immortal.'

'Neither are you. And neither is *she*,' Michael said, gesturing towards Simone. He dropped his arm and spoke with force. 'I want to help Leo out. Let me come along and talk to him.' He glared at the Tiger. 'He was like a father to me. I think he'd listen to me.'

'Oh, thank you *very much*.' The Tiger pulled a chair out and flopped to sit. 'What does that make me?'

'Irrelevant,' Michael said.

'Big words,' the Tiger shot back. 'Harvard must agree with you, preppy boy.' He leaned over the table. 'Rhonda's ready to move back into the Palace, boy, you know that? If she remarries me, then I'll *really* be your fucking father, not just this "biological" business that you keep carrying on about. You'll be obeying *me,* not some fucking black *gay-lo.*'

'Tiger,' Simone said mildly, 'I've had about enough of this. You've been swearing far too much the last few days, and it shows a lack of respect for both me and Emma. And lately you've been very insulting to Leo, who isn't here to defend himself. If you say the f-word one more time, or insult Leo one more time, you will be banned from this household. Is that understood?'

The Tiger's mouth flopped open and he stared at her.

Her voice became sharp. '*Is that understood, Bai Hu?*'

He rose, leaned on the table and glared at her. 'Until you reach majority, Miss So-Fucking-Clever, I have precedence over you, and don't you forget it.'

'Emma?' Simone said.

'Bai Hu, take yourself out of this household and don't come back until called. That's an order,' I said.

The Tiger opened and closed his mouth a few times, then slammed his fist into his hand in the salute and disappeared.

At twenty-four, Michael's muscular frame had filled out and his intelligent face was stunningly good-looking under his short blond hair. He towered over me, as tall as his father, slightly under two metres. He fell to one knee in front of me. 'Lady Emma, permission to assist you on your sortie to Hell.'

'We can't risk it, Michael. You may never be able to come out again.'

He looked up at me, full of hope. 'You're not Immortal, you're an ordinary human. If you can come out, I can come out.'

I sighed. 'Michael, you know that I'm not an ordinary human, far from it. Only Immortals and demons can come out again. Simone's so powerful it doesn't really apply to her, and you know she's done it before. I'm a demon. You? I don't know.'

'Is there a way of finding out?' he said, still on one knee.

Simone and I shared a look.

'I'll ask around,' I said.

'Promise me, Emma, you will ask.'

'I promise, Michael. I know you love Leo as much as we do. I'll see if you can come.'

'Thanks, Emma.' He smiled shyly and stood. 'It's good to see you looking so well.'

I rose and quickly embraced him, then pulled back to smile up at him. 'Thanks, Michael. Is your mother really going back to your father?'

'Not if I have anything to say about it,' he said grimly.

'It's possible she could be happy as Empress of the West,' Simone said. 'And she'd become Immortal, Michael.'

'He'd treat her like ...' He shrugged. 'You know how he treats his women.' He gestured towards where the Tiger had been sitting. 'You heard how he talked about Leo. How could he be like that? Leo's one of the noblest people I've ever met. I'd be *proud* to call him father, not that *beast*.'

'How long did it take you to come from Harvard, Michael? It's a long way,' I said. 'I hope you didn't miss any classes.'

'It's about eight hours; I stop over in Honolulu and rest on the way. I've just about finished for the term, Emma, my papers are in and the exams are finished. Can I stay in one of the student rooms until we hear whether I can come to Hell? Do you have room for me?'

'Of course we do — you can have your old room back. You're part of the family. How long are you planning to stay?'

'I wasn't planning to come for another couple of weeks, until after I had my results,' he said. 'But I heard about you two going to Hell and I wanted to be in on it. Let me stay until we know whether I can come, then I'll go back to the States and collect my gear.' He paused. 'Can I spend the summer brushing up with the Masters at the Academy?'

'I thought you were supposed to go to the Palace,' I said.

'I'm staying here,' he said firmly. He winced. 'I'm sorry, my Lady, I didn't ask you before. Is that okay with you?'

'Sure, spend the summer here. We'd be delighted to have you.' I had a sudden idea. 'How about you take one of the small apartments at the New Folly? I think we have two or three free. You'd have more privacy.'

He smiled shyly. 'Really?'

'Sure. Teleport down there, report to Lok, the building manager. He's the big German shepherd on the first floor, Flat B. Tell him you're taking one of the empty apartments.'

'The building manager's a dog?'

'Yep. I think he's really a dragon, but somebody cursed him. He won't talk about it, just turned up on our doorstep looking for work. He minds the armoury during the day, so if he's not at the Folly he'll be there. He's terrific, you'll really like him. I think your clothes and stuff are still in your room.'

He fell to one knee and saluted me again. 'Thank you, Lady Emma.'

'Oh cut it out, Michael, there's no need for that. Get up off the floor and disappear.'

He rose, smiled, and disappeared.

* * *

'My goodness,' Meredith said, her hands on Michael's shoulders where he sat on a chair in front of her, her eyes unseeing. 'Don't let your father look inside you, Michael, he'll order you to stay in the Palace.'

'I'm that big?' Michael said.

'Short answer: yes. And well on the way.' She released his shoulders and smiled down at him. 'The fact that you can stay in the US for such a long time is a dead giveaway, my friend. You are very big indeed. If I didn't know Rhonda personally, I would say that your mother was definitely something very special.'

'She is,' Michael and I said in unison, and shared a smile.

'Leave now, please, Michael, I need to speak to Lady Emma alone,' Meredith said. 'Wait outside.'

'That means I'm big enough to go to Hell and come back out, and you want to tell Emma that it's a bad idea to take me,' Michael said. 'If that's the case, then I'm coming anyway.'

Meredith watched him, expressionless.

'Good,' Michael added.

'You are about as intelligent as Lady Emma,' Meredith said.

'Oh, I sincerely hope that he's smarter than me. Look at the number of stupid mistakes I've made,' I said.

'That's true, Meredith,' Michael said. 'If she has me along she may not make as many stupid mistakes.'

'You are very cheeky,' I said. 'And probably right.' I sighed. 'The Tiger will go ballistic when he hears.'

'No need to tell him, it's nothing to do with him,' Michael said. 'Keep him out of it.'

'What about your mother, dear?' Meredith said.

Michael's face went expressionless.

'You could be going there to get yourself killed,' she went on. 'I think your mother has the right to know.'

The intercom on my desk beeped and I pressed the button.

'Celestial Messenger for you and Master Michael both, ma'am,' Yi Hao said. 'Do I tell him to wait?'

'Don't make him wait,' I said. 'Send him in.'

The door opened and a tiger stood in the doorway. He wasn't white, like Bai Hu, but the standard deep orange with black stripes. He changed into a man in his mid-thirties wearing the white and gold livery of the Horsemen.

'Great, a message from Dad,' Michael said.

The messenger looked from me to Michael to Meredith. 'I have a message for Lady Emma, and also a message for son number Three One Five.'

'My name,' Michael said pointedly, 'is Michael MacLaren, Ronald, and you know it.'

The Horseman smiled slightly, and handed Michael a white scroll tied with a gold ribbon. Michael unrolled it without moving from his chair. The Horseman waited, watching.

Michael glanced up at the Horseman, his face rigid. 'Do you know what this says?'

'Yes, lad,' the Horseman said. 'Even more, though, do you know what it *means*?'

Michael tossed the scroll onto the desk. He rose gracefully and leaned on the desk with one hand. 'Tell my father.' He hesitated, then spoke with force. 'Notice that I am not going to use a single word of bad language here. Tell my father that I am going to Hell. And that as far as I am concerned, so can he.' He gestured dismissively towards the scroll. 'This is either a tremendous honour or a huge insult. Either way, I don't accept.'

The Horseman visibly relaxed. 'So you do know what it means.'

'Damn straight I do.'

'What is it?' I said.

'He's promoted me to Number Three,' Michael said.

'An honour,' I said.

Both Michael and the Horseman grimaced.

'Only if I can defend the title,' Michael said. 'Anyone who wants to can challenge me for the right to be Number Three.'

'Normally a son of that level of precedence would be Immortal,' the Horseman explained. 'The current Number Three is an Immortal. Dad could be deliberately trying to stir up trouble for Michael, or he could be sincere and really want to promote him, because he thinks he's that good. Actually I think he's genuine, because he wants to patch things up with you, Michael.'

'Why, Ron?' Michael said.

The Horseman fell to one knee and saluted me. 'Lady Emma, Regent of the Dark Northern Heavens. I have a message for you as well, and I think this will explain it.'

'If it's about him wanting to come back here, that's up to Simone,' I said. 'She was right about the swearing. He keeps forgetting that she's only fourteen and it's really not appropriate to talk like that in front of her.'

'No, ma'am, I have an invitation.' He rose and passed me a large white card embossed with gold lettering. There was a red 'double happiness' marriage character at the top and gilt around the edges.

I glanced at the card. Rhonda was remarrying the Tiger, and would be Raised at the wedding ceremony and crowned Empress of the Western Heavens. I was invited to the ceremony, to be held in February of next year, just before the Chinese New Year holiday.

'Thank you,' I said. 'Tell the Tiger I'll send him an RSVP as soon as I'm back from Hell.'

'Good luck in Hell, ma'am,' the Horseman said. He nodded to Michael and disappeared.

'What?' Michael said.

I passed him the card. He looked at it and his face went grim. He threw it onto the desk. 'Terrific. To hell with my mother — I'm going with you.'

'You should talk to her first, Michael.'

He ran one hand over his blond buzz cut. 'No, I shouldn't. She's made her decision, and I've made mine. To hell with it.' He smiled grimly. 'And to Hell with me. I'd better go and put my weapons in order.' He saluted me, shaking his hands in front of his face. 'Lady Emma.' He disappeared.

Meredith smiled slightly. 'This is very strange.'

'What?'

'He *is* very big, Emma. Bigger than any half-Shen I have ever seen, short of Simone herself. I would like to examine Rhonda some time soon; she really must be something special. He is bigger than any son of the Tiger should be.'

'If she was a Shen she would have told us,' I said.

'Not necessarily. Many dragons keep their natures a secret from even their closest families. Look at Amy's father — he was typical. Never told her until she found out she was a dragon by herself.'

'You think we may have found one of these pure Western dragons that are so elusive?'

'If she was a Western Shen she would not be able to live in the East for such a long time,' Meredith said.

'Unless she's really big, that is. Michael's big enough to live in the West.'

'If Michael is a cross between an Eastern and a Western Shen, then he is something completely new and may be more powerful than anything we have ever seen.'

'Never happened before?' I said.

95

'Not as far as I know.' Meredith leaned on the desk and crossed her arms. 'Actually, it's good he's going with you. He's extremely talented, well trained and completely devoted to Leo. Leo loves him like a son. If anybody can talk Leo into coming out, it's Michael.'

'Thanks for coming along too, by the way. I'm glad you'll be there to back us up.'

'I'm bound by the rules though, Emma. I can harm no one while I'm there.'

I picked up the invitation card and turned it around in my hands without looking at it. 'I think I should go unarmed, just in case.'

'That might be a good idea. You're there for your brains and your maturity, not your fighting skills. Simone's not bound by the Celestial rules like I am, and she can destroy anything that we may face in there.'

I glanced into her eyes and spoke softly. 'But can she destroy *me*?'

'Do you want me to talk to her?'

I threw the card back onto the table. 'Yes.'

'I'll talk to Michael as well. That's another good reason to take him. If Simone can't do it, then he can.'

'He can't, Meredith.'

'I think he'd be able to. It would be hard, but he could bring himself to do it if it was absolutely necessary.'

'You don't understand, Meredith. I've sparred with him, and even when I'm in human form he can't take me. My Mother form would tear him to bits.'

She hesitated a moment, then spoke softly. 'You should let us look at it so we can work out what level it is, Emma. We need to know.'

'Every time I take the form, it controls me a little more. Every time, it's harder to change back. One day I won't be able to. I'll be a Mother, Meredith. I won't be *me* any more. I have to avoid taking the form as much as I can. Even if it means not being able to touch

Simone.' I quirked a smile. 'I'm accustomed to not touching the ones I love. When he comes back, I'll find it hard to change.'

'Emma.' I looked up at her. She gazed into my eyes. 'Remember his oath?'

I shrugged. 'Yes, and I know where you're heading.'

We were both silent for a while.

It was me who finally said it. 'He vowed to *find* me. And that means I'll be lost.'

CHAPTER 9

'Through the tunnel or around Pok Fu Lam, ma'am?' Marcus asked. He was driving us to Aberdeen, where we would take the boat to Hell.

I checked my watch: 10 am, Sunday. 'Aberdeen Tunnel, please,' I said.

Marcus nodded and pulled away from the kerb.

'You thought about that one for a while,' Michael said with amusement.

'You aren't limited to regular travel,' I said. 'During office rush hour, or race meetings, it can take up to two hours to get through that tunnel. It's quicker to go all the way around the island through Pok Fu Lam.'

Marcus eased out of the cramped Wan Chai streets around the Academy's nondescript building and turned left onto Gloucester Road, the main four-lane traffic snarl from Central to Causeway Bay. He carefully negotiated past speeding minibuses and taxis, then did a U-turn under the massive Harcourt Road overpass to take us back in the opposite direction.

As we neared Causeway Bay, the traffic started to negotiate the complicated lanes system that diverted people to different destinations from the most densely occupied part of the island. Marcus stayed in the second lane from the right; if he drifted into a left lane he would be forced to cross the harbour using the Cross-Harbour Tunnel, and the traffic in that lane was already banked back about a kilometre. If he went into the rightmost lane, he would miss the Aberdeen tunnel turn-off and be diverted through Causeway Bay. I smiled slightly as I remembered many lost hours trying to make my way through Hong Kong's unforgiving traffic system. If you found yourself in the wrong lane too early, you would be locked in by a single line and other drivers would become extremely aggravated if you tried to escape it. Once I'd missed the Aberdeen tunnel turn-off and found myself halfway up the side of the island in Tai Koo Shing before I could make a U-turn and come back again, only to be in the wrong lane when the Aberdeen tunnel sign came up the other way.

Marcus had been driving us since Leo had gone, and he was familiar with the roads, particularly between Happy Valley and Wan Chai where he transported the students between the Academy and the Follies. He took us now up a narrow, steep ramp and onto Aberdeen Tunnel Road. The road was at second-storey height and we could clearly see into some of the older flats on either side; bare concrete walls, iron bunk beds, and dusty door and window frames.

Just before we entered the tunnel we passed behind the Happy Valley racecourse. The stands looked like massive five-storey buildings with a complicated series of stairs and escalators running through them. On the other side, the open stands had layer upon layer of seating and indoor restaurant viewing areas for the race day visitors. Hong Kong's race season was limited to the cooler months, and races only took place on Wednesday evenings in Happy Valley and on Saturdays at Sha Tin. There were no other race meetings in the

Territory at all. The Hong Kong Jockey Club provided accommodation and transport for all the horses in the Territory; and at each race meeting — the only legal gambling allowed in Hong Kong except for the Mark Six Lottery — the entire GDP of a small country would be wagered.

We whisked quickly through the Aberdeen Tunnel. On the other side, the view opened out; we were no longer in the dense urban high rises of Happy Valley. On the left were the prestigious large low-rise apartments of Shouson Hill, mostly occupied by expatriates who didn't mind being a little further away from the action of the centre of the city. Directly in front of us, the hillside above Ocean Park was decorated with an enormous garden in the shape of a sea horse, the logo of the park.

We continued through Wong Chuk Hang industrial area. Factory buildings in Hong Kong usually towered up to fifteen or twenty storeys, with each floor occupied by a manufacturing enterprise. Elevators large enough to hold the trucks that were Hong Kong's transport life blood serviced each floor.

Before we reached the 'fishing village' of Aberdeen, which was actually a tightly packed district of high-rise apartment buildings, we turned off and headed towards the Aberdeen Boat Club. Marcus wound through the back of the international schools and apartment buildings, eventually arriving at Shum Wan pier. A walkway with a traditional, upward-sweeping tiled roof meandered along the side of the long lay-by area, which was occupied by at least six large tourist buses. This was where the tourists were brought to have yum cha at the floating restaurants. They were ferried across from the two piers, one for each restaurant — the Jumbo and the Tai Pak. The Sea Palace restaurant, which had been moored next to the Jumbo on the other side, was long gone, towed away to become a tourist attraction in Manila.

'Is the yum cha here still awful?' Michael asked as we walked down to the old Sea Palace pier, now unused.

'Couldn't tell you. I stay well away from the tourist traps,' Simone said.

'The restaurants have been renovated recently, they're much nicer inside now,' I said.

'You still pay tourist prices though,' Simone said.

I shrugged. 'You pay extra for the "experience".'

Michael peered at the Jumbo restaurant across the water. 'You're kidding. A theme park on the sea?'

'If you're going to have tourists, you have to give them an "experience",' I said.

'And something to buy,' Simone said. 'They put shops in there too!'

No one seemed to notice us as we stepped over the chain blocking off the third pier and walked down towards the water. A number of noisy mainland tourists were on the pier next to us, shouting with excitement as the boat approached them.

Michael chuckled. 'Typical, going over to a huge restaurant for a banquet and they all have food in their hands.'

He was right. Most mainland tourists carried bags of food around with them, usually small snacks such as dried fish or nuts.

'Oh, give it up, Michael, they're enjoying themselves,' Simone said. She gestured with her head. 'That looks like our boat, it's completely non-tourist.'

A five-metre motor launch was docked at the pier, its white sides gleaming. It had no registration or name. When the deckhand saw us approach, he pushed a gangway out to the edge of the pier for us.

We boarded, Simone leading and Michael guarding the rear. As the deckhand prepared to release the rope, a middle-rank demon appearing as a young Chinese man dressed in a smart black business suit came out from the main cabin. He quickly saluted all of us.

'Passage is payment of a black jade coin,' he said.

I handed him the scroll tied with vermillion ribbon that contained the Jade Emperor's edict to let us into Hell. He perused it quickly; this part of the proceedings was just a formality. He returned it to me and nodded. 'Your passage has been confirmed. Please come with me. There is tea and soda inside if you wish.'

As he spoke, the boat and the sky both went black and the surge of waves beneath the boat ceased. The sound of the noisy tourists on the next pier was cut off, as was the noise from the myriad boats moored in the typhoon shelter. The air echoed with the eerie sound of the inside of a huge cavern and darkness surrounded us. The water was completely still and black as ice, and the temperature dropped.

'Come inside,' the demon said. 'It's about an hour's journey and it's freezing out here. And I'm very honoured to make your acquaintance.'

'Yes, I'm well aware of the similarities to the Western legend of the River Styx,' the demon said as he poured the tea. 'I've studied the mythology and I'm interested in the way that theirs — or yours — matches up with ours. I'd love to travel to the West and see for myself, but of course I'm much too small to travel that far from my Centre.'

'Has the King ever said anything about it?' I said.

The demon made a soft sound of amusement. 'I have been lucky enough in my long life to avoid attracting the attention of the King. It is not something I would do by choice.'

He nodded to Simone. 'I remember when you came through as a child, Princess. You scared me to death with the amount of shen energy you were radiating.

You threatened to destroy me if I didn't take you across. Of course, I couldn't take you without the payment of a coin and I readied myself to die.'

'I remember now, it's all coming back to me,' Simone said. 'At the time I was so upset it was just a blur. I was going to destroy you but then I decided not to waste the time.'

'You rose on your shen energy and floated across the water. You were a thing of terrifying beauty, making the water beneath you ripple as you drifted above it.' He smiled slightly and shook his head. 'You should have been destroyed — the water is full of the power of yin itself; one touch is destruction. Being in the centre of the river is like being in a vortex of yin and therefore should annihilate anything except this specially constructed boat. Yet you were completely unharmed. Later I learnt that you had summoned yin, and I understood. You could probably manipulate this water if you wished to control it.'

Simone smiled back tightly. 'I don't think I'll bother. I'm just here to find my Retainer.'

'As you wish, ma'am,' he said, and we continued in silence.

The landing on the other side was a rough-hewn alcove cut out of the dark grey rock with a smooth stone floor. The only break in the wall of rock was a modern black-doored elevator with a single black smoked-glass button next to it. The demon pressed the button and the light went on.

'This is where I leave you. There is only one destination for this lift,' the demon said. He saluted us. 'Ladies. Sir. Good luck on your sortie and I hope that I will be able to ferry you on your return.'

We saluted back. The demon returned to the boat and it pulled away, disappearing into the darkness.

A bell sounded and the lift doors opened.

'Here we go,' Simone said, and we went in.

'How much of this is coming back to you?' I asked as the lift doors closed and we descended.

Simone looked up but there were no floor lights above the door. 'Some of it. They kept telling me you were here by choice; and the counsellor I was seeing acted as if you were dead, but I knew you weren't dead because I could sense you. When Rhonda took me to school on my first day back and the stone told me that this was the way my life would be now, without you, or Daddy, or Leo, I just snapped. I thought, "To hell with this, I'm getting back the person I can get, and that's Emma".'

'The stone did that on purpose?' I said, incredulous.

The stone didn't reply and I moved to tap it. It spoke before I touched it. 'Some of us had the brains to realise what the King was doing when he manipulated Simone into coming down here, destroying Wong and freeing you.'

'Rubbish,' Simone said. 'You just wanted her back as much as I did, and you didn't give a damn either.'

The stone didn't reply.

'Simone isn't as much fun to torment?' I said.

'She's getting there,' the stone said. 'Give her some time.'

Michael quirked a small smile and shifted his sword, the White Tiger, more comfortably where it lay diagonally across his back. I saw his face; it was strained with tension.

'Are you okay, Michael?'

He nodded, serious. 'I can feel the nature of this place and how it wishes to reject me, but I can tolerate it.'

'I don't feel that it wants to reject me,' Simone said. 'I don't feel anything much.'

'You're probably too powerful, Simone,' the stone said, and Michael grimaced slightly. 'Emma?'

'I don't feel rejected,' I said quietly.

The doors opened and we stepped out of the lift into a large bright courtyard full of small trees and flowing water. The water ran in narrow channels between paths of light tan pavers and raised garden boxes. Small pavilions with white-tiled pillars and traditional roofs were scattered around the garden. The whole area gleamed, and a fresh breeze full of the scent of jasmine lifted the air. A bird sang nearby, and I looked up. There was no ceiling, but neither was there a sky; it was just bright above us, and nothing else was visible. It was impossible to tell how high the ceiling was, if there was one.

An official wearing a traditional black silk robe and a high, square hat with long extensions either side appeared. Meredith was with him. He bowed slightly to us and saluted. 'This way, please.' He turned to our left and led us through a large moon gate. On the other side of the gate was a landing with stairs leading down to the right.

We all stopped on the landing and watched in wonder. The ground below — about a hundred metres away — spread before us to the sandy edge of a large, still, brilliantly blue lake that stretched to the horizon. The beach was bordered by a metre-high tan stone wall, and on its near side was an expanse of manicured lawn dotted with bauhinia trees, their pink and white blooms covering the ground around them. The courtyard we had been in had an open rooftop and the building below us had ornamental arches for windows in its light tan stone walls.

A white marble causeway led out across the lake, with traditional cloud-patterned balustrades on either side. It was about three metres wide and disappeared into the misty distance. Similar causeways could be seen about two hundred metres away on either side of it, spreading out from where we were and stretching across the lake.

Next to our causeway stood a two-storey mansion with red pillars and wooden screens, a large veranda around it, and an upward-sloping roof of green tiles. Identical mansions stood next to the other two visible causeways.

'This is an island, and there are nine of those bridges spreading out across the lake in all directions,' Michael said. 'We're in the middle of a huge wheel and those are the spokes.'

'The Wheel of Rebirth,' the official said. 'Down these stairs are the cells, further along on the right.'

He indicated a row of villas facing the lake, each with a tiny fenced garden that opened onto a white pathway that skirted the edge of the water. The villas were two storeys high and had traditional Chinese roofs with white tiles. The fencing around their gardens also had a small tile roof with decorative fan-shaped, square and circular windows cut in them.

'Leo's cell is the second one,' the demon said.

'Tell me that you see these as luxurious houses,' I said to Simone and Michael.

Simone nodded.

'Yep,' Michael said. 'If this is Hell, then to hell with Heaven.'

'This is the tenth level, Celestial side of Hell,' Meredith said over her shoulder as she walked down the stairs in front of us. 'Not all of Hell is this pretty, believe me.'

The sky was still the same; just a universal warm, white glow. It was bright enough that it seemed to be the middle of the day but completely without glare. We reached ground level and walked along the white path towards the villas. People sat on the grass and strolled on the pathway, all of them seeming happy and relaxed. A couple waved to Meredith and she waved back.

'Don't ask, because we cannot tell you,' the official said before I could speak. 'You are here to collect your Retainer. Please convince him to take the Elixir and fulfil his destiny. It saddens all of us to see him like this.'

As we approached the villas we saw Leo. He was sitting in a wheelchair on the path outside the second house, watching the water.

'Leo!' Simone called, and raced to him. He looked up and saw her but his dark face was expressionless. When she reached him, she crouched to throw her arms around his neck and held him.

Michael put his arms around Leo's neck from behind and rested his cheek on the top of Leo's head. I crouched next to the chair and held his arm.

Meredith stood back, letting the family have its moment.

'God, Simone, you've grown up so beautiful,' Leo choked. His restraint dissolved and he smiled up through his tears at Michael. 'You're a fine young man.' His smile turned wry. 'Hey, Emma, you guys don't know how long I've hoped you'd come and visit me.'

'They wouldn't let us,' I said. 'I've been fighting the Celestial bureaucracy for eight years to let us down here.'

Simone raised her head so she could see into his face. 'Come home with us, Leo, we need you.'

Leo gestured slightly with one hand. 'No, you don't, beautiful. I can see that you can look after yourself just fine.'

She traced his cheek where the tears fell. 'I miss you so much, Leo, please come home.'

Michael spoke to the top of Leo's head. 'Come home, old man, back where you belong.'

107

Leo shook his head. 'I've been hoping for so long that I'd see you all again. They kept telling me to take the Elixir and go back.' He sighed and rubbed his hand over his face. 'Emma, can I talk to you alone?'

'Whatever you want to say, you can say in front of all of us, dear Leo,' Simone said gently. 'Don't worry, I understand. You loved Daddy. But we love you.'

Michael placed one hand on Leo's shoulder. 'You're more of a father to me than the Tiger ever was.'

Simone put her head on Leo's lap and spoke softly. 'We need you.'

Leo stroked Simone's hair. 'Please let me talk to Emma alone.'

Michael straightened. 'Come on, Simone, let's go skip stones or something.'

Simone glared at him. 'I'm not a little kid, Michael.' She smiled up at Leo. 'Okay, you talk to Emma, and then we're taking you home.'

Leo waited until Simone and Michael were out of earshot. 'Let's go inside.'

He grasped the wheels of his chair to wheel himself inside, but I moved to the rear of the chair and took the handles. I wheeled him past his two demon guards into his villa.

I sat on the rosewood couch and he sat in his wheelchair facing me, fidgeting in his lap. I waited for him to start, but he didn't say anything. Eventually I said, 'I know you've been asking to die for eight years, Leo.'

He sighed and tilted his head without looking up. 'That's all I want, Emma. An end to it. That's all I've ever wanted.'

'There's no way we can convince you to come back with us?'

He just shrugged.

'Simone and Michael need you.'

He smiled slightly. 'They're already grown-up, look at them. What do they need me for?' He gestured towards his legs. 'I'm useless.'

'Immortals can fly; you could probably learn to levitate, or even make use of your legs. Iron Crutch doesn't have to take the form of a cripple all the time, and probably neither would you, unless you chose to.'

Leo bowed his head. 'A *cripple*.'

I raised my hands. 'Disabled. Disabled. Geez.'

He rubbed his hand over his face again. 'No, you're right, Emma, I'm a cripple. And here you are, wanting to sentence me to an eternity of being like this and pining after him?' He heaved a deep sigh. 'No, thanks. Go and wait for him, and when he comes back for you, be happy together. Simone and Michael are grown-up now. None of you need me. Please. Let me go.'

I hesitated, then dealt my trump card. 'I know what you want more than death, because I want it too.'

He looked away.

'I want to be his Serpent, Leo. I want to join with him when he comes back, be one with him. I want him to absorb me.' I reached out and touched his hand. 'And I know you want him to absorb you too. It's what you asked him to do when you thought you were going to die.'

He still didn't look at me.

'What if you had the chance to be drained by him?'

His head shot up so he could see me.

'Be one with him forever?' I went on. 'I know that's what I want. I'm sure you want it too. Would you wait for him to come back, to have that chance?'

'That would be wrong, Emma. He loves you.'

'He loves you too, Leo, and I'm sure he'd be merciful enough to do this for you.' I smiled and shrugged. 'My husband and my best friend in one gorgeous package. How could I lose?'

He chuckled. 'That sounds so wrong.'

'Shen only seem to follow human rules when it suits them.' I held his hand tighter. 'So what do you say? Come home with us and spend the time with us, your family, until he returns. Simone's only fourteen and has a lot of growing to do. Michael could really use your advice; he isn't on speaking terms with his father. They really do need you, and I could use your common sense sometimes. And when he returns, both of us can ask him to do this for you. You know he won't say no to me. So how about it?'

'That would be a dream come true, Emma, you know that,' Leo said softly.

'I know, my friend, I know,' I said, and squeezed his hand. 'I want it too.'

'He would do it for me?'

'He already did, but Kwan Yin grabbed you. Remember? He started to drain you. He'd do it again if we asked him, I'm sure.'

'But I have to drink this stupid Elixir of Immortality. Then he won't be able to drain me.'

'He will. I know he will — he was concerned about draining Meredith. Take it, Leo, and come back with us for a little while longer.'

Leo gestured towards the sideboard in his dining room. 'It's over there. It's been there the whole time; I could have used it any time I wanted. Wanna get it for me?'

I couldn't contain the huge smile. 'Sure.'

I rose and went to the sideboard, where an elegant silver and glass jug held the Elixir of Immortality. The liquid was the colour of red wine but its sour, unpleasant smell was discernible from quite some distance. I grabbed a glass as well and took both to him, placing them on the coffee table next to him.

'Smells awful,' I said.

'Yeah,' Leo said. He grinned. 'Must mean it's very good for you.'

'Don't do it yet — I'll get the kids,' I said.

'Does Michael still object to being called a kid?' Leo said.

'Oh, very loudly,' I said, and went to the door of the villa. *Call them for me*, I said to the stone.

Done, the stone replied.

Simone and Michael hurried back to the house, Meredith and the official following.

'He's really going to do it?' Simone said, flushed and excited.

'Yes,' I said.

'This will be your first time to see this then,' Meredith said. 'Come and watch.'

Simone raced to Leo and hugged him around his shoulders. 'Drink it, Leo. I want to see what happens.'

I took the jug and poured him a glass of the crimson, foul-smelling liquid. 'Drink it quickly if it tastes as bad as it smells.'

'Yeah,' Leo said, and raised the glass in a toast to all of us, then drank.

'Wait ...' Meredith said, but it was too late.

Leo dropped the glass, his mouth opened in a silent scream, his eyes wide. He shredded quickly, like a demon, his edges disappearing into black feathery streamers. It happened too fast for me to react; he exploded and was gone.

CHAPTER 10

'You killed him!' Michael shouted, rounding on Meredith and the official. 'You murdered him!' He sagged against the couch and rubbed his hand over his face. 'What happened?'

'This is not possible,' the official said weakly. 'This cannot have happened. He was an ordinary human.' He drifted to the side of the room and fell to sit on a chair against the wall. 'I am contacting the Master.'

Meredith went to Michael and looked into his eyes. 'That wasn't Leo, Michael, believe me. Only demons react like that to the Elixir. Only demons say it smells and tastes bad; to everyone else it tastes very good. That was some sort of demon copy or replacement or something, and the Elixir destroyed it.'

'So where's Leo?' Michael said, glaring at her.

Meredith turned to the official. He snapped back from whoever he had been communicating with, obviously stricken. 'The Master is on his way. We have no idea how this happened. Mr Alexander must have been replaced some time recently. That copy was undetectable though, which is very disturbing.'

'*So where is Leo?*' Michael stormed to his feet.

A middle-aged man in traditional maroon robes appeared. 'We don't know,' he said.

The official bowed and saluted him. 'Yanluo Wang.'

'Come with me to my office and we'll work out what to do,' Yanluo Wang, King of the Underworld, said. 'The demons may know something — we will contact the demonic side of Hell. It appears that Leo has been taken.'

He took us back to the main building, where we'd arrived on the roof, and we went inside the ground-floor entrance. The interior was like a modern office. He led us past sleek designer cubicles containing staff in traditional robes working on computers, and to his office at the other end. It overlooked the lake and contained a meeting table, an executive desk and a computer. A whiteboard to one side was covered with indecipherable symbols and scribbled Chinese characters.

He saw me looking at it and grinned. 'Recent strategic planning session.'

'This really is Hell,' I said wryly.

'Oh, absolutely,' Yanluo Wang said. 'Some residents are punished by being forced to sit in on the sessions. If they are to be punished more severely, they are made to take the minutes of the meetings.' He sat at the large conference table and gestured for us to sit. 'Let me call in the contacts and see what I can discover. Please, give me a moment.' His eyes unfocused.

There was a tap on the door and a man opened it slightly. 'Wong Mo wants to help,' he said.

'I don't want the Demon King having any part of this,' Simone said. 'He caused all this trouble in the first place by putting a price on my father's head.'

'If any demonic influence is involved, then he will be able to help, Princess,' Yanluo Wang said. 'He has equal jurisdiction down here in Hell.'

'It's a good idea,' Meredith said. 'The demons may have some ideas. They can't get up to anything here on the Celestial side. Let them come, Simone.'

'Emma?' Simone said.

'The King has to vow not to try anything,' I said. 'Don't ask me what I mean, just tell him that and make him agree.'

I know exactly what you mean and I vow I will not try anything, the King said into my ear. *I vow I will not try to make you change or convert you. But I'd love it if you were to show me, darling Emma. I dream about your Mother form at night.*

'He can come,' I said, and the Demon King appeared at the other side of the room, with a long-haired Chinese man who looked like John at his side.

Simone moved so quickly she was a blur. She held out one hand, summoned Dark Heavens, and as she ran towards the two men she ripped the sword from its scabbard and threw it aside. She stopped with the point of the blade against the long-haired man's throat.

It was John's son, Martin. He stood with the sword at his throat and smiled slightly, his eyes full of amusement as he looked down at Simone. The King didn't move; he just stood beside Martin with a similar small smile.

Michael drew the White Tiger and stood behind Simone, the sword to one side. 'If you're going to do it, let me help,' he growled.

I stood behind Simone but didn't attempt to call my weapon; she was doing quite nicely by herself.

Simone quivered with rage but her voice was soft and icy and the tip of the sword didn't move from Martin's throat. 'You disgusting piece of scum-sucking pond slime. You lied to Leo, you kidnapped me, you killed a demon child that was used to nearly kill our father, and in the end you did kill our father because you took me to One Two Two and Daddy had to trade his head for my safety.'

'This really is not necessary, Princess,' the King said. 'He is here as my emissary and right now you cannot harm him.'

'It's true, Simone,' Meredith said. 'Don't try anything, it's a waste of time. As an emissary he has protection.'

Simone barked with frustration and swung Dark Heavens to take Martin's head off. The sword passed through without hurting him.

'Didn't know you had it in you, Simone, well done,' Martin said, still smiling slightly. 'There is hope for you after all.'

Michael put the White Tiger away but his gaze didn't shift from Martin. 'You will pay for what you did, Ming Gui,' he said, his voice a rasping growl. 'You'd better not leave Hell because if you do —'

'We … will … find … you,' Simone finished with him.

She held out her hand and Dark Heavens' scabbard flew into it. She sheathed the sword, raised her hand and dismissed it. 'I swear that you will taste my blade, betrayer of my father,' she said softly.

'If it means anything at all, I was honestly misled and thought that we'd be going somewhere safe to spend some more time together,' Martin said. 'I didn't know that the demon child wasn't you — I really did think I'd managed to get you out. That's why I fought alongside you, Simone.' He nodded to me. 'Emma. And my feelings for Leo were genuine.'

'Then what are you doing here with *him*?' I said, gesturing towards the Demon King.

'I have my reasons,' Martin said, the smile fading. 'I have dug my grave and now I must lie in it.'

'He's all mine, and a most desirable trophy,' the Demon King said. 'The Mothers adore him.'

Martin winced.

'You give him to the *Mothers*?' Simone said.

The King spread his hands and shrugged. 'When I'm not using him. Have to keep him busy, you know. Come, little Simone, sit. Let's see what we can do about finding your pet lion.'

The Demon King and Martin moved to the conference table, saluting Yanluo Wang as they sat. Yanluo Wang saluted back. Simone hesitated, then she and Michael sat at the table as well, and I joined them.

'Okay,' the Demon King said, leaning on the table. 'I hear that Leo was replaced. This probably happened while those kids were guarding him and got lured away. Did you destroy them when I sent them to you, Emma?'

I remembered the three demons who had come to the offices a few days before. 'Two ran, but I tamed one.'

'Bring it, I'll have a look inside,' the King said. 'It may have some information for us.'

'Don't destroy it,' I said.

'It will look bad if I don't destroy a demon that's been tamed, you know that.' He smiled slightly. 'But for you, anything.'

Nigel tapped on the door and poked his head around. 'The demon, ma'am.'

'Bring him in, Nigel.'

Nigel opened the door and Four Seven Three, still appearing as a teenager, entered. The demon saw the King and froze. It changed into True Form: a green humanoid of about three metres tall, with scales, tusks and bulging eyes. Red tufts of hair sprouted from its head. It stood frozen in front of the King for a moment, then scurried around the opposite side of the table and crouched behind me.

'Come here, little one,' the King said kindly.

The demon made a small keening sound of terror and slowly rose. It moved like a puppet towards the

King, still making the keening sound. 'Protect me, Lady,' the demon said, its voice pitched high with terror.

'It's all right, I won't let him hurt you,' I said.

The King swivelled in his chair and raised one hand towards the demon. 'Take human form and come sit in my lap.'

The demon didn't stop its quiet wail of fear, but it changed back into a teenager and lurched to the King. It flopped into his lap and he wrapped his arms around its waist and spoke into its ear.

'Emma told me not to destroy you, child. We need some information. Where is Leo?'

The King tightened his grip and the demon threw its head back and screamed.

'Where's Leo?' the King said, his eyes bright with pleasure as he held the writhing demon. 'Where did they take him?'

'I don't know,' the demon wailed. 'Stop. Stop. Make it stop. Lady, please, make it stop.'

'Emma, you only asked him not to destroy it. He can still hurt it if he likes,' Simone said urgently.

I didn't reply; I was engrossed in the demon's agony. It was fascinating.

Simone turned to see me. 'Emma?'

'Emma's enjoying the show,' the King said. 'Look at her face.'

'Emma!' Simone shouted.

Something inside me clicked and I realised what was happening. 'Stop hurting it! There's no need for this, just get the information.' I ran my hands through my hair. 'God.'

The demon's screams turned into gasping sobs.

The King turned his attention back to it and spoke into its ear. 'The look on your face is something that will keep me going for a long time, dear Emma.'

He glanced at me, his eyes full of sly amusement. 'We could have so much fun together, you and I.'

'Geez, Emma,' Simone said softly.

'What the hell?' Michael said.

'Does it know where Leo is?' I said.

The King concentrated. 'Nope.'

He released the demon and it fell off his lap to lie unconscious on the floor. Simone, Michael and myself all jumped up and ran to it.

'Let me,' Meredith said, and we moved away to give her room. She touched the demon, then glared up at the Demon King. 'That was totally unnecessary.'

'I know,' he said, his voice mild. 'But it was so much fun!' He gestured towards me. 'Don't you agree, Emma?'

I didn't reply.

'What now?' Simone said. 'Someone's taken Leo, and we have no idea where he is.'

'Let's go have a look in his cell, see if they left anything when they took him,' Martin said.

'Good idea,' I said. 'Meredith, put the demon to one side and let it recover.' I glared at the King. 'That demon is mine. Do not touch it.'

Meredith picked up the demon like a child and put it on the floor at the side of the room. Demons were generally tougher than humans, and could take much more physical abuse because of their almost liquid insides. An hour or so on the floor and this one would be fine again.

We all went back to the villas. Someone was sitting on the porch of the first one — an elderly woman, her face serene as she watched the lake. She smiled slightly at me as we went past.

We went into Leo's villa. Downstairs were a small living room with a television, a kitchen and a dining room. Upstairs were two small bedrooms and a bathroom. Leo's clothes were in the closet in the bedroom; it was disturbing to see exact replicas of his clothes in his room back at the Peak hanging here.

Simone went to the drawers in the closet and pulled one out. 'Look, Emma.' There were a few pairs of pink boxers at the bottom of the drawer. I shook my head.

'I know what happened to them — I heard you talking about it when we were in Australia,' Simone went on.

'What happened?' Michael said.

Simone turned to him and lowered her voice. 'When we were in Australia, Emma and Leo were playing jokes on each other non-stop, and Emma got into the laundry room and dyed all his undershirts and boxers pink.'

'He did stuff like that to me too sometimes.' Michael turned away. 'Damn but I miss him.'

'I can't believe he kept them,' I said, glancing back down at the underwear. 'He kept a pebble from the beach too, from the looks of it.'

Simone looked into the drawer. 'That's not a pebble, that's something strange.' She pulled out a small golden stone about a centimetre across. 'This is some sort of demon.'

'George?' I called to the doorway. The Demon King, Yanluo Wang, Meredith and Martin entered.

'What is it, Emma?' the King said.

Simone held the stone out to him. 'What do you make of this?'

The Demon King took the stone and stared at it, then grimaced and made a gesture of frustration. 'Six!'

'You destroyed that one,' Yanluo Wang said.

'I thought I did,' the Demon King said grimly. 'It was part of a posse of four demons helping —'

'Helping One Two Two,' I broke in. 'They had meetings when I was held in his apartment in Hell. There were four of them. I remember.'

'I thought I'd tracked them down and destroyed them all,' the King said. 'Looks like I missed this one.'

'Do you know where it is?' Simone said. 'It has Leo!'

'I have a pretty good idea where he is,' the King said. 'These demons were messing with stones before. Even if they're not still in the same place, you'll be able to pick up an idea of where they've relocated if you go there. But I'm quite sure they'll still be in the same nest.'

'Where?' Simone said eagerly.

'I will agree to tell you on one condition,' the King said.

'Oh God, George, is there always a catch?' I said.

'Yes, of course there is,' the King said. 'Michael's mother, Rhonda, must spend a week down here in Hell, here on the tenth level, so I can attempt to talk her out of marrying the Tiger.'

'We can't wait that long. What if they hurt him or kill him while they have him? We need to go find him *now*,' Simone said.

'They won't hurt him, Simone,' the King said. 'He'll be fine.'

'Of course they'll hurt him!' Simone said, frustrated.

The King waved a hand at Meredith and turned away. 'Tell them, Gweipoh.'

Simone and Michael waited, staring at Meredith.

Meredith and Yanluo Wang shared a look, then Meredith sighed and her shoulders sagged. 'You're here now, you might as well know. Leo is a Celestial Worthy; all he needs is to take the Elixir. He's between life and death right now, so they can't hurt him or kill him. He doesn't feel pain, and any wounds they inflict will heal immediately. They can hold him, and that's about it.'

'What do you think they want?' I said.

Meredith turned to the King. 'Tell us about Six.'

'Six,' the King said, and smiled slightly. 'Six was

involved with little One Two Two when Simon was in charge of the Triad activity here. He may have taken over. I hear that your students have fun practising on Triad operations, safe in the knowledge that any supernatural means they use to break up the criminal activities won't be reported?'

Meredith and I shared a look, then Meredith spoke. 'We let the students practise their Arts on any criminals they find, yes. Apparently they've put a huge dent in the income from organised crime in Hong Kong.'

'I wouldn't be surprised if Six has taken over One Two Two's empire, ladies,' the King said. 'He'd probably like you to back off. As I said, give me Rhonda for a week and the information is yours to do with as you please. You will know where they are, and you can go in and sort them out.'

'Maybe *they're* giving *you* a chance to have Rhonda for a week,' I said.

'Oh, very good, my Lady,' the Demon King said. 'Most worthy of you, but I can assure you, I swear, that I myself have nothing to do with them. They have done this on their own and I am merely taking advantage of the opportunity. I've wanted to have a chat with Ms MacLaren for quite some time now. All she has to do is come down and spend a week here, something of a small holiday. That's all.'

'Demonic or Celestial side?' Meredith said.

'Demonic.'

Meredith leaned back and looked at the King appraisingly, then at Michael.

'You want to steal the Tiger's fiancée?' I said incredulously.

'I want to steal his Queen,' the Demon King said.

'It's up to Mom,' Michael said.

'If you ask her to do this she will, Michael, you know that,' the King said. 'If she truly loves the Tiger then a week here will not be such a trial. And if I can talk her out of marrying him, it's a bonus for you.'

'No tricks,' Michael said grimly.

The Demon King spread his hands. 'I vow I shall not use any mind control at all. Just the power of persuasion. Hopefully you and I together can make her see exactly what she would be getting into if she were to marry this asshole.'

'Do you want her for yourself?' I said.

'Of course I do, that's why I'm doing this,' the King said. 'But more than that, I don't want to see this remarkable woman with beauty and courage become the plaything of a man who will only treasure her until he has her in his possession. Once they are wed he will ignore her like all the others and go off in search of a new prize.'

Michael sighed and ran one hand over his face.

'See? He knows,' the King said with a grin.

'Vow that you won't hurt my mom and I'll go talk to her,' Michael said.

'She will be accommodated as the princess she is. She will experience nothing but beauty and pleasure while she is in my care. That I vow.'

Michael studied the King appraisingly, then nodded once. 'Deal. Let me see what I can do. How do I contact you?'

The King focused on Michael and Michael nodded. 'Okay, got it. Take us back up and I'll talk to her.'

CHAPTER 11

'You sure about this, Michael?' I said, as we appeared back in the kitchen at home.

Monica was frantically mopping the floor, which was awash with water, at least five centimetres deep. It flowed into the hallway, leaving a dark stain on the carpet. Gold's child was hovering next to her but she didn't seem to notice it. 'Oh no!' Simone said, and skipped through the water to the kitchen doorway.

'I'm glad you're back, Aunty Emma. It was awful and it hurt Uncle Marcus,' the stone child said.

'Did it hurt you, Monica?' Simone said.

'No, ma'am, just Marcus, but Master Gold says he'll be okay.' Monica mopped more briskly but her shoulders were shaking.

I went to her and put my arm around her. 'Stop, Monica, go rest. Is Marcus in your room?'

She nodded through silent tears.

'Gold is with Marcus in their room, checking him over,' the stone in my ring said.

'Go to him,' I said. 'We can fix this.'

I gently prised the mop out of her hand and led her to her room, which ran off the back of the kitchen.

I tapped on the door and opened it a crack for her. 'Go inside, Marcus is there. Everything will be fine.'

'Daddy said to stay out here, Aunty Emma,' Gold's child said, sounding concerned. 'It was pretty bad.'

'You stay out here with us, we'll look after you,' I said to the child. 'Do you need anything?'

The child dropped to rest on the kitchen bench. 'No, I'm okay.' It hesitated, then, 'It was really scary.'

I held my hand out and the stone flashed over to snuggle into my palm. 'Thanks, Aunty Emma,' it said softly.

'What the hell happened here?' Michael said, looking at the water in bewilderment.

'Simone, it would be a good idea to send it down the drain before it completely destroys the carpet,' I said.

Simone's face went rigid, then she relented and raised her hand. The water on the floor coalesced into a large glistening sphere that formed a funnel and gushed into the kitchen sink and down the drain. 'Elemental,' Simone said. She concentrated again and the remaining water lifted out of the carpet into a brownish lump, leaving the wool completely dry. 'Wow, our carpet's dirty. We should have it cleaned, Emma.'

'Water elemental?' Michael said.

'Yes,' I said, carefully holding the stone child in my hand so that I wouldn't wake it; it had fallen asleep almost immediately. 'They're annoyed that Simone won't summon them. She doesn't have any control over what they do. This one probably sensed she was in Hell and came here to find out what happened.'

Gold came out of Marcus and Monica's room. 'They'll be fine, ma'am. Marcus nearly drowned though.' He turned to Simone. 'Princess, you really need to train with us. Learn how to summon and control these elementals.'

Simone turned away and headed towards her room.

'Talk to her, Lady Emma, please,' Gold said. 'This can't go on. Marcus was nearly killed. It's only the fact that he's half-Shen that saved him; any ordinary man would have drowned.'

He saw the stone in my hand and his face softened. 'My baby was very scared by the whole thing.' He reached out and I passed the stone to him.

'Hold me, Daddy,' the baby said sleepily.

'I won't let you go, bebe,' Gold said. He looked up. 'Everything's under control now, ma'am, it should be fine. But please talk to Simone.'

'She could control water elementals and she doesn't want to,' Michael said grimly. 'Typical. 'Bout time she grew up.' He fell to one knee and quickly saluted me. 'By your leave, Lady Emma, I'll go talk to my mom.'

'Say hello to her for me,' I said, and he disappeared. 'Take the baby home, Gold. I'll talk to Simone.'

'Can I talk to you in your office, after you talk to her?' Gold said.

'Sure, wait for me there.'

I went to Simone's room. She sat at her desk, working on her homework. I entered and sat on the bed.

'Simone, if Marcus wasn't half-Shen, that elemental would have killed him. Both he and Monica are lucky to be alive.'

'Why can't those elementals just go away and leave me alone?' Simone said without looking up from her homework. 'I hate them.'

'That's part of the problem, sweetheart, and you know it.'

She turned and glared at me. 'I don't want any of this, Emma. I just want to be a normal kid. These elementals are freaking everybody out.'

'Learn to control them then.'

'Yeah, sure.' She turned back to her homework. 'I'll learn to control them and be even more powerful. I'll walk through the Academy and people will be *more* scared of me.'

'Nobody's scared of you, Simone.'

She threw her pen onto the exercise book. 'Don't lie to me, Emma, I can sense it. Some of the students are terrified of me. Like I'm some sort of monster or something. And after what happened in Heaven, it'll be twice as bad. The ones that know about your serpent are terrified of you too.'

'The serpent is the least of it. I'm terrified of myself.'

She dropped her head and her voice became small. 'Me too,' she said. 'Do you have any idea how much damage I could do with even a small amount of yin? And my control of it isn't that great either.' She shook her head. 'When I bring it out, it wants me to destroy everything.'

'You need to learn to handle the elementals, Simone. Next time we may not be so lucky. Go down to the Academy and have the Masters teach you.'

'I *hate* the Academy. I hate the way everybody bows to me, and is scared of me, and some of them freaking want to be my friend just because of who my father is. I hate it.'

'I can have one of the Masters come here, if you like. You won't even have to go down to the Academy. Just learn to control them so they don't hurt anybody.'

She sighed and turned back to her book. 'Okay, Emma, I s'pose you're right. But please, talk to the school. I don't want to repeat Year Nine. I've made some great friends there and they treat me like an ordinary kid.'

'I'll talk to them for you.'

'Thanks.' She tapped the book with her pen. 'This biology homework is due soon. I need to finish it.'

I rose to go. 'Okay, sweetheart. Let me know if you need anything.'

'Do me a favour?' she said without looking up from her book.

'Hm?'

'Don't call me sweetheart, Emma, I'm not a little kid.'

I bowed slightly. 'Princess.'

She spun and threw the pen to hit me right between the eyes. I caught it easily and returned it to her desk.

'Leo's gonna call you sweetheart,' I said. 'He called me that all the time.'

'Leo can get away with it 'cause he's gay.'

'Nothing to do with it.'

'Out, Emma.'

'Ma'am.'

'Humph.'

I went into John's office, where Gold was waiting, his baby cradled in his hands. The stone drifted out of my ring across the desk, then took human form and sat in the chair opposite me. It was a slim European gentleman in his mid-sixties with a shock of white hair, wearing a smart dark green suit and tie. He leaned his elbows on the desk and rubbed his hands over his face.

Neither he nor Gold looked at each other but both appeared concerned.

'Well?' I said.

Gold glanced at his parent and shrugged.

'Normally we stones stand aside from the ...' the stone from my ring searched for the word, '... the organic community. We keep ourselves to ourselves, serve the Celestial as we should, and have our own network. But things have been happening.'

Gold touched his child thoughtfully and it made a soft squeak of sleepy contentment. My stone's face softened as it watched.

'We have problems,' Gold said. 'And although we would like to solve them ourselves, I think this time we need help.'

'We're disappearing,' the stone from my ring said. 'Without a trace.'

'Show her, Dad,' Gold said.

A haphazard web of glowing white lines, about sixty centimetres across, appeared floating above the desk. The lines connected hundreds of tiny black dots. It was like looking at a virtual map of the internet.

'The black dots are Eastern stone Shen — there are about a thousand of us altogether,' Gold said. 'The lines are our network.'

'This is what the network looked like six months ago,' the stone from my ring said.

About fifty of the dots blinked out, taking the glowing lines with them.

'Five months ago,' Gold said.

Another twenty dots blinked out and the lines representing the network thinned.

'Three months ago,' the stone said.

Another fifty dots blinked out. About a tenth of the lines had disappeared.

'Last month,' Gold said.

'We lost another twenty in the last two weeks,' the stone said.

'About a fifth of the stone Shen have disappeared in the last six months?' I said, incredulous.

'Slightly less, about fourteen per cent,' Gold said. He placed his hand over his child. 'Most of them were our younger progeny, less than a thousand years old.'

'And now the Demon Prince Six has reappeared,' the stone said. 'And this was the one that was messing with stones before.'

Gold held his child closer. 'Six is once again stealing our children.'

'Please tell me the Celestial knows about this,' I said. 'I'm not the first person you've made aware of this, am I?'

They didn't reply.

'The Jade Emperor has to know,' I said.

'He probably does, but unless we ask for Celestial intervention, this is an internal stone matter, as we have an agreement with the Celestial to …' The stone from my ring smiled slightly. 'Butt out of our business.'

'Then get onto the JE and tell him about this, because something is obviously going on,' I said. 'What's happening to them anyway?'

'That's the thing, Emma,' the stone from my ring said, his voice gravelly with stress. 'We have no idea.'

'We were hoping that, as Dad's owner, you could bring this up with him on our behalf,' Gold said.

'Why don't you go to him yourselves?' I said, then nodded as I understood. 'Of course, lose too much face asking him to come in and give you a hand when you've already told him to butt out.'

'Face has nothing to do with it,' Gold said indignantly.

'You know she's right,' the stone from my ring said with resignation. He glanced up at me. 'So will you talk to him?'

'Prepare a memorial. I'll look at it and sign it and chop it and send it on as FHG,' I said.

'FHG?' Gold said, confused.

'First Heavenly General,' the stone said.

'Oh.' Gold shook his head. 'You don't show the same amount of respect for Celestial matters that others do, Emma. Sometimes it's … strange.'

'Try spending all your time with her,' the stone said dryly. 'I thought my attitude was perverse.'

'I've written the memorial for you; it's on your hard disk in the Celestial Matters folder,' Gold said.

'I'll take a look,' I said.

Gold saluted me. 'Ma'am. By your leave.'

'Go home. If I need you I'll contact you.'

Gold disappeared. My stone folded up its human form and returned to the ring.

I opened the email program on John's computer.

'There's an email there from Simone's teacher; I sent her one making an appointment for you to see her day after tomorrow, after school,' the stone said. 'I've changed the computer records of Simone's absences from school, so all you have to do is claim that they have the absence rate wrong.'

'You shouldn't have done that, it's dishonest,' I said.

'It's a Celestial solution to a Celestial problem. If she wasn't the daughter of Xuan Tian this would not be an issue.'

'Anything else important there?'

The stone's voice softened. 'You have five challenges, but this is pretty bad. Er Lang has called you out.'

'What?'

'I don't know why he wants to match skills with you. He's one of the most powerful warriors on the Celestial, and I'm sure he could defeat you easily. He definitely doesn't want Simone's hand — he's a confirmed bachelor.'

'He's gay?'

'Nobody really knows; he's never been seen in the company of anyone, male or female. There's some speculation that he has something going on with his dog.'

'*Ew*. And his dog's *male*.'

'Oh come on, Emma, look at the Tiger. You know that he gets together with his wives sometimes in Tiger form and —'

I raised my hands. 'Stop. Stop. Way too much information. You are thoroughly squicking me out here.'

'Okay, Emma, think for a moment. What if your own true love, the Turtle, were to return to you in full possession of his senses but in such a weakened state that he could only take True Form?'

I dropped my hands.

'What if you were swimming, and the Turtle were to drift through the water to meet you, told you in John's voice that he loved you with all his heart, then held you gently with his flippers and —'

I interrupted again. 'Cut it out. Enough. Whatever. I'll cross that bridge when I come to it.'

'It might happen, Emma ... Oh. Incoming message.'

The stone was silent for a moment and I waited for it. When it spoke its voice was full of amusement. 'Typical of the Tiger. Lady Rhonda's engagement ring just contacted me. The Tiger has given her a sentient diamond Shen as the centrepiece of the ring. Nothing nearly as precious as me, but diamond Shen are quite rare. This one is arrogant to the extreme. Lady Rhonda wants to know if you are free for lunch tomorrow so she can discuss the ramifications of going to Hell, and what she can expect there.'

'Am I free?'

'I've already confirmed it for you. Now, we need to look at your diary, because you have five challenges you need to take care of sometime in the next two weeks.'

'And Er Lang.'

'Him above all.'

CHAPTER 12

'I feel like Persephone,' Rhonda said over her salad. The years had been kind to her and she radiated intelligence and confidence. 'Kidnapped by Hades, and having to spend half her life in Hell because she ate six pomegranate seeds.'

'He won't keep you there, don't worry,' I said. 'He's trustworthy.' I rested my chin in my hand. 'Actually I trust him more than some Celestials. He won't try anything.'

'He won't expect me to sleep with him or anything?'

'No. Absolutely not. Nothing like that. He just wants to talk to you.'

'I know. He wants to talk me out of remarrying Ah Bai.'

'Congratulations, by the way. The ring is gorgeous.'

She held the engagement ring up for me to see. The central diamond must have been at least two carats and it was surrounded by more large diamonds in a glittering circle. 'It's way too big and a pain most of the time, but it's the thought that counts, I suppose. And you're right, these stones can be extremely useful.'

'I am honoured to be able to serve the Lady Rhonda and to act as the symbol of her troth,' the stone in her ring said, sounding like a young Chinese woman with a soft Putonghua accent. 'As a stone that will never decay, I represent the Emperor of the West's unfailing adoration of her.'

'Nice to meet you,' I said. 'Do you have a name?'

'I was not graced with a name until the Lady Rhonda took possession of me. She has chosen the name of Zara for me, and I am honoured.'

Rhonda shrugged. 'She's a sweetie.'

'I am proud to serve, my Lady,' the stone said.

Rhonda leaned on the table, serious, her salad forgotten. 'What will it be like down there?'

'On the demonic side? I have no idea.'

'But Simon Wong kept you imprisoned there for a few weeks. What was that like?'

I leaned back. 'It was exactly like a posh apartment on top of Harbour City. I could even see the cars parking on the roof of Ocean Terminal. The windows were an illusion, and they were sealed, but it was just like an apartment.'

'All indoors?'

'The Celestial side of Hell appeared to be outdoors, even though there was no sun. I couldn't tell you, Rhonda, but my guess is that it'll be pretty nice.'

'Hell. Nice.' She shook her head. 'Lovely.'

'It's good of you to consider doing this for Leo, Rhonda. I really appreciate it.'

She shrugged. 'The Tiger said I should be fine, and it will prove to everybody on the Celestial that I'm serious about marrying him, so he supports me a hundred per cent.'

'All the best for both of you then. It'll be a tough job for you, being Empress of the West. You'll have a lot to manage.'

She picked up her fork and moved her salad around. 'You have no idea. He's putting me in charge of a massive palace and a hundred women who are all baying for my blood.'

'They're not. They wouldn't.'

She smiled up at me. 'Well, you know — we all like to think that we're his special wife, the one he'll leave all the others for. Now I've stepped up and I *am* the one he nearly left the others for — they hate me. Your friend Louise is probably going to come down as soon as she can and ask you to do something about me.'

'She knows you're my friend. She wouldn't ask me to do that.'

'The others are pushing her. I've already been attacked a couple of times.' She nodded over her shoulder to where two burly sons of the Tiger stood near the door of the restaurant. 'The Tiger's had to give me a personal guard.'

'*To protect you from his other wives?*'

She nodded, amused. 'He's said I should start disciplining them the minute we're married. Apparently during Imperial times it was quite common for the Empress to order misbehaving concubines beaten or executed.' Her smile became wry. 'Sometimes he really needs to be dragged tail-first into the twenty-first century.'

'Good luck managing that,' I said with disbelief. 'I'm glad all I have is a Heavenly realm falling to bits and about four hundred young and unruly Disciples skilled in Arts that give them the ability to maim and kill without even thinking. What you have is much worse.'

'Hey, Zara,' Rhonda said.

'Hmm?' her stone replied.

'Who has it worse, me or Lady Emma?'

'Oh, definitely Lady Emma,' the stone said. 'She has to deal with that ugly piece of worn-out jade on her finger on top of all her other trials.'

134

'It was me that wore you out, baby,' the stone in my ring said slyly.

'Pig-dog,' said Rhonda's stone.

'Look, if the cheating works both ways then it's still cheating and the win isn't valid,' Marshal Meng said, looking and sounding more like an exasperated grandfather than a Heavenly General.

'I cancelled out the cheats they used. I wasn't cheating myself, just making it fair,' Marshal Liang said, his huge whiskers bristling.

'You are all contributing to the wealth of the casino lords, you know that,' I said as I entered the conference room.

'What do you think, Emma?' Marshal Meng said, gracefully indicating his heavy-set companion. 'Liang here uses his abilities to cancel out the cheat on the roulette wheel. That's still cheating and invalidates any wins he makes.'

'I just make it fair,' Liang said, indignant.

'Do you lose then?' I said. 'As if the wheel wasn't weighted?'

Liang nodded. 'Perfectly fair if I win.'

'Then when you lose you're still adding to the wealth of the casino lords and you doubly lose,' I said, to a chorus of chuckles from the other Generals. 'Some of that wealth is siphoned into the Triads, some of the Triads are controlled by demons, so if you lose at the table you're helping the enemy. If you win at the table you're cheating. Give it up.'

Liang opened and closed his mouth, then smiled wryly. 'You have a point, Lady Emma.' He looked around at the other Generals. 'I suppose we should have this meeting now.'

The Generals sat down good-naturedly at the conference table and waited for me. In the past they had kept their forms reasonably standard, but as they'd come to realise that I didn't really care what they looked like, they'd taken a variety of interesting — and sometimes nondescript — forms.

The highest-ranking General present was Marshal Ma, who was a slim, elegant gentleman in his mid-thirties, his hair cut short in the modern style, wearing a pair of slacks and a polo shirt. He seemed too refined to be involved in killing demons but was a fierce and talented fighter.

Next to him sat Marshal Gao, wearing traditional silvery Tang-style robes and armour, his long hair bound in a topknot. He was concentrating and so, for a change, wasn't glowing gently, but as the discussion became heated and he forgot, the glow was guaranteed to return, much to his embarrassment.

Marshal Liang sat next to him, a fierce, heavy-set man with huge sideburns, wearing a short yellow robe and large cloth boots in the Mongolian style. He still looked put out at having his gambling habits called into question.

Marshal Meng was on the other side of the table, looking more like a fifty-year-old bureaucrat than anything else in his black robe and old-fashioned plain cloth cap. He smiled serenely, still appearing like a kindly grandfather.

Closest to me was Marshal Zhu, who, although seeming a pretty, fresh-faced young woman of about sixteen, was much tougher and wiser than her appearance suggested.

As the one with highest precedence, I spoke first. 'Four main things,' I said. 'Leo's kidnapping. Northern Heavens.' There was a chorus of groans around the table. 'Me getting called out by Er Lang —'

'*Er Lang* called you out?' Ma said, shocked.

I nodded. 'Simone and elementals. Anything major from you guys?'

'Nothing as bad as that,' Ma said. 'Leo first, this is important. We heard about the stone left in his cell in Hell — this is disturbing.'

I leaned on the table. 'Why are Simon Wong's little friends who could manipulate stones becoming more active now? You'd think they'd have tried us right after Lord Xuan left. But they've waited eight years, and all they've done is take Leo.'

'Of course it's a trap,' Marshal Liang said. 'The Demon King will probably tell you where they are so you can walk right into it.'

'Do you think he's helping them?' I asked. 'He vowed that he wasn't, but I don't know if I can trust him any more. With Lord Xuan gone, he's making more and more attempts at us. And he's used Leo's disappearance as a way of getting Rhonda into Hell for a week. It almost seems too convenient.'

'I strongly doubt he's in league with them,' Ma said. 'Given half a chance these stone-controlling demons would probably put a knife in the King's back. He's hoping you can destroy them without him having to do anything, same as when Simone destroyed One Two Two for him.'

'God, he's always manipulating me into doing his dirty work for him,' I said, frustrated. 'Recommendations?'

'Do we have any ideas on his location?' Marshal Zhu asked, her firm voice counterpointing her sweet façade.

'We have demons in Hell, and stones all over the place with their ears to the ground looking for something unusual or a new nest,' I said.

'So far nothing has come up,' the stone in my ring said.

'Well, then, there's nothing we can do until we obtain some intelligence,' Ma said, sounding like a corporate CEO in a board meeting. 'As soon as you have news, call us in for an emergency session and we'll work out what to do then. In the meantime, they can't hurt your Retainer, they'll just hold him as a bargaining piece and bait for their trap. We need to find out where he is.'

'I hope the stones get something soon,' I said.

'We should be able to spare some agents as well,' Meng said. 'Many of our foot soldiers are demons.'

'Thank you,' I said. 'What's next?'

'Er Lang,' Liang said, his voice loud and deep. 'Do this one quickly, my Lady, he could injure you. You'll need to get all your current challenges out of the way in the next week so that you can be ready when the Demon King gives you the information about Leo.'

'Are any of you close enough to Er Lang to ask him why he's doing this?' I said.

The Generals looked at each other around the table, then they all shook their heads.

'Let me ask Ah Yu,' Ma said. 'Give me a second.'

'Er Lang's a bit of a loner,' Yang said, as General Ma unfocused, talking to Guan Yu. 'Wasn't so antisocial before the Monkey King defeated him. After that, he spent a lot of time off doing stuff by himself.'

'That really happened, just like in the legend?' I said. 'The Monkey King beat him?'

'Thoroughly spanked his ass,' Zhu said, amusement lighting up her face. 'We weren't called in, the Dark Lord wasn't called in, but the Monkey King caused chaos in the Celestial Palace for some time. The legend is quite accurate; it was only the Lady in the end who could subdue him.'

'Big blow to Er Lang's massive ego,' Liang said with similar amusement. 'Spanked by a monkey.'

The other Generals laughed.

'And spent a lot of time by himself since,' Meng finished. 'Dunno whether he has issues about women in positions of power, but this might be the problem he has with you, and the reason he's called you out.'

'He called me out too,' General Zhu said, the silver pins in her hair glittering as she moved her head. 'When I received my investiture, he was onto me almost immediately to test my Celestial Worthiness. He does seem to have issues with women in power.'

'Oh, *wonderful*,' I said, and rested my chin in my hand. 'He's gonna take out his humiliation on me and give me a lesson at the same time. Is he honourable enough to hold to the ground rules?'

'Yes, it'll be fine,' Meng said. 'You have Celestial backing on that. He's a Shen of honour, he'll respect the limits that are in place.'

'True,' Zhu said, and the other Generals nodded agreement. 'He was completely controlled when I faced him, and in the end he admitted that both me and my sister Bo Niang are more than qualified to hold our rank.'

'I'll arrange to face him right after I've talked to Simone's teacher,' I said. 'I don't know which one I dread more.'

Ma snapped back. 'Ah Yu says that he hasn't spoken to Er Lang in about seventy-five years, except on formal Celestial business to do with the administration of the City of Hell.' He smiled wryly. 'I think he has issues with our ...' His voice trailed off and the other Generals glared at him. 'Well, he has no issues with Guan Yu, but he doesn't like the company that Ah Yu is keeping, so to speak.'

'He has that much of a problem with me?' I said. 'The fact that I'm a lowly human and he has to report to me?'

The Generals all quickly shook their heads. 'No, no, not you, ma'am,' Marshal Ma said. 'Er Lang has issues with the nature of some of the Dark Lord's officers.'

General Zhu snorted delicately with derision. 'It's been a thousand years already, he should *get over it*!'

'Get over what?' I said. 'More information!'

The Generals shared a look over the table, then General Ma deliberately changed the subject.

'Simone and elementals,' he said. 'She *must* learn to control them, Lady Emma, this is becoming very difficult. They appear out of nowhere, sometimes damaging property, other times threatening any Shen who they feel have slighted Simone. It's only a matter of time before they either hurt a Shen or appear before a non-Celestial.'

'Simone's agreed to have lessons with one of the Wudang Masters to learn how to control them,' I said, to a concert of relieved sighs. 'Problem solved.'

'How about bringing down a couple of teachers from Celestial High to talk to her while we have the door open?' Meng said, and the other Generals nodded. 'She could learn so much more at CH; her current school really doesn't cater for her special abilities. She could make friends with other Shen —'

'She refuses point-blank to discuss this possibility,' I said. 'Look at it her way. She's one of the most powerful creatures on the Celestial Plane. People are either scared of her or try to cultivate her because of who she is. At the International School she's just another kid.'

'But she's not learning to use her full capabilities,' Zhu said. 'There is probably so much more that she could do. She is such a valuable asset in the battle against the forces of Hell. Allow us to call her into battle more often. The more of us women kicking demon ass, the better.'

'She's growing up as an ordinary teenager — as far as I can make it anyway,' I said. 'She uses her abilities when she has to, but she's in a reasonably normal Earthly household, and I think this is what the Dark Lord wanted for her. She's not a child soldier fighting

140

demons; she's as much as possible just a fourteen-year-old girl.'

There was silence around the table for a moment, then Zhu said softly, 'You are very wise sometimes, my Lady.'

'True serpent,' Meng said. 'Impressive, ma'am.'

'Northern Heavens,' I said. 'Tell me how bad it is.'

They shifted the papers to bring up the Celestial budget.

'And you *will* tell me what the issue is with Er Lang.'

They ignored me.

The next morning Marcus dropped me outside the Pedder Building so that I could go to the Celestial Combat Arena to face my first challenge. The street was close to the middle of Central District and always packed with pedestrians and cars. The Pedder Building was one of Hong Kong's few remaining old colonial buildings: a multistoreyed mall with a delightful old-fashioned lift and a vintage-themed tea house on the first floor among the clothing factory outlets.

I went around the corner and crossed Queen's Road at the busiest pedestrian crossing in the Territory. It was at least fifteen metres wide and always packed with people jostling to get across the road. The government had made a pedestrian overpass part of the conditions for the developers who'd built on either side of the road, but they'd never bothered to put it up and had never been penalised for it. People were regularly struck by cars as they dashed across the road against the lights.

I walked up D'Aguilar Street, also packed with pedestrians, past the Wellington Street intersection, and turned right onto Wo On Lane. This was a narrow, near-deserted street, only wide enough for one car, and a tiny oasis from the crush of people. I walked to the end of the lane, passing some closed-up restaurants, a laundry and the back of the buildings facing Wellington Street. The lane was a dead end, with a small altar to a local god at the end, and a gate opening onto a park with a circular arena-shaped paved area — the Earthly analogue for the Celestial Combat Arena. Stairs ran up the side of the park to the streets of Central high above, showing exactly how steep the mountainside could be in some parts of Hong Kong.

I nodded to the local god and turned right at the end. An alley, only about a metre wide, ran from the lane to Wellington Street. At its end, on the corner with Wo On Lane, there was a simple metal door with a single blank deadlock.

I touched the door and its voice chimed in my head, sounding like high-pitched bells. *Name and authorisation?*

Lady Emma Donahoe, First Heavenly General, the stone said.

Right on time, the door said. *Good luck, ma'am.*

The door disappeared and a dark corridor was visible in its place. I took a deep breath and walked through.

The corridor was completely silent as I trudged along it. The floor was plain grey and the walls around me red brick. Closed doors appeared on my left and right, about three metres apart. A young man in full traditional armour appeared in the corridor in front of me and saluted. 'Madam General. This way.'

I saluted back and followed him. He led me further down the corridor and stopped to open a door on the left. 'Ma'am.'

I nodded to him and went into the preparation room. It had a large wooden screen on one side, gorgeously decorated with a scene of cranes and pines made from semi-precious stones. A couple of traditional rosewood chairs sat against the wall with a rosewood side table between them holding a pot of tea and four upside-down cups. A small rosewood altar stood against the wall, a burning stick of incense in front of its statue of Xuan Wu.

My armour was ready for me, fitted onto a mannequin made of rosewood that looked very similar to a dressmaker's dummy. A demon servant, appearing as a young woman, stood silent and attentive next to the armour. The weapons rack was empty; nobody but myself could call the Murasame.

I dropped my handbag onto one of the chairs and shook my shoulders out. Then I nodded to the demon and she peeled the armour off the dummy and helped me to place it over my plain jeans and shirt. She carefully checked the buckles and straps, ensuring that the armour was secure.

'Good luck, ma'am,' she said, bobbed her head and disappeared.

I turned to the altar and studied it for a while. Then I said, 'Wish me luck as well, John,' and exited the room.

The same young man in armour waited for me on the other side of the door. He bowed slightly and held his right arm out to indicate the way.

'No weapon, ma'am?' he said as he led me down the corridor. 'Your opponent is armed.'

'Only if needed,' I said.

'A shame,' he said, smiling over his shoulder at me. 'I have never seen the Destroyer.'

'The blade must be fed if it is released,' I said.

. He stopped for a second, hesitating, then continued walking along the corridor. 'I apologise, ma'am, I was unaware. Usually only demonic blades require feeding.'

'It is yin,' I said.

. He nodded understanding. 'Ah, the Dark Lord's blade, of course. It is a wonder you are able to wield it at all, ma'am, such a blade must be a very difficult to control.'

'We have reached an understanding,' I said.

'It is sentient?'

'Not as such. It is not intelligent but it does have a will.'

'Fascinating.' He stopped and gestured; the corridor ended and a moon gate led to a wider corridor to the left. 'Ma'am.'

I nodded to him and went down the corridor, leaving him behind. The corridor brightened at the end and opened out into the Arena.

It appeared as an open area in a glade of bauhinia trees, the dirt floor covered with their pink and white blossoms. Sunshine sparkled through the leaves of the trees, rippling over the ground in bands of light and shade. A sweet breeze heavy with the scents of plant life and damp earth brushed my face.

My opponent stood on the other side of the clearing next to the officiator for the match. He had the nut-brown skin of a Chinese who had spent a great deal of time in the sun, and the square, heavy-set features shared by those from the North. He was at least half a metre taller than me, large and strong. He wore traditional lacquer armour similar to mine — square plates held together with wires — but his armour was as brown as his features. He held a spear that was at least two metres long with a slender, sharp tip surrounded by a red horsehair fringe and decorated with a piece of green silk.

A small young woman in traditional Tang robes in a similar shade of brown, intricately embroidered with green leaves and pink flowers, stood behind him as second, her expression concerned.

I moved to about two metres from them and saluted, bowing slightly. 'Sirs and madam. I am Emma Donahoe, answering a challenge.'

My opponent released his spear and it remained

144

vertical beside him without being held. He saluted me and spoke, his voice deep and rich. 'I am Sang Shen. This is my sister, Sang Ye, who will act as second.'

I bowed slightly to him and his second. 'I am honoured.'

Sang Shen took hold of his spear again and both of us turned to the officiator.

He unrolled a scroll and read from it. '*Tai Ren* Sang Shen challenges Regent General *Da na huo* to a test of martial skills. This test will not be to the death, and will be considered satisfactorily concluded when either combatant yields. Are these terms agreeable?'

I saluted the officiator and spoke first, as I held higher rank. 'I hold these terms agreeable with a request for the further consideration of light contact, and restraint from injuries that cannot be healed by a mortal such as I.'

Sang Ye, the second, hissed under her breath.

'This creature is not a mortal, she is a serpent,' Sang Shen said. 'There should be no consideration for such as her.'

'This matter has been questioned and adjudicated already,' the officiator said. 'It has been resolved by edict from the Celestial that General *Da na huo* is indeed both mortal and unable to recover from major injury such as disseverment of limbs and removal of vital organs. Her request is upheld by the Celestial.'

Sang Ye made a short, angry gesture with one hand but remained silent behind her brother.

'Who is your second, madam?' the officiator asked me.

'The Jade Building Block of the World,' I said.

'I will act,' the stone said.

Sang Ye turned away quickly, then turned back. She opened her mouth but, without turning to see her, her brother raised his hand to stop her speaking. 'The terms are acceptable.'

I nodded to Sang Shen. 'You will use the spear only?'

Sang Shen grimaced and raised the weapon. 'I will use the spear that was my father.'

Oh dear, the stone said. *The search is starting to bring back results and they are all bad.*

Tell me quickly, we're beginning, I said, and moved into the middle of the clearing. I stood and saluted Sang Shen, who grunted and nodded back.

'*Oh dear*' *is right if he's showing this much disrespect for someone of my rank*, I said to the stone.

That spear is *his father*, the stone said. *This is very bad. His father was a tree spirit —*

Resident in the Northern Heavens, right?

Sang Shen moved about two metres across from me and raised the spear in a guard. I responded with an open-handed guard; usually I loaded my hands with chi, but in this case they were empty of energy. I would have to rely on purely physical, and as a last resort call the Destroyer. I didn't have enough chi left to wield it predictably in battle any more.

Precisely, the stone said. *His father died three months ago due to the energy drain resulting from the absence of the Dark Lord. And so, of course —*

He blames me. Lovely.

And, completely pissed that you have a stone as second, Emma. You know how plant spirits feel about us stones.

Oh wonderful, icing on the cake. I didn't know why plants and stones had so many issues with each other — neither side would discuss it — but the enmity had been around for a very long time. I knew what I had to do.

No, you can't take that risk. You don't have good enough control.

Help me out here.

Sang Shen spun the spear over his head in an

impressive arc, then leapt forward with the point of it aimed straight at my left eye. The red horsehair fringe around the tip of the spear was designed to fool the enemy into thinking that the point was further away than it actually was, but I had extensive practice with the Wudang spear and knew what to expect.

I slid my head sideways to avoid the tip, and he swung the spear in an arc to slam the side of my head. I ducked underneath the blow and quickly delivered a side kick to his abdomen as he regained enough leverage to bring the weapon back again. Because of its length it was difficult to wield in a circle quickly. My kick had no effect; it was like hitting a tree.

Is his tree in the Northern Heavens too?

Yes. He's dying as well, Emma, and so is his sister.

Dear Lord, I'm killing both of them without doing anything at all.

You are not killing them, you are fighting to save them.

Sang swung the spear through a long underarm arc, again trying to take out my eyes with it. I feigned unbalance, acting unprepared for the attack, and he pressed home the advantage by jabbing at my eyes. I made a show of regaining my balance, used quick movements to avoid the jabs and leapt back.

Sang stopped and lowered the spear, studying me appraisingly.

He's picked you, the stone said.

Ready?

Please don't do this.

Too late.

I moved as fast as a well-trained human could and went for his face. I ducked under the guard of the spear and managed a couple of good blows at his tanned cheeks, bouncing off ineffectually, before he managed to swing the staff around to knock me to the ground.

He raised the spear with its tip pointed at my abdomen and plunged it straight through the armour into me. I managed to roll slightly to the right so that the tip entered the far left side of my abdomen. At first it felt like I had just been hit with it, then the pain seared through me.

Sang's face went hard with satisfaction and he pulled the spear out.

'She yields!' the stone shouted. 'Desist!'

Sang Shen held the spear above my throat, his face fierce with pleasure.

I gasped for breath. 'I don't want you to die ...' My voice trailed off and I tried to speak, but the air wouldn't come. 'Help me. Tell me what we can do.'

'You have done quite enough,' Sang Shen said, and raised the spear for the killing blow.

He disappeared, and the face of the officiator appeared above me. 'I will seek medical attention for you.'

I gripped my side where the spear had entered. I couldn't do anything about the pain while the officiator was watching.

'No need,' the stone said. 'We have our own transport and medical care.'

The stone took human form, lifted me easily like a child, and carried me out of the Arena. Every move made me want to wail with the pain. I clenched my jaw against it, but couldn't avoid the occasional whimper as the stone's feet hit the ground.

'You can stop the pain now,' the stone said a moment later as it carried me down the hall back to the preparation room.

I concentrated, moved the demon essence through myself, and blocked the pain from the wound. I sighed with relief and relaxed into the stone's arms.

'You can put me down now,' I said.

'No need,' the stone said, and opened the dressing

room door. 'Out,' it said to the demon servant, and lowered me gently into one of the rosewood chairs.

'Is the blood black?' I said.

Its face was creased with concern. 'No.'

'How deep?'

'About three centimetres. I nearly didn't make it inside you to block it in time.'

'Close enough.' I attempted to rise but my muscles didn't want to cooperate. 'Damn, I'm going to need a minute before I can walk.'

Simone appeared next to the stone. 'Oh my God, Emma, what happened?'

'Don't touch me! I can walk out,' I wheezed.

'Let's see you do it,' the stone said.

I struggled to rise then fell back. 'Don't touch me, Simone. Give me a few minutes to get myself together and I'll be fine. Go back to school.'

Simone took my hand and everything disappeared.

'I entered her body and became an internal shield against the point of the spear,' the stone was saying. 'But it went in further than I wanted — that tree spirit was mightily fast.'

'Why did she permit herself to be pierced anyway?' Meredith asked. 'She is much better than he is. How did this happen?'

'He is a tree in the Northern Heavens and he is dying,' the stone said. 'She wanted to give him a measure of satisfaction by drawing her blood.'

Simone sighed with feeling. 'Well, the injury is fixed now, but I'm not going back to school until she changes back.'

'Emma,' Meredith said. 'Can you hear us?'

'Yes.'

Simone squeaked, and Meredith put her hand on Simone's arm.

'Emma, change back to human form.'

'Why? I like being like this.' I thrashed my tail and rose to sit upright. I held my skinless arms in front of me, admiring them. 'I should do this every time I'm injured, it would save everybody a lot of trouble. Healing a small wound like that is easy.'

They didn't reply, just stood around the hospital bunk staring at me, so I flipped my coils to one side and slid off the bed. I slithered around the room, checking the furniture. The Mountain infirmary was quite small and I had to coil my snake end around me to fit.

'It feels good to be so powerful,' I said, looking at my skinless face in the mirror. I flicked my long, forked tongue. 'I don't have to worry about touching Simone, or the demon essence getting out of control, or anything like that. I can just be *me*.'

'I'd rather have you in human form, Emma,' Simone said, her voice small.

I glared at her. 'You're supposed to be in school. I'm seeing your teacher this afternoon to try and fix this up, and here you are skipping school again. You said you didn't want to repeat Year Nine.'

She shrugged. 'It's only Mrs Stupid Wilder's biology class. She hates me.'

'Go back to school,' I said.

'Change back to human form and I will.'

'You should do as I tell you, Simone, I'm your guardian.'

'I don't like your demon form, Emma, and I'm not moving until you're human again,' Simone said, stubborn.

'All right. Have it your way, but this form really is much more powerful.' I grinned at Meredith. 'You wanted to have a look, Meredith. Go right ahead.'

Meredith turned her Inner Eye on me but I barely felt it. She gasped.

'Well?' I said.

'Eighty-one or eighty-two. Somewhere around there,' she said softly.

'Nice,' I said.

'Change back now, please, Emma,' Simone said.

'If I have to.'

I concentrated and returned to human form. Meredith tried to catch me but Simone was in the way. I hit the floor hard.

I came around with Meredith looking down at me. Simone was gone. I pulled myself upright.

'All right?' Meredith said.

I nodded. 'I'm fine. I feel terrific actually. Full of energy, raring to go.' I smiled with regret. 'Ready to kill the next challenger I face.' I ran my hands through my hair. 'Meredith, we can't go on —'

She cut me off. 'Don't try to resign again, because we won't have it.'

'But I'm a *demon*!'

'So are some of the students. So is the Dark Lord's Heavenly Army.'

'I'm totally incapable of doing this job. I'm not an Immortal. I don't have the experience.' I sighed with exasperation. 'You're a great help, Meredith, all of you are, but this stuff is really out of my league.'

She sat on the bed. 'True. You're not Immortal. You don't have the experience. Sometimes the Dark Lord made his most brilliant decisions on the spur of the moment. He chose you because his love clouded his judgement, and it was a brilliant decision. You are detached from any of the Heavenly political rivalry. You are his chosen, and therefore to be obeyed in all things. And now you have Celestial Endorsement, so we have no choice.'

'Of course you have a choice. Take the job from me, please, Meredith. I can't do it.'

'No, thanks. The job's a bastard, and none of us want it. And once you have Celestial Endorsement, we must obey. You're probably aware that many of the past Emperors of China were bloody lousy rulers, but the people followed them anyway, unless they lost Celestial Endorsement and were toppled.'

'That's just what people said when the Emperor sucked badly enough —'

'No.' She cut me off again. 'If you have Celestial Endorsement, your subjects must obey you. That's the way it is. We have no choice; we have to do what you say. That's what kept many dynasties on the throne.'

'No *way*,' I said.

'Yep. We'll help you and advise you, but if you tell us to do something, we'll do it.'

'But what if the demon nature takes over?'

'I assume the Jade Emperor knows what he's doing.'

I opened my mouth to protest but she continued over me. 'That's the way it is. You have endorsement, we'll obey you. And we're thrilled to bits that we don't have to do the job, 'cause it's a bitch.'

'Oh, thank *you*.'

'You are most welcome, my Lady. We in the Academy don't give a damn about anything except that you are doing your damnedest to protect and administer the place as best you can, and we are going to do our damnedest to help you.'

'The Shen outside hate me.'

'Hate is too strong a word. They are suspicious of you. You're only an ordinary mortal; and for some your gender is an issue as well. You're young and really haven't found your way around yet. I wish the Dark Lord was here to help you, but as he isn't, we Celestials in the Academy are here to assist.'

'If anybody discovers my demon nature it'll be all over, Meredith.'

'Then we just have to ensure that they never do.' She rose. 'Now up you get, Missy Emma, and go practise the meditation techniques we've covered. Clear the demon nature as much as you can, control the chi flow, restrain the demon essence, and call me when you think you have it.' She concentrated for a moment. 'Meditation room on the seventh floor is free, all yours.'

'Thanks, Meredith,' I said quietly.

'Feel like tearing the limbs off things rather than meditating right now?' she said.

I nodded.

'Let me know when you don't.'

'Yes, ma'am.'

CHAPTER 13

The Australian International School had significantly grown in the nine years that Simone had been attending. It had spread onto two campuses and its population had doubled.

Marcus parked at a meter near the school and I headed up to the roof. The swimming pool and netball court were up there, and Simone was still at practice. She gave me a cheery wave when she saw me. She was playing the position of goal attack and neatly took the ball that was passed to her by another girl. She turned, lined up the shot, and missed.

'Pick it up, Simone,' one of the other girls said. 'You should be doing better!'

'Tiffi's right, Simone,' the coach called from the sidelines. 'Spend some time on the hoops, please.'

Simone raised her hands and laughed. 'Yeah, I've been slacking off. I'll come up and practise tomorrow, I promise.'

One of the other girls threw her arm around Simone's shoulder and gave her a friendly squeeze. 'That's our star shooter.'

The coach blew her whistle. 'That's it, ladies, we're done.'

Simone trotted to me with a huge smile. 'So what's the go with my teacher?'

'I'm seeing her now. Marcus is waiting downstairs in the car.'

'Okay, I'll take a shower, then meet you down there.' She dropped her voice. 'At the moment I'm getting about one in three to two in five in. Think I should ramp it up? They're starting to complain that I've done a lot of practice but I haven't improved.'

'If you've been practising then you should be getting about three in five or slightly better, I think,' I said. 'And don't make it predictable, have some good and bad patches as well. Just make sure you aren't unnaturally good.'

She nodded. 'Sounds about right.' She grinned. 'I'm counting on you, Emma. I've made a lot of friends in this grade and I don't want to repeat. Fix it up with the teacher, please.'

'I'll do my best,' I said.

We headed down the stairs together, her to the showers and me to the meeting room in the school office.

Simone's home-room teacher was a thin woman in her mid-forties with brown hair immaculately blow-waved into a large teased hairdo. She frowned when I entered the meeting room and gestured for me to sit across the table from her.

'I'm Mrs Wilder.' She pulled out some paperwork, put on her reading glasses and pointed the frown at me. 'Actually, this meeting is far too late to fix anything, Mrs Chen. You may not be aware of it, but Simone has been consistently skipping school all this year. Despite all our attempts to warn you, she's been expelled. You need to find a new school for her.'

I sat there for a moment, stunned, then pulled myself together. 'Are you sure about those attendances?' I said.

'Can you check the records again, because I'm sure she's been coming to school.'

Mrs Wilder raised a sheet of paper. 'I've been keeping watch on her attendance and noting down all her absences, Mrs Chen. She's been absent far more than the permitted ten per cent and we tried to warn you that she was skipping. She even missed my science class this morning, skipped it completely, and joined the English class after that without giving any reason for her absence.'

'I'm not Mrs Chen, I'm Emma Donahoe, call me Emma,' I said, frustrated. 'Simone is an orphan. I'm her guardian.'

Mrs Wilder shuffled the papers. 'This may explain her truancy, and why you aren't aware of it, then. Maybe you should find counselling for her.'

'She does receive counselling, and some of it is during school hours.'

Mrs Wilder removed her glasses and glared at me. 'You should be notifying the school about it then.'

'Simone went through a lot when her parents died, but she doesn't want special treatment so she asked me not to tell anybody,' I said.

'She has you thoroughly worked out, doesn't she?' she said. 'You don't know she's skipping, and you don't let the school know that she has problems purely because she asked you not to.'

'Simone's mother was murdered by a gangster when she was a baby, and Simone herself was kidnapped by the same gangster when she was six years old,' I said. 'When her father went in to try to release her from the kidnappers, they killed him.'

The teacher sighed with exasperation. 'She told you this story and you believe it?'

'I was there,' I said. 'He had his head cut off by a Triad gangster right in front of both of us.'

She studied me appraisingly, then picked up some glossy leaflets. 'Now I see where she gets the ability to tell lies about missing school. It's too late anyway. If we'd been able to talk to you about Simone's truancy earlier we may have been able to avoid expelling her. I doubt you would have believed it though. Anyway.' She pushed the leaflets across the table to me. 'Here is some information about some excellent girls boarding schools in Australia and Malaysia. I think a more disciplined environment would benefit her greatly.'

'She's lost both her parents, one of them in front of her, and you're suggesting that I abandon her as well?' I said in disbelief.

'The schools would probably provide her with more care and attention than you obviously do,' she said snidely. 'You weren't even aware that she was skipping school, and I've been trying to talk to you about it for six months. If you'd made the effort to come in the first time I called you, this would not have happened.'

I was silent. She was right.

Oh, come on, Emma, the stone said into my head. *Don't let this bitch get to you. You're doing a great job of caring for Simone.*

She's been expelled from the school she loves, I replied. *Wait until I tell her. Isn't there anything we can do?*

This woman has a vendetta against you, she's convinced you are an inadequate carer, the stone said. *In her own ridiculous way she wants the best for Simone. Nothing I can do because she's been tracking Simone's attendance on paper, and all I can change is computer records.*

'Is there anything I can do to avoid this?' I said. 'Simone loves this school.'

'School policy,' Mrs Wilder said. 'You've had plenty of opportunities to fix this over the last six months and have made no effort.' She closed her folder with a snap. 'She'd be much better off in a boarding school where they're going to give her at least a small amount of attention.'

I opened my mouth and closed it again. This woman would not believe any story I spun.

You've lost, Emma, the stone said.

I sighed with resignation. 'Mrs Wilder, I'll be talking to the principal in the hope I can sort this out,' I said. 'This is a fabulous school and it's really the best place for Simone.'

'Going over my head will not solve anything,' she said. She rose and opened the meeting room door. 'Good day to you, Mrs Chen.'

I hesitated, then decided that it wasn't worth the effort to point out my name again. 'I hope we can fix this, Mrs Wilder.'

'The best way to fix this would be for someone else to be looking after this poor child,' Mrs Wilder said as she closed the door behind me.

Simone was waiting for me outside the office. 'How did it go?'

I didn't reply, I just pressed the button for the lift. Simone stood behind me, waiting for me to say something.

'Well?' she eventually said.

I went into the lift, turned and pressed the button for the ground floor.

'I don't have to repeat Year Nine, do I, Emma?' Simone said. 'All my friends will leave me behind. Tell me you fixed it.'

I didn't look at her. 'You've been expelled for not attending enough classes, Simone.'

'*What?*'

'I'll talk to the principal, but I don't think I'll be able to change it. We'll have to arrange a home tutor, or get another school for you. We'll work something out.'

The lift doors opened and we walked out of the school towards the car.

'Didn't they give you any warning or *anything*?' Simone said as she walked beside me.

I ran one hand through my hair. 'Apparently they've been trying to talk to me for a while. This looks like it's mostly my fault. They've been attempting to contact me and I've been ignoring them.'

I got into the front passenger seat of the car, and Simone got into the back. 'We can go home now, Marcus.'

'This is the thanks I get for being a freaking battle machine for them,' Simone said, resentful. 'I protect these little assholes from demons that would happily tear them into small pieces and they take away the only thing that makes my life worthwhile.' She slapped the seat next to her. 'Dammit, Emma, why didn't you talk to them sooner? Can't we fix this up by messing with their heads or something? *Do* something! This is your fault!'

'I had no idea you were going to be expelled, sweetheart —'

'*Don't call me sweetheart!*'

Suddenly the car was full of water. It pressed in around me, squashing me. I took half a breath and my lungs filled with water. I was vaguely aware of an impact, but I was suffocating. I panicked, trying to breathe, then made a frantic attempt to open the window of the Mercedes. The electrics didn't work. I scrabbled at the door handle but I was choking. Everything started to fade.

Then I could breathe and I was coughing up water in the front of the car. Marcus was unconscious next to me, and the Mercedes had run into a parking meter on the wrong side of the road.

'Emma! Marcus!' Simone cried from the back. 'Are you okay?'

159

'I'm okay,' I gasped through the coughs. 'Marcus looks bad.'

'Freaking stupid elementals,' Simone said, and got out of the car. She came around and opened the door on the driver's side. 'Marcus? Marcus!'

'Get the water out of his lungs,' I gasped. 'Doing the same for me would be a good idea too.'

The water gushed out of Marcus. I nearly choked as water charged up out of my throat. It flew through the air and splashed outside the car.

'He's not breathing, Emma,' Simone said, frantic. 'Oh my God, he's blue. Do something!'

'You've had training in CPR,' I said. 'Do mouth to mouth on him. I can't breathe enough to do it.' I struggled to turn in my seat and removed the seatbelt. I put my hand on his chest over his heart. 'His heart is beating, he just needs a kickstart on the breathing. Breathe into him, let's get him going.'

She put her mouth over his and breathed into him. His chest rose.

'Keep it up,' I said, still choking. The water had hurt my throat and every breath was difficult.

Meredith appeared behind Simone. 'Move back.'

She did, and Meredith put her hands on Marcus's face. 'Don't leave us now, Marcus,' she said.

Marcus took a huge shuddering breath.

'I'll take him home,' Meredith said. 'Let me send someone with another car for you, and we'll tow this one.' She studied me. 'You'll be fine, you just need some healing on that throat.'

She leaned out to speak to Simone. 'Stay here with Emma, we'll send a car and a truck for you. Pick up the car and move it so that it's aligned with the kerb and make it appear that it's just parked here. Make the damage on the front invisible, so it doesn't attract any attention.'

'Okay,' Simone said weakly.

Meredith put her hand on Marcus and both of them disappeared.

I collapsed backwards into my seat. The interior of the Mercedes was soaked and my clothes were drenched. Simone extracted the water from the interior and my clothes and it funnelled outside the car and splashed onto the ground. Then she sat in the driver's side next to me and leaned back.

'I think I need a lesson in controlling the elementals.'

'I'll arrange it.'

'Thanks.'

The phone rang that afternoon right after I'd put it down from booking an appointment with the school principal. 'Hello?' I said.

'It's the Sparrow.'

'Oh, hi, Zhu Que, is everything okay?'

She chuckled. 'You always assume something's wrong when one of us calls you.'

'That's because it usually is,' I said.

'True. In this case it's not a new attack. I heard that Simone finally agreed to learn how to summon and control her elementals, and about time. I was wondering if you wanted any help teaching her.'

'One of the Masters is going to teach her.'

'Won't work, Emma. Only we Winds and the most powerful of our children can control the elementals. Anyone else who tries it is putting themselves at risk. I have a great deal of respect for your Masters, they've taught some of my best Red Warriors, but you need someone who can do it themselves. You should have asked one of us before.'

I sighed. 'I know how busy you guys are with the demon attacks happening all the time. You have far better things to be doing than teaching a teenager.'

'I have a daughter who seems to have the talent, and I'll be teaching her. I was wondering if Simone would like to join in and both of them can learn together?'

'You can teach Simone how to manipulate water even though you'll be doing fire?'

'Elementals are elementals. The skills are the same.'

'When can you start? Can you come after school ...' My voice trailed off. 'Damn.'

'There's a problem?' she said, concerned.

'She's been expelled for not attending enough classes. I'm talking to the principal of the school tomorrow but it's looking bad. They've been tracking her attendance.'

'Humph,' the Phoenix said. 'The child is helping to protect these ungrateful humans from the demon horde and this is the thanks she gets. She'll be much happier at CH anyway.'

'People are scared of her, Phoenix.'

'With good reason.'

'And she knows they are.'

'Oh.'

'At the International School she's an ordinary girl — she has a lot of good friends who think she's perfectly normal and aren't afraid of her. Even down at the Academy the students are frightened of her, and some of them befriend her purely because they think it'll help them progress.'

'Such students are not worthy of the title Disciple of the Dark Lord.'

'What about the students at CH? They'll know exactly who she is as well.'

She hesitated for a moment, then, 'Let me come with you and help fix this. I can clear it up so she won't be expelled from her Earthly school.'

'I'd prefer not to mess with anybody's head at this early stage; you know how the Jade Emperor feels about that.'

'True.'

'So let me talk to the principal and we'll see what we can do.'

'Good luck with that, Emma,' she said. 'So, since Simone will be free in the near future, we'll do some elemental training. It'll keep her mind occupied anyway.'

'You can use the training room if you promise not to burn down the apartment block.'

'That I cannot guarantee. I have a place that is suitable; it is high and clear of any vegetation. How about tomorrow, say about 10 am?'

'I'm seeing the principal tomorrow morning. How about just after lunch?'

'Sounds good. The training ground is in the Western District.' A scroll appeared on the desk in front of me. 'Give this to Simone, it's directions. We'll be waiting.'

'We'll probably come by car; you know I can't travel.'

The scroll disappeared and was replaced by another one. 'Here you go. Just park on the road leading up to the building, I've marked it on the map. Oh, and can I watch when you face Er Lang?'

'No!'

'But the other two Winds said they'll be there.'

'*What?*'

'See you at the Arena. This should be good.'

'Bring a first aid kit, Phoenix, I may need it.'

'As you wish, ma'am.'

'Oh, please, don't give me that.'

'Madam Regent Heavenly General.'

I sighed into the phone.

'See you tomorrow, Emma,' she said, her voice full of amusement.

The next morning there was a tap on the door as I worked through the day's admin. The Tiger, Marcus and Monica came in. The Tiger and Marcus sat down on the other side of my desk, looking grim, and Monica stood behind them, clasping her hands together.

'You're seeing Simone's teacher this morning?' the Tiger said, subdued and gruff.

'Yes, I'm seeing the principal of the school to try and let Simone stay on. Marcus will have to drive me there in half an hour or so. What's up, everybody?' I said.

Marcus shifted uncomfortably. 'I'm sorry, ma'am, but I've had enough.'

'Enough?' I said.

He made a gesture of helplessness. 'This is my home. It always will be. But things are just too ...' He looked to the Tiger for help.

'They're worried they're gonna get killed if they hang around much longer,' the Tiger said, still gruff. 'And I really don't blame them. Before, they had Ah Wu's protection, and they felt safe knowing that the demons wouldn't hurt them. This time,' he glanced at Marcus, then back to me, 'this time there isn't anybody to protect them from Simone.'

'She's having training on controlling elementals later today,' I said.

Marcus made the helpless gesture again.

Simone charged through the door, nearly hitting Monica with it. She stood panting, hesitating, then said, 'I won't hurt you guys any more, I promise.' She threw her arms around Monica's neck, taking her by surprise. 'Don't go, Monica, I love you. I need you. I don't want a demon looking after me, I want *you*.'

'They'll come back when they're sure they'll be safe,' the Tiger said. 'Let them go. They're scared.'

Simone pulled back to see Monica, and shook her head. 'I promise I won't hurt you again.'

Monica didn't look at Simone, she looked down at the floor.

'Simone,' the Tiger said, 'could you control what happened with the elementals the last couple of days? Could you stop it from happening?'

Simone released Monica and glared at the Tiger. 'I'm having lessons!'

'Fine,' the Tiger said, and rose. 'When you can make that promise and know for sure that you can deliver on it, then I'll bring my son and his wife back. Until then, I'm going to keep them safe. Go to Celestial High and learn to control your power, Simone, 'cause as long as you refuse to do it, people are going to get hurt.'

'I don't *want* to go to Freak Central!' Simone shouted, and ran out again. Her bedroom door banged shut.

Monica started to cry and I gave her a tissue from the box on the desk.

'Go get packed,' the Tiger said. 'I'll take you as soon as you're ready.'

'Bring us back when it's safe again, please,' Monica said.

'I know, she's like a daughter to you,' the Tiger said kindly. 'Go and pack. It'll all work out.'

'Is that all right with you, ma'am?' Monica said. 'We don't want to go, but we're scared. We love you and Miss Simone, but we don't want to die.'

'I won't stop you, guys,' I said. 'Go back to the Palace. Things will get messy around here soon anyway, with this Leo thing happening.'

'Thank you, ma'am. We won't go to the Palace, we're going to spend some time back in the Philippines visiting our families,' Marcus said, and rose. He bobbed his head to me, and he and Monica went out.

'Was this your idea?' I asked the Tiger.

'No. They called me. And as members of the household they have the right to invite me in, so I'm not breaking Simone's stupid rule of me not visiting.'

I sighed. 'They're afraid, and they have good reason. Damn.'

'Do you have some demons that can do the job?'

'Ah Yat can take over the house again, and we'll find someone to drive the Academy bus.'

'What about you?'

'What about me?'

'Who's going to drive you around?'

'Me.'

'Oh, come on,' he said. 'All of us spend our time in the back of the car catching up on work. You need that time to get things done, and I know you meditate and chill too. Take a Horseman.'

'Which one?' I said suspiciously.

He waved a hand airily. 'I dunno, one of the Two Seventies or Eighties. Trained, strong, faced demons before, more than human. They'll probably fight over the opportunity to do it.'

'We're going to have Leo back as soon as we find him, so it's only for a short time.'

He snorted with amusement. 'You think Leo will accept Immortality, then come back here and be your driver again?'

'I'm sure he will,' I said.

'Pfft,' he huffed. 'Whatever. We'll see what happens when it happens. Any word on where he is?'

'Demons and stones are looking. We have spies in all the major demon haunts. So far nothing has turned up.'

'Let me know when you have the information. I want a piece of whoever took the Lion. Thoroughly unacceptable.'

'Done,' I said. 'I'd better prepare for this meeting.'

'My Lady,' the Tiger said, and saluted me. 'I'll take Monica and Marcus when they're ready. Neither of them have seen their families in the Philippines for a while, and Marcus's mother, Wife Sixty-Three, is going too.'

'You never call Marcus by number,' I said.

'No. He's not Shen enough. He's way too human to have a number.'

'Good.'

'I might go talk to Simone,' he said. 'She really should be going to CH, Emma, otherwise she's going to remain a danger to herself and others.'

'I'm beginning to think it might be the best choice for her,' I said.

'Wonder if they're having any interesting classes at CH right now. Let me take Simone to have a look. Is that okay?'

'Sure. If we could get her to go there a lot of our problems would be solved,' I said. 'But first thing after lunch, she and I are heading to Western for a lesson in elemental summoning, so make sure she's here when I get back.'

'None of your Masters can teach that.'

'No, so the Phoenix is doing it.'

'Good idea. Maybe she can talk missy into CH as well.'

The principal, Mr Barrow, was a small, portly man in his mid-forties wearing a pinstripe suit. He invited me into his office and sat me at the small conference table. 'I'm afraid I can't do much to help Simone, Ms Donahoe, it's a matter of school policy. Many parents seem to think that school is an optional activity for their children and give little thought to the fact that the absences are causing their child's education to suffer.'

'Most of Simone's absences are because of her past, Mr Barrow,' I said. 'She's lost both parents and another close family member, and has received a great deal of counselling for it.'

'And you never notified the school?' Mr Barrow glanced at Simone's file. 'There are more absences here than can be explained by her need for counselling. And Mrs Wilder tells me that you didn't even know about most of them.'

'Simone has suffered a great deal in her life, Mr Barrow, and I want to give her everything possible to help her recover from that,' I said. 'Skipping school is just a symptom of her distress. I can provide you with a medical certificate if you like. She asked me not to arrange for her to have special treatment, but in this case it looks like she needs it.'

'I just wish you'd told us all of this before,' he said, closing the folder. 'The paperwork has gone through, Ms Donahoe, and I'm afraid your daughter will have to find a new school. With the large legacy that Simone has at her disposal, I'm sure many of the other international schools would be delighted to take her.'

'Could that legacy be used to help this situation?' I asked.

Whoops, very much the wrong thing to say, the stone said.

He stiffened. 'I don't think so. This is far too late. School policy stands. I'm sorry, Ms Donahoe, but Simone is out.' He rose to show me out. 'If she has any younger brothers or sisters, they are welcome to apply, but as you know the waiting list is closed.'

'Yes,' I said with grim humour. 'There's a waiting list to go onto the waiting list.'

He shrugged. 'You're not the only parent who regards this as an excellent school for their child.' He opened the door and held out his hand for me to shake it. 'Maybe you should have sent her along to school more, if you regard it as so good. I'm sorry we can't help you more, Ms Donahoe. Goodbye.'

CHAPTER 14

Kwun Lung Lau was one of the oldest government housing estates in Hong Kong. When large numbers of refugees had fled across the border from China into Hong Kong in the 1960s, they had settled in shanty towns on the hillsides of the island. A large fire had swept through one of these settlements, killing thousands, and the government had been forced to act. It had built the housing estates.

A 1960s-era housing estate dwelling was a far cry from anything considered an apartment in the West. Each flat was a single room with a balcony, about three by five metres, housed in a large rectangular slab of a building with a long central corridor running through it. The bathroom was about a metre square at the end of the balcony and held a plain porcelain toilet and a stainless-steel sink with a cold-water tap. The kitchen was a low brick bench about a metre from the balcony window with another stainless-steel sink and cold tap, and a ledge for holding the standard gas-powered two-burner Hong Kong stove. If residents wanted bedrooms, they had to partition off the area themselves. In an area of fifteen square metres this made the living area tiny. Hot water was provided by a gas flow-through water heater with its own shower head for the microscopic bathroom, but residents had to purchase these themselves.

The buildings had been thrown together in a hurry, and the low concrete ceilings bore the rough markings of the plywood formwork used to create them, without any smoothing or attempt to cover it. No lights or floor coverings were provided; each resident was renting a bare concrete box with cold running water and a single electrical point.

Many Hong Kong residents chose to remain in these flats long after they could afford to move to something better because the rent on them was ridiculously cheap — three thousand Hong Kong dollars a month instead of twenty to twenty-five in a private apartment that could be similarly tiny. It amused me to see high-end Mercedes, owned by the residents, parked in the car parks of these estates.

Kwun Lung Lau had been built on the side of a steep hill above Western. In its heyday its five connected blocks had held more than a hundred flats to each of its twenty-two storeys, putting nearly two thousand five hundred households in an area covering less than two hectares. The retaining walls around the building weren't thick enough, however, and during one of Hong Kong's enormous rainstorms the retaining wall on the playgrounds at the base of the estate had failed. A huge wash of mud and concrete had swept across the walkway next to the playground and five people had been killed. The estate had been tagged for demolition shortly after, and the thousands of residents had been resettled, but the demolition was proceeding slowly even though the huge estate was empty and fenced with construction fencing.

I parked the Mercedes behind the Phoenix's red Lotus just down the hill from the estate. Simone and I walked up to the entrance; the area was eerily quiet and devoid of people.

'I wonder if the Phoenix made everybody go away,' Simone said. 'They should be still working on it, shouldn't they?'

The Phoenix walked out of the ground-floor corridor and up to the gate, accompanied by a girl of about sixteen. 'They had an extremely convenient gas leak and fire at lunchtime,' she told us. 'It was a huge mess and in the end they just sent all the workers home for the day.'

The Phoenix appeared as a slim, long-haired Chinese woman of about thirty, wearing a scarlet polo shirt and a pair of tan pants. Her daughter was half-black and half-Chinese; her long hair was braided into cornrows and her dusky face was fine-boned and intelligent. She saluted me and then Simone, bowing slightly. 'Lady Emma. Princess Simone. I am honoured.'

Simone and I nodded back.

'This is Evangeline, she's a couple of years older than Simone,' the Phoenix said. 'She's showing a great deal of talent, so we're going to try summoning. Come on up to the roof and let's see if we can't damage it any further.' She concentrated and the gate swung open with a squeak. 'Let's go up.'

We walked along the road through the estate, down a small flight of stairs, and into the central foyer. The lifts only stopped at every fourth floor and residents had to walk up or down stairs to reach the other floors.

The Phoenix pressed the filthy button to call the lifts so we could travel up to the roof using the sixteenth to twentieth floor lifts.

'Call me Eva,' the Phoenix's daughter said as we waited for the lift. She grinned at Simone. 'This should be fun. If I can bring out fire and you can bring out water, we should be able to throw them at each other and see who wins.'

'I'm not into competition,' Simone said stiffly.

Eva shrugged. 'Whatever. Anyway, Mom says for a human I'm pretty good. I hear you're human too? You can't take any animal form? I used to feel left out when I couldn't take bird form.'

'I'm human all the way through,' Simone said, her demeanour still icy.

Tell Simone to cut it out. Eva's trying to make friends, I said to the stone.

Simone glared at me.

The lift doors opened and we went in. Eva and Simone promptly put their hands over their noses; the smell of urine was overpowering and the metal walls were rusting away, revealing the plywood beneath.

'They put cameras in the lifts with monitors in the foyer to try to discourage people from peeing in them,' the Phoenix said, 'but late at night it made no difference — there was nobody in the foyer to see the monitor. And many people had dogs, even though they weren't allowed, and never controlled them.'

'That is *so gross*,' Simone and Eva said together. Eva broke out into giggles behind her hand, and Simone grinned behind hers. The Phoenix shot a fleeting smile at me.

We exited the lift on the twentieth floor and walked up two flights of worn and cracked concrete steps to get to the roof.

The roof had a high chain-wire fence around it, and a floor of plain concrete tiles. A tired, half-fallen basketball net stood at one end against the large tanks that provided the water for the residents of the estate.

The building was quite high up on Hong Kong Island and gave an impressive view over the harbour to the misty hills of Kowloon beyond. The hillside behind the estate was still largely untouched, its steep slope covered with jungle growth and dotted with occasional old graves — concreted platforms with a concrete back indicating the number of generations in the grave. Each was about three metres wide, shaped like the back of a sofa, with a large red circle in the centre.

The Phoenix took us to the middle of the stained rooftop. 'We'll have Eva summoning first, and you can watch, Simone. If Eva has it, then you'll be able to see how she does it and then you'll probably be able to do it too.' She studied Simone. 'If I were to engulf you completely in flames, would you be hurt?'

I opened my mouth to protest but Simone answered first. 'Nope,' she said with a shrug. 'Wouldn't bother me.'

'Sure? It would be hotter than standard fire. There'd also be nothing to breathe, it'd take all the oxygen out of the air.'

'I don't know,' Simone said, unsure now.

'Kids at CH get tested for this sort of thing, Simone, but since we don't know I'll test you myself. Come a little closer.'

Simone appeared reluctant but she moved closer to the Phoenix.

'I'll ramp it up slowly; let me know if you get into trouble,' the Phoenix said, and raised one hand towards Simone.

Simone was encased in a cage of fire, the flames dancing around her. She was unharmed, so the Phoenix moved the fire closer to her. Simone nodded, and the Phoenix made the flames appear to be incinerating her. Simone stood quietly, a shape of fire.

'I'm going to take it to full,' the Phoenix said.

The flames went from red to blue then to white. The sound of the fire changed from a crackle to the dull roar of a blowtorch. I moved back; the heat coming

173

from the flames was almost painful. The fire snapped off and Simone stood there quietly, completely unharmed.

'Wow,' Eva said softly.

'Yes,' the Phoenix said. 'Not many can take that much direct fire. That was more than just flames, it was pure Fire Essence. Nicely done, Simone.'

Simone let out a small sigh. 'Can we start the summoning now?'

'Of course. Ladies, if you will. Eva, hold my hand and observe what I do. Simone, you can watch from the outside, but if you need to, just touch one of us to see what we're doing.'

The Phoenix took Eva's hand with her left. She raised her right hand and a fire grew from the ground, a metre high and about two metres from them. 'A seed of fire. Eva, repeat.'

The fire blinked out, then Eva did the same thing, making a small fire in front of them, then making it disappear.

'Emma, move back now,' the Phoenix said. 'Watch carefully, Simone.'

She lowered her head and made a similar small fire appear in front of them. Then she made a low keening noise, similar to the noise made by a night bird, and the fire abruptly changed. It grew and twisted, becoming white, and took the form of a bird of flames.

Mother, sister, the elemental said into our heads. *I am needed? How may I serve?*

'Just a summoning lesson for Eva here,' the Phoenix said. 'Would you like to help?'

The bird spread its wings of flame and lowered its head. *More than happy to.* It turned its fiery head towards Simone. *Hello, Princess. I have not tested my strength against any of my watery brethren in a while. Please free them, and allow us to play once again.*

'Free them?' Simone said.

It is like a prison not to be called to serve, the bird said. *They wish only to be with you, their sister, and serve you any way they can. We exist to serve.*

'When you're not out causing trouble by yourselves,' the Phoenix said with amusement.

Not our fault if you don't give us enough to do, the elemental shot back, and both Eva and Simone giggled.

The Phoenix waved her hand at the elemental and it disappeared.

'I will give you a starter,' she said to Eva. She took Eva's hand and engulfed both of them in blindingly hot fire. They became two shapes within the flames. 'Now you've met that elemental, ask him to come.'

'Any particular way of asking?' Eva said.

'Not really. If you are aligned enough with the Pure Flame, the elementals will run to you the minute you desire their presence. Once you have the skill, we will need to spend some time teaching you *not* to summon them, as they'll be coming to visit you every time you think about them, wanting something to do. Keeping them occupied is a chore sometimes; they never have enough to do and if they're bored they get into trouble.'

'Oh,' Simone said softly.

The bird-shaped fire elemental appeared in front of us, raised its fiery wings and trumpeted. 'Evangeline, Forty-third Child of the Phoenix, is given the Pact.'

The fire around the Phoenix and Eva blinked out and they stood watching the elemental.

'Dismiss it,' the Phoenix said.

Eva concentrated on the elemental. The bird lowered and turned its head to gaze with one eye at Eva, but didn't disappear.

'*Please*,' Eva said with emphasis, and bowed slightly to the elemental.

It disappeared.

'Well done. Bring it again.'

The elemental reappeared.

'You have the skill, Eva,' the Phoenix said. 'I think we can do more at home, practise dismissing and bringing more than one, have a couple of battles. Just remember the rule about battles at CH — no summoning elementals at school to fight.'

'Sounds like Pokemon,' I said.

'Exactly the same,' the Phoenix said. 'The Tiger's kids are always trying to see if they can beat one of mine. If they can it's terrific kudos. Metal is weak against fire so it takes some skill to beat one of ours.'

'I can take them,' Eva said grimly. 'Assholes,' she added under her breath.

'No you won't, because if I hear about you summoning at school you'll be in serious trouble,' the Phoenix said. 'Now it's your turn, Simone. Eva, to one side. This will be water and we're weak to that, so there is a slight chance of injury. Simone, over here with me.'

Simone moved to stand next to the Phoenix.

'First, encase yourself in water,' the Phoenix said. 'Fill yourself with it; attune yourself to it.'

A glistening, moving sphere of water appeared around Simone, about three metres in diameter, its sides gently moving in and out in time with her breathing.

The Phoenix moved slightly away to give the water room. 'Good. Now, do what we did: place a seed of water in front of you.'

Another sphere of water, about a metre across, appeared in front of them.

'Feel for the spirits of those who seek you, and guide them into the seed.'

It all happened at once. The sphere of water around Simone froze with a loud crack that resounded through the hillside, then went black. The smaller sphere of water also froze, then shattered and fell into a pile of ice.

Eva, DOWN! the Phoenix shouted into my head. *Emma, Eva, JUMP! Get out of here!*

I ran, grabbed Eva around the waist and leapt over the chain-wire fence around the rooftop. As I took us off the edge, an explosion of blackness erupted behind me, nearly sucking me back. I was struck by a blow of heat from behind, almost losing my grip on Eva, then we were falling.

I used my energy centres to slow our fall, and felt Eva doing the same thing. We drifted gently to the ground, touched down, then quickly turned and looked back up to the roof. It was engulfed in a blinding, pulsing light, the heat from it easily felt from the ground.

Eva's eyes went red and she gasped. 'Simone summoned yin! Mom's making yang and feeding it.'

'Is she all right? She's not hurt?'

We're fine, the Phoenix said. *I'm helping Simone take control of it. Give us a couple of minutes. You should be all right to head back up now; by the time you get here we'll be done.*

When we got out of the lift on the twentieth floor I stopped. A hole had been blown in the ceiling, going through the two storeys of flats above, as well as to the level below us. Twisted reinforcing steel rods bent around the edges of the hole; their ends looked as if they'd liquefied and then solidified again.

'Check that it's safe for us to go up, Eva,' I said.

Come on up, Emma, Simone said.

We walked up the two flights of stairs, now littered with gravel and concrete, to the roof. Simone and the Phoenix stood near the basketball hoop at the end of the rooftop with a pair of water elementals next to them. The hole in the roof was about ten metres across; nearly the width of the roof itself. The walls and floors of lower storeys were visible beneath.

'Wow,' Eva said softly.

Simone appeared stunned, her face pale, and I moved closer. 'Are you all right, Simone?'

The Phoenix smiled wryly. 'Completely my mistake, Emma. I told Simone to feel for the spirits of those that seek her, and she did. She pulled the essence of the one who seeks her the most.'

Simone lowered her head. 'Daddy.' She turned away to hide the tears.

'Yin itself,' the Phoenix said. She shrugged. 'Elementals heard the call as well. You did it, Simone.'

Simone sniffled and wiped her nose on her sleeve. I went to my bag, found some tissues and handed them to her. She accepted them with a nod.

'That was yin?' Eva said, breathless.

'The real thing,' the Phoenix said with amusement. 'I think we need to bring Qing Long, the Lesser Yin, in to do some yin training.'

'He can't help me,' Simone said into the tissue. 'He says I'm much more yin than he is and the only one who can do it is Daddy.'

'Lazy bastard,' the Phoenix said under her breath. She raised her voice so Simone could hear. 'Let me talk to him.'

Simone nodded into the tissue.

Eva went to Simone and put her arm around her shoulders. 'That must have been awful. Yin is really scary.'

'This was nothing. This was the yin under control with your mom helping me.'

'Well, you have your elementals now, Simone,' the Phoenix said briskly. 'Let's do some practice.'

Simone sniffed into the tissue, nodded and straightened. Eva released her with a final friendly pat.

'What about the roof?' I said.

The Phoenix shrugged again. 'Not much we can do

about it, I'm afraid. I'll need to find a new training area here in Hong Kong.'

'What is the construction company going to say?'

'They'll probably scratch their heads and then blame the gas leak,' the Phoenix said. 'Highly unlikely that someone would drop a bomb on an unused building, but they will be wondering about it for a while.'

We can fix it, one of the water elementals said. *We can put it back together so that it appears nothing has happened. The concrete won't have the reinforcing metal, but that shouldn't be a problem as it's being demolished soon anyway.*

'You can do that?' Simone said.

Both elementals, appearing as human-shaped globs of water, bowed to Simone. *It would be our pleasure to serve.*

Simone waited for them to move, but they just stood there before us.

'You must order them to do it, Simone,' the Phoenix said. 'Tell them exactly what you wish them to do.'

'Please fix the roof up so it looks like nothing happened,' Simone said.

Sister, the elementals said, and disappeared.

The bent reinforcing rods sticking out from the edges of the hole straightened and the concrete grew like an organic creature from the edges of the hole. Below us, the walls inside the hall were visibly growing back. It was like watching a slow-motion recording of a flower opening, strangely natural. The concrete slid together on the roof and the tiles reappeared on it.

'Is it strong enough for us to walk on?' the Phoenix said.

The water elementals reappeared near us and bowed to Simone. *Sister.*

'You'll have to ask them for me, Simone,' the Phoenix said. 'They won't talk to any other now that you have summoned them.'

'Can we walk on it?' Simone said.

It is strong enough to walk on, one of the elementals said. *Princess, we have a request now that we have performed this task for you.*

The Phoenix made a soft sound of amusement. 'Pushy. You need to discipline these little fellows, Simone.'

Neither of the elementals had any facial features but both appeared to be staring, disgusted, at the Phoenix.

'How do I discipline something made of water?' Simone asked.

'Easy,' the Phoenix said. 'When they make their request, it'll be obvious.'

'What do you want?' Simone asked the elementals.

A battle, Princess, the elemental said. *We have not fought worthy opponents in a very long time. The Princess Evangeline has just gained the Pact, as have you. Why not test your skill at summoning against hers?*

'How can we match skills?' Simone said, intrigued. 'We call you, you do as we say. How much skill can there be in that?'

Without moving, both elementals radiated amusement. *If she defeats you, you will know. Particularly since fire is weak to water.*

'Let's try!' Eva said, excited.

'How does it work?' Simone said, unsure.

Eva explained, still excited. 'We call our elementals, then direct the battle. Just like Pokemon, as Emma said. The more aligned you are with your ellies, the more you can get out of them. You can also learn which abilities they have to use in battle, and teach them new abilities that you make up yourself.'

'Hold on a minute,' I said. 'That sounds *way* too much like Pokemon to be a coincidence.'

'There have been a number of pet-fighting games over the years, Pokemon was the most popular of many,' the Phoenix said. She grinned. 'Yeah, one of the Dragon's kids in Japan invented the concept, based on elementals. Made a fortune.'

'Elementals are *way* more fun though,' Eva said. ''Cause they're a natural intelligence, they can help you in battle, give you suggestions. You work as a team.'

'This is much more complicated than I expected,' Simone said. 'I thought I would just summon and control them.'

You do not control us, the elementals said. *You can only will us to do your bidding.*

'Dismiss and resummon them, Simone,' the Phoenix said. 'Just bring one. Then you and Eva can match skills.'

'How do I dismiss them?' Simone said. The elementals disappeared. 'Oh.'

'Summon one only,' the Phoenix said.

Simone made a seed of water in front of her.

'Without the seed,' the Phoenix said.

The seed disappeared. Simone concentrated for a moment and five elementals appeared in front of us.

'Looks like you need some practice,' the Phoenix said wryly. 'Dismiss all but one, if you can.'

Nothing happened.

'You may have to do it out loud,' the Phoenix said, 'until you are more skilled.'

'All but one of you disappear, please,' Simone said.

All of the elementals disappeared.

'They're being deliberately difficult,' Simone said, exasperated.

The five elementals reappeared.

'Tell them which one,' the Phoenix said. 'They can't decide themselves.' She raised her voice and spoke pointedly at the elementals. 'They're too stupid.'

Four of the elementals disappeared. The remaining one appeared to be glowering at the Phoenix.

'So what sort of thing can they do?' Simone said, studying the elemental.

'That's entirely up to you,' Eva said. 'You are only limited by your imagination and your knowledge of what your element is capable of.'

Simone thought for a moment. 'Freeze,' she said.

The water elemental froze with a loud crack.

'Very good,' the Phoenix said.

'Steam,' Simone said.

The elemental changed from ice to a human shape of steam with no water transition.

'Very nice, sublimation,' the Phoenix said. 'Eva, Simone is using the different states of water. You don't have access to that.'

'I want to battle!' Eva said, still enthused. 'I've seen the kids at CH do it, I want to try!' She raised one hand and a fire elemental, a glowing sphere of flame, appeared next to Simone's water elemental.

'It's something of a status symbol to be able to do it,' the Phoenix said with amusement.

'And they obviously do it at CH despite the ban,' I said.

'Just like they still play AIPets at the Australian School even though it's been banned for a long time,' Simone said, still pensive. 'Orb.'

The water elemental changed to a glistening sphere of water.

'Bird,' Eva said. The fire elemental changed to the fiery shape of a phoenix, about one-and-a-half metres tall.

'Snake,' Simone said.

The elemental changed form to a snake, but it had long tendrils coming from its head and large, bulging eyes, similar to a dragon. Scales appeared along its length, even though it was obviously still made of water.

'Simone has better control, Eva,' the Phoenix said. 'She's added the details of scales and whiskers.'

Eva stared, concentrating, at her fire elemental and its form appeared more polished, with glowing feathers of red tapering to orange tips.

'Oh, wow, that's really pretty,' Simone said.

'Thanks,' Eva said, and she and Simone shared a smile.

'You could colour the scales on yours if you like,' the Phoenix said to Simone.

Simone studied the water elemental, and its scales changed from transparent to opaque, glistening from dark blue-green to the pure turquoise of sunshine in clear water. It swayed on its tail and turned its head to admire itself. *I like.*

'Yours is pretty too,' Eva said.

'Both of you have an artistic streak,' the Phoenix said, pleased. 'You can use your elementals as works of art as well as battle creatures, if you prefer. There are competitions for the most elegantly decorated elementals on the Celestial Plane. A metal elemental has won the last two years in a row — I think the Tiger's arranged for his children to receive special training. A water elemental has never won; the Turtle's children aren't really interested in this sort of thing.'

'Not good enough,' Eva said. 'Fire or water need to win some.'

Simone concentrated and her elemental changed to a bird with glittering royal blue and purple feathers and a crown of peacock-like feathers on its head.

'I'm not trying to outdo you,' Simone said quickly. 'I just wanted to try it.'

'No, no, that's fine,' Eva said. She changed her fire elemental to a glowing orange serpent, its flat triangular head more snake-like than Simone's had been. Its scales had feathery edges of flame, glowing with heat.

'I wonder if there's a way we could combine them,' Simone said. 'Make them two creatures, but like yang and yin.'

'That's an interesting idea,' Eva said.

'There's never been a combined work of two elementals entered into the Decorative Elemental Contest,' the Phoenix said. 'It would be an interesting innovation.'

'Want to try?' Eva said, her smile to Simone now shy. 'We could work together, make something really pretty, and put it into the competition.'

'When's the competition start?' Simone said.

'The judging is held just before Chinese New Year, in a couple of months,' the Phoenix said. 'The elementals are displayed as part of the New Year celebrations on the Celestial.'

Simone turned to me, bright with pleasure. 'Is that okay, Emma?'

I nodded.

'Hey, Simone,' Eva said, and Simone turned back to her. 'My art teacher at CH might be able to help us with the design, she's a phoenix too. I don't know if she can do ellies, but she can help us with colours and designs and stuff. What do you think?'

Simone quickly turned to shoot an angry glare at me.

I raised my hands. 'I had no idea. Don't look at me.'

Simone stood thinking for a moment, then turned back to Eva. 'Sounds like fun.'

I recall an agreement to battle, Simone's water elemental said. *Also, please release me from this GODAWFUL form!*

Me too! Eva's elemental said. It turned its serpent head to the Phoenix. *Mom! They're making me into something that's WATERY!*

184

Simone and Eva collapsed laughing. The elementals lost their shapes and became roughly human-shaped fire and water forms.

'I don't really want to battle; I'd rather play with your form,' Simone said.

'It'll be fun, Simone, have a try,' Eva said. She gestured towards her elemental and walked to the other end of the roof. 'Target the elemental, not the summoner. It's very bad form to injure your opponent, but sometimes the Tiger's kids do it if they're losing.'

'Wow, they *are* assholes,' Simone said.

'That would not be an issue for Simone,' the Phoenix said.

Eva turned to face Simone from the opposite end of the roof. Her elemental glided to stand about two metres in front of Simone, facing her. 'Position your elemental the same way.'

'Water elemental, I choose *you*!' Simone said, and giggled. She made her elemental take the form of a large turtle with a spiked shell and water cannons coming from its shoulders, and it moved into position in front of her.

'It's a Blastoise!' Eva said, laughing. 'I used to watch Pokemon when I was a kid too!'

Lame, the elemental said. *Change me back*. Simone nodded and the elemental returned to its human shape of water.

'The objective is to make your opponent's elemental so uncomfortable in its position that it leaves,' the Phoenix said. 'Whatever it takes.'

'I don't want to hurt yours,' Simone said, unsure. 'That's wrong.'

'They don't feel pain, but you can put them in a situation where they're unhappy,' Eva said. 'Like when we made them take the form of animals that were the opposite of their essence, it made them unhappy. If you make them do something like that for long enough, they'll take off.'

'Any rules apart from not hurting the other summoner?' Simone said, intrigued.

'Nope,' Eva said, and her elemental sent a blast of fire, like a flame-thrower, directly at the water elemental.

Simone's water elemental took the shape of a doughnut with a hole through its centre, and the flame passed through it. The edges of the hole boiled.

'Good job, Simone, quick thinking,' the Phoenix said.

'The ellie suggested it,' Simone said.

The water elemental retook its human form and raised its arms. It sent a wave of water over the fire elemental.

Eva squeaked and raised her arm towards the fire elemental. It changed from red to white flame within the water, then glowed very bright and hot. The water around the fire turned to steam.

'Plasma!' Eva cried, her voice hoarse with effort.

The elemental took the form of an arc of glowing liquid light and arched over to strike the water elemental, vaporising it. The water elemental turned to steam, then dissipated.

'Eva wins,' the Phoenix said. 'Well done, Eva, using the different states that fire is capable of; I never even thought of plasma. That would be very useful against the Tiger's children; plasma is an electromagnetic force as well.'

'We just did plasma in physics,' Eva said, subdued. 'It was hard to get the elemental to do it.' She turned to Simone. 'You okay? I promise I didn't hurt it, I just made it go away.'

Simone grinned broadly. 'I did plasma in first semester. Did you play with plasma lamps too?'

Eva nodded, smiling back.

'That was great, what a good idea.' Simone paused, thoughtful. 'I wonder how cold I could make my elemental go. Plasma won't be much good when the water it's facing is only a few degrees above zero ...'

'It'll still destroy it, I think,' Eva said.

'... Kelvin,' Simone finished.

Eva stopped, then, 'Oh.'

'No destroying the world for fun,' the Phoenix said.

'Awww!' Eva and Simone whined at the same time, then collapsed in giggles together.

CHAPTER 15

Simone and Evangeline chatted excitedly about what they would like to do for their elemental quasi-sculpture as we headed back downstairs. Simone stopped directly in front of me at the bottom, making me nearly crash into her. Both she and the Phoenix raised their hands and their eyes unfocused.

'What's going on?' I said.

'Demons,' Simone said, as if from a million miles away. 'Something's up.' She gasped. 'They think they've found Daddy!' She snapped back and stared at me, eyes wide. 'There's a whole bunch of demons in Sai Kung at the seafood restaurants, and there's a freaking enormous black loggerhead turtle in one of the tanks!'

'There are a large number of extremely small demons there, only level three to five, some as low as one,' the Phoenix said. 'And what appears to be a natural turtle in one of the tanks.'

'Go,' I said, but Simone was already gone.

The Phoenix bowed slightly to me. 'By your leave, ma'am.'

'Go,' I said again. 'Can you teleport?' I asked Eva.

'Not yet, Mom says I'm not ready,' Eva said. 'Can you drive the car? Or have someone pick us up and teleport us?'

'Can one of your elementals carry you?' I said.

Eva's face cleared. 'I think so. Just a sec.'

She concentrated a moment and a fire elemental appeared in its human-type form.

Eva turned to me. 'It will take me, but how will you get there? One of these would burn an ordinary human like you down to nothing.'

Emma, I need you here now, Simone said into my ear. *I don't know what to do! All these little demons want sanctuary! There are big demons here, and I'm not even sure if this is Daddy or not. It's sending out some very strange vibes.*

Take the Lotus, the Phoenix said into my head.

'Tell your mother I couldn't drive one of those things in a million years,' I said to Eva, 'and my own car is too slow. I need to be there now. I'll get a Celestial from the Academy to take me. You go.'

'Okay,' Eva said, took the elemental's fiery hand and disappeared.

'Stone,' I said, turning back to the building. 'Call a Celestial Master to take me.'

The stone was silent for a moment, then said, 'I'm looking, but there are three attacks happening right now. They are probably timed to coincide with this to separate you from your protection. I'm trying to find someone to guard you or take you, but all the Celestials are tied up.'

'It could be *John*,' I said desperately. 'And that place is full of demons. Find someone!'

'Edwards says to wait, he's bringing a car. Gold is on his way in his Boxster but he was in Kowloon. We're doing our best.'

For some reason my voice sounded deeper and stronger. 'Get Simone back then, she can carry me.'

'You'll fall into demon form if she touches you ...' The stone sounded desperate. 'Emma, control it!'

Suddenly I was perfectly calm and in control, and more comfortable than I'd been in ages. 'Never mind, I'll take myself there.'

'Emma ...'

'Yes?'

'You still in there?'

I slithered through the hallway to the lift lobby. 'Yes, of course I am. I'm fine. Don't worry. Tell Simone I'll be right there. Oh, hold on, I might be able to do it myself.' I concentrated, trying to contact Simone directly. 'Nope, have to work on that. Tell her for me, will you?'

I stopped at the lift lobby in front of a large fung shui mirror and saw myself. A lot of good a fung shui mirror would do against something as big as me — I had slipped into Mother form, about two metres long from head to black snake tail. I turned to see my back; my spinal column appeared as bony ridges poking through the skinless muscle. Damn.

Thank you so much, Simon Wong and Kitty Kwok. If I ever laid my hands on Kitty Kwok, that bitch would definitely see exactly what she had done to me. There had been rumours of her appearing and disappearing, sometimes in Hell, other times on Earth, but none of them had been definitive.

'Find a safe spot for me to land, will you?' I asked the stone.

The stone hesitated for a moment, then a map appeared in front of me, projected into the air. 'Here should be good. Is that still you, Emma?'

'Of course it's me.'

I took off, and landed where the stone indicated — an alley behind some particularly fine-smelling dumpsters. I was at the back of the Sai Kung market: a typical purpose-built two-storey building with tiled walls and floor running with blood and water.

'Turn left, head to the end of the alley, you'll come out onto the promenade next to the ocean,' the stone said.

I cast around with my demon senses: there were a number of humans nearby. Although they would be good sport to play with, right now I was more interested in the contents of the tanks at the seafood restaurants.

I gathered my demon energy, my dark chi, and focused it. I made the twenty or so humans along the waterfront suddenly feel nauseous and convinced them that they'd smelt a gas leak from one of the restaurants. They didn't bother calling the authorities; they were too panic-stricken and ill. They just fled, some of them not even aware of what they were fleeing from except a general feeling of foreboding. This was a lovely powerful demon ability that could be used both to lure people towards me and to frighten them away; a shame I couldn't use it in human form. I should really take demon form more often; there was great fun to be had with unsuspecting humans.

I slithered to the end of the alley, feeling the cracked tiles beneath my coils, the water and rubbish sliding away from my snake back end. The Sai Kung waterfront looked much as it usually did: a raised concrete waterside promenade with seafood restaurants lined up opposite the water. Their tanks held a variety of seafood, and tables and chairs were set up on the worn concrete, thin disposable plastic tablecloths their only cover.

Then I saw the tanks, and my tongue flicked out at the banquet spread before me. They weren't full of the usual prawns, fish and shellfish; they were full of demons in the form of seafood. Tiny ones, only levels two or three, some as small as one. I grinned. Demons this small couldn't teleport; they were trapped in the tanks. If their Lord had made them take this form, they couldn't change to run either, and as seafood they probably wouldn't be able to leave the water anyway.

A feast.

I slithered to the nearest tank. The demons inside, in the form of mantis prawns, squealed with terror and climbed over each other in an attempt to get out of the tank. The walls were clear Perspex, about twenty centimetres high, and they had no chance of escaping.

I reached out with my skinless hand, grabbed a particularly fat and juicy prawn, and brought it, legs waving pathetically, to my mouth. I bit it in half and savoured the flavour. These small demons didn't taste like seafood; they tasted like warm roast meat rich with wine and herbs and a dash of something spicy, a robust and satisfying taste. I realised I was starving; it had been such a long time since I'd eaten properly and I needed more, now! I swallowed the remaining half of the demon, unlocked my jaw, and grabbed a handful more out of the tank to make one huge, delicious swallow. They squealed with terror as I held them in front of my skinless face, their fear adding to the pleasure of eating them.

Suddenly I couldn't move; I was bound. Someone with a will greater than my own was holding me.

Well, to hell with that, these demons tasted good and I was hungry. I fought the binding but whoever had me was immensely powerful. I turned my attention behind me, using my demon sight, to find out who was messing with my dinner.

I saw her with my demon vision: dark and blue and gold. That little cowardly bitch Simone, who didn't even have the guts to summon elementals. A bird spirit stood behind her, nearly as powerful as she was; essence of pure flame. A fire child cowered behind the fire spirit, its strength minuscule compared to the two larger entities.

'You don't know what you're doing, Emma,' Simone said.

'That's *Emma*?' the fire child said.

'It's a long story, Eva,' the bird spirit said. 'Simone, we have to change her back.'

'Leave me alone, I'm hungry,' I said.

'Emma, you protect demons that request sanctuary; you don't hurt them,' Simone said in a maddeningly calm tone. 'Change back to human, please. We need to work out what to do about this turtle.'

'Fuck the turtle, I'm eating,' I said.

Ha! The use of the foul language shocked her and she released me slightly. I resisted her binding, but she brought it up again. Damn.

'If you can't hold her I may have to take action, Simone,' the bird spirit said. 'She will continue to eat these and we must stop it.'

'Don't do anything!' Simone said. 'Don't hurt her!'

Ha, the little girl was protecting me. Stupid.

'You know, you're such a coward, Simone.' I spoke conversationally, adding to the cruelty of my words by being calm and mature. 'You're scared of your own father's Celestial Form, and you're scared of the Jade Emperor; hell, you're even too frightened to summon your own elementals. Your father will be *so* ashamed of you when he gets back.'

She hesitated for a moment, then said, her voice small, 'Please change back, Emma.'

'Make me, bitch,' I said with amusement. 'You don't have the guts to wield your full power. Look at you, capable of summoning yin and too scared to do it. You could go to the Celestial school and learn to make the most of your powers, but you're too worried that,' I changed my voice to a teenage whine, 'the other kids will be *scared* of you.' I chuckled. 'You are pathetic.'

Simone's will pressed harder on me. She was trying to make me change back to human. I fought her.

'Not this time, sweetheart. I like the lifestyle, and the food is great. Let's go have some fun together, just you and me. You were always my favourite. We could have some real fun playing with some of those humans that you resent so much.'

'We can't let this go on much longer, Simone,' the bird spirit said. 'Make her turn back, or I'll have to call in some Red Warriors to contain her. She is much too dangerous to leave like this.'

'I can't do it by myself,' Simone said, her voice strained.

'I'll have to step in if you can't,' the bird spirit said grimly. 'Emma, if you don't change back, I'm going to contain you, and I may severely injure you with my Fire Essence if I do. It's in your best interest to take your human form now.'

'You can bind me for a short time, but you can't contain me,' I said with pleasure. 'Try me. You know you don't have the power.'

The bird spirit's essence moved through me and I blocked her out. I swallowed my handful of demons whole. Delicious.

'I wonder if there are any humans nearby,' I said. 'Now there's some *real* fun.' I cast around with my demon senses — why had I made them run away before? I pressed against their bonds, managed to slither a few metres left, and turned around to see them. 'You're tiring, and then I'll be able to find something interesting to play with. Come on, Simone, let's find you some friends.' I leered at the small fire spirit. 'Hello, little girl, want to play?'

'I can't control her, Simone,' the bird spirit said.

'I don't know what I'm going to do — she's out of control and we need to stop this. A Mother as big as her could cause untold damage.'

'Don't even *think* about destroying her, Aunty Zhu, she's all I have left!' Simone cried. 'Help me, Lady of All Mercies!'

'Oh shit,' I said, but it was too late.

Kwan Yin appeared in front of me and put her hand on my forehead. I tried to duck away, but she had me. Her serene presence radiated through me.

'There is a chance that the one you love is in this place,' Kwan Yin said, her voice gentle and sad. 'But while you are like this he cannot love you.'

Her words hit me like arrows. The one I loved? Xuan Wu?

'John,' I gasped. 'Where?'

'There's a big turtle in a tank here, Emma,' Simone said. 'Please, change back, we need to check if it's him.'

Kwan Yin helped me. I forced my demon essence down and sucked the darkness into me, bringing my yang out to fight it. I concentrated on yang: bright, hard, life-giving and pure. The demon essence spiralled down inside me and compacted into my dan tian. I changed back and leaned on the edge of the seafood tank, gasping.

'She has it,' Kwan Yin said, and released me. 'The way to control this demon is to focus the yang side of yourself, Emma. Your serpent. It will help you; do not be afraid to call upon it when you are in need.' She disappeared.

'Have you tried that?' Simone said. 'Using the snake?'

'No,' I said.

'Contact some serpent-type Shen and see if they can assist,' the Phoenix said. 'The Lady's suggestion has merit.'

'Let's check this turtle.' I looked down at the demons in the tank. They sat frozen in the water, watching me with their crustacean eyes. 'We'll come back to free you,' I told them, and shuddered as I remembered exactly how delicious they were. A stab of hunger pierced me. 'I won't hurt you now.'

We went to the large tank holding the sea turtle. It was obviously distressed to be in such a small tank, full of polluted water from the harbour and its own waste. It floated in the tank barely moving, its eyes dull.

'It's not Daddy,' Simone said, 'but it's not natural either. I'm not really sure what it is.'

A demon in human form, appearing as a very elderly man grinning through his long beard and stooping over a cane, came out from the back of the restaurant. 'Greetings, Ladies. Please do not harm me, I have information for you.'

None of us replied, and he continued. 'I have information as to the whereabouts of Mr Alexander.'

Simone made a sudden grasping move towards him, then pulled away. 'Where is Leo? Do you have him?'

'I do not have him,' the demon said, still grinning. 'But I know where he is, and if you were to go in and kill those who are holding him, I would be very pleased indeed.'

Demon politics, the stone said. *Wonderful.*

'Where is Leo, and what do you want in return for this information?' I said.

'Golden Arcade, Sham Shui Po, and nothing,' the demon said.

He speaks the truth, the stone said. *But that last bit is suspicious. Leo's whereabouts are certainly worth more than nothing.*

'Golden Arcade is a maze,' I said. 'Where in there is he? Any particular store?'

'Down the far southern side in the deepest part of the mall, where there are many stores selling peripherals, there is a corridor under the stairs, where they keep their stock in cupboards. There's a metal roller door there that is always closed. Go inside and there are stairs down into the demon's nest. That demon is holding Leo.' He waved one hand over the turtle in the tank. 'I have taken the liberty of rescuing this one from the cooking pot — it was scheduled to be chopped up and served to the public in a money-making feast this weekend. You would probably like to remove it; it is yours.' He grinned at us again. 'Good luck on your sortie, ladies, and I hope you find the Black Lion.' He disappeared.

Simone went to the tank and put her hand on the turtle's head. 'Aunty Phoenix, could you help me? I don't know whether this is a natural turtle or a demon or what.'

When the Phoenix put her hand into the tank to touch the turtle it was like a hot iron hitting the water; steam exploded everywhere. 'Whoops,' she said, and the steam stopped. 'Nearly had turtle soup.' She concentrated. 'I have no idea what it is, but it doesn't seem to be a natural turtle.'

I bent to see the turtle's face in the tank. It seemed to have some intelligence in its sad eyes. 'Can you talk to us?' I asked it.

The turtle didn't move.

I sighed and stood up again. 'We can't take it back to the Academy, we don't have a tank or a pond or anything to put it in. I suppose you'd better take it somewhere safe and release it, and we'll keep an eye on it.' I bent to speak to the turtle again. 'If you're a Shen, that will be suitable for you. If you're a demon, it will also be okay. If you're just a natural turtle, then it's the best option. Do you have anywhere in particular you would like us to drop you?'

The turtle still didn't move.

'Nothing coming from it,' the Phoenix said. 'I think it may be some sort of hybrid demon. Take it out and let it go. It'll be fine living as a turtle; anything's better than a life in Hell for them.'

'I'll take it somewhere a long way away where there's plenty of stuff for it to eat,' Simone said. 'How are you going to get home, Emma?'

'I'll take a taxi,' I said. 'You guys go.'

The Phoenix concentrated. 'Eva's father is on his way here with the Lotus, Emma. He can give you a lift home.'

Eva lit up. 'Daddy's coming?'

The Phoenix touched Eva's arm. 'Yes, we were going to have dinner here in one of those Western places that he likes so much.'

She said 'Western places' with such scorn that both Simone and I stifled a laugh.

'Don't bother him, you guys have your dinner. I'll just take a cab,' I said. 'Simone, take this poor thing out and let it go.'

Simone and the turtle disappeared.

'Stay here and have dinner with us, Emma,' the Phoenix said. 'Phil would love to meet you. He'd probably like to compare notes on dealing with Shen relationships.'

'Daddy's human,' Eva said with amusement. 'Mom drives him nuts.'

'I'm sure she does,' I said, and gestured towards the tiny demons in the tanks. 'Stone, get a team in here to clean this up, will you?'

'I have two teams of four juniors on their way; excellent training in carrying for the youngsters,' the stone said. 'Nigel is coming as well, to see if we can't change them to something a little less difficult to handle. We also have six seniors who were having dinner here this evening — they alerted Simone in the first place. She asked them to guard the perimeter so they didn't see your demon form.'

'Thank you,' I said.

The Phoenix smiled slightly. 'Good delegation. Well done.'

I shrugged. 'Let's go eat. Western, you say? I haven't had a good vegetarian pizza in ages.'

Eva jiggled and clapped her hands. 'Pizza, yes!'

'Cheese,' the Phoenix said grimly. 'You people are so strange.'

'Chow dau foo,' I retorted, 'stinky bean curd, and you complain about eating cheese.'

'Chow dau foo is great once you get past the smell,' the Phoenix said, indignant. 'Cheese is just yuck.'

'I like them both,' Eva said. 'Now let's find a pizza!'

Eva's father was a tall slim African-American with an intelligent, good-humoured expression. He shook hands with me over the table. 'Nice to meet you. I've heard a lot about you.'

'Nice to meet you too,' I said. 'How long have you known the Phoenix?'

'I met her at an IT conference here about twenty years ago,' he said. 'I applied for a transfer here to Hong Kong — I'm head of the Asia-Pacific division of Binary Computer Systems.' He smiled at the Phoenix. 'Don't get to spend nearly as much time with her as I would like, her being an Empress and all.'

The Phoenix waved him down. 'I'm an ordinary Hong Kong housewife, I just happen to have some good investments that keep me comfortably well-off.'

Eva nearly spat out her soft drink. 'You make me laugh every time you say that, Mom.'

'You have to deal with this too?' Phil said.

'All the time,' I said. 'I suppose it's too late to warn you about forming a relationship with a Shen.'

'Far too late,' he said.

Emma, Simone said into my head. *Um.*

199

'Um?' I said. 'Pass this on to the rest of us here in a conference call, please, stone. We're waiting for you, Simone.'

'What is it?' Phil said.

'She's talking to Simone Chen through the stone in her ring,' the Phoenix said. 'Apparently there's some sort of problem.'

Um, Simone said. *This is ... funny.*

Phil shook his head.

'What?' I said. 'Tell us.'

Well, I let the turtle go. There's a lovely deserted island here, a reef just offshore, plenty of sea grass to eat, perfect spot. I dropped the turtle in the water and stood on the beach to make sure it was okay.

'It's not okay?' I said.

It swam up to the beach, climbed out of the water and came up to me.

'Did you drop it back in the water?'

Yep, and it did it again! Do you have any idea how long it takes a turtle to climb up the beach like that?

'I have some idea,' I said.

And it grabbed the bottom of my jeans in its mouth and wouldn't let go. So I'm sitting on the beach here, with this turtle next to me, and it has its head in my lap and it's sorta holding on to me with its flippers, and it won't let go.

'Are you sure it's not your father?'

Absolutely positive.

'Um,' I said.

That's what I said.

'Stone,' I said.

'On it,' the stone said. 'Simone, Liu is sending two dragons to you. They will escort the turtle to the Northern Heavens, where it will be appropriately cared for by some of the clergy from the Mountain.'

Oh, good idea! Thanks!

'It's obviously intelligent, has it made any attempt to communicate?' I said. I gasped. 'Good Lord, it's not *Martin*, is it?'

Not Martin. Not anyone I know. I don't think it can communicate, but it's obviously intelligent.

'Poor thing,' Phil said. 'I wonder if it pissed anybody off.'

'Probably,' I said. 'Want to come and have some pizza with us after you drop the turtle off?'

I'll get something in the Heavens, Simone said. *It will take me a good hour to get there and back again.*

'The dragons can handle it,' I said.

I want to make sure it's okay. See you back home when we're done. We need to arrange a little trip to Sham Shui Po.

'Sham Shui Po?' Phil asked.

'We think we've found Leo,' the Phoenix said. 'The demon that gave us the turtle gave us a lead.'

'I'd offer to come,' he said, 'but I think that's slightly out of my league. I'll let you martial arts experts handle it.'

'Mom doesn't do martial arts,' Eva said with amusement. 'She just barbecues stuff.'

'Nothing in the world beats the sweet fragrance of roasting demon,' the Phoenix said with relish.

'Not even this?' Phil said, waving one hand over the groaning table of pizza, ribs and salad.

The Phoenix wrinkled her nose. 'It's a million times better than the smell of that awful cheese.'

Simone was already home when Phil dropped me off. I waved a cheery goodbye to him and headed up to the front gates of the building. The workers who had been repairing Simone's swimming pool had left for the day, and the pool sat empty and forlorn with a large puddle of green water from recent rain at its bottom. It had been poorly constructed from the start, and the concrete had cracked about a year after they'd finished it. And we'd used one of the more *reputable* construction companies and paid extra for them.

I took the lift up. At the top floor the gate hung open in front of the closed wooden front door. Simone often left it open when she was home. We didn't need to worry about anything entering as long as she was there; just her presence was enough to terrify away most demons.

I didn't feel the familiar uncomfortable buzz of the seals hitting my demon nature as I walked through the front door, and I stopped. 'Stone, you awake?'

'Hmm?' the stone said.

'Seals are still down. Did the Tiger send someone?'

'Not yet, he probably forgot.'

'Send a reminder please.'

'Will do.'

'While we're on the topic, how's Rhonda? Can you ask her stone how she is?'

'She's underground, Emma,' the stone reminded me gently.

'Oh, yeah. Any word through on the network about how she's going?'

'No news. In this case it means that everything is fine.'

'Good,' I said with feeling. 'Ask Lok to get someone over here and reset these damn seals, please.'

'Already done.'

I went through to my bedroom and dumped my bag on the floor, then headed into John's office and checked the email quickly. I glanced at my diary. Damn. I had a challenge the next day, and I wanted to head to Sham Shui Po this evening. Looked like another night without much sleep.

'Cancelling your appointments for tomorrow; all you

have now is the challenge,' the stone said. 'You can have a granny nap tomorrow afternoon.'

'A *granny nap*? You've been around those kids too much.'

Ah Yat tapped gently on the door, then came into the office with a cup of Ceylon tea for me. 'Your new driver has arrived, ma'am. I put him in the second student room.'

'What's his name?'

'Two Eighty-Three.'

'No, Ah Yat, what's his *name*?'

Ah Yat looked blank. 'I have no idea, ma'am.'

'I'll talk to him when he's settled in then.'

'I'll tell him, ma'am,' she said, and went out.

Simone came in and flopped to sit in one of the visitors' chairs. 'The turtle's fine, it seems to have settled in the lake in the Northern Heavens. The Celestials are arranging for it to be fed regularly. It let me go and pushed me away with its nose, so it's happy for now. We need to find out more about it though.' She sat up straighter. 'I want to go to Sham Shui Po tonight, when the stores are closing. Take them by surprise.'

'Me too. Call up Liu — let's see who we can round up to go.'

The phone rang and Ah Yat picked it up in the kitchen.

Simone unfocused, talking to Liu, and I waited for her. The intercom beeped on the phone on my desk and I picked it up.

'Call for you, ma'am, it's the fung shui man,' Ah Yat said, and put the call through.

'Ronnie,' I said with pleasure. 'Good to talk to you.'

'Ms Donahoe,' Ronnie Wong said. 'Good to talk to you too. Just wondering when you'd like me to come in and have a look at your seals? I hear that you're having some difficulty with them. Lok gave me a call.'

'What an excellent idea,' I said. 'How soon can you be here?'

'If I hang up now I can be there in about three minutes. I need to collect some stuff.'

'Simone and I are going out as soon as we can get a suitable group of warriors together — we're going to raid a nest. Can you handle things without us?'

'Certainly. I'll be right there,' Ronnie said, and hung up.

'Same situation as when you went into One Two Two's nest, Emma,' Simone said, still unfocused. 'The Winds can't really spare any of their armies because of the danger of attack right now. There's something of a feeling of being besieged at the moment, with the Demon King and the higher-ranking demons attacking just about everything Celestial all the time.'

'I understand that completely,' I said. 'A couple of Celestial Masters and a few seniors from the Mountain should probably do us for this, unless the demon that tipped us off has warned our target.'

'Liu is putting a team together, and suggests that you start heading out that way now since you can't teleport,' Simone said.

'Right after I talk to Ronnie.' The front doorbell rang. 'There he is.'

I went to the front door. Ah Yat had already opened it and let Ronnie in, and he was giving her a warm hug.

'Hi, Ronnie,' I said.

Ronnie released Ah Yat and saluted me. He appeared to be a thirty-year-old Chinese wearing a plain white shirt with no tie and a pair of tan slacks with loafers. He grinned at me through his thick plastic-rimmed glasses. 'Hi, Emma, your seals are completely down. What's causing this? The ink is still damp on the paper!'

'I have no idea, and if you could find the cause I'd very much appreciate it,' I said.

Ronnie concentrated, and moved into the living room. 'Something weird here. I may have to change and check it after I've reset the seals.'

'Warn Ah Yat before you do.'

Ronnie grinned at Ah Yat. 'This one knows exactly what I am.'

Ah Yat smiled back at Ronnie and returned to the kitchen.

Simone came into the living room. 'Hi, Ronnie. Emma, we have fifteen, and we're good to go. Did you talk to the new driver yet?'

'Not yet,' I said.

Simone concentrated. 'Done.'

The new driver came out from the students' quarters at the other end of the flat, and fell to one knee, saluting Simone and myself.

'Up you get,' I said, and he rose. 'What's your name?'

'Two Seven Three, ma'am.'

'No, your *name*.'

'Oh. Denis.'

'Welcome to the insanity, Denis. The keys to the big Mercedes in the number one car park downstairs are on the hall table. Please bring it round the front. We're going to raid a nest in Sham Shui Po.'

He grinned broadly. 'Excellent. I'll meet you downstairs.'

I nodded. 'Be right there.' I raised my hand to stop Denis before he walked out the door. 'Denis, this is Ronnie, he's resetting the seals on the apartment for me.' Denis nodded to Ronnie, who nodded back. 'You can probably sense his demon nature; he's half-demon, which makes him particularly skilled in this. He may have to change later to check some stuff for us; please don't destroy him.'

Denis nodded to me. 'Understood, ma'am. I'll get the car out for you.'

'Be right down.'

'See you at Sham Shui Po, Emma,' Simone said, and disappeared.

Ronnie placed a large, battered briefcase on the coffee table and opened it. He pulled out a fung shui mirror with the complicated direction and elemental symbols around the edge, and a stack of paper seals held together with a rubber band. 'These won't cut it for this type of job. Need hand-made ones.'

He scrabbled through the case and pulled out a smaller, ebony case that he flipped open. It contained an ink brush, a stone tablet for mixing the ink, and an ink block. The ink block was a solid black block, square in cross-section, that had been intricately carved and highlighted with gold paint around the edges. Ronnie summoned some water into the cavity of the tablet and ran the ink block in circles over it, dissolving the block to make the ink.

'I heard you spoke to my father recently,' he said. 'How is he?'

'Alive,' I said. 'Has he gone after you lately?'

'Still alive? Oh well, can't have everything. No, he hasn't. He might be busy with something else.' He glanced up at me through the plastic-rimmed glasses. 'Actually, it occurs to me that I should keep you updated when he's trying me out, because he only tries to kill me when he has nothing better to do. If he's not trying to kill me, then he's plotting something.' He glanced down at the stone. 'And he hasn't tried to kill me at all since about the middle of September.'

'He's certainly been trying the Celestial,' I said. 'We are suffering constant attacks from Hell from both your father and his assorted children. With the Dark Lord gone, it's becoming very hard to hold things together.'

'You can do it, Emma,' Ronnie said, and picked up the brush. He squinted at a piece of rice paper that was about twenty centimetres long and five wide. 'Now go and get your Retainer.'

'Damn, Ronnie, is there anything that goes on that you *don't* know about?' I said.

He grinned up at me. 'Not much.'

'You *sure* you don't want a job at the Academy?'

He snorted with derision and began the complex process of writing the symbols onto the paper that would create the seal. 'No, thanks. I've managed to remain solo and avoid the King's assassination attempts for close on three hundred years now. I quite like being a free agent.' He nodded to me. 'I appreciate the offer though, Lady Emma, and if there was any organisation I would join, it would be Wudang.'

Ronnie rose with the paper in one hand, the ink still slightly wet. He waved it to dry the ink, then went to the front door. He stood in front of the doorframe and concentrated. He flashed brilliant white for a second, then the white energy coalesced onto the paper, making it almost too bright to see. The paper was ripped from his hand and smacked into the left-hand doorframe, glowed painfully white, and disappeared.

'One down, six more to go,' he said.

'There are more windows than that,' I said.

'That's just this door alone,' Ronnie said. 'If I do my job right, both of us are going to feel mighty uncomfortable every time we go through this door.'

'That's what I like to hear,' I said. 'I'd better go, they're waiting for me.'

He returned to the coffee table, knelt on the carpet again and pulled out another seal. 'Go. Let me know how it ends.'

'Somehow I have the feeling that I won't need to,' I said.

Ronnie grinned at the seal he was working on. 'See you later, Ms Donahoe.'

CHAPTER 16

Denis double-parked on the busy Sham Shui Po street to let me out of the Mercedes. 'Do you want me to park and join you, or circle the building?' he said. 'There's a government car park across the road.'

'Park on the street if you can, otherwise cruise,' I said. 'Hopefully this won't take long, but we may need to get out fast if we find what we're looking for.'

'Good luck, ma'am,' he said as I closed the door, and he pulled away to find a park.

Although it was 9.30 pm, the street was full of young Hong Kong locals, some driving souped-up Lancers and Nissan imports. People crushed the sidewalks and overflowed onto the streets, a typical evening in the busy area around the Golden Arcade. This part of Hong Kong was one of the most densely populated areas in the world; the buildings were all packed high rises, stacking minuscule apartments with tiny windows over sprawling block-sized shopping malls full of similarly tiny shops. The sidewalks and gutters overflowed with trash; it had been a long time since the morning pass-through by the street sweepers.

The Golden Arcade filled the basement and first two floors of one of these apartment complexes. About three hundred metres long and a hundred wide, it twisted through narrow passageways from two entrances. The large entrance on the corner was for the basement and ground floor; a tiny entrance halfway along the building allowed access to the first floor.

None of the Disciples in our team were visible. They had all merged into the crowd. We would meet up inside.

The interior of the mall was low-ceilinged, with small shopfronts on either side of the meandering narrow corridors. Each shop, only about two metres square, had its speciality laid out on the counter: video cards or network cards, the prices written large in marker on cardboard cut-outs. Shoppers would cruise from store to store seeking the best price for the particular piece of hardware they were looking for.

As I entered, a young man called to me, 'Copy software, ma'am?' but I ignored him and headed down the stairs and further in. If I'd said yes he would have taken me to a shopfront around the corner further away; the mall was closely watched by customs officers. There would be a small shop selling handbags or candy with a false back wall, and behind that would be another store selling cheap mainland-made copies of any software or game the user could imagine.

The Academy kids occasionally practised their skills on these copy CD shops, running through and closing them down using the more advanced energy and Arts techniques. There was no fear of them being reported because they were shutting down criminals. The underworld outlets were excellent targets and we'd probably decimated the income the Triads received. If the demon Six had inherited Simon Wong's underworld empire, it looked like the backlash was finally catching up with us.

I moved down the stairs to the basement. The lower stores contained stacks of DVDs in shrink-wrapped bundles of a hundred, colourful novelty peripherals such as mice and keyboards, and cheap computer accessories — mouse pads and printer paper. The store holders glanced curiously at me, but none accosted me to buy. Wrong race, wrong gender, wrong age.

As I went further in, the stores became smaller and their goods cheaper. The floor hadn't been washed in a very long time and piles of dirt and dead insects crusted the corners. Some of the fluorescent lights buzzed and flickered.

Simone was waiting for me at the end of the corridor. A small flight of stairs led up to street level, with a metal chute next to them for throwing boxes of stock down into the basement. The corridor the demon had mentioned was on our left, stretching the complete length of the arcade. The ceiling was low and angular in places where it fitted under the stairs. There was a single pull-down roller door halfway along, with boxes containing computer cases stacked in front of it.

As I neared the door, the Disciples came into view. Simone had hidden them with a simple charm that only made them visible as they were approached. They weren't wearing Mountain uniforms, just jeans and T-shirts, but their T-shirts were black in unspoken acknowledgement of their Master. Nobody told them to wear black; they did it out of a sense of unity. I smiled inwardly; without thinking, I'd worn a black T-shirt too.

It was something of a crush with fifteen Disciples, Simone and myself. I went to stand next to Simone and the Masters and looked at the door.

'Will anybody see if someone uses PK to break the door?' I asked.

'No need, Emma,' Simone said. 'Michael's here.'

Michael shimmered into view behind Simone, strikingly different in his white T-shirt. 'Sorry, forgot you can't see much. I'll take down the door for you.' He nodded to the Disciples around us. 'Be ready, there may be something on the other side. Nobody can sense anything.'

'Wait,' I said, raising my hand. 'You can't sense anything?'

Both Simone and Michael shook their heads.

'Might be similar to what happened under Kowloon City Park, Emma,' Simone said. 'But I don't remember that well, and that charm dissipated shortly after the demon was destroyed, so we couldn't study it. We'll just have to play it by ear.'

I tapped the stone in my ring.

'What now!'

'Stone, they can't sense what's on the other side of the door.'

The stone sounded chagrined. 'Oh. I see.'

'I hate to ask this, but ...'

'No,' the stone said. 'All my children are accounted for. So if this demon has used stone essence to line the walls and make them spyproof, he's used Shen outside of my family.'

'Are your kids the most powerful stone Shen?' Michael said.

The stone hesitated for a moment, then said, 'No. The children of other Building Blocks, and direct descendants of the Grandmother herself are more powerful than mine.'

'Could one of their kids defeat one of yours?'

The stone hesitated again, then, 'Yes.'

'Bad news all around,' I said, studying the door. It was plain grey steel. In human form I couldn't check any further.

'Let's just do it and see what we get,' Liu said. 'The other shops are closing, the ones nearby are deserted. Let's go.'

'Everybody,' Michael said firmly, and the Disciples stilled to hear him. 'I'm going to change this door to mercury to make it open silently for us. Just hold your breath until it solidifies at the bottom — mercury is pretty toxic and you don't want to inhale any.' He glanced around. 'Got it?'

The Disciples nodded.

'Okay, doing it now.'

Michael raised one hand towards the roller door and it changed from dull steel to shiny mercury, then slid into a puddle on the floor. The mercury splashed against an invisible force field — he had ensured that it wouldn't touch us — then solidified into a grey lava-like lump on the floor.

'All clear, it's steel again,' Michael said.

The interior of the store was obviously a front. The shelves were unoccupied except for a couple of empty display boxes for hardware more than ten years old. The counter was a tired-looking office desk with no chair, and the cash register's power cord hung forlornly down the back of the desk, not even plugged into the wall. There were no other doors or apparent entrances to the demon's nest, however, and the Disciples began to search for the way in.

'Nothing,' Simone said, casting around. 'Michael?'

Michael concentrated. 'Nothing here either. Appears to be just a room.'

'Stone?' I said.

'Strange.' The stone was silent for a moment, then Lee, one of the Disciples, stepped forward. The stone drifted out of my ring and grew to about the size of my fist, still square and polished green. Lee took True Form, a red granite stone about the same size. The two stones circled the room, occasionally moving to the centre of the room and then drifting out again — an elegant dance that seemed to have no pattern to it. Finally they drifted only millimetres above the floor, side by side, and covered nearly every square centimetre.

Lee stopped just inside the shop door and hovered slightly above the floor.

The stone returned to my ring. 'Under there.'

'There is a hollowness of some sort directly beneath me,' Lee said. 'Other than that, we can't really be sure, ma'am.'

Simone and Michael stepped forward and both crouched to put their hands on the floor, concentrating. They shared a look, then stood again. Lee returned to human form and joined the silent group of Disciples.

Michael shrugged. 'Concrete. Too much for me, unless we go for physical force, which will rock the building and probably bring the authorities.'

'Isn't there a latch or something?' I said.

'If there is, it isn't anything obvious,' the stone in my ring said. 'Probably something only a demon could open.'

Simone shot me a look. *Don't even think about it. The last thing we need is you running out of control right at the entrance to a nest.*

I stood on the spot the stones had indicated, then crouched and put my hands on the floor, wondering if my demon nature could detect anything. I jumped back as the floor slid smoothly open, revealing a black stone ramp leading down. A strong breeze came from the hole, surprisingly fresh with the smell of mown grass and greenery.

The Demon King, in his usual human form of a mid-twenties Chinese with maroon hair in a short ponytail, poked his head through the hole and grinned at me. 'Hi, guys, just got here. Mind if we tag along?'

'We can handle this ourselves,' I said. 'Get lost.'

His smile didn't shift. 'This is demon business. By rights I could tell *you* to get lost, but in the interests of Hell–Celestial relations, we'll just come along and see what happens.' He raised his hands. 'Strictly hands off, we'll just observe. I promise.'

He's right, Emma, the stone said. *This is a demon matter. The demons in this nest haven't attacked anyone as far as you know, and the King is within his rights to claim territory.*

'I'm well aware of that,' I said.

I proceeded down the black stone ramp, ducked to pass under the floor and crouched until the ceiling of the tunnel was high enough to stand. The walls quickly closed in around me, leading to a narrow, low-ceilinged black stone passage, its sides unfinished and rough.

The King had brought Martin along. He stood behind him, waiting in the tunnel.

Simone hissed under her breath when she saw him. 'I don't want him here.'

'My choice, Princess,' the King said. 'You don't have much say in the matter, I'm afraid, dear.'

'Don't call me dear,' Simone said, and moved to push past the King.

Martin leapt forward, hands out, to block her way. 'Mei Mei, take care, we don't know how much damage your touch will do to the King. Please stay back.'

Simone gestured angrily to push Martin away from her. 'Don't call me *Mei Mei*!' Her eyes flashed black then returned to normal, still full of fury. 'You are no brother of mine!'

The King's and Martin's faces went blank with shock, then Martin recovered and bowed slightly. 'As you will, Princess. All I ask is that you take care with touching Wong Mo.'

'Go then,' Simone said, gesturing down the tunnel. 'We can't sense anything up ahead, so you first.'

The King and Martin turned and headed down the tunnel. It was just high enough for us to stand without bending, but the sides were so narrow that we had to squeeze through, the walls brushing against us.

'I hope nobody's claustrophobic,' I said. 'This is intense.'

I am, the stone said. *This is awful.*

The black tunnel carried us down and further in for a hundred metres, still not becoming any larger. The silent Disciples moved behind us in single file, with Michael bringing up the rear. As the light behind us receded the tunnel became darker.

'I can't see,' I said. 'I don't have any sort of Inner Eye right now. And some of the Disciples are human, they'll need light too. Simone, can you help?'

A glowing ball of light appeared just above Simone's left shoulder, floating in the tunnel.

'It's cold light, you can touch it,' she said. 'Just walk right through it. I'll leave a trail of them.'

Martin stopped in front of us. 'There is something here.'

The King inhaled deeply. 'Smell that, Emma.'

The tunnel was rich with the pungent aroma of spices and warm bread. I breathed deeply, savouring the scent. Even though I'd eaten before I left home, this food-rich fragrance struck something inside me and I felt a deep gnawing hunger that normal food would not satisfy.

Simone inhaled and gagged. 'God!'

The Disciples made some distressed sounds behind us.

'Does that smell awful to you?' I said softly.

'It's like a combination of burning tyres and something that's been dead for a long time,' Simone said.

'There is a dead demon here,' Martin said.

The King wasn't visible on the other side of Martin in the narrow tunnel. 'Been dead a while. Don't tread

215

on it, it's probably liquefied inside.' His voice filled with amusement. 'Can't stop to eat right now, sorry, Emma.'

'You are *disgusting*,' Simone said, and moved forward. 'Why didn't it dissolve into essence?' She picked her way past the corpse. 'Ugh.'

The dead demon lay on the floor of the tunnel, an insect-type, about a metre long, looking like a large dead cockroach. It lay on its back with three of its legs curled up, the remaining legs detached and lying further down the tunnel. The delicious smell of bread and spices was coming from it, even stronger now that I was close, and the empty hungry feeling inside me became almost painful. I slapped it down.

'Any idea why it didn't dissolve?' I said.

'We'll take it back later and study it,' Liu said. 'We'll need some brave-hearted Disciples to handle that little job.'

'I claim it,' the King said. 'It's mine.'

'Damn,' I said under my breath. He was within his rights to claim any demons we encountered that didn't attack us.

'It was a guard,' Martin said. 'Here we are. Step carefully, there is a large hole here down to the nest.'

The tunnel led to a round room, about four metres across, made of the same black stone. The floor was nonexistent except for a ledge of about a metre wide around the perimeter of the room. We moved in and stood on the ledge around the central hole.

'Got it, Liu?' I said.

'Yep,' Liu said. 'Only two require carrying.'

'How deep, Simone?' I said.

'I can see down about twenty metres,' Simone said. 'I can't see the bottom.'

'Same here,' Michael said. 'I'd like to know what's blocking our vision.'

'How far can you see, George?' I said.

'About the same,' the King said. 'Let's go, shall we? I'm sure there's a bottom to this hole eventually.'

I stepped off the ledge and into the darkness. One of Simone's glowing light balls followed me. The sides of the hole glittered with crystalline fragments that sparkled in the light, and a fresh breeze, again full of the fragrance of mown grass and spring blossoms, blew up from the bottom into my face. This had to be one of the most beautiful places I had ever been; the fragrance, the cool darkness and the sparkling walls all called to me, welcoming me home. I felt that I would never want to leave.

We fell at a steady rate, all together, two of the Disciples guided by Celestials that held their hands.

Did Simon Wong's nest smell this bad? Simone said into my head.

Tell her no, I said to the stone, not wanting to share that the whole place smelled warm, welcoming, and homely to me.

It's your demon nature, Emma, the stone said. *We need to get this stuff out of you.*

I know, I said.

We fell about fifty metres and the floor loomed below us, black rough stone, the same as the walls. We drifted to the bottom.

A single bare fluorescent tube hung on the wall above a square entrance on the side of the hole. As Michael approached the tube, it flickered into life.

The warm bread aroma hit me again; there was another dead demon here. Simone sent the glowing ball into the tunnel and the dead cockroach-type came into view.

'I can't sense any demons here,' Simone said. 'My vision is still partially blocked though.'

'Anybody else?' I said.

'I think there is something further inside. Some of mine,' the Demon King said. 'If you want, I can just tell them all to die.'

'We always give them a chance to turn first,' I said. 'And you swore not to interfere.'

'That I did,' the King said. 'They are all yours.'

'I haven't killed a demon in nearly six months. My skills are rusty,' Michael said. 'Let's go.'

The tunnel with the cockroach was larger than the tunnel above, but with the same black stone walls. It was high and wide enough to walk three abreast. We passed openings on either side that led to more corridors to the right and left, each of which appeared to go for about five metres and then turn a corner.

'Let's split up,' Michael said. 'We can cover the ground faster.'

'Humph,' Liu said. 'You have been spending too much time in the United States watching Hollywood movies, my friend. We will spend some time on tactics later.'

'Both Simone and I are capable of taking anything we find down here,' Michael said, indignant. 'We can each take a group and keep in touch.'

'Let's just stick together for now,' I said. 'The fact that your vision isn't clear is a bad sign, and I wouldn't want us to lose contact.'

'Ma'am,' Michael said.

We slowed as we reached the end of the corridor, about twenty metres from the bottom of the hole. The change in the texture of the air allowed us to feel what we couldn't see: the room beyond was a huge cavern with a ceiling so high it was invisible. The sides curved away from the corridor, their angle suggesting that they would meet again at the other end of the room fifty or sixty metres away.

Simone gasped softly. 'A nest cavern.'

'I can't sense any Mothers, but there may be other stuff here,' the Demon King said. 'I think it's abandoned.' He moved to the end of the corridor, stopped and looked around. 'Nice nest though. Some of my smaller Mothers would like it.' He turned to me and his maroon eyes glittered. 'Want to join them?'

We moved forward, a couple of Simone's glowing lights following us. The cavern had indentations in the floor where the Mothers would tend their eggs. Each indentation was five metres across, and they were ten metres away from each other, a total of five indentations in the whole cavern. The first indentation had a couple of eggs in it, and I approached them.

The eggs were round, sixty centimetres across, and had transparent shells. The demons inside were visible through the milky shells, appearing as small humans. The shells were wrinkled and dull and the demons inside were obviously dead.

The King approached an egg and turned it over. The demon inside remained curled up in the same position as the egg moved.

'Interesting,' the King said. 'This appears to be a copy of Simone.'

Simone moved forward quickly and studied the demon inside the egg. 'Oh my God,' she said quietly.

The King summoned a dagger and split the shell open. The contents were like a watery jelly, oozing from it and spreading over the ground. The strong fragrance of jasmine and sweet lemon came from it.

Simone covered her nose and moved back quickly. 'Did you *have* to do that?'

'Dammit, why does *everything* down here smell like shit?' Michael said, exasperated.

'Doesn't smell bad at all to us demons,' the King said with pleasure. He grinned at me. 'Right, Emma?' He sucked some of the gel off his fingers. 'Not too bad at all.' He glanced down at the demon. 'Now let's have a look at this.'

He pulled the tiny demon from the shell. It was only forty centimetres tall, a miniature and perfectly formed copy of Simone when she was around twelve years old.

'It's so *tiny*,' Simone whispered.

'Interesting,' the King said. 'Obviously designed to grow to full size outside the egg. Love to see the Mother they used to make this.' He rose, wiped his hands on his jeans and looked around the cavern. 'All gone though — looks like they were tipped off.' He grinned at Simone. 'You were very pretty when you were twelve, Simone. You're even more beautiful now. Wonder if there's any naked fourteen-year-old Simones around here?'

Simone blanched and I opened my mouth to protest, but Martin interrupted me. 'There is a dead Mother here,' he said from further into the cavern. 'My Lord.'

The dead Mother lay sprawled across the floor of the cavern, stretched out in True Form. Her back end was the usual large black snake tail, but her front end was different: she appeared as an ordinary Chinese human female, naked from the waist up, her pale skin shining eerily in the darkness of the cavern.

'Oh, now this is interesting,' the Demon King said, and crouched to study her.

'Was she in transition to human form?' I asked.

'No, this is her True Form all right. Never seen anything like her,' the Demon King said. 'I claim.'

'Dammit!' Michael said softly behind me.

Something whispered above our heads, the flutter of large wings, and we all quickly stood and looked up.

'Flyers up there, Emma,' the King said. 'We usually keep flyers in the nest ventilation shafts to stop anything from trying to get in. I'd say they'd be pretty hungry by now. They haven't tried this Mother, she's too big for them to eat.' He looked from the Mother to me. 'Does she smell like food to you?'

Leo's deep voice drifted across the floor of the nest from the other side. 'Emma?'

'Lion,' Martin gasped, and raced towards the voice, the rest of us trailing him. As we ran there was a clatter of wings above us and the flyers attacked.

I summoned the Murasame and stepped back to face them. The air flashed brilliantly white and gold as Simone used shen and Michael used chi energy in destructive blasts. There were about fifteen of them, appearing like black dragons with glowing red eyes, wings and four legs. They were each about a metre long. One of them swooped down on me, raising its legs to rake my face with its claws, but I sliced it in half with the Destroyer before it could reach me. It disappeared into black feathery streamers; at last we'd found some demons that were behaving as they were supposed to. I moved back quickly to avoid being hit by the demon essence.

The students dealt with a couple of flyers on the floor, one holding the demon down and the other using bare-handed techniques to break its shell with swift punches and make it dissipate. Simone and Michael handled the last couple with energy, and they were all gone.

'Emma,' Leo said. I turned and Leo grabbed me, pulling me into a fierce hug. 'Thank God you're here. I thought you'd never come.'

I pulled back to see him, grinning like an idiot, then my smile disappeared as I realised what I was seeing. It was Leo, but he was naked and didn't seem to know it. He looked the same age as he had been when he'd been taken by Kwan Yin, and he was walking and speaking without any impediment.

He raced to Simone and engulfed her in a massive embrace, pulling Michael in to hold him as well. 'Look at you kids, all grown-up. Damn, but I missed you guys.'

'Yep, one of mine, Emma,' the King said with compassion. 'Demon copy.'

'He could be the real Leo,' I said. 'They could have healed him.'

'And kept him the same age for eight years?' the King said. 'I sincerely doubt it. And I thought that spinal injuries like his were beyond anyone but the Dark Lord's Serpent.'

'I can't tell, Emma,' Simone said. 'He seems human to me.'

'He's a demon, and I can prove it,' the King said. 'He should come with me.'

'The Hell I'm a demon,' Leo said. 'I'm Leo goddamn Alexander from Chicago, and they've been holding me here for ages. These kids,' he gestured towards Simone and Michael, 'are like my own children, and Emma here is like a sister to me. You're not taking me. I'm going home with them, to serve them and the Dark Lord. I'm a sworn Retainer of the House of the North.' He turned to me and became more serious. 'Is Mr Chen still here, Emma? Is he okay? He still has some time, doesn't he? Why didn't he come with you?'

'Leo, take Emma's sword,' the King said.

Leo strode to me, grabbed my sword hand with one hand and attempted to pull the Murasame from it with the other.

'Don't try to take it, Leo, it'll hurt you,' I said.

'I don't have a choice,' Leo said, his face blank with shock. 'Give me the sword.'

I pulled my hand away and moved back, but Leo followed me. He made a few quick attempts to grab the sword by the blade, and I moved quickly enough to evade him.

'Give me the sword!' Leo said. 'I'm going to take the blade if you don't give me the handle!'

I flipped the sword in my hand so that he could take the handle, and he wrenched it from me. He howled with pain, then went silent, panting, holding the blade. He gritted his teeth, but a small sound of pain escaped him.

'Give me the sword back, Leo,' I said. 'It hurts anybody who tries to hold it.'

'I can't!' Leo said. He shook his hand that was holding the blade. 'Dammit! It hurts!'

'Kill Simone,' the King said.

Leo spun and made a lightning-fast swing at Simone's head. She easily evaded him, stepping out of the way. He swung the sword the other way to take her in the midsection, and she blocked his sword arm with her forearm without difficulty. She took his arm in both hands, twisted, and dropped him onto his back on the floor. Then she slid my sword from his hands, grimaced with pain, and threw it to me.

Leo struggled beneath her and she held him down.

'Let me go!' Leo gasped. 'I need the sword!'

'Leo, sleep,' the King said.

Leo flopped unconscious.

'As I said, one of mine,' the King said. 'I'll take it.'

'It's ours,' I said. 'It attacked Simone.'

'Oh, damn, you're right,' the King said, chagrined. 'Shouldn't have told him to do that, should I? That was dumb of me.'

Martin knelt to study Leo. 'It doesn't appear to be a demon to me, my Lord. I see it as human.'

'I do too,' Simone said. 'But the King can control him, so he has to be a demon.'

'I don't believe anything to do with you, George,' I said. 'There's a chance that this is the real Leo.'

The King snorted with derision. 'Look at it. It's not injured, it hasn't aged a day, it's naked in a nest where they were making copies, and it obeys me. That's four strikes. I'd say three strikes and we have a demon. Don't take it with you, Emma, it's probably a construct controlled by whoever held this nest. It'll turn on you later. Leave it with me; it's too dangerous.'

'You're not having it,' I said. I turned to Liu. 'Can you summon some clothes for him? Let's keep moving and see what else we can find.'

'Wake up, Leo honey,' the King said.

Leo grunted and shook his head, then rose from the floor. 'What happened?' He saw me and his face split into a huge grin. 'Emma! Finally! Where have you been? I've been stuck down here for ages!'

Liu handed Leo a pair of black cotton pants and a black jacket, the traditional Mountain training uniform. Leo put them on unselfconsciously, not seeming to notice that he had been naked in front of everybody.

'Whoa, I must have been in a coma or something,' he said. 'Is that you, Simone?' He looked around. 'Michael? What the hell is happening here? What am I doing here?'

'What's the last thing you remember?' I said.

Leo stared at me for a moment, ran one hand over his bald head then dropped his hand to his side. 'I don't know.'

'You're a demon copy of the real Leo,' the King said. 'You probably hatched not long ago.'

'No,' Leo said.

'Raise your right arm,' the King said.

Leo watched, wide-eyed, as his arm seemed to move by itself.

'Emma, tell him to drop his arm. If he can't, then he's mine,' the King said.

'Lower your arm, Leo,' I said.

Leo grimaced with effort, then exhaled a huge breath. 'I can't.' He glanced at the King. 'I'm a *demon*? Then where is the real me?'

'That's what we want to find out,' the King said. 'Drop your arm. Tell you what, love, come to my nest with me, I'll look after you.' He smiled slightly. 'I'll even take the Dark Lord's form for you; such a shame to waste something as beautiful as you.'

Leo's face didn't shift, he just silently watched the King.

'Come with me, and we will extract as much information as we can from you, then you can live out the rest of your short life being cared for as only a prize member of the King's harem can. Believe me.' He smiled slightly again. 'You will be gracing my bed nearly every night until you fade.'

'Fade?' Simone said.

'I doubt this demon has more than a couple of months to live,' the King said. 'It's way too complex. Should never have been made. Probably can't ingest anything except plasma.'

'What do you mean?' Leo said.

'He's saying you're a vampire and that you will only live a couple of months,' I said. 'And I don't believe him. You're coming with us.'

'Just kill me and be done with it,' Leo said. 'That's the kindest thing right now.'

'We need you,' Michael said. 'Come with us. Even if you're not the real Leo, you still have information about these demons that we can use.'

Leo hesitated, then frowned and nodded once sharply. 'Sounds like the best option. Let's get me back, restrain me, and get the information out of me. The real me is out there somewhere and we need to find him.'

Michael turned to the King. 'You still have my mother, and you say you have definite information on the location of the real Leo. You'd better not be guessing here, demon.'

The King raised his hands. 'On my honour, and you know I have some. I will give you a first-class lead on the location of the other Leo.' He glanced around the nest. 'I'll send in a clean-up team, this place is done.'

'I want my people to check it out first,' I said.

'No need, Emma. If I find anything I'll pass it on to you, word of honour.'

I turned to the Celestials and Disciples behind me. 'Liu, get a couple of teams in and do a sweep, please. We'll take this Leo copy home.'

'Bad idea, Emma,' the King said.

'I'm Queen of the Bad Idea,' I said.

The King raised one hand towards Leo. 'Obey Lady Emma in every way. If you feel the urge to harm her or Lady Simone, die first.'

'I thank you,' Martin said softly.

Leo stared at the King, his face full of conflict, then said, 'As Your Loathsome Majesty wills, so I will obey.' He turned away. 'Damn.'

'I think we have what we came here for,' I said. 'Let's go home.'

'Mind if I stay and have a look around?' Michael said. 'I need some practice.'

'You can lead a clean-up team,' I said. 'All yours.'

Michael grinned and saluted me. 'My Lady.'

CHAPTER 17

Icalled Denis on my mobile as we walked back out through the mall, and he met us outside the arcade. Simone sat in the front of the Mercedes, and I sat in the back with Leo.

'Lion,' Denis said, nodding in the rear-view mirror. 'Welcome home.'

'I'm a demon copy, not the real Leo,' Leo said. 'But thanks anyway. You're one of the Tiger's?'

'Two Eighty-Three.'

'More than able to take me down if you need to. Good,' Leo said.

Denis glanced at Leo in the rear-view mirror as he pulled away, shot a look at me, then concentrated on the road.

'How old are you, Simone?' Leo said. 'You're all grown-up!'

'Fourteen,' Simone said. 'You've been gone eight years. The real you was in Hell refusing Immortality all that time, but was somehow replaced by a demon copy that exploded when we went to get him out. Now we don't know where he is.'

'This could be the real Leo,' I said.

Neither Simone nor Leo replied.

'Anyway, the Dark Lord is gone,' I continued. 'I'm managing the Academy and the Heavens very poorly, the Demon King is attacking the Celestial all the time, John hasn't been heard of in ages, and basically things are falling to bits.'

'Oh, give it up, Emma,' Simone said patiently. 'We're doing the best we can in the circumstances, and everybody says you're doing an okay job. The King hasn't won yet, and we won't let him as long as we can fight.' She turned in her seat to see Leo. 'And we'll find the real you and be a family again.'

'What's the last thing you remember?' I asked Leo.

'It's really vague, sort of a blur,' Leo said. 'I remember waking up on the floor of the nest when I heard your voices. Before that ...' He paused, thinking. 'Before that I sort of remember being in the Peak apartment, and something about Martin, and Mr Chen being mad at me for something, but that's about it.'

'Nothing from inside the nest?' I said.

'Not really,' Leo said. 'I'll do my best to remember so that we can find the real me. You can't afford to waste your time searching for me if you have so many issues at the moment.'

'Ma'am, I'm sorry, but I really can't stay quiet here,' Denis said. 'Are you *sure* this is a good idea? This is a demon!'

'Does he scan as a demon to you, Denis?'

Denis was quiet for a moment, then, 'No.'

'It's had a compulsion put on it, Denis,' Simone said. 'The King's told it to die before it hurts me or Emma.'

Denis shook his head. 'You should not be taking this back to your home, ma'am.'

'Actually I think home is the best place for him,' Simone said. 'Emma thinks he's the real Leo, and I don't. Either way, he'll be close and we can watch him.'

Denis shook his head again but didn't argue any more.

'If it means anything at all, Denis, I agree with you, and I think I should be destroyed on the spot,' Leo said.

'We have tame demons at home all the time,' Simone said. 'One more won't make much difference.'

'This one's not tamed,' Denis said.

'Tame me then,' Leo said. 'Whatever it takes. I want you two to be safe.'

'Say, "Protect me, I am yours",' Denis said.

'Protect me, I am yours,' Leo said.

Simone shrugged. 'Okay, I'll finish it up at the Peak.'

'I don't feel any different,' Leo said. 'Should I?'

'Don't know,' Simone said. 'Let's see what happens when I complete it at home.'

'Yeah, the pool's been like that for a year,' Simone said as we approached the front door on the eleventh floor of the apartment building. 'The concrete cracked shortly after it was built and it's been unusable for a long time.'

'Just get a Celestial in to fix it,' Leo said.

'I'm going to use elementals, I think,' Simone said. 'We have to be careful — the first and third floors are leased out to ordinary humans and we can't have them seeing anything weird or the Jade Emperor goes stupid at us.' She keyed the numeric code into the keypad on the front gate and the gears inside meshed. 'Haven't changed the key code, Leo, it's the same one.' She opened the front door, entered and kicked off her shoes. 'Ah Yat?'

'I don't remember the door code,' Leo said, then stopped at the doorway, bewildered. 'What the hell?'

I made it through the new seals, but it was more than an unpleasant buzz, it was like walking through a high-voltage electrical field. My legs collapsed under me and Denis caught me.

'I'm okay,' I said before they could ask. 'New seals.'

Denis effortlessly raised me to stand on my feet and then took a couple of steps back to study me. He looked from me, to Simone, to Leo, who still stood on the other side of the door, bewildered because he couldn't go in.

Denis turned back to me and opened his Inner Eye on me — another electric jolt that blinded me and felt like it had split my head open. I staggered back against the wall, seeing nothing but red, my ears roaring, my brain pierced with a massive burning spike.

The pain switched off and I slid down the wall to sit on the floor, still unable to see.

'Don't hurt her!' Simone shouted. 'She's not a demon! It's all right, the demon who killed my father did this to her.'

'I think I'm going to throw up, Simone,' I said. 'Help.'

A bowl was thrust into my hands and I retched over it, too weak to move. Nothing came up and I collapsed back against the wall, trying to breathe, heavy nausea churning my stomach. I took deep breaths.

'You okay, Emma?' Simone said.

I nodded, still taking deep breaths. 'I'll be all right. That's a hell of an Inner Eye you have there, Denis.'

'That's right, take a good look at me too, Denis,' Simone said. 'I'm not a demon, I'm the real Simone. This household hasn't been taken over or anything. Emma was injected with demon essence when One Two Two held her and she's been transformed into a horrible demon … *thing*. She can control it, and we're going to get this demon stuff out of her.'

'Sorry, Princess,' Denis said, sounding rueful. 'Your housekeeper is a demon, this Leo is a demon copy, the fung shui man was half-demon, and now Lady Emma is struck down by demon seals — it's not a difficult conclusion to make.'

'The house has been taken over by demons,' I gasped.

My vision began to clear and I saw Denis and Simone were standing over me looking concerned. 'And Simone is the biggest one of all.'

'Well, I'm a teenager, what do you expect?' Simone said. 'I can't help you up, Emma. Do you want Denis to help you to your room?'

'Leave me here, I'll get over it,' I said. 'Let Leo in. He's standing there looking as confused as ever.'

'You may enter, Leo,' Simone said.

Leo entered, and quickly crouched next to me. 'Are you okay, Emma? What happened?'

'It's a long story,' I said.

'What's this thing with the door?'

'Obviously the demon seals that Ronnie put in are exceptionally good ones,' I said. 'I'm going to pay him double when he sends his bill.'

'But why is it affecting *you*?' Leo said. 'Me I can understand, I'm a demon. I couldn't even come in. But why you?'

'Simon Wong turned me into a Snake Mother,' I said. 'If Simone touches me I'll fall back into that form. I'm just as much demon as you are, mate.'

'You're a copy too?' Leo said.

'Nope.' I raised my hand and he helped me up. I placed the bowl on the hall table, pleased that I hadn't had to use it. 'I'm the real Emma all right — snake, Snake Mother, demon, the whole works.' I turned to Denis, who was watching me like a predatory creature. 'I hate to do this, Denis, but I'm ordering you not to tell anybody about my demon nature. If some of those assholes on the Celestial Plane found out about this I'd lose the Academy and the Northern Heavens.'

'Snake?' Denis said.

'Snake. I'm a big black snake as well. Only seems to come out when my family are threatened.' I shook my head. 'John thought it was cool.'

'Remember what Kwan Yin said,' Simone said. 'It could be useful in controlling your demon nature.'

'I don't want to pull my demon nature out to try it,' I said. 'Well, we have Leo here — let's settle him in, and try to get some rest. I have another challenge tomorrow.'

'I know, and I'm sorry I ever said that, Emma,' Simone said. 'This is a pain in the neck for you. You go; I'll tame this Leo.'

'I want to watch,' I said. 'I want to see what happens when you complete the process.'

Simone waved Leo closer and held her hand out. He took it. Simone's eyes unfocused and her brow wrinkled. She frowned. 'Um.'

'Say "Protect me, I will serve you, I am yours",' Denis said.

'Protect me, I will serve you, I am yours,' Leo said. 'Is something supposed to happen?'

'Yes.' Simone dropped his hand. 'And it isn't. It's like trying to tame a human being.' She focused on him again. 'Maybe you are the real Leo.'

'Is he too big for you to tame, Princess?' Denis said.

'I've tamed a level eighty-nine, Denis,' Simone said. 'I don't think so.'

Denis whistled softly between his teeth. '*Eighty-nine?* Damn.'

'Tomorrow, we're going to take you to the Academy and we're going to clear up once and for all whether you are a human being or a demon copy,' Simone said. 'Go get some rest, Leo. If you're hungry ask Ah Yat for something.' She picked her little backpack up from the floor. 'I'm going to bed. If any demons attack the Celestial Plane, or Hell erupts and demons take over the world, or the Celestial Palace starts to fall from the sky,' she grinned at me, 'tell them to get lost.'

'Sounds like a very good idea. Night, Simone,' I said.

'Come on, Leo, your room is the same, pink underwear and all.'

'Pink underwear?' Leo asked.

'Never mind,' I said. 'This way.'

Leo stopped just inside his room. 'This feels very strange.'

'How much do you remember?'

'It's weird.' He went to his television unit in the living section and fingered his R&B CDs. 'I can remember all of this and yet it's all new.' He looked around. 'Which is not surprising since I'm a copy. I have Leo's memories, but I've never been here before.'

'Get some rest,' I said. 'We'll go to the Academy tomorrow. Regina and, if we're lucky, Meredith can check you out.'

'I don't know what the Academy is but I know that I want to be there, it's one of my favourite places,' Leo said. He pulled me into a warm embrace. 'It's good to see you again, Emma.'

I held him close and buried my face into his huge chest. 'I've missed you so much. You're like a brother to me.'

He held me close for a while, then pulled back to see me. His expression became intense, and he raised his hands to circle my throat. I felt a moment of concern but he smiled slightly, pushed one hand behind my neck, and raised the other to brush my cheek.

'I could never hurt you, Emma,' he whispered, pulled me closer, and lowered his face to mine to kiss me. I kissed him back, a chaste kiss, but he wanted more. He opened his mouth on mine and turned the kiss from gentle to passionate and full of need. I freed myself and stared at him, bewildered. 'What are you doing?'

He raised his hands and smiled ruefully. 'Sorry. My hormones got away from me there, my bad.' He dropped his hands. 'Won't happen again, Emma, I promise. But you really can't blame me — you are still just as attractive as ever.'

'You find me *attractive*?'

He shrugged. 'Of course I do. Always have. Must be exhausted or something, because I never acted on it before.' He smiled ruefully again. 'Don't worry, I know that the Dark Lord has your heart.'

'Get some rest, Leo, we have an early start tomorrow,' I said, and went out, closing the door behind me. I hesitated for a moment, then tapped on Simone's door.

'Come on in, Emma.'

Simone sat on the bed wearing a cute set of 'I hate boys' pyjamas she'd bought on our last trip to London. 'What happened? You look like you've just seen a ghost.'

I went in, pulled out her study chair and sat on it. 'Leo just made a pass at me.'

She didn't seem surprised. 'I know, the elementals told me. More evidence that he's a demon copy, Emma.' She waved one hand at me. 'Go to bed. Don't worry about him — I have a couple of elementals standing guard over him. If he tries anything I'll know about it.'

'The elemental thing working out okay? It was just today you learned to summon them.'

She quirked a small smile. 'Actually, it's really easy. And they're quite fun to talk to as well, they travel around a lot. Must thank Aunty Zhu for teaching me.'

She held out one hand and a tiny water elemental, only about ten centimetres tall, appeared on her palm. The little elemental waved to me, then turned into a streak of water and shot up into the air, separated into droplets that spread horizontally in a circle, and disappeared.

'That's great, Simone.' I took a breath to ask about Celestial High, then changed my mind and rose from the chair. 'I'm going to bed. Night.'

'Night, Emma. Sleep well. Don't worry, we'll find the real Leo. This fake one wants to help.'

The next morning I took Leo with me to the Academy and Regina checked him out. She was as confused as everybody else was.

'Human, not demon, as far as I can see, Emma,' she said. 'Even his blood is red.' She sighed and leaned on her desk, studying Leo. 'What we have here is a perfectly normal forty-one-year-old human male, HIV positive, exactly the same as when he left, except he is no longer a paraplegic with a speech impediment.'

'Still HIV positive?' I said. 'He's a demon, he can't be!'

Regina nodded. 'His blood is human, and he has AIDS.'

Leo sagged and leaned his elbows on his knees where he sat. 'Wonderful. Back exactly the way I was, but now I'm a demon that has a maximum of twelve months to live, probably less, and I can't be trusted to protect you or Simone.' He glanced up at me. 'We need to find the real me in a hurry, before I turn or die.'

'I suggest you ask a Celestial to look at him,' Regina said. 'Leo, could you wait outside for a moment?'

Leo nodded, went out and closed the door softly behind him.

'What?' I said.

'This isn't about him, this is about you,' Regina said. She pulled another file across the desk towards her. 'You're due for another set of blood work, Emma. I want to make sure you're all right.'

'Okay, I'll come back in this afternoon and you can take it,' I said.

Regina rose, went to the cupboard and pulled out a hypodermic syringe. She pushed the needle onto the end and took the cap off. 'Sure you will. I know you're lying, Emma, you're not planning to come back at all. So let's do it right now.'

I was about to argue but gave up. She was right. She tightened the rubber hose around my arm and slipped the needle into my vein. Red blood filled the syringe and I sighed with relief.

'Roughly how much of your dan tian is demon essence, do you think?' she said as she watched the syringe fill.

'Dammit, Regina, leave me some, I have a challenge in half an hour,' I said. 'Still just over half-full of demon essence.'

'It shows up on the blood work as toxins in your blood,' Regina said. 'The White Tiger's been giving me some assistance about demon physiology, but you're something completely different.'

'Yeah. "Never seen anything like you before, Emma." Heard that so many times now I'm sick of it.'

'Are you writing down your dreams?'

I nodded. 'I don't know what's at the top of this hill that my snake is always climbing, but the snake sure as hell wants to get there in a hurry.'

'Any ideas on where this home place is?'

'All I know is that it's very green with a sky that's sort of pastel blue, not brilliant blue like the Plane. Mostly rolling gentle hills, and the village on top of the hill has views for miles over meadows. There's two places: the hill that the snake is racing to get to the top of, and the village on top of the hill. I don't know how I know, but they're two different places. Every time I have that dream I search the web trying to find any sort of place on the planet that looks like that — thatched cottages, low stone walls, rose gardens. Most of the places are in Europe, but none are on top of a high hill like that.'

'But your family is Australian?'

'My father is thinking of checking the family tree, doing a family history, to see exactly where we came from. May be able to trace the source of the Serpent Essence.'

'Interesting,' Regina said. 'Good luck with that.' She plastered a small bandage over the puncture wound on my arm. 'I'll let you know the results of the blood work as soon as I get them.'

'Thanks, Regina.'

I used the same changing room at the Arena, and the same demon helped me with my armour, bowed and left the room. I nodded to the small statue of Xuan Wu and went out into the hallway. The same young man guided me down the hall to the Arena.

'We have been seeing quite a lot of you lately, Madam General,' he said. 'I have heard of Princess Simone's announcement. I hope it does not cause you too much difficulty.'

'What is your honoured name?' I said.

He bowed slightly. 'Chan. I am one of the Arena facilitators.'

I nodded back. 'I thank you for your concern, Mr Chan. I've yet to be seriously injured, and it's good practice for me.'

'My Lady,' he said, and raised his arm to indicate the entrance to the Arena.

This time the challenger had chosen a hilltop clearing as the setting. The high, thin mountains of China's Guilin area surrounded us, mist at their bases.

My challenger and the officiator stood together at the other side of the clearing and I approached them. As I neared my challenger I stopped and studied her. She was obviously trying to look like a boy, in cotton martial arts pants and a brown jacket, her hair tied back into a topknot. She appeared to be about fifteen years old, and even to my limited vision she was completely human, no Shen or demon essence about her at all.

I raised my arms. 'This is ridiculous. How can a woman challenge for Princess Simone's hand?'

'Woman?' the officiator said.

'Put your glasses on, Mr Zhou,' I said. 'This is a fifteen-year-old girl.'

A pair of spectacles appeared on the officiator's head and he pulled them down to peer at my challenger. He did a double-take as he realised I was right. 'This is highly unusual, young lady. You are obviously under age and the wrong gender to be challenging here.' He bowed slightly to me. 'Apologies, Lady Regent. This challenge is forfeit.' He took his glasses off and cleaned them with the edge of his silk robe's sleeve. 'Sorry, ma'am.'

The young woman stepped forward. 'I want to fight you! I'm good enough for the Mountain and I want to prove it!'

'You're too young for the Mountain,' I said. 'You know we only take adults.' I moved closer and patted her arm. 'Keep training, and come and try out when you're seventeen or eighteen.'

She pulled her arm away. 'I'm from Rabbit Village. I'm sixteen, I'm old enough. But the sexist assholes in charge of recruitment there won't approve me for the Mountain.'

'Sexist, eh? Stone, how many female Rabbits did we get last year?'

'Six.'

'How many male?'

'Eleven.'

'Year before?'

'Four, and thirteen.' The stone was quiet for a moment. Then, 'What's your name, Rabbit?'

'Tu Men Jiu,' the Rabbit girl said, defiant.

'What's your email address?'

She hesitated, then said, 'Fire horse twenty-three at sinoconnect dot com dot cn.'

'You're not a fire horse,' the stone said. 'You're a fire rat.'

'I want to be a fire horse,' she said, still defiant.

'You want to be the only zodiac sign that's regarded as completely unsuitable for women, making them bad-tempered, argumentative and difficult?' I said.

She raised her chin. 'Yes.'

'More power to you,' I said. I moved to the side of the Arena and pointed to the ground across from me. 'Okay, let's see how good you are.'

She grinned broadly and saluted me. 'Thank you, Lady Emma.'

'I will also have my people check whether your allegations are correct about the officials at the Rabbit Village,' I said. 'If what you say is true, there will be something of a shake-up.'

'Kick their asses, ma'am,' she said.

I put my hands up into a standard long defensive position, and she moved with fluid grace into a similar position across from me.

'Light contact, we don't want to do any damage, please. I've had enough crap kicked out of me the last week or so.'

She smiled tightly. 'I find that hard to believe, ma'am. You're famous for being one of the best, completely unbeatable.'

I shook my head. 'Just about every single Master, human and Shen, on the Mountain has beaten me, Men Jiu. I'm not really that good.'

Suddenly there were two of her. One of them lunged at my head, and the other jumped completely over me and attempted to attack me from behind.

239

I did a quick side-flip and the two Men Jius passed through each other as they tried to strike me.

'Stop,' I said, and raised my hands.

One of the Men Jius disappeared, and the other bowed and saluted me.

'That was shadow casting. I know that the Rabbits are experts in this sort of thing, but it's an advanced energy technique and, at sixteen, I'm surprised you know it.'

'My mother taught me, because the Masters in Rabbit Village don't teach it to girls,' she said.

'I think they don't teach it to people who are too young, actually,' I said, 'because it requires extremely good energy control, and that usually only comes with a degree of maturity.'

She didn't reply.

'I've seen enough, leave it with me, Men Jiu,' I said. 'I will discuss your case, and that of women in general at Rabbit Village, with the elders.'

'Promise?' she said.

I nodded. 'You have my word.'

She grinned. 'Did you stop the match because I could beat you?'

'Defend yourself,' I said, and before she was even into the defensive position I had gently turned her over and flipped her onto her belly on the floor of the Arena, her arms pinned behind her.

I moved back and let her up.

'Try again. This time you tell me when to start,' I said.

She was already moving before she said, 'Now.' Once again she formed a copy of herself and tried to take me from behind, with the copy distracting me in front.

I spun to face the real Men Jiu behind me and used a simple weight transfer manoeuvre to knock her off her feet again. The shadow's foot passed harmlessly through my head. She landed on her back and stared up at me.

'You're very fast, Lady Emma,' she said, gasping.

'I don't rely on it though, Miss Tu, the way that you rely on your shadows,' I said. 'Obviously this gift has helped you to win many times, but when you find someone who can deal with it, you have no skills to fall back on.' I held my hand out and she took it so that I could help her up.

'That's why I want to learn at the Academy, ma'am,' she said. 'I want to gain more skills! I want to cast more than one shadow. I've seen the Masters cast twenty or more!'

'I understand completely. I've seen how good you are, Men Jiu, leave it with me. Are there any other women in your group who have skills as good as you and would like to come to the Academy? We just had the intake from Rabbit Village two months ago.'

'I think there are a couple, ma'am.'

'I'm sending you an email, Rabbit. Reply with the names of the good students in the Rabbit Village,' the stone said.

'You should call her by name, not just "Rabbit", stone. Don't mind the stone, it's very rude sometimes,' I said.

She smiled and glanced down at my ring. 'I know, ma'am, your ring is famous.'

'Of course I am,' the stone said.

'Famous for being an asshole?' I said.

Her smile widened. 'Ma'am.'

'Humph,' the stone said, and went quiet.

The officiator came to us with a clipboard. 'May I speak with you, Lady Regent?'

Men Jiu fell to one knee and saluted me. 'I hope to see you at the Academy, ma'am.' She rose, saluted me again, and went out through the tunnel.

'What's up, Mr Zhou?' I said. 'I know these challenges have been a pain. Hopefully they'll settle down soon.'

'It's about Er Lang,' Mr Zhou said. 'Your challenge with him is scheduled for Saturday afternoon, two days from now. The Arena will have to be extended for the period of the match; we have a large number of people who have requested entry to watch.'

'I'd prefer this be a closed challenge,' I said. 'He's going to kick my butt, and although I'm not bothered about people seeing me beaten, it's not good to display such division at the highest levels of the Celestial Bureaucracy. The Second General shouldn't be calling out the First; we should be working together.'

'The challenger has the choice of venue and whether the match is open or closed,' Mr Zhou said.

'I know, I know.'

'Oh, and the tree's trial is scheduled for next week. You'll be called to testify. Your stone too.'

'Tree?' I said, confused, then remembered. 'Sang Shen is on trial?'

'He tried to kill you, ma'am. That's really not allowed.'

'Stone, clear the time in my diary. I want to be there to make sure nothing happens to him.'

'Done.'

I saluted Zhou. 'Thanks, Mr Zhou. See you at my next challenge.'

'Hopefully, ma'am, there won't be another before Er Lang.'

'I don't want another at all,' I said ruefully, and went out.

CHAPTER 18

I took the MTR back to the Academy after the non-event challenge; it was actually quicker to take the underground train from Central to Wan Chai than having Denis drive me through rush-hour traffic in Hong Kong's busy streets. I entered my office, dropped my bag, and sagged when I saw a Celestial box on my desk. My in-tray was overflowing, I had this Rabbit thing to deal with, I had to find a tutor for Simone, the real Leo was out there somewhere, and now the Celestial was bugging me. Great.

'Stone, ask Yi Hao to start researching schools and tutors for Simone,' I said. 'And order me some ho fan, please.'

'Done,' the stone said. 'Might need to import a tutor. There's a shortage here; most of them have moved over to China where there's more work.'

I flipped through the in-tray: mostly minor administrative matters, more requests for assistance for students travelling home for Christmas or Winter Solstice, and the press cuttings. Nothing urgent, so I sat at the desk and thumbed the clasp on the box.

I pulled out the single vellum scroll. It was tied with a scarlet ribbon. I opened the scroll; it was a direct edict from the Jade Emperor himself, written in red in his distinctive English script.

Hi, Emma. This business with Er Lang is getting out of hand. You have precedence here, and I suggest you summon him immediately and have it out. See if you can make him back down.

'This has the weight of an edict, doesn't it,' I said to the stone.

''Fraid so, Emma. Even though he says he's suggesting it, it's effectively an order.'

'The Jade Emperor expects me to make Er Lang, who is a hundred times older than me and a zillion times more powerful, back down,' I said. 'He should talk to Er Lang himself.'

'The Jade Emperor always knows what he's doing,' the stone said.

'You know, when we met him I thought that he actually liked me,' I said. 'Now I'm not so sure. Summon Er Lang, ask him to be in my office this afternoon, please.'

The stone was silent for a moment, then, 'He says he is busy and he can come next week when he is free.'

I looked back down at the edict. 'Immediately'. Dammit.

'Tell him to be in my office at three this afternoon, on the dot, and that's an order,' I said.

'Done. My goodness, Emma, but you just pissed him off.'

'I think that's the whole idea, stone. I just hope that you're right and the Jade Emperor knows what he's doing.' I pulled my in-tray closer. 'Now, let's see what we have here.'

One of the press cuttings was a three-paragraph column about the explosion at Kwun Lung Lau; the reporter noted that safety was being reviewed on the site as people had witnessed a second explosion after the first gas leak had cleared the building. A scathing comment was also made about the poor construction standards of these early estates, as it had been found that parts of the roof were lacking their steel reinforcement rods. The reporter brought up the 1997 demolition of an entire Sha Tin housing estate that had been constructed with insufficient foundation pilings, but moderated her anger by saying that construction standards in the Territory had improved dramatically since those bad times.

My desk intercom buzzed and I pressed the button.

'I have a couple of students here who've been waiting in the office to see you, Emma,' Yi Hao said. 'They want to speak to you urgently.'

'Send them in.'

The two students entered my office; both of them were slim, blond and European, in their mid-twenties. Scott was Canadian and his best friend, Tymen, was from the Netherlands. Tymen looked like he'd been crying: his eyes were red and his face was swollen.

'Scott, Tymen,' I said. 'Take a seat, gentlemen, how can I help you?'

They shared a look, then Tymen leaned forward over his knees. 'Ma'am, I need your help. I'm desperate. You're the only one who can help me.'

I put down the press cutting I was holding. 'What's the matter?'

He looked down at his hands and took a deep breath. 'It's my mother. She has ovarian cancer. They diagnosed her six months ago and operated, but they couldn't get it out. It's already spread, ma'am.' He wiped one hand over his eyes and looked away. 'She doesn't have long.'

'I'll arrange the plane tickets for you,' I said. 'Go home to her.'

Scott clasped Tymen's hand and Tymen held it. 'Actually, ma'am, she's on her way here.'

'Your training is not more important than your mother, Tymen,' I said. 'That's ridiculous. You should have gone home instead of bringing her here.'

'I didn't bring her here so I can train, ma'am,' Tymen said. 'The doctors in the Netherlands say it's too advanced to treat, and you're our last hope.'

'I can't cure cancer, nobody can,' I said. 'Not even Meredith has that sort of ability. I know you're desperate, but energy manipulation isn't that accurate, and it's very hard to pinpoint cancer cells and clear them all. The Dark Lord's Serpent has been known to cure cancer, but he's the only one.'

'*Your* Serpent might be able to cure her,' Tymen said.

I leaned back and stared at them. Most of the longer-term students at the Academy knew about the Serpent, from the times I'd changed when Simone was younger. There was a sort of blanket agreement that none of the newer students were to know, however, because many of them were freaked out if they found out about it.

'Your Serpent has immense healing powers,' Scott said. 'I've looked it up.' He glanced at Tymen. 'Both of us have been researching healing, and whenever we bring up a medical site, there's the Serpent, right on the top.' He squeezed Tymen's hand. 'Please help, ma'am.'

I opened my mouth and closed it again. I hadn't brought the Serpent out often enough even to try this sort of healing; I had enough trouble holding back from changing to demon form, and trying to change to the serpent might make me slip into a Mother.

'I don't know if I can take the Serpent form on demand,' I said. 'And even if I can, there's no guarantee it can heal her.'

'All we ask is that you try, ma'am,' Scott said. 'We don't need any more than that.'

'Let me think about it,' I said. 'Tymen, have you organised a hotel room or something for your mother?'

'She'll stay with me and Scott, I'll sleep in the living room,' Tymen said. 'She thinks we're going to try some sort of ancient Chinese remedy that I've heard of here.'

'Stone, ask Lok to arrange something for her, please.'

On it, Lok said into my head. *I will move some kids around. Cow's heart! Come on, woman! You promised!*

'When does your mother arrive, Tymen?' I asked.

'Four this afternoon.'

I checked my watch. 'Okay, it's one thirty now. Denis can run you out to the airport in my car, but could you pop up to the markets near Ruttonjee and buy a fresh cow's heart for Lok before you go?'

Lok's voice echoed triumphantly in my head. *YAY!*

'Who's Denis?' Scott said.

'Marcus is taking some time off, and we have a White Horseman acting as driver for a while,' I said.

'Thanks, ma'am,' Tymen said.

'Not a problem. Let me think about this snake thing while you two go and buy the heart and go to the airport. Stone, talk to Denis about taking them, please.'

'Done.'

The two students rose, fell to one knee to salute me, and went out.

The intercom buzzed and I pressed the button again. 'Master Leo is here with your noodles, ma'am.'

'Send him in.'

Leo came in holding a couple of foam takeaway bowls. He put one on the desk in front of me with the cheap paper napkin, plastic Chinese spoon and disposable chopsticks, and cleared a space on the desk for a similar bowl for himself. He flipped off the top and stirred the noodles with the chopsticks. 'Vegetarian for you.'

'Thanks.' I took the lid off and stirred my own ho fan: slender white rice noodles in vegetarian broth with baby bak choy and fried bean curd. 'What did you get?'

Leo hesitated, then picked up a dark red cube on his spoon. 'The Demon King was partially right. I can eat the noodles and the soup, but I really crave this. I'm surprised how easy it is to get.'

'It's hard to find anywhere else in the Territory; people are more aware of health issues after the SARS thing,' I said. 'But the restaurants around here sell it because we have so many demons working here, who love it.' I gestured towards his bowl. 'You never liked that before.'

'Well, it wasn't me, it was the real Leo.' He slurped the cube of pig's blood off the spoon. 'Meredith's had a look at me, and she says there's something weird going on and that I look like a human. She can't find anything in my memories. Then she was called away by something happening in the Northern Heavens, they needed her energy skills or something.'

'Without John to provide the Centre of Power for the Northern Heavens, it's like the entire place is running out of batteries,' I said. 'It's often in complete darkness and very cold. The plants are dying. Meredith, other senior energy workers and dragons from the Academy try to connect to the life force there, the stream of chi, and bolster it, but it's a losing battle. The temperature drops a couple of degrees every year.'

'How long before it's unliveable?'

'They give it about three to five years before everybody will have to move out and all the plants die.' I forced myself to eat the noodles; suddenly I wasn't hungry. 'Some of the trees in the Northern Heavens are sentient Shen, and they're dying too. Some of them have already died.'

Leo saw the stack of private school brochures on my desk. 'I thought Simone went to the Australian School.'

'You remember that?'

'Yeah.' He grinned. 'We had a huge argument about

it — you wanted her to go to the American school, I wanted her to go to the Australian one. Only argument I had with you that I ever won.'

'Not true.'

He gestured with his chopsticks towards the brochures. 'So what happened?'

'The Demon King and his assorted children are attacking the Celestial all the time. Sometimes Simone is called in to help. As her father isn't around, she's one of the most powerful demon slayers in existence right now. She's been skipping school to help out, and was expelled for not attending enough classes.'

'Poor Simone,' Leo said. He hesitated for a moment, concentrating on his noodles, then changed the subject. 'I was wondering how Rob was after all these years.'

'You remember him?' I said.

He smiled gently. 'Yeah. I treated him real bad. I hope he found someone.'

'Do you remember the relationship you had with him?' I said.

He shook his head over the noodles, still smiling gently. 'He knew how I felt about Mr Chen, but he stuck with me anyway. That guy deserves to find real happiness with someone else.'

I put my chopsticks across the top of the bowl and glared at him. 'Leo, are you straight or gay?'

He stared at me, incredulous, then said, 'What a dumbass question, Emma. I think you outed me like five minutes after you joined the household, when I brought Rob home.'

'You made a pass at me last night.'

He snorted. 'Yeah, sure I did. Like I'd be interested.' He leaned over the noodles and grinned. 'You got the wrong equipment, sweetheart.'

I opened my mouth to protest, then returned to my noodles.

'Oh my God, you're serious,' Leo said.

'Do you remember anything about what happened when I showed you into your room last night?'

Leo stared at me, then shook his head, his face blank. 'Not a damn thing. I remember ...' He thought for a moment. 'I remember us coming home, and Simone trying to tame me ... After that, nothing.'

'It's not surprising that you have some problems. You've been gone a long time.'

'No, I haven't. I've been alive a very short time, and I'm a — what did the King call it? A fragile copy. Imperfect.'

The intercom popped; it was Yi Hao. 'You asked me to remind you, ma'am. Er Lang will be here in less than an hour, and you have to prepare.'

Leo scooped his noodle bowl off the desk. 'I'll get out of your way.'

'What have you been doing with yourself? You keeping busy?'

'Some of the kids from my old classes have been showing me photos, trying to help me remember things,' Leo said. 'I think I have about half of the real Leo's memories.' He rose and took my empty bowl. 'You get ready to meet with Er Lang. I've heard that he's challenged you. He'll kick your ass if you don't make him back down.' He turned and opened the door. 'Good luck.'

An hour later I sat behind my immaculately clean desk waiting for Er Lang. I'd showered, washed my hair and tied it back into a neat bun, even though it kept threatening to come out again. I wore the standard Mountain uniform of black cotton pants and jacket with a mandarin collar and toggles and loops down the front, but my uniform was freshly laundered, starched and pressed by the demon staff of the Academy. I was so nervous I felt ill.

Yi Hao tapped on the door, opened it, and moved back for Er Lang to come in. I rose to meet him.

Yi Hao closed the door softly behind Er Lang and he and I sized each other up for a moment. He was in human form: a handsome man in his mid-thirties, well-built and stern. His dog, who appeared as an enormous black Doberman, stood at his heels. Er Lang wore a jade-green traditional mandarin-collared Chinese robe that fell to the floor over his black trousers. He wore his hair long in the traditional style, with a topknot wrapped inside a Tang-style filigree gold crown, only about five centimetres across.

I politely and formally saluted him. 'My Lord Er Lang, Second Heavenly General. Welcome to New Wudang.'

Er Lang saluted back. 'My Lady Regent, First Heavenly General. I thank you.'

Okay, this was going to be three hundred per cent formal. Lovely. I moved around the desk and opened the door. 'If you will come with me, my Lord, we have a more suitable meeting room for a dignitary such as yourself.'

He bowed slightly to me. 'Any place is suitable, ma'am. Here is acceptable, if you wish.'

I gestured with one hand towards the door. 'I have a much more suitable place. This way, please.'

He bowed again and stiffly walked through the door. I followed him, then guided him through the corridor to the conference room on the other side of the building, suddenly feeling that the entire top floor needed to be renovated.

The conference room had been reconfigured to suit the occasion. The large table had been moved out and Chinese-style meeting chairs, side by side with a tea table between them, had been installed. Gold and Jade stood behind my chair to act as Retainers. Er Lang glared at them. I gestured for him to sit at my left. He stopped and glared at the chairs, then stared around the room without moving.

I waited for him to ask me to sit, but he didn't. Eventually I had to break the impasse. 'Please, my Lord, sit,' I said, again gesturing towards the chairs.

He grimaced, then flipped the hem of his robe out and sat stiffly in the armchair. I sat next to him, and his dog took up position at his left next to his chair.

He sat down before you did, Gold said into my head. *Be careful, ma'am, that's a huge breach of protocol. The one with highest precedence traditionally sits first, and he should have stopped and asked you to sit first anyway. Emperors have had people beheaded for less.*

I nodded to indicate that I'd understood what Gold meant as I poured some Tikuanyin tea. 'This tea is from one of the plantations in the Northern Heavens, my Lord. I hope it is suitable.'

He nodded, took a sip and grimaced slightly. 'Is it stale? It does not taste fresh.'

Jade and Gold shifted slightly behind me without speaking.

'It may be, my Lord,' I said. 'I shall have it replaced if you wish.' I nodded to Jade, who moved between us to take the pot and cups.

'No need,' Er Lang said, waving Jade back. 'I do not expect better.' He put down his teacup and sat back in the chair. 'Why have you summoned me, my Lady?'

Jade was leaning between us to take the tea. She shot an expressionless look at Er Lang, looked quickly at me, then moved back. She didn't need to say anything, I knew what she was thinking.

'You have challenged for Princess Simone's hand,' I said. 'As part of this challenge, you must face me in the Arena. I feel that it is damaging to the harmony of

252

the Celestial to have the First and Second Heavenly Generals locked in combat like this.'

'That may be so, but it is one of the conditions that Princess Simone has set, therefore it must take place,' Er Lang said.

'Are you really after her hand in marriage?' I said.

'I would not challenge otherwise.'

'But she hardly knows you. You'll definitely win, and then you'll have to fight her. Why don't you just get to know her instead of battling your way through like this?'

'She is the one who has set these conditions,' Er Lang said. 'I am merely following her directions. If she did not want to have her suitors follow this course, then she should not have set it.'

'She only did this because suitors are continually harassing her and she wants to be left alone,' I said.

'Then she should have thought more before making the announcement. She has paved the way for all to challenge, and made herself available for marriage.'

'But she's just a *child*,' I said, exasperated. 'She's only fourteen! Surely you have more integrity than this?'

He shot to his feet. 'What are you suggesting here, madam?'

I rose as well. 'Please, my Lord, do not take offence. In modern times it is considered unsuitable for women under the age of eighteen to be married.'

He stared at me for a moment, then sat. 'I would not pursue the matter until she was considered old enough. Of course I would not seek to marry a child under the age of eighteen. I am aware that in modern times such a thing is without honour.'

I sat as well. 'I know that it was acceptable in the past, my Lord, and I know that you are senior to me in years. But Simone is a child of the twenty-first century and does not expect to be forced into marriage.'

'If she did not want this to be a possibility then she should not have set the conditions in Court before the Celestial Himself,' Er Lang said.

'Do you think you can embrace the yin?' I said. 'You are that powerful?'

'It will not come to that. This matter will be resolved before there is any need for me to touch yin.'

'How?' I said.

He took another sip from his teacup, grimaced slightly again and put the cup down. He moved to sit straighter in his chair and looked away from me. After a minute or so it became apparent that he wasn't going to reply.

'My Lord Er Lang, all I ask is that we resolve this matter privately, without going into battle with all of Heaven watching us. If you wish to pursue Simone's hand, then you are most welcome in our house to speak to her, anytime.' He didn't move or look at me. 'There's no need for us to fight.'

'I will follow Princess Simone's directions regarding this matter, Lady Emma.' He rose, turned and saluted me. 'Is there anything else you wish to discuss?'

I stood as well. I hesitated, then saluted him in return. 'No, my Lord. Since you obviously wish to drag this battle out into the view of the entire Celestial, there isn't much I can do about it. I will see you on Saturday in the Arena.'

He bowed slightly, then he and his dog disappeared.

I flopped to sit back in the chair. Jade and Gold came around to face me, looking concerned.

'Has Simone *ever* spoken to him?' Gold asked.

I shook my head in reply.

He glanced at Jade. 'How many times has he even *seen* her?'

'I think two or three,' Jade said. 'He definitely saw her when she was presented as a baby, and then again when she and Lady Emma visited the Celestial, but apart from that I don't think he's seen her at all, unless he's stalked her in a different form.'

'Stone, get Simone to ask her elementals, who've probably been following her all her life, if she's ever had a stalker,' I said.

Simone's voice appeared in my head. *Um, no, why?*

'I'm asking her if she knows Er Lang,' the stone said.

Simone appeared in front of me. 'I hardly know what the man looks like. He's way too old anyway, and his dog is creepy.'

'It's possible that he was impressed by your Celestial Form, Princess, and he's basing his actions on that,' Jade said.

'Kicking my ass is just a side benefit?' I said. "Cause it's obvious he hates me.'

Simone made a sideways chopping gesture with one hand. 'Whatever. Let him face you. He can't hurt you too badly because even though he's acting like a freak right now, he at least has some integrity and will follow the rules. I don't mind facing him. I've never stood against anybody higher on the list than Liu and Meredith, and it would be interesting to try my skills against a General. And if he wants to embrace my yin, then he has a nasty surprise in store.'

'He said that it would never get to the yin stage, but wouldn't say why,' I said.

'Maybe he just wants to challenge Simone and see how good she is,' the stone said.

Simone and I shared a look. 'He gets to take me down a peg or two, and he gets to try out his skills against the daughter of the only Shen on the Celestial who's regarded as more skilled than him in martial arts,' I said. 'Is that really enough of a motive to do this, particularly when it's putting Celestial Harmony at risk?'

'From his behaviour I'd have to say yes,' Jade said. 'But I'd like to believe better of him. I wish he really had some higher motive for this.'

'Not much we can do about it, either way,' I said. 'We will see if he's happy on Saturday after he's kicked my ass, and whether or not he wants to take it a step further and fight missy here.' I rose from my chair. 'Can you take him down, Simone?'

Simone thought for a moment. 'I have no idea.'

'Wonderful. There's no chance he'd actually hurt you, is there?'

'Nah, I don't think so. Like I said, he has some integrity, and it would be completely without honour to hurt a little girl.' She made a wide-eyed, coy face. 'And I'm just a harmless little girl.'

Gold made a strangling noise.

Simone thumped him on the arm. 'Jerk. I really am completely harmless.'

Gold bowed in reply. 'If you say so, ma'am.'

'I'm going back to my office to try to find you a tutor, Simone,' I said. 'I'll see you at home later.'

'Is it okay if I go visit Aunty Zhu?' she said.

'As long as you're back at dinnertime.'

'Okay,' Simone said. 'I'm bored as anything at home by myself — thought I might see if Eva wants to go shopping or something.'

'Good idea, but she's probably at school.'

'Hurry up and get me a tutor or a school, Emma. If you could get me a new Earthly school that would be great.'

'I'm trying, Simone.'

She turned to disappear, then stopped. Her face went pensive for a moment, then she turned back again. 'Um, Emma, I was just about to head south to Aunty Zhu's place ...' She pointed behind us. 'And south is *that* way.'

I dropped my head into my hand. 'Oh, *shit.*'

'Emma! Language!' Simone said with humour, and disappeared.

Jade and Gold fell to their knees.

'We are so sorry, ma'am, we've completely failed you,' Gold said with remorse.

'I cannot believe the stupidity of this small Shen,' Jade said.

I sighed. 'Well, you can help me pick up the pieces when he kicks the shit out of me on Saturday. Lovely. I should have known as well; the roads here go east–west. What an insult, to have him facing *north.*'

Meredith was waiting for me back at my office.

'Everything okay in the Northern Heavens?' I said.

'Not much we can do, Emma, we're trying our best,' Meredith said. 'One of the dragons fell sick from overdoing it, and I had to fill in for a while.' She straightened. 'Scott and Tymen asked you about using the serpent?'

'This wasn't *your* idea, was it?'

'Not mine alone. We had something of a brainstorming session and the concept was raised.' She lifted her hands. 'Not by me.'

'I'd love to be able to heal Tymen's mother, but not if it costs me my humanity.'

'Maybe practise summoning the serpent with some assistance first.'

'What if I fall into Mother form?' I winced. 'I could go on a rampage.'

'Ronnie Wong's been in training room eight for the last twenty minutes setting seals,' Meredith said. 'Not much chance of that.'

'I may be able to break anything he puts up.'

'Blood seals, Emma.'

'That's against policy!'

'*Celestial* blood seals. Believe it or not, the blood actually burnt Ronnie when he spilt a couple of drops on himself.'

'You can't be donating when you're already draining yourself to keep the Northern Heavens alive.'

She shrugged. 'Plenty more where that came from. Oh.' Her eyes unfocused. 'Oh, this is very good news. We've found a serpent who's willing to help.' She snapped back to me. 'Ten tomorrow. Can you do that?'

'Sure, I have nothing on tomorrow morning.'

'Okay. Go home now, and do at least an hour of yang sword form, then an hour of yang-style Tai Chi, then into bed early. I've contacted Ah Yat; she'll have some barbecue bean curd on the table waiting for you, and some other reasonably yang-type food — as yang as she can find for a vegetarian anyway. Have coffee with breakfast, and mango and lychees. Yang stuff. When you come in tomorrow, I want to see you so yang you shine.'

'That food will heat up my blood so much, my throat will clog up and I'll break out in pimples.'

'If you do, it means we've achieved our goal.'

'Can I have something to cool my blood back down afterwards? I hate it when my blood's too hot.'

'We'll see how we go.'

I shook my head. 'Before I came here, I had no idea about all this stuff. Now it's obvious to me when my blood's too hot and I crave chrysanthemum tea to cool it down again. My throat clogs up with mucus, I break out in pimples, I even feel overheated.'

'I think you go too far in the other direction, taking your blood too cold, making you sluggish and chilly. Right now, what we are aiming for is to have you extremely yang so that the Serpent will have an easier time appearing.'

I pulled my bag out of the bottom drawer of my desk. 'I'll see you tomorrow then.'

'We'll take care of things,' Meredith said. 'I want to check on Tymen's mother, and then do another run through the students in the Follies to make sure we have no demon impostors.'

'Don't overstretch yourself, Meredith, we need you strong,' I said. 'Ask someone else to do the demon checking. All the seniors know what to look for and it's good practice for them in finding the fakes.'

'I'm fine,' Meredith said.

'You just want to be one hundred per cent sure that there are no copies in the Follies,' I said, and she nodded. 'Stone, is Denis back from the airport?'

'Yes, he's waiting for you in the car park with Leo. I asked them to take you home.'

'Thanks. Meredith, take a couple of seniors with you to share the workload, okay?'

She bowed slightly. 'Ma'am.'

Leo and Denis were standing beside the black Mercedes in the basement car park.

'Want to drive, Leo?' I said. 'The road hasn't changed at all, there's only a couple of new tunnels to the New Territories. Around Central and Wan Chai is the same traffic headache it always was.'

Leo opened the rear door for me and closed it after I'd sat inside the car. He sat in the front passenger side and Denis took the wheel.

'I don't know how to drive,' Leo said. 'I didn't even know that you turn the key to start it. My demon creators mustn't have given me the skill; they probably thought I'd never need it.'

'Geez,' I said softly.

'I also have no skills in martial arts, so don't even think about sending Denis back to Bai Hu. I can't guard you or Simone, much as I would like to. I remember none of the moves at all.'

'Do you remember actually *doing* the moves?' I said. 'Maybe if you run through them in your head —'

'No. Nothing. Like I said, I only have a fraction of the real Leo's memories.'

'We also found a tattoo inside his left wrist,' Denis said as he drove to the exit and the smiling demon guard opened the large gate to let us out of the building and into the fading russet light of the polluted early evening air. 'It's hard to see, because of his black skin, but he has a number tattooed there.'

'Four,' Leo said grimly.

'The death number,' Denis said. 'Not a good sign, ma'am. You sure you want this in your house?'

'Dear Lord, there are three other copies of you out there?' I said with horror. 'Did they find anything else in the nest in Sham Shui Po?'

'The sweep only found dead insect-types. Michael tried to bring a couple of the roaches back to study, but the minute they hit open air they exploded. The Mother was gone, the King must have taken it,' Leo said.

'Any paperwork?'

'Not a thing. No hint of whose nest it was.'

'Damn.'

'Stones are on it, ma'am,' Denis said. 'They're searching the entire internet looking for anything that is even remotely connected with this nest. Bank records, immigration, all the government departments, rental records for the Golden Arcade. They will track this demon down.'

'Get someone to look inside me, Emma,' Leo said.

'Meredith already did.'

'Deeper.'

'That could damage you.'

'So?'

'My father says that on Saturday, after the challenge, he can look if you like,' Denis said. 'But he wants the option of taking the Leo copy to the West to have a closer look at it if he finds something. He has a lab over there that can do some very detailed work on it.'

'No,' I said.

'I already said yes,' Leo said.

'Leo, I —'

'I'm the one they'll hurt, I'm the one who'll be pulled apart, and I'm the one who wants to find the demons who created me and are obviously planning to use other copies against you. This is my choice, Emma, I'm the one it'll be happening to. I said yes.'

'Demons don't have free will. You don't have the will to agree to this; you're just going along with Denis because he's half-Shen and you're programmed to obey.'

'I have enough free will to know that I want to protect you and Simone, and if I'm in the Western Palace there's no chance of me turning on you.'

'But I like having you around,' I said.

'You'll like having the real Leo around more,' Leo said. 'You need to find him. This might be the only way.'

I sighed. He was right.

CHAPTER 19

Next morning I went to the Academy, but Leo stayed back at the Peak and went out for a walk with Simone. He said he'd never seen the view from the Peak before, and Gold said it would be a good idea for him to walk around there, as it might spark some memories.

Training room eight was one of the smaller ones, about three metres to a side, with windows along one wall. It was only on the fourth floor, so the view from the windows was of a forest of neon signs, their rusted metal frames appearing very flimsy up close, and the windows of the buildings across the street. We'd had one-way tinting installed on our windows so people couldn't see us practising the Arts.

Meredith and a young woman were in the room already when I arrived. I didn't even attempt to enter; the seals were obvious and painful even from a metre away. I waited for Meredith to invite me in.

'Come on in, Emma, this is Sylvie,' Meredith said, gesturing towards the young woman. 'She's a snake, and she's agreed to try to help you.'

Sylvie was a Chinese woman appearing in her late teens. She wore a short black pleated skirt, a long black jacket, and her black hair was shoulder-length. She looked like an anime character, with the scowl to match.

I nodded to her. 'Pleased to meet you, Sylvie. I hope you can help me, 'cause I'm in a lot of trouble.'

'Anything that will give us a chance to prove everybody wrong about snakes,' she said.

'I know the feeling,' I said with grim humour. 'It's worse for me — I'm a Snake Mother on top of everything else.'

'I heard,' she said. 'I also heard that the Serpent side of you may be able to help you to control it. But you're scared to change.'

'I don't want to slip into demon form,' I said.

'That's why I'm here, to help you avoid that.' Sylvie approached me and held out one hand. 'Give me your hand.'

She took my hand and stared into my eyes. Suddenly it felt like my entire circulation system was full of tiny electric worms, frantically wriggling inside me. I shivered violently, trying to control the sensation, when it snapped off.

Sylvie scowled and turned away. 'There is nothing to fear from your Serpent nature, that is *you*. What you should be afraid of is your demon nature, which is even more *you*.' She turned back to me. 'I will help you.'

'Thanks,' I said.

She raised her hands. 'Give me yours.'

I raised my hands, and she clasped hers to mine, palm to palm, our fingers twined together. She lowered her head.

'I will take it slowly,' she said. 'What you must learn is not to fear your Serpent side. Although it is capable of great harm, you will have complete control over it. The demon is another matter. It is almost pure Mother and hates all that lives.'

Her hands went limp in mine. 'Relax,' she said. 'Look inside yourself for that which is pure.'

I closed my eyes and relaxed, and felt her there with me. She moved slowly and sinuously through me, her scales sliding through my consciousness. Something within me rose to meet her and I pushed it down.

'Do not deny it,' Sylvie said softly. 'It is you.'

She did something and the snake rose within me, answering her call.

'Let it come,' she whispered. 'Do not fear.'

I heard soft voices, but didn't understand what they were saying; then I realised Scott and Tymen had entered the room with Tymen's mother. I concentrated on the serpent rising within me. It was smooth and cool and bright, full of intelligence and humour, but at the same time a destructive force ready in a second to crush those who would attempt to hurt the ones I loved.

The floor shook beneath me and Sylvie let go of my hands. I opened my eyes and saw the snout of the biggest, blackest snake I had ever seen in my life. It must have been more than five metres long, curled up to fit inside the small training room. Its head hovered in front of my face, its glistening hard eyes staring into mine. It was John's Serpent, and something inside me rose with joy to greet it.

'The Xuan Wu has heard your call,' Sylvie said with wonder. 'God, it's so *beautiful*.'

I raised one hand and touched its snout. It ducked its head so that I could feel it; cool and smooth, its scales like satin. It flicked its tongue over my hand and tasted me, and my heart leapt again.

'You need to find your Turtle,' I whispered to it. 'You need to be complete.'

It gently butted me with its nose, then raised its head and looked around. I knew what to do.

'Tymen,' I said, 'bring your mother here. I think today is her very lucky day.'

Tymen brought his mother to stand next to me. She had obviously been sedated because she just stared dully at the Serpent. She had lost most of her hair from the chemotherapy; only a few grey wisps remained. She was thin and frail and something about her shrieked *unwell* to my newly activated serpent senses, even though I hadn't changed form.

The Serpent lowered its head and gazed into her eyes. It glanced at me and I nodded. It touched its nose to Tymen's mother and she sighed and sagged. Tymen had to catch her and hold her up.

The Serpent pulled away from Tymen's mother. It turned back to me and slowly slid itself around me. It coiled up my body, wrapping me within it, holding me tight.

'Master Liu,' Scott said urgently behind me.

'Don't move,' I said. I relished the feeling of being held within the Serpent's coils. 'I'm fine.'

The Serpent squeezed me gently, all around me, soft and black and cool and wonderful. Then it disappeared and I fell to my knees, suddenly weak.

'Take your mother out, Tymen,' Meredith said behind me. 'Scott, go with them. She probably needs some time to recover. She will come out of the trance in half an hour or so. Be ready for her to be extremely agitated at what she's just experienced; she will remember all of it.'

Sylvie crouched and looked into my eyes. 'Are you okay?'

I sat on the floor and ran my hand over my forehead. 'I feel like I've had way too much to drink, and been heavily sedated, and at the same time been given the most amazing upper ever.' I rubbed my hands over my face. 'Give me a minute.'

Sylvie touched my arm. 'This is the perfect time to bring out your own serpent then. Take a moment to recover, then we can concentrate on what you just felt.'

I glanced up at her. 'I'd like that very much. The serpent is ...' I searched for the words. 'The serpent inside me is ...' I smiled and shook my head.

'I think the word you're looking for is "cool",' Sylvie said. 'Because it is.'

'Is she yang enough?' Meredith said.

'More than enough,' Sylvie said. 'A little too much, perhaps.'

'My face will be like the surface of the moon tomorrow,' I said ruefully. I rose from the floor. 'Let's try it again.'

Sylvie nodded, and we clasped hands.

'You don't want to do this as Serpent?' I said softly.

'The Serpent doesn't have hands,' she replied, just as softly. 'Relax.'

I relaxed and let her guide me. The snake within me moved much more easily, somehow triggered by the appearance of John's Serpent.

'The Serpent within her is awake,' Sylvie said.

'... to control the demon essence,' Meredith was saying.

'Welcome back,' Sylvie said to me, her voice full of humour. 'You are very handsome.'

I concentrated on the Serpent Essence, but it had subsided. 'It's gone,' I said, disappointed. I opened my eyes. 'I don't think I'll be able to summon the serpent, it's escaping me.'

'You just changed, Emma,' Meredith said, full of quiet approval. 'Well done, that was remarkable.'

I shook my head, dropped Sylvie's hands and turned to see Meredith. 'I didn't change.'

'You did,' Sylvie said. 'As I said, you are very handsome.'

I went back through my memories and gasped with shock. 'I blacked out. I didn't do anything dangerous, did I?'

Meredith's smile disappeared. 'You don't remember?'

I shook my head.

'But you remembered what happened all the other times you changed, right?'

'The first time I blacked out, but every other time I remembered being the snake. I was just unable to control what I did,' I said, still dumbstruck at my memory loss. 'That means it's possible I've changed into a snake and not been aware of it? I could have gone out on a rampage and not known anything about it!'

'You do not need to concern yourself about your behaviour as the Serpent,' Sylvie said. 'Your Serpent is noble and gentle. It is you without the demon inside you.'

'You sure about that?' I said. 'I'm not in there — it may not even be *me*.'

Both Meredith and Sylvie smiled slightly.

'It's you, Emma, it called me by name,' Meredith said. 'After you changed, you asked if Tymen's mother needed another dose of healing, and offered to try even though you weren't sure you could help her.'

That filled me with relief. 'Okay, that's me.'

'It's very much you,' Meredith said. 'Don't be concerned. I'd like to try this again soon. When are you free next?'

'Ronnie's coming to the Peak this afternoon to have another look at the seals; he says there's something weird going on. I have the challenge with Er Lang tomorrow morning, after that Bai Hu's looking at the copy Leo. Monday, Rhonda comes back and the Demon King will give us his lead on the real Leo. Probably the only time I'm available is Sunday.'

'That's fine, I'll come and help you Sunday,' Sylvie said. 'I have homework I want to catch up on Saturday, and back to class on Monday.'

'Do you go to CH?' I said.

Sylvie nodded.

I checked my watch. 'Aren't you supposed to be in school now?'

Sylvie shrugged. 'I took some time off to do this.'

'One of the reasons we'd like Simone to go there,' Meredith said. 'They're extremely flexible about attendance.'

'But I *do* need to catch up on some classes on Monday,' Sylvie said. 'So Sunday, if that's okay.'

'Fine with me, I'll be here,' I said.

Sylvie saluted me. 'Lady Emma.' She lowered her hands and grinned. 'Your snake is *hot*. I'm *very* much looking forward to seeing it again.' She disappeared.

I turned to Meredith and pointed at where Sylvie had been. 'Did she just …?'

Meredith nodded, smiling slightly.

'Are all snakes like that?'

'No, the ratio's about the same as the human population.'

I dropped my hand and shook my head. 'I need to head home, Ronnie'll be there already.'

Meredith saluted me. 'I told Denis you're ready. See you tomorrow at the Arena, if not before then.'

'Oh, God, Meredith, you're not going to watch too, are you?'

She sobered. 'I am concerned about Er Lang's behaviour. Liu and I will be there as a backup just in case.'

I hesitated, then said, 'I appreciate it.'

'No trouble at all. See you tomorrow.'

* * *

Ronnie turned up at 2 pm to check the seals. He carried his usual battered brown case and a long, flexible stick with him, and proceeded to set up on the living room coffee table.

'Before you start, Ronnie,' I said, 'I didn't get a chance to ask you the other night — how much do you know about the Demon Prince Six?'

Ronnie stopped moving, stared at the contents of his case, then glanced up at me. 'That one's dead, isn't it? I was sure Dad took it out a long time ago when One Two Two was yinned.'

'Apparently the King missed it,' I said. 'It had a stone planted in Leo's cell in Hell; it seems Six is the one holding the real Leo.'

Ronnie closed the case with a snap and rose. 'If Six is still around, that's bad news for all of us. That little posse were quite possibly more dangerous than One Two Two and the Pussycat together.'

'I remember,' I said. 'There were four of them. They had several meetings in Simon Wong's apartment when I was there.'

'Six and his consort Three are the ones that mess with stones,' Ronnie said. 'I don't know the numbers of the other two, but one had a lab in Guangzhou that experimented with elementals. The other one — I think it was a female — was making the demon copies for One Two Two.'

'Stones. Elementals. Demon copies,' I said. 'That fits. We're still finding demon copies in the Academy. It's like they're continually testing the copies on us to see if we can detect them.'

'As soon as you stop detecting them, bring me in,' Ronnie said.

'Because they'll have produced copies that we can't detect,' I said. 'Thanks.'

'There was one more demon in that group,' Ronnie said. 'Did weird things with energy. Had demons producing some sort of black energy blast.'

'I saw Simon Wong use that energy when I was in Hell,' I said, remembering. 'It completely shredded Xuan Wu in True Form. I know he was weakened at the time, but it was extremely scary.'

'Yes. Ordinary demon energy would not have been able to do that.'

I held my hand out and generated some black chi. 'Is this the same stuff?'

Ronnie inhaled sharply and moved closer to peer at the chi in my hand. 'I'm going to change, is that okay?'

I nodded, and he changed to his demon form: two metres tall with black scales, bulging eyes, and tusks at the corners of his mouth. In demon terms he was considered extremely good-looking, and I was glad that I wasn't demon enough to agree.

He studied the chi carefully, looking at it from all angles, his red eyes glowing. He held one large clawed hand above the energy. 'Fascinating.'

'Same stuff?' I said.

'No,' Ronnie said. 'That's just black chi. I've heard of it, but I've never seen it before.'

'Where have you heard of it?' I said. I absorbed the chi into my hand.

'Wow, that was cool,' Ronnie said. 'Your hand went black. Only extremely senior demons, those that have blood instead of essence, ones that are close to human, can make that energy. I've seen my dad do it.'

'Yes, Ah Yat said she'd seen the King do it too. So who's the demon behind this new energy that Simon Wong was using?'

'Nobody knows,' Ronnie said. 'He talked about the energy as if it was his idea, but everybody knew he didn't have the brains to produce anything like that.

There was talk that he had a partner who taught him how to do it. That's about it.'

'Another one,' I said. 'Great. If the King didn't manage to get rid of Six after the business with Simon Wong, then they're probably all still out there. Messing with stones, elementals and copies.'

Ronnie picked up the slender switch. 'And if it's Six that's behind all of this, then I know exactly what your problem with the seals is. It's just a matter of finding it.'

'What?'

'Six used to boast about the number of stone Shen he'd experimented on.' He held the switch out in front of himself. 'Let's find the pebble that he's planted here.'

'There's no way anything could be planted here,' I said.

Ronnie slowly walked around the living room, the switch quivering in his hands. 'Ever had an ordinary human workman in here, ma'am?'

'Nope,' I said, then, 'oh wait, I had an electrician in here about four months ago. And a plumber, when the toilet in Monica's bathroom backed up and it turned out that someone downstairs had renovated and put the pipes back together wrong ...' My voice trailed off.

'Monica's bathroom, eh?' Ronnie said. 'And where is that?'

I pointed towards the kitchen. 'Monica is the domestic helper. Ah Yat's filling in for her.'

'She should have sensed the stone in her bathroom,' Ronnie said. 'Is it possible she was in league with them?'

'She's an ordinary human, can't sense anything,' I said.

Ronnie stopped and stared at me. 'You have an *ordinary human* domestic helper?'

'It's a long story,' I said. 'Xuan Wu has more than one human staff member.'

'Oh yes, I remember,' Ronnie said, grinning to fully reveal his tusks. 'For a while there he had an ordinary human nanny as well.'

'And bodyguard,' I added.

'Nothing ordinary about the Black Lion, he has always been exceptional,' Ronnie said. 'Fortunately for him, the Dark Lord was never old-fashioned about people's preferences.' He glanced at the kitchen door. 'I assume the helpers' quarters are in the usual place.'

'Past the kitchen, yes,' I said, and opened the kitchen door for him.

He entered the kitchen, where Ah Yat was sitting at the table noting the expenses and sticking receipts into Monica's household budget notebook.

'I need to check the servants' quarters' bathroom,' Ronnie said.

Ah Yat nodded. 'I have not been in there to clean yet, so it will be as they left it.'

'They?'

'Monica met one of the Tiger's sons when she was being kept safe at the Western Palace,' I said. 'They were married on the Plane, and he came back here to live with her. He worked as the family and Academy driver.'

'How Shen is he?' Ronnie said, concentrating on the switch and moving through the kitchen towards the servants' quarters. 'He should have sensed the stone too.'

'Not much Shen about him at all,' I said. 'The Tiger hasn't even given him a number.'

'Unusual,' Ronnie said. 'Must be very human then.'

He stopped near the apartment's back door, which opened onto the stairwell. The domestic staff used the back door for coming in and out, and the rubbish was left outside there in the stairwell for the janitor to collect nightly. Ronnie indicated the grey metal box on the wall next to the door. 'Is this the circuit box?'

'Yes,' I said.

He opened the box and appeared to be sniffing it. 'Doesn't smell of demon.' He closed it and opened the door to Monica and Marcus's room. 'Probably in here somewhere.'

The minute he walked in the door the switch began to quiver in his hands. He concentrated and its movement became more lively. As he approached the bathroom, the switch leapt out of his hands.

'This is interesting,' Ronnie said, opening the bathroom door and peering inside. 'I can't sense anything, but the rod went wild.'

He went into the small bathroom. Monica hadn't cared too much about the décor and it was nearly original from when the apartment had been built in the 1970s — pale green wall and floor tiles, with a green toilet, sink and green bath with a shower over it.

Ronnie looked inside the bathroom cabinet. 'And of course nobody else besides your non-Shen staff would come in here, so nobody sensed it.' He went to the bath and studied it. 'Hard to find anyway, might need the stick again. Oh, hold on.' He ran his clawed hands along the shower curtain rail to the end. 'Nope.' He lifted the top off the toilet cistern and peered inside. 'Toilet was backed up, you say?' He glanced at me. 'Can I have a plastic supermarket bag, one without any holes in it?'

I went back into the kitchen and pulled a bag out of the recycling bag hanging off the back of the kitchen door. I checked that it had no holes and returned to give it to Ronnie. He took it from me, put his hand inside it and reached into the toilet cistern.

He quickly wrenched his hand out again, splashing water everywhere. 'Ow, ow, ow!' He dropped the stone he'd been holding onto the floor and shook his hand, showering more cistern water everywhere. 'Dammit!'

Ah Yat poked her head in the door. 'Master Ronnie, that water is dirty, take care.'

'I know,' Ronnie said. 'Sorry, Ah Yat.' He took the bag off his hand and dropped it into the bath, then crouched to study the stone sitting on the floor. 'Let's see what we have here.'

The stone was about two centimetres across, smooth and golden brown, and didn't appear to be anything special.

'This is what's been killing your seals,' Ronnie said. 'My guess is that it's a segment of some sort of dead demon, manipulated by Six to become this stone hybrid thingy.'

I moved to pick it up but when my fingers closed around it, it felt like acid. I quickly dropped it.

'Wash your hands. The seawater they use for flushing toilets is usually heavily contaminated,' Ronnie said.

'I was going to rinse it, but I can't even pick it up,' I said. I rose and carefully washed my hand in the green sink. 'It's like touching a Shen when they don't protect you.'

'Exactly,' Ronnie said. He stood up. 'I'd be passing this little gem to the Tiger, Lady Emma. He has an interesting facility out there in the West and can probably find out more about it than anyone else in the Celestial.'

'He'll be here tomorrow to see me fight Er Lang,' I said. 'I'll give it to him then.'

'In the meantime, perhaps a Shen will be able to handle it. Princess Simone is the obvious choice, due to her mixed parentage of both Heaven and Hell. She can probably —'

'Wait,' I said raising my hand. 'What do you mean, *Heaven and Hell*? She's half-Shen, half-human, no demon at all.'

'You didn't meet her mother,' Ronnie said with grim humour. 'But that's not what I meant. Her father is unique, and has qualities of both Heaven and Hell. If she's inherited some of his essence, then she will be able to travel to places that no other Celestial can.'

'Heaven and Hell, Ronnie? Tell me more.'

Ronnie changed back to human form and washed his hands in the sink. 'I don't think it is my place to be discussing the Dark Lord's true nature with his Chosen.'

'True nature,' I said, remembering. 'That's what the kitsune said.'

'Stay away from fox spirits, they're bad news,' he said.

'This one's dead. One Two Two got her.'

'Oh, the one that whelped the demon child,' Ronnie said. 'That was a terrible shame.'

'Our fault too,' I said morosely.

Ronnie shrugged. 'We all make mistakes.'

'Yeah, but not all of us make mistakes and have people die because of them.'

'Did you intend for her to die?'

'No, we tried to protect her. Unfortunately we called attention to her and she died as a result.'

'Then that's life, and stuff like that happens to the best of us.'

I ran my damp hands through my hair. 'That's very easy for you to say.'

'I'm a Demon Prince, it's the easiest thing in the world for me to say,' he said. 'Conquering my nature has given me nasty insight to the creature that I once was. I have a burden of guilt that will live with me for many centuries to come.'

'I know how you feel, my friend.'

'You have control over your nature. You've never tortured or killed anyone for sport and then had to live with that after you have turned to the other side. You have no idea how it feels.'

'The demon nature has taken me over and I've eaten small demons,' I said with misery, but he didn't respond, his features impassive. 'But I've never killed anyone for sport. You have my sympathy at having to live with that.'

'That's more than I deserve,' Ronnie said.

He collected his stick and we went back to his case on the living room coffee table. 'Until you can remove that stone, it's a waste of time setting new seals. Leave it where it is for now, it's not really hurting anything, and when you see the Tiger tomorrow bring him round and see if he can take it with him.'

'I understand. Thanks, Ronnie.'

He grinned, lifted his plastic glasses off his nose and dropped them back down again. 'You may not be thanking me so much when you get my bill. I always charge extra if I get hurt.'

'I'll pay you double whatever you charge me, you know that.'

He shook his head. 'And you want me to come work for you. I think the arrangement we have right now suits me very much.'

'As long as I know I can call on you.'

'Any time, Lady Emma.' He saluted me and went out.

CHAPTER 20

The next morning, while I was in the Arena's preparation room, I worked with what little chi I had left, trying to move it through me and provide some energy-based protection. It wasn't going to be enough though if Er Lang decided to go all-out on me.

I summoned the Murasame and carried it through the tunnel to the Arena. For this challenge I wasn't going to mess around, even if it did mean feeding the blade.

I heard the crowd before I entered the Arena; they were talking loudly among themselves and the rumble echoed on the walls of the tunnel. As I walked into the Arena itself, the roar subsided, there was a smattering of applause and then people started loudly discussing the match again.

I felt a jolt of shock when I realised what form Er Lang had chosen for the Arena: it looked like the Demon King's throne room. The crowd sat in stands on either side of the large area, and Er Lang and the officiator stood where the throne would normally be. The ceiling was very high, held up by red pillars that were covered in good-luck motifs — stylised longevity and 'double happiness' characters. The room was fifty metres across, plenty of room for us to face each other. The pillars, each a metre round, were ten metres apart. They'd be in the way, and I made a mental note to stay aware of their locations so that I didn't accidentally back into one.

Er Lang was in his usual human form: mid-thirties, wearing green scaled armour and a war helmet. He wore his long hair unbound and it flowed down over his shoulders, nearly to his waist.

I went to him and the officiator and saluted them. 'I am Emma Donahoe, answering a challenge.'

Er Lang nodded to me instead of saluting; a shocking breach of protocol. The crowd didn't miss this and their voices rose slightly, then subsided.

'I am Er Lang, Second Heavenly General. I call you out as I am in pursuit of the hand in marriage of Princess Simone of the Northern Heavens.'

'My Lord,' I said, saluting him again just to rub it in. He glared at me with disdain. I turned to the officiator. 'My second is the Jade Building Block of the World.'

Emma, Er Lang just told me that I should know better than to serve you, the stone said into my head. *What is going on?*

'My second will be my companion,' Er Lang said, nodding to his dog, who looked up at him and nodded back. 'Let us begin this.'

The officiator read from the match scroll. 'Er Lang, Second Heavenly General, challenges Regent General Da na huo to a test of martial skills. This test will not be to the death, and will be considered satisfactorily concluded when either combatant yields. Are these terms agreeable?'

Er Lang saluted the officiator. 'I find these terms agreeable.'

There was a shocked gasp from the crowd. Er Lang had once again shown disrespect by speaking first.

I saluted the officiator. 'I hold these terms agreeable with a request for the further consideration of light contact and restraint from injuries … Oh hell.' I turned to Er Lang. 'Look, I'm mortal. I can't take much of a beating. Could you do me a favour and not kill me, please? I'd like to be alive when the Dark Lord comes back for me. He promised he would.'

Er Lang glared at me, then shook his head and moved to the other side of the throne room. 'Defend yourself, woman,' he said as he walked away.

'That's what this is about?' I said loudly to his back. 'You don't like working for a *chick*?'

'I do not work for you.' Er Lang turned, faced me and summoned his halberd. The blade wasn't the flimsy type that made a noisy snap when flexed; this one was eight millimetres thick and honed to a sharp edge down one side of the blade and on both sides of the tip. 'I serve the Jade Emperor and assist him when he is busy, engaged in the protection of his Kingdom. Because of the Dark Lord's absence, His Celestial Majesty is fully engaged in directing the Celestial armies to keep the demon horde at bay. He does not have time to dwell on details such as you.'

'I'm a *detail*?' I said, incredulous.

'Not for long,' he said, held the blade in front of him and rushed me.

I stepped aside, moving faster than was humanly possible, and he easily matched my speed. He swung the halberd in a quick arc and smacked me square in the side of the head with it.

I didn't fall, but I reeled back, the ground moving beneath me. I didn't see the next blow but I felt it; he caught the blade under my chin and knocked my head back. He was so skilled that he struck me with the blade of the polearm without cutting me.

I somersaulted back, shaking my head to clear it. He stood and waited for me, his halberd still held in front of him in a defensive position.

Yield, the stone said.

I don't think he's hurt me enough to let it go yet, I said. *But at least we know now that it's about my gender and nothing to do with pursuing Simone.*

You say that like it means he's not going to kick your ass, the stone said.

I drew the Murasame and dropped the scabbard. I held the sword above my head in a defensive position, my left hand in front of me with two fingers raised, ready to use chi if necessary. Not that I had much chi left.

'The Destroyer. The sword that thirsts for the blood of its victims. Fitting,' Er Lang said, and came for me again. He swiped my sword out of the way and, before I had a chance to do anything, once again smacked me on the side of the head.

I reeled back again, disoriented, and shook my head. 'Are you trying to damage my brain?' I said. 'Because you're wasting your time. Everybody in the Academy knows I don't have one.'

He tried to hit the side of my head again, and the Murasame swung around, almost by itself, and blocked the blow. The blade bit slightly into the wood of the halberd's handle and we were locked together for a moment, both of us fiercely pulling at our weapons to free them.

Er Lang grimaced with anger. 'The demonic weapon of destruction assists you, woman.'

I ripped the blade free and stepped back. 'It's not demonic. It's just yin. Same as the Dark Lord.'

He swung the halberd at my head again and I ducked underneath it.

'The Dark Lord overcame his true nature,' Er Lang snarled. He swung the blade back again and struck me on the side of the abdomen, knocking me two metres sideways so that I slid along the polished wooden floor. 'But his eyes were still clouded by you, woman.'

Yield! the stone said. *This is getting serious!*

I used the sword as a lever to help me up. 'Get over this thing with women already! I've been given this job that I don't want and I'm doing my best to serve the Celestial!'

'Resign. That would be the best service you could do Heaven,' Er Lang said. He spun the halberd in his hands and used the end of the pole to knock my feet out from under me before I was even fully upright. He really was at least three times faster than I was, and I was inhumanly fast. He spun the halberd again and held the blade over my throat.

'I yield,' I said, looking him right in the eyes.

The blade quivered above my throat. I was surprisingly calm; he was going to kill me quickly and cleanly. I was dead. I waited for the blow to fall. Sorry, John, I really wanted to be here for you, healed and whole.

He wrenched the halberd away from my throat, spun it in his hands, and turned his back on me. He strode away down the tunnel, his dog following.

The officiator scurried after him, waving the scroll that contained the match details.

I pulled myself upright, the beginnings of a massive headache building behind my eyes. I retrieved the Murasame's scabbard and hesitated about whether the blade would still require feeding. To hell with it. I shoved the blade into its scabbard. If it was mad at me later then it could feed then. Right now I'd had enough.

Simone, Jade and Gold appeared next to me. Gold moved to take my arm and assist me, but I waved him away. 'I'm fine.'

'Meredith wants to check to see if you have a concussion,' Simone said. 'Come through to your prep room and we'll have a look.'

I was about to protest but the stone said, 'Go, Emma, he landed some very square blows there.'

I shrugged. Someone took my arms on either side and I was half-lifted, half-guided back down the tunnel to the prep room.

Half a dozen people were crammed into the room when I returned; I was too disoriented to distinguish them all. Someone pushed me into the chair at the side of the room and hands worked to unbuckle my armour and lift it over my head.

Meredith's face appeared in front of me, her features concerned. She put her hands on either side of my head and concentrated, gazing into my eyes.

I moved weakly to protest. 'I'm okay, really, he didn't hit me that hard.'

Meredith released me, straightened and looked away. 'No permanent damage, but I'd like her to take a couple of days off and rest. I think she's going into shock.'

'I don't have time to rest, Rhonda comes back day after tomorrow,' I said, but nobody seemed to hear me.

'Good idea, Meredith,' Simone said. Her face was now in front of me, then her hand. 'How many fingers am I holding up?'

'Meredith just said I'm fine, Simone,' I said. 'If I'm going into shock, isn't having a zillion people and a lot of noise and excitement here a bad idea?'

'She's right. Out,' Meredith said.

I dropped my head in my hands; the headache wasn't building any more, it was towering, and my skull throbbed with pain. Thankfully the noise subsided as people left the room.

I glanced up. Only Simone, Meredith and the Tiger in human form remained, and all were silent.

'You have no idea how much I wish ordinary human painkillers worked on me right now,' I said.

'Is it that bad, Emma?' Simone said, distraught.

'I feel like I've been hit by a truck,' I said, 'that ran backwards and forwards over my head.'

'Let's get her home and see what we can do there,' the Tiger said. 'Is her car nearby?'

Simone concentrated. 'Denis is at the end of Wo On Lane, double-parked. He's made the car invisible.'

The Tiger nodded sharply with satisfaction. 'Good lad. Let's get her home.'

Meredith and the Tiger took one arm each and lifted me, but I shook them off. 'I'm *fine*.' I took a couple of steps and the floor rolled beneath me. They grabbed my arms again before I toppled over.

'That was completely unfair and totally unnecessary,' Simone said, her voice full of quiet anger. 'He's way more powerful than she is, and that was just … *wrong*.'

'I hope he's happy now,' I said as they guided me out the door into the tunnel. The officiator, Mr Zhou, was waiting for us there.

'Er Lang is satisfied and says that he does not wish to pursue this matter further,' Mr Zhou said.

'Well, *I do*,' Simone said. 'Can I challenge *him*? Beating up ordinary humans just because they're female is *wrong*!'

'Deal with it later, Simone,' Meredith said. 'I can feel Emma's headache from here; this whole thing is catching up with her. Let's just get her home.'

'Sounds good to me,' I said weakly. The world was beginning to fade and I felt vaguely nauseous. I leaned more heavily on Meredith and the Tiger; my legs weren't strong enough to hold me up.

The Tiger lifted me and carried me like a child, and I didn't have the strength to protest.

'Got you where I wanted you, finally,' he whispered in my ear as he carried me gently down the corridor.

'Asshole,' I replied, and relaxed into a half-conscious daze in his arms.

'It's definitely an effective way of dealing with this. All you need is more practice,' Meredith said.

I was in the training room back at the Peak, with Meredith and Simone standing across from me, watching me. My headache was gone and I felt fine. I stared at them, disoriented.

'Are you okay, Emma?' Simone said.

I tried to remember what had just happened: one second the Tiger had been carrying me out of the Arena, injured; the next I was here and healed. Realisation jolted through me.

'Did I just bring out the Serpent again?' I said. I raised my hands. 'Never mind, that's obviously what happened. How long have I been home? What time is it?'

'We've been home about an hour,' Meredith said. 'We walked you through the transformation again. You said it was easy.'

'Now all I need to do is work out how to remember when it happens,' I said.

'That will probably come with time and practice,' Meredith said.

'And I still have no idea how I did it,' I said, frustrated.

'I wouldn't worry too much about that, Emma,' Simone said. 'Even though you were pretty out of it, you just concentrated and brought the Serpent out easily. Meredith didn't even need to help you much.'

'And you're fully healed from that thrashing that Er Lang gave you,' Meredith said.

'The Tiger is in Monica's room checking out that stone thingy,' Simone said. 'Want to have a look?'

'Sure.'

'I'll head out,' Meredith said. 'I'm needed in the Northern Heavens, it's my shift.'

'Spend some time with your husband!' I said.

'He's coming with me,' Meredith said with a grin. 'Don't worry, after three hundred years we don't need to be together every minute of the day.'

'That's a lie and you know it,' Simone said.

Meredith shrugged and disappeared.

Although Monica and Marcus's room was enormous by the standards of most domestic helpers in Hong Kong, the three of us with the double bed and the wardrobe made it something of a squeeze.

'Simone, can you pick up the stone?' the Tiger said, studying it from the entrance to the bathroom without touching it. 'So far it's burnt me, Ronnie and Emma — a Shen, a demon and a human.'

Simone went to the stone and crouched to see it. She hesitatingly held out one hand, then picked it up. She held it in her palm and studied it. 'Feels really, really weird.'

'Bring it to the living room,' I said.

We moved to the living room and sat on the couches. Simone put the stone on the coffee table.

Leo came out from his bedroom and into the living room. He saw all of us sitting on the couches and approached us, curious. 'What's going on?'

The stone flew up into the air, hovered about a metre off the ground and disappeared.

Simone and the Tiger both jerked their heads up and their eyes unfocused, then they disappeared as well.

'They're tracking it,' the stone in my ring said.

'That stone was destroying our seals,' I told Leo. 'We think the Demon Prince Six planted it here.'

Leo flopped to sit on the couch and put his head in his hands. 'And it took off when I moved near it. Wonderful.'

China, Simone said. *Just a sec.*

Homing, the Tiger said. *Dammit!*

I'm helping out, Michael said into my head. *This thing is fast!*

Lost it! the Tiger said.

I'm on it ... Simone's voice trailed off. *Heading northeast ... still going ... I'm nearly past Guangzhou already ...*

I see you, Michael said.

Got you, the Tiger said.

Still going northeast, Simone said. *Gah! This pollution is awful!*

Industrial centre, Michael said. *I'm having trouble with the pollution.*

Me too, Simone said. *I'm losing it! Uncle Bai?*

Gone, Michael said.

I lost it a while ago, the Tiger said.

It went underground, everybody, the stone in my ring said.

There was silence for a moment.

Somewhere around here, Simone said.

Simone, where was the last place you saw it? Michael said.

Here.

This is my last location, it was moving in this direction ... it disappeared somewhere around here, Michael said.

Emma, we have an area of about twenty kilometres to a side, Simone said. *We're going to have a poke around. Tiger, where exactly are we?*

That's Shantou, Eastern Guangdong seaboard, northeast corner of Guangdong Province, the Tiger said. *Nothing terribly exciting there, just a lot of noise and pollution. Not even famous for good-looking chicks.*

'Do you think I can be transported in serpent form?' I asked the stone.

'I have no idea, but there's nobody here to take you,' it said. 'And it's a good four hours' drive from Guangzhou to Shantou.'

I'll send you a cloud, hang on, the Tiger said.

She can't ride clouds, she can't make herself invisible, Simone said. *Hang out there, Emma, we'll be fine.*

After a few minutes of nervous waiting I said, 'Any news, stone?'

The stone didn't reply, and I glanced down at it. The setting in the ring was empty; the stone was gone. I threw myself up and went to the training room to do a Tai Chi set to remain calm. Intellectually I knew that the three of them were some of the most powerful demon destroyers in this part of the world, but my heart wouldn't stop reminding me what my head already knew: Simone and Michael might have been powerful but they were still mortal, and if they ran into more than they could handle there was a very real chance they could get themselves killed.

Leo didn't move from his position on the couch as I headed to the training room.

I had already completed a forty-eight-form yang set and was halfway through a full eighty-eight-form set when the doorbell rang. I took a deep breath, centred what remained of my chi, and went out to answer it.

Leo had already opened the door. A huge demon stood there, nearly as big as any Number One. He was in human form, a man in his mid-sixties with long grey hair held in a topknot, wearing a traditional robe of grey silk. When the demon saw me he raised his hand, pointed at me, and said, 'Hold her.'

I turned to run but Leo grabbed me and spun me around to face the demon. I should have been able to shake him off, but he was vastly stronger than me and held me easily.

The demon entered; the seals were completely down. He stopped and looked around the living room, then turned back to me and grinned. 'Lady Emma. Let's go.'

CHAPTER 21

Leo marched me out of the apartment, holding my arms behind me. A huge Chinese human, at least six five and a wall of muscle, stood in the lift lobby pointing a gun at me.

'Don't try anything or Chang here will shoot you,' the demon said. 'Come quietly, please, Miss Emma.'

The Leo copy released my arms, and I hesitated. I was inhumanly fast, but I wasn't fast enough to risk getting shot. I raised my hands.

'Oh, very good,' the demon said. 'We won't hurt you, we just want to talk. Please, come with us, have a small chat, and we'll be happy to let you go.'

'Jade Building Block,' I said.

The demon's grin widened. 'Nice try, ma'am, but you're with *me* and I am an expert in dealing with stones. Your little green friend is a long way away and cannot hear you.' He nodded towards the lift. 'Let's go, shall we?'

They took me down to the car park. A bucket of soapy water stood next to the front wheel of my Mercedes and a sponge sat on the hood.

'Where's Denis?' I said.

'Who?' the demon said.

'My driver.'

'Oh, he was *fun*,' the demon said with pleasure. 'Horsemen are *good*.'

'You will pay for that,' I said.

'Yes, of course I will,' the demon said. 'The car's out here.'

They guided me outside the building and pressed the button to open the pedestrian gate at the end of the drive. A white Mercedes waited at the side of the road, its engine running. Another demon was standing next to the car, in the form of an elderly Chinese woman in a blood-red cheongsam with gold trimming.

'Miss Emma in the middle in the back,' the male demon said. 'I will sit on one side, Three the other. Leo in the front.'

The man with the gun moved it slightly to indicate that I was to get into the car. The male demon opened the door for me and watched me carefully as I entered. I sat in the middle, and the demons sat on either side of me. Leo sat in the front next to the big Chinese, who passed the gun to him. Leo turned and pointed the gun at me.

'Let's go, Chang,' the male demon said. 'We have a suite at the Shang, on Pacific Place. Please, ma'am, just come quietly. We won't hurt you, we just want to talk.'

'I won't try anything,' I said. 'I want to hear what you have to say.' I nodded towards the Leo copy. 'Did you make him?'

The demon settled more comfortably into his seat. 'No.'

'Who did?'

The demon hesitated slightly, then said, 'Who made you, Leo?'

'My mother and father,' Leo said, the gun not moving from my head.

'Very good answer.'

Leo nodded. 'Thank you.'

'Do you know who I am, Leo?' I said.

'Emma Donahoe. Promised of the Dark Lord. Known as the Dark Lady, you also turn into a goddamn huge snake and a Snake Mother.'

'Who is the Dark Lord?'

An expression of bewilderment swept across Leo's face. 'What?'

'Disengage, Leo Four,' the demon said.

Leo's face went blank.

'Nice try, ma'am,' the demon said. 'Let's just wait until we're at the suite before we talk any more, shall we?'

'Your choice,' I said.

We drove in silence down Garden Road, past the office buildings of Admiralty, and up the ramp onto the top of Pacific Place, where three of the Territory's most luxurious hotels and serviced apartment blocks were located. We travelled past the bottom of Hong Kong Park, with its manicured gardens and fountains, and pulled up at the entrance to the hotel.

'Please don't try anything as we take you up, ma'am,' the demon said. 'I would have to use force.'

'You won't use force on me in plain view of everybody,' I said.

'Ah, you see, that's the thing,' the demon said, as if he was telling a charming story to a small child. 'Nobody can see us.'

The female demon opened the car door and guided me out. They took me through the lobby of the hotel, the gun at my head, and nobody seemed to notice. We went up in the lift to the club suites on the highest floors. The suite they took me into had a living room, two separate bedrooms and overlooked the harbour. The winter day was fading and the neon lights on the buildings across the water were beginning to come on in a colourful spectacle.

A couple of bodyguards were waiting for us inside, and the big driver nodded to them as we entered. They stationed themselves on either side of the door.

'Sit, Miss Donahoe,' the demon said.

I didn't say anything, I just sat.

The demon nodded to the bodyguards and spoke in Putonghua. 'Order some Western tea from room service.'

One of the guards nodded and picked up the phone.

The elderly female demon led Leo into one of the bedrooms, then returned and sat on the couch across from me.

'You may call me Six,' the male demon said. 'This beautiful lady is my consort, Three.'

I took a good look at Three and felt a jolt of shock. She was bigger than Six; she was upwards of a high-level eighties Snake Mother, one of the biggest I had ever seen. She watched me with amusement as I recognised her.

Six raised one hand and the big driver opened the door to the second bedroom, went in and brought out Billy, the stone in my first-year class. The kid was in human form and had his hands bound in front of him with a plastic zipper slide, the newer alternative to handcuffs and impossible to wriggle out of. I shot to my feet and the driver immediately pulled out his gun and pointed it at Billy's head.

'Sit down, Ms Donahoe,' Six said amiably. 'We won't hurt the kid, we just want to talk. We thought you'd need convincing.'

'Tell me what you want,' I said.

'Don't do anything for them, ma'am,' Billy said. 'Just kill me and then run.'

'Have they harmed you in any way whatsoever?' I said.

'No, ma'am.'

'Not at all?'

'Not at all, ma'am,' he said. 'They did something to me that meant I couldn't use energy; I couldn't change form. I fought back in human form and they took me down without harming me. This guy,' he gestured with his chin towards the big driver, Chang, 'must have trained at Shaolin. Real Shaolin. Has to be ex-monk. He's like rock.' His voice dropped with shame. 'He took me down without even hurting me. I thought I was better than that.'

Chang smiled slightly and nodded.

'These demons control stones somehow, Billy,' I said. 'Besides, you've only been learning a few weeks. In a year you'll be able to take down anyone who's learned from any other school on Earth. But right now there's no shame in losing to someone like him.'

Chang frowned.

'I think we should do the deal.' Six leaned back on the couch, relaxed. 'Miss Donahoe, your students make our lives miserable. They catch our …' He hesitated, looking for the word. '*Operatives* —'

'Gangsters,' I said.

He ignored me. '— who are working their livelihoods and the students use their talents to shut them down. We're losing at least a million dollars a week because of your kids. The copy DVD and software sales where a group of people will go past and all of the disks are suddenly ruined. The illegal fuel stations where the fuel goes bad. The drug deals where the drugs simply disappear. Frankly, Emma, we've had enough, and we'd like your help.'

'I don't think I can give you any help,' I said.

'We just want you to ease up on our members only, please. Since Three and I left Hell, our activities here have kept us in an extremely comfortable lifestyle, one we could not otherwise afford. One Two Two was stupid and went after more than he could handle. All we want is to be left alone.' He gestured towards Billy. 'As a show of good faith you can have this one. Lay off us for a week, promise to continue to do so for good, and you can have your retainer, Mr Alexander, back.'

'Remember, Miss Donahoe,' Three said, 'your students are trained to defend themselves against demons. Our Little Brothers are humans, they have guns, and there is no Art that can defeat someone with a firearm.' She smiled like a kindly socialite. 'We have no desire to make trouble, ma'am, we just want to be left alone to make a small living doing what we do best.'

'Were you two together with One Two Two?' I said.

Their smiles widened slightly but neither of them replied.

'I don't remember seeing either of you in the meetings with him.'

Six spread his hands. 'We may take many forms, ma'am.'

'So, Miss Emma, do we have a deal?' Three said. 'Lay off our Little Brothers, and you will have your Leo back, and your students will not be in danger.'

'What happens in a week?' I said.

'We make a final pact for both our benefits,' Six said, his wide grin not moving. 'Your students gain the protection of one of the most powerful demons outside Hell; no other demon will challenge them. And you will gain the return of the Lion.'

I grimaced when he said *protection*. I was being drawn into one of the oldest Triad games in the book — protection money. Wonderful. I needed to stall them for the week and use the time to find out where their nest was, because if I hadn't taken them down in a week I would have to renege on the deal, my students would be targeted by humans with guns, and Leo would die.

'Why wait a week?' I said. 'Why not just do the deal now?'

'Two reasons,' Six said. 'First, the real Leo is so deeply hidden it will take that long to get him out. Second, we want to see a show of good faith from you so we'd like to see our activities untouched for a full week.'

'I want a way to identify your gangsters so my students can still practise on other Triads,' I said.

Six and Three visibly relaxed. 'That we will provide as early as tomorrow, ma'am. Does this mean that we have a deal?'

In two days the Demon King was going to provide me with the location of these demons' centre of operations. Doing the deal would give me some breathing space to gather the resources I needed to take them down. And, more than anything, I needed to protect my students, who had no defence if someone came after them with a gun.

'Agreed,' I said. 'We'll lay off for a week. After that, we'll see.'

'We'd rather die than see you make a deal with them, you know that,' Billy said.

'And you know that I'd do anything to keep you safe, Billy,' I replied.

'An excellent result all around, I think,' Six said. 'Chang will take you and your student home, and we will provide you with an identification method first thing tomorrow, delivered by demon to your Academy. We will contact you in seven days to arrange the final agreement and handover.'

'I want the Leo copy too,' I said.

Six and Three both stiffened with shock, then shared a concerned look.

Six turned back to me and smiled patronisingly. 'Emma, dear, why do you want that around you? It's completely controlled by us. It's just a demon.'

'Sentimentality,' I said.

They shared another look, and this time appeared to be communicating.

'How about this?' Six said. 'The Leo copy will be the one to deliver the identification tomorrow.'

'I want it to come home with me now,' I said.

'Very well,' Six said. 'Either the Leo copy or the student. Or wait until tomorrow and you can have both — the student now, and the demon then.'

'While we have your student I don't think there's much you can do about anything,' Three said.

I sighed and ran my hands through my hair. 'Okay, have the Leo copy deliver the identification tomorrow. Make it something simple, large and obvious, like having all your gangsters wear those goofy women's golfing hats — the fold-up ones with flowers. Something the other gangsters won't even think about copying.'

'Good idea,' Six said.

'I like those hats,' Three said. 'They keep my skin white and beautiful, and they fold up to a fan that's very handy when the weather is hot.'

'I think we're done here,' Six said. 'Chang will take you home, ma'am, and we'll see you in a week.'

They rose from the couch and I rose as well.

'The tea never arrived,' Three said sadly. 'Sometimes service in these places is so slow.'

'Chang,' Six said, and the huge driver nodded. 'Take Miss Emma and young Billy here home, please.'

The driver surprised me by speaking in lightly accented perfect English as he opened the door to the suite. 'Please, ma'am, come this way.'

'Oh,' Six said. 'The little gift just outside the door is an example of what we can do. Nobody heard anything, nobody saw anything, and that could very easily have been one of your students.'

I went to the door of the suite and stopped. The room service tea trolley was just outside, and the bellboy who had been pushing it was lying next to it on his stomach, with a huge bleeding hole in his back. He'd been shot from the front at close range and we'd never heard it.

'Holy shit,' Billy said softly when he saw it. 'They killed him.'

'Just as we might have killed you,' Chang said. He gestured towards the lifts. 'This way, please, sir, ma'am.'

'Release Billy,' I said.

Chang pulled a knife from his pocket, flipped it open and cut Billy free. Billy lunged for his head with a basic attack and Chang grabbed his hand, wrenched it down with an audible snap, then took Billy's feet out from under him with a quick swipe. Billy fell heavily and yelled in pain.

'His technique is very good,' Chang said, looking down at the writhing student. 'With more training he could be good enough for Shaolin.'

I crouched to check Billy. Chang had broken his wrist. 'That wasn't necessary,' I said, 'we're coming with you.'

'He attacked me, ma'am,' Chang said. 'I merely defended myself.' He reached down, grabbed Billy by the collar and pulled him to his feet. 'Stop crying, I'm taking you home.'

Billy went quiet, pulled his injured wrist into his chest and held it.

I patted him on the uninjured arm. 'Are you okay to make it home?'

He took a few deep breaths and nodded.

'As soon as we're home, take True Form and fix yourself up,' I said softly.

He nodded silently.

Chang bowed slightly and gestured with one hand towards the lifts. 'I suggest we go.'

'Your English is very good, Chang, where did you learn?' I asked as he drove us back up to the Peak.

Chang hesitated, obviously deciding whether to answer me, then said, 'At the monastery, ma'am. They wanted to send me overseas, as part of the show.'

'Did you go?'

'Yes. I performed in the show, and acted as interpreter for the media. I saw people who took riches beyond my imagination for granted. People who lived in huge luxurious houses with gardens, who owned their own cars, who always had more than enough food to eat. They considered this normal! Even the *poor* had houses to live in! I wanted to live like that too. So when Master Six approached me and offered me similar wealth, I took it.'

'You come from a poor family?'

'No family at all,' he said. 'Nobody. That's why I was in the monastery. I was taken in when I was a year old. My parents died of AIDS, nearly everybody in the village died. Nobody could care for me; they didn't even have the strength to sell me. So they just abandoned me, and a wandering monk found me and took me to Shaolin.'

The AIDS problem was well known in China. Blood buyers had travelled from village to village preying on desperately poor peasants. They only wanted the platelets; they returned the plasma to the donors. But the plasma was stored in a single large holding vat, which meant everybody who gave blood received plasma from everybody else. The blood buyers had travelled all over the countryside, spreading AIDS from a single infected donor. And without the correct drugs cocktail, most of the villagers died very quickly. Whole villages had been decimated.

298

'Six is a demon, Chang.'

He nodded. 'I know.'

'I care for Zhen Wu's daughter.'

That silenced him for a moment, then he said, 'Zhen Wu? Xuan Tian Shang Di?'

'Xuan Tian.'

'You do not look like a Shen.'

'I'm not. I'm an ordinary human. Xuan Tian hired me to mind his little girl. I help look after Wudangshan as well now, as he's out of the picture for a few years.'

'Wudangshan?'

'Yes. We have a Shaolin-style school within Wudangshan as well. The head is Liu Guang Rong.'

'He died six hundred years ago.'

'No, Chang, he attained Immortality six hundred years ago.'

He let his breath out in a long gasp.

'I think you're fighting on the wrong side, my friend,' I said.

'I am sworn, ma'am.'

Billy piped up. 'Vows to a demon are worth nothing.'

'Vows are vows, son,' Chang said. 'It does not matter who you give your word to, because it is *your* word you are giving.'

'Chang is correct,' I said.

'You have given me much to think about, ma'am,' Chang said.

'I am glad, Chang. Pass me your mobile, I'll give you the Academy's number.'

He hesitated again, then reached inside his jacket and passed me a garishly gold-plated designer mobile phone in a crocodile-skin case. I entered my secretary's direct phone number into the phone book and handed it back.

He pulled up at the end of Black Road, in front of the apartment building.

'Will you do something for me, Chang?' I said.

He nodded slightly without looking at me.

'Don't decide you've wasted your life and kill yourself, please. I think there is hope for you. You have my number. If something goes wrong, call me and I will help you.'

He didn't reply, just nodded again.

'Come on, Billy, let's get that wrist fixed,' I said.

As we opened the car doors, Chang turned. 'Billy.'

Billy hesitated with the door still open.

'I am sorry I hurt you,' Chang said. 'I hope one day to make it up to you.'

Billy leaned into the car to reply. 'I hope one day to spar against you and win, my friend. Trust Lady Emma.'

Chang nodded and turned back. We closed the car doors and he drove down the hill.

'What would happen if we went back and tried to take out Six?' Billy asked.

'He'll serve Six faithfully until either he or Six dies,' I said. I gestured for him to follow me. 'I hope we can free him.'

Simone ran out of the lift lobby. 'Emma! Where have you been? Denis is dead!' She saw Billy. 'What happened to you? I can feel your pain from here.' She looked around. 'Where's Leo?'

'Round up Michael, any of the Winds you can, Generals Ma and Li Number Two, and either of the two Lius,' I said. 'I have very bad news.'

'Wow, this sounds serious,' Simone said.

'It is. Let's go upstairs, so Billy can take True Form and fix himself up.'

We headed back inside and she pressed the button for the lift.

'What happened to Denis?' I said.

'Shot,' Simone said. 'They wouldn't let me see him, he was a mess apparently.'

'The Tiger must be monumentally pissed,' I said. 'Poor Denis.'

'Actually the Tiger just said, "Damn, I need to find you a better one."'

'Where's my stone?' I said.

'Right here,' the stone said, and I looked down. It was back in its setting. 'I went to help them.'

'And left Emma by herself,' Simone said with scorn.

The stone didn't reply.

We entered the lift and went up to the top floor. Ah Yat was waiting for us in the living room.

'You okay, Ah Yat?' I said.

'I'm fine, ma'am. I was at the market doing the afternoon shopping when this happened.'

Billy took True Form. 'If you don't mind, ma'am, I'd like to let Lok know I'm okay. A few people were worried about me.'

'That's fine, you go.'

Simone and I went to the dining room. The Tiger and Michael were already there.

'Meredith and Liu are still in the Heavens, they can't make it,' Simone said. 'General Ma is the only one that's free at the moment — he's on his way. None of the Winds are free; there seems to be some sort of attack happening at the Eastern Palace.'

'Just pass the information along then,' I said. 'They don't really have to be here; we have at least twelve hours before things start to go stupid.'

I sat at the dining table and told them all that had happened.

'And they kept the Leo copy,' Michael said. 'Just before Dad was going to take it and look at it.'

Ma appeared, saluted me, and sat at the table. He and the Tiger shared a look, obviously transferring information, then he grimaced. 'Letting demons have the upper hand over you is not a preferable state of affairs, ma'am.'

'As soon as I find out where these two have their nest, I am gathering every senior Disciple I can and we will put all of our training and practice to good use,' I said. 'I will not do deals with demons.'

They all stared at me for a moment, then Simone grimaced. 'Please don't do that, Emma.'

'What?'

'You sounded exactly like Ah Wu,' the Tiger said. 'You haven't been playing with your serpent lately, have you?'

'Meredith said that it might help control the demon nature,' I said.

'Does it?'

'Yes. I can transform and heal any injuries that I've sustained.'

Ma leaned back and put his hands on the table. 'That is good news, ma'am. If you can control your demon nature, we do not need to be concerned about you running out of control. You may even be able to clear it.'

'The downside is that I don't remember anything that happens when I'm a snake,' I said.

'Yeah, well, I'm not surprised — snakes have extremely small brains,' the Tiger said.

'At least their brains aren't in their gonads,' Michael said quietly.

The Tiger glared at him, then opened his mouth to let loose.

I cut him off. 'We have more important things to worry about than you two bickering.'

The Tiger subsided, glowering at Michael. Michael ignored him.

'Tomorrow morning they will drop the Leo copy off

with information on how to identify their gangsters,' I said. 'Can you pick it up then?'

'My pleasure,' the Tiger said. 'Shame I didn't get the stone; we couldn't find where it went to ground.'

'Bet you anything you like, the King gives us the location of Six and Three in Shantou,' Michael said.

'On Monday, day after tomorrow, the King will return Rhonda and give us the information,' I said. 'We'll see if you're right, Michael. Until then, I'm going to lock down the Academy and keep the students safe.'

'I'll give you another driver — that one sucked,' the Tiger said.

'He was your *son*, Uncle Bai,' Simone said.

The Tiger waved one hand dismissively. 'Bah. Got plenty of them. One less, one more, who cares.'

Michael rose and saluted me. 'If you please, ma'am, this worthless son of the Devil Tiger of the West was originally chosen by the Dark Lord as a replacement for the Black Lion, to be your bodyguard. He would be honoured if you would let him take up this duty. Of course, it makes no matter whether this worthless son dies, because one more or less makes no difference at all to the Devil Tiger, his father.'

'Oh, come on, I didn't mean you,' the Tiger said, exasperated.

Michael glared down at the Tiger with disdain. 'That is even more disturbing; it means that you value me over your other sons. And I think that value is based purely on who my mother is — the only woman that could leave you.' He leaned on the table to speak more closely to the Tiger. 'I am only a tool for you to get something that you want.'

The Tiger opened his mouth to argue but Michael turned to me and saluted again. 'Please let me serve you as bodyguard, ma'am.'

'You've come a long way since Mr Chen chose you, Michael,' I said. 'You have a degree in business. Weren't you planning to help your mother with her antiques chain?'

'She's going to sell it when she moves to the Western Palace,' he said without emotion. 'I am no longer needed there, but I am needed here. I would be honoured.'

'You can always come and be my Number Three,' the Tiger said.

Michael ignored him.

'I am the one who's honoured, Michael,' I said.

'I'll bring my stuff over and move into one of the student rooms,' he said.

'You can do the job from the Folly,' I said.

'If I'm going to do it, I'll do it right and be live-in.' He saluted me again. 'By your leave.'

I nodded to him and he disappeared. The Tiger banged the table with frustration.

'Ma'am.' General Ma saluted me. 'We are under attack from two fronts at the moment. The Eastern Palace is being attacked by Demon Prince Fifty-five and a small army, including three Mothers. Rat Village is also under attack by a small troop of low-level demons.' He nodded to Simone. 'The Princess's help at the Eastern Palace would be most appreciated. The Rats have their attack under control with the help of Third and Twenty-fourth Divisions.'

Simone sighed and her shoulders slumped.

'You don't have to go if you don't want to, Simone,' I said.

She straightened. 'No, it's fine. They're after the baby dragons at the Eastern Palace again. I'll help.'

'Before you go,' I said, 'call Ronnie for me and ask him to come up and reset the seals on the apartment.'

Simone's mouth dropped open. 'I never thought of that. You're completely unprotected here.'

'I'll stay here until Michael returns; no demons will try anything with me around,' the Tiger said.

Ma nodded to Simone. 'Princess?'

Simone rose, raised one hand and summoned Dark Heavens. 'Show me the way,' she said, and they disappeared.

'Hmm,' the Tiger said. 'Never seen a demon slayer go into battle wearing a pair of jeans and a Hello Kitty T-shirt.'

'It's her way of being the opposite of the Academy,' I said.

Ah Yat poked her head through the door from the kitchen. 'Hungry, ma'am? You haven't eaten since breakfast, and I have some vegetarian noodles here for you.'

Suddenly I was starving. 'That would be great, thanks, Ah Yat.'

'Ronnie is here,' the Tiger said.

I went to the front door to let Ronnie in.

'I heard what happened,' he said. 'I hope my father gives you a good lead on where Six is.'

'You seem to know an awful lot about what goes on,' the Tiger said.

Ronnie hesitated, looking at the Tiger, then said, 'I have my informants.'

'How?'

Ronnie went into the living room and put his battered case on the coffee table. 'I'm pretty big, Tiger.'

'That doesn't explain how you know so much,' the Tiger said.

Ronnie opened the case, then leaned on the table and glared at the Tiger. 'I have fifty-five level thirty to fifty kids. They're my network.'

The Tiger opened his mouth and closed it again. Then he said, 'You can sire spawn on a *Mother*?'

Ronnie pulled his ink and brush set out of the case, and some rice paper ready to be made into seals. 'I can sire spawn on up to a level sixty-five Mother. As I said, I'm pretty big, Tiger.' He summoned some water to make the ink on his stone tablet.

'Damn, man, we should get together, kill the King and set you up as Demon King,' the Tiger said with awe.

Ronnie didn't look up from his tablet. 'That's the dumbest idea I've ever heard. Besides, it wouldn't work.'

I went to the couch and sat. 'Why not, Ronnie?'

He smiled up at me through his plastic-rimmed glasses. 'The Demon King must by nature be opposed to the forces of the Celestial. That's the way it is. As I have changed allegiance, I cannot take over the demonic side of Hell. Things just don't work that way.'

'You have a point,' the Tiger said. 'If the Celestial were to upset the balance so strongly, the resulting imbalance — and the backlash from setting things to rights — would be devastating.'

Ronnie grinned at the Tiger. 'You can be very erudite when you want to be, sir.'

'Dunno what the fuck you're talking about,' the Tiger said. 'I'm getting some tea. Come and finish your noodles, Emma, you've had a hell of a rough day. Take tomorrow off, or I'll take a horsewhip to you.'

'I have too much to do,' I said. 'Sylvie's coming back and we'll do some more serpent transformation.'

We went into the dining room together. The Tiger summoned some Chinese tea and I returned to my noodles.

'You don't need any more training on this snake business, you got it down,' the Tiger said. 'Tomorrow's Sunday, the Academy's closed, nothing's going to happen. Take some time off.' He hesitated, concentrating. 'Done.

The Lady will be here at eleven to take you to the Garden for the day, and I told that snake chick you don't need her.'

'Six is delivering Leo to the Academy tomorrow morning.'

'Fine. Take the delivery, then I'll take the Leo copy straight to the Western Palace.'

'I have a charity thing tonight.'

'That has no relation to what you'll be doing tomorrow.'

I sighed and returned to my noodles.

'Good,' he said.

CHAPTER 22

Later that evening Simone tapped on my door. 'Ready yet, Emma?'

'Just about got it,' I said.

Once again I was running out of make-up and had the distasteful task ahead of me of shopping for new lipstick. After hours of finding the best colour it was usually discontinued next time I went looking for it. I straightened my bun and went out. Simone checked me up and down, then gave a small nod of approval.

'Glad I pass inspection,' I said.

She smiled slightly. 'Well, you don't have Leo to organise you any more.'

'Leo never organised me,' I huffed and went out to the living room.

Michael was waiting for us there, smartly dressed in a business suit.

'This event is humans, right?' he said.

'Yeah,' Simone said. 'Although the occasional demon turns up, just to try and intimidate us.'

'Okay,' Michael said. He reached inside his jacket, pulled out a small revolver and checked it.

'What are you doing with that?' I said, incredulous.

He smiled at me. 'There are some advantages to

being a Horseman: they have firearms training in the West as well as training in traditional demon-fighting weapons. Sometimes the wives are attacked because human crims think they're the wives of rich Middle Eastern princes and prime targets for holding for ransom.'

Simone pointed at the gun. 'You can use that?'

Michael nodded and put it away. 'Yes, ma'am.'

'Oh, don't give me that,' Simone said. 'I was wondering, could we go somewhere private together …'

Michael's face went blank.

'… and see if I can disable it from a distance, like Daddy used to? It would be a useful skill and I've never tried it.'

Michael appeared relieved and nodded. 'But if you can wreck them, I might have to take a few along.'

'Don't worry, I'll pay for the replacements,' Simone said. She checked her watch. 'Time to go.'

'What's this dinner about?' Michael said as he drove us down the hill to the same hotel where I'd been held hostage earlier that day.

'It's a standard fifty-thousand-a-table dinner and show for the orphanages that I support,' Simone said.

'Orphanages?' Michael said.

Simone nodded. 'Hn. In China. Mostly for baby girls who are abandoned because of the one-child policy, but they have a lot of disabled kids of both sexes in them as well. We arrange for them to be adopted out to overseas families.'

Michael glanced back at her. 'You organised all of this?'

'No, I just help out as much as I can. I've only really been contributing the last couple of years, since I heard about it,' Simone said. 'I was sort of "meh" and didn't really care enough to be doing anything, until my friend Josie told me her story.'

'What happened to her?'

'Well, she's from a wealthy Hong Kong family,' Simone said, settling further back into her seat. 'She's the third daughter in her family, and her mom can't have any more kids now. Apparently, when she was born, her mother's father went to her father's father and bowed and humbly apologised for his daughter's failure to produce a son for the family. It's ten times worse in China, where you only really have two chances. Have one kid and you get concessions; try to have more than two kids and they'll be down on you hard. Have two girls and it's a disaster.'

'Having daughters is not a disaster,' Michael said vehemently.

'I know that, you know that, but try telling that to the people who want to continue the family name in a very male-dominated society,' Simone said. 'It'll take a long time for attitudes to change, I think. Look at Josie; her mother's father went to freaking Harvard, same as you, and still felt the need to apologise.'

'Hong Kong is very modern now, Simone, there isn't that sexist attitude around as much any more. There are a lot of women running companies here,' Michael said.

'We'll see what you say if the Nemesis latches on to Emma,' Simone said with amusement.

'Oh, no, please don't wish that on me,' I said with misery.

'The Nemesis?' Michael said.

'Just a guy,' Simone said, still amused. 'You'll see.'

'Calling the Nemesis "just a guy" is like calling Typhoon Victor "just a storm",' I said. 'I think I'd rather cross swords with Six.'

'Be careful what you wish for, Emma,' Simone said. 'I've seen some very big demons at these things, and Six is probably at them all the time being as he's so senior in the Triads.'

'Here we are,' Michael said, and pulled up outside the hotel entrance. He hopped out and opened the door for me, letting Simone get out herself. He passed the keys to the bellboy, surreptitiously checking him over at the same time, then nodded and moved behind us to guard us as we walked into the lobby.

The area had been lavishly decorated with pink balloons and streamers and large screens with photographs of baby girls and boys from the orphanages pinned to them. The usual socialite mishmash was present, smiling artificially, drinking expensive champagne out of oversized flutes, and talking about nothing at all. I steeled myself; I hated these things, but at fifty thousand dollars a table for ten, the profit for the orphanages was enormous.

I looked around at the patrons of the dinner; as far as I could see, all of them were human. I glanced at Simone, but she was concentrating on the crowd too. I looked back at Michael and he had a similar look on his face. They both snapped back at the same time and shared a look, then Simone spoke into my head.

Two big demons and four small ones present. Large demon twelve o'clock — could be Six but it's taken the appearance of a young businessman. The other big one's on his arm, looking like a Malaysian-Chinese princess. The four small ones are scattered around the room looking like ordinary middle-aged —

Michael's voice overrode her. *Heads up! We've been spotted. Incoming.*

'Here she is, our favourite little heiress,' the big demon businessman said as he approached us with a huge grin. The demon princess stayed on the other side of the room, chatting with some overdressed middle-aged socialites. 'Wonderful job you've done to get your little schoolfriends to make their parents come, Simmie.'

311

Simone's smile froze. 'Having fun?'

The demon looked around and gestured expansively. 'Oh, absolutely.' He pointed the grin at me and it became more artificial. He changed from cheerful to menacing. 'Having wonderful fun with your little friends as well, Miss Donahoe. I hope we can work out a very profitable partnership that will see us move towards a bright and golden future together as old friends.'

Careful, Emma, Michael said into my head. *You know that 'old friend' means very much more to Chinese than it does to Westerners; it means that you each have the* guanxi *to ask anything of the other.*

I nodded to let Michael know that I understood. Nobody had ever had the hubris to attempt to claim old friend status with me, and the minute the words were said to me the relationship, as far as I was concerned, no longer existed. My oldest friends didn't need labels.

I dropped my voice. 'Whatever arrangement we have it will never reach the status of old friends. It will be business, and hopefully I will need to have as little contact with you as possible.'

'*Emma!*' A loud voice blasted halfway across the room, and I jumped.

Six's face hardened when he saw that a human was approaching. 'See you tomorrow, Emma,' he said, and returned to the Malaysian princess, who was probably Three in a different form.

Nemesis to the rescue, Simone said wryly into my head.

The Nemesis, Peter Tong, glided towards me. It was his signature to wear traditional Chinese robes, and on his portly figure they looked like a black silk embossed tablecloth. He threw his arms wide and air-kissed me on both cheeks, then pulled back to grin at me like a predator.

He turned the grin on Simone. 'Simone, honey, tell your stepmother that she needs to look after you better, those clothes are awful. Where did you get them — China Wall Shopping Centre in Lo Wu?'

'London,' Simone snapped.

He waved one hand dismissively. 'Harrods, I'll bet. Home of all things kitsch.'

She opened her mouth, probably to say something about his retail outlets offering a wide variety of incredibly kitsch Chinese goods for the Western tourists, then shut it again and smiled. She'd had a great deal of diplomatic training for her role as Celestial Princess and some of it had sunk in. 'I like them,' she said.

'Only good thing about Harrods is that Princess Diana, who came through my store more than once, was going to marry into their family,' the Nemesis said. 'Now, Emma, I've been thinking. It's just not right what you have to deal with.' He waved one hand to indicate the crowd of socialites. 'All these ugly men after you *all the time*. Having to manage the estate. You need a *man* around to handle the money for you; you simply can't do it by yourself.'

'Emma has an MBA, she's quite capable of managing the estate's affairs,' Simone said.

'Simone, I'm sorry, darling, but your judgement really isn't mature yet, you're just a child,' the Nemesis said. He turned to me. 'It's wrong that you are managing poor Simone's money; you can't possibly be doing it right. You shouldn't have to do any of that. Let me come in and I'll take it all off your hands, and you won't need to worry about anything.'

'I'm quite capable,' I said.

'Emma, dear, with all due respect, it doesn't matter how many pretend correspondence degrees you have from bogus universities, you still aren't capable of managing a large enterprise like Chen Corp.'

'Why not?' Simone said, pinning him down.

He opened and closed his mouth a few times, then raised his hands and grinned. 'Let's just face it, men are *so* much better at business. Look at my corporation; you know I'm not after your money, I probably have more money than you do. I just want to add my *expertise* to your family, so that it isn't all handled by ... handled by —'

'*Women*,' Simone said cuttingly.

'If I were to marry you as you've suggested, would you arrange for people to dress me so I look more publicly acceptable?' I said.

'Yes!' he said, the grin becoming wider. 'I'm glad you know you need that!'

'And I wouldn't have any input on the way the corporation is run? Basically, all I'd have to do all day is the same thing most of the Tai Tais do, go shopping and have long lunches in Central?'

'*Yes!*' he said, sounding more excited.

'And I'd be able to sit back and be pampered, while you run everything for me so I don't need to make a single decision myself?'

'Doesn't it sound *wonderful*?' he said expansively.

'No,' I said. 'I know what I'm doing, and I know what you're doing. You want a trophy wife. Fine. Go find one.' I nodded to Simone. 'I need to use the bathroom. Be right back.'

'I think that's a "no",' Simone said. 'And the last time you asked, it was a "no" as well.'

The Nemesis stood there, stunned for a moment, then his grin returned. I heard his reply as I walked away. 'She just needs some time to think about it, darling Simone. You should talk to her about how much better things would be if I were to help.'

'I will. I'll make sure she knows every detail of exactly what her life would be like with you,' Simone said.

The bell rang for everybody to go into the hall. 'Hurry up, Emma, it's starting,' she called to me, and I raised one hand to indicate that I understood.

When I came out of the ladies room Michael was waiting for me, posted at the end of the corridor.

'What about Simone?' I said as he fell into step behind me.

'I'm in constant contact with her, and she can take down just about anything that tries her,' Michael said. 'She's more powerful than me. You, on the other hand, I need to watch. You have to be careful not to destroy any demons and get their essence on you, so it's more important that you never fight them.'

I hesitated for a moment, then nodded. 'I guess you're right.'

'What is it with that Nemesis guy?' Michael said. 'He doesn't look like the type that'd even be into chicks but he asked you to *marry* him?'

'Ultimate trophy wife,' I said. 'More than just a European trophy, I'm the wealthy partner of a famous dead billionaire. He wants to be Onassis to my Jackie.'

'Jackie had some fashion sense,' he quipped.

'True, and I have none at all. He's definitely into girls, he's just a big nancy boy. He's dated every young brainless starlet that's appeared on a TVB variety show. He has at least three of them set up as mistresses. He's looking for something a little more upmarket for a wife.'

Michael shook his head as he opened the hall door for me. 'Designer wife. You're real quality, Madam Emma, very haute couture.'

'I wish,' I said.

I steeled myself for three hours of banal name-dropping self-aggrandisement from the other members of our table. 'Here we go.'

*　*　*

The next morning I waited on the first floor of the Academy with Lok and the Tiger. I ran through the armoury to pass the time, checking the status of some of the rarer and more powerful weapons. The Murasame resided here when not called upon by me, on a special rack in a small heavily sealed area at the back of the armoury. Now that Michael had returned, his sword, the White Tiger, had also returned to its custom-made white and gold weapons rack. Seven Stars and the weapons possessed by the Celestial Masters lived in the armoury at the Mountain, although when they were being used in regular training they occasionally took a space here as well.

The Murasame hadn't made my life miserable about not being fed after the Er Lang battle, which was unusual. Normally if it required feeding, it made itself so heavy that it was almost unliftable. The first time it had done this, I'd been confused for a week as to why I couldn't use it, until the sword sorted out the problem itself by becoming so heavy I dropped it and then flying up and slashing me on the upper arm. This time it didn't need feeding, however, and it was possible that the blade was beginning to accept me as its master, something that was both relieving and a little disturbing.

Lok came over as I checked the blade for nicks and ran the whetstone over it a couple of times.

'Did you know that a lot of students come in wanting to see the Destroyer and asking questions about it?' he said.

'What's there to see?' I said. 'It's a completely plain katana with very little decoration.'

'They ask if the legend about it is true. About the Murasame, and the swords produced by the Masamune school.'

'What, that Murasame was the crazed student of Masamune?' I said.

'That, and the stream thing.'

'Well, first of all, Murasame live a good two hundred years before Masamune, so it's impossible that the two knew each other,' I said, sheathing the blade and returning it to its rack. 'But I think it's quite true that Murasame, the man, was pretty demented and intent on creating the ultimate destructive weapon.'

'And the stream thing?'

I glanced down at him. 'They know about that?'

Lok nodded, then ran his tongue over his canine chops. 'They ask if it's true.'

I brushed my hand over the black lacquer scabbard. 'Yeah, I tried it. I got a bag of leaves from the gardeners and took a Masamune and the Murasame to the stream at the back of the house on the hill in Guangzhou. I put the Masamune in the water and dropped the leaves in upstream. It's true, they all moved away from the blade of the sword. Everything moving down the stream moved away from the sword. The Masamunes are preservers of life.'

'And the Destroyer?' Lok said.

'When I put the Murasame's blade into the water,' I said, 'I didn't even need to add the leaves. Things started coming up from the bottom — shrimps, small fish, weeds — everything alive in the stream. All of it was sucked straight into the blade, sliced in half, then ran past it. I pulled the blade out of the water before it could start drawing things from further away.' I took my hand away from the sword. 'The legend is true.'

Lok studied the sword. 'That's a little scary, Lady Emma.'

'More than a little,' I said.

'Stop playing with Ah Wu's toys and come down,' the Tiger said loudly from the lift lobby. 'Your demon is here.'

Lok made a small doggy whining sound. 'Ronnie Wong just told me he's found a stone on floor six that's been eroding our seals.'

'It's not your fault,' I said.

Lok shook his head, the shake carrying through to his whole body. 'I should be aware of such things within my building, ma'am. By your leave, I'll go up to Ronnie and have a look with him.'

I nodded to Lok, and we both headed to the lift lobby. Lok jumped up on his hind legs and pressed the 'up' button with his nose. I pressed the 'down' button when his head had moved away.

The Tiger looked up at the lift floor indicators above the doors. 'That explains why the lift buttons on this floor are so gross.'

The bell to go up pinged and the left lift doors opened. Lok went in, then turned around and stared at the Tiger. 'Up yours, Devil Tiger,' he said just as the doors closed.

The Tiger grunted with amusement. The right lift arrived and we stepped inside. A couple of students were in the lift already, and fell to one knee to salute both me and the Tiger.

I indicated that they could rise. 'You are supposed to be at home today,' I said.

One of the students nodded. 'Just collecting some books,' he said. 'We wanted to catch up on some study this weekend.'

The Tiger moved like lightning. He slammed the stop button on the lift, then pinned both students by the throat against the wall, one in each hand. He moved his face very close to the gasping student on the left, then turned his attention to the one on the right. He hesitated a moment, then released them and stepped back. The two students sagged, breathing heavily.

'I'm sorry, I thought you were demons,' the Tiger said without a hint of remorse. 'You okay?'

The students nodded, obviously unable to speak.

'How are you getting to the student accommodation?' the Tiger said, waving one hand over the lift panel so the lift could move again.

'We were planning to take the bus, sir,' one of the students gasped.

'Don't,' the Tiger said. 'Wait in the lobby of this building with us. I'll take you home.'

I spoke silently to the stone in my ring. *Ask him if he still finds them suspicious, and explain about the copies. If he's not sure about them maybe we should have a closer look.*

Nothing happened, so I tapped the stone. 'Yes, Emma?' it said.

I explained the situation silently to it, but before I was done, the Tiger spoke into my head.

I'm still looking at them and I'm still not sure. Permission to take them West?

Tell him provided he doesn't hurt them, I said.

The lift doors opened and the two students bolted out of the lift, through the lobby, pushed past the surprised security guards and Leo, and disappeared into the crowd.

The Tiger raced to follow them. *Stay here and get your Leo.* Then he reappeared next to me and spoke out loud. 'I changed my mind. That could be a diversion to get you alone. You're in an unsealed area here and I don't want to leave you by yourself.' He gestured towards the door the fleeing students had passed through. 'How long have they been here?'

'About a month,' I said. 'Latest batch.'

'Let's find the stones that are wrecking your seals, and see what happens when we get the seals set up again,' he said. He concentrated for a moment. 'I'm bringing one of my guys in as well.'

He stepped forward to where Leo was waiting with the security guards, looking completely bewildered. 'Let's check out this demon copy.'

As soon as I approached Leo I knew it was a demon.

'This isn't the same one,' I said. I took its right hand and turned it over. There was no tattoo on the inside of its wrist. 'Definitely not the same Leo; they've used a different one to drop off the identification. This one scans strongly as demon.'

I looked up at Leo. 'Do you know who I am?'

The Leo copy stared down at me, but didn't speak.

'I see this as about a level twenty, and the only unusual thing about it is that it looks like the Black Lion,' Bai Hu said. 'Definitely not the same one. They went back on their deal.'

'Any way to contact Six and Three?' I asked the stone. 'They haven't fulfilled their part of the deal, so the deal is off.'

'I will put feelers out through the network, but most of us would prefer not to have any contact with that pair,' the stone said, 'after what they did to my children.'

'Understandable,' I said.

I smiled reassuringly up at the Leo demon, which still looked completely confused, and gestured towards its left hand, which was holding a scroll. 'Is that for me?'

The demon appeared to notice the scroll for the first time and stared at it silently. Then it raised the scroll and held it out to me.

'Can you speak?' I said.

The demon just stared impassively at me.

'I don't think so,' the Tiger said. 'This is extremely basic, whatever it is. I suspect that it's a very thin shell of a façade with a half-formed low-level demon inside.'

I took the scroll out of the demon's hand and opened it.

The demon exploded all over me. I was thrown back

by the shockwave and found it difficult to breathe. I quickly realised I'd been injured — and it felt serious. Dazed, I looked at my arm and it was covered in black demon essence.

'Snake! Now! Snake, Emma, snake!' the Tiger yelled. 'Quickly change before you absorb it all!'

I concentrated on bringing out the serpent as I watched the essence disappear into me with a quiet liquid sucking sound.

'Shit,' the Tiger said softly. 'Get that snake out, woman.'

Snake. Snake. Serpent. I tried to concentrate.

Bright light dazzled me through my eyelids. I opened my eyes to a brilliantly blue sky, then shaded them with my forearm and closed them again. I could hear the gentle sound of water on sand and opened my eyes again, squinting against the brightness.

I pulled myself up so I was sitting. I was on a beach of pure white gritty coral sand, and the water before me was perfectly flat, aqua, clear and shallow — a tropical lagoon. I could see breakers on a reef further out and then the deeper blue of the true ocean. I looked behind me and immediately recognised the place — the Phi Phi Islands in Thailand. Simone and I had travelled there a couple of years before, and she'd taken me for a swim on the reef to share her underwater abilities — her 'mermaid skills' as she called them.

The beach I was sitting on was only about a hundred metres long and about twenty metres wide at its widest. Behind it was a sheer rock face, overhanging near its base, a jungle high above me on its top — at least twenty metres up. The only way anyone else could visit this island was by boat.

I saw a flash of movement at the end of the beach on the left. Ms Kwan stood there in her white swimsuit and matching white over-shirt, wearing huge sunglasses and an enormous white floppy hat. She caught the hem of her shirt and waved it at me, smiling broadly.

I rose, staggered slightly, then gathered myself and walked over to her, already sweating in the tropical warmth.

'There is a bure here,' she said as I approached. 'Relaxation, deep tissue, hot stone or shiatsu?'

I gently embraced her and pulled back. 'Relaxation sounds exactly what I need.'

'I completely agree,' she said, and led me through the palms to a thatched-roof cottage. A smiling young demon appearing as a Thai woman in a sarong was waiting for me with a handful of fluffy towels.

I sat on the massage table and took a thorough look at myself. I had absorbed some more demon essence, but not a whole demon's worth — I'd been lucky.

'Yes, the serpent training could not have come at a more opportune time,' Ms Kwan said. 'I think your snake has, in its own way, rescued your humanity.'

The demon handed me a thick white robe and gestured to the left. 'There is a screen there, ma'am.'

'Is this place real, Ms Kwan?' I said as I moved behind the screen to change into the robe. 'And is everybody okay?'

'No, and yes,' Ms Kwan said. 'You are still in my Garden, but this is a very special place that I think is exactly what you need right now.'

'You have no idea,' I said as I pulled the robe around me. The demon helped me onto the table and used the towels to cover me as I eased the robe off again. 'It's been so full-on the last couple of weeks I haven't been able to take a breath.'

'I understand,' she said. She sat next to the edge of the bure and a white fan appeared in her hand. She waved it lazily in front of her face. 'The Tiger requested some breathing time for you. You can always ask for my help yourself, remember, Emma.'

'There is one thing I would like to ask you,' I said.

'Hmm?'

'Tell me about the Xuan Wu's true nature.'

Her fan stopped.

'Mixed heritage of Heaven and Hell. Is he a demon that changed sides, Ms Kwan?'

'Have you read *Journey to the North*, Emma?'

'No,' I said. 'I gave up about halfway through *Journey to the West*. The classics are just so damn *hard*, and I have so many other things happening right now that I don't have the time they deserve to study them properly.'

'And no crib notes on them either,' she said wryly.

'I wish.'

The stone in my ring piped up. 'It is my understanding that the Dark Lord forbade his Retainers from giving Miss Emma any sort of education in the classics.'

Both I and Ms Kwan made disgusted sounds of derision.

'But of course you women would ignore such an edict,' the stone said.

'Read *Journey to the North*, then ask to see me again. We will talk,' Ms Kwan said.

The demon worked her smooth hands over my shoulders and I collapsed into the relaxation with a small gasp of pleasure.

'Good,' Ms Kwan said. 'Enjoy the massage. Lie in the deckchairs on the beach. The demons can provide you with anything you need. Swim in the ocean; I have made it warm and calm for you. I will return later.'

I glanced up from the table. 'Ms Kwan?'

'Hmm?'

'Why don't you do this for people who are really in need — the poor, the abused, the disadvantaged? Why for me and not for them?'

'Who says I do not provide this for them?' she said. She smiled gently. 'But for those who are truly suffering, coming here would not be a gift. Nobody can stay here forever. All must return.'

'I see,' I said. I dropped my head onto the silky soft towel. 'And thank you.'

'You are most welcome,' she said.

'Is this Potakala Island?' I said, but she had gone.

'I have some messages from home for you,' the stone said.

'I don't want to hear anything except that Simone and everyone at the Academy are okay.'

'They are. Louise is planning to come down and visit you this afternoon and bring her kids to say hello, and wants to know if that's all right with you.'

'No, thanks,' I said. 'She wants to bitch about Rhonda before Rhonda gets back tomorrow. Tell her I'll have lunch with her later in the week, when things have settled down.'

'You mean never,' the stone said. 'Things never settle down.'

I shook my head into the towel. 'No, I really do want to see her, I haven't seen her in ages. I just don't want to get stuck in the middle of this Rhonda thing right now.'

'Perfectly understandable, ma'am,' the stone said.

'Anything else?'

The stone made a soft snoring noise.

The masseuse raised the towel covering one of my legs and began to work the tension out. A large bird flew overhead. The water rippled in front of me. I sighed and closed my eyes.

CHAPTER 23

The next morning, I waited with the Tiger, Michael and Simone in the Chinese restaurant of one of the hotels in Causeway Bay. We'd filled in the order sheet and the dim sum were arriving steamer by steamer at the table, but nobody had the appetite to eat much.

The Demon King walked in accompanied by Rhonda and Martin. Rhonda raced to where Michael had risen to greet her and was engulfed by his huge hug. She then embraced the Tiger, who kissed her loudly on the cheek and grinned at her, his tawny eyes sparkling with delight. She smiled around the table, and Michael quickly moved so that she could sit between him and the Tiger.

The Demon King sat at the table, waved for Martin to follow suit, and examined the dim sum baskets with interest. 'Any fish cheeks?'

Simone silently slid one of the steamers over to him. He looked at the small dish of steamed fish heads sliced in half and dotted with black beans, then pulled out a piece with relish.

'Love this place,' he said through the fish. 'Great fish heads, and they do excellent frog's legs.' He grinned at me, his blood-coloured eyes full of amusement. 'Emma knows just how much I love those.'

'I've seen you watch the frogs being killed,' I said. 'I have never seen you eat them, and frankly I'd be happy if I never did.'

His amused expression didn't shift, and he spat the fish's skull onto the saucer below his rice bowl. 'Excellent.' He put down his chopsticks. 'To business.'

He waved one hand at Martin, who pulled out a Chinese street map from the pocket of his tan slacks. 'I've marked the location of Six's nest on the map. The real Leo is there. Be aware when you go in that there are at least five and probably more fake Leos.' He turned his maroon eyes on me again. 'I think you ran into one of them yesterday. Some of the fakes are very easy to pick, others will be harder. If you're not sure just bring all of them out and let me look at them, I can tell you which is the real one.'

Martin silently passed the map to me. I studied it; it wasn't a map of Shantou as we had expected, but a map of Guilin region. I glanced up at the King. He was watching me, his eyes full of humour.

I passed the map to Simone, who glanced at it, gasped, and then shot a look at the Demon King. '*Seven Stars Cave?*'

The King nodded, then pulled another dim sum basket towards him. 'Any fung jao — phoenix claws?'

'You're sure the demon's nest is under the cave?' I said.

'Only about an hour by plane from Hong Kong — a good central location if you're going to be based in Guangzhou. Pretty too.' The King pulled a chicken foot out of the steamer and sucked at one of the toes. 'Good fung jao. Calling them "chicken feet" doesn't capture the delicate essence of this dish — trust you Westerners to give them a name that is so much less glamorous.' He spat some toe bones onto his saucer. 'Probably chose Seven Stars Cave because of the irony of the name. That's it.'

'Like we can trust you,' the Tiger said gruffly.

The King shrugged and spat out the last of the chicken foot bones. 'Suit yourself. You can check them out yourself in your labs or whatever you have in the West, up to you.' He rose, went to Rhonda, knelt and kissed her hand. 'My Lady. You are welcome to visit again, any time. I will treat you with the respect that you deserve. Please, do yourself and your son a favour and do not marry this ugly cat.'

Rhonda hesitated, watching the King, then shook her head, smiling slightly.

The King rose again. He saluted us around the table. 'Celestials. It's been fun.' He and Martin disappeared.

'You okay, Rhonda?' I said.

Rhonda shrugged. 'Just fine. It was easy.' She ruffled Michael's hair, then turned and took the Tiger's hand. 'I'm glad to be home though.'

'And we're glad to have you back,' the Tiger said gruffly. 'I missed you.'

Michael made a show of studying the steamers in front of him.

'I wonder who we can round up to take to Guilin this afternoon,' I said. 'Stone, ask around.'

'How will you get there, Emma?' Simone said.

'Check flights as well, stone.'

'No need, I'll take you on a cloud,' the Tiger said.

'Oh, no, I *hate* riding on clouds,' I moaned.

'Scary?' the Tiger said, grinning.

'No,' I said. 'Ridiculous.'

'Humph.' The Tiger pulled a steamer of siu mai closer, dug one out with his chopsticks, then dunked it into a bowl of chilli sauce he had appropriated from the wait staff. 'Travel by cloud is the traditional, classical and most respectable form of transportation for all Celestials.'

'I am finding people who are willing to accompany you, ma'am,' the stone said. 'We are working on a meet-up place.'

Michael rose. 'Let's go.'

The Tiger waved him down. 'Let the ladies eat, son. The nest will still be there in an hour or two.'

'What if the Demon King tips them off?' Simone said. 'I think Michael's right and we should head out now.'

'I agree,' I said.

'Humph,' the Tiger said. 'Both of you need to spend some time reading the Tao. Okay, we'll go. Do you need to get anything before I take you, Emma?'

Michael saluted me. 'Lady Emma, if you don't mind, in my role as driver I have the capability to take you to your destination on a cloud, hidden from view. Please permit me to fulfil my duties and do this for you.'

'Oh will you *cut it out* with the formal Retainer bullshit,' the Tiger said, exasperated.

'Thank you, Michael,' I said. 'If you can bring a cloud here to Causeway Bay without being seen, go right ahead, and we'll head out immediately.'

'That I think nobody can do,' Michael said wryly. 'Far too many heads to mess with.'

'I can do it,' the Tiger growled.

Michael ignored him. 'How about I drive you to the top of Braemar Hill and we head out from there?'

'Let's go.'

'I'll come too,' Simone said. 'Top of Braemar Hill is a good spot to start out from.'

'I'll bring the car around, you wait for me downstairs,' Michael said. He kissed Rhonda on the cheek. 'It's good to have you back, Mom. Dinner tonight at the flat? We have some catching up to do.'

Rhonda hesitated, then said, 'I'm sorry, Michael, but while I was away we re-leased the apartment and I moved out. I'm staying at the Palace now.'

Michael shot a swift glare of contempt at the Tiger, then smiled again at Rhonda. 'Whatever you're happy with. Maybe I can drop by the Palace later?'

'You are more than welcome, son,' the Tiger said.

Michael ignored him, smiling only at Rhonda.

'I would love that,' she said. 'I have a lot to tell you about what happened after you left Hell and came back up to the Earthly.' She looked around the table. 'You are all most welcome to drop by after ...' Her voice trailed off, as she realised that I couldn't travel to the Plane. She turned to the Tiger. 'Maybe we can organise something at the Sheung Wan or Shatin hotels?'

The Tiger bowed his head slightly to her. 'Your wish is my command, my Empress.' He swept his tawny gaze around the table. 'I'll fix this up — you guys head out. Meet you on top of Braemar Hill. Let's see who we can find to help.'

Michael effortlessly guided the Mercedes through the packed streets of Causeway Bay near the entrance to the Cross-Harbour Tunnel, then north towards North Point and Tin Hau. He slipped through the underpass to Tin Hau Temple Road and headed up the hill above North Point and Quarry Bay. The only other vehicles on the road were red Island taxis, dropping people to the exclusive apartment blocks clinging to the hillside.

'Who do we have?' I said.

'Just us so far,' Simone said. 'We can't take any human students, it's too far for them. There's no Celestials free at the moment, and the Demon King went straight from lunch to the Southern Palace to try out some real phoenix claws instead of the mundane ones you find in yum cha.'

'Are the phoenixes okay?'

She shrugged. 'Sure. They don't need my help; it's just the King and a lot of lower-level stuff.'

'Na Zha wants to come along,' Michael said.

'He's welcome,' I said. 'We haven't seen him in a while. What's he been up to?'

'No idea,' Michael said. 'I haven't seen him for a while either.'

'You, me, the Tiger, Michael, Na Zha — I hope it's enough,' Simone said.

'If it's too much we just leave,' I said. 'And return with reinforcements.'

'You underestimate yourself, Simone,' Michael said. 'The combined force of you and your elementals is more than enough to take down anything we face.'

'Oh yeah, I keep forgetting about them,' Simone said. 'And every time I do, they come and spray me with water. I'll bring a few of them.'

We climbed to the top of the hill, passing the highest high-rise housing estate and then parking near the three schools on top of the hill: a Chinese International School, a small English Schools Foundation school, and one of the campuses for the Japanese International School.

'You have an appointment with the people at the Chinese School later in the week, Simone,' I said. 'They may be able to find a place for you.'

'They should be able to,' she said with scorn. 'That school is freaking enormous.'

'Are those the only types of school you can find, Emma?' Michael said. 'The kids who go to those are all rich and spoilt.'

'I'll fit right in then,' Simone said cheerfully.

'You know how hard it is to find a space if you don't start at grade one,' I said.

Just be careful, Michael said into my head. *Some of these schools have drug problems — the kids are given way too much cash for their own good. I've heard of bullying as well.*

'That is *so rude*!' Simone exclaimed. 'If you have something to say, say it *out loud*!'

We climbed out of the Mercedes and walked the couple of hundred metres up the hill to the end of the road. School was in and the sounds of children in the classrooms was a background murmur. We stopped a little into the scrub on top of the hill where we couldn't be seen. From this high vantage point all that was visible were the roofs of the buildings below us, covered with washing lines and air-conditioning towers, and stained with damp. The busy harbour traffic caused white trails across the water far below.

Simone brushed her fringe to one side of her face and studied the Chinese International School. 'Is this the best you could find? It's *huge*.'

'You're being interviewed to go on the waiting list,' I said.

She turned away from me.

The Tiger appeared next to us. 'Let's go.'

'Na Zha's coming along,' I said.

'He won't join us here in Hong Kong, it's too damn Western for him,' the Tiger said. 'Head out, he'll probably meet us along the way.' He stuck his fingers in his mouth and whistled loudly.

'You don't need that, Lady Emma is using mine,' Michael said, and raised one hand. A cloud coalesced next to him, about three metres long, two wide and a metre tall. 'Hop on, ma'am.'

The Tiger changed to a slightly smaller than usual version of his Celestial Form: two metres tall with furred face and clawed hands, and a huge mane of white hair held in place with a gold ribbon. He wore scaled armour of white and gold, and carried a large two-handed katana, also white and gold, loose in his right hand. A cloud swept in from above us and he stepped onto it with dignity.

331

Simone raised one hand and summoned Dark Heavens. 'You ready to go, guys?'

I stepped onto Michael's cloud. Although it appeared insubstantial, it was a steady platform with vapour around it.

Michael stood on the cloud as well. 'I won't go too fast, you need to be able to breathe,' he said. 'But you might like to take a seat, otherwise you could lose your balance.'

I sat cross-legged on the cloud, not a moment too soon. My stomach fell out as we shot into the air.

Michael grinned and sang the first few lines from the *Aladdin* magic carpet song in a surprisingly pleasant baritone. Simone floated up from beneath the cloud and flew next to us on our right side, her hair ruffled by the breeze. She scowled at Michael. 'Dork.'

He gestured towards the cloud, still grinning. 'Plenty of room for all the ladies.'

She tossed her head and looked away. 'I prefer my own methods of transport, thank you very much.' She drifted away, then closer again. 'I have about six elementals who are coming with us.'

'Nice,' Michael said, nodding.

Simone flew closer. 'Can you pull out metal ellies?'

Michael shook his head and his smile became rueful. 'I've tried, but they ignore me. There's something about me they just don't like.'

'Has your dad spoken to them about you?' I said. 'Told them to stay away?'

Michael appeared thoughtful for a moment. 'Don't think so. Actually I think he'd prefer it if they *did* come to me.'

'He is trying hard, Michael,' I said.

Michael looked away, then gestured towards the north, the direction we were travelling. 'Na Zha.'

Na Zha screamed through the air towards us,

creating swift-forming clouds of vapour as he broke the sound barrier. He wore his usual human-like form of a Chinese teenager wearing black skinny jeans and a white T-shirt three sizes too big for him, a nano clipped to one sleeve with earphones in his ears.

'Heard you were heading to free the Black Lion. Count me in.' He raised one hand to Michael. 'Mikie bro.'

They high-fived, then Na Zha spun in mid-air on his fire wheels and kept pace with the cloud. Simone ducked under it and reappeared on the other side, away from him.

'Hello, gorgeous,' Na Zha called to her, leering.

Simone flew slightly higher above Michael and myself so that she could be heard. 'When did *you* go emo?' she said.

Na Zha's face went blank with shock and he stopped in mid-air, then hurried to keep up with us. 'I'm no emo!'

Simone pointed at his jeans. 'Black skinnies, emo boy. Kissed any nice boys lately?'

'Simone!' I said.

She poked her tongue out at me and disappeared under the cloud again. 'Nice view, have a look,' she called from beneath us.

A cloud came down from above and slotted into position behind us. It was the Tiger. He nodded to Na Zha. 'Third Prince.'

Na Zha half-heartedly saluted. 'Emperor.'

'I have sent some metal elementals to scout ahead,' the Tiger said. 'They have entered the Seven Stars Cave and have yet to find the entrance to the nest. But they say that something appears amiss.'

'Exactly what?' I said.

Simone popped up on my left again. 'Oh, good idea, Uncle Bai, I'll send some water ellies too. They can slide through the limestone in the caves.'

The Tiger nodded to Simone then turned to me again. 'It is extremely quiet in the caverns. Very few tourists there; the humans seem to sense that something is wrong.'

'Do you think the demons know we're coming?' I said.

He bowed his shaggy head. 'It seems to be that way.'

'I'll fly on ahead and have a look,' Na Zha said.

The Tiger raised one clawed hand to stop him. 'That you will not, Third Prince. We will do this together.'

'Fine,' Na Zha said, resentful. He dipped below the cloud so that I couldn't see him.

Both Simone and Na Zha were invisible beneath the cloud for a moment, then Simone shot out to the left, drew level with my cloud, then fell back to about fifty metres behind us.

'Is he hitting on her again?' I said.

'Let him try,' the Tiger said with amusement. 'She hates him.'

'Are there any boys she doesn't hate?' I said, mostly to myself.

'Oh, one or two,' the Tiger said with a knowing grin.

I opened my mouth to ask and then shut it. Simone's love life was her business, and if she chose not to share it with me, that was also her business. I could only hope that when it came to advice on relationships she would come to me or someone else that she trusted, because it really was a minefield out there, Celestial or not.

'Don't worry, Emma, she talks to the Phoenix and the Lady and Master Liu,' the Tiger said. 'She says she doesn't want to embarrass you.'

'Humph,' I said. I moved to a kneeling position so that I could see over the edge of the cloud. 'Nothing she could possibly say could embarrass me.'

Simone streaked up beside the cloud and yelled with delight into my head. *Hey, Emma, are you pre-menstrual*

right now? 'Cause you sure are hard to get along with!
She grinned with mischief and disappeared again.

I could feel my face reddening and flopped back down so I was sitting on the cloud.

'Eavesdropper,' I said loudly.

We passed over the massively huge city of Guangzhou.

'The city is probably a hundred and fifty kilometres north to south, Emma,' Michael said as we flew. 'If you include all the smaller cities that have joined up with it.'

'It makes Hong Kong look tiny,' I said.

'True. But Guangzhou has ten million people, and Hong Kong has nearly seven, all crammed into that tiny space.'

'Making Hong Kong even more tiny.'

The scenery changed. We were no longer passing over the grey tiled roofs of village houses and concrete apartment buildings; the mountains became more rugged and the population less dense. An occasional valley village stood out as a grey scar across the landscape where all of the trees had been removed.

As we approached Guilin, the famous mountains swept into relief before us. The slender, nearly vertical mountains that appeared in Chinese brush paintings weren't an artistic affectation; they were real, and the district around Guilin was crowded with them, making the area as splendid as any painting.

Simone drifted up to fly next to me, watching the mountains unfold below us. 'Seven Stars Park is in the city, across the river from the Elephant Nose Mountain,' she said. 'There are seven mountains in the park, supposedly taking the positions held by the stars in the Seven Star constellation, the Big Dipper.'

'I've often wondered if a Celestial put them in Guilin as a sort of backyard feature,' Michael mused. 'They do mirror the constellation very closely, and there are caves underground that look like Guilin above ground. Mom and I did the Li River cruise thing a couple of years ago, it was great.'

Simone giggled. 'Oh look, a theme park!'

I looked over the edge of the cloud but couldn't see anything except brown scars of construction and long dirt roads below me.

'It has a mock Polynesian village, with local people painted black and dressed in grass skirts, banging drums,' Michael said with amusement. 'Very culturally sensitive.'

'You went there?' Simone asked with delight.

'We took a group of disadvantaged Mainland kids with us,' Michael said.

'You didn't mention that,' I said.

He shrugged. 'Not really worth mentioning. Mom and I used to do it often, take disadvantaged kids on holiday, give them time away from the concrete jungle.' He glanced back towards the Tiger's cloud. 'I dunno whether I'll want to continue doing it if Mom doesn't want to.'

'If she doesn't want to, can you and me keep it going?' Simone said. 'It sounds really worthwhile.'

Michael hesitated for a moment, then grinned at her. 'Sure.'

'Okay!' Simone yelled. She nodded towards the ground. 'Seven Stars Park, Guilin, everybody off!'

'I'm going to take us pretty much straight down, Emma,' Michael said. 'If you feel uncomfortable let me know.'

I peered over the edge of the cloud. 'We're there?'

Michael nodded, and pointed towards a green swathe next to the river that stood out against the grey of the urban sprawl. 'That's it.'

'Thanks for the ride,' I said, and threw myself off the cloud.

I used the energy centres to slow my fall, and Simone came down to match my speed.

'You have enough energy control, Emma?' she called over the noise of the wind.

'I thought —' I started, then hit something with a thump that knocked the wind out of me. I lay, gasping, on a cloud that had appeared under me and swooped up to catch me.

I rounded on Michael. 'That was totally unnecessary. I'm quite capable ...' My voice trailed off as I saw the Monkey King grinning at me from the back of the cloud. I pulled myself to a sitting position and saluted him. 'Great Sage.'

The Monkey King was in Celestial Form. He was about five feet tall, his appearance part monkey and part human. His face was like that of a chimpanzee, and he stood upright without difficulty the same as a human would, but his simian feet were bare. He wore a traditional bright red cotton jacket with toggles and loops, and brown cotton pants. The circlet that the Buddha had given him was around his brow and he held his magic wishing staff in his right hand. I nearly laughed; he was a caricature of how he appeared in popular culture. Humans didn't often get the appearances of Celestials exactly right, but the way that the Monkey King was portrayed was uncannily accurate. Probably because he was such a glory hound and helped them out.

'Thanks for the lift, Great Sage, but I was taking myself down,' I said, and threw myself off the cloud.

I drifted down for about fifty metres, but the Monkey King swooped behind me and collected me on his cloud again.

'Was there something you wanted to say to me?' I said.

'No, not really,' he said, grinning and leaning on his staff.

'Then how about letting me have a fly?' I said.

He shrugged.

I dropped off the cloud and spreadeagled on the air, again slowing my fall and enjoying the light sensation of drifting downwards. The mountains below were like jagged teeth sticking out of the ground towards me, and the Li River glistened with reflected sunlight. South of the city of Guilin the landscape was green and unbuilt because of the steep mountains, but around the area of the city there was extensive urban development and many terraced rice paddies.

The Monkey King flew his cloud beside me, then dipped below and up again to collect me.

I stood up and put my hands on my hips. 'What are you doing?'

He just shrugged again, leaning on his staff. I did a huge backflip off the cloud and soared a good eight metres backwards. I landed on his cloud again.

'Okay, whatever,' I said. I turned to face the direction the cloud was moving, away from the Monkey King, and sat cross-legged on the cloud.

He did a barrel roll, turning the cloud upside down and tipping me off.

His choice to be an asshole if he wanted, so I ignored him. I looked down as I slowed my fall; I was only about a hundred metres above the ground. Simone reappeared next to me and gently guided me with PK to the exact area where we needed to land: a small walkway halfway up the steepest hill in the park.

You should order him out, Simone said into my head. *You deserve more respect than this.*

Tell her he's a valuable fighter, I said to the stone. *And besides, his behaviour is his business, and the repercussions of his behaviour will also be his business.*

Michael, the Tiger and the Monkey King guided their clouds next to the walkway, then soared from them to meet us. Na Zha swooped in from above, then dismissed his fire wheels and joined us. Night was falling and the local and foreign tourists had left the park, leaving empty drink bottles and snack packets all over the ground, and newspapers covering the concrete outdoor chairs and tables.

Simone shook her head. 'I don't know why people sit on newspapers, they make your bum blacker than the chairs would anyway.'

'It makes them feel better about the dirty chairs without actually doing anything,' Michael said.

We gazed up at the side of the mountain. The walkway up to the entrance to the cave was a switchback of stairs and paths that led up the nearly vertical rockface.

'Anyone sense anything?' I said as I started up the stairs and through a moon gate towards the cave entrance.

'Demons, no,' the Tiger said. He gestured towards the entrance. 'Them, yes.'

The cave entrance was as big as a hall, with rough rock walls carved with the Chinese version of graffiti — many poems in elegant calligraphy etched into the rock by visitors over thousands of years. Some of the poetry was by famous historical poets, making the graffiti true works of art. A modern Communist Party slogan, at least fifty metres long, in large red simplified characters had been carved into the wall about five metres above us.

Within the cave at least twenty and possibly thirty Shen stood quietly, waiting for us. They appeared to vary in age from about ten years old to well over ninety. Gold stood at the front of the group, wearing a pair of tan slacks and a beige polo shirt. His child floated next to him.

He raised his hand and approached us. 'Before you say anything,' he said, 'we want to come along, so don't try to stop us. We want a piece of this asshole demon that's been messing with our nature. We never forget when one of our own has been hurt, and in this case this demon has hurt many of us.' He saluted us quickly. 'By your leave, Celestial Masters, please allow this group of stones to assist you in your quest.'

'But don't try to stop you, eh?' the Tiger said.

All of the stone Shen except for Gold transformed at the same time. They took the form of tiny pebbles, each only about half a centimetre across, and swirled into a cloud of stones hanging in the air.

'We can go as small as dust motes if you like,' Gold said. He grimaced. 'Well, they can.'

'I can't allow the children to come,' I said. 'But I won't stop the rest of you. You're right, this is just as much your business as it is ours.'

'Listen to the white chick giving orders,' the Monkey King said with amusement.

I turned to face the Monkey King, summoned the Murasame and stood with it in my right hand. 'I'm First Heavenly General, Sage Sun. I have precedence over everybody here. Including you. If you have an issue with doing as you're told,' I gestured with my sword away from the mountain towards the long drop below, 'the clouds are that way.'

I turned and walked towards the group of floating stones. 'No juveniles can come along; feel free to leave them here with someone to mind them. Adults only, please. I won't be held responsible for putting children in any sort of danger.'

'But I *want* to *come*!' Gold's child whined.

I stooped so it was at my eye level. 'If they chop you, little one, you'll be killed. Your dad and the other adult Shen would survive. You wouldn't. Wait until you're bigger, and then you're welcome to come to everything we do.'

I nodded to Gold. 'You don't have to come, Gold, you can stay here with your child.'

Gold's child settled onto the floor and turned black. 'I hate you.'

I bent to grin at it. 'I hate you too. And both of us know we're lying. So wait out here for us with the other kids, and we'll be back soon.'

Gold's child rolled into a corner and stayed there, silent.

'There aren't any other kids,' Gold said. 'The stones who take the appearance of children aren't children at all. We're all adults here, except for my little one, and I'd prefer not to leave him out here by himself.'

'Let me *come*!' Gold's child said.

'It'll be fine, ma'am,' Gold said. 'Any trouble and I'll take it out.'

'All right, you can all come,' I said with resignation. 'Don't make me regret this, Gold. Children deserve our protection.'

I walked through the cloud of stones towards the tunnel entrance to the cave itself.

'You take orders from this little girl?' the Monkey King said behind me as the rest of the group moved to catch up.

'Yeah,' the Tiger said. 'Do you?'

'Ah Ting's really pushing it,' the Monkey King said.

'*Due le*,' Na Zha said in Putonghua, agreeing with him.

I didn't turn to see them, I just gestured backwards with my sword. 'Clouds are that way, fellas.'

They made some displeased noises and followed me in, the cloud of tiny stones behind them.

CHAPTER 24

As soon as the Tiger entered the cave it lit up with splendid coloured fairy lights highlighting all the interesting limestone rock formations.

Simone gasped. 'Pretty!'

'Vandalism,' Gold said dryly.

'We do not exist for entertainment, and we do not need to be "prettied up",' one of the stones said in a sarcastic female voice. 'These "enhancements" have damaged the surface of the rock, and the "emissions" from so many visitors are eroding the limestone.'

'The tourists are damaging the very things they want to see,' Gold said.

The Monkey King shrugged, looking around at the stone formations. 'It'll take years for the damage to show. And as long as you get to see the rocks before they're gone, who cares?'

'That's a slash and burn attitude,' I said without looking back.

'Slash and burn is a good way to get new farmland,' the Monkey King said.

'What if you run out?'

'World's a big place.'

342

I rounded on him. 'Why are you here anyway?'

He leaned on his staff and grinned at me. 'Black Lion owes me a one on one.'

'Oh, now that I would like to see,' the Tiger growled. 'But you can't use the wishing staff.'

The Monkey King grimaced. 'That's not fair.'

The Tiger moved further into the cave, studying the walls. 'No, that *is* fair, and that's why you don't like the idea.'

'Anyone sense an entrance to the nest?' I said. 'This place doesn't seem anything unusual.'

'Probably further in,' Michael said, studying the formations. 'They like to be as far from the surface as possible.'

'Boy's right,' the Tiger said. 'Let's head further in.'

'My elementals say further in too,' Simone said. 'They're looking but they haven't found it yet.'

We followed the damp path through the cave, the walls dripping moisture from the limestone around us. As the Tiger approached each area the coloured lights blazed into life, then faded as he moved away again.

'When you go on the tour through here, the guide stops at each formation and goes into a detailed background story or description of it,' Michael said. 'If you didn't stop I think the whole cave would take about twenty minutes to walk through, but they can stretch it into an hour.'

'I'd prefer not to be told what to see,' Simone said.

'Makes life a lot easier if you just go along with what you're told and see what you're told to see,' I said. 'Thinking for yourself is the hard way.'

'Then I choose the hard way.'

'That's what makes you special,' the Tiger said, his voice full of approval. 'Only those marked for the highest levels of consciousness have the strength of character to decide such things for themselves.'

'Bah,' the Monkey King said. 'Females are unable to attain Enlightenment, they're still one step below the ultimate Earthly incarnation of male form. Scriptures say so.'

Simone stopped and stared at him.

'This is not the place to be arguing this, Simone,' I said.

'Yeah, I'll take it up with him later,' she said.

'Bring it,' the Monkey King said without looking away from the rock formations.

We arrived in a cavern with limestone ribbon formations standing vertically along the ground. They'd been lit up to make them appear like the Great Wall. The Celestials all stopped and looked at the formation.

'This is it,' the Tiger said.

'So many demons on the other side of this,' Simone said. 'So *many*!'

'How big are they?' I said.

'All sorts,' Na Zha said. 'Like a hotel buffet.'

The limestone ribbons only stood about twenty centimetres tall, but they were at least five metres long, curling through the base of the cave in a pond of water. We all took a step back as the ribbons rippled, then rose out of the water to coalesce into a fake stone elemental demon with a body and limbs of large, rough rocks that floated together without any physical joins between them.

Simone shot a blast of shen energy at the demon. It dropped slightly then rose again.

Na Zha summoned his throwing ring and threw it at one of the stone demon's limbs; it severed the limb and returned to Na Zha. The limb quickly rose and reattached itself to the body.

'Oh, quit playing with it,' the Tiger said. He shot across the water so he was floating above the demon, and drew his sword to engage it. Simone, Na Zha and the Monkey King followed, all of them descending on the demon.

Michael gently took my arm and held me. 'I know you want to have a try at it, Emma, but if it explodes on you it could be very bad.'

'Let me go. I won't try for it.'

The demon threw its arms wide, hitting each of the Celestials, knocking them backwards to the ground.

'You okay, Simone?' I called, moving towards her. Michael took my arm again and I shook him off. 'Let me *go*!'

'You stay right there,' Simone said, spreadeagled in the water. 'We can take it.'

'How big is this thing anyway?' I asked Michael. 'I can't sense anything at all from it.'

'No idea, it's one of the new stone elementals.'

'Water's weak against stone,' I said, concerned, 'and Simone's the daughter of water itself.'

'Metal's not weak against stone though,' the Tiger growled, and rose from the ground. He shot towards the demon and ran his sword straight into the middle of its body. The demon somehow ejected his sword, throwing him back again.

Simone filled Dark Heavens with shen energy and ran towards the demon. The Monkey King did a huge leaping dive towards the centre of the demon with his staff. Simone sliced through the demon's torso, and the Monkey King broke each of the limbs off, then the head. Na Zha finished the job by sending his flying ring through all four of the legs, making them fall into shards of stone.

Simone turned to walk across the water and back to me, and was struck in the back of the head by one of its arms, sending her sprawling towards me. The demon proceeded to re-form.

I didn't attempt to help Simone up, much as I wanted to; Michael still held me. She shook her head and rose, then rubbed the back of her head and turned to face the demon.

Na Zha, the Tiger and the Monkey King all stood just out of reach of the monster, studying it.

'Any ideas?' the Tiger said.

'Stones?' I asked our companions.

The cloud of stones swirled and coalesced into a solid, then split apart again. Gold, who was still in human form, smiled slightly. ''Bout time you asked the experts.'

The stones moved so fast through the air that they were a blur. They latched onto the stone demon, then grew into larger rocks, pinning it down. It fell to the ground, its limbs thrashing as it tried to fight the stones off. They held it spreadeagled on the ground and its writhing became weaker.

'Okay, you got it. Now what are you going to do with it?' the Monkey King said, his voice heavy with sarcasm. 'Can you actually destroy this thing, or are you going to be in bed with it for the rest of your lives?'

Gold approached the stone demon and waved the Monkey King closer. 'Run your staff right through ...' He studied it carefully, then pointed at the stone body. 'Right there.'

The Monkey King swaggered to the stone demon, swung his staff in his hand and ran it through its body where Gold had indicated. The demon's limbs went completely straight, then flopped, lifeless, onto the ground.

The stones lifted in a cloud above the demon, and Gold shrugged. 'Sorted.'

'The entrance to the nest is behind this room,' Simone said, still rubbing the back of her head. 'There are plenty more demons in there to play with.'

'More stones like this?' I said, picking my way through the water to the back wall. I considered whether I should send Simone home.

'No, most of them are standard Hell-type humanoids,' Simone said. She saw my concern. 'I'm okay, just getting a mighty fine bump.'

'You sure you can handle this?' I said.

She shrugged. 'Had worse. You don't see some of the stuff the Generals throw at me.'

I dropped my head and shook it. 'If you're getting injured like this, I want to stop them calling on you to help them.'

'I'll be healed in about ten minutes, don't worry about it, Emma.'

We stood at the back wall of the cave, studying it. Na Zha put one hand out and felt the wall. 'Seems solid.' He punched it hard, making chips of stone fly from it. 'Very solid.'

The Tiger raised his hands and a circular metal blade appeared in front of him, spinning in the air. He ran it into the wall, and moved it through, creating a doorway. He pulled it out again, but the wall flowed back together as if it hadn't been damaged.

'This wall is at least a metre thick,' he said. 'Maybe our oh-so-clever stones have an idea for getting through it … What the fuck?' He suddenly shot into the air and hit the ceiling with a bang.

I turned and saw that the arms of the not-so-dead demon were holding Tiger and Simone by the throat. The Tiger seemed unfazed, but Simone was obviously choking and clutched at the stone tentacles strangling her.

Michael leapt to cut off the tentacle holding her and it broke to the floor. It re-formed and grabbed him around the throat as well; now it had all three of them. The stone Shen gathered into a cloud and coalesced onto the body of the demon, trying to stop it, but it ignored them. Simone's struggles became more frantic, and the pool of water on the ground rose as a sphere and attacked the arm where it held her.

Na Zha and the Monkey King attacked the demon, but their blows bounced ineffectually off it.

'Move *away* from the body *now*!' I yelled. 'Do it!'

The stones and Shen hesitated, then moved back. I saw the body of the demon through the cluster of stones, and moved quickly, driven by Simone's strangled cries of distress. I concentrated, planted my feet, pulled the Murasame from its scabbard and lowered my head. I pulled the demon energy out of the stone demon and into the Murasame. The demon quickly folded up into a small black bead and fell, rolling slightly, into the water.

The Celestials dropped to the ground and I raced to Simone. I couldn't touch her, but Michael could. He held her by the shoulder and studied her. 'Are you okay?'

The Tiger came over and knelt next to her, but Na Zha and the Monkey King stood back and stared at me.

'You okay, little one?' the Tiger asked Simone gently.

She nodded, then took a deep breath, closed her eyes and concentrated. Her face went completely peaceful for a moment, then she snapped open her eyes again. 'I'm fine. All fixed.'

'You need practice in that,' the Monkey King said with disdain. 'A little bit of choking never hurt anyone.' He pointed at the demon bead on the floor. 'And I want an explanation *quick smart* on why you could do that, lady.'

I rose and shrugged. 'I just can. You know I can do some stuff that humans aren't supposed to do, like white and black chi, and multiple chi balls.'

'That's just because you're talented and were trained by the Dark Lord,' Na Zha said, studying me as closely as the Monkey King was. He nodded to the demon bead. 'This is way different. How come you can do this?'

I shook my head, confused, and moved to collect the

bead. 'It's just one of the things I can do that's a little different from normal. Can someone call a jar here and I'll pop it inside?'

The Tiger summoned a small jar with a wire-clipped lid to hold the demon. 'This isn't a little different, Emma,' he said. 'This is major. They're right. Why didn't you tell anyone you could do this?'

Na Zha took a step closer to me and turned his Inner Eye on me. I felt as if I was being squashed flat and fell to sit in the water, dropping the sealed jar containing the demon.

'No Inner Eye! Stop it, stop it!' Simone yelled.

The squashing feeling left me and I gasped for breath, still sitting in the water.

The Monkey King stood in front of me. I was still weak and could only see up as far as his staff and simian feet.

'Why can you make demon pearls?' he demanded.

'I just can, it's nothing special,' I said. I made an effort and glanced up at his suspicious face. 'Isn't it?'

'Only the Dark Lord can create the demon pearls,' the Tiger said gruffly. 'Many of us have tried to collect the essence as he can, and only end up destroying the demons. Only he can do it, because of his true nature.'

'Jointly of Heaven and Hell,' I said, understanding. I rose from the floor and took some deep breaths. 'He's the *only one*?'

Na Zha glared at me. 'We thought he was.'

'What the fuck are you?' the Monkey King said.

I nearly laughed at the irony. 'Damn, Monkey, if I knew that I'd be a very happy Serpent indeed.'

'I know what the Dragon would say if he was here,' the Tiger said. 'He's said for a long time that you're some sort of demon.'

'I know,' I said. I pointed at the wall. 'But right now, I have a Retainer in there who's an ordinary human and

349

marked as Worthy. How about we concentrate on getting him out, and then later you can have fun with the usual sport of Emma baiting?'

The Monkey King hesitated, then raised his staff. 'Works for me.' He jammed the staff into the wall again, chipping the rock.

'Oh, move back and let us do it,' Gold said with resignation. 'Why are you constantly ignoring us and our abilities?'

'Ego,' I said, and the Monkey King and Na Zha glared at me. 'Go right ahead, Gold.'

'Give us a couple of metal elementals,' Gold said, studying the wall.

The Tiger raised one hand and the metal elementals appeared as glowing silvery globes, each about twenty centimetres across, floating in the air.

'Why didn't you get help from these when the demon had us?' Simone said. 'Mine came to help.'

'*They* don't help *me*. I'm the boss,' the Tiger said. 'I help them, and I use them for mundane tasks. I never need rescuing.'

'You are so full of shit it's surprising your eyes aren't a darker brown,' Na Sha said, watching the stone Shen as they worked on the wall.

They scrabbled at the rock like insects, scratching away at its surface, a visible dent appearing as they worked. Then an enormous *whoomph* came from the other side of the wall that made dust rise and knocked off a few of the stones. The Shen still on the wall shrieked and scattered away from the large crack that had appeared down its centre. The wall was hit from the other side again, and we all took a step back. The stone Shen rose and floated to hide behind us.

'Any ideas?' I said.

'I do not believe what I am seeing,' the Tiger said as a hole a metre across opened in the wall. A black turtle's head poked through and tore at the edges with its beak. When it had enlarged the hole slightly it grinned at me. 'Hello, Emma.' It turned to see Simone. 'My little one.' Its dark eyes sparkled at me. 'Come on through.'

'*Daddy!*' Simone shrieked and threw herself at the wall, tearing at the rock to break through.

There was a large open area on the other side, an underground complex of two-storey buildings with red wooden pillars and doors like a traditional temple. John, in True Form, stood in the middle of the large courtyard. Although underground, it was brightly lit even though there was no visible light source.

Simone fell to her knees and clutched his head. She put her forehead against his. 'Daddy, Daddy, Daddy,' she said through the tears.

He butted her with his nose. 'I can't stay long, sweetheart. I was brought by your suffering and I don't know how long I'll be able to stay conscious.' He glanced at me and grinned his tortoise grin. 'What happened to you, Emma? You're full of demon essence.'

I knelt in front of him and raised my hand to touch his nose. He was completely black and about three metres long. His shell rose in a graceful arc from his sides, but was covered in intimidating spikes. His head was like a cross between a lion's and a dragon's, but much uglier, with a large black shining frill around his neck. He smiled at me with the eyes I'd loved for so long and I nearly joined Simone in weeping to see him.

'Simon Wong injected me with the essence,' I said, stroking his turtle nose. 'I change into a Snake Mother if Simone touches me or if I get really mad.' I touched my forehead to his as well, joining Simone. 'I'm trying to control it, and I hope to be rid of it before you come back for good.'

'Don't worry, you will be whole again, love,' John said, and I nearly wept again to hear his voice. He glanced up at the Tiger. 'Ah Bai.'

The Tiger, Na Zha, the Monkey King and Michael all dropped to one knee and saluted him.

'Xian Tian,' the Tiger said.

'Nu Wa, and the Three,' John said.

The Tiger's face went blank with shock.

'Emma is to see Nu Wa. If she cannot help, then go to the Three Pure Ones. They may be able to help.'

'Nobody's visited Nu Wa in a thousand years,' the Monkey King said with scorn. 'Remember what happened last time an asshole Emperor went up there.'

'This does not concern you,' the Turtle said, glaring at the Monkey King, who dropped his head. John turned back to face me. 'Go see Nu Wa, love, she will have some ideas.' He butted Simone with his nose again. 'This place was full of demons. I had some fun and cleared it up for you. Why are you here?'

'We think Leo is here,' Simone said.

The Turtle raised its head and its gaze unfocused. 'There are three copies of Leo here, all demon. There are some stone Shen being held here as well.' It pointed with its nose. 'Down that way, down some stairs, there's more demons below. I only took out the biggest ones on the top here.' He concentrated. 'None of those Leos is the real one.'

'Dammit!' Bai Hu said.

'How many Shen? And where is the real Leo?' I said.

John's eyes unfocused again, then he snapped back to me and grinned. 'Five stone Shen are held here. Leo: no idea. Listen,' he rubbed the side of his face on my hand, 'I don't have long. Once I revert I'll probably be gone for a while again.' He glanced from me to Simone. 'But I am slowly returning, my beloved ladies. Still no idea what happened to the damn Serpent though.'

His dark eyes studied me with amusement. *Hope I can see yours soon, it really is incredibly hot.*

'Anyway,' he said, switching back to out loud, 'there is probably some clue here to where the real Leo is, but remember, Emma, more than anything, Leo wants to die. He felt that he failed me in not protecting Michelle, then again when not protecting Simone, and he does not feel worthy to share this world with us.'

'He's been judged Worthy,' I said.

'Of course he has,' the Turtle said. Its eyes glazed over slightly, then it shook itself. 'Damn, I'm fading.' He looked around, and smiled at me and Simone. *I love you both. Thank you for waiting for me. Simone, I am so proud of you ...*

Simone released a huge sob that made her shoulders shake and buried her head in her father's enormous black frill.

Emma, I love you ...

And he was gone.

CHAPTER 25

'They're here!' a voice yelled from the other side of the hole in the wall. We all turned to see who it was. A group of warriors from Rabbit Village were visible there, about five or six of them, all wearing a polo shirt with a small rabbit on the front where the designer logo usually sat. They clambered through the hole, then knelt on one knee and saluted us.

'We heard you were clearing a nest in here, Exalted Ones, and wanted to help,' the senior Rabbit, Tu Gong Wei, said. 'It is an insult to the honour of the Rabbit Village that this nest exists so close to our home.'

'That's right, Rabbit Village is in the mountains south of here,' Simone said. 'We flew right over it.'

'These yours?' the Monkey King asked me.

'They're from one of the Twelve Villages of the Arts,' I said. 'Rabbits are the shadow casters.'

'Useful if we have to face a large number of demons,' the Tiger said. 'Bring 'em.'

The Rabbits, still kneeling, saluted him.

'We would be honoured,' Tu Gong Wei said.

I looked around. With the stones and the Rabbits along, our force was close to thirty, all skilled in Arts and stone magic. I shrugged. 'Fine.'

'What do we have here, sir?' the head Rabbit asked the Tiger.

The Monkey King replied without looking away from the courtyard. 'Lot of demons holding some stone Shen and a few Black Lion copies that we're here to get out.'

The Rabbit leader nodded. 'Let's go then.' He saluted me. 'We can take it from here, ma'am.'

'I'm sure you can,' I said, and hefted my sword. 'Let's go. We need information on where they're keeping the real Leo, and how they're making the stone copies.'

The two-storey building surrounded the courtyard on three sides, with a rock wall on the fourth side. The building was made of grey bricks with red wooden pillars holding up a balcony with a red railing all around the inside. Red wooden doors and hexagonal windows opened out from the rooms to the courtyard.

'Run a sweep through all these rooms and see if there's any strays,' I said. I turned to Gold. 'Assign a couple of stones to each Rabbit and work as teams.'

Gold nodded. 'Ma'am.' He turned and raised one arm, speaking telepathically to the stones and Rabbits.

'That's not the right way to do it,' Tu Gong Wei said. 'It would be better to have stones together and Rabbits together rather than mixed groups.'

'I think a mix of skills is a better way,' I said.

Tu Gong Wei grimaced. 'As you wish.'

The Rabbits grouped into teams of three and entered the ground-floor rooms, some of them jumping from the ground level to the balcony. The stones floated in True Form beside them.

There was a brief yell and sounds of fighting, then the Rabbits and stones reappeared. Tu Gong Wei saluted the Tiger. 'One demon, only level eighteen. All clear.'

'Good job. Where are the stairs?' I said.

'This way,' Gold said.

Can I thump Gong Wei? Simone said into my head. *And did you notice that all of these Rabbits are guys? That Rabbit girl you told me about was right!*

There was a standard stairwell inside the building through a pair of red wooden doors. We took the stairs down, the stones floating with us. At the bottom was a corridor with rooms on either side, looking very much like an old-fashioned high school. The walls were plain dark grey stone and the doorframes were the same red wood.

The first room on the left held a mah-jongg table, a couch and a television. There were weapons racks on the wall, but they were empty. A table to one side held a large Chinese-made metal hot-water flask, and a teapot and cups black from constant use. The room across the hall on the right went almost the length of the corridor, about fifty metres, and was obviously a training room, with more empty weapons racks but no mirrors — small demons couldn't stand the sight of their reflections. Neither of the rooms had any windows or visible light sources, but they were still brightly lit.

'Looks like our little friends were tipped off,' the Tiger said. 'They've either taken off or they're further in, waiting for us.'

'Can anyone sense anything?' I said.

'No,' Simone said. Michael shook his head. The Celestials didn't reply — their way of saying 'no'.

We went to the end of the corridor to another stairwell, again leading down. The rooms we passed on the left were empty — no furniture or weapons. Demon resting rooms — they didn't require furniture, they just shut down and stood motionless, like automatons.

The stairwell at the end didn't go anywhere, just down a couple of steps into a rock floor.

'Dead end,' I said, confused. 'That's all there is here?'

'That's not the floor, that's a demon,' Simone said, studying the rock. 'Some sort of stone thingy.'

The Tiger was standing behind me, and his musky big cat scent filled the stairwell. 'Can you pearl it?'

I shook my head. 'I can't do it to really big stuff, and this might be too big. I have no idea what size it is.'

'That one in the cave was pretty big,' Na Zha said.

'That one in the cave was killing Simone,' I said.

The Tiger raised one furry clawed hand and a lance of shining metal appeared in the air above the stone demon, then fell to skewer it. The demon appeared unharmed.

'Wish the Turtle had hung around a bit longer,' the Tiger said.

'We need a dragon,' I said. 'Stone is weak to wood.'

'*Now* she works it out,' the Monkey King said.

I glared at him. 'Don't see *you* being terribly useful right now.'

He bared his teeth at me in a simian threat. I turned back to the stone demon blocking the stairwell. 'Stone, ask a couple of dragons to come and see what they can do about this. Maybe Silver and Precious?'

'On their way,' the stone in my ring replied.

Simone walked the few steps down to the stone demon and stopped, thoughtful. She crouched and put her hands on it.

'Move back, Emma,' she said, as if from a million miles away.

The Tiger grabbed my arm, dragged me out of the stairwell and shielded me with his body, just as the demon exploded into a huge mass of feathery streamers all over the rest of the group.

'Oh *yuck*,' Simone said. I peered around the Tiger to see her; she was covered in black demon essence. She summoned an elemental, and it enclosed her completely in a sphere of water, then disappeared, leaving her clean and dry. She raised her hand and similar spheres of water appeared around the rest of the group, cleaned them, then disappeared.

'That worked,' Na Zha said, studying the staircase stretching down. 'Nice Third Eye. Looks like a long way down.'

The dragon Silver appeared in the corridor behind us in Celestial Form, tall with silver-scaled armour and holding his spear. He was accompanied by Precious, another of the Academy dragons. She was about thirty centimetres shorter than him, and wore traditional Tang-style robes of pink and lilac, with her hair elaborately pinned in twining braids adorned with enamelled silver birds and flowers.

The Tiger grinned at her. 'Well, hello, *gorgeous*! What are you doing wasting your time in Wudang?'

Precious replied in her high-pitched, almost little-girl voice. 'Learning how to kick the shit out of assholes like you.'

The Tiger leaned towards her and his grin widened. 'I'd love to see you try. Wanna meet up later? My shit will be open season for you, honey.'

Sylvie appeared on the stairs behind us, and ran down them to stand next to Precious. She was in human form, wearing her black pleated mini-skirt and a long black blazer. 'I'm sure this cat generates enough shit for both of us to kick, Precious.'

Precious nodded, still gazing coolly at the Tiger. 'More than enough to bury us.'

The Tiger changed to female form: a tall, Amazonian-looking white woman with platinum blonde hair. 'I see how it is. Like me better like this?'

Precious generated a small ball of chi energy, about the size of a baseball, and threw it to hit the Tiger right between the eyes. He continued to leer at her, unfazed.

Sylvie took a couple of steps towards the Tiger and glared at him. 'Back off, asshole.'

The Tiger changed back to Celestial Form and raised his clawed hands, still grinning. 'Point taken. Backing off, lovelies. But,' his grin widened, 'any time you want some fun, you know where to look.'

'I'd rather play with a Snake Mother,' Precious said.

The Tiger placed one hand over his heart. 'I'm wounded.'

'Oh, good,' Sylvie said, and moved closer, saluting me. 'Lady Emma. What do we have here?'

I opened my mouth to reply but was interrupted by Michael striding to the Tiger and punching him so hard in the mouth that the Tiger reeled back, stunned.

Michael remained staring at the Tiger, standing in a long defensive stance.

The Tiger glared at him, shocked, then raised one clawed hand in dismissal. 'Whatever, kid. You can't stop me from being what I am. Deal.'

'Gold, please do me the favour of relaying these events just past to my mother's stone, Zara,' Michael said through his teeth. 'I'm sure my mother would like to see exactly what she is committing herself to.'

'Won't do you any good at all, boy,' the Tiger said with malice. 'She knows how I am and loves me for it. And I love her, as much as I love any of my wives. Like I said ...' He leaned closer to Michael, grinning. 'Deal.'

Michael drew his sword, ready to attack. The Tiger's grin widened with anticipation.

'Stand down, Michael,' I said loudly. 'I acknowledge that he's insulted you, but unfortunately right now we need his claws. Feel free to call him out later though, and have it out in the Arena if you have to.'

Michael resheathed his sword, glowering at the Tiger. 'Ma'am.'

'Precious, Silver,' I said. 'Looks like this is the nest of Demon Prince Six. He's the one that's been messing with stones for the last ten years or so. I've called you in because of your alignment.'

Silver nodded. 'Understood, ma'am. We should be able to help control anything stone-based that we encounter.'

Precious concentrated. 'I was present when we investigated the seals on the nest in Kowloon City, ma'am, and this is something similar — stone essence used as a barrier that not even a powerful dragon could pierce.'

'That is very bad news,' the stone in my ring said.

'This time we're going to nail Six down,' I said. 'It has Leo, and it's been experimenting on and killing stones.' I gestured to the stairwell at the end of the corridor. 'Let's go.'

We went down the stairs together. Each flight was about six steps, then they turned ninety degrees and went down a further six steps. They seemed to spiral down for a very long time.

'I feel like I'm in an Escher drawing,' Simone said.

Gold gasped behind me and rushed down a couple of flights ahead, then stopped, staring at the wall. He looked stricken.

The wall had been splashed with black mud, like an inkblot. The stones all gathered in front of it, hovering at eye level.

'That isn't what I think it is, is it?' I said.

Gold dropped his head and shook it. 'I knew him.'

'I'm scared, Daddy,' Gold's baby said.

'Take him out,' I said, just as Gold said, 'I want to take him out.'

Gold turned and saluted me. 'By your leave.'

'Go.'

Gold turned and he and his child headed back up the stairs together.

'Two stones as escorts, please,' I said.

A couple of stones detached themselves from the group and floated up the stairs with Gold.

'And a Rabbit,' I added, remembering the nature of the demon we were facing. 'No, two Rabbits. One stone, two Rabbits.'

'Are you sure you can spare that many of us?' Tu Gong Wei said. 'There are only six of us here; that would cut our numbers by a third.'

'How about,' the Tiger growled, 'you stop questioning every single order you're given and do as the First fucking Heavenly General orders you, human.'

'I was merely saying —' Tu Gong Wei began, his voice rising in pitch.

'I respect your suggestion. Two Rabbits to accompany Gold,' I said.

'All right, all right,' Tu Gong Wei said, and gestured for a couple of the Rabbits to go with Gold. He sighed with resignation. 'And she's just as human as I am.'

'That's debatable,' the Tiger said.

He proceeded down the stairs, the rest of us following. At the bottom, we entered another corridor, similar to the one above, with grey brick walls and red painted-wood doorways. The floor was plain stone and, although there were no windows in the classroom-sized rooms to the right and left, the entire area was as brightly lit as if we were in daylight.

We stopped when we heard a scrabbling sound at the end of the corridor.

Before we could investigate, the Tiger shouted from the next room, 'Come and see this.'

The room was obviously a basic laboratory; a dark green metal tube, about a metre across, filled one corner of the room from floor to ceiling, and a bank of 1950s style gauges and meters with an old-fashioned monotone monitor sat against the wall next to it. On the other wall were metal shelves holding a number of small green boxes, each about ten centimetres square. They appeared to be made of jade.

'That's a scanning electron microscope, a real vintage one,' the Tiger said.

He strode to the shelves and peered at the jade boxes. He opened one and a stone flew out, then took the human form of a middle-aged Chinese man. He knelt before us and saluted, then quickly moved to the shelves and opened other boxes, releasing other stone Shen.

When the stones were freed, each of them took one of the jade boxes and smashed it on the floor, one of the female stones stamping on the pieces to make sure they were completely destroyed.

'The demons knew you were coming and started clearing out about two hours ago,' one of the stones said. 'They had a few very unusual demons with them.'

'Any clue where they went?' I asked the stone.

'They did not say where they were going, but they didn't seem terribly concerned,' the stone said. 'Apparently they were very excited at the prospect of collecting something more valuable than all of us put together.'

'Simone?' I said.

The stone shook his head. 'No idea.'

'They were experimenting on us, ma'am,' said one of the female stones that had just been freed.

There was a spark from the electron microscope in the corner of the room and the Monkey King yelled.

'Sticking your fingers in, eh?' the Tiger said with amusement. The Monkey King growled something unintelligible at him.

'There is another of us in there,' one of the freed stone Shen said.

The Monkey King ducked to check the sample

chamber of the microscope. He pulled his wishing staff out of his ear where he had been storing it, expanded it to normal weapon size, and tried to prise the sample chamber open.

The Tiger swaggered to the microscope and flipped a switch, causing a hiss of escaping air that made the Monkey King jump back. The Tiger pushed a button on the side of the chamber and it opened like the drawer of a filing cabinet. He and the Monkey King peered inside the chamber, then the Tiger reached in and pulled out a golden stone.

'Pure gold?' the Monkey King said. 'There aren't many of them.'

'No,' the Tiger said. 'They coat them in gold to get better resolution through the microscope.' He turned to the other stones that had been held captive. 'Were any of you put inside this?'

They shook their heads.

The Tiger went to the oldest stone Shen and held out the golden stone. 'I think being cut in half, coated in gold, put in a vacuum and bombarded with electrons ... has killed it.'

'No,' one of the stones moaned softly.

The room suddenly became very still and quiet. I recognised the silence that happened when a large number of Shen were discussing something telepathically.

'I would like to know what's being discussed,' I said.

'Although they don't appear very emotional, all the stone Shen are extremely agitated at what's happened here,' Michael said. 'Some of them knew the black stone that was put up as a warning outside, and those that were held captive in the boxes are wailing with horror at what's happened to their companion. They have been held here together for a couple of weeks, and the other Shen have been searching unsuccessfully for them. Apparently three or four other stones that were also held in the jade cages were taken out and probably killed in a similar way.'

'You guys can leave if you don't think you can handle it,' I told the freed stones. 'We need to find where the demons are headed, and gather a force to stop them.'

They ignored me.

'Listen!' I shouted, and the thick silence eased. 'Let's not just stand around here wailing about what has happened to our friends. Let's find any others that are being held captive, and track down the owner of this nest! Don't you want to find Six?'

They all stared blankly at me.

I gestured towards the door. 'Let's go find our friends, and then hunt down the one that did this.' I didn't wait for them; I went out into the corridor, turned left and followed it to the end, then stopped.

There was a gaping hole leading into a cave about two metres wide and high, roughly carved out of the limestone rock. It smelt of sweet flowers and mown grass. I hefted my weapon and walked in.

The Tiger hurried to join me on my right, and Simone appeared on my left.

'This nest is *huge*,' she said softly. 'And the Tu Jia had no idea it was here.'

'That guy in charge of your Rabbit Village needs a good kick up the ass,' the Tiger growled. 'Regardless of the fact that you're a chick, he needs to show more respect.'

'As if being female had anything to do with it,' Simone huffed.

'Whatever,' I said. 'Can you guys sense anything?'

'No,' Simone said, and the Tiger shook his head.

The corridor changed from oval to square, with stone tiles on the floor and more polished walls.

'They built this first, and then linked up with the

complex under the cave,' Simone said. 'I wonder if this is an invasion, demon against demon.'

Suddenly everything went perfectly dark and quiet. My own breathing was loud in my ears. I attempted to move but found myself in some sort of casing that was stopping me from doing anything. I had a moment of panic and then realised that I had no difficulty breathing.

'Stone?' I said.

The stone wailed with terror in my head.

'Stone, calm down. Where are we?'

If the stone could have panted it would have. 'We're going to die, we're going to run out of air, we're locked up, it's closing in, we're going to be crushed —'

'Stone!' I shouted. 'We're not dying, it's not closing in! *What is holding us?*'

The stone made a high-pitched ringing noise.

'Get a hold of yourself!' I shouted. 'You're not helping. *Where are we?*'

I felt a blow on the side of my abdomen, but couldn't move to avoid it. To hell with this. I concentrated, and filled the Murasame with chi, making the interior of my prison glow. It was a stone Shen, holding me inside it.

'Are you holding me inside you?' I asked my stone.

'No!' it shouted. 'Someone else is holding us, and they're going to crush you!'

'I'm not being crushed. Let me see if I can burn my way out,' I said.

I loaded the Murasame with chi energy, making the blade glow with an eerie black flame. I levered my hand so that the blade touched the stone surrounding me. Nothing happened.

'Try demon essence,' the stone said, sounding desperate. 'Get us out of here!'

'Absolutely bloody useless in a crisis,' I grumbled under my breath. I loaded the blade with demon essence, touched it to the walls of my prison, and they exploded outwards in a shower of gravel.

I looked around. I was in the same place, the cavern under the nest, and the Tiger and Simone were standing next to me, their faces fierce with desperation. Some human-shaped stone figures stood nearby — obviously this had happened to a few of our group.

I kept the Murasame loaded with demon essence and went to the nearest figure. I shaded my eyes and touched the blade to the stone.

'No, Emma, wait!' Simone shouted, but it was too late. The stone shape exploded outwards in a shower of gravel, releasing Precious, who blinked at the light.

I turned to Simone. 'What?'

'Those stone prisons are the stone Shen that were held here,' the Tiger said. 'You just killed two of them.'

I turned back to the stone prisons. 'Oh *no*.'

'They turned on us,' Simone said. 'They enveloped you in casings. We've been trying to talk sense to them, and even strike them to make them come around, but they won't budge.'

'Touch me to one,' the stone in my ring said.

I went to one of them and touched the stone to it.

'I can't talk to it,' the stone said. 'It's controlled. They've done something to it. Destroy it.'

'No.' I turned. 'Precious, come and have a look.'

Precious approached the stone prison and put her hand on it, concentrating. 'Silver is in here,' she said. 'Give me a moment, we're talking about options.' She lowered her head. 'Nothing.'

'Move back,' I said, then loaded the Murasame with demon essence, and blew up the stone Shen.

'What are you doing, Emma?' Simone cried.

The Tiger attempted to take my arm as I loaded the sword again, but he jerked back and shook his hand. 'Shit!'

I went to each of the stone Shen in turn, blowing them up with demon energy, and freeing Michael, Na Zha, Sylvie and the Rabbits. When I was done, I turned to face the rest of the group.

'Is that you, Emma?' Simone said, sounding forlorn.

'Of course it's me.'

'You *killed* them!'

'That's right. I killed them. So that means they're on the tenth level of Hell now, freed from the control, right?'

Simone hesitated, then turned to the Tiger. 'Uncle Bai?'

The Tiger didn't reply for a moment, then said, his voice gruff, 'She's right. They're in Hell, and they'll be back soon.'

'Ordinary humans aren't really supposed to know about the existence of Hell,' the Monkey King said.

'Well, since I've been there under Celestial sanction, I guess the rules have changed,' I said.

I studied the group of stone Shen that had come with us. 'Are you guys sure you won't be controlled by this demon as well?'

The stones were silent; probably discussing among themselves. I waited for them. We didn't need about fifty of them turning on us.

'Since we haven't been held by this demon, we shouldn't be affected,' one of the stones said. 'Let's go. We have unfinished business here.'

We continued into the nest, down the tiled grey stone corridor. It reminded me unpleasantly of the nest under Kowloon City where Simon Wong had held Simone.

The corridor opened out into a nest cavern, with indentations for Mothers; but it was deserted, not even eggs left behind.

'Looks like it's been evacuated,' Na Zha said.

'The King tipped them off,' the Tiger said.

On the other side of the nest cavern was another corridor, and we all went down it. It started to slope downhill and the sides became rougher. We arrived at a smaller cavern, only about fifteen metres across, with rough walls but a tiled floor. A dead Mother in True Form lay on the floor near one wall. The three Leo copies that John had mentioned lay on their stomachs in the centre, dressed in old-fashioned paisley cotton pyjamas. The room smelt strongly of frangipani flowers, pungent and sweet.

The rest of the group, except for the Monkey King and the Tiger, put their hands over their noses.

'Oh my God, that is awful,' Michael said. 'I thought out in the cavern was bad, but this is enough to make you throw up.'

I went to one of the Leo copies and turned it over. The frangipani smell was coming from it. It seemed uninjured, but its stomach was bloated from death. I checked the inside of its wrist — it was number two.

'Do the other two Leos have numbers?' I said.

Michael and Na Zha checked them.

'This is number three,' Na Zha said.

'Five here,' Michael said.

'That's two, three and five here, and the one that we rescued from Sham Shui Po was four. I wonder if number one is the real Leo,' Simone said.

'We'll know when we find it,' I said. I glanced at the Tiger. 'Can you take these copies to the West and have a look inside?'

'Good idea. I'll take them with me when we're done here,' the Tiger said.

I rose and brushed off my jeans. 'We need to find more information than this. Let's have a look around.'

CHAPTER 26

The corridor didn't have any other junctions or tunnels off it; it just headed straight and slightly downwards.

'If we continue down here far enough, we'll end up in Hell,' the Monkey King said with amusement.

After about four hundred metres we reached a pair of red wooden double doors with the Door Gods painted on them. We stopped.

'I can't sense anything on the other side,' Simone said.

'Is this an entrance to Hell?' Michael asked Na Zha.

'Nah, man, Hell's a lot further down,' Na Zha said. 'Doors would be the same though.' He paused, thoughtful for a moment. 'Tell you what. Everybody move back, and us big Shen will open it up and have a look.'

'Sounds like a plan,' the Tiger said. 'Everybody back. Just me, Sun Wu Kong and Na Zha to have a look.'

'And me,' Simone said, moving to stand next to them.

The Tiger opened his mouth to say something to Simone, then smiled slightly and closed it again.

Simone turned to speak to the rest of the group. 'Move back, everybody.'

I ushered them about fifty metres back along the stone corridor. We turned and stood, grouped together, waiting to see what would happen.

The Tiger opened one of the doors and stuck his head through. 'Can't see a damn thing.' He opened it wider, and Na Zha opened the second door, both of them pulling them all the way back so they were flush with the walls. They took a few steps through, disappearing into the darkness.

The room flared into visibility in front of us; Simone had generated one of her balls of light. She made it larger until it was about a metre across, and raised it so that it was more than ten metres above us.

It showed us a large rectangular hall, about fifty metres to a side. At the other end stood an army of demons, appearing as young humans in brown cotton pants and jackets. They weren't in any particular formation; they just stood as a clump bristling with weapons.

'How many?' I asked.

'About fifty,' Simone said.

The Tiger glanced back at us. 'Everybody but us big Shen — me, Na Zha and Sun Wu Kong — hold off. We'll start by mincing them.'

'And me,' Simone said. She raised her hand to the side and Dark Heavens appeared in it.

The rest of the group moved further back. The demons waited for the command to attack.

I stepped forward, brushing Michael aside as he tried to stop me. I stood next to Simone and the men. 'Six, if you can hear me,' I said loudly, 'this would probably be a good time to negotiate. You went back on your deal last time. Now you're —'

The demons raced towards us, and the Shen drew

their weapons. The Tiger had a large white and gold traditional one-handed Chinese sword; the Monkey King pulled his staff out of his ear; and Na Zha raised his hands and his chain whip appeared in his right hand and his throwing ring in his left.

'Back up, Emma,' Simone said, readying herself to face the onslaught.

I moved back, out of the way of any possible demon essence.

As the demons approached, a couple of the Shen concentrated and the demons hesitated, then began to struggle to move.

'How big?' Simone said.

'Big enough to resist our Inner Eyes,' the Tiger said. 'Let's go.'

He raced forward and swung his sword, slicing through demons so fast he was a blur. Na Zha spun, using his chain whip with deadly effectiveness and hitting the demons with his ring without throwing it, slicing pieces off them and making them dissipate into black streamers. The Monkey King whooped with delight and pole-vaulted on his staff right into the middle of the demons, then swung it with wild abandon and destroyed everything around him.

Simone filled Dark Heavens with shen energy, making it glow almost painfully white. Everything she touched disintegrated. She carved a path of destruction through the demons, her tawny hair flying.

As the demons closest to us were destroyed, more sprouted out of the ground behind them, joining the existing group from the rear. Simone, the Tiger, Na Zha and the Monkey King continued to fight, but with the reinforcements we had more to face than we'd started with. Another group of demons sprouted from the ground on either side, tripling the army we were facing. Simone continued to blast shen energy, but she couldn't destroy them faster than they were replaced.

Na Zha raised his hands and an energy barrier stopped the demons in their tracks. *Shen Barrage*, he said. *Anyone who knows, move up.*

Simone hesitated, confused. 'Shen Barrage?'

'If you don't know what it is, move back, girly.' He glanced back. 'Anyone who knows what it is, move up quick, 'cause I can't hold these forever.'

Precious, Silver, Michael and Sylvie moved forward.

Simone came back and stood next to me. 'I've never heard of this,' she said.

'Part of the advanced energy curriculum at Celestial High,' Sylvie said over her shoulder to us. 'Watch.'

They stood in a line in front of us, each about two metres from the other. They raised their arms, lowered their heads and radiated shen energy. The energy linked between them, crackling like lightning and moving in vertical bars from person to person, so bright it was almost painful.

The energy coalesced into a barrier in front of them, a wall of brilliant bright light, then expanded out from them in a large arc from wall to wall, destroying everything in its path. The demons didn't explode as it hit them; they dissolved into black goo that boiled into nothingness. The shen energy hit the far wall and disappeared.

The group in front of us dropped their arms and waited. The only sound was a couple of pebbles dropping to the floor.

'I think that did it,' the Tiger said.

'Why don't they teach that at Wudangshan?' Simone demanded. 'That's so useful!'

'Only Shen can do it, and a very senior Celestial has to be present to guide it,' the Tiger said, walking back to us. 'And Shen learn to do it in high school before they go to Wudang. They teach more advanced energy work at Wudang; they assume you already know basic guided stuff like this.'

'But nobody taught me!' Simone said.

The Tiger put his hands on his hips and glared at her. 'That's 'cause you're never there to learn it!'

Simone's eyes widened and she didn't reply.

The Tiger continued, hands still on hips. 'You should have taken me up on the offer to have a look at CH. You'd like it.'

Simone turned away. 'I don't want to go to Freak High!'

'You calling me a freak?' Sylvie said with amusement as she returned to us.

'But you are a freak,' Precious said behind her.

Sylvie turned to face the other end of the hall. 'I s'pose you're right, Precious. So are we going in to have a look around? This place is fascinating.'

She was right. The hall we stood in was about fifty metres wide and long, and had a tiled slate floor and smooth rock walls with a ceiling of rough-hewn stone. The far end looked like a village; there were two-storey buildings on either side with a narrow cobblestone road down the centre, leading a long way away from us.

The Tiger whistled through his teeth. 'Shit, look at that. This nest is fucking enormous.' He glanced around at the Rabbits. 'And it was right under your feet, eh, humans?'

'We did not know that this existed,' Tu Gong Wei said. 'We rely on you Celestials to inform us that Hell is growing beneath our feet; we are only human, after all, and cannot see ourselves.'

'Nobody can see under here,' Simone said, studying the small town before us. 'They've done something with stones that makes it invisible.'

'She is correct,' one of the stone Shen said. 'We are blind in here.'

'This is an evil place, full of the death of stones,' another stone Shen said.

We walked to the other end of the hall, where the buildings and road began.

'How were the demon reinforcements teleported here?' I asked.

'Dunno,' the Tiger said. 'That's a new one on me, never seen demons travelling when they're that small.'

'Someone moved them?' Simone said.

'Demons can't be moved by other demons,' Na Zha said. He rounded on Simone. 'Don't they teach you *anything* in school?'

'She goes to a human school,' the Tiger said.

'Well, *that's* stupid,' Na Zha said. He grinned menacingly at me. 'You worried that she'll be more powerful than you if she's trained properly?'

'It was my choice, not Emma's,' Simone said.

'That's even *more* stupid,' Na Zha said.

'Just shut up,' Simone said, and stormed towards the village in front of us.

The narrow street was lined with two-storey inns and tea houses all constructed of stained hardwood. Most of them were open on the ground floor, with a wooden bar as serving area, and a number of round old-fashioned rosewood tables with round stools, and stairs to the next floor up. Large red lanterns decorated with birds, flowers and good-luck characters provided lighting.

'This looks like an Ancient China theme park,' Simone said as we approached the first tea house.

'It's completely deserted,' Precious said.

The restaurants had wooden bowls and chopsticks on the tables, apparently left behind when the demons had fled. The inns had closed-in lower floors, with paper windows and wooden doors, and signboards next to the doorways.

'Brothels,' Na Zha said with amusement. 'Demon brothels.'

'And gambling houses. This is an entertainment district for demons,' the Tiger said. He opened the door to one of the buildings and peered inside. 'All the demons are gone though.' He came back out. 'The demons that owned this place must have been making a killing.'

'Demons spend money like this?' Simone asked.

The Monkey King nodded. 'They even use normal human currency. Rob people to get it.'

'But where are all the demons?' Simone said. She stopped and gasped. 'Oh my God.'

The third restaurant along the lane had a vat of food out the front, with wooden bowls scattered on the ground. I could smell it before I saw it; the vat was emitting the strong smell of roast beef. It was full of cow's blood, and the bowls had spilled some blood on the ground. Inside the restaurant on the left, hung the cow's raw innards, lungs and intestines from hooks off metal racks. The head was on a spike at the front door with the character for 'cow' splashed in blood on a sign underneath it.

The next building on the left was also a restaurant, but instead of blood it served demon eggs; each about twenty centimetres across, the shells opaque with age. A couple of eggs lay broken open, the tiny demons inside dead on the ground.

'This is creeping me out,' Simone said.

Three stone elemental demons grew out of the floor in the demon egg restaurant and lurched towards us. They were about two-and-a-half metres tall, made of several rocks that floated together in a roughly human form.

Silver and Precious both took two steps back and raised their hands towards some rosewood dining chairs in the restaurant behind us. The chairs shattered into wooden pieces, which flew into the dragons' hands. The dragons strode up to the stone demons and shoved the shards of wood into them, then concentrated. The wood sprouted buds and leaves that quickly grew like a time-lapse movie. The demons' stone faces seemed to register shock for a moment, then they shattered where the wood had been inserted into them.

Precious dusted her hands against each other. 'That was easy.' She looked around. 'Any more?'

'Let's keep going,' the Tiger said. 'I want to see what's at the end of this.'

The next restaurant smelt strongly of stinky bean curd. Inside was a charcoal-fired cylindrical pottery stove with a large flat frying surface holding the rectangular bean curd pieces. Another stove held a large soup boiler with a flat metal lid and the flat spoon used to scoop out sweet bean curd. Behind the counter a large number of catering-sized jars of peanut butter stood on a shelf.

'I didn't know demons liked bean curd as well,' Simone said. 'And look at all the peanut butter.'

'They really go for chau dau foo and dau foo fa,' the Tiger said. 'And you would know this if you went to CH.'

'Shut up about CH already,' Sylvie said. 'She's already said she doesn't want to go to school with us freaks, and I don't blame her.'

'You're not freaks,' Simone said, her voice more gentle.

'We snakes are used to being on the outside, Princess,' Sylvie said.

'My father's a snake,' Simone said. 'And he's a wonderful person.'

'Then you're lucky that you know him. Usually our

parents lay us as eggs and then ditch us. No snake ever has a family,' Sylvie said.

'Emo bullshit,' Na Zha said. 'You snakes only complain about being alone when it suits you. The rest of the time you're off by yourselves anyway.'

Sylvie grimaced at Na Zha, then turned towards the end of the street. 'There's a mansion there.'

The street ended in a traditional Chinese gate, with a single character — the number six — on it. Instead of statues of fu dogs or lions flanking the gates, there were stone images of Snake Mothers.

'Well, we know who lives here,' the Tiger said.

'The Demon King was right,' I said.

'Looks like he had a demon entertainment business going here, and decided to expand upstairs,' the Monkey King said.

'He inherited One Two Two's crime empire,' I said.

The Monkey King glanced at me. 'And you let him?'

'My students regularly shut down their operations,' I said. 'That's what brought us here in the first place. He got annoyed with us and took Leo.'

The Monkey King turned back to check out the mansion. 'And you've known that a demon was running the show in your own backyard for so many years and you've never done anything about it?'

'You know we can't interfere in demon matters unless they attack us,' I said.

'The King was right,' Simone said. 'They've cleared out. I hope we can find a lead on where they went.'

We approached the mansion. It bore an unsettling resemblance to the paper house effigies that were burnt at funerals: two storeys with a veranda over the entrance. The stone-paved front yard had a few silk flowers in pots placed around the edge. The front door hung open.

Directly inside was the entrance hall, with stairs leading up and around to the first floor. On the left a living room held a couple of hard-backed square rosewood couches with red silk cushions and a rosewood tea table, still with teapot and cups on it. A widescreen plasma television stood on a more modern-looking veneer television unit across the room.

Simone ducked her head to check out the library of DVDs. 'He really likes Canto soaps,' she said. 'These are all pirate copies.'

The Tiger grunted with amusement. 'I own one of the production houses — he's been taking money off me.'

'The Dragon's gonna get pissy at you owning so much stuff in the East,' the Monkey King said.

'Fuck the Dragon,' the Tiger said.

'Dragon Tiger Energy Connection Golden Lotus Tao!' Na Zha said, clasping his hands together in the prayer position, holding one foot against the other knee, and swiftly making an expression of bliss.

'You insult the True Path,' the Monkey King growled.

'I insult everything,' Na Zha said. He went further into the dining room, which held a round rosewood ten-seater table inlaid with mother-of-pearl. 'Nice table. Looks like it came from one of those furniture shops in Wan Chai.'

'Surprised he hasn't upgraded to something garish and European,' Simone said. 'They usually go for expensive-looking ultra-rococo with lots of gold.'

'Six is old demon, first generation, he'll be a traditionalist,' the Tiger said. 'Won't go for that modern rubbish.'

The strong smell of smoke filled the room. Simone unfocused for a moment, then snapped back. 'The top floor's on fire!'

We raced up the stairs to the first-floor landing, which was filled with smoke billowing from one of the rooms. The room was completely ablaze with huge flames from the floor to the ceiling. The human members of the group, myself included, started coughing uncontrollably and raced downstairs to get away from the choking smoke.

A gush of water surged down the stairs behind us, nearly knocking us off our feet, and we heard the hiss of steam. The smoke dissipated.

'Safe to come up,' Simone said.

The stones vacuumed the smoke into themselves, clearing the air. Simone gingerly picked her way into the burnt-out room, the walls dripping around her.

'It was a fake fire elemental,' she said, looking around. 'It ran when I hit it with a real water one.'

The room appeared to be a study; the walls were covered in bookshelves but only a few books remained after the fire: old-fashioned Chinese books, flimsy pages bound by large stitches along the edges. The Tiger picked one of them up off the floor. 'These are lab notes.'

'What about?' I said, fascinated. I couldn't read any of the flowing Chinese cursive script; my ability to read was limited to standard printed characters, and even then not many because most Celestial documents didn't need translation.

'From what I can make out from what's left of it, experiments on stones,' the Tiger said. He flipped through the remains of the book. 'This one is about different ways of making stones into slaves.'

The Tiger moved from shelf to shelf reading out their brass labels. 'Fake stone elements, making of. Planting stones on humans to make them obedient ...' He turned to me. 'Isn't that what happened to the Lion?'

'Yes,' I said. 'At that school thing. You were there — they planted a stone on him and he did what they told him. He nearly killed Michael.'

'I remember,' the Tiger said. He continued to look at the shelves. 'They have more advanced control techniques — implanting stones in people ...' He glanced at me. 'I'd be checking your students to see if they've got any stones implanted in them.'

'Any sign of where Leo is being held?' I said.

The Tiger checked through the few remaining books. Most of them dissolved into ash as he touched them.

One of the stones moved forward. 'We would like to scan the pages of these books and distribute them to the network,' it said.

'There's not much left,' Simone said, sounding disheartened.

'Try anyway,' I said.

'Then email the results to my lab in the West,' the Tiger said.

'Of course,' the stone said.

The stones moved in a greyish cloud over the books and they floated up to the sodden worktable. The pages began to flip rapidly.

'While they're doing this, let's go out the back and see what's further along the road,' the Monkey King said. 'Might be something interesting down there.'

We headed back down the stairs and through the living room and dining room to the kitchen. It was extremely old-fashioned, with neither a gas nor an electric stove; instead it had two cylindrical ceramic charcoal burners with large woks on top of them.

A narrow path led away from the rear door. Surprisingly, there was vegetation here; real live plants as opposed to the silk flowers shoved into the pots at the front. It formed a jungle barrier at the back of the house, except for the path leading away.

We walked up the path, which curved to the right, narrow with overhanging azalea bushes. The air smelled less fresh here, more full of damp and plant decay.

'This reminds me a lot of Hong Kong,' Simone said. 'Up on the Peak, where all the jungle is.'

'That's because that's where we are,' Na Zha said as the path led us to an open grassed area surrounded by steep jungle-covered hillside. On the summit of the hill above us stood a tower covered in a complex tangle of mobile phone boosters and satellite dishes. 'This is Mount Austin. You walk down the hill a bit, you're at the Peak Tower.' He turned and pointed west. 'I think I can see the top of your apartment building from here.'

I looked behind us; the path we'd followed had disappeared.

'One-way trip,' Michael said.

'And this was so close to us!' Simone said. Then: 'Oh my God, Gold!'

Gold lay dead on the ground, the two Rabbit warriors lying next to him. The stone that had accompanied them was nowhere to be seen and I felt a jolt of horror.

'Where's his baby?' Simone cried.

'Look inside him. Is it in his human body?' I said.

The stone in my ring was silent for a moment, then, 'No.'

'Can you trace it?'

'We're searching. We can't find it,' the stone in my ring said.

Tu Gong Wei crouched next to his dead Rabbit warriors. He grimaced up at me. 'If you had listened to me, this would never have happened.' He rose and jabbed his finger at me. 'I *knew* that having you in charge was going to be a disaster.' He shook his head, then gestured towards the other Rabbits. 'Let's get out of here. Shen or not, this ...' He hesitated, then spoke with force. 'This *woman* is leading us all into destruction.' He turned away and gestured behind him without looking back. 'Bring our fallen comrades.

No more Rabbits will die because of this woman's incompetence.'

He turned his back on me and approached the Tiger, falling to one knee. 'I request your assistance in guiding us home, Highness.'

The Tiger gestured behind him. 'Go wait over there. I'll finish up with Lady Emma, and take you home.'

The Rabbits lifted their fallen comrades, glared at me, and went to one side of the park, squatting next to the bodies to wait for the Tiger, all with their backs to me.

'Asshole,' Simone said, hands on her hips.

'He just lost two members of his clan, I don't blame him,' I said. I looked down at Gold. 'This is very bad. Tiger, is there any way we can contact the Courts and find out if Gold's child went with him when he went to be Judged? We need to find his baby!'

'It will take at least three days to make our way through the bureaucracy to find out what happened to them, and in that time Gold could very well be back,' the Tiger said. 'If his child was taken, the Courts will probably be lenient and permit him to return almost —' My mobile phone rang. 'See?'

I answered it; it was Gold, ringing from the Peak apartment.

'I don't have my child, ma'am, something happened. I was controlled. They ...' His voice broke. 'They took it. We have to find it!'

'Do the Celestials in Hell have anything for us to go on?' the Tiger said.

'No,' Gold said, his voice full of misery.

'Don't worry, we'll find it for you,' I said. 'We're coming home now.'

'Wait there, I'll bring the Merc down and pick you up,' Gold said. 'Dad's told me where you are.' He hung up.

'I want to send a sweep through the demonic side of Hell,' I said to the Tiger.

The Tiger grimaced. 'We can't. Their business is their business, that's the term of the treaty that Ah Wu worked out all that time ago. Either you have to send in demon agents, or you have to negotiate with the King.'

'We *have* sent in agents and they've found nothing.'

'Then I suggest you contact the Demon King.'

'Shit.' I turned away. 'Stone, summon the four most senior Celestial Masters — the Lius, Chen and Wong — and the four most senior Generals — Yu, Ma, Gao, Zhou. Let's get together and plan for a cleanout of this nest, and a negotiation with the forces of Hell.'

I turned to the Tiger. 'Want to be in on this?'

'You betcha,' he growled. 'I'm sure the other Winds will want to be involved as well.'

'Where, Emma?' the stone said. 'The conference room in Wan Chai?'

'No,' I said. 'Book our usual conference room at the Hyatt. Let's do this right. I want to invite the Demon King along, and we'll thrash something out. He wants Six dead as much as we do.'

The Monkey King gestured towards me. 'You cannot do this. You don't have precedence.' He turned to the Tiger. 'She's a goddamn human!'

'She's fucking First Heavenly General,' the Tiger rasped. 'You gonna argue with the Jade Emperor? 'Cause for some reason the old bastard's on her side.'

'Shit,' the Monkey King said. He raised one hand and summoned his cloud. 'Let me know if there's any demon killing involved and I'm in. Otherwise, this is all your show, Gweipoh.'

Na Zha saluted me cursorily and disappeared without saying a word.

'You've made *so many* friends in your time as First Heavenly General,' Simone said. 'But don't worry, Emma, you're doing the right thing.'

I sagged slightly. 'I hope I am.'

The Tiger slapped me on the back. 'It's what Ah Wu would have done. You even sounded like him. Don't worry.' He grinned with malice. 'You're doing fine, *Gweipoh*.'

'Rude bastard,' I said. 'Take the Rabbits home, my friend. I appreciate your help.'

'You really should be a snake more often, 'cause you sound totally like Ah Wu,' the Tiger said, then turned and strode to the Rabbits. They all disappeared.

Gold appeared at the bottom of the road driving the Mercedes.

'Don't worry, Gold, we'll find it,' I said as we climbed in.

'I trust you, ma'am,' he said.

'The conference room is booked; they will be there in ninety minutes,' the stone in my ring said. 'Let's go home and see what we have.'

CHAPTER 27

Meredith and Marshal Ma were waiting for us when we arrived home.

'I heard what happened,' Meredith said. 'But we have other things happening, Emma. I need to give you an update.'

I raised my arms. 'I'm covered in dirt and ash. Can you make it fast?'

'When we removed the stones that had been eroding the seals, we reset the seals and fourteen students were destroyed trying to run out.'

'Fourteen students were copies?' I said, horrified.

'Yes, and two of them had been in the Academy for more than a year.'

'Damn!' I said. 'Do you think the originals are dead?'

'Demons do not normally kill humans without provocation,' Marshal Ma said.

'But it's quite likely that our students provoked them when they tried to take them,' Meredith said. 'I don't think there's much chance that our students are still alive. We need to find the demon that's making the copies.'

'We will,' I said.

'Oh, and there's one other thing. Just FYI, we are having problems with a dragon,' Meredith said.

'What?'

'One of the little prostitutes was a dragon, remember?'

'I remember,' I said. 'Her name was Hien, she's Vietnamese.'

'She's a drug addict,' Meredith said. 'Her captors put morphine in their food to keep them placid. We didn't find out until she changed to a dragon, broke into the infirmary and held Regina hostage. She's threatening to kill Regina unless we give her something for the pain.'

'And Regina hasn't given her something to calm her down?' I said, then I realised. 'Nothing will work on her in dragon form.'

'And she doesn't know how to change back,' Meredith said.

'I need you to handle that while I work on getting Gold's child back,' I said. 'Can you guys put some dragons on it?'

Meredith nodded once, sharply. 'We'll manage. Talk to the Demon King about Gold's baby. This is the most important thing.'

'I'll be at the Hyatt in forty-five minutes. Michael is bringing the car around now. I just need to change out of these filthy clothes.'

'Good,' Meredith said. She nodded to Marshal Ma. 'If I'm not at the meeting, it's because I've been delayed.'

'Don't worry, Meredith, we'll help Emma sort this out,' Ma said. He saluted me. 'By your leave, ma'am, we'll secure the conference room for the meeting with the King.'

'Thanks, Hua Guang. Most appreciated,' I said, and he and Meredith disappeared.

* * *

The doorbell rang while I was pulling on some clean jeans and a shirt.

Ah Yat shrieked, 'Ma'am!'

'Emma!' Gold shouted. 'Come quickly!'

I raced out to the hallway. Ah Yat had opened the front door, but the gate remained closed. On the other side stood a demon in True Form, human-sized but black with bulging eyes, tusks and long bright red hair.

'Protect me, ma'am!' Ah Yat cried, and scurried into the kitchen.

I summoned the Murasame and stood just inside the door. 'State your business here, demon.'

'It's Martin,' Simone said from where she'd come up behind me.

I lowered the sword. 'No way.'

The demon nodded its massive ugly head. 'I am Ming Gui. I have taken this form to avoid detection by the Demon King. Please, let me in, I have important information for you.'

Simone laughed without humour. 'Like I'll let you in after all the times you've betrayed us.'

The demon glanced from Simone to me. 'I give you my word, I have information on where Leo is.' It glanced backwards, as if expecting someone to follow. 'Let me in! I vow I will not hurt you.'

'Can you take him down?' I said.

'Yes,' Simone said. She strode to the door and pushed the gate open. 'You may enter.'

The demon bowed slightly and walked inside, grimacing as it passed through the seals. It changed form to Martin: tall, with long black hair, wearing a dark green polo shirt and tan slacks. He looked like a younger, slimmer version of John and my heart ached to see the resemblance.

Martin strode to one of the couches and sat, leaned his elbows on his knees and clasped his hands together.

'We must be quick, before the Demon King finds that I have gone. You have to kill me.'

'*Kill* you?' Simone said.

'It is the only way to free me from my servitude.' He sat straighter. 'Once I am dead, I am free from my oath, and I can be Judged and return to assist you.'

'What oath?' I said.

'I cannot tell you. You must work it out yourself.'

'You made an oath to the Demon King?' I said.

'That ...' Martin grimaced. 'I am bound and cannot answer that question.'

'Great, a game of twenty questions while someone has Gold's child,' I said. 'Can you tell us *anything*? And if not, why are you here?'

'Simone must kill me. Then I will be free.'

'Why Simone?'

'She vowed I would taste her blade. I will give her the chance to fulfil her oath and free me from mine.'

'Okay, you swore some sort of oath. Probably to the Demon King, and that's why you've been following him around. Why?'

Martin grimaced. 'When Father returned to True Form, he was in two pieces and so weak ...' His voice trailed off and he pulled himself together. 'Simone was so tiny! The Demon King wants more than anything to be able to return to the world above. If he were to destroy Father, or hold Simone to control Father, he would be able to do this. I had to protect them both. I swore an oath ...' He struggled to continue, then obviously gave up.

'You made a deal with the King to protect me and Daddy?' Simone said.

'I cannot answer that.'

'So you're saying that the reason I'm alive today is because you've gone off with the King to live in Hell,' Simone said with scorn.

'You've never been attacked, Mei Mei,' Martin said. 'They've defended themselves if you attacked them, but no demon has ever come after you.' He slashed one hand through the air. 'But all of this is beside the point. You need to kill me now so that I can come back and take you to get Leo out.'

'I seem to recall you coming here with a certain Number One Demon Prince in a similar situation offering us help,' I said.

Martin leaned on his knees again. 'That was before I met Leo.' He looked up at me, his eyes full of pain. 'Leo taught me the path of true nobility; he taught me what it is to truly love.' He glanced at Simone. 'I would do anything to keep you, my sister, and him safe. We must bring him out of Six's nest before they use him in any more ...' His voice trailed off again.

'In any more what?' I said. 'Experiments? Duplications? What?'

'I cannot tell you until I am freed.'

'And you've just decided that I don't need protecting any more, eh?' Simone said.

'We need to find and free Leo and Gold's child. The stone baby will be destroyed if we do not move quickly. I do not want to risk your safety, Simone, but I could not live with the death of this child on my conscience.'

'I think you know way too much and this is all a trap,' Simone said.

Martin raised one hand, palm-up. 'Ask Gold. I can see him.'

Gold had taken the form of a tiny pebble and hidden in the corner of the room, helping to guard us. 'He's telling the truth,' he said, his voice full of misery. 'All of it. He sincerely wants to help.'

'What are they planning for Leo and Gold's baby?' I said.

'Leo was just a way of making you come out to find him. What they were really after was the stone child,' Martin said.

'Why?' Gold said, almost a wail of grief.

'They are banished from Hell,' Martin said. 'As long as they are outside Hell, they are dying. They feed off the energy ... I cannot tell you more.'

'They feed off the energy of stone children?' I said. 'That's why they wanted Gold's child?'

He hesitated, choosing his words carefully. 'If you break a stone, the small piece becomes a stone child. If you do this in an artificial situation, you create an artificial child. But artificial is never as good as the real thing.'

I was silent, appalled.

'I cannot say more. I will be able to tell you more after you kill me and I return. You must do it right now. I will request a quick return to the Earthly to assist you.'

'We can shelter you here. You don't need to die, Martin,' I said.

'I am bound into servitude, Emma. If I am ordered to kill you, I will obey. The only way for me to break this bond is to die.' He nodded to Simone. 'Is there a private place where you can do this?'

Simone ducked her head into her hands, then ran her hands through her hair. 'Is this really necessary?'

'Yes.' Martin quirked a small smile. 'You vowed I'd taste your blade, sister. Here is your opportunity.'

'How long will you be gone?' Simone said, desperate. 'If you're gone too long, they'll kill Gold's child before you're back to take us in! You should just show us where it is.'

'I can't tell you until I'm released,' Martin said. 'I'm bound by a vow of silence. I can only tell you once I've died.'

'Damn!' Simone said, and turned away.

'One last thing before we do this,' I said.

'We need to hurry,' Martin said. 'The meeting is soon. The minute the King leaves Hell, he will know I am here. If he orders me back, I will obey, and then our chance is lost.'

'Why can you take demon form?' I said. 'That wasn't an illusion, that was *you*.'

'It is because of my mixed heritage of Heaven and Hell,' Martin said. 'Because of the nature of my father. When I return, I will tell you more. Now.' He rose. 'Please, the King will be here soon. Do it, Simone, quickly.'

I gestured. 'In the training room.'

'You do it, Emma,' Simone said, her voice small.

Martin rose and touched Simone's hand where she sat on the couch. 'I'd prefer it was you, Mei Mei. Show me what you have learned. Free me from my bonds.' He touched the top of her head. 'I know you can do it.'

Simone threw herself up off the couch and summoned Dark Heavens. 'All right!' she snapped. 'Let's just do it and get it over with, and then slap the living daylights out of the Demon King for letting this happen!'

'He said he'd killed Six,' I said as we walked down the hall to the training room.

'He probably phrased it so that he wasn't telling a lie,' Martin said. 'He can be very clever with words. If you can pin him down and force him to state the truth, he will. Otherwise, he will use words to twist a lie to make it sound like the truth.'

'I'll remember that,' I said.

I opened the door of the training room and let them in. 'This will completely ruin the mats.'

'Do it in a bathroom?' Martin said. 'I'll take the body with me, but I can't guarantee that there won't be some … spillage.'

'No way am I showering in a room I killed someone in,' Simone said. She took the sword from the scabbard, and glanced at me. 'I don't think I can do this, Emma.'

Martin strode to her and held her with one hand on either side of her face, staring into her eyes. 'Please, Mei Mei, be brave. Free me. I will feel nothing. I will return as soon as I can, and we will bring out Leo who we both love so much.'

Simone hesitated for a moment, staring at him, then threw herself at him to hug him, one hand with the sword behind his back.

Martin buried his face in her hair. 'I love you, Mei Mei. Be strong.' He stepped back and smiled slightly, then dropped to one knee and bent his head. 'Free me.'

Simone didn't say another word, she just raised the sword and, with an effortless, elegant swipe, took his head. She looked away as his head hit the floor and rolled away slightly, then his body crumpled, blood pumping from the arteries in his neck. The body disappeared, leaving a bloodstain on the mats.

Simone bent and walked, devastated, out of the room, the sword dragging behind her.

'You don't have to come to the meeting,' I said to her back.

'I'll come,' she said. 'Wait for me. I need a tissue.'

'I'll meet you downstairs,' I said.

'I think Martin must have been passed over when it came to the brainy genes in the family,' Simone said, looking out the window of the Mercedes as Michael drove us down the hill. 'He keeps doing really dumb things, with the best intentions in the world.'

'He kept you safe, Simone,' Michael said.

'He let the Demon King boss him around, and he let himself be thrown to the *Mothers*!' Simone cried, anguished. 'What an *idiot*!'

'We need to contact the Celestial to arrange for him to be released from Hell as quickly as possible, so we can find Leo and Gold's baby,' I said.

Michael took the overpass from Garden Road to Harcourt Road next to the harbour, then went straight up onto another overpass that took us towards the Convention and Exhibition Centre on the water's edge. It was 8 pm — we'd been running since lunchtime — and the traffic was still very busy through Central and Wan Chai. The laser light show on the top of the buildings around us had started, sending brilliant green laser beams across the harbour and making the buildings shine with a variety of different colours and patterns in a splendid display.

The Hyatt was part of the Convention Centre complex, one of two hotels that flanked the Convention Centre building. John had always booked a room there for meetings with senior Celestials and I'd followed the tradition. We left the car with valet parking — they recognised us after so many meetings held there — and went through the lobby to the meeting rooms on the same floor, next to the exhibition centre at the back of the hotel. There weren't any other functions taking place; only our people were waiting in the meeting room lobby with its plush tan carpet and elegant deco lights — Celestial Masters Chen, Liu and Wong, and Generals Gao and Ma, all in normal human form wearing business suits.

We shook hands Western-style all around and went into the meeting room. It had beige walls, no windows, and the U-shaped table and chairs around it were covered in cloths that went to the floor.

Michael took up position as guard outside the room, but I waved him inside. 'You're part of this. Come sit.'

He hesitated, then shrugged and came in.

Master Chen, the Wudang Weapons Master, was in the form of a mid-sixties woman in a tailored navy business suit. Master Nigel Wong, the Demon Master, was an Immortal who looked like a twenty-something yuppie with slicked-back hair. Shaolin Master Liu also wore a business suit, but it didn't really suit his bushy eyebrows, long white beard and completely bald head. Meredith wasn't there yet.

Marshal Gao had done his best not to glow, but seemed distracted — probably from the effort of retaining the form. Marshal Zhou hadn't changed his appearance very much; he had his usual long, scruffy black beard and dark skin, but he had made the effort of wearing a Chinese black silk robe with cotton trousers underneath instead of his usual armour.

The White Tiger came in, glowered at Marshal Zhou, saluted me, saluted around the Generals, then went to the end of the table and sat. He summoned a jug of wine for himself and poured it without talking to anybody.

One of the hotel staff, a tall man in his early twenties, stuck his head around the doorway. He glanced around, trying to work out who had booked the room, and Master Chen went to him to discuss the meeting arrangements.

Marshal Ma came in, looking middle-aged and serene as usual. He touched the hotel staff member's jacket as he passed and the young man nodded. Ma smiled around the room, nodded to the salutes of the more junior generals, saluted me, and sat.

The young hotel staffer appeared confused by all the formality and saluting, but Master Chen quickly took his attention with a complicated order for drinks and snacks. He went out, closing the door behind him. Master Chen opened it again and left it open for the Demon King, then came and stood beside me.

'Meredith's held up with the dragon, she may not make it,' she said softly. 'Guan Yu's on his way. The Demon King we haven't heard from yet, but he's not attacking anybody at the moment so he should be here.' She turned to face me so she could speak softly into my ear. 'But this is interesting, Emma, apparently Er Lang is on his way as well.'

I tried not to communicate my frustration through my body language. 'Wonderful.'

She turned back to the group. 'Don't panic.'

Marshal Ma approached us. He stood between me and the rest of the group, blocking their view of me, and spoke casually. 'I don't know what's going on with Er Lang, but we can handle it, Emma. Stay aloof. He's beneath your attention.'

'Can I slap him upside the head with my little sword?' I said, just as quietly.

Ma grinned at me. 'One day you're going to give him the beating that he deserves.'

Everybody who had been sitting quickly rose, and everybody present fell to one knee: Guan Yu had arrived. He saluted me, nodded to those saluting him, and approached us.

To hell with protocol. I held my hand out to Guan Yu and we shook. He grinned at me. Guan Yu didn't often have time to come down from the Celestial because of his role as Guardian of the Gates, but whenever he did he was warmly welcomed by all. He'd taken his usual human form of an exceptionally tall, extremely muscular man with a thin black beard, his black hair in a buzz cut that made it stand straight up. Surprisingly it suited him, even though he appeared in his mid-forties. He turned to the group and waved one hand. 'Is that everyone?'

'I believe you're waiting for me,' the Demon King said from the doorway.

He wore a black T-shirt and a pair of maroon jeans, his black hair held in a short ponytail. He came into the conference room flanked by a pair of Snake Mothers in the form of tall, slender, gorgeous women, one black and one a redhead. He sat at the table, saluting everybody around it, and the women sat on each side of him, grinning with menace. The Celestials saluted back and I joined them at the table, a few of them rising to sit after I did in formal Chinese protocol.

'You've failed me, Emma,' the Demon King said with humour. 'You were supposed to destroy Six, and all you did was run him to ground. Nobody will ever be able to find him now.'

'We have help now …' Simone said, then her voice trailed off as she realised she'd said too much.

The Demon King shot a short, appraising glance at her, then smiled broadly again. 'I'm sure you do have help. You have me as well.'

'Is Six in the demonic side of Hell?' I said, and some of the Generals stiffened and leaned back from the table, shocked at this appalling breach of protocol.

'Always straight to the point, so refreshing, Emma,' the Demon King said. 'Yes, he's in my side. Do you want my permission to go in after him?'

'Yes,' I said.

The King shrugged. 'Sure thing. Is that all you needed?'

'Provide Simone with directions to Six's nest,' I said.

The Demon King's face froze, emotionless, for a second, and the Snake Mothers hissed quietly. Then he grinned broadly. 'Oh, this is *very* good news for you!' he said with delight. 'Was it *you* that killed your brother, Simone?'

All of the Generals glanced sharply at Simone and she blushed at the attention. 'I may have,' she said.

The King spread his hands over the table. 'Well, it's about time. I never really had a use for him, except to entertain the girls, but when he offered himself in exchange for your safety it was too good an opportunity to refuse. It's really about time he got the courage to ask someone to kill him and free him from the oath. He always was a shocking coward.'

Simone raised her chin, defiant. 'I think what he did was very brave.'

'Of course you do. I'm so glad for you, dear, you have a member of your family back. And soon you'll have Leo as well! This is marvellous news.'

'We need to know where Leo is so we can bring him out,' I said.

The King shrugged. 'Sorry, Emma. That one has been very quiet under the radar for the last eight years. You have my permission to enter the demonic side of Hell, but I'm afraid it is not within my ability right now to tell you where he is. Martin may be able to help you though.'

'We just had fourteen demon copies turn up at the Academy,' I said. 'They were destroyed when we removed the stones that were eroding our seals, and put the seals back up. Is it the same demon making the copies?'

'Excellent, you've found the problem with your seals,' the King said. 'I'd love to have a look at these stones that are causing the problem, must be extremely advanced breeding techniques to produce something like that. As to your question, I don't think it's the same demon making the stones and the copies. There may have been more than one of them in league with One Two Two, but I thought I'd destroyed them all.' He shrugged. 'Pain in the ass. We'll have to do something about it, eh?' He grinned around the table. 'Sorry I couldn't be more help, but you have Martin to help you now, and he certainly knows his way around Hell. Is that all?'

I glanced around at the Generals to see if they had anything to add. They all either sat impassively or shook their heads.

'That's all,' I said. 'If you gain any info on where Six is, we'd appreciate the help.'

'Anytime, Emma, anything for you, you know that.' The King rose, came to me, took my hand as if he was going to shake it, then kissed it. I snatched it back with revulsion when I felt his tongue on my skin. He moved closer to speak softly to me. 'I'd give you anything at all if you came to me for one night in Mother form. Anything in Hell would be yours.'

He nodded around the table and spoke more loudly. 'See ya, fellas.'

He and the Snake Mothers were about to leave when Er Lang appeared in the doorway, blocking their exit. Er Lang took a step forward into the King's personal space and the King backed up, glaring up at him.

Er Lang stared down at the Demon King. 'You are constantly attacking the Celestial. You should be punished.'

'I live in Hell, and cannot see the light of day without permission,' the Demon King said. 'Is that not punishment enough?'

'Stay in your own part of Hell, demon,' Er Lang said. 'Do not meddle in Celestial affairs.'

The Demon King backed up. 'Whatever.' He grinned at me. 'Later, darling Emma.' He turned back to see Simone. 'Congratulations on finding your brother, little one. It is good to see you with family.' He shoved past Er Lang and went out, the Snake Mothers following.

'What was all that about?' Marshal Ma said.

I sat at the table. 'Ming Gui, the Xuan Wu's son, gave an oath to the King of the Demons and was bound in servitude to him. In return, I think the King agreed not to harm either Simone or Xuan Wu.'

'That was a monumentally stupid thing to do,' Guan Yu said, 'but I can understand him wanting to make this sacrifice to keep his baby sister safe.'

'She killed Ming Gui before we came to this meeting. He is free from his oath. He says he can help us, but we need to bring him out of the tenth level as soon as possible.'

The Generals turned to study Simone appraisingly.

'She killed him?' Marshal Ma said.

'My brother is free; we just need to bring him out of Hell as quickly as we can,' Simone said.

We need to get rid of Er Lang and we can discuss a sortie into the demon side of Hell, Marshal Ma said into my head. *Close the meeting.*

He's right, Emma, Master Liu said. *The Generals can help with this, but not while Er Lang is here.*

I rose. 'Let's head to Hell immediately. I believe that I still have sanction. We'll prepare for a full-on nest raid, and meet at the docks in Shum Wan.'

The Masters and Generals saluted me, and rose to go out.

'One moment, madam,' Er Lang said as the Generals and Masters walked out.

I nodded to him. 'My Lord. Will you join us?'

'I am needed on the Celestial,' Er Lang said. 'I believe it would be unwise for the Princess to accompany you. She is too valuable to wander around Hell; it is too dangerous.'

Simone strode to Er Lang, put her hands on her hips and glared up at him. 'I'm a better demon killer than just about every other Celestial put together. I'm Princess of the Dark Northern Heavens, and Leo Alexander is my Retainer. Gold's also my Retainer, and his child has been taken. It's my *responsibility* as their

399

Lady to make sure that they're okay. Just because I'm young and female doesn't mean that I can't kick some demon ass.'

Er Lang smiled slightly down at her. 'You're right, Princess. You are young and female, and it really shouldn't be necessary for you to endanger yourself by going to some of the most disturbing parts of the Underworld.' He gestured with one hand to encompass the departing Generals and Masters. 'Some of these Celestial Worthies have fought demons for hundreds of years. Let them handle this for you. Go home, where you are safe.'

'Tell you what, Er Lang,' Simone said. 'How about you contact Yanluo Wang for us and arrange for my brother to be released from the tenth level quickly?'

'I really don't think that's necessary.'

She cocked her head at him. 'How about I *order* you to do it? Do I have precedence over you?'

His face went fierce with anger for a moment, then he made a visible effort to relax. 'That will not be necessary, Princess. Although you do not have precedence, we will see what we can do about releasing Ming Gui from the Underworld.'

She nodded to him. 'I thank you, sir. Now, if you will excuse me, I need to prepare for a sortie into Hell to release my Retainer's child.'

He nodded back to her. 'Madam.' He disappeared.

Simone sagged. 'I thought I would never get rid of him!' She turned back to me. 'They're coming back. I'd like to know what they want to say that he wasn't supposed to hear.'

The rest of the group reappeared around the conference table.

Marshal Ma gestured to me. 'Sit, Emma. Let's work this out.'

'Why did you need to get rid of Er Lang?' I said.

The Generals shared a look, then Marshal Ma said, 'That's not really important. What is important is finding this stone child and destroying Six. This has gone on for long enough.'

Martin appeared in the doorway. 'I can help.'

I waved him in. 'Come and tell us everything.'

CHAPTER 28

The hotel staffer appeared with a trolley of drinks and snacks. We waited impatiently while he carefully placed the platters of sandwiches and sushi on the table, presented everybody with small plates and napkins, then proceeded to set glasses for soft drinks as well as cups and saucers on the conference room sideboard.

'Leave that, we'll do it ourselves,' I said.

He nodded and went out, obviously relieved to escape the tension.

Martin saluted around the table. 'It is good to be free.' He nodded to Simone. 'Thank you, sister. Now I can take you to Six's nest. But you must know — there is more than just Six.'

'Four demons altogether, right?' I said. 'I remember them having meetings when I was held by One Two Two.'

Martin nodded. 'There are actually five — but nobody seems to know who the fifth is. Six and Three — male and female together, mother and son, who are the experts with stones. Then there is Fourteen — the Death Mother — she is the one that has made the demon copies. She escaped from the nests shortly after being promoted to Snake Mother and has created her own nest of vipers somewhere in the south. She is extremely cruel and dangerous. Thirty-Three, the technological expert, has been making the fake elementals for them. He is lazy and has no real ambition for himself except to survive and have an army of demon servants. There is one more — the expert with the energy. Nobody seems to know who it is.'

'I saw that energy destroy Xuan Wu in True Form,' I said.

'No energy should be able to destroy Xuan Wu's True Form,' Marshal Guan said.

'It's black and very scary,' Simone said. 'I saw it when I was little — Simon Wong used it on me, but I was full of yin and just absorbed it. It starts out a really pretty shade of blue, then turns black, and then just destroys everything. It's different from yin but it's still nasty stuff.'

'And you have no idea where the demon that produces this is?' I asked Martin.

'Nobody does,' Martin said. 'Maybe Kitty Kwok does, but she's keeping very much to herself.' He saw my face. 'Yes, Kitty is still alive, and working as a go-between for these four demons.'

'What's in it for her?' I said. 'She's lost all her assets on the Earthly Plane, and as a human she can't go anywhere on the Celestial.'

'Immortality,' Martin says. 'She is helping these demons because she thinks they can give it to her.'

'Immortality cannot be purchased,' Guan Yu said with disdain. 'It can only be earned with cultivation and merit.'

'She saw what Six and Three were doing with the stone Shen and adapted their methods to herself,' Martin said.

'Exactly what are they doing?' I said.

'They are in exile outside Hell, and any untamed demon that stays too long outside Hell will eventually weaken and die,' Martin said. 'To keep themselves alive, they kidnap stones and carve pieces off them to make children. But the children they create are artificial, because of the imprisonment of the parents. They are able to keep themselves alive using these artificial children, but to return to full strength they need the energy from a real stone child. It is possible that this is what they planned from the start when they sliced a piece off Gold eight years ago. Stone children are only born from the Grandmother once every thousand years or so, and born from the damage to a parent stone even less frequently.'

'And Kitty is using this stone energy too?' I said.

'No, Kitty is using the energy of human children to keep herself young. She believes that if she can take the energy from a Shen child, she will have Immortality.'

'Oh my God, the kindergartens,' I said.

'Yes. She was using the essence of the children to keep her young. The kindergartens were just a way of accessing them.'

'She wasn't young though, she looked mid-forties,' I said.

'She is one hundred and twenty-eight years old.'

'Dear Lord, I just thought she had an excellent plastic surgeon.'

'No surgery. Just draining children.'

'What about the legal implications of her being older than is humanly possible?' I said.

'Easy to change your birth details when people born in the Mainland in the past never had any sort of birth certificate,' Martin said.

'How would she drain the children?' Simone said. 'I was there, and she took samples off me — but I never felt drained.'

'Blood,' Martin said. 'The essence of life.' He nodded to me. 'You are probably aware of the thirst that demons have for blood. It is how they stay alive — draining the essence of other demons. To become extremely strong, they drain the blood and essence of humans.' He shook his head. 'But doing this to humans is not permitted under the terms of the treaty that Father brokered with Hell. Any demon caught doing this to humans is tried and destroyed by the Demon Courts.'

'But Kitty's not a demon,' I said.

'Exactly. She can work with impunity.'

'So Six and Three have Gold's child and copies of Leo — and probably the real Leo — in their nest,' I said. 'Let's worry about these two demons now, and then hunt down the other three later. We need to get Leo and Gold's child out *now*.'

I turned to the gathered Celestials. 'Now what did you want to share that Er Lang wasn't to hear?'

'Quite a few of the Generals have a demon form as well as their Celestial Form,' Marshal Guan said. 'They can enter Hell in that form without alerting the demons.'

'But that means Simone and I can't go,' I said.

'No, it just means you can't go,' Simone said, her voice small. 'I can do it too.'

I turned and stared at her. '*What?*'

'As a child of the Xuan Wu, it is not surprising that she has a demon form,' Martin said. He nodded to Guan Yu, who nodded back. 'Only four or five of the Generals do not.'

'But I can't go, I don't have one,' I said.

'Can she go as a snake?' Simone asked Martin. 'There are snakes in Hell.'

'I won't remember anything if I do,' I said.

'You have no choice,' Martin said. 'Humans and Celestials are not welcome there and will be attacked on sight. If you are a large enough demon, you will be kowtowed to — and there are snakes there.'

'So who of the Generals can come?' I said.

Guan Yu and Marshal Ma stopped and concentrated.

Ma snapped back first. 'Me. Zhou Gong Ming. Liang Tian's form is a little extreme, but he's willing. Marshal Shi of the Divine Thunder —'

'Lord *Shi* has a demon form?' I said. 'His normal form is an elderly scholar.'

'Wait till you see it, it's thoroughly over the top,' Ma said with humour. 'That should be enough; the four of us, you and Princess Simone.' He bowed to the White Tiger. 'Are you willing, my Lord?'

'Sure,' the Tiger said, his voice quiet and gruff. He'd reappeared at the end of the conference table with his wine. 'For these girls, I will.'

'That should suffice. I will guard the Gates while you are gone,' Guan Yu said.

Ma nodded. 'Guan Gong doesn't have a demon form.'

'I want to come too,' Michael said.

'Don't be ridiculous,' the Tiger said. 'You need a demon form to come along, and you don't have one. You're half-Tiger, half-human.'

'I have a demon form,' Michael insisted. 'It's a very big cat-looking thing, but —'

The Tiger interrupted him, quickly standing. 'You have a demon form? What the shit?'

Michael glowered at the Tiger for a moment, then said, 'Don't sound so surprised. You're a demon yourself.'

'I am not!' the Tiger roared, then grimaced and lowered his voice. 'I may have been fond of more variety in my diet in the past, but that's behind me, and I am *not* a demon.'

'Michael,' I said, and they both stopped to look at

me. 'Has Rhonda ever said anything about being more than human?'

'Yes,' Michael said, and the Tiger shot him a quick, stunned glance. 'She's often said that she wishes she was more than human so she could kick Dad's ass. And complained that she isn't.'

'So she's sure she's an ordinary human?' I said.

Michael nodded. 'Everything I have, I got from my dad.'

'Well, you didn't get a demon form from me,' the Tiger said gruffly. He saluted me. 'See you in Hell, babe.' He disappeared.

I turned to Marshal Ma. 'Is it possible Michael got his demon form from his father?'

'Of course it is,' Ma said. 'The Tiger may protest — and notice he protests very loudly — but he has very much more in common with the demons than he does with Celestials. Everybody knows that, and he's been trying to live it down for hundreds of years.'

'Well, let's head to Shum Wan and go to Hell,' I said. 'The quicker we depart, the quicker we find Gold's child.'

'Get your armour from the Academy first, ma'am,' Ma said. 'You may decide to fight in human form, and the Murasame could be a great asset.'

'I'll drive you,' Michael said.

The Generals and Celestials rose, their faces grim with satisfaction. Everybody saluted and they disappeared.

Simone grabbed a piece of sushi and wolfed it down, then gulped a quick drink of lemonade. She took a couple of sandwiches and rose. 'Let's go.'

We went up to the infirmary to check on the dragon before we departed. It was very quiet. Everybody was gathered in a semicircle in the waiting room, facing Hien who was in dragon form and holding Regina's head in her mouth. Her dragon was dark cobalt blue with lighter purple fins. Blood ran down Regina's face where the dragon's teeth had pierced her scalp and she seemed only semi-conscious, her eyes open and her body limp.

'Have we found her mother?' I said.

'Nobody knows who her mother is,' Amy said. 'You know what dragons are like. Even her mother probably has no idea who she is.'

Jim Edwards entered. 'Heard you were having some trouble with one of the little girls.' He saw Hien. 'Oh, my.'

He moved to the front of the group to face Hien. 'Hello, Hien. Remember me? I helped you out of that awful place you were in.'

'It hurts!' Hien wailed, her voice muffled by Regina's head. She shook Regina and the doctor flopped like a rag doll.

'Regina can take the pain away. You just need to let her go, honey,' Edwards said.

'She tried!' Hien said, her voice still muffled. 'It didn't work!'

'I'm not surprised — you're a reptile,' Edwards said with humour. 'You probably need some special reptile medicine.'

Hien stopped moving and concentrated on him. 'There is special medicine that can fix me?'

'How about you let Regina go, and we can have a look?' Edwards said.

Hien's bright blue eyes focused on him for a moment, then she dropped Regina.

'Good girl,' Edwards said. 'Now, what I want you to do is go into one of the treatment rooms and wait there, and we'll get someone who specialises in dragons to see what we can do about this.'

Hien jumped forward and took Regina's head in

her mouth again. 'Don't make me wait! It hurts too much!'

Edwards raised his hands. 'We won't make you wait. We just need to find someone who can help. Now drop Regina …'

Hien lowered her head, looking at him, then gently released Regina.

Edwards stepped forward and put his hand on Hien's head. 'Good girl. You're a very pretty dragon, you know that?' He opened one of the treatment room doors. 'Come in here and wait with me while they find someone to help you. I'll stay with you.'

'You'll stay?' Hien said, her voice full of hope.

Edwards stroked her head. 'I'll stay with you. Did you know, I know what you're going through because I used to have a daughter just like you, who was on this stuff too? I know how much it hurts.'

'You know?' Hien said, sounding more like a little girl than a dragon.

Edwards cupped her face with one hand and nodded. 'I know exactly what it feels like, and I know how to fix it. So come with me in here, and they'll find someone with the right stuff for you.'

Hien ducked her head and then gazed up at him again. 'Okay.'

He led her gently into the treatment room. As he closed the door, he grimaced back at us and mouthed, 'Better find something fast.'

As soon as the door closed we raced to Regina. She seemed unconscious. A couple of the students lifted her and carried her to the bed in the other treatment room.

'Find a dragon who is an expert in either transforming or, as Jim said, in healing,' Meredith said. 'Someone find Regina's sidekick, Edwin. He can take a look at her.'

She put her hands on Regina and concentrated. 'Never mind. Regina's dead.' She dropped her head and shook it, then gathered herself and looked up. 'Move, people! Dragons — find someone who can help.'

She saw Simone and me. 'Why aren't you in Hell getting Gold's baby out?'

'We're going now. We wanted to make sure Regina was okay,' Simone said.

Meredith sighed and looked down at Regina's limp body. Regina didn't seem dead; her eyes were open and her skin still had a normal flush. I touched her hand and it was still warm. A horrible heartless voice inside me commented on how alive she still looked, and an even more horrible voice lamented the loss of so much warm rich human blood.

My phone rang and I answered it. 'Emma.'

It was Edwards. 'She changed back. She's human. Get someone in here in a hurry, Emma.'

'Did you hear that?' I asked Meredith, but she'd already grabbed a syringe.

'Go, Emma,' she said as she filled it. 'We can handle the rest. We'll keep her sedated until we work out what to do.'

I touched Regina's hand again. 'I am so sorry, dear Regina. You worked so hard for all of us.'

'The Celestial Judiciary is going to be down on this poor little dragon like a ton of bricks,' Meredith said, her voice crisp. 'Hurry back, Lady Emma, she'll need a great deal of assistance to avoid a death penalty. Jim lost his daughter to drugs; let's not lose this little one too.'

'Let's go to Hell and find the demons that gave her the drugs in the first place,' Simone said. '*They're* the ones who are going to pay. For Regina, and for Hien.'

I turned to the door. 'Good idea, Simone. Some demons need to suffer for this.'

* * *

The lift to Hell once again let us out on the roof of the main administration building. Nobody else was there. We went down the stairs to the side of the lake and saw a large black Mercedes van parked on the road.

I stopped and stared. 'They have cars in *Hell*?'

Marshal Ma, still in human form, leaned out of the driver's side window. 'Of course we do. How else do we get around?'

'Float, fly, I don't know; however demons get around?' I said as I slid the side door open and pulled myself into the van.

Liang Tian, Marshal Zhou and Marshal Shi were already inside, looking like serene Confucian gentlemen in their traditional black robes. Martin sat in the front passenger seat, staring out the window. The Tiger was in the back row, scowling.

Simone and Michael climbed in behind me and seated themselves, we closed the door and Marshal Ma started the van.

'Not taking demon form yet?' I said.

'Not on the Celestial side, Emma,' Marshal Ma said as he pulled the van away from the kerb. 'We'd get ourselves killed.'

'Tell me more about this demon business,' I said as we drove along the side of the lake. 'Why do you all have demon forms?'

'You've obviously never read *Journey to the North*,' Marshal Zhou said, his bushy beard bristling. 'Have you read *Journey to the West*?'

'Got about halfway through, then it started getting really repetitive,' I said, ashamed. 'They go over a mountain, they get captured by demons, the Monkey King frees them, the monk admonishes everybody, and they journey to the next mountain where exactly the same thing happens again.'

The Generals chuckled.

'That's about the gist of it,' Marshal Ma said from the front. 'But you may have gleaned from the text that the Pig was a Heavenly General who was cast down from Heaven, and accidentally reborn from a pig's womb.'

I stared around at them. 'You were all cast down from Heaven? Is that why you have demon forms?'

'Something like that,' Marshal Zhou said.

'I have to read *Journey to the North* now,' I said, almost to myself.

'Would probably be a good idea,' the Tiger said from the back of the van. 'What I've done is *nothing* compared to what some of these guys got up to.'

'Oh, I wouldn't say that,' Marshal Ma called back. 'You've done some pretty despicable things in your time, my friend.'

The Tiger dropped his head and glowered. 'And we've all gained redemption.'

'I really need to read it,' I said.

'Me too,' Simone said. 'And *Daddy* did this too?' She turned to Martin. 'What about you?'

Martin's face went rigid. 'I have never been cast from Heaven.'

'What about —' the Tiger began, but Martin cut him off.

'I have never been cast from Heaven,' he repeated. 'I have been exiled from my clan, thrown from my family, but I have always acted with honour.'

We came to a causeway and Marshal Ma slowed the van. He turned left and the Judge's mansion at the Celestial end of the causeway appeared in front of us.

'We drive to the end, then we have to walk,' Ma said.

'Will there be issues with us going through the Gates?' Michael said.

'We take demon form inside the van, park it at the

end, and stroll out like we own the place,' Zhou said. 'We won't be questioned.'

'We just eat anything that stops us,' the Tiger growled.

'You will be with me. You will not be questioned,' Martin said.

'I can't change in here, there isn't room,' Liang Tian said. 'You'll have to park the van so it blocks their view of me, so I can change after I get out.'

'Not a problem,' Marshal Ma said. He picked up speed as he drove along the causeway across the absolutely waveless lake. 'It's about a fifty li drive. I suggest you do any preparation now; we have at least half an hour before reaching the demonic section.'

I turned to Marshal Zhao. 'Tell me about *Journey to the North*.'

Both the Generals in the back of the van grimaced. Martin remained impassive.

'Tell her, it's about fucking time,' the Tiger growled.

'Tigers don't tell me what to do,' Zhao snapped back.

'No, but we do,' Simone said, her voice sweet and childlike. 'And cut it out with the bad language, Uncle Bai.'

'Humph,' the Tiger said. He summoned a can of beer, opened it and took a swig, then settled back into his seat to look out the window.

'Some aspects of the story as it has been retold are wrong,' Zhou said. 'Lord Xuan Wu is not a soul of the Jade Emperor.'

'He's said that himself,' I said.

'The Turtle and Snake are not separate entities — well, not separate in the sense of separate from *him*. They *are* him.'

'In the story they are separate from him?'

Zhou nodded. 'And Avalokitesvara had very much more to do with this than is hinted at in the book —'

'Who?' Simone said.

'Avalokitesvara is Kwan Yin's Sanskrit name,' I said. Zhou nodded again.

'She's *Indian*?'

'She's a Bodhisattva, Simone. She isn't anything,' I said.

'That is correct in many more ways than one,' Ma said from the front of the car.

'He fell. He was redeemed. When he returned to Heaven, his Generals had also fallen and he made the journey to retrieve them,' Zhou said.

'Whoa, that's the *Reader's Digest* version of the *Reader's Digest* version,' the Tiger said.

'We're nearly there,' Zhou said.

'Some of you guys didn't fall,' the Tiger said.

'This is true. Guan Gong — I mean Guan Yu, Gao Yuan the Heavenly Star —'

'Is that why Gao Yuan glows all the time? He's a *star*?' Simone interrupted.

'Yes. His story is very sad, but I can't go into it. Ask him later. Marshals Deng and Zhang of the Thunder Gates, Heavenly Lord Xin, Grand Marshal Xiao of the Hours, Wang Tie of Tiger Peak —'

'Yeah, a few of you guys just went off and did your own thing but didn't eat people,' the Tiger said with humour. He swigged his beer. 'But a few of you went off — and *did* eat people.'

'No *way*,' Simone said. She stared at Marshal Zhou, wide-eyed. 'You *ate* people?'

The Generals were silent, all of them obviously embarrassed.

Simone turned to Marshal Ma, who was suddenly concentrating on driving. 'You *ate* people, General Ma?'

Ma grimaced, dropped his head, then raised it again, concentrating on the road. He sighed heavily, then replied, 'Okay, so sometimes presidents of countries have their sordid pasts brought up. Some of them may have done drugs when they were in high school —'

'But they didn't *murder people and eat them*!' Simone said.

'It's much the same thing though, my Princess. It's easy to become addicted to the blood of humans. We're all reformed addicts.'

He glanced over his shoulder, saw my face and smiled slightly. He knew my cravings.

Simone turned to look out the window. 'I'm consorting with murderers and cannibals.' She leaned her head on the glass. 'And my father was the biggest one of all.'

'Reformed, judged, punished and redeemed,' Zhou said. 'He gave us the Fire Pill and enabled us to control our addiction —'

'Holy shit, that means you're all tame demons,' Simone said, her head snapping around to see him. 'That's what we do to tame them — give them the Fire Essence Pill. It took me a long time to learn that at the Academy!'

'That's the point they're trying to make, honey,' the Tiger said. He dropped his voice. 'And you complain about *me* using bad language.'

Simone turned back to the window. 'What about Daddy — is he a demon too?' She turned to gaze at Zhou. 'Am I half-demon? Is that what it means that I can take this demonic form?' Her eyes went wide. 'And who gave *him* the Fire Pill?'

'Nobody needed to,' Martin said, breaking in. 'He met Avalokitesvara and decided on this path himself, the path to redemption. He attained the Tao with her assistance. He is the mightiest creature ever to have shaken off his past and turned to the Celestial.'

'Will he revert to demon when he becomes whole?' she said, her voice small.

'There is no chance of that at all,' Ma said with conviction. 'He has changed more than any of us. He will never return to that path, it cannot happen. He is either the Xuan Wu the animal spirit, or Xuan Tian the Celestial General.'

'We're here,' Ma said.

There was a small car park with space for about ten cars at the end of the causeway. Ahead was a towering craggy black cliff seemingly made of some type of shining glass, with enormous red doors, about fifty metres high, adorned with black metal studs, much like the doors of the Celestial Palace. Demon guards in armour carrying swords stood on either side of the gates, like statues.

Ma parked the van sideways to the gate — there were no other cars there — and turned off the engine. He turned to speak to us. 'Who is bigger than the inside of the van?'

'Just about all of us, Ah Guang,' Marshal Zhou said.

Ma peered out the front windscreen. 'Only two guards on the Gates, and they look parked. Might as well go for it. Use the van as cover.'

We slid the door open and got out. Everybody stood there, obviously hesitant at changing. Martin didn't bother waiting: he took his demonic form again — black skin with long bright red hair, bulging eyes, and tusks. He raised one clawed hand and summoned the Silver Serpent, the sword that Xuan Wu had originally given to me.

He grimaced. 'I still have your sword. Do you want it back?'

'Was it yours originally?' I said.

He nodded his massive demon head. 'Father had it forged for me. When I was disowned, he took it from me.'

'Keep it,' I said.

Marshal Ma grew and thickened and his skin turned green. His clothing changed from a business suit to a traditional black silk robe, and his face became longer and his eyes round and bulging. His mouth thickened and became redder. When he was about two-and-a-half metres tall he stopped growing, and visibly relaxed.

'Haven't done that in a while,' he said.

'You look nearly human,' I said.

He bowed slightly. 'I thank you, madam.'

Zhao Gong Ming and Shi Cheng shared a look, then both changed at the same time. They took similar demonic forms: Zhao was red all over with scales and tusks, and Shi went completely white. They both wore traditional black lacquer armour. Shi Cheng carried a long, narrow sword with characters along its length. Zhao held a golden leather strap in his left hand, and in his right a sword embellished with tigers on the hilt.

The Generals bowed slightly to me, and Zhao grinned, revealing his fearsome tusks.

Liang Tian, who usually appeared as a middle-aged scholar with a refined, elegant face, grimaced. 'They're right. My demon form is a bit extreme.' He appeared embarrassed. 'Please don't take fright at it — and you need to move back, it's large.'

'Let's see it,' I said, curious.

Liang Tian changed quickly, the transformation taking only a few seconds. His body went from human to long and serpent-like, then to that of a dragon on all fours with black scales and claws, three metres long. But his head was like a Chinese lion, all fangs, bulging eyes and a mane of large scales. He shook his head and opened his mouth, revealing his huge red tongue.

'Frankendragon,' Simone said. 'You look like two monsters glued together.'

Liang Tian bowed slightly to her. 'I shall take that as a compliment, miss.'

'Your turn. Let's see it, ma'am,' Ma said. 'I've heard an awful lot about this famous serpent form.'

I gestured towards Simone, the Tiger and Michael. 'Me last. You guys first.'

'Why?' the Tiger said.

'Because I might slip into demon form,' I said.

None of the Generals seemed surprised.

General Ma nodded his huge green head. 'I understand. You last.' He turned to the Tiger, Simone and Michael. 'Any chance of the demon side taking over on you three?'

'No guarantee I won't eat anything,' the Tiger said gruffly, and changed. He grew taller and his head became much larger, turning into a full tiger's head with long fangs. His body filled out, still remaining reasonably human, and his clothes shrank to a simple tiger-skin loincloth. His hands grew and spread into paws with fearsome long claws that hung level with his knees. He shook his head. 'Been a while for me too.'

Michael's change was sudden. His body lengthened and grew pale gold tiger fur with black stripes, and as it lengthened he fell forward to stand on all fours. His head also became a tiger's head, with a shaggy mane. He must have been at least three metres from nose to tail.

'That's not too different from your tiger form,' Simone said.

'Different enough,' Michael said, his tiger vocal cords making his voice a rough growl. He raised his black nose to her. 'Your turn.'

Simone concentrated, and suddenly grew so that she was at least thirty centimetres taller, and her skin went completely black. Her jeans and T-shirt changed to flowing black robes, and her fingers lengthened and grew long nails that were almost claws. Reptilian scales appeared all over her body, and her face became more narrow and reptilian, her nose disappearing and her large green eyes showing slits instead of pupils. Her legs stayed in normal human shape but were black and covered with scales. She bent forward, stretched her scaled arms in front of her, then, with a growl, threw herself back again to complete the form.

Everyone stared at her in awe.

She rubbed her clawed hands over her face. 'I *hate* this form. It's really itchy.' She gestured towards me. 'Your turn, Emma.'

'I really don't want to do this. I don't remember anything that happens while I'm in this form,' I said.

'You can always stay behind,' the Tiger said. 'Wait here for us.'

I didn't reply, I just changed. I concentrated on taking the serpent form, and slid into it easily; nearly as easily as demon form. When I lifted my head it was about the same height as Simone's.

'You there, Emma?' Simone said.

'Yeah,' I said. I flicked my tongue and tasted the air. It smelt/tasted foul: the presence of the demons and the demonic side of Hell close by. 'This place really stinks.'

Michael raised his head and sniffed. 'That it does.'

Martin hefted his sword. 'Follow me. I will guide.'

Ma raised one arm. 'Lead on, Gui Dai Ren.'

CHAPTER 29

We followed Martin to the base of the gates and the demon guards changed from inactive automatons to living creatures. They raised their pole arms, then saw Martin and lowered them again, falling to their knees. Martin raised one hand and the gates opened slowly and smoothly inwards. A blast of foul-tasting stale air hit us and we went in.

The tunnel was the same craggy obsidian as the cliffs the gates were set into, as high and wide as the gates themselves. We travelled along the smooth floor for some distance and Martin obviously relaxed.

'I still have the King's endorsement,' he said. 'I wonder how long it will be before he removes it.' He dropped his head. 'Then there will be no place for me, in either Heaven or Hell, again.' He raised his head. 'I will return to the ocean.'

'Don't lay a guilt trip on the girl,' the Tiger said. 'You chose this path. You have a lot to prove.'

'Don't worry, Uncle Bai,' Simone said, her voice hissing. 'I wasn't about to feel sorry for him.'

Martin shot a quick, appraising glance at Simone, then turned back. 'It is a long way, past the Pits, to Six's nest. It is beyond the edge of Hell, in caverns under Shantou.'

'Avoid the Pits if you can,' the Tiger said.

Martin nodded once sharply. 'We will.'

'I can see the Pits anyway,' Simone said. 'The King said he didn't know where Six had his nest. How come you do, Martin?'

'Exactly what words did the King use?' Martin said.

'He didn't say that at all, Simone,' I said. 'He knows exactly where the nest is, he just doesn't want to be involved. He wants us to do all his dirty work for him.'

'I was sure he said he didn't know where the nest is,' Simone said, sounding unsure.

'Stone?' I said.

The stone was embedded in my flesh roughly where my shoulder would be if I wasn't a snake. It didn't reply.

I shook myself. 'Stone!'

'Hmm, Emma? What?'

'Don't fall asleep on me now,' I said. 'We're going to Six's nest. Replay the King's words where he said it wasn't within his power to tell us where Six is.'

The stone replayed the King's voice. *'I'm afraid it is not within my ability right now to tell you where he is. Martin may be able to help you though.'*

'Oh, that bastard,' Simone said. 'He didn't say anything of the sort.'

'He says that it's "not within his ability" when he doesn't want to do something,' I said.

'Why didn't you call him on it?' Simone said.

'What would be the point? We have Martin, who I trust twenty times more than I trust the King.' I waved my serpent head at him. 'But that's twenty times nothing, Ming Gui.'

Martin shrugged. 'I have a great deal of atonement to perform.'

'That you do,' the Tiger said. He straightened slightly. 'Heads up.'

The way was blocked by a couple of demon dukes, both of them with the bodies of heavily muscled men and the heads of horses. They turned when they saw us and took positions of alert.

'What are all of you doing here?' one of them said. 'I have never seen you on level six before.'

'They are with me,' a voice behind them said.

They both dropped to one knee and lowered their horse heads. 'Da Shi Yeh.'

The Generals and the Tiger quickly dropped to one knee as well.

Kowtow quick, the Tiger said, and Simone dropped, lowering her serpent-like head. Michael knelt with one foreleg, and I did the same as Simone, lowering my serpent head.

The demon Da Shi Yeh — Ancient Demon Grandfather — appeared as a bent, wizened old man wearing a tattered sackcloth shift that came to just above his bony knees, and leaning on a long knotty wooden staff; the only sign of his demon nature was his bright blue skin. He grinned at the demon dukes. 'Let them come with me. I asked them here to help out with some of the Mothers. An *extremely large* Mother's clutch is about to hatch and these serpent demons — and their guards — may be able to assist.' His grin widened slightly. 'Do you want to come help?'

The demon dukes rolled their eyes like terrified horses.

'That will not be necessary,' one of them said.

The other waved us on. 'Go with the Venerable Grandfather.'

Da Shi Yeh led us further down the corridor. It narrowed, and other passages appeared on either side, but the walls were still black glass.

'Thank you, sir. We can go the rest of the way ourselves now,' General Ma said.

Da Shi Yeh grinned over his shoulder at Ma. 'Not that easy, my friend. You must pay a price for my assistance.'

'What price is that?' Martin said, suspicious.

Da Shi Yeh continued walking down the corridor. 'I really do need your help. I did not lie to the dukes. There is a very, very large Mother in the nest cavern up ahead, and her clutch really is about to hatch. I need the assistance of the beautiful serpent ladies here to help me salvage a couple of the spawn. I think they may very well be the most powerful demons that Hell has seen in a while — perhaps even a future King.'

'Do you know why we're here?' I said.

Da Shi Yeh shrugged. 'Of course I do, but that is inconsequential to me. I am here to ensure that the spawn hatch successfully. Apart from that, I do not care for the politics or power plays. The King leaves me alone to do my work, and I return the favour.'

'If you stopped assisting the hatchlings, would demon reproduction stop altogether?' Simone said.

Da Shi Yeh stopped and turned to her, smiling broadly. 'Oh, you *are* your father's daughter, dear!' He turned back and raised his staff. 'The cavern is just up ahead.'

Simone looked down. 'I've had about enough of nest caverns.'

'Me too,' I said.

'Holy *shit*,' the Tiger said in front of us.

'Whoa,' Michael said.

We reached the end of the tunnel and stopped. It opened into a nest cavern that had to be at least four hundred metres across, with a ceiling so high it was invisible. Snake Mothers writhed across the floor, some in their nest indentations with their eggs, others

423

appearing to be chatting, or sitting on piles of cushions watching the several widescreen plasma televisions standing around the edges. A couple were in human form, sitting on the stone floor playing handheld video games; but the rest were in True Form, at least four metres long.

'These things are *huge*,' the Tiger said under his breath.

'The eggs that are about to hatch are in the middle,' Da Shi Yeh said, and walked without hesitation towards the centre of the cavern.

Simone sidled closer to me. 'This is very scary.'

Michael, the Tiger and the Generals moved to form a protective shield around Simone and me. When the Mothers nearby saw us they dropped what they were doing and quickly slithered closer to examine us.

'Ignore them. This way,' Da Shi Yeh said from the darkness.

'That's very easy for him to say,' Simone said.

One of the Mothers raised herself on her serpent tail to see us more clearly. 'Oh, look, girls, snake soup,' she said.

'I adore snake broth,' another said, her voice hissing.

'Perfect for the winter, heats up the blood,' the first one said.

We continued walking, trying to ignore them, but they matched our pace. As we passed more Mothers they joined the group.

'Did Little Grandfather bring us some toys?' one said. She reached out to the Tiger and he slapped her hand away. Her voice changed to petulance. 'Little Grandfather only brings toys to the biggest. *We* want some too!'

'Ooh, toys, really?' another Mother said as we passed her. 'I *love* playing with snakes! And these are big demons too!' She clapped her hands. 'Little Grandfather brought us some *toys*!'

'Me first, me first, I haven't played with anything in ages,' one of them said. She had a small scuffle with another Mother that was blocking her from moving closer to us. 'Mine!'

Some of the other Mothers heard her and approached. We now had at least fifteen enormous Mothers hovering on their serpent tails over us, arguing over who would be the first to play with us.

Da Shi Yeh stomped back to us and waved his staff at the Mothers. 'These aren't toys for you, girlies. Go back to your soap operas. They're with me; you can't play with them.'

One of the Mothers poked her tongue out at him — all thirty centimetres of it. 'You're no fun at all. Bring us *toys*! Tell the King we want toys.'

'Yes! Tell him to send us toys or no sex for him!' one of the other Mothers said, and laughed.

A third nudged her. 'Don't be silly, Fifty-Three. You deny him and he kills you.'

'I know that,' Fifty-Three said. 'I was just joking.'

'These demons are with me. Leave them alone,' Da Shi Yeh said, and gestured for us to follow him.

A very large Mother, with a thickly scaled black tail and a heavy-set human torso, spoke with a deep, almost masculine voice. 'Is Seventeen's clutch about to pop?'

The Mothers suddenly stilled. Those who had been moving away stopped to listen as well.

'Don't you worry about what's happening in the middle,' Da Shi Yeh said. 'You stay away from those big ones, they'll eat your tails for breakfast.'

'But their babies won't,' the big Mother said.

'Ooh, babies,' Fifty-Three said. 'I love babies.'

'Nearly as good as snake broth,' one of the other Mothers said.

'You going to fight a Mother in the centre for her clutch?' Da Shi Yeh said with amusement.

The Mothers hesitated at that, then most of them wandered back to their cushions and televisions.

A couple stayed. 'You would protect us, Little Grandfather,' one said. 'Let us see.'

'I want to see,' the other said.

'I cannot protect you from something as big as her,' Da Shi Yeh said.

'You both wanna die? Go right ahead,' the older Mother said. 'I'm going to watch TV.'

The two smaller Mothers shared a look, then both turned and slithered away.

'So restless right now,' Da Shi Yeh said. 'Let's go.' He led us through to the Mothers in the centre of the nest.

'How many in here?' I said.

'About fifty. The King has been extremely productive,' Da Shi Yeh said. 'Might have to move some of these out; we're beginning to lose the ones around the edges.'

'They kill each other?' I said.

'Don't ask obvious questions like that in here — you're supposed to be a demon,' General Ma said very softly into my serpent ear.

'Why didn't they recognise Martin?' I said. Martin had remained at the back of the group, quiet and cowed, during the whole episode.

'I only came here in Celestial Form,' Martin said. 'They wanted me as a Shen.'

'Or you didn't come here at all and the King was lying,' I said.

'I can change to Shen form and have them recognise me — and then play with me, if you like,' Martin said.

'I don't think that will be necessary,' I said.

The number of Mothers in the cavern thinned as we approached the centre.

'Here's the clutch,' Da Shi Yeh said.

A group of Mothers stood in a circle around the eggs that were about to hatch. They were really big ones, at least five metres long, some of them even longer. They towered over us in their True Forms.

Da Shi Yeh casually hit a few of them with his staff and they moved back for him, hissing with menace.

Seventeen was wrapped protectively around her eggs, glaring at the Mothers hovering over her nest. She relaxed slightly when she saw Da Shi Yeh. 'I thought you'd never get here, Grandfather.'

Da Shi Yeh raised his arms at the other Mothers. 'You girls go away *now* and let us do this.' He waved his staff and they hissed at him. 'Shoo!' He grinned over his shoulder at me. 'Give me a hand, people.'

Simone grew another sixty centimetres so that she was as large as the biggest Mother. She slapped a few of them on the head and shoulders, easily avoiding their retaliatory blows. 'You heard him! Move back.'

The Mothers retreated, making swipes in the air in Simone's direction, but she wasn't intimidated by them. She grabbed one around the middle, lifted it easily and tossed it away from the nest cavity. 'Move *back*!'

The Mother she'd thrown raised herself and slithered quickly away. The other Mothers moved back to form a wall of waiting demons, just out of her reach.

'That'll do nicely, thank you, missy,' Da Shi Yeh said. 'Now, let's see what we have here.'

He approached the clutch and Seventeen hissed at him, rising on her coils. He slapped her snake end — 'Don't try that with me' — and she subsided. The clutch was five eggs, each about forty centimetres across, the slightly translucent shells showing the dark shapes of the baby demons within. He put his hand on one of the eggs and concentrated for a moment, then summoned a stethoscope from the air and put it in his ears. He

427

listened to the egg, then nodded, satisfied, and made the stethoscope disappear. 'Right on time.'

He gestured for us to gather and listen. 'When they start to hatch, we won't have much time. You'll have to move fast, people. Let her have the first one or two, they'll keep her busy, but once her immediate urge is satisfied she'll be paying more attention and she'll try to stop you. So as soon as one hatches — even if part of it emerges from the shell — grab it and move way back. Then you'll have to stop the other Mothers from eating it.' He straightened. 'Piece of cake really.'

'Why don't you just take the eggs away from her and let them hatch in a safe place?' Simone said.

'They die,' Da Shi Yeh said. 'If they spend more than a couple of hours away from her, they lose energy and die. And if we tried to take them now, she'd just smash them anyway.'

One of the eggs rocked. The baby demon inside hammered at the shell, and Seventeen raised her skinless body, staring transfixed at the egg.

A piece of shell broke away, punched out by the tiny black demon hand inside. Seventeen swooped on it, but Simone was faster. She pounced on Seventeen, grabbed her by the throat and stared at her. Seventeen stared back, flicking her long snake-like tongue, but didn't move otherwise.

'I have her bound,' Simone said. 'She can't move. Take the demon spawn.'

'How long can you hold her?' Da Shi Yeh said.

'I dunno, five or six minutes?' Simone said, staring at Seventeen.

'Should be long enough,' Da Shi Yeh said.

He went to the egg, grabbed the demon hand that had appeared through the shell and yanked the demon out. He lifted it by the arm as it hissed and kicked, trying to bite him. It was about ninety centimetres at full length, a black humanoid with bulging eyes and small horns protruding all over its head. He smiled up at Seventeen. 'It's a girl.'

Three of the eggs began to hatch at the same time, the shells cracking.

'Move quickly,' Da Shi Yeh said.

'That would be a good idea, 'cause I can't hold this Mother forever,' Simone said.

'Let us know when you start to lose it and we'll let her have the rest,' Da Shi Yeh said. 'We're lucky to have even one from a clutch this big.' He raised the spitting demon he was holding. 'You are so *cute*!'

The Tiger strode into the clutch, pulled a cracked shell away, and lifted out a red demon child that was a similar size to the black one. He yelled and shook his hand as it bit him, then changed his grip so he held it by the throat. The demon struggled furiously in his grasp, clawing at his arm as he threaded his way out of the clutch to the edge of the indentation next to Da Shi Yeh. 'Cranky little bastards.'

'Get that wound cleaned up later,' Da Shi Yeh said. 'Otherwise it'll go septic — their saliva is toxic.'

The Tiger checked his clawed hand. 'Charming.'

An egg in front of me cracked open and a tiny naked twenty-year-old man, only about a metre tall, emerged.

'A human, grab it!' Da Shi Yeh said.

I lashed out with my serpent head and took it by the abdomen in my mouth, carefully not squeezing hard enough to hurt it. I pulled my head back out of reach of the other eggs while it kicked and raked at me with its fingers. The fluid from the egg that still covered the baby demon hit my sensitive taste buds. 'God, it tastes *awful*.'

'Let me see how *you* taste, bitch,' it said, still flailing at me. 'Let me *go*!'

'A real prize,' Da Shi Yeh said.

Another egg burst open and General Ma reached in and pulled out another black baby demon. He brought it to Da Shi Yeh.

'The King will be very pleased,' Da Shi Yeh said.

The demon I was holding was slimy from the egg fluid and it slipped out of my mouth. I lunged forward to grab it, but I was too slow. It moved faster than any human could, ran to Da Shi Yeh, scrambled up his leg to his torso, reached the demon he was holding, and bit it on the face and throat repeatedly, making it howl.

I made another lunge and grabbed the human-like demon again, this time with a stronger grip. I pulled it with difficulty off the demon that Da Shi Yeh was holding, and moved back.

Da Shi Yeh studied the injured demon.

'I can't hold her much longer,' Simone said. 'You have twenty seconds.'

'On the count of three, let her go,' Da Shi Yeh said. 'One ... two ... three!'

Simone released the Mother and scrambled back. At the same time, Da Shi Yeh threw the injured baby at the Mother, and she caught it with one hand then raised it to her face. She unlocked her jaw, opening her mouth wider than was humanly possible, shoved its head in, then snapped her jaws shut.

'Well done, everybody,' Da Shi Yeh said. 'Salvaging three from a clutch this big is unheard of — and particularly one that is a human-shaped demon. The King will be very pleased.'

The Mother lowered herself on her coils, crunching the baby's head in her mouth. The final egg hatched and she grabbed the baby out of it, holding it with her other hand.

A few of the other Mothers sidled towards us, and Seventeen hissed at them. They retreated, intimidated.

'Let's take these to the nursery,' Da Shi Yeh said. 'Then I'll show you the way to where you need to go.'

He led us away from Seventeen towards the other side of the cavern.

'Oh, Little Grandfather!' Seventeen called from behind us, her mouth full of demon baby.

Da Shi Yeh turned back. 'Yes, sweetie?'

Seventeen gestured to one side, still holding the half-eaten corpse. 'Some Mainland *slut* went and blocked up the toilets again — probably throwing her sanitary pads down there. Teach those cows how to use civilised bathrooms, for God's sake!'

'At least we're not spoiled helpless *bitches* like you Hong Kong scum,' one of the other Mothers shouted.

Seventeen rounded on her. 'You Mainland whores throw trash everywhere and shit all over the bathroom. You're *animals*.'

'We are not!' another Mother shouted. 'At least we know how to clean up after ourselves, and don't squeal for servants to wipe our precious little asses!'

The Mothers started squabbling, some of them trading blows. Demon guards in the form of human eunuchs appeared out of the darkness and lashed at the Mothers with bullwhips, cracking them loudly and making the Mothers howl with pain. The fighting Mothers scattered.

'Let's get this done quickly,' Da Shi Yeh said, 'so I can come back and sort this out.'

He led us to the side of the cavern, where a simple pair of large wooden double doors, painted green, were set into the obsidian wall. He raised his staff and the doors opened in front of us, leading into what appeared to be a hospital corridor.

'Nursery's this way,' Da Shi Yeh said, gesturing with his staff.

He took us to the end of the corridor where another pair of double doors opened to a room that looked like an animal-testing lab. Large barred metal cages, each about a metre cubed, lined the walls of the room, stacked three high. Some of the cages held small demons, which threw themselves at the bars trying to reach us, clawing at the air, screeching with frustration. A stainless-steel veterinary examination table stood in the middle.

A small Snake Mother, only about three metres long, came in holding a clipboard. 'This Seventeen's baby?'

Da Shi Yeh gestured expansively. 'We got *three* out, and one of them is human!' He waved his arms with glee. 'Three babies!'

The Snake Mother stared at him, then glanced at the struggling babies we were holding. 'Unusual.' She opened three cage doors, the metal squeaking. 'Toss them in here.'

'Help me close the door on it,' I said, my voice muffled by the demon in my mouth.

Michael raised himself on his hind legs and put one paw on a barred door. 'Go ahead.'

I tossed the human-shaped demon into the cage and Michael slammed the door shut before it had a chance to escape.

The Snake Mother went to the bars and studied it, just out of reach of its grasping hands. 'And the King sired this on Seventeen?'

Da Shi Yeh shrugged. 'I don't ask their parentage, I just stop their mommies from eating them. But the King's the only one big enough to sire spawn on Seventeen, you know that.'

The Snake Mother continued to study the baby demon. 'I know. But still ... never seen a human come from this pairing before.'

'Whatever, we have places to go,' Da Shi Yeh said. 'We'll take some flyers.'

The Snake Mother indicated behind her with her chin. 'There's six or seven next door; you can take them if you like. Just make sure they come back in one piece; they're to be handed to the troops later this week.'

'Why?' I said.

The Snake Mother glanced at me, then pointedly ignored me and spoke to Da Shi Yeh. 'They're well trained, they just need their final battle training, so don't get them destroyed, okay? A lot of work went into them.'

'Don't worry, we're not going anywhere particularly dangerous,' Da Shi Yeh said.

The Snake Mother nodded. 'I trust you, Little Grandfather.'

'This way,' Da Shi Yeh said, and took us into the next room.

It looked very much like the stables at the Jockey Club riding facility: concrete stalls, the floor of each thick with rice straw. The demon flyers were black and similar to dragons, but more lizard-like, with four legs and two bat-like wings. Some were standing in their stalls; others were lying down half-asleep.

'Flyers aren't intelligent?' I said as the demons saw us and rose with curiosity, poking their heads out of the stalls. They seemed completely unafraid of my serpent form.

Martin dropped his voice so that nobody nearby could hear his answer. 'No, they're just like animals, but they are occasionally used for crossbreeding with low-level demon thralls.'

I dropped my voice as well. 'I should know that, shouldn't I.'

'There's a lot that you and I don't know, Emma,' Simone said, her voice similarly soft. 'I s'pose I really should spend more time finding this stuff out.' She rounded on the Tiger. 'And don't mention CH!'

The Tiger raised both clawed hands. 'Never said a word, sweetheart.'

'You ride these to Six's nest,' Da Shi Yeh said. 'Just hop on and I'll tell them where to go. Wherever they land, that's the destination. Jump off; they'll come back here.' He shrugged. 'Easy.'

'You're not coming with us?' Simone said.

'No, I'd better sort my girls out,' Da Shi Yeh said. 'I don't like to see them fighting. Then I have some other places I need to be.'

'I can't ride something like this, I'm a freaking snake,' I said.

'Just wrap your body around it, it'll be fine,' Da Shi Yeh said. 'They're used to it.'

I gestured towards General Liang, with his dragon-like body and monstrous head, and Michael in demon form, on all fours. 'What about them? They can't ride like that.'

'I can fly myself,' General Liang said.

'So can I,' Michael said.

'Go into a stall and hop on top of one.' Da Shi Yeh bowed slightly to me. 'Or wrap yourself around one and then just hold on. I'll do the rest.'

Ask General Ma if we can really trust this guy! I said to the stone.

I don't need to, the stone said. *You can trust him.*

How do you know?

I'll tell you later.

I hissed under my breath with frustration, and carefully went to one of the stalls. The flyer inside watched me suspiciously as I neared it, but didn't make a move to attack me. I cautiously moved to its left side, hoping that they were trained to be mounted from the near side, the same as horses, then put my chin on its back. It stayed unmoving, not attempting to fight me, so I slid my head to rest on top of its, then wrapped my body around it, carefully keeping my coils free of its wings so that it would be able to fly unobstructed.

I raised my head to see the rest of the group.

Everybody except for Michael and Liang Tian was mounted astride.

Da Shi Yeh looked around at everybody. 'Ready?'

Nobody replied, in the typical Chinese way of indicating yes without saying anything. 'Ready,' I said.

Da Shi Yeh concentrated. 'Okay, I'm telling these little fellows where to go. Just hold on tight, you'll be travelling through the air ducts. It may get a little ...' He hesitated. '... Tight.'

Oh, wonderful, the stone said. *Can I go home now?*

The gate of the stall opened by itself and the flyer carefully walked out, as if testing my weight. The other flyers carried their riders in a coordinated queue towards the large doors at the end of the stable. Mine moved more easily as it worked out my weight.

'How far is it?' I said.

'About four hundred li,' Da Shi Yeh said.

'That's a couple of hours' travel,' the Tiger said, glaring back at Da Shi Yeh. 'No *way* is the Hell ventilation system that big!'

'Shows how much you know, Mr Pussycat,' Da Shi Yeh said. He waved to us and turned away. 'Have fun, and give my regards to the Black Lion. The Japanese have a word for such as he — *Samurai.*' He grinned knowingly over his shoulder at me, then went back to the nursery, closing the doors behind him.

Holy shit, that was —

Don't even think it! the stone said. *And don't say anything out loud to anybody — anywhere! He helps the Mothers hatch their clutches, and he visits with the longer-term residents of the Pits to give them some comfort. He is who he is and nothing more. Anything said anywhere could put him in peril.*

I was silent for a moment, then, *I understand.*

We are not going to dwell on this matter any longer. Oh, and hold on.

CHAPTER 30

We went through the doors to a large domed room with holes at irregular intervals in the ceiling. I coiled my body slightly tighter around the flyer as it took a few running steps forward, then launched itself into the air, surrounded by the other flyers. With each beat of its wings it fell then jerked upwards again. I had never ridden a flying creature with wings before and the sensation was rough and unsteady, each tiny gust of wind seeming to throw it sideways, its wings making it lurch clumsily through the air.

The flyer rose quickly and I clutched its body, hoping I wouldn't slide off in the steep ascent. It rapidly approached one of the holes and I raised my head slightly. It wouldn't fit into that hole; no *way* it would fit in that hole.

I know, I know, but it will fit. Unfortunately it will fit, the stone said.

The flyer approached the too-small hole at collision speed, then was deafened by a wall of pressure as it entered the hole. I was sure that its wingtips had clipped the sides as we went in.

Actually, it had at least a metre on each side to spare, the stone said. *But I hate it too.*

We were now in a perfectly dark tunnel, with flashes of light appearing and disappearing down the sides; I wasn't sure if they were really there or if the darkness was tricking my eyes.

Are the rest of the group okay and with us? I said.

They are.

We lurched sideways in the darkness, then fell almost straight down for two hundred and fifty metres. I clutched the flyer and it bent its head back to nip at my coils, then levelled out. I released it slightly and it took a huge breath.

Don't strangle it, Emma, the stone said.

Hard not to when it feels like we're falling out of the air.

Just try to relax, Simone said. *I know it's hard for you 'cause you can't see, but it's really very interesting for us who can — you should see all the stuff below us!*

I raised my head and peered down past the flyer's head, but I couldn't see anything. It suddenly veered left, went up fifty metres, then veered right.

The tunnel disappeared, and I was in human form riding the Blue Dragon over the water towards the city of Kota Kinabalu. I was wearing a gorgeous pale blue cotton gi that the staff of Qing Long's undersea palace had provided me with when John had ripped my clothes off in one of his enjoyable fits of passion. I leaned slightly right and looked down; John was sliding through the water below us, stretched out as if he was flying, matching our speed through the dark water. I straightened and looked up to see the star-filled sky.

'Thank you, stone,' I said.

'Just remember to keep holding on tight, dear,' the stone said. 'I'm sharing this recording because I'm finding this whole dodging-blind-through-narrow-tunnels thing as distressing as you are.'

The Blue Dragon's frill was like a soft chamois, glittering blue and silver in the moonlight.

'Tell me, Qing Long,' I shouted over the wind whistling in my ears.

'You do not need to shout,' the Dragon said, as if his mouth was next to my ear. 'You are sitting close to my lizard ears and they just need the vibration of your voice for me to hear you. Talk normally.'

'Lizard ears?'

'I don't know how they work, but they do. Ask your questions.'

'Sorry,' I said. 'So tell me, you have an undersea palace, but your nature is wood?'

'That it is, madam,' the Dragon said. 'All serpents are aligned with water. Some of us have wings, some of us have legs, but all of us are aligned with the life-giving rain that feeds the world.'

'I'm a serpent too,' I said. 'Why are you so afraid of what you saw inside me?'

The Dragon stiffened slightly beneath me, then relaxed again. 'What I saw was not pure serpent. Serpent is life-giving water, the rain that allows things to grow. Serpent is the power of healing and poisons to bring both life and death. Serpent is the weather that moves the world. What I saw was not like that. It was just destruction, not life-giving.'

'Hopefully one day we can find out what it is — and remove it.'

'I'm sure Ah Wu is working on it,' the Dragon said.

'So the serpent is the bringer of life. I can see the connection with wood, with growing things, now.'

'I have a Wood Palace as well, same as the Phoenix has her Fire Palace,' the Dragon said. 'It is more in the East, off Japan. You must come and see it some day.'

'I would love to,' I said.

The Dragon flew lower, writhing with ease through the air and providing me with a completely smooth ride. John's long hair flew behind him as he moved through the water just beneath the surface, the reflected light of the stars rippling above him. He saw me and smiled slightly; then lifted just out of the water and turned onto his back. Then he dived backwards under the water again.

I felt a pang of pain. I hadn't spent every precious second that I could have with him; I'd spent far too much time working on my degree and teaching at the Academy. I'd wasted time that I could have spent with him, and it could be a very long time before I would see him again.

'I am telling him that he would make a fine exhibit at Sea World,' the Dragon said with amusement. 'Do you like the gi?'

I raised one hand from the Dragon's frill and touched the soft pale blue cotton of the gi. It was decorated with white stylised cherry blossoms, some as small as a centimetre across and others as wide as ten centimetres. It was held together with a wide sash — an obi — made of dark maroon silk with similar white cherry blossom patterns. 'It is lovely,' I said. 'Thank you.'

'Come visit my palace in Japan,' the Dragon said. 'I have many fine kimono and gi there. Some are worth a small fortune and have been worn by royalty.'

'I would like to one day.'

I peered down at John, who was obviously enjoying this time in the unpolluted water. I looked up; the lights of Kota Kinabalu started to show over the curve of the earth before us, Mount Kinabalu a dark majestic shape behind the city.

'We are nearly there,' the Dragon said. 'I hope you have enjoyed my hospitality.'

'I have,' I said.

'Hurt my friend Xuan Wu and your life will be both painful and short,' he said, his conversational tone not changing.

'If I hurt him I would wish nothing else for myself,' I said.

'Then we are in agreement,' the Dragon said, and we skimmed over the water in silence, John enjoying himself below us.

I have to bring you back now, Emma, the stone said. *Be ready: it'll go from smooth to rough, human to serpent.*

Ready.

The change was like a drop of about ten metres, and I was a snake again. No time for regrets now, Emma, the tears of loss can come later; and besides, never forget that he's promised to come back for you.

Snakes can't close their eyes so I just held on.

The final tunnel was straight and narrow and we seemed to be travelling through it forever. I'd often joked that Hell was being stuck in one of Hong Kong's interminable tunnels under the harbour in a traffic jam, choking on fumes, and this was an unpleasantly similar experience.

Another pressure wave deafened me as we shot out of the tunnel into a wide, low-ceilinged cavern. The cavern's only feature was a concrete box, about a metre high and four hundred metres square. The flyers all descended quickly, landed in front of the box, and waited restlessly while we dismounted. I loosened my coils and slid off; the flyer took off before my tail was completely free of it.

We regrouped in front of the monolith.

'Well?' I asked Martin.

'There are two entrances, front and back,' Martin said without looking away from the concrete box. 'While I was bound to the King, I would often spy for him, and one of my tasks was to see what they were doing inside here. I have some idea of the floor plan.' He turned to speak to us. 'We are not visible to them right now, but the minute we try to remove the stone child and Leo, they will know.'

'So we need a diversion,' I said.

Martin bowed his head slightly without speaking.

I turned to the Generals. 'How about a loud violent attack from you guys in the front, while we sneak in the back?'

'Sounds like a plan,' General Ma said. He grimaced and dropped his voice. 'Are you sure that Ming Gui is trustworthy in this? He could be leading you to your destruction while we are preoccupied.'

'I once asked Xuan Wu if I could trust him,' I said. I turned back to face the building. 'He said yes.'

'That's good enough for me,' General Ma said. He nodded to Martin. 'Do you know where they are holding the Lion and the stone child?'

'I have an idea,' Martin said. 'The King asked me to investigate the research they were carrying out. At the far end of the building, behind the residential quarters and breeding nest, there are some laboratories that they used for experimentation on stones. I believe that they will be in there.'

'Leo wasn't in there when you investigated before?' I said.

'No,' Martin said. 'If he had been, I would have tried to get him out.'

'Let's do this,' the Tiger said. 'We Immortals at the front door; we can fight to the death. You run round the back and someone let us know telepathically when to make a lot of noise.'

'Let's go,' I said. 'Martin, you can hide us right until we're at the door?'

'They don't have any external guards. They think they're impenetrable,' Martin said. 'Last time I went in and stayed inside for about thirty minutes undetected.' He shrugged. 'Six is up himself.'

'He'll be on his guard now that we've attacked the Guilin nest,' the Tiger said. He raised one huge demon paw and his sword appeared in it. 'We'll stay back here and wait for your word. Let us know when to bring the roof down.'

I saluted the Immortals. 'I'll see you on the other side.'

They saluted me back.

Michael, Simone and I followed Martin to the back of the facility. Martin was right; there weren't any exterior guards and there didn't appear to be any surveillance cameras either.

The Tiger ran up behind us. 'Wait for me,' he said. We slowed so he could join us. 'If anybody is getting killed in there, it's me. If something happens, you guys get out as fast as you can. I don't like the idea of leaving all of you with Mr *Turtle* here.'

'Suit yourself,' Martin said.

We went around the corner to the back of the building. Martin led us about halfway along, stopped, and put one hand on the wall. The wall slid towards him, like a cube coming out of the side of the building. It extended a metre and a half, then stopped. It seemed to be made of the same featureless concrete as the rest of the building.

Martin went to one side, then walked straight into it. 'It is an illusion,' he said. 'This is the entrance ...' And then he grunted loudly.

We rushed to follow him. He was right: the concrete was an illusion, and on the other side was a white room with smooth walls and floor, about three metres square. Martin was battling two stone fake elementals in the middle of it. The fake elementals were roughly human-shaped and made of skull-sized rocks that floated in the form, without visible faces or hands.

Michael changed to human form but Simone remained a demon, summoning Dark Heavens and holding it in her clawed, scaled hand. Michael, Martin and the Tiger slashed ineffectually at the stone elementals, not even chipping them with their weapons. Simone held Dark Heavens point up in front of her, lowered her head and concentrated for a moment, then slashed the sword sideways through one of the elementals. It fell into two pieces and collapsed into its component stone parts on the floor, some of the stones rolling to the sides of the room.

Simone raised the sword to do the same thing to the second one, but I was faster. Finally, I was able to fight a demon myself without worrying about absorbing any demon essence. I slithered to the demon, climbed up its body, wrapped myself around it and ripped its head off with my mouth. I spat the head to the side of the room, then proceeded to dismantle it piece by piece, extracting the demon essence from each piece before I discarded it. It quickly turned to a similar lifeless pile of rock.

The men stood there panting, watching us. Then Michael said, 'Nice.' He turned to Martin. 'Where to next?'

Martin gestured towards the door. 'This way.'

I tasted the floor with my tongue. 'This is very similar to the lining of the walls and floor of the nest in Kowloon City.'

'It's infused with stone babies?' Simone said with horror.

I rolled onto my back, giving the embedded stone a closer look at the floor.

'No,' the stone said. 'It isn't infused the same way that nest was, but it is still a very unusual ceramic material that blocks my senses.'

'Would you say that it's a type of baked stone demon?' I said, righting myself.

'That's exactly what it seems to be,' the stone said.

'Lovely,' I said. 'The Phoenix would adore it.'

'I heard she prefers her demons barbecued rather than baked,' Simone said. She went to the door, put her hand on it and concentrated. She shook her head. 'Can't see a damn thing.'

'Language, missy,' the Tiger said. He hoisted his sword, gestured for us to move to the sides, then pulled the door open, theatrically hiding behind it like something out of a Hollywood movie.

'That was completely unnecessary,' Martin said. 'There is only a corridor on the other side of this, that leads to the holding cells and the laboratory.'

'Holding cells? We'd better shut down all the trash compactors in the detention level,' Michael said with amusement as he followed Martin.

'Trash compactors?' Martin said, confused.

Michael waved him on. 'Just a lame fanboy joke.'

'Extremely lame,' Simone said, rolling her eyes.

'Oh, I dunno, I have a very bad feeling about this,' the Tiger said.

'We're surrounded by lame fanboys, Simone,' I said.

'That you are, ma'am,' the Tiger growled, bringing up the rear.

The corridor had three cell doors on either side that looked like something out of a horror movie version of a lunatic asylum — small barred windows and thick metal rims. Michael pulled at the first door on the left but it didn't open. Simone grabbed the handle, hesitated for a moment, then pulled the door completely out of the doorframe. She stood for a moment holding it as if she didn't know what to do with it, then placed it against the wall next to the open doorway. The cell was empty.

Simone and the Tiger went from door to door wrenching them open, pulling some of them completely off their hinges. Each cell was empty. When we'd opened the last cell, we all shared a look.

'Well?' Simone said to Martin. 'Is this all the cells? And if it isn't here, then where is it?'

'It may be in the laboratory,' Martin said. 'These are the only cells.' He gestured towards the end of the hallway. 'Through there.'

We went through the door and stopped. It was another white room, covered in shiny white tiles on the floor, walls and ceiling. The room was about five by three metres, with green metal cabinets along the walls and a more modern electron microscope than in the Guilin nest in one corner. A large stainless-steel workbench littered with a variety of tools, including scalpels, rasps, hammers and hacksaws, stood in the middle of the room.

Six was there, in the form of a young twenty-something Chinese with a short ponytail. He was wearing a white coverall with a clear safety screen over his entire face, and holding what appeared to be a circular saw over something held in a vice on the table. Gold's child!

His partner, the Snake Mother Three, was in the form of a teenage girl wearing a micro-mini, a bikini top and a pair of moon boots all in black. 'Fuck!' she cried, went to the side of the room and pressed a fire alarm button. Bells started ringing outside the room.

Snakes can't jump, much as I tried. Instead I moved as fast as I could, launched my head at Six and slammed into his midriff, knocking him flat. He brought the circular saw up and tried to take my head with it, but I evaded him, moving my head out of the way with each swipe of the saw. He released one hand from the saw and grabbed me by the throat, holding me tight, then moved the saw to try and take my head with it again. I swayed back, fighting his grip, then opened my mouth and spat poison in his face, moving with the pull of his hand. I tried to bring my fangs out and bury them in him, but it was no good; the poison didn't seem to have any effect on him except make his grip stronger. He easily held me off, shifted his grip so that it was slightly tighter, then raised himself with difficulty, leaning on his elbow to get up. He was still holding the buzzing circular saw next to my head.

'I think you should stop now,' he said, 'or the snake will lose her eyes.'

I couldn't see what was happening behind me but I heard the weapons hit the floor and hissed with frustration.

'Let go of Three,' Six said. 'Slowly, please. Thank you.'

Three came to stand behind Six facing me, still in the form of a teenager.

'You disappoint me, Emma,' Six said. 'I'd heard you were unbeatable, particularly in snake form.'

'Stories always grow with retelling. I'm actually not that powerful in any form. I get my ass regularly kicked by both demons and Celestials,' I said.

'What are we going to do now?' Three said. 'We need that damn stone! We'll die without it!'

'We'll die if we try and take it,' Six said. 'You guys have been such a nuisance. You destroyed our little stone farm under Guilin, and now you're here ruining our last chance at a life outside Hell. You really are a pain in the ass, you know that?'

'If you turn, you will be safe,' the Tiger said.

Three barked with laughter. 'If we turn we'll be dead the minute we step outside your doors. Slavery? No thanks, we had enough of that in Hell. When my lovely Six was born, I was already tired of the nests and catering to the whims of the King. My son is a better lover than the King ever was, so we ran away together.'

'It's a terrible shame that my darling Three is too big for me to sire spawn on,' Six said with regret.

'You things are sickening,' Simone said. 'You're mother and son, how can you do that?'

'Emma should have told you, dear. Very common among demons. Frankly, we're all related. It makes no difference to us. Most of the King's harem are his aunts and cousins. A couple of them are his daughters. Of course, he killed his mother and all his brothers and sisters when he became King.'

'How many times has the King tried to kill you, Three?' I said.

'He stopped the serious attempts after about two dozen, Emma. He'll still have the occasional go at me when he's in a bad mood.'

'We are a powerful partnership,' Six said. 'Only problem is the issue we have with being outside Hell.'

'Let's cut some sort of deal here,' Three said. 'How about we trade the stone for the Lion?'

'No,' Simone and I said in unison.

Six tightened his grip around my throat. 'How about a trade of the snake's life and the Lion's for the little stone?'

'You might as well kill me then, because I won't trade my life for a child's,' I said.

'All right,' Three said, and concentrated for a moment. She began to glow, a pale blue aura that surrounded her. Her face slackened and became peaceful. The blue glow intensified and crackling bolts of electricity writhed through it. The blue glow moved, writhing up towards her head, and encircled her emotionless face.

'Is that it?' the Tiger said to Simone.

'That's it,' Simone said. 'Completely wiped out Daddy in True Form.' She held out her hands and yin writhed around them. She concentrated the yin at her fingertips and launched it at the Snake Mother. It hit Three between the eyes and she was sucked into a tiny dark vortex. It grew from a centimetre across to twenty across as it absorbed her, then grew even more, to twenty-five centimetres, then thirty. Six was drawn towards it, still gripping me; he tried to move away but was sucked back, sliding across the floor. All the air in the room began to swirl into the vortex, pulling us into it as well.

'If I go she goes!' Six shouted over the roar of the air rushing into the yin.

'I lost control!' Simone shrieked. 'Help!'

The Tiger and Martin moved quickly. Martin grabbed Simone's hand and concentrated, and the yin began to shrink. The Tiger raised his hands, his fur all stood on end, and he generated a white blast of pure heat and light that burnt me like radiation as it flashed past me to be sucked into the vortex.

Six released his grip on me and ran out the door, slamming it behind him. I fell to the floor, blinded and burnt by the yang that the Tiger had generated. The yang disappeared into the vortex, making it shrink until the yin disappeared. I raised my head, blinded by the brilliance of the yang, feeling as burnt as if I'd been lying in Australia's summer sun all day.

'Is everybody okay?' I said.

'I nearly destroyed everything,' Simone said, her voice full of tears. 'I nearly killed everybody!'

'You need some lessons on controlling that, girly,' the Tiger said.

I heard him moving but was unable to see, my retinas burnt as if I'd been looking straight at the sun.

'Are you okay, Emma?' Simone said. I felt her cool hand on my head and raised it.

'I can't see, the yang blinded me,' I said. 'How is everybody?'

Simone was quiet for a moment, then, 'Martin?'

Another cool hand touched my head. 'It's not permanent. Her vision will return.' As Martin said it, my sight began to clear, like sun blindness wearing off. 'Is that better?' he said.

'Yes,' I said. 'Thank you, my vision is returning.'

'Oh fuck, Michael, no,' the Tiger moaned. I turned to see: he was on one knee next to Michael's prone body.

'The Mother hit him hard on the head,' Simone said. 'Is he all right?'

'Major brain haemorrhage.' The Tiger rubbed one hand over his face. 'He's done for.'

I slithered to Michael and touched my nose to his face. I could see the bleeding without needing my eyes; the demon had hit him very hard and burst a large number of blood vessels around his brain. His system couldn't clear the blood from the damaged area fast enough, and the pressure of the blood build-up was destroying his brain. He was dying.

I opened my mouth, releasing my long fangs which hinged forward. I raised my head, mouth open, and readied to bite him.

Simone's hand snaked out and held me by the throat. She lifted me clear and stood with me, so tall that my tail only just touched the ground. 'I don't know what you're trying to do there, Emma,' she said, her voice mild. 'But I don't think I'll let you.'

'Heal him,' I said with difficulty through her grip.

She released me slightly. 'You can heal him?'

'Let me go, silly Simone,' I said. 'I'm the only chance he has. You may not want to watch though.'

She hesitated, still holding my head high above the floor.

'He's going to die anyway. Let me save him,' I said.

She gently lowered my head and released me.

'I'm going to drain the blood out of his brain, like a shunt, and stop the bleeding,' I said. 'It will probably be messy and you may not want to watch.'

'Just do it, Emma,' Simone said, her voice small.

Michael lay with his head slightly to one side, his expression peaceful. I raised my serpent head and dropped it quickly, slipping my fangs through his skull and into his brain cavity. Blood welled around the fangs, staining his short blond hair. I hesitated as I tasted his blood. I'd never been addicted to anything in my life but I knew what it felt like; *this* was what it felt like. Michael's blood was like a cold blast of pleasure in my mouth, a sweet and pure flavour full of liquid clarity, ringing with sweetness and slight acidic tones. It tasted very much like some sort of sweet, alcoholic, lemon-flavoured tea and filled my entire serpent body with a hungry, desperate need for more.

As I held down the desire to siphon all of this wonderful pleasure into me, the more logical parts of my brain were fascinated. Michael didn't taste like a Shen; Shen blood was sweeter and fresher. He didn't taste like a human; humans were like Shen, but not quite as fresh, more full of greenery and earthy tones rather than the heavenly sky flavour of Shen. He didn't taste remotely like demon either; demons always tasted like a warm satisfying meal of spiced meat and bread.

I shook myself out of it. Michael was dying here, and I was meditating on the way his blood tasted. Wrong, Emma, healing time. I had to extract the blood from the gap between his compressed brain and his skull without puncturing any brain tissue.

'Don't touch me, this is very tricky,' I said, my voice muffled by the blood and my fangs.

I moved slowly and with care, keeping the tips of my fangs between his skull and brain. I siphoned the blood out without drinking it; if I was to actually swallow any, I didn't think I could control the urge to finish it all. I pulled the blood out and released it through the punctures in his skull; just a small amount, enough to relieve the pressure; he couldn't afford to lose too much. Then I moved my consciousness into the area, finding each ruptured blood vessel in turn and repairing it. The flow of blood slowed, then stopped. I waited to make sure that no more blood was entering the cavity, and closed a couple of smaller vessels that were still leaking. I withdrew my teeth and healed the wounds in his skull and scalp. The rest of the blood would drain by itself. Only time would tell if there was any permanent damage.

I pulled my head back slightly and touched him with my serpent tongue, then immediately regretted it as I tasted his heavenly essence again.

'I did my best. I think he'll survive. I hope he won't have any permanent brain damage. Damn, but that bitch hit him hard.' I looked around; I could see clearly now. It appeared that the taste of Michael's blood had been more than delicious; it had aided my own healing. 'Is Gold's baby okay?'

'I'm okay!' the stone child said from the vice. 'You guys saved me! Where's Daddy and Grampa?'

'I'm here, little one,' the stone in my ring said, its voice unmuffled even though it was embedded inside me. 'Daddy couldn't come — he can't come to the demon side of Hell. So we came to get you out. He's waiting for you back home, and he's really worried.'

'Can you let me out of this?' Gold's baby said. 'It kinda hurts.'

Martin swung the handle of the vice around a few times and the baby flew out of it. 'Thanks, guys!' it said. 'Is Uncle Michael gonna be okay? His head is bleeding.'

'We hope he'll be okay,' I said.

'You're a big snake, Aunty Emma,' the baby stone said.

'I know,' I said. 'Don't be afraid, it's really me.'

'I'm not afraid, I know it's you,' the stone said. 'You look *way cool*! And so do you, Simone!'

Simone smiled, revealing surprisingly human teeth in her serpent demon mouth. 'Thanks, kiddo.' She looked around. 'We need to take him and Michael out, but we still have to find Leo.'

'You go out, I'll look for the Lion,' the Tiger said.

'No way,' I said. 'We started this, we'll finish it. You take your son out.'

The Tiger looked down at Michael and grimaced. 'His mother'll kill me if he dies.'

'Take Michael and the stone to the West, keep them safe,' Martin said. 'I will guide Simone and Emma the rest of the way, and meet you there.'

The Tiger grimaced again. 'This is what I *don't* like. Leaving you two girls in the care of someone that really can't be trusted.'

'I can take him down, Uncle Bai,' Simone said. 'And I won't hesitate to do it if he messes us around. But we need to find Leo, and you need to get Michael to safety.'

The Tiger raised his head and concentrated. 'The Generals are keeping the demons occupied out the front. You should hurry.' He strode to Martin and glared into his face. 'You get either of these girls hurt, and I will hunt you down and pull your shell off while you are still alive.' He poked Martin in the chest. 'Very, very slowly.'

Martin wasn't fazed. 'I swear that I will keep them safe; as long as I live I will protect them.'

'How will you get out?' I asked the Tiger.

'Same way we came in, through the ventilation shafts that the flyers use. There has to be one to the outside near here; all I need to do is find it. And if the worst comes to the worst, metal can cut through earth.'

He changed to a huge True Form of a white tiger at least four metres long, his shaggy head nearly touching the ceiling. He waved his nose at the stone child. 'Come and sit somewhere on my back and I'll take you out, little one.'

'Okay,' Gold's child said. 'I wanna go home to Daddy.'

The Tiger bent and gently picked up Michael in his mouth like a cat holding a kitten. 'Don't worry about us, we'll find a way out,' he said, his voice muffled around Michael. He glanced from us to Martin. 'Just get your Black Lion and get the fuck out of here. Don't worry about the demon; without its energy it'll eventually die anyway.'

The stone child rested on the back of the Tiger's neck. 'Good luck finding the guy you're looking for, everybody,' it said. 'Be careful, 'cause this demon …' Its voice cracked slightly and filled with tears. 'This demon is a real bad one. The lady demon was mean, but that man demon,' its voice was full of pain, 'is *really* mean.'

The Tiger nodded to us and left.

CHAPTER 31

'Do you have any idea where they're holding Leo?' I asked Martin.

'None whatsoever,' Martin said, 'but he has to be somewhere around here.'

'Then let's go find him,' Simone said. 'And I want that demon's head.'

'Just no more yin without the Tiger around,' I said.

'Don't worry, Emma, I don't think I'll ever do that again.' Simone lowered her voice. 'I nearly ruined everything.'

'You just need some training in the control of it,' Martin said. 'The Blue Dragon should help you, he is the Lesser Yin.'

'I've asked him a few times and he's always too busy messing with his companies in Japan,' Simone said, frustrated.

We went out of the lab and into the corridor. Two stone elemental demons were blocking the way, impassive and unmoving. Before Simone or I could do anything against them, Martin held the Silver Serpent vertically in front of him, point up. He concentrated, and his bright red demon hair rose to float around his head. The sword glowed white and began to sing; not the crystalline whine that I had produced with chi, but a purer and more brilliant sound, even more beautiful than Simone had produced when she filled the sword with shen energy. The sound was both deep and high at the same time, a perfect harmonious chord that made the air ripple around it. The ripples hit the demons and they shattered into gravel, falling onto the floor.

Martin lowered the sword. 'It still resonates.'

'Daddy should never have taken that off you,' Simone said with wonder.

'He had his reasons,' Martin said. He concentrated for a moment. 'Our friends are still keeping most of the guards busy. Let's find that demon and our Lion.'

We continued down the corridor, and nothing stopped us. The bells still rang throughout the complex, and occasionally there were yells and the sounds of doors banging in the distance. The corridor was still all white, glistening ceramic on the walls, floor and ceiling. At the end of the corridor, there was a sharp turn left and a small atrium with a lift.

'There's no up, so we have to go down,' Simone said, and pressed the button. She looked up at the ceiling. 'No security cameras. You're right, Martin, this guy is up himself. How many floors are there?'

'Only two, it's mostly a horizontal facility,' Martin said. 'Spread out.'

'Why is that?' I said. 'All the buildings in Hong Kong and China are more vertical; why is this one more horizontal?'

'Less digging,' Martin said.

The lift doors opened and we went in. The numbers on the buttons were in English: G then B1. I pressed B1 with my serpent nose and the lift went down extremely slowly then the doors opened.

We moved into a corridor that looked completely different from the floor above. Instead of white ceramic, the walls and floor were all plain grey concrete. Five or six rusting galvanised-iron pipes ran along the corner of the ceiling from one end of the corridor to the other, with another few pipes along the corner of the floor. The floor was caked with sticky dirt, and the pipes were covered in a thick layer of dust. But the floor was only dirty in the corners; it was obviously often walked on.

Steel cabinets, each about a metre high and padlocked, with a thick layer of dust on the top, lined the left side of the corridor. Each cabinet door had a demon-proof seal, the complicated sigils painted by hand on the rectangular rice paper glued to the front.

Martin studied one of the seals. 'This isn't to hold demons,' he said. 'It is to hold Shen.'

Simone bent the bar of the padlock like plasticine and pulled it away so that she could open the door.

The cabinet was about fifteen centimetres deep and held two shelves with holes in them that looked like they were designed to hold wet umbrellas. The shelves, however, were empty. Simone closed the cabinet again, and we followed Martin down the hallway, moving as quietly as we could and listening for any sound.

At the end there was a T-intersection and we had a choice between going left or right. I flicked my tongue out, then quickly pointed left with my nose. 'That way.'

'Why?' Simone said.

'I can taste it. It went this way.'

Simone raised one hand and scraped her demon claw on the wall, leaving a slight mark. 'Okay, let's go.'

'No need to do that, I can taste the way we came,' I said.

Simone shrugged without replying.

This corridor had rooms on the left and right, each with a standard wooden door. Simone concentrated then shook her head. 'My Inner Eye isn't blocked down here. All these rooms are empty. They look like barracks.'

'That's probably what they are,' Martin said.

We walked down the corridor, which seemed to run the length of the facility; the end wasn't visible. I flicked my tongue out every so often, tasting the air, and then stopped. 'Leo.'

'Where?' Simone said, and concentrated. 'I can't see him.'

I raised my snout and flicked my tongue again. I moved my head left and right, tasting the air. 'Further along somewhere. It's so faint that I can't get a good fix on it.'

'Is your sense of taste really that sensitive?' Simone asked.

'I think it is,' I said. 'I can taste the Generals, far away. Six is around here somewhere, hiding. I can definitely taste Leo somewhere ...' I moved my head from side to side. 'Up ahead. Let's go.'

We moved down the corridor, both Martin and Simone checking inside the rooms with their Inner Eyes. The taste of Leo strengthened and I quickened my pace. Leo was getting stronger, but Six wasn't; the demon was travelling away from us as fast as we were approaching him.

'Six is running,' I said.

'Leo is our first priority,' Martin said. 'Without his source of energy, Six will eventually die anyway.'

'I'd still like to take that demon's head after all it did to those stones,' Simone said, her voice mild.

'We can always track it down later. Emma has the scent.'

We neared the end of the corridor. An occasional vibration shook the ceiling; they were fighting above us. I quickened my pace again; Leo was very close ahead.

His scent was coming from a large pair of double doors on the left, close to the end of the corridor, which turned right.

'There he is, I see him — oh, there's two,' Simone said.

She threw the double doors open and we rushed in. The walls and floor were tiled with small square bathroom tiles, and the ceiling was bare concrete with a couple of unshaded neon tubes in the middle. There were two operating tables in the centre of the room, and both of them held bound Leos. Each Leo was completely identical and looked the same as when he'd been taken to be Judged eight years before. Both were lying on their stomachs, wearing pyjama pants and nothing else, their arms and legs bound to the edges of the table.

'Don't release them just yet,' I said. 'They may be more copies. Check their numbers.'

Martin and Simone went to each of the Leos and bent to see their wrists from underneath.

'This is four,' Simone said.

Leo Four came around. 'Simone?' he said, sounding groggy. 'Is that you?'

'Simone?' the other Leo said.

'This is number one,' Martin said. 'Should we destroy the four and take the one? Four is the one that attacked you.'

'Why do you look like demons?' Leo One said.

'We're sneaking in the back door, these are disguises,' I said. 'The serpent lady is Simone, the black demon is Martin, and I'm Emma.'

'Kill me,' Leo Four said. 'I'm a copy.'

'Kill both of us,' Leo One said. 'We're both copies.'

'Then where's the real Leo?' I said.

Neither replied.

'Destroy Four, take One,' Simone said.

'We're not sure!' I said.

'Destroy both of us, Emma,' Leo Four said. 'You can't trust either of us. We're both copies.'

'That's the best plan, guys,' Leo One said. 'Just kill us both. That would be the kindest thing to do to us; we're demon copies anyway.'

'How do you know that?' I said.

Leo One gestured with his head as best he could towards Leo Four. 'He told me what happened. You found him in a nest and took him home, and when Six turned up, he found he had to obey Six. He's been beating himself up about it since, and asking Six to let him die.'

'We don't have time to mess around with this,' I said. 'Free them and take them with us. We'll work out what to do with them later.'

'Just take them to the Celestial,' Martin said. 'If they are demons, they will be destroyed.'

'And if they both die?' I said.

'Then there's an original around here somewhere,' Simone said, 'and we're going to find him.'

'Does Six have any other nests apart from this one?' I asked Martin.

'Not any more,' Martin said. 'You drove him out of his other two nests.'

'And we've kept an eye on them and they've stayed vacant,' I said. 'Good. Any other Leos have to be somewhere in here. Let's go.'

Martin and Simone freed the Leos and helped them off the tables. Both of them were slightly unsteady on their feet.

'What is this one doing with you, Emma?' Leo One said, gesturing towards Martin. 'He betrayed you. I remember that much.'

'He's trying to make good,' I said.

'I hope you don't trust him,' Leo Four said.

'No more than I trust you,' I said. 'I'm ready to destroy either of you the second you attempt anything.'

'Good,' both Leos said in unison.

'This is very freaky,' Simone said.

We went out of the room and back into the corridor that seemed to run the length of the facility. Doors opened on the right side but not the left, where there were more of the narrow cabinets against the wall. I lifted my snout and tasted the air. 'Something's dead around here.'

We went to the first set of doors on the right; the smell of death was coming from this room. 'In here,' I said.

There was a large stainless-steel vat in the centre of the room, much like a commercial-sized mixing or cooking vat, at least a metre tall and around. There were shelves all around the edge of the room, which was about four metres by three. The smell of death was almost overpowering, but it was tempered by the scent of something, like talcum powder.

Simone went to one of the shelves and studied its contents. 'Stones,' she said.

I moved to stand next to her. 'These are what's dead,' I said. 'They were once alive. I think they're stone Shen.'

'These are the missing stone Shen,' the stone in my ring said quietly. 'This is where he made the essence to line the walls and the stone tools he used. They're all dead.' Its voice went hoarse with grief. 'They're all dead!'

I raised my head to see. There were at least two hundred stones, of all sizes and colours, on the shelves, and all dead. The mixing vat was full of what appeared to be white clay-like mud; the ceramic lining before it was baked and placed on the walls.

'They weren't using stone demons to make lining,' the stone in my ring said. 'They were using adult stone Shen.

'We have to take them with us, to return them to the Grandmother. We can't leave them here.'

'Look around for something to put them in,' Simone said.

Martin raised a bucket that had been sitting next to the vat. It was a typical cheap red plastic bucket used by many householders in China to hold trash. 'This will do.'

'This is most unfitting,' the stone grumbled as Martin, Simone and the two Leos went around the shelves and carefully placed the dead stones in the bucket. I didn't help, and nobody questioned me. They probably knew that I didn't want the taste of dead things in my serpent mouth.

'This building is kinda square, with a corridor all around the edge,' Simone said as she put the last of the stones in the bucket. 'I can see about twenty metres, and all the rooms are empty. The kiln's two doors down.'

'Let's check everywhere else then,' I said. 'But Six's scent has gone, he may have taken off already.'

Martin placed the lid on the bucket and we went back out of the room. We turned right and followed the corridor; there were still cabinets all along one side.

'These cabinets are everywhere. What were they for?' I said.

'I think they held the stones,' Simone said. 'Kind of like little jail cells for them.'

'And the seals held them in,' I said, understanding.

'But the cabinets are empty now. All the stones are dead,' Martin said.

'If you don't mind, Emma, I would very much like for us to track this demon down later and rip its throat out,' the stone in my ring said.

Martin and Simone stopped and both turned their unseeing heads to the right.

'The kiln room,' Simone said.

'That's where your students were,' Martin said.

I tasted the air; it tasted of death and ash. We moved down the corridor and opened the door on the right. The room contained a large kiln of the type used for firing pottery, and a plastic storage bin stained black from holding ash.

'That bin contained the remains of your students,' Martin said. 'They baked them and combined them with the stone Shen to make the ceramic lining.'

'That's what happened to the students that were replaced by the demon copies,' Simon said. She wiped her eyes. 'This demon needs to *die*.'

Heads up, I'm the only one left, General Ma said into our heads. *There are about three big demons remaining, and I only have one working arm and internal injuries that will kill me in the next five minutes or so. I may lose consciousness and die soon, so I suggest you hurry it up and get out of here.*

'Let's move,' I said. 'Sweep the corridor. Look with your Inner Eyes — above and this level. Let's see if there's anything left.'

We moved quickly down the corridor. Simone and Martin swept their heads from side to side, their eyes wide and unfocused. At the end of the corridor we turned right again, and walked as fast as we could down it. We reached the middle, which led to the lift lobby, and passed it.

'Ma is down,' Martin said.

'Still nothing in any of the rooms,' Simone said. 'The demons are above us, they'll be coming down in the lift any minute.'

We turned right again: final corridor. When we reached the middle, another corridor branched to the right and three big humanoid demons charged down it towards us. Simone raised her hand and Dark Heavens appeared in it. Martin did the same with the Silver Serpent. I raised my head and opened my mouth, swinging my fangs out.

The demons were standard humanoids, about two-and-a-half metres tall and black with scales and tusks. They carried a sword in each hand, and at level seventy-five were a formidable challenge.

'Leo stay back,' I said. 'Guard the rear. These are too big for you.'

'Yes, ma'am,' both Leos said in unison.

Martin took the one in the centre. He filled the Silver Serpent with shen energy, making it sing, and swung it at the demon's head. It blocked with both of its swords, swung Martin's blade down, and attempted to take his head. Martin made a few fast attacks that unbalanced it slightly, making it give ground and move back along the corridor.

I raised my head to strike, watching the location and direction of the swords carefully. As the demon swept both swords left — obviously its strong side — I evaded them, went through underneath, opened my mouth as wide as I could and buried my fangs in its abdomen. I injected it with poison, then quickly released it and pulled back out of the way of the reverse swing of the swords.

The poison seemed to have no effect on the demon. I checked Simone — my eyes were on the sides of my serpent head — and she was battling her demon with no difficulty, just waiting for it to open its guard and allow her to finish it.

My demon swung at my head. I dodged under its guard, swung my head up with my mouth open and gripped its wrist. Before it had a chance to take my head with its left hand, I bit its right hand off and snapped back out of reach again.

This was enough. The demon essence spiralled out of the injury in its hand, destroying it. I siphoned the essence into me; again it turned into something bright, dark and powerful.

Martin's demon struck him in the side, its blade cutting through his armour and burying itself at least fifteen centimetres into his abdomen and lodging there. The demon lifted the other sword to take his head, but he blocked it with his own. They were deadlocked. The demon tried to finish Martin with the second sword as it attempted to free the first, but he was fast enough to block every blow.

Simone finally found an opening in her own demon and sliced it through from shoulder to hip, tearing it open to release its demon essence. It spread out into feathery black streamers, sticking to Simone where they hit her and dissipating into the air where they didn't. She raised Dark Heavens and threw it like a spear at the remaining demon's head. The sword travelled straight through it and destroyed the demon, which exploded all over Martin.

Martin fell and the bucket holding the stones toppled, scattering them everywhere. He held his side where the demon's sword was still lodged in it; it was a Japanese-style wakizashi dagger, at least forty centimetres long. He gripped the handle and winced with pain, then gasped as he yanked it from his side and threw it sideways. He fell back clutching his side, which was now dark with blood.

'Rinse him off, then I'll heal him,' I said. 'I don't want any venom inside him when I seal the wound.'

Simone concentrated and a small cloud, dark with moisture, appeared above Martin. A tiny deluge fell from it, warm and salty, and Martin gasped again as it hit him. He raised himself so that his side was flooded with the water, his face stiff with pain.

Simone moved behind him to hold him up. 'Sorry, Ge Ge, I can only do salt water.'

'Salt is better for me,' Martin said, his voice hoarse with effort. He focused with difficulty on me. 'You can heal it?'

'I can try,' I said. I waited for Simone's rain shower to finish rinsing him clean, then touched my serpent snout to him. 'Lower him gently,' I said.

Simone returned him to the floor, then looked behind her. 'Leo, can you collect the stones back up, please?'

'We already are,' one of the Leos said behind me.

I concentrated on Martin. I didn't even try to touch him with my tongue; the taste of a Shen would definitely push me over the edge. I knew that this was the demon inside me, not the serpent; the snake liked the taste of blood, but didn't have this raw, gnawing addiction to it that my demon side had.

We need to clear —

We need to clear this essence out of me, I know, I said before the stone had finished. *John said I was to visit the Three Pure Ones. I hope they can help.*

Anything's better than going to the Demon King, and don't pretend you haven't thought about it, the stone said. *Can you heal him?*

I can give it a damn good try.

'Can you heal him?' Simone said.

'If you can't heal me, just leave me here,' Martin said.

'If we leave you here, there's no way for us to get out,' I said. 'Simone can't carry all of us.'

'Simone can touch you while you're a snake,' Martin said. 'She can carry you out. Leave us and go.'

'Not an option,' Simone said. 'Can you do it?'

'Will everybody stop asking me if I can do it and let me see if I can?' I said irritably, and they went quiet. The only sound was the stones hitting the bottom of the bucket as the Leos collected them.

I moved my consciousness through Martin. His only injury was the slash in his side; the demon had caught him with a lucky blow.

'I thought you could take down just about anything if you had a weapon,' I said.

'I'm out of practice,' Martin said. 'I haven't had to fight a demon in eight years.'

'You can still do the katas,' I said.

'Wasn't allowed to,' he said, and flinched as I touched the wound with my nose. 'Just go and let me die here. It's all the same.'

I checked the depth of the wound; it had clipped his large bowel — ugly. Bacteria from his bowel would contaminate his abdominal cavity and cause infection. He needed hospital care, where they could cleanse the wound and fill him full of antibiotics — both inside the wound and through his bloodstream. If I closed it up with that amount of bacteria in him, he would die within a week without hospital care, Shen or not.

I raised my head. 'I can fix the wound now, but he will need to go to hospital later. The wound is contaminated and needs antibiotics.'

'Close it up, and I'll take you out,' Martin said. 'Then we can either let me die or take me to a hospital. Your choice.'

I touched my nose to him again and healed the bowel wound, then closed up the exterior slash, knitting the muscles as best I could. I didn't need to do a thorough job as it would have to be opened again and cleansed.

'It needs binding,' I said. 'The join is weak and may split open again.'

Simone used Dark Heavens to tear away part of the bottom of her flowing demon robes and wrapped the fabric around Martin's abdomen to cover the wound. He watched, impressed, as she worked with precision and competence.

'Nice job,' he said.

'I did first aid as part of an adventuring award program they have in Australia,' Simone said. 'I want to do it all the way up to the gold award — it's a great learning experience. I hope my new school has it.'

Martin leaned on her and she helped him to his feet.

We exited the room and turned right again.

'Is there any more ground we need to cover to find another Leo?' I said.

Simone nodded. 'We have about another fifty or so metres of corridor to check.'

'Can you make it that far, Martin?' I said.

Martin nodded, but his face was fierce with pain. 'I'll make it.'

'Let us carry him,' one of the Leos said. 'He can go between us.'

'Good idea,' Simone said, and passed Martin to the Leos, who stood one on either side of him with his arms over their shoulders.

About halfway down the corridor Simone stopped. 'There's something on the right here.'

'Anything we'll need to fight?' I said.

'No, nothing alive. It just feels … strange.'

I pushed the double doors open with my nose and went in. There was another rack of shelves in this room, again covered with dead stone Shen but these ones didn't smell dead. They flew up off the shelves and grew to take the form of fake stone elementals; so many of them that they completely filled the room, forcing us back out the doors and into the corridor.

'There are at least fifty of them, and more growing!' Simone said. 'We need to get out of here — I can't destroy that many!'

'Come to me,' Martin said, and put his hand out from where the Leos were holding him. 'Touch me. I'll take us out.'

'Go with him,' the stone in my ring said. 'Get out of here!'

Simone raised her hand and touched Martin's; I touched his hand with my snout. There was a flash of light, a feeling of disorientation, then we were on a grassy lawn next to a wide lake. It was night; the stars above blazed brighter than any I'd seen before. To our left, further along the shore of the lake, were the lights of a city, golden and welcoming. A fresh breeze full of the scent of the water and the mown grass blew from the lake, but it was chillingly cold.

One of the Leos stiffened as if he'd been struck, then exploded into a mass of black feathery streamers, disappearing quickly. The other Leo gently lowered Martin to sit on the grass, holding him so that he could see around him.

Simone changed back to her normal human form and put her hands on her hips. 'You stupid *asshole*! You could have killed Emma!'

'How?' Martin said. 'It's just the Celestial Plane. It can't hurt her.'

'Because of the demon essence in her, travel to the Celestial Plane in human form will destroy her,' Simone said, furious.

Martin nodded to Simone. 'My apologies. I didn't know. But she seems to be all right.'

'We're on the Celestial Plane? Where?' Leo said.

'We're in the Northern Heavens,' Simone said. 'That's why the other Leo died; he wasn't the real one, he was a demon copy. Obviously you're the real …' She hesitated, then threw herself onto the grass to hold him. 'You're the real Leo!'

'I'm not, sweetheart,' Leo said sadly. 'I'm Leo Four.'

Simone pulled back to see him, confused. 'You're the one that attacked Emma?'

Leo nodded.

'The demon must have been controlling you, same as when you attacked us at the school concert,' Simone said.

Leo's face cleared and he grinned. 'I remember that. You wore a tiger mask and said a little poem in Putonghua.'

'Check to see if there are any stones planted on you,' I said. 'When you attacked us after the concert, a stone was put in your pocket to make you obey.'

Leo rose and felt his pyjama pants. 'No pockets here.' He grimaced. 'They may have … it could be …' He shrugged. 'If there's one on me, we have to take it out.'

'We'll have someone check when we get home,' I said.

'What?' Simone said. 'You think they shoved a stone up your *ass*?'

'He was on his stomach on the table,' I said.

Leo stared at Simone for a moment, then said, 'You are growing up way too fast, missy.'

'I'll take that as a compliment,' Simone said. She knelt and took Martin's hand. 'We can take you to the hospital here, Ge Ge. The physicians will treat you; there's no need for you to make another journey through Hell.'

'I just need to take True Form and rest in the lake for a while,' Martin said. 'But I am not sure that I am welcome here.'

'I am Regent, Simone is Princess,' I said. 'We say you are welcome. You are.'

We heard a splash from the lake and turned. The turtle that we had found in Sai Kung had pulled itself out and was making its way laboriously to us.

'By the Heavens, Jie Jie,' Martin said with wonder. 'What are you doing here?'

The turtle crawled up to Martin and rested its head on his knee.

'This is your sister?' Simone said.

469

'This is our big sister,' Martin said. 'I am Ming Gui, the Bright Turtle. This is Yue Gui, the Moon Turtle.'

'A demon gave her to us,' I said. 'She can't speak.'

Yue Gui nudged Martin with her nose.

'I wonder what has happened to you,' Martin said. He put his hand on her head. 'She cannot speak at all, not even mind to mind. I have never seen anything like this before.'

The turtle raised its head from his knee, turned away, and crawled back down to the lake. It hesitated for a moment, looking at the moon, then slid into the water and disappeared.

'I will take True Form and join her,' Martin said. 'She may be able to talk to me that way.' He moved to rise, then grunted and clutched his side.

'Good idea,' Simone said. 'Meet us at the city later.'

Martin nodded. Leo and Simone helped him to the edge of the water. He took a couple of steps into the lake, then raised his head and concentrated. He shrank and changed into a green sea turtle. He turned his head back to see us. *I will return to the city in an hour. I will see you there.*

Simone waved to him. He turned away and slipped further into the water, disappearing beneath it.

'My family keeps growing all the time,' Simone said. 'Now I have a sister too. I wonder how many other children Daddy had.'

'He was going to tell me but I asked him not to,' I said.

'I don't blame you,' Leo said.

Simone gestured towards the city. 'You guys up to walking? I can't summon a cloud.'

'I'm going to crash badly when we get there,' I said. 'I think we've been going for nearly twenty-four hours straight.'

'You'd better go back home before you do that,

Emma,' Simone said. 'If you change back to human form while you're asleep, you could be destroyed.'

'Good point,' I said. I lowered my serpent head. 'I'm buggered. I hope we can find someone to take me home. I just want to sleep.'

Leo choked with laughter and I rounded on him. 'It means something else in Australia!'

'I know, you told me when we were there,' Leo said.

I slithered away to follow Simone around the edge of the lake towards the city. 'You are the real Leo. Only you would remember that.' I turned my head to see him. 'But some stuff you don't remember. What did they do to you?'

'I don't know,' Leo said.

'Is your ass sore?'

'Not even in a good way.'

Simone put her hands over her ears. 'La, la, la, la, I can't hear you.'

I nudged Leo with my serpent head. 'It's good to have you back, my friend.'

'You still can't trust me, ladies,' Leo said grimly. 'You should lock me up until you're sure you can.'

'Simone is one of the most powerful ...' I hesitated, searching for the word.

'Creatures,' Simone said. 'I'm one of the most powerful creatures on the Celestial Plane. Don't worry about hurting me, Leo, you would never even get close to me.'

'You're still my little girl,' Leo said.

Simone went to him and put her arm around his waist. He put his arm over her shoulder and they walked together. 'I'm glad,' Simone said. 'Leo, you're shivering like crazy, you must be freezing!' She raised one hand and conjured a big padded parka, like those worn by Hong Kong people when there was even the slightest chill in the air. 'Here, put this on.'

Leo shrugged the jacket on and nodded. 'Thanks, sweetheart.'

'He's barefoot too, Simone,' I said from behind them. 'He could probably do with a pair of ugg boots as well.'

Simone conjured a pair of big white sheepskin boots and passed them to him. He quickly pulled them on. 'That's way better.'

Simone looked back to see me. 'You okay, Emma? You're slowing down.'

'It's hard to move,' I said. 'It's like something's draining my energy.'

'Is it the Celestial Plane?' she said, concerned. 'Is it hurting you?'

'I think it's the cold,' I said. 'I'm cold-blooded. Reptiles get really sluggish if they get too cold.' I stopped and dropped my head on the grass. 'I just want to sleep.'

'Emma, make yourself smaller,' Simone said. She came to me and lifted my serpent head in both hands. 'Make yourself smaller. I can carry you and warm you up.'

No way could I make myself smaller, just the effort of talking was more than I could manage. 'Too ... hard ...' I said. 'Just ... sleep ...'

Emma, the stone said, *I know you're coming around. It is most vital that you don't take human form. Stay a snake.*

Huh?

Stay a snake, Emma, don't change.

'She's coming around,' the stone said out loud.

It was a very strange feeling waking up with no eyelids. My vision was blurry, but the thing I felt the most was the warmth. Delicious spreading warmth, all over my back, filtering through to my belly. My tail wasn't under the warmth and I moved it. Somehow I spread myself wider to catch every single ray of the wonderful warmth. I flicked my tongue and tasted the air. Simone was there; Leo was there, and Gold and his baby were there too. I raised my head; my vision was still unclear and my head fuzzy, but the warmth didn't shift.

'Mind out, Emma, you'll touch the ray lamp with your head,' Simone said.

'Warrrmmm,' I said.

'You have no idea how much she is enjoying this,' the stone said.

I dropped my head again. 'Blissssss.'

Gold's baby floated to settle in front of my snout. 'Thanks for helping to get me out, Aunty Emma.'

I flicked my tongue and touched it. It tasted of gold and talcum powder. 'You are welcome,' I said.

It flew up out of reach. 'Ew, she *licked* me!'

I chuckled in my throat and turned my head to see everybody. 'How long have I been out?'

'Twelve hours,' Simone said. 'It's 2 pm. The stone told us you were waking up.'

'Is Martin all right?'

'Martin is fine. He's downstairs eating.'

'Did his sister talk to him?'

'No. She's still in the lake, not talking.'

'Did we find Six?'

Simone hesitated, then, 'No. But we will find it.'

'It's probably gone to ground with one of its little friends,' I said. 'The other demons in that posse.'

'We'll find them,' Simone said.

'We need to head home,' I said. 'I have a diary full of appointments. Is the Sang Shen trial today or tomorrow? I want to be present for that. And you have an interview with the Chinese International School on Thursday.'

'Whoa, slow down, Emma,' Leo said. 'How about you take a break? You've just been to Hell and back — literally.'

I raised my head carefully; as Simone had said, there was a ray lamp above me, providing the warmth. 'I feel fine. You okay, Simone?'

'Don't you even want to see the Northern Heavens, Emma?' Simone said. 'As far as I know, you've never been here.'

'When's the trial?' I said.

'In an hour, 3 pm,' the stone said.

'How long to take me home?'

'About that long.'

I slithered off the bed onto the floor. 'Let's go.'

'Umm, Emma,' Simone said. 'The trial's here.'

That stopped me. 'No way.'

'Sang Shen is a resident of the Northern Heavens. He's under this jurisdiction. It's here,' Gold said.

'Oh damn,' I said, and dropped my head.

'The evidence is cut and dried, Emma,' the stone in my ring said. 'You don't need to attend.'

'That's why I *do*!' I said. 'If I don't go and testify on his behalf, they'll execute him.'

'But he's already dying,' the stone said.

'Asshole,' I said.

'It's the truth, my Lady,' the stone said.

'Do *not* give me that bullshit now,' I said. I slithered backwards and forwards on the floor of the elegantly decorated traditional bedroom with its rosewood four-poster bed and side tables inlaid with mother-of-pearl peonies. 'I can save his life.'

Simone raised one hand palm-up towards me. 'Emma, you can't testify. You can't take human form here; it will kill you. If you go to the trial, you have to go as a snake, and you have to identify yourself as Emma Donahoe. All of Heaven will find out that you're a snake. You can't do it.'

I slithered out of the bedroom. The house was a traditional two-storey Chinese courtyard style. Outside

474

the bedroom was a balcony that ran along the entire interior perimeter of the house, looking down into the courtyard, which was paved with cobblestones and had a small tree with a well beside it. I turned left and slithered along the balcony to the stairs in the corner, raised my head to grasp the balustrade, and slithered down the handrail to the floor below. The courtyard had doors opening onto the living room on the right and the kitchen on the left, with a dining room visible on the back wall.

I went into the dining room with the rest of the group following me. Martin was sitting at the round twelve-seater rosewood dining table eating a Japanese-sized bowl of noodles — easily twenty centimetres across. He saw me, placed his chopsticks on the table, rose, saluted me, then sat and waited for me to speak.

'Can you hide my serpent nature?' I asked. 'I want to attend Sang Shen's court case.'

'Yes,' Martin said. He picked up his chopsticks and stirred the noodles. 'But it would be against the law, so the answer is also no.'

'Can you attend in my place, stone? You were there,' I said.

'If I wasn't a possession, I could. But I was given to you as a gift, so I cannot testify on your behalf,' the stone said.

I went out to the courtyard, slithered up the trunk of the tree, and rested in one of the branches, needing a place to think. It was still night and the cold began to sink back into my bones. 'Wait, it's dark ... Didn't you say it was 2 pm right now?'

'The Northern Heavens are dying,' Martin said from his seat in the dining room. 'Most of the time it is dark. Only when a dragon or a Celestial comes to top up the energy do they have something approaching daylight, and even then it is like dusk, not day.'

I rested my chin on the branch. 'No wonder the trees are dying.'

'Sang Shen is also dying,' the stone in my ring said. 'Do not open yourself to political homicide by revealing your serpent nature, Emma. It would be futile in the end to try to save his life. He has no life to save.'

'I'll come and back you up, Emma,' Simone said.

'Thanks, Simone.'

'You don't know she'll do it,' the stone said.

'I know my Emma,' Simone said. 'And she wouldn't be able to live with herself if she let this tree be executed. As long as he has a chance, she'll fight for it.'

I slithered down the trunk of the tree. 'Simone is quite correct. Let's go.' I raised my snout. 'You guys want to come? There may be some backlash; I'd understand if you didn't want to.'

'If you don't mind, ma'am,' Gold said, 'I'd like to stay here with my child and make sure it's safe.'

'I'll stay here. Gold can keep an eye on me,' Leo said. 'Don't trust me enough to take me around with you.'

'I understand,' I said. I lifted my head towards the dining room. 'You coming, Martin?'

Martin slurped the last of his noodles, grabbed a tissue out of the large box in the centre of the table and wiped his mouth. He took a sip of some black tea in a glass sitting next to his bowl. 'Of course.'

I looked around; the house was white concrete, with a flat roof above the second storey holding a roof garden of potted plants — azaleas and bonsai trees. 'Whose house is this?'

'One of ours,' Simone said. 'Apparently it's a guest villa, and Gold and Jade stay here when they're in the Heavens.'

'As you've never been able to travel here, the occupation of this house has been a null point,' Gold said. 'Now that you are here, I will move out if you require.'

'It's being put to good use. Why would we change it?' I said. 'How far is it to the Court?'

'About five kilometres,' Martin said. 'One of the demons will drive us.'

'They have cars in *Heaven* too?' I said in disbelief.

'Of course we do. How else are we supposed to get around?' Martin said. 'Horse and cart?'

'Up until ten years ago this house *did* have a horse and buggy as its main form of transportation,' Gold said. 'The Dark Lord only bought the car recently.'

'He always was behind the times,' Martin said. He gestured towards the front door. Just inside it there was a large rosewood screen carved with turtles and snakes, blocking a view of the street. I stopped when I saw it.

'That's a demon barrier. That's a concern here?'

'No, of course not,' Martin said. 'But fung shui principles must be followed even in Heaven, and a barrier such as this will stop evil from entering the house.'

'There's evil in Heaven?'

'We're going to a trial for someone who attempted murder,' Martin said. 'So I think the answer is: yes.'

CHAPTER 32

O ne of the demon staff drove us to the hearing in a
1980s' vintage black Mercedes. I curled up on the
back seat looking out the window.

'How did they get a Mercedes up here?' I said.

'He carried it himself,' Martin said. 'They removed
the engine; it's powered by whichever demon drives it.
The demon moves the car.'

'I have a sudden image of *The Flintstones*,' Simone
said.

'That's what your mother called it,' Leo said. 'The
Flintstones car.'

'She came here?'

'Yes. Not often, because she hated coming to the
Celestial.'

Simone settled into her seat. 'That I can understand.'

The driver took us along wide avenues, each road
two lanes in each direction with a strip of garden in the
centre, the streetlights blazing in the darkness. Chinese-
style mansions, all with upwards-sweeping roofs and
complicated wooden windows, sat in the centre of their
own Chinese gardens complete with rocks and streams.
But all the grass was yellow, and the trees were brown
in the streetlights — everything was obviously dying.

'These houses are much larger than the one we just came out of,' I said.

'That's because they're not guest villas,' Martin said. 'Many extremely senior Shen live here. Or lived here. Many have moved out because of the energy drain.'

'Not much fun to live in a place so cold and dark,' I said.

The road ended in a roundabout with a fountain depicting the Xuan Wu in the centre. Behind a two-metre-high fence stood a complex of mansions, all two storeys high, with up to nine little animals on the corners of the roofs. There were two sets of gates, side by side, and the ones on the right slid smoothly open to allow the car entry to the paved forecourt.

Simone leaned on the armrest in the door and put her chin in her hand, looking out at the Palace complex. 'I suppose when Daddy comes back I'll be expected to live here.'

'Father hardly ever lived here himself,' Martin said. 'He spent some time here helping out with the running of the place, but he much preferred Wudangshan.'

'If you had a choice, where would you live, Emma?' Simone said. 'Would you like to go back to Australia? You often complain about the awful pollution and crowding in Hong Kong, and how life is so much easier in Australia.'

I turned my serpent head to see Simone. 'Ask me that again after I've seen the Mountain. In the photos, it looks truly wonderful. But for the moment ...' I looked out the window again. 'I choose to live where my family is. And that is you; and when John returns, it is him too.'

'Stop sounding like Daddy,' she said, her voice mild.

'What, wise?' Martin said.

'Yes,' Simone said.

The car came to a halt in front of the main Palace building. 'This is it, my Lords, my Ladies,' the demon driver said. 'The Central Yamen of the Northern Heavens — the Hall of Dark Justice.' He got out of the car and bowed as he opened the doors for us. 'I am profoundly honoured to serve the family of the Dark Lord himself.'

We exited the car. The building was nearly as big as the main audience hall in the Celestial Palace, with a set of steps going up to the massive front doors but no ramp in the middle. A veranda skirted the perimeter of the building with a carved wooden balustrade at waist height around it. The balustrade was decorated with snakes and turtles, and fairy lights had been strung all along the edges adding to the brilliance of the existing illumination.

A pair of demons in True Form, blue with bulging eyes and wearing helmets and armour, stood on either side of the doorway holding spears. They raised the spears when we approached.

'Stand down,' Simone said.

The demons dropped to one knee and bowed their heads.

We went into the hall. There was a lobby, about five by five metres, with two sets of double doors on the far wall, and another set of doors on each of the left and right walls. A large desk stood in the middle of the room, between the doors. A middle-aged Chinese woman and a young Chinese man were sitting behind the desk; both of them Shen. When I flicked my tongue, she smelt like a standard Taoist human Immortal, and the young man was a dragon. They rose as we approached them, their faces full of shock.

Martin bowed slightly to them and saluted. 'Greetings, Lily, Firebrand. It is good to see you again.'

Both of them fell to one knee and saluted us. 'Princess. Wang Chu.'

'I am no longer Wang Chu,' Martin said. 'I am nobody. And this …' He gestured towards me.

'Is Emma Donahoe, your Regent,' Simone said.

Lily and Firebrand stared at me, dumbstruck.

'Kowtow!' Martin said sternly.

Both of them dropped to their knees and touched their heads to the floor, as if pulled by strings. Then they rose again and stared at me.

'I know I am a snake. So is your Emperor. Is this an issue?' I said.

Firebrand saluted me. 'A thousand pardons, madam, but I was led to understand that you were an ordinary human.'

I raised my serpent head. 'I am.'

Lily saluted me. 'If you say you are, then you are, madam. How may we poor stupid subjects be of assistance?'

'You can start by not calling yourself stupid,' I said. 'If Xuan Wu gave you this job then you are competent. I am here for the trial of Sang Shen; I wish to testify.'

'You sound very much like the Dark Lord,' Lily said with wonder. 'Are you his Serpent, ma'am?'

'I hope not,' I said.

'This way, ma'am,' Firebrand said, gesturing towards the doors on the left. 'The trial has yet to begin.'

'Put us up the back of the room to start off with,' I said. 'I don't want to take attention away from the trial itself and turn it into a circus until I'm ready to speak.'

'I understand, ma'am,' Lily said. 'We will not announce you.'

They led us into the room. It was nothing like a Western courtroom; it was a simple rectangular room with the judge's desk on a dais at the far end and a wooden bench at the back for spectators. A guard stood on either side of the judge's chair, and four more guards stood on each side of the dais. They looked curiously at me at first, then saw Martin and Simone and fell to one knee, saluting.

'Rise,' Simone said. 'Continue.'

The guards pulled themselves to their feet and took their positions again.

The judge appeared seated behind the desk and the guards fell to one knee again.

'All kowtow in the presence of Judge Pure Sky,' one of the guards on the dais said loudly.

We kneel and salute, Martin said. He and Simone stood up and saluted the judge. I lowered my head.

The judge nodded to us. 'Welcome to my court, Gong Zhu, Tai Zi, Prince and Princess of the Northern Heavens.' He banged the desk with a block of wood. 'The court demands the presence of the tree spirit Sang Shen.'

Sang Shen was brought in by two more guards. He wore the simple white jacket and pants of the convict, but the character for 'convict' didn't appear on his back as it was depicted in many Chinese period dramas. His hands were chained behind his back. The guards led him to the middle of the floor and pushed him to his knees.

Sang Ye, his sister, followed him in. She glared at us, then went to the other end of the bench to stand waiting. Five or six more people followed her in. I tasted the air — yep, all tree spirits. Moral support, probably.

'All sit and listen to the words of the honoured judge,' one of the guards on the dais said.

Everybody sat on the benches. Sang Shen remained kneeling on the floor, his hands chained behind him.

'You have confessed to the attempted murder of your Regent,' the judge said. 'Do you have anything to say in your defence before I pass sentence?'

'My only regret is that I did not make a killing blow,' Sang Shen said.

You really don't want to waste your time helping this

one, Emma, the stone in my ring said. *It's not worth revealing yourself when he pleads guilty.*

I already revealed myself, I said.

Those two out the front work for you; they'd keep quiet, you just have to give the order.

I slithered off the bench and stood in front of it, raising my serpent head to human head height. 'If I may, Your Honour,' I said, hoping that the English term would be translated correctly by the language charm in Heaven. 'I am Emma Donahoe, Regent of the Northern Heavens, and I wish to make a statement.'

'Emma Donahoe is a human,' the Judge said. He glanced at Martin for clarification.

Simone rose. 'This is Emma Donahoe, previously my nanny, now my guardian. She also takes the form of a serpent.'

The Judge didn't turn away from Martin. 'My Prince?'

Martin also rose. 'I vouch for the fact that this is the Regent of the Northern Heavens, Acting Director of New Wudangshan Academy, the Dark Lady Emma Donahoe.'

I bobbed my head. 'I thank you.' I turned back to the Judge. 'I am the one that Sang Shen nearly killed, and I ask the court to be lenient with his sentence, as he had every right to be angry with me.'

'That may be so, madam, but he does not have the right to kill you.'

'As Regent, may I choose to pardon him?'

Sang Shen pulled himself to his feet and turned on me. 'I don't want a pardon! I want to die, and you will be the one to kill me! Chop my tree down, cut me into firewood, and burn me alive. I do not care! You are destroying us all!' He spat on the floor in front of me. 'You are destroying these Heavens, bitch. It does not surprise me at all that you are a snake, you evil

483

monster. You are worse than Da Ji, blinding the eyes of our Sovereign with your evil ways and leading him down the path of destruction for all of us. Any day now we expect you to order the making of hollow pillars of iron, so you can build fires inside and tie your subjects to them, watching with delight as they roast to death.'

'I want to preserve the Heavens, not destroy them,' I said.

'A fine job you are doing,' Sang Shen said, and turned back to face the Judge. He fell to his knees again. 'Sentence me. Make it quick, my Lord, because right now I am dying slowly. I would prefer to die quickly.'

'As Regent I wish to pardon him,' I said to the Judge.

'As Regent you cannot do such a thing,' the Judge said. 'The Northern Heavens are different from all the others. Our judicial system is separate from the monarchy. Nobody is above the law; not even the Dark Lord. You cannot decide to change the judgements that have been handed down. The Dark Lord set this up himself. He is the only one of the Four Emperors that has not set himself above his Court system.' He took a wooden slat with a character on it and threw it to the floor next to Sang Shen. 'Death. Tomorrow at noon. Cut down his tree.'

'Thank you, my Lord,' Sang Shen said. He turned back to see me as he was pulled to his feet. 'I only hope that the Dark Lord returns soon to see what you have done to his dominion.' He glared at Martin. 'And you were always too spineless to take control, you brokeback.'

Martin jerked back and his eyes widened.

'Take him away,' the judge said. He pulled open a book and took a brush from a stand on the desk. He inked the brush on an ink stone and wrote the sentence into the book. Then he nodded to us. 'Regent, Princess, Prince. It has been a pleasure seeing you in this courtroom.' He disappeared.

I dropped my head onto the floor, discouraged. I'd opened myself to all sorts of trouble by declaring my existence as a snake and it had been for nothing.

Told you, the stone said.

Shut up.

I raised my head again. Sang Ye had come to stand in front of me, the other tree spirits in a group behind her.

'I will die soon as well,' Sang Ye said. 'When I do, chop my tree into firewood and burn it in your kitchen.' She spat at the ground in front of me. 'I am the last of our line to live. Our trees have graced the Northern Heavens for thousands of years. I die without seed; there will be no more of us.'

She turned on her heel and strode out, the other tree spirits following.

Simone touched the back of my neck. 'Let's go home, Emma.' She saw how upset I was and threw her arms around my serpent neck. 'It'll be fine. It's not your fault.'

I rested my head on her shoulder. 'He's going to die, Simone. If it wasn't for me, he would be alive.'

'No way. It's nobody's fault. If anybody's, it's Daddy's. Definitely not yours.'

'I just wish I was Immortal and he could have had the satisfaction of killing me.'

'I wish you were Immortal too, dear Emma. Just remember, Daddy promised. Now let's go home.'

'He promised I'd get lost.'

'He promised he'd find you.'

'He'll only have to find me if I'm lost.'

There was a flash and a moment of disorientation and we were in the living room at home. Simone released me and stood back.

'See if you have any trouble taking human form,' she said.

485

I concentrated and slid easily into my human form. Every time I changed I wondered how we conjured the clothes. Maybe my subconscious didn't want me to be naked or something, and I was only naked after changing if I was too weak. Nobody seemed to know how it happened or care too much.

'Do you remember what happened?' Simone said.

'Did we go to Hell, visit a nest full of really big Snake Mothers, find Leo in a block of concrete, then go to the Northern Heavens and try to save Sang Shen?' I said.

'You remember all of it,' she said.

Leo and Martin appeared on the other side of the living room.

'Before I leave the Lion here, he has requested that I look for a stone that may have been planted on him,' Martin said.

'Go into his bedroom, we won't disturb you. Shout if you find anything,' I said.

Ah Yat came out of the kitchen. 'Welcome back, everyone. Is this the real Leo? He looks like the real Leo.'

'We hope I am, Ah Yat,' Leo said.

Ah Yat nodded and returned to the kitchen. 'This is good news. I will need to buy some steak for you.'

'That sounds absolutely awesome,' Leo said. He turned back to Martin. 'Let's check me out.'

Simone raised one hand and headed to her bedroom. 'I need to take a shower. This is all too freaky for me.' She stopped and turned to me. 'Are you sure you're all right?'

'I'm fine, go take a shower,' I said.

I went into the office and checked the email. Once again we'd been gone for more than twenty-four hours and the messages had piled up. The rest of the schools I'd contacted apologised and suggested she go on the waiting list. None of the tutors in China that I had contacted had bothered to reply. Louise wanted to see me, she sounded snarky in her email. I replied that I'd have lunch with her the next week if she liked. My parents had sent me an email from the Western Palace, skirting the issue of why I never visited them — again — and asking if I was available for dinner the following week. There was a thinly veiled suggestion that I was avoiding them. I replied and suggested dinner the following week as well.

'While we're on the subject of my social life, please contact Venus's secretary to book a lunch with him sometime in the next three weeks,' I told the stone. 'He's right, we need to keep in touch.'

'Where?'

'Mandarin coffee shop. We both love the cheesecake there.'

'Done.'

'Oh, ask Ah Yat to bring the messages in please.'

'Done.'

'Contact the White Tiger, ask him how Michael is.'

The phone rang and I answered it. It was the Tiger.

'Too early to know yet,' he said. 'The doctors say that you saved him from death or major brain damage though. Thanks. Rhonda says thanks too.'

'Is he still out?'

'Yeah, they have him in a drug-induced coma to let his brain heal. They say that they are cautiously optimistic, and we should know in about twenty-four hours.'

'Simone will want to know too, but now is not a good time.'

'Simone already asked about him.'

'Oh, okay.'

'Now, if you will excuse me, madam, I have a quarter of the sky to attend to.'

'Please excuse me as well, sir, as I do too.'

He hung up without another word.

'Now, do you need to get some rest?' I asked the stone. 'I think you've been awake since we entered Hell. That's an awfully long time for you, old man.'

'Actually, if you don't mind, Emma,' the stone said, 'I'd like to go spend some time with Gold and my grandchild. They're back in Happy Valley.'

'Wait.' I raised my head. 'I had no trouble at all coming in. Are the seals on the apartment still good?'

The stone was quiet for a moment, then, 'Yes. They're still as strong as ever, not eroding. Looks like removing that stone has fixed the problem.'

'So how could I get in without throwing up?'

'You came in as a serpent, Emma.'

'Oh. So the seals don't see the serpent as a demon? And the serpent doesn't see the seals as a demon?'

'Apparently not. By your leave, ma'am.'

'Off you go.'

The stone disappeared.

Ah Yat came into the office. 'I have put the mail and some noodles in the dining room for you, ma'am.'

I had a sudden memory of John eating noodles and opening the mail in the dining room a million years ago, when he had asked me to work full-time for him. I hesitated, then said, 'Okay, Ah Yat, there's plenty of room in there. Please ask Simone if she would like to eat as well. Thank you.'

Ah Yat bowed slightly and went out.

I went into the dining room, sat at the table, and picked up my chopsticks and spoon. For some reason vegetarian noodles didn't really appeal; what I truly craved was ... meat. Probably a backlash from being a snake for such a long time. I wondered if my snake would eat things alive the same way John's would. Lovely.

When I was about halfway through my noodles, Martin came in. He saluted me, then sat at the table.

'Ask Ah Yat if you want some,' I said, pointing with my chopsticks at the noodles.

'No need, what I had in the Heavens was more than sufficient,' he said. 'I found nothing in Leo's body cavities. Perhaps they had something in his clothes when he was here the last time.'

'Not really possible, we found him naked,' I said. 'He seemed disoriented; maybe he had a stone inside him then.'

'Possible.' He rose. 'I will leave you now. I hope you do not mind if I come to visit my sister occasionally. I missed Simone terribly while I was in Hell. I truly do want to be a good brother for her.'

'Wait,' I said. 'I would like you to do me a favour. You said you weren't welcome in either Heaven or Hell. Well, I have a job for you. Don't go back to the sea; stay and help us.'

'After what I've done?' he said.

'Gold said you were telling the truth. You really want to help. Would you like to help us by being a liaison between myself and the staff of the Northern Heavens? Particularly since now everybody knows I'm a snake.'

He bobbed his head. 'I would be honoured.'

'I remember you being offered a position like this before, and messing it up completely by falling for Number One son of the Demon King,' I said.

'That was before I met Leo.'

'Actually, you met Leo when you were infiltrating us on behalf of One,' I said.

'This is true. It was one of the hardest things I have ever done to bring One to the household. But I gave my word to him.'

'Seems making dumb promises runs in the family,' I said.

'That it does,' he said. 'I will take up residence in the lake.'

'No, you won't. I'll give you an edict from me to the senior staff of the Northern Heavens to give you an apartment in the Palace complex.'

He was taken aback. 'That is not necessary!'

'Yes, it is. You are my representative there and you need to be treated accordingly. I bet you had an apartment in the Palace before, when you lived there as Crown Prince.'

'I did,' he said. 'It is probably still there.'

I put my chopsticks down. 'Good. Let's go into the office and I'll write you something to make sure you can stay there. If they give you any shit, get them to call me.'

He grinned. 'I'm looking forward to working with you.'

I patted him on the upper arm as we went out to the office.

Just after dinner the doorbell rang. I opened the door to a visitor from home — an Australian who I vaguely recognised. I hunted through my memory while she stood in the doorway, waiting.

I smiled. 'Hi, I'm trying to work out where I remember you from.'

'Humph,' she said with a strong rural Australian accent. 'Never met you before in my life.'

I studied her, desperately trying to remember where I knew her from. She was obviously Aboriginal; she appeared to be in her mid-sixties, only about a metre-and-a-half tall, and wearing a plain tan-coloured sleeveless cotton shift that swept halfway to the floor. She had the extremely dark skin and strong features of a pure-blood Aborigine, a flat nose and wide mouth, and short dark curly hair shot with grey.

I shrugged. 'Sorry, no idea where I know you from. Can I help you? What's this about?'

She had no difficulty entering through the seals without being invited, and stopped in the living room to look around as I closed the front door. 'Nice.'

'I'm Emma Donahoe, lovely to meet you ...' I let my voice trail off to encourage her to give me her name.

She pointed at the stone in my ring; the stones had returned after dinner. 'Is that little asshole giving you any trouble?'

The stone in my ring yelped, then said into my head, *Kneel, Emma, kneel — it's HER!*

'Too late for kneeling, little asshole,' I said to the stone, and I grinned at the Grandmother of All the Rocks. 'Sorry I didn't recognise you, Grandmother Uluru ...' My voice trailed off as I placed where I knew her from. 'Holy shit, you're a professor of comparative literature at Brisbane Tech! I attended one of your lectures while I was doing my undergrad degree.'

She clasped her hands together and sat on the couch. 'Then I have met you before.' She patted the cushion next to her. 'Come and sit. I think we have a few things to talk about. One of them being an Eastern demon that's been messing with my kids.'

Gold entered from the kitchen, accompanied by his child who was floating at eye level. Gold froze when he saw the Grandmother. He quickly changed to stone form, zipped into the living room and settled onto the floor. 'My Lady Grandmother.'

'*Nanna*!' Gold's child shrieked, and shot to the Grandmother, hitting her in the stomach with an audible thump. It settled into her lap with a delighted squeal and jumped up and down. 'Nanna, Nanna, Nanna, Nanna, *Nanna*!'

The Grandmother touched Gold's baby. 'It's good to see you too, little one,' she said with affection. She waved one hand at Gold. 'Up you get, Trouble, and take your proper form. You're not done with your punishment yet.'

Gold took human form, and fell to one knee, bowing his head to the Grandmother. 'I look forward to completing my sentence and rejoining you.'

'I hear you have something for me,' the Grandmother said to me.

'Gold, go and get them,' I said.

'Ma'am,' Gold said, and went into my office.

'I'm glad you stopped this demon,' the Grandmother said. 'My children were living in fear because of it. I was hoping someone would stand up and assist us; the stones have been fighting a losing battle against it.'

'I didn't finish it,' I said with remorse. 'It's still out there, and it probably joined up with the rest of its little friends. But I will track it down and destroy it.'

Gold came in with a carved camphorwood box that we'd moved the dead stones into. He knelt in front of the sitting Grandmother and lowered his head. 'I am glad that we could return them to you, Mother.'

She took the box, opened it, and her face went grim when she saw how many dead stones were inside. She closed the box again and wiped her eyes. 'So many. So many.'

She held the box in her lap, and Gold's baby floated to sit on top of it. She turned to study me. 'So you're the famous Emma Donahoe. There's something of a ruckus around the traps at the moment — seems you turned into a great big black snake right in front of everybody.'

'I've been a snake for a while; nobody seems to know why,' I said. 'Only just went public with it yesterday. The Jade Emperor said that it might have something to do with my Australian nature. Do I look like a Rainbow Serpent?'

The Grandmother took my face in both her hands

and concentrated on me, then released me. 'Nope. I vaguely remember seeing something like you a couple of hundred years ago, among the first waves of white settlers, but you're definitely not one of ours.'

'Well, that's a start,' I said. 'My father's tracking down my family tree; he may find out who this first settler was, and where they came from, and we can trace it back from there.'

'Any other members of the family snakes?' the Grandmother said.

'No,' I said. 'But I have to admit I'm in a unique situation ...'

'Sleeping with one, I understand,' she said.

'Also, if they could turn into snakes, I don't think they'd want to anyway.'

'Perfectly understandable,' she said. She rose, holding the box, and Gold's child floated away from her. 'I suppose I'd better take these poor dead things home.'

'Do you mind if I come and visit you sometime?' I said.

She touched my arm. 'Dearie, I would like that more than you could possibly know. Just come to Uluru, and touch me. I will take this form and show you around the nurseries, and make you a really nice cuppa and some lamingtons.'

I gasped with pleasure. 'I have *not* had a halfway decent lamington since I left home.'

'Yeah, all this Chinese muck they eat here, pig's snouts and chicken's feet, don't understand any of it,' she said, and winked at me. 'But I do like their Chinese veggies.'

'Me too,' I said. I went to the door to show her out. 'I can't tell you what an honour it is to meet you, Grandmother.'

'Likewise,' she said. 'You're an Aussie girl who's gone out and made the world your home, and that always makes me proud. I see the students at the uni working so hard, and it pleases me when they take their studies and go out and do great things.'

'Thanks,' I said, feeling my face redden.

'Oh, look, now I've gone and made you blush,' she said, delighted. 'Typical young people — talk about sex like it's nothing, but you hand them a compliment and they're lost for words.'

'I'm not that young any more — I'll be forty soon,' I said.

She leaned closer. 'You're young compared to one of us,' she said confidentially. She went out the door and stood in the lobby. 'Come and talk to me soon. I'll see if I can find out more about that snake with the first settlers for you.'

'I will!' I said, and she disappeared.

CHAPTER 33

I was woken that night by a touch — then by someone strangling me. I grasped the hands around my neck and tried to pull them away, but they were way too strong for me. I opened my eyes and saw Leo, his face blank, his hands around my throat. His thumbs pressed against my voice box; if he broke it I was dead.

I used a lock break move and freed myself, then attempted to Push him into paralysis by touching the side of his throat. He slid to the side and I missed him, but felt a large lump on the back of his neck, just at the bottom of his hairline. Usually he had a fold of skin there on his bald head, but this was more.

I changed to a snake of natural size, less than a metre long, and wriggled away, sliding across the floor to the other side of the room. I changed back to human form and readied myself as he came at me. One chance at this, Emma, be fast. I pointed the first two fingers of my right hand at him, as if I was pretending to hold a gun, and hit the right spot. He fell like a dead tree face-down in front of me.

I knelt to check the back of his neck. Yes, there was a lump about two centimetres across just at the base of his skull. It wasn't very noticeable because of the folds of skin. I touched it and he didn't move. I changed to serpent form and touched it with my tongue, then pulled back with revulsion. It tasted of death and talcum powder.

I reverted to human form and summoned the Murasame. I had never attempted anything like this before and hoped I could do it. I carefully placed the sword horizontally over the lump and ran it lightly along his skin. The sword fought me, trying to make more than a shallow cut, but I managed to keep control of it. His black skin parted easily, revealing a layer of fat that quickly began to ooze blood. The stone was visible, shiny black and smooth. I took a deep breath, reached in and pulled it out, bringing some blood with it. I rose to put it on the other side of the room.

I turned back to Leo and stopped. He was shrinking, losing weight all over his body, his muscles becoming smaller. Hair sprouted from his head, grey over the black, but only around the base of his skull, leaving the top bald. He'd aged from late-thirties to late-forties. He turned his head to see me, groggy, and he had grown a salt and pepper beard.

I knelt next to him. 'Don't move, I still need to heal up this wound on your neck. It's bleeding.'

'What happened?'

'You had a stone planted in there. It was controlling you, I think. But now that it's gone, you've aged eight years.'

He dropped his head on the carpet. 'I feel like it.' He raised his head again. 'I can't feel my legs. I can't move them.'

I flopped to sit next to him. 'Oh dear Lord, no.'

'No, Emma, it's a good thing,' he said. 'It means that those demons aren't controlling me any more, and that you're safe.'

'Let me change back to a snake and see what I can heal.'

'Don't you bring that reptile anywhere near me, lady,' he growled into the carpet.

'Okay, you're definitely back,' I said, and changed to a snake. I touched my nose to the back of his neck and healed the wound, then checked his spine — the bones were crushed and the spinal column completely destroyed. Perhaps another snake with greater healing abilities than me could do it, but I couldn't.

I changed back to human and the ground hit me hard.

I came around with Simone's concerned face above me. 'How many times did you change back and forth?' she said.

'About three,' I said. 'I needed to be human to cut him open. Then I needed to be the snake to heal him.'

Leo was next to her. He was very much older, and in a wheelchair. 'Changing too much wears you out?'

'Yeah,' I said. I rose so I was sitting upright. 'And you had a stone embedded in the back of your neck. I pulled it out and put it on my desk.'

'I saw it,' Simone said. 'I've never seen anything quite so evil before. The Tiger said that he wants to have a look at it in his lab in the West.'

'Tell him he can,' I said.

'I already did. He came and took it about half an hour ago, and left us a wheelchair for Leo.'

'Okay.' I rotated so that my legs were over the side of the bed. I was still wearing my pyjamas. 'Now I have to change to the snake again and you have to take me to the Northern Heavens, Simone. I think there may be a similar stone embedded in Yue Gui.'

'Who is Yue Gui?' Leo said.

'Our older sister,' Simone said.

'Our?'

'Me and Martin.'

'That bastard betrayed you; you should not be trusting him,' Leo said.

'Some of your memory is gone,' I said. 'I think the stone in your neck was messing with your head.'

'It was messing with a lot of things,' Leo said. 'Look at me. Eight years older and a paraplegic.'

'You're still our Leo,' I said.

'I'm not taking you up to the Northern Heavens at 3 am,' Simone said. 'I'm taking Leo back to his bed, and then I'm going back to bed myself. We can do it in the morning.'

'We should do it now,' I said.

Simone took the handles of Leo's chair and moved to wheel him out. 'That's nice for you, Emma, but I won't take you till you've had a decent night's sleep. So go back to bed, and I'll take you after breakfast.' She opened the door to my room. 'And, stone, don't let her call anyone else to help, 'cause she needs her rest.'

'Don't worry, Princess, I do too,' the stone said. 'Emma, go back to bed.'

'They're right, Emma, deal with it in the morning,' Leo said as she wheeled him out.

I took the ring off my finger and put it on the side table, then pulled myself out of bed.

Simone stopped halfway through the door and glared at me. 'Go back to bed!'

'I need to go to the bathroom first, Miss Bossy Pants,' I said. 'It's the middle of the night and I just woke up.'

Simone smiled slightly, embarrassed. 'Oh, okay, sorry. Night, Emma. Tomorrow morning, okay? First thing.'

'Okay,' I said, and she went out, closing the door behind her.

I went into the bathroom and closed the door. I changed into a snake and concentrated on the Northern

Heavens. I focused all my thoughts on the grassy lawn next to the lake where we'd encountered Yue Gui.

Nope, couldn't do it.

I changed back, did what I'd said I was going to do, and went back to bed.

'Didn't work, eh?' the stone said from the side table.

'Shut up,' I said, and turned off the light.

We usually had breakfast at the small four-seater table in the kitchen, just Simone and me, but when I went out the next morning Ah Yat indicated that we were eating in the dining room. Leo had his usual huge mug of black coffee in front of him but wasn't eating the breakfast Ah Yat had made for him. Simone was sitting with white coffee and scrambled eggs but also wasn't eating. Both of them looked miserable.

I sat down to my tea and toast and opened the peanut butter jar. 'What?' I said.

'Leo still wants to die,' Simone said.

'I'm HIV positive. I have AIDS. I'm a danger to all of you. I don't want to live. How about letting me go?' Leo said. 'I want to go back to Chicago, see my family one last time, and then disappear for good.'

'After all the trouble these two went through to get you out, you want to die,' the stone said. 'Fine way to thank them.'

'Stone, he has a point. If I was in his situation I'd probably want the same thing,' Simone said.

'As far as your family is concerned, you're dead,' I said.

Leo's face went grim. 'I'll be dead in a year anyway.'

'If you take the Elixir of Immortality you will be cleared of the AIDS,' I said.

'You want to commit me to an eternity of pining ...' Leo didn't finish.

'For something you can't have. Yes,' I said.

'Emma, you said something to the Leo copy in Hell that changed his mind. What was it?' Simone said.

'Something extremely personal that you probably don't want to hear.'

Simone stared at me, silent for a moment. She hesitated, then said, 'I thought Daddy was straight.'

'Are you *sure* you want to explore this, Simone?' Leo said.

'No, no, I'm fine with it,' Simone said. 'Did you offer him the chance of sharing Daddy with him? 'Cause Leo's like a father to me, and having two dads is okay.' She shrugged. 'Two dads, two moms, a sister who's a turtle, a gay emo brother — I'll fit right in with most of the kids at school.'

'I think I need to give *you* a gold coin,' I said.

'Your father is the straightest man I have ever met,' Leo said. 'It's probably why I fell for him so hard.'

'Leo has no chance whatsoever in that direction,' I said. 'What I offered was for your dad to drain him when he returns.'

'Oh,' Leo said softly. 'That makes it different.' He stared at the table, thinking. 'That makes it all different.'

'Don't you even consider it!' Simone said.

'I'm sorry, sweetheart, but it sounds too good to be true,' Leo said.

She rose and leaned on the table with one hand. 'Oh, thank you very much. So when I get one father back, I'll lose the other?'

'You won't lose Leo, he'll merge with your dad. They'll be one,' I said.

'I'll lose him!' She rounded on Leo. 'Haven't I lost enough people I love already?' She swept the air with her hand. 'Am I such a bad daughter that you want to *die* to be away from me?' She glared at him. 'All right. When Daddy comes back, he can drain you, and good riddance.' She stormed out, slamming the door behind her.

'She has no trouble with the idea of us being in a threesome, but when she hears about this she panics,' I said.

'He wouldn't do it,' Leo said.

'He would if I asked him to.'

'God, Emma, that would be a dream come true.'

'I know. I want it too.' I smiled wryly. 'Déjà vu. I said that to your demon copy in Hell.'

'You're *absolutely certain* I'm not a copy?' Leo held up his wrist with the number four tattooed on it. 'That's the death number.'

'That's why I'm sure you're the real one,' I said. 'You're the one we were supposed to kill.' I pointed at his wrist. 'You're marked for death.'

'But a *demon* told you where I was.'

'If we find a stone in Yue Gui's neck, then I know who that demon was,' I said. 'I think it was Six himself. He gave us Yue Gui to put into the lake at the Northern Heavens and spy for him. He cleared out his nest in Sham Shui Po and left you there ready for us to collect. We were supposed to think you were a demon copy and bring you back here for examination. Then you'd kill me with the strength of a demon from that stone inside you. Then Simone or someone would kill you, and she'd be left with nobody. Six would do the hands-off-our-gangsters deal with a heartbroken Simone and give her one of the other Leo copies, telling her that it was the real Leo — which would be another spy controlled by them.'

'But I didn't try to kill you,' he said. 'I wasn't controlled until Six turned up at the front door.'

'You had your hands around my throat, then you said you couldn't hurt me and changed it into a kiss,' I said. 'You were confused, but you still wouldn't hurt me — your will was stronger than they expected. Six needed to get you back to make sure that you did the job right, so he made the desperate move of kidnapping me and pretending to make the deal — just to get you back.'

'And when you found me in Hell ...'

'They were putting the stone in the back of your neck — and into the back of the neck of the Leo they were going to give us after we destroyed you. You tried to kill me last night. But they didn't know I'm a snake. My human form wouldn't have been able to stand against you with that stone in you — you were way too strong — but my snake form could do it.'

'So Martin betrayed you again by leading you to me,' Leo said.

'I don't think so,' I said. 'He really is genuinely trying to help. And you were still on the operating table when we broke in. Six's nest is destroyed, and he's on the run.' I rested my chin in my hand. 'The only one who hasn't been any assistance whatsoever here is the Demon King. All he did was lead us into Six's nest in Guilin to clear it out for him.'

'It's all way too complicated for me,' Leo said, and took a sip of his coffee. 'I'm just glad that their plans didn't work out. And that you're smart enough to know what's going on.'

'Most of the time I have no idea what's happening until it's happened,' I said. 'This is all speculation. I'll only know I'm right if Yue Gui has a stone embedded in her as well.'

He smiled wryly. 'You sound like him. What's that expression he used? Played like a pipa.'

'That's the way I feel,' I said. 'They've played me. I'm really not up to this job.'

'If he thought you were up to it, you're up to it,' Leo said. 'Let me think about this draining thing. I need some time.'

'Take as long as you need. But if you do go for it,

then it would be best to take the Elixir of Immortality. It will clear you of the disease and give you abilities beyond the norm as well as the Immortality thing. You'll be able to wait for as long as it takes.'

'I don't care about any of that, but I would be willing to do it for the chance to be one with him,' Leo said.

I buttered my toast. 'So would I.'

'Simone needs to eat her breakfast,' the stone said.

'Send it to her room, she can eat in there,' I said.

Her scrambled eggs disappeared.

'You forgot the coffee,' I said.

'She took it, I didn't,' the stone said.

'You forgot your coffee,' I said loudly, but the coffee had already disappeared.

Martin met us at the grassy lawn next to the lake. It was 9 am but it was still dark, the stars in the sky blazing brighter than any I had seen.

'Let me see if I can call her,' he said. He went to the edge of the water, raised his head, and concentrated.

She emerged from the water, pulled herself onto the dark sand at the edge of the lake, then waited patiently.

'Take care, she isn't sentient,' Martin said. 'Don't frighten her.'

'What if we find a stone and have to cut her open?'

Martin hesitated. 'I suppose one of us will have to hold her.'

I carefully approached her and could see that she was watching me. I curled up next to her, Martin and Simone with me, and touched the back of her neck with my serpent snout.

'She has one,' I said. 'There's a stone here, where her neck meets her shell. It's almost invisible under the front of her shell.'

Simone grabbed the front and rear of her shell, lifted her, and sat with Yue Gui in her lap. 'Okay, I have her.'

'I can't do it in serpent form,' I said. 'Martin, you'll have to do it.'

Martin nodded. He summoned the Silver Serpent and knelt next to Yue Gui. He felt the back of her neck and she struggled, her flippers striking Simone on either side of her body.

'Do you have her?' Martin said, his focus not moving from the back of Yue Gui's neck.

'Yes. Do it,' Simone said.

Martin placed the sword on the back of Yue Gui's neck and sliced it. Yue Gui struggled harder, and Simone grunted with the effort of holding her. Martin pulled out a black stone identical to what had been in Leo's neck, quickly rose, and took it about five metres away, dropping it on the grass as if it was toxic.

'That is nasty!' he said, brushing his hands on his slacks. He dismissed the sword. 'Can you heal her, Emma?'

Yue Gui changed form, becoming thinner and larger and longer and freeing herself from Simone's grip. She changed into a young Chinese woman in a silvery Tang robe, lying across Simone's knees. She rolled off onto her back on the grass, her eyes glazed.

'Roll her over,' I said, and Martin turned her over.

I touched my snout to the back of her neck. Martin had done well; the cut was shallow and hadn't even broken any large blood vessels. I sealed the wound. 'Fixed.'

Martin gently put her on her back, took her hand and gazed into her eyes. 'Jie Jie. Do you hear me? Yue Gui.'

She gasped and her eyes went wide. She shuddered and her body went stiff, then she relaxed. She cast around, confused. 'What happened?'

Martin pulled her up to sit on the grass and she saw me. 'Father?'

I bobbed my serpent head. 'Hello, Yue Gui, I'm pleased to meet you. My name is Emma Donahoe.'

Her face filled with understanding. 'You're Father's promised. I remember.' She saw Simone. 'Are you See Mun?'

'My English name is Simone.'

Yue Gui moved to rise and Martin helped her. She looked around. 'I don't remember what happened. How I came to be here.'

'A demon planted a stone in your neck. It forced you to stay in turtle form and locked out your sentience.'

'How long have I been like this?' she said.

Martin held her hands. 'We don't know, Jie Jie.'

She smiled at him. 'Di Di. It is good to have you back in the Northern Heavens.' She turned to Simone, who had risen to stand next to them. 'And you are my new Mei Mei, my new little sister.' She smiled at both of them. 'Our family has grown. I am glad.'

Simone reached for Yue Gui's hand and Martin released it so that she could hold it. The three of them stood in a ring, holding hands, and immediately the sky changed from black to the pure dark intense blue of the Celestial Plane. The air warmed and filled with the scent of living things. Martin, Simone and Yue Gui raised their heads, apparently revelling in the feeling of bringing the energy to the Heavens.

I spread out on the grass, opening my ribcage to make myself flatter to absorb the warmth. An orange glow appeared on the horizon — the sun was about to rise.

'The sun has not risen in the Northern Heavens in six years,' Martin said with wonder. 'See if we two can do it; Simone needs to go to school — when we find one for her.' He released Simone's hand and gestured for Yue Gui to give her other hand to him. The rising sun's glow disappeared, but the sky didn't go dark again.

'I need to come back in,' Simone said, and they took her hands again. The warmth and feeling of growing things filled the air and the sun peeped over the horizon. 'Needs all three of us.'

'Three of us to build the energy for a few hours, then the two of us can keep it going, Mei Mei,' Martin said. 'You don't need to be here all the time.'

'You can restore the life to the Northern Heavens?' I said.

They nodded.

'The trees won't die?'

'No,' Martin said. 'Life will return to the Heavens. No more trees will die.'

'Can you stay and do this, Yue Gui?'

'Of course. I have always been part of the administration here.'

'Yue Gui is a member of the Council,' Martin said.

'That's a relief,' I said. Suddenly I remembered. 'We need to go see Sang Shen! See if he will change his plea now that we can assure them the trees won't die!'

'The judgement has been recorded, Emma. It cannot be changed.'

'I have to try,' I said.

'Is this the one that cannot resist a challenge?' Yue Gui said.

'That she is,' Martin said.

'Sang Shen has a sentence recorded against him?'

'He tried to kill Emma,' Martin said.

'Why?'

Martin raised one hand to indicate the sky, which was fading again without their energy. 'Revenge for the death of his father.'

'Sang Da Ren died?'

'Not six months ago.'

Yue Gui dropped her head. 'That is sad news. I knew

Sang Da Ren for a very long time.' She raised her head. 'Let us save Sang Shen.'

We found Sang Shen standing under his tree with the guards, one of whom carried a petrol-powered chainsaw and another a large axe. He was still in the white of a convict with his hands chained behind him and his expression defiant.

He was a mulberry tree, and enormous, at least fifteen metres high and a similar amount around, spreading like a huge umbrella. His branches were bare, with yellow serrated leaves covering the ground beneath them.

'Mulberry trees are practically indestructible once established,' Yue Gui said sadly. 'Conditions must have been extremely bad to kill him.' She glanced at Martin. 'How many more plants have died?'

'Not many. Most of them are like Sang Shen, however, with only a year or so to live before the darkness and cold kills them.'

Sang Shen saw Yue Gui. 'Mother!' He struggled with his bonds for a moment, then gave up and ran to us, falling to his knees in front of her. 'Mother, I thought you were dead.'

Yue Gui touched Sang Shen's head and the chains fell away.

Simone raised her hands. 'Wait, wait, wait. You're his *mother*?'

Sang Shen pulled himself to his feet and took Yue Gui's hands, gazing down at her with adoration. 'It is a long story.'

'That is his way of avoiding embarrassing me,' Yue Gui said with amusement.

The guards approached us and Yue Gui raised her hand to stop them. 'Hold until we are finished talking to him, then you may have him.'

The guards saluted and moved back.

Yue Gui nodded to them and turned back to Sang Shen. 'I was walking through the Palace grounds one autumn day and one of the mulberry trees was heavy with dark fruit. They looked so delicious that I ate some. Later that evening, the spirit of that tree came to me and asked me if it was as good for me as it was for him.' She dropped her head, coy. 'I could not lie to him.'

'This tree sprouted the day I was born, and I have been that tree ever since,' Sang Shen said. 'I am the tree child of a turtle.'

'That means that you're my *nephew*,' Simone said in shock.

Sang Shen nodded to her. 'That I am, I suppose.'

'What about Sang Ye?'

'She is not mine, she is all tree,' Yue Gui said. 'My time with Sang's father was short. I felt the call of the sea and left him, and when I came back he had found a new love. But what we had together was very special.' She held her son's hands harder. 'Sang Shen, you will not die. We can save you. We can save all of you.'

'Yue Gui, Ming Gui and Simone together can bring warmth and light to the Heavens again,' I said.

Sang Shen gazed down at her. 'No more trees will die?' He released his mother's hands. 'Show me. Show me that this is true.'

Martin, Simone and Yue Gui joined hands, raised their heads, and the sky immediately filled with light and warmth. The breeze changed from chill to comforting, full of the scent of life.

Sang Shen raised his face and arms to the light, his expression beatific. His tree sprouted shoots, turning green all over, and the grass beneath our feet turned greener and grew as I watched.

'Can you hold it though?' Sang Shen said. 'It will not

drain you? You will not plunge us into darkness?' He shook his head. 'It feels so *good*! My sap is moving for the first time in *years*.'

'Too much information,' Yue Gui said with amusement. 'Yes. We can charge it like a battery, and it will last at least two weeks. We will need to top it up every now and then, but it will not be a serious drain on us.'

'By the Heavens, I think I'm going to flower,' Sang Shen said, embarrassed. 'I can't control it. Right in front of everybody too.'

The tree sprouted greenish-grey flowers, each long and narrow and hanging in bundles off the branches. Sang Shen's face was full of rapture.

'Spring has arrived in the Northern Heavens,' Simone said. 'It's a good feeling.'

Sang Shen nodded to her. 'You have returned my mother, and with her, life to the Heavens. I thank you.' He turned back to the guards. 'I am ready now.'

'Let us try to save you,' I said. I gestured with my nose towards his tree. 'You are full of life, we can't cut you down now!'

Sang Shen ignored me and walked back to his tree.

'The sentence must be carried out, my Lady,' one of the guards said. 'You may not want to watch. Whatever happens to the tree happens to the Shen as well.'

Yue Gui released Martin's and Simone's hands, but the warmth remained. She came to stand next to me. 'He will be the first Shen tree cut down in living memory.' She glanced down at me. 'And when somewhere is populated by Immortals, that is a very long time.'

I lowered my head. 'I don't want to watch.'

'You can't close your eyes, you're a snake, same as our father,' she said. She touched the top of my head. 'Come. All will be well. The Heavens are just.'

She reached out and took Martin's hand and the sky flared to life again.

Sang Shen knelt under his tree, his head bowed and face expressionless. One of the guards pulled the cord to start the chainsaw and approached the tree.

Simone looked away. 'I don't want to watch either.'

'Take our hands and add energy to the Heavens, See Mun,' Yue Gui said. 'And watch what happens.'

'Okay,' Simone said, and joined hands with them. The sky visibly brightened and the guards looked up, then returned to the tree.

'Did you know that some of Heaven's finest silk is produced by worms that eat the leaves from his tree?' Yue Gui said as the guard approached the tree with the chainsaw. 'One of his main sources of income was his own leaves, carefully harvested and sold at a premium to silk producers in the Eastern Heavens.'

'They did not tell anyone that their mulberry leaves came from the north; they wanted the legend to stand that their own trees were better,' Martin said, and winced as the chainsaw hit the tree.

The guard stood with the chainsaw against the trunk of the tree and an expression of confusion swept across his face.

'It is enough,' Yue Gui said. 'We just need to hold it.'

The chain on the saw broke, and the guard turned it off and stared at it, confused. The other guard hefted his two-handed axe, took a deep breath and swung it into the trunk. It bounced off ineffectually. He tried again twice more; each time the axe made no mark on the bark.

The guards stood back and stared at the tree, perplexed.

Yue Gui released Simone's and Martin's hands and stepped forward. 'Report this matter to the judiciary. I will take custody of the prisoner until a solution to this problem has been reached. Suggest to the magistrate that the best option might be a suspended sentence until the execution can be carried out.'

The guards knelt and saluted Yue Gui, then walked back to the Palace complex.

Yue Gui turned to us and smiled broadly with her arms out. 'I hope the demons in my residence have maintained it while I was away. Who is hungry? I believe it is lunchtime. And after lunch, Ming Gui, See Mun and myself have some more trees to save.' She threw one arm around Martin's shoulder. 'I think I still have some really *ripe* whale in my freezer that I found in the South Pacific about twenty years ago. This is a special occasion, I hope it is still good.'

'You eat *whale*?' Simone said with horror. 'Hunting whales is barbaric!'

'Only whale that has died of natural causes,' Yue Gui said, her smile not shifting. 'Do not be concerned, little sister, I think the human hunting of whales is barbaric too.'

'A treat I haven't had for a very long time, sister,' Martin said. 'Lead on.'

'What about me?' Sang Shen said.

'You are released into my custody,' Yue Gui said.

'No.' He didn't move. 'I deserve to be punished.' He turned to return to the Palace complex. 'They can put me in jail.'

'Ah Shen,' Yue Gui said, but he didn't stop. She went after him and took his arm. 'You are released into my custody. Obviously you don't understand. You'll be living with me. Full-time.'

He stared at her for a moment, then turned back to the Palace. 'I'd rather go to jail.'

'I know, that's why you're coming with me,' Yue Gui called after him. 'Don't make me put the chains back on you.'

He stopped, dropped his head and shook it, then returned to us. 'You are a cruel woman, Mother.'

She bowed slightly to him. 'Thank you. Now let's go find some lunch. I might be able to send someone to the market for some lemonade for our tree.'

'It is good to have you back, Mother, Uncle.' He grinned at Simone. 'Auntie. I will ask Sang Ye to join us for lunch; she did not want to watch this.' He lowered his head and shook it. 'She will not die. None of us will die.' He raised his head. 'This is a great day!'

'My family just keeps growing all the time,' Simone said with wonder.

'This is not a bad thing,' Yue Gui said.

'I guess it's not.'

'I'll go back to the guesthouse and wait for you,' I said.

Martin gestured towards the Palace. 'There is an Empress's apartment in the Palace, and I believe that is yours.' He stopped and turned. 'But please, come with us.'

'No, this is for family only, I think,' I said. 'And I don't want to lord it over the Palace staff as a snake; it's not right. Sang Shen has a point: I'm the cause of most of this and it would probably be a good idea if I kept a low profile. You're a much more acceptable representative.'

Simone came to me and touched my serpent head, then threw her arms around my neck. 'You're family too, Emma, you're like my mother.' She turned to Sang Shen with one arm still slung over my neck. 'Don't hate her. The only crime she's committed is falling in love with Daddy. The rest of it is his fault more than hers.'

'This is true,' Martin said. 'Come to Jie Jie's house, and we'll tell you the whole story and you can decide for yourself.'

Sang Shen hesitated, then shrugged. 'I don't think I have much choice.'

'Oh, excellent idea,' Yue Gui said with enthusiasm. 'While you stay at my house, you will have to listen to Di Di's jokes and stories every day you are there.'

'What's wrong with my jokes?' Martin said, indignant.

'You really are a very cruel woman indeed,' Sang Shen said. He spread his arms. 'Let's go. Lunch with the family sounds good.' He nodded to me. 'I suppose I am willing to give you a second chance if they all say you are genuine.'

CHAPTER 34

I went into the kitchen the next morning to find breakfast and once again Ah Yat shooed me into the dining room. Simone and Leo were sitting there together, talking as if a day hadn't passed since he left. Martin was intent on his soup noodles and didn't notice me come in.

I stopped for a moment, watching them, revelling in the feeling of having some of the family back. One more member to return and we would be whole again.

'Hi, Emma. Anything important that's happened since Leo left that we need to tell him about?' Simone said. 'I can't really think of anything.'

I sat at the dining table, and Ah Yat brought me my toast, tea and the newspaper. 'Tsim Sha Tsui is a disaster area,' I said.

Simone's face cleared. 'You're right, it is.'

'What, an earthquake or something?' Leo said.

'It looks like it, but it's all just development,' I said. 'The KCR's been combined with the MTR, and the KCR has a station in East Tsim Sha Tsui now. So what they did was make a massive series of underground walkways all through TST, and block off a buttload of roads for roadworks —'

'I don't think I remember a time when TST wasn't full of roadworks,' Leo said with amusement. 'Kowloon Park Drive has never *not* had roadworks on it.'

'Now you can't even cross Kowloon Park Drive down near the Star Ferry,' Simone said. 'You get routed through this stupid complex series of underground walkways that make you walk a mile out of your way to get to Harbour City.'

'Wan Chai's the same,' I said. 'We're renovating the exterior of the Academy building, and I think it's a sign of the times that instead of tiny stationery shops and computer outlets, we have a big comfortable coffee shop downstairs that makes really nice lattes.'

'The rest of it isn't rented out yet though,' Simone said. 'America broke the world economy or something in 2008 and it's taken everybody a long time to recover.'

'Oh, you have a black president,' I said.

'No *way*,' Leo said with delight. '*Really*?'

'Yeah,' Simone said. 'Anyway, after breakfast we're going down to the Academy. Wanna come?'

Leo didn't hesitate. 'Sure.'

'I would like to come too, if you don't mind,' Martin said. 'I need to brush up on my Arts, and I would like to talk to some of the Masters about some tutoring.'

'Good idea,' I said.

'You need to think about whether you want to move the Academy back to Wudangshan now that you can go to the Heavens,' Simone said.

'Not until the demon essence is removed,' I said. 'I want to be able to run it as a human; the damn snake can't type.'

'Understandable,' Martin said.

'What demon essence?' Leo said.

'One Two Two injected me with demon essence. Somehow it filled my dan tian, and when I lose control

515

I turn into a really big Snake Mother,' I said. 'John gave us a suggestion on who to talk to about clearing it, and we'll go see them soon.'

'Wait, you said Mr Chen gave you a suggestion — he's back?'

'No,' I said. 'He comes and goes. He appears in my dreams, he's met us in True Form — he appears to be returning. It might take a while.'

'Did he fall into True Form and disappear?'

'No. One Two Two took his head in exchange for Simone's safety.'

'What happened to that bastard One Two Two?' Leo said.

'I yinned him,' Simone said.

'What, just ... yin ... destroyed ... gone?' Leo said.

'Exactly.'

'And I'm left stuck as a half-demon, half-snake thing,' I said.

'Yep, sounds like you,' Leo said.

'I love you too,' I retorted.

'It's good to have you back, Leo,' Simone said.

He didn't hesitate. 'Absolutely.' Then he remembered. 'How's Michael?' Leo said.

'He is in ... what's the term? A serious but stable condition,' I said. 'Basically, he's not going to die, and they're waiting to see if that clout on his head has caused permanent brain damage.'

Leo was quiet for a moment, then said, 'Do you think I could visit him?'

'We'll contact the Tiger when we're down at the Academy and see what we can arrange,' I said.

He nodded. 'Sounds good.'

'I've organised to go shopping with Eva and Sylvie after lunch, Emma,' Simone said. 'Can I take Leo with me?'

'No,' Leo said.

'Come on, Leo. All your outfits are way out of date, and I need you along to help me choose,' Simone said, wheedling. 'Please?'

He hesitated for a moment, then said, 'Okay, why not. I suppose I have to get used to being in a wheelchair.'

'Yay! We can help each other buy stuff, sounds like great fun,' Simone said. 'Emma can sort all that out at the Academy, get the stones to set up an identity for you, and we can just use my company expense card until you get your own. How long will that take, Emma?'

'Shouldn't take more than a week to get all that sorted out,' I said. 'Don't worry about cash, we'll set you up with a corporate expense card and your own bank account. You'll never have to worry about money again.'

'I hope you have a limit on your monthly spending, young lady,' Leo said sternly to Simone. 'I don't want to see you wasting your money like those spoilt local girls who wheedle money from their fathers to buy expensive designer handbags all the time.'

Simone tossed her head at me. 'Emma's a cow. She won't give me nearly enough money to buy a Kelly.'

'Well, that's different, that's just child abuse.' Leo glared at me. 'If the Princess wants a Kelly, the Princess should have a Kelly.'

'She had a Coach bag last year that she completely destroyed within six months,' I said. 'Dragged it around in the rain, then didn't dry it properly and it got mouldy. Ruined. No way am I spending fifty grand more on another bag that'll last a similar amount of time.'

Leo rounded on Simone. 'You destroyed a Coach? I don't think I want to go shopping with you now.'

'We can buy a couple of new outfits for Emma,' Simone said in a stage whisper.

Leo hesitated, looked at me, then turned back to Simone. 'It's a deal.'

Simone jiggled and clapped her hands. 'Yay!'

'Don't you dare!' I said.

'Can't hear you, Emma,' Simone said. She tucked into her scrambled eggs. 'Can't wait. This will be *so* much fun.'

'Have you spoken to any of the staff or students of the Academy since you returned from the Heavens, Emma?' Martin said.

'No,' I said, then I understood. 'Oh dear.'

'What?' Simone said, then realised. 'The snake thing.'

I put my toast down. 'I don't think I want to go down there now.'

Martin raised his head and concentrated, and Meredith appeared sitting at the table with us. Ah Yat brought in a pot of English tea for her.

'Tell us the worst,' I said.

'You have an energy work class at ten, Emma, better get a move on,' she said.

'Is everybody as freaked out as I think they are?'

She sipped her tea. 'No.'

'That's not possible, Meredith. I'm a *snake*. Half the students probably didn't show this morning.'

She put her tea down. 'Emma, the most common reaction amongst the students is "oh, she is something weird after all".'

Simone choked on her coffee and spluttered for a few moments. She grabbed a tissue from the centre of the table and wiped her mouth.

'She's laughing because it's true,' Meredith said.

Simone nodded, obviously unable to talk.

'Nobody's left the Academy?' I said.

'Nobody.'

'What about the Celestial?'

'Ah.' She put down her teacup. 'That has been slightly different. Snakes have a reputation for being untrustworthy and shiftless. They are loners who don't socialise with the rest of the Celestial fraternity. They are also without family and some of them don't even know their ancestry; this is very shocking.'

'So me being a snake just pounds home the point that I'm an outsider,' I said. I ran my hands through my hair. 'Wonderful.'

Meredith nodded to Leo. 'Welcome back.' She nodded to Ming Gui. 'Both of you.' She turned back to Leo. 'Are you planning to come down to the Academy?'

'I want to see my old students,' Leo said. 'I'd like to catch up with them.'

'Good. When you are down there, ask Emma's secretary to call me. I'll have a look at your back, see what we can do about it.'

'I don't think there's anything you can do, Meredith,' Leo said. 'It's wrecked.'

'We will see.' Her voice became brisk. 'Well, missy, you have an energy class at ten, regardless of how long and narrow you are. Your kids need you and the Academy needs you.' She put down her tea and rose. 'Oh, Jim took off with Hien. We don't know where they went. He left a sealed envelope in your pigeonhole for your eyes only. We have a good idea what it says. Apart from that, things are relatively normal down there. See you soon, don't be late.' She disappeared.

When I arrived at my energy class, the juniors were sitting silently on the mats in a circle around Billy, their eyes unseeing. Billy was in True Form: a stone of rough-hewn granite about the size of my fist.

'Is Billy showing them a recording?' I said.

'Yes,' my stone said.

The students all jumped as if stung, and a couple of the girls squeaked. Esmerelda's eyes went wide with horror.

'Oh my God,' Chelsea whispered. 'Oh my God.'

'I'm here, Billy, you can turn off the horror show now,' I said loudly.

The students sagged and looked at each other, guilty. Billy took human form and rose, also looking guilty.

'You should all have been standing when I came in, guys, this really isn't good enough,' I said, attempting to break their mood. 'Let's start with about fifteen minutes of meditation, then we can do chi flow.'

The students sat cross-legged on the floor and shared another look. Obviously from the Shens' expressions a silent conversation was taking place. Billy grimaced at Apple, and Apple gestured with her head back at him. All of the students looked guilty. A couple of them shifted slightly away from me.

'How did you get a recording of me being a snake?' I said. 'Only the guards and the tree spirits were there; there weren't any stones!'

'My parent was one of the guards,' Billy said quietly.

I ran my hands through my hair. 'Does everybody in the Academy know?'

'I think everybody in the *world* knows now, ma'am,' Billy said. 'It's number one search parameter on the stone network.'

I rose, turned and went out. I didn't go up in the lift; I went to the stairwell and ran up the stairs from the third floor to the twenty-sixth. I slammed the door open and stormed into the offices. The minute I entered, everything went silent. I felt everyone's eyes on me as I rushed to my office.

I closed the door behind me and leaned on it, then fell to sit at my desk and put my head in my hands.

Dear God, everybody in the Celestial had seen it.

Somebody tapped on the door and I ignored them.

'Ma'am?' Yi Hao said softly on the other side of the door.

I shuffled papers on my desk. 'Come in, Yi Hao.'

She opened the door a crack and peered around it. She opened it further and sidled in. She stood just inside the door and wrung her hands.

'What, Yi Hao?' I said.

Yi Hao hesitated, then, 'Your juniors are here, ma'am, they want to see you.'

I spun away on my chair. 'Maybe later.'

Something clattered on my desk and I turned to see. Billy sat there in True Form. 'Ma'am, could you come back down to the training room? We're very sorry if we offended you.'

'I'm not offended, Billy,' I said. 'I just don't like the idea of you having to see what you saw.'

'Actually ...' Billy's voice trailed off. 'Actually, ma'am, we were wondering if you would show us again. In the training room. We want to see it.'

'You don't want to see it, Billy.'

'Uh, ma'am.' Billy paused again, as if taking a deep breath, and plunged on. 'Ma'am, we think that your serpent form is absolutely the coolest damn shit any of us has ever seen in our entire lives, and we humbly ask you, as your students, to come and show us. Please. In the training room.' His voice took on a wheedling edge. 'Please?'

I couldn't help myself: I laughed quietly. 'Cool shit, eh?'

He sounded delighted. 'Yes, ma'am!'

'We have a phoenix in our class, Billy. You know how the birds feel about snakes.'

'Esmerelda thinks you're cool shit too, ma'am, provided you promise not to eat her,' Billy said. 'Please?

We really want to see.' He obviously had a sudden idea. 'You won't attack us or anything, will you? You're not poisonous and going to bite us?'

'No. Even though I *am* poisonous, I won't bite you, and I definitely won't attack you,' I said. 'Even though I change shape I'm still one hundred per cent me.'

'Are you his Serpent, ma'am?' Billy said.

I was silent at that.

'That would be even cooler.'

I sighed with feeling. 'I don't know, Billy. I really have no idea what I am. I'm not a Shen; I'm a human being that changes into a snake. Why I change, I don't know. In fact, anybody who has any ideas as to what I am is most welcome to make suggestions.'

'I hope you are his Serpent, that really would be excellent,' Billy said. 'So, you coming down to show us? We have plenty of time left. Please say yes.'

I rose and pushed my chair away from the desk. 'I suppose.'

'Woot!' Billy said, and disappeared.

He reappeared on the desk. 'Uh, can we move it to training room four, because the other juniors want to come and see? No, some of the seniors too. Whoa, about fifty people want to see this, ma'am.'

'Training room four it is then.' I shook my head. 'Cool shit?'

'Cool as hell, ma'am, and I apologise for the language,' Billy said. 'But there's really no other way to say it.' He disappeared.

After the energy work class I went back to my office. Yi Hao had cleared my pigeonhole and there was a pile of memos about the Academy in my in-tray. Most of it was standard stuff; a few were memos of support from the staff saying that snakes were just as good as anybody else and not to take anything personally.

I opened Jim's letter. It looked like it had been written in a hurry.

Hey Emma,

They're after her and it wasn't really her fault. I can't see any other option here; as a rep of the Celestial you're obliged to turn her in. She reminds me too much of my own daughter and I can't believe I didn't see the addiction a second time around. Looks like the pine nuts and spring water will have to wait.

Jim

I wondered where he'd taken her — could have been anywhere. He was an expert at infiltration and could possibly still have some of the fake identities that the British Special Services had set up for him. All I could do was wish them the best.

At about 6 pm Leo and Simone slammed open my office door and she pushed him in in his wheelchair. Simone put her hands on her hips. 'You come home right now.'

I gestured towards the computer screen. 'When I've finished these sheets. You guys go, and I'll give you a call when I'm ready.'

'No,' Simone said. 'It's dinnertime soon, and we're all having dinner together. You, me, Leo and Martin. Like a family.' She gestured towards the computer. 'That can wait.'

I hesitated, then shrugged. She was right. I saved the sheet and rose to accompany them. 'Where are all the shopping bags? I can't believe you two went out with two of Simone's girlfriends and didn't buy anything.'

'The trunk of the Merc is so stuffed full I nearly needed to pull out a bungee cord like the taxi drivers do when they have too much luggage,' Leo said with amusement. 'The demon driver the Academy gave us laughed himself sick.' He sobered. 'You'd better review the receipts, Emma, I think we went slightly overboard on the spending.'

'Did you have fun?'

They shared an evil grin.

'Then it was worth it,' I said. I gestured towards Simone. 'This is the happiest I've seen you in years, Simone. It's good to see.'

'All we need is Daddy home and everything will be perfect,' she said. 'Oh, and a school for me.'

'One of the interviews is tomorrow, remember,' I said. 'The school on top of Braemar Hill.'

'I'd like Leo to come as well,' Simone said.

'That's not really appropriate —' Leo began, but Simone cut him off.

'You're not a Retainer, Leo, you're part of the family. My ... kinda second father, or weirdo gay uncle or something. Whatever. You count.'

Leo's face darkened. 'Weirdo gay uncle.'

'Matched set with my weirdo gay brother,' Simone said, unfazed.

Leo shook his head. 'I guess you're right.'

We went down to the car and Simone helped Leo into the back seat.

'I want to drive you two around,' Leo said, frustrated. 'I want to be useful. I want to be the driver again.'

'If you take the Elixir —'

He cut me off. 'I will be stuck for all eternity as a paraplegic, don't pretend I won't. I know that's how it works.'

'Don't let it stop you, Leo,' Simone said. 'Immortals can change their forms and fly and everything.'

'That's not the issue for me. Do you think we could have the car adapted so I can drive it anyway? Can they do that?'

'I'll get Yi Hao onto it right away,' I said.

'Now you're talking,' Leo said with enthusiasm.

* * *

'How many schools do you have lined up for me?' Simone asked as I drove us up the steep road to Braemar Hill the next day.

'Just this one at the moment. They're interviewing you for the waiting list.'

She hesitated a moment, then, 'Maybe if I can't get something, I could go to Celestial High for a while. Sylvie and Eva say they have great fun there, and they don't get any trouble about missing classes 'cause they have to fight demons or anything. And besides, it would make it easier for Eva and me doing our elemental thing.'

'That might be a good idea,' I said. 'I'm having trouble finding a tutor for you, and we can't stop your education because of this.'

'Yeah, I don't want to fall behind. But I still want to go to a normal school!'

'This elemental thing you'll be doing sounds great,' Leo said. 'Can't wait to see them.'

'I'll show you some when we get home,' Simone said. 'They've been pestering me lately 'cause they don't have enough to do. I rotate them on swimming-pool duty, but they've started to complain that it's boring.'

'They're in the *pool*?' Leo said.

'It leaks like a sieve otherwise,' Simone said. 'I got sick of waiting for the construction company to get around to fixing it, and just filled it with elementals instead.'

'So the water in the pool is elementals?' I said. 'You never told me that. I thought they'd just fixed it and the building management hadn't told me.'

Simone shrugged. 'I sent the management company a letter from the construction company saying that it was done, and a letter the other way saying that the construction company were fired. I filled the pool with elementals and made the lifeguards too. I've been practising on colouring them, and the lifeguard model I have them taking is nearly completely opaque. You only notice that they're transparent if you get really close. They'll be all ready to go when the swimming season starts.'

'I'm not sure I want to go swimming now,' I said.

'Me either,' Leo said.

Simone made a derisive noise. 'They're like rocks. They don't care.'

'Well, I'm not and I do.'

'They'll keep the water warm when the season's changing, and make it nice and cool in the middle of summer,' Simone said. 'Most pools are disgustingly warm in the middle of summer. Not refreshing at all.'

'I still don't feel right about swimming around in a sentient creature,' I said.

'We'll see what you say when summer comes and that water is clear and blue and really nice,' Simone said.

I managed to find a parking spot on the school grounds. We had some trouble explaining our mission to the security guards, but in the end they rang up to the office, then let us sign the guestbook on the condition that we gave our Hong Kong ID card numbers, and provided us with guest passes.

'This is like entering a military base,' Leo grumbled as we wheeled him through the cavernous open areas to the main office.

Like most schools in Hong Kong, this one was mostly vertical, with classrooms along two wings on either side of an administrative core. There was a small concreted area underneath for breaks, probably used in shifts by the students as there wasn't enough space for all of them to be out there at the same time. The gymnasium was the bottom two floors of one of the wings, and I peeked inside before we entered the core building. It had nearly new, extremely expensive equipment for basketball and gymnastics, a full electronic scoreboard system and air conditioning.

I checked the appointment letter and we went up the lift to the third-floor reception. A Filipino woman was behind the reception desk, and asked us to sit in the waiting area. It was bright and decorated with artwork produced by the students.

The registrar, Mrs Cowan, came out of her office. She was mid-fifties, overweight and had short permed hair. She spoke with a definite British accent and smiled with welcome when she saw us. 'Miss Donahoe. Simone?'

'That's us,' I said. I gestured towards Leo and used the cover story. 'This is Mr Alexander, my half-brother, Simone's step-uncle.'

She didn't seem impressed. 'I see.' She flipped through the file in her hand. 'Ms Donahoe, may I talk to you first? Then I can see Simone.'

I rose and followed her into her office. It was small and cluttered, with a stained brown computer on her desk; all beige hardware gradually turned brown in Hong Kong's humidity and pollution. She sat behind the desk and threw the notes onto it, then reached under the desk to a filing cabinet and pulled out a glossy cardboard folder containing a prospectus. She handed it to me. 'Did you receive one of these?'

'No,' I said.

'Take a copy then, it will provide you with all the information you need if Simone is put onto the waiting list.' She leaned her elbows on the desk. 'But you must be aware that there is a very long waiting list. This school is quite prestigious and,' she looked me up and down and I was suddenly aware of my faded jeans and tatty T-shirt, 'the fees are extremely high. Simone is an orphan — can you afford them? Are you sure you wouldn't prefer to take her back to Australia where you can care for her in your own country, and she can go to a free public school?'

'It's Simone's choice to stay here,' I said.

'Please look over the prospectus carefully,' she said. 'There are a large number of extracurricular programs that all add considerably to the cost of attendance. Please decide carefully that this is the right place for her.'

'She might be an orphan, but she has a considerable legacy,' I said. 'Her father was John Chen of Chen Enterprises, and her mother was Michelle le Blanc, the famous —'

'Her mother was Michelle le Blanc?' Mrs Cowan said. 'She's *Michelle le Blanc's* daughter?'

'Yes.'

Mrs Cowan went misty-eyed. 'I wasn't in Hong Kong when she was singing here, but I heard her when she came to the Albert Hall back in '93 — wonderful voice, sang like an angel!' She leaned over the table to speak closely to me. 'Does Simone sing?'

'Not a note,' I said. 'She inherited more from her father than she did from her mother, I'm afraid. She plays the piano but she doesn't really sing at all.'

'Such a shame,' she said, shaking her head. She looked down at Simone's application, then up at me. 'And you say she has a large legacy?'

'I think the word I'm looking for here is immense,' I said. 'I'm her guardian, and the funds are held in trust until she's an adult.'

'All right, for Michelle's daughter we can do this,' Mrs Cowan said. She opened the prospectus that was in front of me on the desk and pointed. 'You pay two million into the school building fund and she has a place automatically.'

'I asked about that and was told that option was closed,' I said.

'For her I think we can make an exception.'

I pulled my handbag into my lap and shuffled through it. 'Personal cheque okay?'

She waved me down. 'No need to rush, just fill out the forms in the folder.' She reached under her desk again and gave me another couple of forms. 'And these. When you bring them back, attach a bank cheque for two million. You can do two million no problem?'

'No problem at all,' I said.

'Good.' She pointed at the forms. 'Fill these in, bring them back, and she can start as soon as the money clears — probably as early as the end of next week, or the beginning of the week after. I do need to interview her though, to make sure that her English is up to standard.'

'Her English is fine.'

'It's just a formality, Emma — may I call you Emma? Were you Mr Chen's second wife after he lost Michelle? I heard about that, such a tragedy, must have been terribly hard on little Simone. We must make sure that she takes all the time and care she needs to get over this.'

'We were engaged when the gangsters killed him,' I said. 'Simone regards me as a stepmother more than a guardian, and I do miss him terribly, even after eight years.'

'Oh, so you've suffered too, such a tragic family,' Mrs Cowan said. 'I hope you find some solace in the school community.'

'I'm sure we will,' I said.

I gathered up the documents and she opened the door of the office.

'Simone, dear, if you don't mind coming into my office and having a chat with me?' the registrar said. 'We need to check how good your English is. Just a formality.'

Simone nodded and went into the office with her. She was so intent on being 'normal' that she didn't even make the mind-to-mind comment I was expecting from her.

I sat next to Leo and opened the prospectus.

'Well?' he said softly.

I held the document open for him to see and pointed at the bursary option.

He quickly scanned it, glanced up at the receptionist, then turned back to the document. 'I thought you tried that and it didn't work?'

'I did. But I hadn't factored in the registrar being an opera fan.'

He stared at me blankly for a moment, then said, 'Oh, Michelle.'

'A huge fan. Absolutely thrilled to be having Michelle's daughter in her school.'

'Well, how about that.' He sat back more comfortably. 'Problem solved then.'

I flipped through the rest of the documents, which were standard school information sheets, glossy and glowing in their descriptions of the standard of education on offer. 'Looks perfect.'

'As long as she's happy,' Leo said.

'Precisely.'

I silently perused the documents while we waited. After about five minutes, Mrs Cowan and Simone emerged.

'Her English is fine,' Mrs Cowan said. She touched Simone's arm. 'I have one of your mother's CDs, dear — she was a wonderful singer. Terrible tragedy; of course, we'll do anything we can to make sure that you have all the help you need to get over this situation.'

Simone glanced at me. 'I'm in?'

'Yes, as soon as we have the correct forms filled in and the cheque is cleared, you can start,' Mrs Cowan said. 'Probably as soon as the end of next week.'

Simone could barely restrain herself from jumping with glee. 'That's wonderful! Thank you!'

Mrs Cowan smiled with genuine pleasure. 'I'm looking forward to having you here.' She held her hand out to me. 'Miss Donahoe.'

I shook her hand. 'It's been a real pleasure, Mrs Cowan. I am awfully busy managing Mr Chen's estate, but don't hesitate to contact me if you need anything with regards to Simone's education.'

'You wouldn't possibly have any more of Miss le Blanc's CDs, would you?'

'I'll drop a couple of signed ones in on Simone's first day of school,' Leo said.

Mrs Cowan appeared to notice Leo properly for the first time. 'Signed?'

'I have a boxful of signed CDs somewhere around, I'll give you a couple,' Leo said.

Mrs Cowan was obviously delighted. 'Thank you!'

'Looks like we all won today,' I said.

'I think we did,' Mrs Cowan said, beaming.

CHAPTER 35

The next day I met Louise for lunch at one of the Tiger's hotels in Mong Kok. He had a shiny new demon-driven white Mercedes pick me up and take me there, as our Mercedes was still in the workshop being altered so that Leo could drive it. The bellboys at the hotel seemed to be expecting me; they provided me with more obsequious service than could normally be expected at a four-star establishment like this.

I was led through the lobby, which was packed with Mainland tourists, all wearing distinctive sticky labels on their jackets indicating their tour company so they could not be lost. A couple of them were wearing business suits purchased in Hong Kong, the brand label still prominent on the jacket sleeve so they could show off their luxury purchase back home.

The bellboy indicated the escalators up to the first floor, where the reception desk and the Western restaurant were situated. I took the marble stairs up another floor to the Chinese restaurant and presented myself at the entrance.

The receptionist checked the book when I arrived and asked for Louise, then her face cleared and she smiled at me, welcoming. She led me into the restaurant and gestured towards the end, where Louise and her two children sat at one of the large, comfortably set out tables. They were spread far apart in an elegant dining room setting. Louise waved when she saw me and gestured for me to come sit at the table. She had the yum cha order form in front of her, and the children were bending over it to see what she was choosing. Louise still had the same servant with her: a demon called Beanie who took the form of a mid-forties Filipina.

When the kids saw me they both went serious and said, 'Aunty Emma,' then returned to the menu.

Kimberley was ten years old now, as precocious and cheeky as her mother. Her half-Chinese heritage only showed in her eyes; her complexion was fair and her hair was platinum blonde. Her brother, Lucas, was five, his hair a darker shade of blond.

'Sit, Emma, we're working out what to order,' Louise said. She held the menu in front of Kimberley's face between us. 'Delicate shark fin dumpling with crab roe. That's siu mai, isn't it?'

'No, Mom, it's yu chee gow,' Kimberley said. She pointed at one of the boxes. 'Fresh pork mince with shrimp, that's siu mai.'

'Two!' Lucas said.

'Yeah, order two,' Louise said, and ticked the boxes. She glanced up at me. 'Oh, that's right, you're vegetarian. We'll order something for you too.'

She waved to the waiter, who was standing to one side with his hands crossed in front of him. He quickly approached us and she handed him the order form. 'Anything in particular, Emma?'

I took the menu and flicked through it, then turned back to the waiter, wondering how good his English was.

'Something completely vegan, completely vegetarian, no meat products at all,' I said.

He nodded, smiling. 'Noodles? Vegan ho fan? Fried or soup?'

'Fried,' I said. 'Mushrooms.'

He nodded and scribbled on the order form. 'Drinks?'

'Coke!' Kimberley and Lucas said in unison.

'We'll stick with the tea,' Louise said.

The waiter poured more tea for us, then took the order form away.

'Beanie,' Louise said, turning to the demon, 'take the kids out to look at the fish tanks or the fountain or something.'

Beanie nodded and rose to take the children out.

'Are you going to change into a snake, Aunty Emma?' Lucas said, loudly enough for those at nearby tables to hear.

'Not in the middle of all these people!' Louise hissed at him, and his face fell.

'Sorry.'

'Go with Beanie, have a look around, and then come back.'

'Come on, Lucas, there's a couple of computers with internet next to reception,' Kimberley said.

Lucas stopped next to me on the way out and leaned close to whisper to me, his eyes wide, 'I wanna see the snake, please, Aunty Emma.'

'If your mum brings you up to the Academy I might show you,' I said.

'I don't want to see it,' Kimberley said. 'Snakes are icky.'

'Thank you very much,' I said.

'I didn't mean you,' she said quickly.

'It doesn't matter. Go for a walk, and Beanie can bring you back when the food is here.'

Kimberley leaned in to speak to me. 'I know Mummy just wants to talk to you without Lucas hearing, so I'll keep him busy for a while, okay?'

I lowered my voice to reply. 'Thanks.'

She nodded to me, her face serious.

'Kimberley! Hurry up! The computers are free!' Lucas called to her. She smiled conspiratorially at me and followed him out.

'She is ten going on fifty,' I said.

'Part of being half-Shen, they say,' Louise said. 'They grow up way too fast.'

She poured tea for both of us, and put the teapot down. 'Emma, I know you've been real busy being a superhero lately, but we have a major problem that only you can fix.'

'A *superhero*?' the stone in my ring said, incredulous.

'Shut up, this has nothing to do with you,' Louise said. 'Up until recently, all us wives were the same, nobody was a favourite — well, okay, when we were new we were favourites, but things settle down and you go on the roster —'

'If this is about Rhonda, I really don't want to hear it,' I said desperately.

'No, hear me out,' Louise said. 'Before, we were all *equal*. You move down the list as you get older, but he still looks after you. Equally. Now this American bitch has moved in and she has him all confused. He doesn't know what he's *doing*, Emma. It's just not fair to us! Who does she think she is, taking over the place? We don't want someone else lording it over us. He's our *husband* and we do what *he* says, not what *she* orders us to!'

'I can understand how this is pissing you off, Louise, but it has nothing to do with me,' I said.

'You're his boss!' she said. 'You can tell him to cut this bullshit out and come to his senses!'

'I can't tell him what to do in his own household.'

'You have to stop this, Emma. It's just not right.'

I spread my hands. 'There's nothing I can do. What he does in his own household is his own business.'

She stared at me for a moment, then turned back to her tea, sullen. 'Jesus, Emma, you are his freaking snake.' She looked up at me. 'Cold-blooded.'

'You have no idea,' I said miserably.

She shook her head. 'Well, I tried. They all came to me and offered their spots on the roster if I could pull this off.' She studied her teacup. 'Looks like I'll be out in the cold for a few weeks now.'

'How often do you see him?'

She shrugged without looking up. 'About once every six weeks.'

I opened my mouth to say something but she cut me off. 'Yes, I know, just like April. And when she told us that, I was horrified. At least he's not going to use me as a rent-a-womb for farming a baby, then kill me and chop me into little pieces.'

'If ever you want to find a place for yourself in the world, Louise —'

'No.' She tapped the table between us. 'I am happy where I am. He loves me, and I love him. Seeing your husband every six weeks or so isn't terribly uncommon in Asia, and I have two beautiful children and a Palace in Heaven. I have it good.' She rubbed her hand over her face. 'But when this Rhonda chick moves in, it'll all change. We'll see him a lot less, 'cause she'll be there *all the time*. She'll be setting the roster, and controlling who goes where, and bossing us around. We don't want that.'

I sighed with exasperation. 'Rhonda's one of my best friends too.'

'I was your friend first!' she snapped.

The food arrived. Surprisingly, the waiter had fully understood my order and placed a large dish of stir-fried ho fan with vegetables and mushrooms in front of me. I nodded my thanks.

Louise pulled out her mobile phone and pressed a

button on the keypad, then put it away again. 'That's a remote control for the demon; it tells her to bring them back.' She put her hand on top of mine. 'Talk to Rhonda, let her know that it'll be awful if she does this. None of us want her. We'll make her life miserable, Emma. This is a bad idea. Tell her.'

'I'll tell her,' I said. 'But I think she already knows.'

She nodded. The children came in with Beanie and she smiled at them.

'Can we buy some cakes to take home with us?' Lucas said as he clambered into his seat.

'That's typical of you, Lucas, want to buy food when there's a whole table of it in front of you,' Kimberley said. She picked up the black serving pair of chopsticks from the double white/black sets in front of her and studied the steamers. 'This looks very good.'

'We'll go down and have a look at the cakes when we're done here,' Louise said. 'But you can get cakes anytime at the bakery back home.'

'They don't have Hong Kong cakes there,' Lucas said. 'And they have dan tart!'

'Let's see how much room you have when you're done,' Louise said with amusement.

'So, how's school going, you two?' I said.

Both of the children grimaced at me. I did my best to keep the conversation as mundane as possible and not mention any American women for the rest of the lunch.

After lunch I had no classes so I went home and curled up on the living room sofa with a copy of *Journey to the North*. This version had been translated and annotated by a professor from a prestigious American university, and was no longer in print; it had taken me a year of hard searching to find it. For a classic of Chinese literature it was surprisingly short, and it didn't take me long to become engrossed in it.

The first part told the story of how the Dark Lord had fallen from Heavenly grace and had taken a thousand years of incarnations pursuing the Tao to regain Immortality. General Ma was right: Kwan Yin was hardly mentioned.

The second part told how, after the Dark Lord had regained his place in Heaven, he sent for his Generals and they weren't there. The Heavenly bureaucracy told him that they had gone down to Earth and were wreaking havoc — there was a 'cloud of evil' over the world.

The first two demons he subdued were the Snake and the Turtle. The demons were the transformed stomach and intestines of Xuan Wu himself, which he had ripped out when he attained the Way, vowing to remain vegetarian and disgusted with the idea of having eaten meat. They lived on Wudang Mountain and ate any travellers to the mountain. They kidnapped a couple of young women and kept them as sex slaves, and only then were pursued by Xuan Wu and subdued by him.

I looked up from the book. 'Stone.'

The stone didn't reply and I tapped it.

'I don't want to talk about it,' the stone said.

'The Xuan Wu was an evil snake-turtle demon that ate people, and kidnapped women to hold them as sex slaves on Wudang Mountain,' I said. 'Later, he attained the Way and tossed aside his demonic ways. Tell me I'm wrong.'

The stone was silent.

'Shit,' I said softly, and returned to the book.

After the Dark Lord had subdued the Snake and Turtle demons, he travelled through the world, subduing or finding each of his thirty-six Generals in turn, and giving them the Fire Essence Pill to tame them if they had become demons, making them obedient to his order.

'Stone,' I said.

'I'm asleep,' the stone said.

'Have all of the Generals been fed the Fire Essence Pill?'

'No,' the stone said. 'As you can see, some of them weren't actually causing trouble. Guan Yu was doing his job guarding the Gates of Heaven; only his sword needed to be subdued, as it had taken on a life of its own and was killing people for sport.'

'Wait,' I said. 'His sword came alive? That's not made up?'

'It can happen. It's only a matter of time before that bastard black blade of yours turns around and starts telling you how much it loves the taste of blood.'

'Then you can just put me away in a mental institution,' I said.

'No, it happens,' the stone said. 'Any artefact used by a Celestial for long enough becomes something greater. Heavenly Lord Xin's writing brush is an example. You talk to it all the time.'

'I don't know his brush,' I said, confused.

'It's Tian Guai, his secretary,' the stone said. 'You talked to him three weeks ago.'

'That's his *writing brush*?' I said, and flipped to the relevant passage in the book. The stone was right: the brush had been left by itself for too long and had taken on a life of its own, needing to be subdued by Xuan Wu and his Generals with the help of Heavenly Lord Xin.

'If the Murasame ever gains some sort of sentience, I hate to think what sort of artefact it will be,' I said.

'It's only six hundred years old, it probably won't happen for a while,' the stone said. 'And you're not a Shen anyway.'

'So what am I?'

The stone was silent.

I continued through the book, reading with fascinated horror as, one by one, the Generals that

I worked with were described as evil, cannibalistic monsters.

I finished it and put it down. 'John tried to keep this from me.'

'That he did.'

'I'd dearly like to slap him right now, stone.'

'He was concerned that you would leave him if you found out exactly what sort of person he used to be.' The stone's voice became firmer. 'And he left a message for you, for just this situation.'

'Oh, trying to explain himself, is he?' I said with derision.

'Not really. Do you want to see it?'

I hesitated. 'I might cry when I see him again.'

'His photo is in the hallway right there, Emma.'

'You know it's not the same.'

'If you don't want to see it, it's your choice.'

I quickly decided. 'Show me.'

'In your room. It would be best if Simone didn't walk in on it.'

'She's out at the shops —'

'Trust me, Emma, you don't want her seeing this.'

I shrugged. 'Okay.'

I went into the bedroom and sat on the bed. The room expanded and contracted, and there he was. He was sitting on the bed in the Dragon's Palace under the sea. I lay on the white silken bedsheets, sprawled on my stomach next to him, obviously asleep. He moved to sit cross-legged on the bed and I couldn't help but admire him: gold silken skin, toned muscles, the glowing curves of him, naked and relaxed. I missed him so much.

He pointed at his nose. 'Up here, Emma.'

I snorted with amusement.

He shrugged, and brushed his long hair out of the way to one side. 'Sometimes I think my human form should be more plain. But this is how I looked; at the time I was a warrior, trained in the Arts and very fit. I can't help it. And besides,' he smiled, 'I know you like it.'

He sobered slightly, more serious. 'I have asked the stone to take a message for me while you are sleeping here. You are completely exhausted, you won't wake up.' He glanced down at my sleeping form. 'So beautiful.' He looked up, seemingly at me, but he was probably looking at empty air. 'I know I don't have much time. I know what will happen to me after I go, even though I have tried to keep the truth from you. I think you guessed.'

'Of course I guessed.' Of course he didn't hear me.

'You probably noticed when Jade suggested that you learn the classics, I forbade her from employing a tutor for you, and at the time I didn't say why.'

'I remember,' I said.

'Well, if you don't know the reason why, you soon will.' He glanced affectionately at my sleeping form. 'Right now, the stone tells me, you haven't read the classics yet. It is possible that you will become curious later, after I've gone, and if you are there'll be no stopping you.'

He looked up, seemingly right into my eyes. 'One of the classics is *Journey to the North*. This is the reason why I forbade it. At the time, I didn't want you to know.'

'Do you want me to go on, Emma?' the stone said. 'You've read *Journey to the North*. You have an idea what he's going to say.'

'Continue,' I said.

'Tell me to stop if it's too painful for you,' the stone said kindly.

'Just do it,' I said. 'I want to hear what he has to say for himself.'

John looked down at his hands. 'Yes. *Journey to the North* is about me. About the Emperor Zhenwu: me.

The story has two main threads: how I gained Immortality, and how I overcame the demons.'

'It says you're a soul of the Jade Emperor,' I said.

'A lot of the detail is wrong in many ways, twisted to suit the beliefs of the time,' he said. 'The Snake and Turtle demon storyline, particularly, is very different from the reality.'

'They did a lot of very bad things,' I said. 'I think the word I'm looking for here is atrocities.'

'Everything they are accused of having done is true,' he said, his face completely expressionless. 'They did kidnap those two poor girls and hold them as pleasure …' He tilted his head, still looking down at his hands. 'As *sex* slaves.'

'But they were you,' I said.

'Once you've read the story you'll recognise it immediately,' he said, looking at my sleeping body again. 'They weren't demons, they were *me*. I didn't overcome demons; I overcame my own nature, to gain Immortality. I was already a Shen; I didn't need to do it. But Kwan Yin helped me to overcome that side of my nature, to rise above it and attain the Tao.' He looked up at me. 'Everything those demons are accused of doing, they did. *I* did. I did it all. I killed and ate all those people. I raped all those women.' The anguish started to show in his face. 'I did it all.'

'Stop,' I told the stone, and John froze.

'This was such a bad idea,' the stone said. 'I told him not to do it.'

'He talks about them as two distinct entities, separate from himself. Is that the way it was?' I said.

'They *were* two distinct entities, they hadn't joined,' the stone said. 'That was a very long time ago. The Dark Lord was the Turtle. The Serpent was an independent entity. The Turtle and Serpent got together and …' Its voice trailed off.

'Committed atrocities,' I said. 'As two separate entities. Was the joining part of the attainment of the Tao?'

'No,' the stone said. 'It just happened.'

I dropped my head. 'He just gets stranger and stranger.'

'Actually, Emma, I think over time he's become *less* strange. Recently he has been a straightforward Turtle Shen, a simple human man with a family.'

'More human. Continue,' I said.

'No, Emma, really, you don't need to see the rest,' the stone said.

'Continue,' I said. 'Do it. I want to hear it all.'

John continued speaking. 'I am a completely different person now that I have attained the Tao. Those demons have been banished. I could never do any of that again.'

'You're saying that because you're not sure,' I said.

'She'll see through you, my Lord,' the stone said. 'Once she finds out what you become after being so drained for so long, she'll suspect.'

'Damn,' John said with a wry grin. 'That's two of you who can see right through me.'

'Three,' the stone said.

'Four,' I said.

'No, four,' John said. 'My family.' He sighed. 'Something I have never had, in all my history. I have had children, but I am a reptile. Children, family, mean nothing to us.'

'You're just becoming more human all the time,' I said.

'And once I have gone, I will be a reptile again. I will be the Snake and the Turtle. I will be those demons again. The human side of me will be too weak to control them.' He glanced up at me. 'And I am not sure how much of the old nature will emerge.'

I gasped. 'No.'

John froze.

'No, Emma,' the stone said. 'None of that has emerged. The Turtle swims and cries, but it has not gone out into the world. It merely hunts for you and Simone.'

'What if it rejoins with the Serpent?' I said. 'When they get back together, will they start it up again? The Generals said that it couldn't happen, but they sounded as if they were lying. What if it happens?'

The stone didn't say anything, but John unfroze and spoke again.

'I want you to understand, Emma, that the reptiles are not *me*. Not the me that you love. When I have control over them again, I will be me again, the Xuan Wu that loves you, that would never hurt you, that would never be unfaithful to you.'

'Aha,' I said, '*this* is the whole point of the exercise. I should have seen this coming. He doesn't think he'll go off and torture people; he thinks he'll be a *turtle*!'

'You don't need to say anything, stone,' John said, the wry smile back. 'I know. She'll see right through me again.' He appeared to be looking me in the eyes. 'If I am unfaithful to you in True Form, I want you to know …' His voice trailed off. 'What do I say?'

'You don't need to say anything, Turtle,' the stone said. 'Because she already said she'd be happy to share you. She loves you completely, and knows that anything you do while you are a beast is outside your control.'

'I sincerely hope you are correct, stone,' John said. He glanced up. 'I'm finished. She'll probably want to tear raw bleeding strips off me when I come back. I hope she'll have the chance. I love you, Emma. Please forgive me any transgressions while I am a beast; understand I have no control. Goodbye.'

I was back in my bedroom.

'Well?' the stone said.

I shrugged. 'You were right. Of course I understand. Whatever he does while he's like this is entirely outside his control.'

'I knew it!' the stone said. 'I win!'

'What do you win?' I said sharply.

'Whoops.'

'*What do you win?*'

'His shell.'

'His whole shell?'

'Yes.'

'How are you going to get it off him?'

'The usual way.'

'*He bet his shell that I wouldn't understand?*'

'I bet my silence for two weeks that you would understand,' the stone said. 'Stupid Turtle. Of course you'd understand. He underestimated you.'

'I'm going to help you,' I said.

'Help me what?'

'Take his shell off.'

'He was right about you tearing strips off him,' the stone said.

'Oh, I'm not going to tear strips off him,' I said. 'I'm going to turn him upside down and leave him on a beach in the sun for three days, and then you and I are going to take his shell off. Together.'

'Lady Emma?'

'What?'

'Are you *sure* you're not a stone inside?'

'Nope, definitely one hundred per cent snake, all the way through. Except when I'm a Mother.'

'I think you're a Mother all the time, dear.'

'I know.'

Leo, Simone and I met my parents for dinner at a Western restaurant in Harbour City. It was a steak restaurant where each diner cooked their own piece of meat on a hot stone.

After the drinks waiter had left us, my father glared at me. 'Okay, something's going on and I want to hear it.'

'The word's out that you're a snake, Emma,' my mother said. 'And that you were a snake in the Northern Heavens. Is this why you never came to visit us in the Western Palace? You turn into a snake in Heaven?'

I hesitated, studying the menu.

'Don't try to hold back on us,' my father growled.

I dropped my menu onto the table and sighed with exasperation. 'You really don't want to know. Believe me.'

'Try us,' my father said.

'It's not like you're a demon or something, you're just a snake,' my mother said, smiling with encouragement. 'Snakes are Celestials too, they're just not very well understood. It will be fine.'

The abstract illustration on the front of the menu suddenly seemed very interesting. 'I *am* a demon too.'

'No, snakes *aren't* demons, the Tiger's said that many times,' my mother said.

'Simon Wong, the demon that killed John, injected me with demon essence. If I lose control, I become a Snake Mother.'

My mother jerked back with shock. 'What, one of those really big ugly things with no skin and a snake tail?'

'Exactly like that,' I said.

My mother turned to Simone. 'Is she telling the truth?'

Simone nodded silently, then looked down at the table, her head tilted to one side.

My mother turned back to me. 'So why didn't you come to visit us at the Palace?'

'If I travel to the Plane as *me*, I will be destroyed

546

because of the demon essence,' I said. 'We just found out by accident that if I do it as a snake, there's no problem. So up until a couple of days ago, I thought I couldn't travel to the Plane at all. That's why I never came to visit.'

'And you can come as a snake now?' my father said.

I nodded a reply.

'Well, that's wonderful news,' my mother said, grinning broadly. 'I can't *wait* to show you my little garden, and some of the needlework I've done. You have to come up and visit as soon as you can!'

'But I have to do it as a *snake*,' I said. 'I can't take human form on the Celestial Plane. I have to travel as a snake, and stay a snake.'

'And?' my father said.

'It's really big, and black, and ugly,' I said. 'When I changed at the graduation, it freaked both of you out completely.'

'It's not *that* ugly, dear,' my mother said, patting my hand.

'But you were so scared of it!' I said.

'Emma.' My mother waved her menu at me. 'I don't know what I'm going to do with you sometimes. You're our daughter. It took us a while to get used to you changing into a snake, but, darling, it's still *you*.' She glanced at Simone. 'It's still Emma, isn't it? When she's a snake?'

'One hundred per cent bossy, annoying Emma,' Simone said, and Leo choked on his beer.

'Sounds about right,' my father said.

My mother turned back to me. 'So come and visit soon, please. I understand that you didn't want to come before because you would die, but now you can come up as a snake and see what we're doing.' She patted my hand again. 'So please come up and stop being a stranger, okay?'

'Okay, Mum, I'll come up sometime in the next day or so,' I said.

'She's free …' The stone hesitated a moment. 'She's free Sunday after two.'

'Book us in, stone,' my father said.

'Done,' the stone said.

'That's settled then,' my mother said, and opened her menu. 'I've heard great things about this cook-your-steak-yourself-on-the-hot-stone business and I can't wait to try, but goodness look at these prices.'

'Eating out is always ridiculously expensive in Hong Kong,' I said, flipping through to find a vegetarian option.

'It'd want to be bloody good for these prices,' my father growled.

'Well, let's order and see,' I said. Simone was smiling at something behind me. 'What?' I asked her.

She indicated the woman behind me with her head and dropped her voice. 'She's spent the whole time since they ordered surfing the net on her laptop, and she just found an outfit that she likes at one of the outlets here in the mall and she's showing it to the older woman next to her.'

'Better than reading the newspaper and ignoring everybody,' I said, indicating another group with a nod of my head. 'He's been doing that to his wife and children since he got here.'

'Well, none of us are going to do anything like that,' my father said. 'We're all going to catch up and tell each other what we've been doing. And in your case, Emma, I have heard that it is a great deal. You've been to Hell and back, according to the stories.'

'Three times,' Simone said.

'I have no intention of returning there for a very long time,' I said. I gestured towards Leo. 'I found what I was looking for.'

'Well, that's good to hear,' my father said. The waiter came and he raised his menu. 'And right after we order, I want to hear details.'

'This is going to be a lot of fun,' Leo said.

'Damn straight,' Simone replied.

'You mind your language, missy.'

'Yes, *sir*, Uncle Leo.'

'I think Leo's right, this will be a lot of fun,' my mother said to my father.

'Just don't forget to eat, Barbara,' my father said. 'When you get stuck into some really good gossip you always forget.'

'I can't wait to share this with the book club,' my mother said.

'You could write a book, Emma,' my father said.

'I already am,' I said. 'But it's way too fantastic to be believable. I'm doing it just to make sure that I never forget how completely wild my life has become.'

'Don't deny it, Emma, you love every minute of it,' Simone said.

'The Princess Simone is quite correct,' the stone said.

'I hate you all,' I said, and pointed out the mushroom vegetarian option for the waiter.

CHAPTER 36

The next morning I had no classes until the afternoon so I went through my in-tray, trying to sort out some of the issues that had been piling up. The reports had come in from our spies in Hell: nothing had been heard about Six's location. He'd probably gone to ground with the rest of the group. Before I had a chance to arrange a meeting to suggest some search options, Yi Hao poked her nose in my door and said, 'There's a couple of groups of students who made appointments to see you, ma'am.'

I stashed the documents back in the in-tray and gestured towards it. 'Anything majorly urgent there?'

'Nothing that can't wait until after you see them,' she said.

'Who are they?'

She came in and placed a document on my desk with a short list of names and a quick rundown of what they were after.

'Start with Tu Men Jiu,' I said. 'While she's in here, please email me the list of students in the latest intake who are from the Twelve Villages of the Arts. She's from Rabbit Village.'

'Ma'am,' Yi Hao said, and went out.

'Oh, the Rabbit got in,' the stone said.

There was a tap at the door and young Tu Men Jiu came in, this time not pretending to be anything other than herself. She wore a pink T-shirt and a pair of white jeans with sneakers. She carefully bowed to me, saluted, and waited.

'Sit,' I said. I glanced at the computer and the email popped up. 'Give me a moment, Men Jiu.'

I checked the email; the list showed that there were twelve students in the current intake from Rabbit Village, and that six of them were girls. Four were girls that she had said were good enough for the Academy. Three of the girls that she'd mentioned had been assessed as close but not ready and hadn't been brought in. Two were names I hadn't heard before.

I turned back to Men Jiu. 'Are you being treated well by the staff? Settling in okay?'

She smiled slightly, embarrassed. 'I'd never used a microwave oven before, but the other students are showing me how it works. There are so many cars here! It is very different.'

'Are you being ignored by boys from Rabbit Village, and having to ask for help from people who aren't from your village?' I said.

Emma ..., the stone said.

Her mouth flopped open. 'How did you know? The boys from Rabbit Village, even though they've known me all my life, none of them want to help me at all.'

'What, stone?' I said.

Uh ... nothing. That was a very good guess. You asked that out of nowhere as if you knew what the answer would be.

'No guess. I've experienced that sort of thing before,' I said. I raised my hand to show Men Jiu. 'My stone's being an ass, it's talking to me privately. Very rude.'

She moved closer to see the stone. 'I've heard about this stone. They say it's really annoying and to keep away from it.'

'My plan has succeeded then,' the stone said.

She chuckled. 'I don't know, I think I like it.'

'I quite like it too,' I said.

'Oh, spare me the animal emotional bull ... dust,' the stone said, and Men Jiu and I laughed.

'Was there anything in particular you wanted to ask me, Men Jiu, or are you just here to say hello?' I said.

'I wanted to thank you, ma'am,' she said, and saluted over the table. 'Because of you, we girls are receiving attention at the Village. The elders are not happy about it, but one of the Heavenly Generals came to us and said that the unbalanced nature of Rabbit Village had come to the notice of the Celestial, and that if they didn't change their cultural bias, a new leadership would be instated — probably one consisting of all women, similar to the leadership at the Rooster Village.'

'That probably scared the life out of them,' I said.

She sighed and looked down. 'I think what they're doing now is the minimum to keep their jobs and fulfil the requirements handed down by the Celestial. Once they feel that you're not watching them any more, they'll go back to favouring boys.'

'Stone,' I said.

'On it,' the stone said. 'Men Jiu, I will be keeping track of the intakes from the Rabbit Village, and if they show signs of slipping, I will be down on them.'

'Is Meredith busy right now?' I said.

Meredith appeared next to me. Men Jiu shot to her feet and saluted her. 'Lady Master Liu! I am profoundly honoured.'

'Oh, you're the Rabbit girl,' Meredith said. She held

her hand out and Men Jiu shook it, wide-eyed. 'What do you have for me, Emma?'

'Meredith, they're paying lip service to the "change your culture to less sexist or we'll slap you" order,' I said. 'Now that you're free from feeding energy to the Northern Heavens, would you like to go in and do just that?'

'What, slap them?' Meredith said with grim satisfaction.

'Theoretically, yes. But tell them that you're going to provide some advanced instruction on energy work. They can't help but be flattered, and at the same time you can drum a new attitude into them, one brain cell at a time.'

'Shouldn't take long. I hear that the Council members of Rabbit Village only have one brain cell each,' Meredith said.

Men Jiu's mouth flopped open, then she grinned broadly.

'Do you have time?' I said. I gestured towards Men Jiu. 'We just got another new batch of students to replace the copies we lost when the seals were put back up — you might be busy.'

'Let me look at my diary,' Meredith said, and her eyes unfocused for a moment. 'If I can offload some of these advanced classes onto someone else, I can go for a couple of weeks.'

'Sounds perfect,' I said.

'Want to take the classes for me?'

'I can't do advanced energy, you know that,' I said in exasperation.

She leaned on the table. 'You can try.'

'Maybe when you're back.' I nodded to her. 'Thank you, Master Liu.'

'No problem at all,' Meredith said, and disappeared.

'If you don't mind me saying, ma'am,' Men Jiu said, her voice weak with wonder. 'You kick ass.'

553

'Not as much as Meredith does,' I said. 'Your Council won't know what hit them by the time she finishes with them.'

She saluted me. 'I thank you.'

'Better run, Rabbit,' the stone said. 'You have a class in five minutes.'

'Oh!' She jumped up and quickly saluted me again. 'I do! Thank you, Lady Emma!' She saluted me again, bobbed her head, and ran out.

'Ask Yi Hao who's next,' I said.

The intercom popped and Yi Hao said, 'They need you in training room seven right now, ma'am. There's been an injury.'

'What about Edwin? I'm not a doctor!' I said.

'Dammit, Jim!' the stone said, and I rapped it on the desk. 'Ow!'

'Edwin's there,' Yi Hao said. 'Please, ma'am, they say they need you.'

We need you, ma'am, Master Park said into my head.

I went out to the stairwell and floated down from the twenty-sixth to the seventh floor. I stopped at the fire door. 'That was easier.'

'I do believe that being a snake has cleared some of the demon essence from you,' the stone said.

'I must have Meredith check me out,' I said. 'That is good news!'

In training room seven, Master Park had been holding a weapons lesson with blades, and one of the students had been injured. He lay on the floor, bleeding. I went to him and knelt. Edwin was there, examining the wound, with Master Park beside him. Meredith appeared on the other side of the student, and shooed the rest of the class back out of the way.

The student had made a common mistake, guarding

too close to the body, and the blade had rebounded off a fellow student's dagger and sliced him in the thigh. The wound was deep and long, the length of his thigh, and bleeding profusely.

'Oh my God,' I said, and quickly changed to a snake. The kid had hit his femoral artery, one of the biggest blood vessels in his body. He would bleed to death within minutes if it wasn't contained. Edwin was holding the wound closed with both hands, but blood continued to pump out of it.

When they saw the snake, a number of the students reeled back with shock. I touched my nose to the wound: he'd already lost so much blood. I quickly healed the artery, making sure that there was no leakage. I concentrated, making sure that the artery was strong enough to contain the pressure of the blood.

'She did it,' Edwin said in wonder.

'He needs a transfusion,' I said. 'Edwin, I suggest you set one up, and get a stretcher while I fix the rest.'

'You can fix this?' Edwin said.

I knitted the muscles of the thigh, working carefully and thoroughly from bottom to top and ensuring that the long fibres of the muscle tissue lined up exactly. It was delicate, finicky work and I had to concentrate. This wound was at least thirty-five centimetres long; any longer than that and I wouldn't be able to heal it all.

'I can stop him from dying right now, but he's lost a good half of his total blood supply and he needs topping up *now* with fluids and then with blood to make sure that his organs aren't deprived of oxygen by the loss in pressure,' I said. I stopped and raised my nose. 'How did I know that?'

'Understood, ma'am. We have his blood type in the infirmary, we just need to get him down there quickly and infuse him,' Edwin said.

Some students arrived with a stretcher, eased the injured student onto it and took him out to the lifts.

'Stay here and do as Lady Emma says,' Master Park called back from the lift as the door closed.

The students gathered around me, studying me with curiosity. One of them touched me and I jerked back, and so did she. I moved forward again, my head at the height of the students' eyes.

'This is Lady Emma?' one of them said.

'Yes, it's me,' I said.

'She just saved Sean's life,' Meredith said. 'I can heal, but I can't stop blood loss as quickly and effectively as that.'

'Serpents are healers, we learned that,' another student said. She came closer to me. 'Can you cure my pimples?'

'Let me touch your face with my nose,' I said.

She closed her eyes and pressed her face towards me. I put my nose to her skin; the pores were filling with excess oil, and the oil provided a home for bacteria, which caused infection in the pores, leading to the acne. I killed the bacteria and reduced some of the redness and swelling, but I couldn't provide a permanent cure.

'I've eased it a little,' I said. 'But the secret for you is to keep it very clean with a mild cleanser that won't irritate your skin, and to avoid food that makes it worse.'

She opened her eyes and pulled back slightly. 'That's exactly what the doctor said.'

'Lady Emma did make it better,' one of the other students said. She gestured with her head towards the lobby. 'Go and look in the mirror in the toilet. It's gone down a *lot*.'

The student with the acne smiled broadly, bobbed her head to me, and rushed out.

'I have some appointments still lined up outside my office,' I said. I looked around. 'Is everybody okay?'

'Thank you *so* much for saving Sean,' one of the students said. 'We thought he was going to die.' She pointed at the floor. 'Look at how much blood he lost!'

The mats were soaked in blood. I desperately wanted to taste it, but I didn't have the grinding need that usually filled me when I was faced with blood. The serpent form was helping me to control every aspect of the demon infusion.

'He did lose a lot,' I said. 'When Master Park comes back from the infirmary, he can arrange for it to be cleaned. In the meantime, head to the cafeteria and take a break for a short while.'

The students nodded, some of them obviously still shocked by what had happened, and filed out.

'I'll keep an eye on them,' Meredith said. 'You go back to what you were doing.' She turned to me. 'Now that you have this skill, you are going to save us a great deal of trouble.'

'Maybe I should move my office to the infirmary,' I said. I started to slither out the door.

'Aren't you going to change back to human?' Meredith said.

'Not so close to all that blood. I'll change further away from it.'

'Good idea,' Meredith said as I went out.

Scott and Tymen and Tymen's mother were waiting for me outside my office when I returned. They rose when they saw me.

I went to Tymen's mother and took her hands. 'How are you feeling?'

My senses were still heightened from being a snake and I could sense her status without being told. Although she was still desperately weak, she was clean. The cancer was gone. All she needed now was rest.

'I will not be sure until I have returned to the Netherlands and my doctors have checked me over,' she said in her charming Dutch accent. 'But I somehow *feel* more well. I think that the big snake cured me.'

'Did the boys explain to you what happened?' I said.

She nodded, her eyes bright. 'I could not believe it was true. I was touched by a God? Of course not the good Christian God, so some smaller healing spirit, or angel …'

'That is exactly correct,' I said. 'A spirit of healing.'

She nodded. 'I am blessed.'

She turned to look at Scott and Tymen. 'And my son is blessed to have such a good friend.' She touched Scott's arm. 'One day I hope my son finds a man as good as you.'

Both Scott and Tymen rolled their eyes.

'Stop trying to set me up!' Tymen said.

'Well, one day, if you find the right person, you may be able to bring me some grandchildren. Your own or adopted, I don't care.' She spread her arms. 'And now I will live to see them!'

Scott turned to me. 'You see that? She doesn't care if her son shacks up with another guy, she doesn't care *who* that guy is, provided there are kids in the equation. I swear, all mothers are the same.'

'You get this from your mother too?' Tymen's mother said.

'Yes!' Scott said with force. He turned back to me. 'We just wanted to say thank you, Lady Emma. Tymen's mom is going home in a few days, and then later in the year we're going to visit her in the Netherlands.' He shrugged. 'I'm trying to get Cindy to come too.'

'And I want you to come with someone too,' Tymen's mother said, patting Tymen on the arm. 'You have been too long alone, Tyty.'

Tymen leaned down to speak to his mother; she was a good twenty centimetres shorter than him. 'I will never bring anyone unless you promise to stop embarrassing me.'

'Oh, pfft.' She waved him down. 'We are going to lunch, Emma. Would you like to come along?'

'I would love to, but today I am visiting a close friend in the hospital,' I said.

'Well, you wish your friend the very best from us, and tell him that if he is touched by a snake, he is very lucky.'

'He was already touched by a snake, and that's the only reason he's alive,' I said.

'I never thought of snakes as having this wonderful healing power,' she said. 'You have changed the way I see you.'

'I'm not ...' I started, then gave up. 'Thank you.'

They went out, waving cheerfully. I waved back.

'Being a snake isn't such a bad thing after all,' I said as I went into my office to check my email before Simone came to take me to visit Michael.

'If you start doing it all the time, can we put a ring on your tail to hold me?' the stone said. 'I *hate* being in your muscle tissue like that.'

'How about a collar?' I said. 'I'll talk to some of the other transforming Shen about how they work that. Maybe I could change to a snake, have a collar fitted and have a setting in it for you.'

'You wouldn't feel like you're wearing a dog collar?' the stone said.

'Not if I don't choose to. And if it's more comfortable for you, so much the better.'

'Gold or silver?' the stone said.

'I'm black — so silver.'

'Platinum. Filigree.' The stone was silent for a moment. 'I like the direction this is going. How about something that goes over your head as well, like a filigree crown?'

'Oh God, not too complicated. Just a collar will do.'

'Do you mind if I work something out with the other stones? I think a few of them would like to thank you for stopping Six, and this could be a way of doing it.'

'Six is still out there, and we haven't had word from any of our agents.'

'You'll find him. So ... Can I make this platinum collar for you?'

'Go right ahead.'

'It might take me a couple of days to find something suitably elegant for a stone as majestic as me.'

'Oh, I'm sure it will.'

Simone wheeled Leo into my office an hour later. 'Coming, Emma?' she said.

'Absolutely, just let me get my bag,' I said, then stopped. 'Uh, okay, no hands, no bag. Will Leo be all right to go to the Celestial Plane?'

'Yeah, he'll be fine. He's already so damaged that it really can't hurt him more,' Simone said. 'The Tiger wants to have a look at him while we're in his medical centre.'

'And I say the Tiger can keep his goddamn paws off me,' Leo said.

'He may be able to help,' I said.

'We'll see,' Leo said.

'That was the most *hands off me* "we'll see" I've ever heard,' Simone said. She nodded to me. 'Change, Emma, and I'll take us.'

'Can I stay behind?' the stone said.

'No way,' Simone said. 'Apparently there's an opal there that hasn't seen you in ages and wants to catch up with you.'

'Oh,' the stone said. 'That's different.'

'Come on, Emma, chop chop,' Simone said. 'Snake, please.'

'Can I take the normal big size? The small one is much harder,' I said.

'Big is okay,' Simone said, and I changed.

'That seems easier every time you do it,' she said.

'It is. It's almost like second nature now. My chi is flowing again, and the stone says that the demon essence is a little less every time I do it.'

'You should spend time at home as a snake then,' Simone said. She came to me and touched the back of my neck. 'I can touch you and give you hugs. We'll put a beanbag and a ray lamp in your room.'

I was about to protest, then said, 'Ray lamp?'

'Real big warm one,' she said.

'Actually, that sounds pretty good.'

We landed outside the hospital wing of the Western Palace. The building was two-storey, built of the same red stone as the rest of the Palace. A desert garden with winding paths surrounded it, and a large hedge provided some privacy.

'Leo passed out,' I said.

'That's what used to happen to you all the time,' Simone said. 'We should get you some training in teleportation; you could probably do it.'

'Your father was very excited the first time he saw the snake,' I said. 'I don't know if you remember, but he was thrilled at how powerful it was, and thought we would even be able to touch.'

'Did you try? To see if you could?'

I just looked at her.

'Okay, stupid question.'

She wheeled Leo to the entrance. It looked very much like a small private hospital, with a blue vinyl floor and modern, bright furniture. A demon in the form of a young woman stood behind the reception desk.

'They need a doorkeeper?' I said.

'All the wives come here to have their babies,' Simone said. 'And they visit each other. Sometimes too many at a time.'

'I can imagine,' I said.

We approached the reception desk, the demon watching me like a rabbit in headlights.

'We're here to see Michael,' Simone said.

The demon checked the register on the computer, still looking at me now and then.

'Don't be afraid, I won't hurt you,' I said, and the demon jumped.

She turned back to Simone. 'No Michael here.'

'Uh …' Simone began.

'Three One Five,' I said.

'Oh, the good one,' the demon said. She gestured to indicate the corridor behind her. 'Upstairs, ward four.'

Leo shifted in the wheelchair and Simone moved to crouch in front of him, holding his hand. 'Leo?'

Leo rubbed his hands over his face and blinked. 'Huh?'

'Take it easy, Leo, you just travelled to the Celestial Plane and the journey can be difficult sometimes.'

Leo put his hands on the armrests of the wheelchair and tried to stand. 'What's the matter with me?'

'Stay, Leo,' Simone said, pushing him back down. 'You're still disoriented from the journey. We're visiting Michael. Stay in the chair.'

Leo fell back and stared blankly at her.

'Just take it easy,' I said.

'Emma?' He turned his head to see me and nearly leapt out of the chair. 'Holy shit!'

'Maybe I should put him back under,' Simone said.

'No, he's coming around,' I said. 'Just sit back and relax, Leo, it'll come to you. You're safe.'

Leo looked from me to Simone, then relaxed. 'Oh, we're visiting Michael. Are we there?'

'We're there,' Simone said. 'Just sit back and we'll take you up to see him.'

Leo nodded. 'Okay.'

We took the lift up to Michael's ward and went in. It really did look just like a small private hospital; each bed was a standard hospital bed with an oxygen port and an IV stand. Michael was in a two-bed ward, next to the window, the other bed empty. He was watching the wall-mounted television when we went in, and turned it off when he saw us.

Simone went to him, put her hands on his shoulders and kissed his cheek, then turned. 'This is Emma in serpent form. She can travel to the Plane as a snake.'

Michael focused on me and his eyebrows creased. 'Really? Emma, that's you?'

'One hundred per cent me,' I said.

Michael smiled at Leo. 'Hello, old man. I hear you're back. Welcome home.'

Leo wheeled himself closer to Michael and took his hand. 'It's good to see you, pal.'

Simone sat on the bed next to Michael. 'So when are they letting you out?'

'I think that's mostly up to me,' Michael said. 'As soon as I can walk again, they'll probably let me go.'

'You can't walk?' I said.

'It's something to do with the brain damage,' Michael said, gesturing towards a wheelchair at the side of the room. 'I can get myself around in that thing, but I usually just change into a tiger and scare the staff. My tiger form seems to be okay, but they say that's normal, because it was the human form that was damaged.' Michael tapped Leo's hand. 'You should try turning into a lion, old man. You could probably walk in lion form.'

'Is that so?' Leo said. 'I might give that a try.'

'How are you generally though, Michael?' I said. 'You *will* be able to walk again, right?'

'Yeah, I just need to get some practice in. They do physical therapy with me twice a day, and I'll need to continue that once I'm out.' He grimaced. 'That means I have to stay here for a while. I need to keep up the therapy, otherwise I may lose the use of some of my muscles. Is that okay?'

'Don't worry, man. I can look after the girls while you recuperate,' Leo said.

'And as soon as you're well enough, if you want to come back, you can,' I said.

He relaxed. 'That's good to hear. So what happened after Three smacked me in the head? Obviously you got Leo back, and I heard you rescued Gold's child. Did you destroy Six?'

'No,' I said. 'We have agents working on it. We know what to look for, but it seems to have gone to ground with its little friends and we haven't heard anything. We shut down its operation completely though; no more stones are going to be hurt.'

'You'll find it,' Michael said. He raised one hand towards me. 'Nice snake form. I like it.'

I bobbed my serpent head. 'I thank you, Mr Tiger.'

'Are you poisonous?'

I opened my mouth carefully, allowing the fangs to swing down without spitting any poison. Then I closed it again. 'Cobra.'

'Nice. Can you do the hood thing?'

'I don't know, I've never tried.'

He waited silently, watching me.

'Oh, okay,' I said, and raised my head. I concentrated, trying to make my neck wider.

'Nothing,' he said, disappointed. 'You need to work on that.'

'And you need to work on the walking,' I said. 'Let's see who gets there first.'

'First one there buys the other one — and these two,' he said, indicating Leo and Simone, 'dinner.'

'It's a deal,' I said.

'And now,' he said, settling back into his pillows, 'you're going to tell me, in detail, everything that happened after we entered Hell. The last thing I remember is being driven in the van towards the Pits. Everything after that is a blank. So tell me what we did.'

'You don't remember any of it?' Simone said.

'Not a thing,' Michael said.

'Damn, I should have brought my notes,' I said with amusement.

'I can print them out at the nurses station if you like,' the stone said.

'No, Simone can prompt me if I forget any of it,' I said. I looked around for a chair and sat next to Michael. 'Here we go.'

CHAPTER 37

Four weeks later I attended the biggest wedding to be held on the Celestial Plane in a very long time. The Tiger had erected a stage for the ceremony on the desert plain outside the Western Palace, and it was decked with white and gold silk that billowed in the breeze. A stadium-sized LCD screen had been set up above the stage, allowing those further back to see the proceedings in detail. Tiered viewing stands for the guests had been built on either side of the road leading to the stage, and flagpoles lined the road, each of them bearing white and gold flags with the motif of the tiger. An honour guard of Horsemen on horseback lined the road on either side, facing inwards, each of them also bearing a lance topped with a tiger banner.

Simone was in a special box at the side of the stage, with other guests of honour. I was in serpent form, as small as I could make myself without discomfort, curled up under her chair.

The banners over our heads snapped in the strong breeze, and the horses' bits jingled as they shook their heads and shuffled with excitement.

I nudged Simone's foot with my nose. 'You keep moving your feet together — I can't see!'

'Sorry,' she said, and adjusted her position.

There was a fanfare of trumpets and drums, and a flash on the stage. The Jade Emperor had arrived. Everybody rose and, as one, fell to their knees, kowtowing three times to him. They remained kneeling with their heads on the floor until his voice rang out: 'Rise.'

Everybody rose and sat. The large screen zoomed in on the face of the Jade Emperor, smiling benevolently. Er Lang stood glowering at his right shoulder.

'Have you spoken to Er Lang recently?' Simone whispered.

'I just keep out of his way and he keeps out of mine,' I said.

'He should be trying to work with you.'

'As long as I lack the attributes he requires, I don't think he will.'

'And I don't think Emma will grow a penis just to appease his prejudice,' the stone said.

Simone, Yue Gui and Martin all laughed quietly above me.

There was another fanfare of trumpets, and a few of the honour guards' horses danced with excitement but remained in place. The riders quelled them and they stood again.

The Tiger and Rhonda rode up to the stage on horseback, each mounted on what appeared to be a Spanish horse: solid body, fine legs, thick, heavy neck and intelligent, large-eyed face. Rhonda's was a striking palomino with a bright gold body and shining white mane and tail; the Tiger's was pure white. Both horses had manes that nearly touched the ground, falling in long ripples from being plaited. The bridles and saddles appeared to be made of gold, and the bride and groom wore the traditional red Chinese wedding robes. The Tiger was in a mandarin jacket and pants of red silk, and Rhonda rode side-saddle in a traditional wedding dress of red silk jacket and long skirt, the jacket front elaborately embroidered with a phoenix and tiger in gold and silver thread.

Michael and Leo escorted them down the aisle, Michael on the right as a large tawny golden tiger and Leo on the left as a black lion. Each was about twice the size of the natural animal, their shoulders nearly the same height as the horses. Their presence had absolutely no effect on either the horses the couple were riding or on the guards' mounts — an impressive display of training.

'Leo nearly couldn't manage it. He only just got it yesterday,' Simone said.

'I'm glad,' Martin said. 'It is good to see him able to walk without aid.'

The couple reached the stage and dismounted at the bottom of the stairs, passing the horses to a couple of the Tiger's sons, who led them away. They walked side by side up the stairs, flanked by Leo and Michael, and kowtowed to the Jade Emperor. Leo and Michael went to one side and bowed as animals. Demon servants came forward to assist them with crutches and a wheelchair, and they changed back to human.

'Michael says that with hard physical therapy he should be walking in a couple of weeks,' Simone said.

'That is also good to hear,' Martin said.

'They're breaking with tradition: her face isn't covered,' Yue Gui said.

'They're remarrying so it doesn't really matter,' Martin said.

'The big ceremony is more for crowning her as Empress of the West,' Simone said.

'Oh, shit,' I said softly, and Simone giggled. She'd heard me.

'We must ensure that the ceremony to wed and

crown Emma is much larger,' Yue Gui said with enthusiasm. 'With martial arts demonstrations. Mass ones. And dancing. An orchestra. A mix of East and West, martial arts, music, dancing — it must be *bigger*.'

'Oh, *shit*,' I said, even more softly, and Simone laughed louder, struggling to hold it in.

The Tiger and Rhonda moved to stand in front of the Jade Emperor. He sat on a throne that had been prepared for him on a raised dais at the back of the stage, and they knelt before him. Demon servants brought a tray of teacups, and each of them served the Jade Emperor in turn. Then they rose, and the Tiger sat on a smaller throne to the right of the Jade Emperor.

Oh, look, they're facing south, Jade said into my head.

'Tell Jade thank you very much for reminding me,' I whispered to the stone.

You are most welcome, ma'am. I hope you can see okay, because in time this will be you.

'Damn, everybody really hates me today,' I said softly.

Rhonda knelt before the Tiger and served him tea. He took the teacup, sipped from it, then returned it to the tray. She passed the tray to a demon, and took her seat on a throne to the right of the Tiger's. They were officially married.

The Tiger gestured to the demon, and the demon handed him the tray of teacups. He rose, carrying the tray, and turned to kneel in front of Rhonda. The crowd gasped.

Rhonda stared at the Tiger, confused. He said something that wasn't picked up by the microphones and she shook her head. He pushed the tray towards her and she reluctantly took a teacup, sipped from it, and returned it to the tray.

There was a quiet roar of discussion within the crowd.

'Did he just set her above himself?' Simone said.

'More as an equal,' Martin said. 'She served him, he served her. Tremendous breach of protocol; people will be talking about this for a very long time.'

The Tiger rose, handed the tray to the waiting demon, then took Rhonda's hand and kissed it. He pulled her up by the hand, guided her to stand next to him, and raised her hand in triumph. She wiped her eyes with her other hand.

The crowd erupted into a roar of approval, the Horsemen yelling loudest of all. An orchestra at the base of the stage played traditional Chinese marriage music, and the Tiger walked her, hands held high, the length of the front of the stage. They turned as a couple to face the Jade Emperor, still holding hands, and both bowed to him. He stood and bowed back, then sat again.

The Tiger raised one hand and Rhonda's throne, gold and white carved with a pair of phoenixes as the back, floated to the middle of the stage, slightly to one side from the Jade Emperor's, which remained at a higher position at the back. The Tiger guided Rhonda to sit on the throne, and bowed to her, and she nodded back. He turned, and a demon came forward with her crown.

From a distance the crown looked like a simple dome, but on the large screen it was much more complex, made of a delicate filigree of gold that was similar to the stone's setting my snake form now wore. It was embedded with pearls, with a massive pearl in the centre of her forehead, at least three centimetres across. The crown had wings on the sides, like stylised phoenix wings, with strands of pearls hanging down from them to frame her face.

The Tiger took the crown, raised it for the audience to see, and then set it on her head. She used her sleeve to wipe her eyes again as the crowd erupted in more cheering. The Tiger took her hand again, raised her to stand, and led her to the front of the stage. He raised his other hand for the crowd to hush.

He released her hand and stood to one side as silence fell over the crowd.

'Kowtow to your Empress,' he said.

As one, all of the Horsemen thumped their chests with their fists, acknowledging her. The members of the crowd who were residents of the West knelt before her. Simone, Martin and Yue Gui, together with the other dignitaries, rose from their seats and saluted her.

Rhonda stood up and cleared her throat. 'You may rise,' she said, her voice choked with emotion. She turned, her wedding dress sweeping around her, and walked to the Jade Emperor. She fell to one knee before him, saluting, and he nodded to her. The Tiger saluted the Jade Emperor, took Rhonda's hand again and led her to her throne, which had drifted to return to its place next to his. After she had seated herself, he knelt and saluted her, then sat himself.

The Jade Emperor rose and moved to the front of the stage, and the crowd hushed. Simone jiggled in her seat with excitement.

'Bring me Leo Alexander, the one called the Black Lion,' the Jade Emperor said.

Leo wheeled himself to the front of the stage to sit before the Jade Emperor, and saluted him. The Tiger clapped his hands in personal applause.

The Jade Emperor beckoned to Er Lang, who brought forward a tray holding a glass and silver jug and a crystal goblet. While Er Lang held the tray, the Jade Emperor poured the Elixir into the glass. He took the glass, raised it to the crowd, then handed it to Leo, one hand holding the glass and the other supporting the bottom in a traditional show of respect.

Leo took the glass and hesitated, looking at it. He looked around at the crowd.

'Be the real Leo, be the real Leo, be the real Leo,' Simone whispered.

Leo saw Simone and raised the glass to her, then took a small sip, then a larger gulp. He finished it and returned the glass to the Jade Emperor, who nodded to him.

'Nothing happened,' Simone said, sounding disappointed.

'Yes, it did,' Yue Gui said, and as she spoke the change occurred.

Leo was suddenly enveloped in the red-gold light of ching energy and raised from the wheelchair as if pulled by a string from his heart. He floated above the chair, his face full of rapture, the red-gold energy growing around him. He smiled with a mixture of joy and wonder, and a cloud came down from the sky, looking very similar to the clouds that Immortals travelled on. He stepped onto the cloud as if this was something he'd always wanted, and flew off high into the sky, disappearing from view.

The crowd erupted into cheers of joy, clapping and whistling.

'He *will* be back, promise he'll be back,' Simone said.

'You know that it is his choice, Mei Mei,' Martin said. 'I'm sure he will though.'

'He'd better,' she said, her voice choked with tears. 'Oh, Emma, it's wonderful.'

I was silent; I was too emotional to speak.

The Jade Emperor stepped forward. 'Bring me Empress Rhonda MacLaren of the Western Heavens.'

Rhonda rose from her throne, the pearls on the crown bobbing as she moved. She walked to the Jade Emperor, knelt before him, then stood again.

He poured another glass of the Elixir for her, and passed it to her. She nodded to him, and wrinkled her nose as she brought it to her mouth.

'No! Stop her!' I yelled, but it was too late.

She took a drink from the glass and her eyes went wide. She dropped the glass and exploded. She didn't explode like a demon; she was all human, and the drink destroyed her in a cloud of red and white mist that covered the stage with blood. The crowd roared with shock, and the Tiger shot to his feet, his mouth open with horror.

'That wasn't her!' I said.

'It had to be, Emma,' Simone said. 'He had her tested when she came back from Hell. That was *her*. What *happened*?'

The Tiger strode to the confused-looking Jade Emperor, grabbed the glass and sniffed it. He took a large swig and put it back, confused. He turned to walk away, but Michael was behind him, standing without the crutches and holding his white and gold katana.

'You killed my mother!' Michael yelled, his voice booming from the amplified sound system. 'What did you do? You poisoned her!'

'I don't know what happened,' the Tiger said. He raised his hands, palms up. 'That was her. That was the right Elixir. I don't know what went wrong.'

'You *bastard*, you *killed her*!' Michael yelled, and swung the sword to take his father's head.

The Tiger didn't attempt to block the blow and his head was separated from his body. Both parts hit the floor of the stage and disappeared.

Michael fell to his knees in the pool of his mother's blood, weeping. 'He killed her. He killed her.' He rocked backwards and forwards over his knees, his eyes wide and his mouth open. 'He killed her.' He disappeared.

'I'm going after him,' Simone said, and disappeared as well.

The Jade Emperor raised his arms. 'Return to your homes. We will investigate. I call upon the Number One son of the White Tiger to take control of the Heavens while he is incapacitated.' He waved his hands and turned away. 'Go home. Show's over.'

He waved Er Lang closer and conferred with him for a while, then both of them disappeared.

I slithered out from under the seat. People were milling around in shock and talking loudly about what had just happened. No one noticed me. I climbed up into Simone's seat to speak to Yue Gui and Martin. 'Has anything like that happened before?'

'I've never seen anything like it,' Martin said. 'If a demon takes the Elixir, they are destroyed as demon essence. But she disintegrated as a human. It's very confusing.'

'And that was definitely her?'

'Absolutely,' Yue Gui said. 'The Tiger has the most advanced demon research facility in the Celestial. If anybody could pick a demon copy, he could.'

'It's not possible she was a demon; she was human all the way through,' Martin said, and gestured towards the stage. 'That's definitely human blood.'

'I am talking to her engagement ring, and the stone is as confused as everybody else,' the stone in my ring said. 'It swears blind that Rhonda was not replaced, and that was the genuine woman.'

'Maybe she *was* something special,' I said. 'We thought she was a Shen. Maybe she was a demon after all, or something like me.'

'Can one of you take Emma home?' the stone said. 'It could be a while before Michael decides to return, even if Simone manages to find him.'

I felt a jolt of dismay. I was going home alone. I'd lost all of them in one go.

'They'll be back, Emma,' the stone said. 'Simone will definitely be home later, whether she finds Michael or not.'

'How long does it normally take someone who's just attained Immortality to return?' I said.

'That depends entirely on the individual,' Martin said. 'Sometimes only days. Other times they come back a hundred years later, as if no time has passed.'

'I suppose it's worth it to know he's not dying any more,' I said.

'That it is, Lady Emma,' Martin said. He put his hand on my serpent head. 'I will take you home.'

Ah Yat came out of the kitchen when Martin and I landed in the living room. 'Welcome home, ma'am, Ming Dai Yan. I thought you were staying for a party in the Western Heavens?'

I changed to human and flopped to sit on one of the couches. 'It was a disaster. The Elixir of Immortality killed Rhonda, completely blew her up. Then Michael killed his father and took off. Simone's gone after him. Leo's gained Immortality, and he's gone as well.' I dropped my head into my hands. 'It's awful.'

Ah Yat came and knelt in front of me. 'Do not be concerned, ma'am. You are fated for better than this. All will be well.' She rose and went back into the kitchen. 'I will make you tea.'

Martin touched my back. 'I will stay with you, Emma.'

I raised my head and brushed my hands through my hair. 'Do you know where Simone is?'

He concentrated, then snapped back and shook his head. 'She is more powerful than any of us. She could be anywhere.'

'Will Michael be arrested for killing his father?'

'Only if his father wants it. There is a loophole that if someone kills an Immortal and they both claim that it was during training, the student is exempt.'

'But he did it in front of everybody.'

'I do not think anybody will want to commit him for doing what he did. He knows the Tiger is Immortal, and everybody knows that the Tiger is quite capable of defending himself. The Tiger let him do it.'

Simone appeared in the middle of the living room, her face taut with emotion.

'Did you find him?' I said.

'Yes,' she said, and rushed into her bedroom, closing the door behind her.

I went to follow her.

'I will leave you,' Martin said. 'I will return tomorrow, when things have settled. If she wishes, she can tell me where Michael is and I will fetch him.'

'Thanks, Martin,' I said. He disappeared.

I went to Simone's room and tapped on the door.

'Go *away*!' she said.

I opened the door and went in. 'Did anything happen that I need to be concerned about?' I said.

She was lying on her bed crying and glared up at me, full of fury. 'No! Yes! Nearly! Go away!'

'Well, thank God it's only nearly,' I said. 'And you have the commonsense to stop.'

'I didn't stop, *he did*!' she cried, distraught. She rose, pushed me out of her room and slammed the door in my face. 'Go *away*!'

'Is he all right, Simone?' I said to the door.

'Of course he's not all right. He's just seen his father kill his mother, and then killed his own father. He's a wreck. He's going back to the Folly. He says he needs some time and to leave him alone.' The door opened again and she glared at me. 'I need some time too. Leave me alone.' She shut the door again.

'Call the Lady, please, stone,' I said.

'Kwan Yin is already in there,' the stone said.

I listened, and heard Kwan Yin's voice talking to Simone, calm and comforting. I turned and went back to the office.

Kwan Yin appeared in the office after I'd read every twitter on the net twice. She sat across the desk from me in her human form of a mid-forties woman in a white pantsuit.

'She hugged him, he was distraught, he kissed her, that's all,' she said.

'And she's blowing it out of proportion?' I said.

'Completely. You know how she feels about him.'

'Oh Lord, he didn't apologise profusely, call her his kid sister and ruffle her hair, did he?'

'That's exactly what he did.'

'Damn, she'll be impossible for days.'

'Should I talk to him?'

I hesitated, then, 'If anybody talks to him, his attitude will change. It will be obvious that someone told him, and she'll hate me forever.'

Kwan Yin nodded.

'It'll be worse when she finally has a *real* boyfriend, won't it?'

She nodded again.

'I quit.'

She rose and touched my hand. 'I will go speak to him now. What he has been through is very tough.'

'Wait.' I raised my hand. 'What happened? Why did it kill her? Was that a demon copy?'

She hesitated for a moment.

'Dammit, you're doing it again!' I said. 'You're deciding how much you should tell me without giving the future away! You do this all the time.'

'There are some things that you should not know.'

'Was Rhonda a demon?'

'Not in the sense that you mean.'

'What was she?'

'An ordinary human being whose heritage betrayed her. Much as yours has betrayed you.'

I leaned back and stared at her with shock. 'You know what I am. And it's something like Rhonda.'

'If you can clear the demon essence from yourself, the Elixir will not kill you,' she said. 'Now I will go talk to Michael.' She disappeared.

I banged the desk and turned away.

CHAPTER 38

Three weeks passed. On the Friday night, I finalised the records for the new students and put my computer into sleep mode. I shoved some of my notes and a to-do list into my scruffy tote bag, turned off the light and went out to the lift lobby. I was meeting Simone and Michael for dinner at a local Thai restaurant and then we were planning to see a movie together in Pacific Place.

The phone rang in my office and I charged back, turned on the light and grabbed it. 'Emma.'

'Ma'am, it's the guard downstairs. There's a delivery here for you, from Australia. Something about Uluru. Do you want me to escort him up? He says it's a gift.'

'Send him up, twenty-sixth,' I said, and put the phone down. It wasn't uncommon in Hong Kong for deliveries to be made very late. I'd had people knocking on the door at 11 pm with deliveries as if it was the most natural thing in the world. I wondered what the Grandmother had sent me; I really should plan a visit to her very soon.

I went out to the lift lobby to wait for the delivery. The doors opened and the delivery boy stepped out holding a package.

Oh Hell, it was Six. I backed up the length of the lobby.

'My brothers and sisters have removed me from the group,' Six said. 'They say I have failed, that I am a liability. They have the stones I built for us and they no longer need me.' He grimaced. 'You stopped me at every turn, and you didn't even know you were doing it!'

'I guess we were just lucky,' I said, and summoned the Murasame.

Six smiled without humour. 'I have no hope outside Hell. But I plan to take you with me.'

'Thanks, but I don't think I want to come,' I said, and readied myself.

He took True Form: a four-legged creature with long claws, scales, and a snake-like body with a demonic lion-like head. He looked something like Liang Tian's demon form.

'That's the thing, you see,' he said in his usual voice. 'I don't think your snake can take down something as big as me. You need a weapon. That's why you stayed human.'

I backed up slightly. He was right.

'So you have to fight me in human form. And when you destroy me, I'll squirt my essence all over you.'

'Not the choice of words I would prefer,' I said.

'And when it hits you, you'll be turned into a Snake Mother.' He grinned with malice, showing long green fangs. 'You'll become one of us, probably big enough to take on the Demon King. I'd like to see that bastard get what's coming to him.'

'If you turn I will take you in and protect you,' I said.

'Frankly, I'd rather see you changed into a Mother, then go in and kill the rest of my group. That bitch the Death Mother, I gave her the caverns for her nest in

Thailand. *I* funded the geek's fucking research lab in Shenzhen. I gave them all the means to take the King down, you know that? And this is how they show their appreciation. They kick me out and leave me to die.'

'You don't have to die if you turn,' I said.

'I have to die if *you're* going to turn though,' he said, and came for me. He swiped at me with his head, and I backed up to avoid the fangs. I somersaulted over the top of his head and readied myself on the other side of the room.

'Get me some goddamn *help*,' I said. 'Call Simone!'

The stone didn't reply.

'I still have some sway with our little inanimate friends,' Six said as he leapt towards me and swiped at me with his clawed front legs.

I dodged his blows and landed a good strike with my sword on one front leg, severing it, then somersaulted backwards away from the spray of demon essence. He fell onto his belly and howled with pain, but didn't disintegrate. I stopped, confused.

He stretched the leg out in front of him. It didn't bleed, but it didn't leak demon essence either. The end of the limb was just blank and grey, like concrete. He concentrated, and the talons sprouted out of the end of his leg.

'I still have some sway with my own nature, as well,' he said. 'It's amazing what a demon can do when it's combined with the essence of powerful stones.'

I took advantage of his moment of disorientation and moved closer to take off his head, then stopped at the last minute. His leg may not have caused him to explode, but his head probably would. It was a trap to make me explode it on myself. I stepped back, holding the sword in front of me as a guard.

Six came at me again, swiping at my head with his enormous mouth. I ducked under his head and took off two of his feet. He fell screaming again, and I stepped back as he concentrated and again regrew the limbs.

I banged the stone on the wall. 'Wake *up*, dammit!'

The stone didn't respond.

Six stepped forward, swinging with both front feet and his head again. I took off one of the feet but he seemed to be less bothered by it, pushing me back through the lobby as he hobbled on three legs.

I lowered the sword and took some deep breaths. I was still fit but I couldn't keep this up forever. In the end I'd have to destroy this thing or be destroyed by it.

After another ten minutes of dodging his blows and cutting his feet off only to have them grow back, I really was beginning to feel it. My phone in my bag had rung twice; probably Simone trying to find out where I was. Six undoubtedly had some sort of stone shield so that nobody could see what was happening here. I could only hope that she would get tired of waiting for me and come to chase me up. I smiled grimly as I dodged another of Six's attacks. I just had to hold out until the little girl saved me. Again.

He saw that my reflexes were slowing. 'Come on, Emma, finish it. You never know, you might like being one of us. The food is *great* — you said that yourself.' He swiped again at my head, and I was tired enough for him to hit me. I slid across the floor and crashed into the wall. He approached me, grinning with menace. 'Or maybe I just kill you and take you with me. That works too.'

He put one huge paw on my abdomen and held me down, then opened his mouth wide to take my head. I changed into a small snake, slithered out of his grasp and raced to the other side of the room. He clumsily turned; his large bulk made it difficult for him to move in a circle easily, but he was lightning-fast in a straight line. He thundered after me and tried to grab my snake form in his mouth.

I raced to the other end of the room again, turned and faced him. I grew to about five metres long, the same size that he was. I opened my mouth to release my fangs, spitting poison at him. The poison didn't have any effect.

'Bad idea, Emma. I can definitely kill you like this, and I like the taste of snake,' Six said.

He swiped his head at me, trying to grab my head in his mouth, and I moved with inhuman speed to avoid him.

He stamped one foot on my body to hold me down and I fell to the floor, writhing with pain. He had me. He lowered his head to look me in the eye. 'Change into a human and take me down.'

'No,' I said. 'I'll die as a snake.'

'You can kill me with your sword, you can take me,' he said. 'You've cut my feet off so many times. Do it. Kill me!'

'No!' I shouted and buried my fangs in his leg. He ignored it. I ripped them free, and hissed with pain as one of them broke.

He opened his mouth wide and lowered it to kill me, and I sincerely wished that I had eyelids.

His head stopped slightly above me and his eyes widened with shock. Then he was thrown off me and flew across the room. I lifted my head to see what had happened; Leo had appeared next to me.

'Need a hand, ma'am?' he said.

'You're Immortal, you don't call me ma'am now.'

Leo stood facing the demon. 'I don't feel Immortal.'

Six raised himself back onto all fours and shook his head. 'Good. You can come with me too.'

'You just threw that thing all the way across the room,' I said. I changed back to human form and resummoned the Murasame. 'Need a sword? You can ask for Dark Heavens, I'm sure it would come to you.'

'No, it wouldn't,' Leo said, but at the same time the sword appeared in his hand. 'Well, how about that.'

We faced Six side by side.

'This one doesn't look too big for you, Emma. Why haven't you killed it?' Leo said.

'If I absorb any more demon essence, I'll be turned into a Snake Mother.'

'Oh, that's not good.'

'You can take it down, my friend. You're an Immortal.'

He glanced down at me. 'I don't feel any different. If there's anything special I can do, I don't know how to do it yet.'

'Oh, this is wonderful,' Six hissed. 'I get to destroy a shiny new Immortal. It's completely worth it.' He threw himself at us.

Leo wasn't inhumanly fast and Six grabbed his body in his mouth. I had no choice. I jumped up, swung my sword and took off his head, trying to land as far away from the exploding demon as I could. Leo fell to the floor, stunned.

I landed in a long defensive stance and watched as the essence sailed towards me in slow motion. Damn, I should have stayed a snake and let both of us die. My Snake Mother form really was as dangerous as Six wanted it to be. This was going to be horrible.

I turned my sword on myself, hoping I could destroy myself before the essence hit, and the essence stopped. It hung in mid-air between Leo and myself. Then it fell to the floor and disappeared.

I flopped to sit, panting. I'd been fighting flat out for nearly forty minutes and that really was the longest anyone could keep that type of intense activity going without their muscles turning to mush.

Leo got up and came to sit next to me. 'I don't want to learn any more superpowers under such circumstances, is that understood?'

I just dropped my sword and threw my arms around him, holding him tight.

'I don't think I can walk now,' he said into my shoulder. 'The adrenaline's worn off. Do you guys have a wheelchair around here? 'Cause I can't walk home as a lion.'

'You teleported in,' I said.

'I have no idea how I did that. I just knew you were in trouble and came to help.'

'Thank God you killed that monster, Emma, and nothing will be able to control us again,' the stone said. 'I've been trying to get you help since it appeared.'

'Can you ask Simone to come in and help Leo?'

Simone appeared next to us, fell to her knees and threw her arms around Leo. 'Welcome back, Prince Leo.' She pulled back to touch his face. 'Are you ready to come home?'

'That's the best thing anybody's said to me today,' Leo said. 'Is the car all fixed up? I want to drive.'

'It's downstairs waiting,' I said.

'Do you have a wheelchair here?' Leo said.

'Lok is bringing one,' Simone said. 'Let's go home.'

The next evening, the grassy area next to the lake in the Northern Heavens was full of people and brightly coloured lights. A small stage had been erected, also strung with coloured lights, and a band of musicians played Chinese New Year music with gusto. Some of the plum and cherry tree Shen had moved their trees, rich with the blossoms of early spring, to the field to allow them to be decorated with more lights, making the whole area glow with colour. More colour was provided by the elemental sculptures that were spread over the lawn, and the marquees at the sides selling flowers, cumquat bushes in pots, novelty lanterns, hand-made calligraphy banners and all the other requirements for a happy Chinese New Year. There was no moon in the sky above us; Chinese New Year was set by the lunar calendar and always fell on a new moon.

Yue Gui and Martin had met us and now walked with us through the sculpture display, admiring them. Simone and Eva's sculpture was the only one to feature two intertwined elementals: a blue water serpent and a red fire phoenix forming a stylised yin-yang symbol.

'Most of the Tiger's kids' ones are pretty boring,' Simone said. 'Just copies of movie stars and animals.'

'Their execution is almost flawless though,' Yue Gui said. 'They are masters of the technical aspects of elemental sculpture.'

'Boring,' Simone said. 'But the wood ones are so pretty! I've never seen a wood elemental before.'

We stopped in front of one of the wood elemental sculptures.

'Oh,' Simone said, reading the sign next to it. 'This was made by Sang Shen.'

'He's been bored these last two months,' Yue Gui said. 'It's kept him busy.'

'It's so detailed,' Simone said with wonder.

Sang Shen's sculpture was made of glossy dark wood and depicted the life cycle of the silkworm in a stylised large tree. It began with the eggs on the branch of the tree, then showed the worms on another branch eating green leaves, which were so beautifully carved they looked alive, went to the cocoons, then, in a striking departure from the brown and green, showed a vivid purple silk robe draped over a branch, its fabric decorated with glowing white silkworm moths and silver dragons.

'I thought only the Dragon and his children could work with wood elementals,' Simone said.

Yue Gui nodded. 'He traded some of his leaves for the services of a dragon from the East.'

'Wait,' I said. I waved my nose in front of the sculpture. 'Is the dragon aware that this sculpture is pointing out that Sang Shen provides the leaves for his silk?'

'Knowing the dragon,' Yue Gui said with amusement, 'the idea never occurred to him. He is rock-solid in his high opinion of himself, and would never consider that people would think for a minute that his own products — including mulberry leaves — are not the finest.'

'I like Sang Shen more and more all the time,' I said.

'Did I hear my name?' Sang Shen said, approaching us. He was wearing a robe identical to that depicted on the tree, vivid purple with white silkworm moths and silver dragons. He carried a number of white paper bags, and passed them around; in each bag was a Chinese waffle, often sold in the streets of Hong Kong. Batter was put into a mould that was shaped like a bunch of balls slightly smaller than ping-pong balls and cooked over a gas stove. The result was sweet and feather light, and the balls could be torn off and eaten individually.

He hesitated with the bag that was obviously for me.

'Don't worry about it, I've already eaten,' I said.

'How do snakes generally manage?' he said.

'I'll break them off for her,' Simone said. 'Most other snakes can use PK — carrying — to lift and move things.'

'I don't have that,' I said.

Michael approached in the form of a tawny tiger, with Eva and the Phoenix.

'Is that you, Emma?' Eva asked me.

'It's me,' I said. 'Do snakes bother you?'

Eva shivered. 'Just a little.'

'You don't need to come close to me if you don't want to,' I said. 'I understand.'

Eva nodded and stood back from me slightly.

587

Simone broke off a piece of waffle for me and I carefully picked it out of her hand, savouring the sweet flavour. Sang Shen had even asked the stall holder to put peanut butter on it for me, and the melted paste added to the delight. He watched me with barely concealed amusement as I ate the waffle.

In big snake form my head was about the height of the Phoenix's, and she moved closer to see my collar. Despite my protests, the stone had designed it so that the elegant filigree rose up the back of my neck and made a decorative cover over the top of my head, neatly fitting the curves of my serpent skull.

'That's gorgeous, Emma, where did you get it?' she said.

'The stone had it made,' I said. I lowered my head slightly so that she could see. 'Its setting sits between my eyes. Before, it lodged in my neck muscles and it was uncomfortable for both of us.'

'I'm on top of the world,' the stone said.

Michael went to Leo. 'Hey, old man.'

'You still not walking yet?' Leo said.

'Won't be long,' Michael said. He nudged Leo with his nose. 'It's good to have you back.'

Leo put his hand on Michael's head. 'It's good to be back. Looks like I'll be useful here after all — I just helped Emma.'

'They just took Six down together,' Simone said with pride.

'Did it give you any leads on the rest of its group?' the Phoenix said.

'The Death Mother is in Thailand, and the one making the elementals is in Shenzhen,' I said.

The Phoenix nodded. 'That's good to hear. It's only a matter of time before you find them.'

The music on the stage stopped and an old-fashioned PA system crackled to life.

'We have the results of the judging for the Celestial Elemental Artistic Competition,' the MC said. He shuffled some papers, the noise loudly echoing over the speaker system. 'Junior Elemental category. Second runner-up: Tiger Son Number Three Six Three, with "Four Kings".'

There was a smattering of applause.

'Which one was that?' I said. 'I don't remember seeing a Four Winds sculpture.'

'Four Kings of Canto-pop,' Simone said with derision.

'Oh,' I said, and hissed with amusement.

'First runner-up: Tiger Son Number Two Nine Four with "Drunken Master".'

'That's the Jackie Chan one,' Simone said.

'Did he give his permission to be used like that?' I said.

'Probably not,' the Phoenix said. 'But who's going to sue the son of a god?'

'Me,' I said, and Simone chuckled.

Eva gripped Simone's arm and jiggled with excitement; either they'd won or they'd come nowhere.

'Winner of the junior competition is Phoenix Princess Number ...'

The rest of the announcement was lost as Simone and Eva both shrieked with delight and hugged each other.

Simone released Eva and came to hug me, holding my serpent head close.

'... with "Fire Consumes Devil",' the MC finished.

Simone released me and stood back, and she and Eva shared a stunned look.

'My sister Minnie won it,' Eva said in a disbelieving tone.

'The one with the snake demon burning in fire?' Simone said. 'That was *gross*.'

'Apparently the judges liked it,' the Phoenix said. 'With something like this, there's no accounting for taste.'

Eva went to Simone and took her hand. 'We'll win it next year.'

Simone's face went blank and she released Eva's hand. 'I'm going to a human school again now. I don't think I'll have time to do that kind of thing.'

Eva hesitated, then nodded. 'I understand.' She shrugged. 'I s'pose I should go and congratulate Minnie.'

Simone nodded and Eva walked away.

'The results for the Open Celestial Elemental Artistic Competition are ...' the loudspeaker began, but it was drowned out by the sound of cracking wood and shifting earth. We turned to see what was making the noise; Sang Shen's wood elemental had moved, lifting its base out of the ground and walking towards us, making the ground shake with every enormous step it took. Other wood elementals in the display also pulled themselves out of the ground and began to move around.

'What's going on?' Yue Gui said. 'The winner hasn't been announced, they shouldn't be leaving yet.'

The elementals moved towards us, their steps full of purpose. The one closest to us, Sang Shen's sculpture, lost its silkworms and became all wood, a twisted shape that looked more like driftwood than a tree. Its branches writhed and grew, becoming tentacle-like, and it reached towards me.

Snakes can't move backwards so I turned and slithered away as quickly as I could. Something was seriously wrong here.

The elemental swung one branch in a wide arc, hitting Simone in the stomach and knocking her flying. It thrashed its branches, hitting the rest of the Shen and knocking them down.

The Tiger appeared next to us, grabbed a branch and used it as a lever to hold the elemental still. Then he raised one hand and a couple of metal elementals appeared in the form of crescent-shaped blades, each about a metre long. The metal elementals carved up the wood elemental, cutting it into pieces that fell to the ground.

The Phoenix changed to True Form and blew fire from her beak at another wood elemental, but it seemed unharmed by the flames.

She raised her wings, standing in front of us to guard us. 'I have the rear guard. Take them, Tiger.'

Simone pulled herself to her feet, raised her hand and summoned Dark Heavens. She moved to stand beside the Tiger. 'Are these fakes?'

'Very good ones,' the Tiger said. 'Had all of us fooled.' He turned to Simone. 'Hey, you're on the Celestial. Take Celestial Form and pull out Seven Stars. It'll be easier to do up here. Come on, girly, don't be a coward. Get the big sword out and have a go.'

The elementals were about ten metres from us. The rest of the inhabitants of the Northern Heavens had scattered, except for those lying on the ground after being hit by the branches.

Simone hesitated. 'I'm not game, Uncle Bai.'

'Do it.' The Tiger glanced back. 'Everybody else behind Zhu Que. Me and missy here should be able to handle this.' He waved one hand at Michael. 'You too, get back.'

'I want to fight!' Michael said.

The Tiger glared at him. 'With a sword, I'd say yes. Claws only, not good enough. Stay back.' He saw me. 'You too, Miss Snake-In-The-Grass. Weapons yes, fangs no.'

The wood elementals attacked and the Tiger concentrated on them. The water elemental in Simone and Eva's sculpture detached itself from its phoenix-shaped partner and flew in a sparkle of water droplets to assist Simone, but the wood elementals ignored it.

Simone swung Dark Heavens at the first elemental, narrowly avoiding a blow from a second. The Tiger faced three. He swung at the one on his left with his big white katana and sliced it in half. The two pieces each grew limbs and became new wood elementals.

'Seven Stars, girly,' the Tiger said.

Simone ducked under a swinging branch and buried her sword into the trunk-like body of one of the elementals. Her sword lodged in the wood and she was struck by one of the flailing branches as she tried to free herself.

'Come on, Simone, these things are big,' the Tiger said. 'Get out your Celestial Form and pull down the Seven Stars.'

Simone generated a wall of darkness around her and changed into Celestial Form. She grew to be nearly four metres tall, towering over the elementals, which moved back slightly, obviously intimidated. She was in full majestic Celestial Form, with robes of space sparkling with glittering stars, black hair, and huge black eyes with no whites. She dismissed Dark Heavens and the sword disappeared. She raised her hand, summoned Seven Stars, and ripped the enormous dark blade out of its scabbard. It had a hilt of shining white, but the blade itself was black, and down its centre were seven indentations surrounding holes which were about three centimetres across.

The elementals hesitated when they saw the blade.

Simone raised the blade vertically in front of her and closed her eyes. A deep, resounding note echoed from the sword and a red light appeared in the base of her abdomen, then disappeared and appeared in one of the holes in the sword's blade. The rest of the colours quickly followed, each with a higher note than the one before — orange from her pubic region, red from her stomach, green from her heart, blue from her throat, a deep blue from the centre of her forehead, and then a vivid, almost invisible ultraviolet from the top of her head. The lights transferred to the sword, from base to tip, and when the lights were complete she raised her head and lowered the sword. Her eyes glowed completely white, and the blade shone with a similar light, enhanced by the colours in the holes.

Simone moved so fast she was a blur of light and darkness. The sword left trails of light and brilliant colour through the air as it carved the wood elementals to nothingness. She took out the six elementals in less than ten seconds, moving with an elegance and speed only her father could match.

When the elementals were gone she stood in an attack-ready wide stance, left hand out with two fingers raised and glowing with shen energy, and the brilliantly lit sword held in her right hand to one side, ready to sweep away any attackers. She looked around and saw that they had all been destroyed. She lowered her hand, removed the shen energy from it and then raised the sword again. She removed the chakra lights from the blade, starting at the top of her head and moving down through her body until the sword no longer glowed. She picked up the scabbard from the ground, resheathed the sword, and, as she raised the sword and dismissed it, she retook her normal human form.

She came to us to check on us, then stopped, her face full of disbelief as loud cheers and applause broke out behind her.

She turned to see. The residents of the Celestial Plane were cheering her with enthusiasm. Some of them came to her and patted her on the arm and back, but many held back, respectful, and applauded her.

She bowed to the crowd, who cheered louder, then she rejoined our group, blushing furiously.

'Well done, Simone. Your father would be so proud,' I said.

She stopped and stared at me for a moment, her face blank, then shook her head.

'What?' I said.

'That's not what you said in Sai Kung,' she said.

'I can't remember what I said.'

'I can.'

'If it was anything cruel, it was the demon talking, and I want you to know that exactly the opposite is true.'

'No, Emma,' she said. 'Some of what the demon said was very true, which is why it hurt so much.'

I rubbed her arm with my snake head. 'I'm sorry.'

She smiled down at me and put her hand on my head. 'Don't be. And thanks for not calling me "sweetheart". I know you want to.'

'It's only 'cause I love you.'

She put her arms around my neck. 'I love you too, Emma.'

She pulled back and wiped her eyes, then turned to the Tiger. 'You could have taken them easily, couldn't you, Uncle Bai?'

'Of course,' the Tiger said.

'Thanks,' she said.

'You're welcome,' he said. 'Now you know where the demon that made them lives, go find it and use the sword on it. About time that sword came out of mothballs and we saw some fireworks. It's been sitting at Wudang gathering dust for way too long.'

'Thank you for reminding me,' Yue Gui said, and concentrated for a moment.

The fireworks that Yue Gui had organised blasted off from three barges on the lake, filling the sky with a glittering display of light and colour. As one, the crowd said, '*Wah*.'

Someone touched the back of my neck and I turned to see, and looked straight into John's eyes; he was standing next to me with his hand on the back of my neck. I stood transfixed, staring at him, and he smiled, his eyes crinkling up. He bent to kiss the end of my snout, and disappeared.

I turned and opened my mouth to tell Simone and saw her face; it was full of cheeky delight. She quickly turned away, pretending that she hadn't seen, and watched the fireworks. I leaned my serpent head into her, Leo wrapped his arm around both of us, and we watched the fireworks together.

The Serpent raises its head from the water and slides onto the ice, the stars blazing above in the night sky.

The Turtle sinks to the bottom of the rich light-filled water, attempting to avoid the sun's brilliance and find a sanctuary in the dark.

They cry. There is no answer.

GLOSSARY

The Chinese language is divided by a number of different dialects and this has been reflected throughout my story. The main dialect spoken in Hong Kong is Cantonese, and many of the terms I've used are in Cantonese. The main method for transcribing Cantonese into English is the Yale system, which I have hardly used at all in this book, preferring to use a simpler phonetic method for spelling the Cantonese. Apologies to purists, but I've chosen ease of readability over phonetic correctness.

The dialect mainly spoken on the Mainland of China is Putonghua (also called Mandarin Chinese), which was originally the dialect used in the north of China but has spread to become the standard tongue. Putonghua has a strict and useful set of transcription rules called pinyin, which I've used throughout for Putonghua terms. As a rough guide to pronunciation, the 'Q' in pinyin is pronounced 'ch', the 'X' is 'sh' and the 'Zh' is a softer 'ch' than the 'Q' sound. Xuan Wu is therefore pronounced 'Shwan Wu'.

I've spelt chi with the 'ch' throughout the book, even though in pinyin it is qi, purely to aid in readability.

Qing Long and Zhu Que I have spelt in pinyin to assist anybody who'd like to look into these interesting deities further.

Aberdeen Typhoon Shelter: A harbour on the south side of Hong Kong Island that is home to a large number of small and large fishing boats. Some of the boats are permanently moored there and are residences.

Admiralty: The first station after the MTR train has come through the tunnel onto Hong Kong Island from Kowloon, and a major traffic interchange.

Amah: Domestic helper.

Ancestral tablet: A tablet inscribed with the name of the deceased, which is kept in a temple or at the residence of the person's descendants and occasionally provided with incense and offerings to appease the spirit.

Anime (Japanese): Animation; can vary from cute children's shows to violent horror stories for adults, and everything in between.

Bai Hu (Putonghua): The White Tiger of the West.

Bo: Weapon — staff.

Bodhisattva: A being who has attained Buddhist Nirvana and has returned to earth to help others achieve Enlightenment.

Bo lei: A very dark and pungent Chinese tea, often drunk with yum cha to help digest the sometimes heavy and rich food served there.

Bu keqi (Putonghua) pronounced, roughly, 'bu kerchi': 'You're welcome.'

Buddhism: The system of beliefs that life is an endless journey through reincarnation until a state of perfect detachment or Nirvana is reached.

Cantonese: The dialect of Chinese spoken mainly in the south of China and used extensively in Hong Kong. Although in written form it is nearly identical to Putonghua, when spoken it is almost unintelligible to Putonghua speakers.

Causeway Bay: Large shopping and office district on Hong Kong Island. Most of the Island's residents seem to head there on Sunday for shopping.

Central: The main business district in Hong Kong, on the waterfront on Hong Kong Island.

Central Committee: Main governing body of Mainland China.

Cha siu bow: Dim sum served at yum cha; a steamed bread bun containing barbecued pork and gravy in the centre.

Chek Lap Kok: Hong Kong's new airport on a large swathe of reclaimed land north of Lantau Island.

Cheongsam (Cantonese): Traditional Chinese dress, with a mandarin collar, usually closed with toggles and loops, and with splits up the sides.

Cheung Chau: Small dumbbell-shaped island off the coast of Hong Kong Island, about an hour away by ferry.

Chi: Energy. The literal meaning is 'gas' or 'breath' but in martial arts terms it describes the energy (or breath) of life that exists in all living things.

Chi gong (Cantonese): Literally, 'energy work'. A series of movements expressly designed for manipulation of chi.

Chinese New Year: The Chinese calendar is lunar, and New Year falls at a different time each Western calendar. Chinese New Year usually falls in either January or February.

Ching: A type of life energy, ching is the energy of sex and reproduction, the Essence of Life. Every person is born with a limited amount of ching and as this energy is drained they grow old and die.

Chiu Chow: A southeastern province of China.

Choy sum (Cantonese): A leafy green Chinese vegetable vaguely resembling English spinach.

City Hall: Hall on the waterfront in Central on Hong Kong Island containing theatres and a large restaurant.

Confucianism: A set of rules for social behaviour designed to ensure that all of society runs smoothly.

Congee: A gruel made by boiling rice with savoury ingredients such as pork or thousand-year egg. Usually eaten for breakfast but can be eaten as a meal or snack any time of the day.

Connaught Road: Main thoroughfare through the middle of Central District in Hong Kong, running parallel to the waterfront and with five lanes each side.

Cross-Harbour Tunnel: Tunnel that carries both cars and MTR trains from Hong Kong Island to Kowloon under the Harbour.

Cultural Revolution: A turbulent period of recent Chinese history (1966–75) during which gangs of young people called Red Guards overthrew 'old ways of thinking' and destroyed many ancient cultural icons.

Dai pai dong (Cantonese): Small open-air restaurant.

Daisho: A set of katana, wakizashi, and sometimes a tanto (small dagger), all matching bladed weapons used by samurai in ancient times.

Dan tian: Energy centre, a source of energy within the body. The central dan tian is roughly located in the solar plexus.

Daujie (Cantonese): 'Thank you', used exclusively when a gift is given.

Dim sum (Cantonese): Small dumplings in bamboo steamers served at yum cha. Usually each dumpling is less than three centimetres across and four are found in each steamer. There are a number of different types, and standard types of dim sum are served at every yum cha.

Discovery Bay: Residential enclave on Lantau Island, quite some distance from the rush of Hong Kong Island and only reachable by ferry.

Dojo (Japanese): Martial arts training school.

Eight Immortals: A group of iconic Immortals from Taoist mythology, each one representing a human condition. Stories of their exploits are part of popular Chinese culture.

Er Lang: The Second Heavenly General, second-in-charge of the running of Heavenly affairs. Usually depicted as a young man with three eyes and accompanied by his faithful dog.

Fortune sticks: A set of bamboo sticks in a bamboo holder. The questioner kneels in front of the altar and shakes the holder until one stick rises above the rest and falls out. This stick has a number that is translated into the fortune by temple staff.

Fung shui (or feng shui): The Chinese system of geomancy that links the environment to the fate of those living in it. A house with good internal and external fung shui assures its residents of good luck in their life.

Gay-lo (Cantonese slang): gay, homosexual.

Ge ge (Putonghua): Big brother.

Guangdong: The province of China directly across the border from Hong Kong.

Guangzhou: The capital city of Guangdong Province, about an hour away by road from Hong Kong. A large bustling commercial city rivalling Hong Kong in size and activity.

Guanxi: Guanxi is a social concept where people have built a network of others that they can call upon to help them when needed. The more guanxi you have, the more others will be willing to assist you when you are in need.

Gundam (Japanese): Large humanoid robot armour popular in Japanese cartoons.

Gung hei fat choy (Cantonese): Happy New Year.

Gwun Gong (or Guan Gong): A southern Chinese Taoist deity; a local General who attained Immortality and is venerated for his strengths of loyalty and justice and his ability to destroy demons.

H'suantian Shangdi (Cantonese): Xuan Tian Shang Di in the Wade-Giles method of writing Cantonese words.

Har gow: Dim sum served at yum cha; a steamed dumpling with a thin skin of rice flour dough containing prawns.

Hei sun (Cantonese): Arise.

Ho ak (Cantonese): Okay.

Ho fan (Cantonese): Flat white noodles made from rice; can be either boiled in soup or stir-fried.

Hong Kong Jockey Club: a private Hong Kong institution that runs and handles all of the horseracing and legal gambling in Hong Kong. There can be billions of Hong Kong dollars in bets on a single race meeting.

Hutong (Putonghua): Traditional square Chinese house, built around a central courtyard.

ICAC: Independent Commission Against Corruption;

an independent government agency focused on tracking down corruption in Hong Kong.

Jade Emperor: The supreme ruler of the Taoist Celestial Government.

Journey to the West: A classic of Chinese literature written during the Ming Dynasty by Wu Cheng'En. The story of the Monkey King's journey to India with a Buddhist priest to collect scriptures and return them to China.

Kata (Japanese): A martial arts 'set'; a series of moves to practise the use of a weapon or hand-to-hand skills.

Katana: Japanese sword.

KCR: A separate above-ground train network that connects with the MTR and travels to the border with Mainland China. Used to travel to towns in the New Territories.

Kitchen God: A domestic deity who watches over the activities of the family and reports annually to the Jade Emperor.

Koi (Japanese): Coloured ornamental carp.

Kowloon: Peninsula opposite the Harbour from Hong Kong Island, a densely packed area of highrise buildings. Actually on the Chinese Mainland, but separated by a strict border dividing Hong Kong from China.

Kowloon City: District in Kowloon just before the entrance to the Cross-Harbour Tunnel.

Kwan Yin: Buddhist icon; a woman who attained Nirvana and became a Buddha but returned to Earth to help others achieve Nirvana as well. Often represented as a goddess of Mercy.

Lai see (Cantonese): A red paper envelope used to give cash as a gift for birthdays and at New Year. It's believed that for every dollar given ten will return during the year.

Lai see dao loy (Cantonese): 'Lai see, please!'

Lantau Island: One of Hong Kong's outlying islands, larger than Hong Kong Island but not as densely inhabited.

Li: Chinese unit of measure, approximately half a kilometre.

Lo Wu: The area of Hong Kong that contains the border crossing. Lo Wu is an area that covers both sides of the border; it is in both Hong Kong and China.

Lo Wu Shopping Centre: A large shopping centre directly across the Hong Kong/Chinese border on the Chinese side. A shopping destination for Hong Kong residents in search of a bargain.

Love hotel: Hotel with rooms that are rented by the hour by young people who live with their parents (and therefore have no privacy) or businessmen meeting their mistresses for sex.

M'goi sai (Cantonese): 'Thank you very much.'

M'sai (Cantonese): Literally, 'no need', but it generally means 'you're welcome'.

Macau: One-time Portuguese colony to the west of Hong Kong in the Pearl River Delta, about an hour away by jet hydrofoil; now another Special Administrative Region of China. Macau's port is not as deep and sheltered as Hong Kong's so it has never been the busy trade port that Hong Kong is.

Mafoo (Cantonese): Groom.

Mah jong: Chinese game played with tiles. The Chinese play it differently from the polite game played by many Westerners; it is played for money and can often be a cut-throat competition between skilled players, rather like poker.

Manga: Japanese illustrated novel or comic book.

Mei mei (Putonghua): Little sister.

MTR: Fast, cheap, efficient and spotlessly clean subway train system in Hong Kong. Mostly standing room, and during rush hour so packed that it is often impossible to get onto a carriage.

Na Zha: Famous mythical Immortal who was so powerful as a child that he killed one of the dragon sons of the Dragon King. He gained Immortality by unselfishly travelling into Hell to release his parents who had been held in punishment for his crime. A spirit of Youthfulness.

New Territories: A large area of land between Kowloon and Mainland China that was granted to extend Hong Kong. Less crowded than Hong Kong and Kowloon, the New Territories are green and hilly with highrise New Towns scattered through them.

Nunchucks: Short wooden sticks held together with chains; a martial arts weapon.

Opium Wars: (1839–60) A series of clashes between the then British Empire and the Imperial Chinese Government over Britain's right to trade opium to China. It led to a number of humiliating defeats and surrenders by China as they were massively outclassed by modern Western military technology.

Pa Kua (Cantonese): The Eight Symbols, a central part of Taoist mysticism. Four of these Eight Symbols flank the circle in the centre of the Korean flag.

Pak Tai: One of Xuan Wu's many names; this one is used in Southern China.

Peak Tower: Tourist sightseeing spot at the top of the Peak Tram. Nestled between the two highest peaks on the Island and therefore not the highest point in Hong Kong, but providing a good view for tourist photographs.

Peak Tram: Tram that has been running for many years between Central and the Peak. Now mostly a tourist attraction because of the steepness of the ride and the view.

Peak, the: Prestigious residential area of Hong Kong, on top of the highest point of the centre of Hong Kong Island. The view over the Harbour and highrises is spectacular, and the property prices there are some of the highest in the world.

Pipa: A Chinese musical instrument, shaped like a mandolin, but played vertically with the body of the instrument held in the lap.

Pokfulam: Area of Hong Kong west of the main business districts, facing the open ocean rather than the harbour. Contains large residential apartment blocks and a very large hillside cemetery.

Putonghua: Also called Mandarin, the dialect of Chinese spoken throughout China as a standard language. Individual provinces have their own dialects but Putonghua is spoken as a common tongue.

Qing Long (Putonghua) pronounced, roughly, Ching Long: The Azure Dragon of the East.

Ramen (Japanese): Instant two-minute noodles.

Repulse Bay: A small swimming beach surrounded by an expensive residential enclave of high- and low-rise apartment blocks on the south side of Hong Kong Island.

Salute, Chinese: The left hand is closed into a fist and the right hand is wrapped around it. Then the two hands are held in front of the chest and sometimes shaken.

Sashimi (Japanese): Raw fish.

Seiza: Japanese kneeling position.

Sensei (Japanese): Master.

Seppuku: Japanese ritual suicide by disembowelment: hari-kiri.

Sha Tin: A New Territories 'New Town', consisting of a large shopping centre surrounded by a massive number of highrise developments on the banks of the Shing Mun River.

Shaolin: Famous temple, monastery and school of martial arts, as well as a style of martial arts.

Shen: Shen has two meanings, in the same sense that the English word spirit has two meanings ('ghost' and 'energy'). Shen can mean an Immortal being, something like a god in Chinese mythology. It is also the spirit that dwells within a person, the energy of their soul.

Shenzhen: The city at the border between Hong Kong and China, a 'special economic zone' where capitalism has been allowed to flourish. Most of the goods manufactured in China for export to the West are made in Shenzhen.

Sheung Wan: The western end of the Hong Kong Island MTR line; most people get off the train before reaching this station.

Shoji (Japanese): Screen of paper stretched over a wooden frame.

Shui (Cantonese): 'Water'.

Shui gow: Chinese dumplings made of pork and prawn meat inside a dough wrapping, boiled in soup stock.

Shroff Office: A counter in a car park where you pay the parking fee before returning to your car.

Sifu (Cantonese): Master.

Siu mai: Dim sum served at yum cha; a steamed dumpling with a skin of wheat flour containing prawn and pork.

Sow mei (Cantonese): A type of Chinese tea, with a greenish colour and a light, fragrant flavour.

Stanley Market: A famous market on the south side of Hong Kong island, specialising in tourist items.

Star Ferry: Small oval green and white ferries that run a cheap service between Hong Kong Island and Kowloon.

Sticky rice: Dim sum served at yum cha; glutinous rice filled with savouries such as pork and thousand-year egg, wrapped in a green leaf and steamed.

Sun Wu Kong (Cantonese): The Monkey King's real name.

Tae kwon do: Korean martial art.

Tai chi: A martial art that consists of a slow series of movements, used mainly as a form of exercise and chi manipulation to enhance health and extend life. Usable as a lethal martial art by advanced practitioners. There are several different styles of tai chi, including Chen, Yang and Wu, named after the people who invented them.

Tai chi chuan: Full correct name for tai chi.

Tai Koo Shing: large enclosed shopping mall on the north side of Hong Kong.

Tai Tai (Cantonese): Lit. 'wife' but in this context it refers to a wealthy middle-aged Hong Kong woman who spends all her time shuffling between designer clothing stores, expensive lunches, and beauty salons.

Tao Teh Ching: A collection of writings by Lao Tzu on the elemental nature of Taoist philosophy.

Tao, the: 'The Way'. A perfect state of consciousness equivalent to the Buddhist Nirvana, in which a person becomes completely attuned with the universe and achieves Immortality. Also the shortened name of a collection of writings (the Tao Teh Ching) on Taoist philosophy written by Lao Tzu.

Taoism: Similar to Buddhism, but the state of perfection can be reached by a number of different methods, including alchemy and internal energy manipulation as well as meditation and spirituality.

Tatami (Japanese): Rice-fibre matting.

Temple Street: A night market along a street on Kowloon side in Hong Kong. Notorious as a triad gang hangout as well as being one of Hong Kong's more colourful markets.

Ten Levels of Hell: It is believed that a human soul travels through ten levels of Hell, being judged and punished for a particular type of sin at each level. Upon reaching the lowest, or tenth, level, the soul is given an elixir of forgetfulness and returned to Earth to reincarnate and live another life.

Teppan (Japanese): Hotplate used for cooking food at teppanyaki.

Teppanyaki (Japanese): Meal where the food is cooked on the teppan in front of the diners and served when done.

Thousand-year egg: A duck egg that's been preserved in a mixture of lime, ash, tea and salt for one hundred days, making the flesh of the egg black and strong in flavour.

Tikuanyin (Cantonese; or Tikuanyum): Iron Buddha Tea. A dark, strong and flavourful black Chinese tea. Named because, according to legend, the first tea bush of this type was found behind a roadside altar containing an iron statue of Kwan Yin.

Tin Hau (Cantonese): Taoist deity, worshipped by seafarers.

Triad: Hong Kong organised-crime syndicate. Members of the syndicates are also called triads.

Tsim Sha Tsui: Main tourist and entertainment district on Kowloon side, next to the Harbour.

Tsing Ma Bridge: Large suspension bridge connecting Kowloon with Lantau Island, used to connect to the Airport Expressway.

Typhoon: A hurricane that occurs in Asia. Equivalent to a hurricane in the US or a cyclone in Australia.

Wakizashi: Japanese dagger, usually matched with a sword to make a set called a daisho.

Wan Chai: Commercial district on Hong Kong Island, between the offices and designer stores of Central and the shopping area of Causeway Bay. Contains office buildings and restaurants, and is famous for its nightclubs and girlie bars.

Wan sui (Putonghua): 'Ten thousand years'; traditional greeting for the Emperor, wishing him ten thousand times ten thousand years of life.

Wei? (Cantonese): 'Hello?' when answering the phone.

Wing chun: Southern style of Chinese kung fu. Made famous by Bruce Lee, this style is fast, close in ('short') and lethal. It's also a 'soft' style where the defender uses the attacker's weight and strength against him or her, rather than relying on brute force to hit hard.

Wire-fu: Move kung-fu performed on wires so that the actors appear to be flying.

Won ton (Cantonese): Chinese dumplings made mostly of pork with a dough wrapping and boiled in soup stock. Often called 'short soup' in the West.

Won ton mien (Cantonese): 'won ton noodles'; won ton boiled in stock with noodles added to the soup.

Wu shu (Putonghua): A general term to mean all martial arts.

Wudang (Putonghua): A rough translation could be 'true martial arts'. The name of the mountain in Hubei Province; also the name of the martial arts academy and the style of martial arts taught there. Xuan Wu was a Celestial 'sponsor' of the Ming Dynasty and the entire mountain complex of temples and monasteries was built by the government of the time in his honour.

Wudangshan (Putonghua): 'Shan' means 'mountain'; Wudang Mountain.

Xie xie (Putonghua): 'Thank you.'

Xuan Wu (Putonghua) pronounced, roughly, 'Shwan Wu': means 'Dark Martial Arts'; the Black Turtle of the North, Mr Chen.

Yamen: Administration, as in Yamen Building.

Yang: One of the two prime forces of the Universe in Taoist philosophy. Yang is the Light: masculine, bright, hot and hard.

Yang and yin: The two prime forces of the universe, when joined together form the One, the essence of everything. The symbol of yang and yin shows each essence containing a small part of the other.

Yellow Emperor: An ancient mythological figure, the Yellow Emperor is credited with founding civilisation and inventing clothing and agriculture.

Yin: One of the two prime forces of the universe in Taoist philosophy. Yin is Darkness: feminine, dark, cold and soft.

Yuexia Loaren (Putonghua): 'Old Man Under the Moon'; a Taoist deity responsible for matchmaking.

Yum cha (Cantonese): Literally 'drink tea'. Most restaurants hold yum cha between breakfast and mid-afternoon. Tea is served, and waitresses wheel around trolleys containing varieties of dim sum.

Yuzhengong (Putonghua): 'Find the True Spirit'; the name of the palace complex on Wudang Mountain.

Zhu Que (Putonghua) pronounced, roughly, Joo Chway: the Red Phoenix of the South.

CULTURAL NOTES

Animals on the edge of the roof:

Traditional Chinese buildings have upturned roofs and on official buildings there is always the same series of creatures. The point of the roof holds a man riding a chicken (or phoenix), and he is followed by a series of mythical creatures, with a dragon's head at the very back. The more creatures behind the man, the higher the building is in the Imperial hierarchy. Buildings in the Forbidden City have nine animals; in a small province there would be only one between the man and the dragon. The small vignette is a reminder and a warning to those working inside the building, that whatever they do, all of the mythical creatures on the roof are watching them, and will pounce on them and devour them if they stray from their official duty.

Ah Ting:

Part of the legend of the 'Creation of the Gods' involves the raising of all concerned to the Celestial. When it came time to choose the person for the job of Jade Emperor, the leader of the winning side graciously and politely didn't immediately take the position, he just said 'Ting, ting.' ('Wait, wait.') Legend has it that a rogue by the name of Ting jumped up and loudly accepted the post of Jade Emperor, and as it was what the leader had said, he was given the post.

I have expanded my library considerably while researching for the second trilogy, Journey to Wudang, and I have delved deeper into the mythology, as well as the texts and scriptures, of Taoism. Here is a list of some of the works that I have added to my collection, and may be of interest:

A Selected Collection of Mencius, Sinolingua, Beijing, 2006

A Selected Collection of the Analects, Confucius, Sinolingua, Beijing, 2006

Anecdotes about Spirits and Immortals (in two volumes) by Gan Bao, translated into English by Ding Wangdao, Foreign Languages Press, Beijing, 2004

Creation of the Gods (in four volumes), Xu Zhonglin, Translated by Gu Zhizhong, New World Press, Beijing, 2000

Early Taoist Scriptures, Stephen R Bokenkamp, University of California Press, Berkeley, 1997

Journey to the North, Gary Seaman, University of California Press, Berkeley, 1987

Journey to the West, Wu Cheng'En, Translated by W J F Jenner, Foreign Languages Press, Beijing, 1993

Secret of the Golden Flower, Lu Yen, NuVision E-book, 2004

Selected Chinese Tales of the Han, Wei, and Six Dynasties Periods, Translated by Yang Xianyi and Gladys Yang, Foreign Languages Press, Beijing, 2001

The Origin of Chinese Deities, Cheng Manchao, Foreign Languages Press, Beijing, 1995

The Scripture on Great Peace: the Tai Ping Jing and the Beginnings of Taoism, by Barbara Hendrischke, University of California Press, Berkeley, 2006

To Live as Long as Heaven and Earth, a Translation and Study of Ge Hong's Traditions of Divine Transcendents, Robert Ford Campany, University of California Press, Berkeley, 2002